MW00783690

KEVIN PRINCETON

AND THE HOLY LAND OF SOULS

KENNETH VIVOR

Contents

I dedicate this novel to my mother, Paula Salako, who is the big heart in my life. From reading to editing, she has helped me to polish and finalize this enthralling tale. In addition, her strong faith in God, and her spirituality, have been one of the sole inspirations for the story of Kevin Princeton. And I couldn't be prouder to have such a loving dedicated mother who has raised me and my brother from the ground up.

I also dedicate this novel to my big brother, Kelvin Vivor, who is not only my brother, but also a best friend. My source of creativity came from our passion for it. And I am too blessed to having a brother like him in my life.

Emilia Phillips was such an impact on my strive to improve on my writing style and how I wanted to present my story. Not only she helped me to find my definitive writing voice, but a unique way of telling my stories from this day forward.

Finally, I thank my friends, my teacher Brenda Thomas, and relatives for their ongoing support and love they had showed me to continue improving my craft. And most of all, I thank God for shining this light of writing I had yet to see or extract from within. Without his grace, I wouldn't be enthusiastic to put out his story that came from the love of fantasy, drama and artistic quality stories that find a way to tell stories beyond the basics.

All I could hope is for this story to enrich you and intrigue you the best way I know how.

KEVIN PRINCETON

Prologue

I lived three lives. But I only managed to make one right.

And it was a life I neither expected, nor wanted. It was surely not a normal life. But it was another life. A life that shouldn't have existed. But it did. I had to come in terms with it. And I did.

But a bit about me. I came from a bloodline. A bloodline of knights. Edward Carter was my ancestor, a long-lost member of the Christian Hospitallers of St. John, an order of knights who served the ill and weary pilgrims who were on a journey to the Holy Land. From there, our ancestor hoped for his legacy to build upon that foundation in hopes to not only serve the people, but to serve God most importantly. To help others meant to serve and celebrate God. And no matter what, they deserved to be saved in his grace. Do unto others as you would have them do unto you. This was what I knew growing up. These were the stories I was told by my parents. And it was what I wanted to live up to.

This was the first life. And all I wanted was to see it last in good terms. I loved the idea of being knightly. I was set to serve as my ancestor did. I tried to take upon that role to defend our kingdom. Honestly, my kin meant a lot to me more than the world itself. All I wanted was to see that life with them last in triumph.

But it was when they faced evil, when they got burned alive by dragons, that drove me away from that. At the end, I came to realize that those were just fairytales to distract any child from the coldest reality of the world God created (and perhaps wanted). And I failed to see how someone like Edward pursued to serve a world, to serve a God, that didn't want him anymore. I wish I knew how many lives he lived to make it happened. To make his legend known and celebrated within the tradition of my kin.

I know it would be hard or absurd for someone to truly understand. But this is what happened. This is what I had to face. This is my tale. My story. And I promise to explain everything as best as I could. Perhaps I could start here; the last days of my life; those days when I was alive. My second life.

May 17, 2010

Nightfall overwhelmed the mellow blue sky. It filled the sky with the color of coal glazed with stars projecting their glimmer like spotlights. Right after my five-minute smoking break, I stumbled as quickly as I could through the shrouded alleyways of Brooklyn.

Two small headphones were in my ears as I was listening to You on the Run by the rock band "The Black Angels". They weren't my favorite band, but I did like the song. It was good to listen to in the dark cloudy streets. It made it atmospheric somehow. Before implanting both hands in my condensed jean pockets, I placed my hood over my head, making myself scarce from the public. I became breathless due to the nonstop sprints I did to get to where I was. I would stop very often, eagerly looking back and forth to make sure I was not to be seen by any police-man. Sirens rang like an eagle crying in the skies, but very distantly behind the dewy roads glistened with light after rainfall. I was missing for thirteen years. So, I had to move quickly and never stop to not be recognized by anyone else. Especially the law.

Sprawled from side to side, I finally got closer to where I was going to, a church amid other buildings. It stood out from the rest of the avenues on the corner of the street. Sprinting towards the grotesque red building in full speed, I rushed across the car-ran roads to avoid full detection from anyone who might have seen my face on the wanted papers. The streetlamps weren't much help either. As soon as I crossed over to the other side, I paced myself through the crowd. My hands were constantly patting my way through the people, placing my hand on their clothed coats. I was afraid of the number of people that night, knowing that most of them would potentially recognize me.

I was relieved to be on the other side of the street as I then faced the tower that was connected to the church. I rushed across the damp sidewalk.

Getting towards the door, I stopped immediately to catch my breath and to keep myself steady. I removed my headphones and my hood, faced the beige tinted door, and knocked. However, there was no response. So again, I knocked the door. As it creaked whilst it opened, an old man in black formal wear with a white collar around his wrinkly neck showed. His grey hair was circled around his bald spot.

"I'm sorry, but night services are..." His sunken eyes widened as he saw me. "Kevin? Is that you?!"

"I need to ask you a favor, Harris! We need to discuss it inside!" I said in haste.

Turning left and right, he scanned for some apparent reason. Probably to keep a look out since I have been on the other side of the law. He then said to me, "Come inside."

As I entered, the sounds of honking cars and chatting people vanished as the door closed behind me. The halls within the church were lit with a bluish light that glimmered, leaving a little bit of shade on each corner of the tower. Harris then led me towards the staircase on each side of the beige limestone walls, leading towards his rectory that happened to be in a church. Obviously.

When we got to his room, he pulled out his rusty keys to unlock his blocked-up door. It was a small room, containing a bed near the window and a shelf by the right side of the room.

Harris closed the door behind me as soon as I entered. His face was still in shock after seeing me. It's been thirteen years since I've seen him.

So, I felt his arms wrapping around me, but I didn't choose to hug back. He knew about that place and chose not to get me. He got off and the smile he had vanished once he saw my vacant expression.

"I know...it's been long. But I need to make my way around Brooklyn. And if there's any person, I know who was granted to hold accountable for my family's inheritance, it would be you." I said.

"I haven't seen you...in thirteen years. And this is how you greet me." He then asked after letting out a regretful sigh, "Kevin, what happened? Why did you run away?"

"I couldn't stay there, okay?" I said directly. "It was clear that I wasn't welcomed there."

"You could've at least called me! I've called the cops, everywhere in the city, they're tirelessly searching for you." He said almost angrily, gazing up and down at me. He then caught a smell and sniffed my jacket,

"Is that...tobacco?" I would've preferred for him to get off me, but he began to investigate my jacket. He pulled out my iPhone, which he saw a text from someone named Snake. "Snake?"

"Honestly, he's just a friend!" I retorted nervously as I was hoping that he wouldn't find out about my whereabouts. He then stood back as his hands got to his hip. He scoffed and sucked on his teeth. He then concluded, "Snake! You mean Snake the career criminal?" I sighed in a regretful but agitated way.

"Alright! I'm with Snake. So, what?!" I admitted as I then saw him hide his sigh with his hand palming his face. His face shrunk with disbelief and disappointment. I roared, "You're not my father, okay!? You'll never be!"

"You're right! I'm not your father." He then said, gradually raising his voice. He then pointed at me. "But I'm your friend! A friend of your father, who would've disapproved you for being a criminal!"

"Hey, it's a lot better than to be held in a place full of arses." I said.

"I didn't know they would hurt you! If you'd call me, I would've known! I'm very sorry!" Harris said defensively.

"No, you're not! You're not sorry! You would've done something if you were, but you didn't!"

He then wandered off and said, "So...the massacre...that robbery that happened at the foster care and Dime Community Bank two weeks ago... the news that was televised...were you responsible?"

I slightly chuckled, "Yeah. What of it? Hm. It's not like you gave a damn anyway! My father's money never should've been held in that place he financed! And for suits...they don't deserve that kind of money in banks."

"Kevin, I know you! You're better than that!! I know you are better than this!"

"No, you don't! I expected you to come back and help me! But you were never there! You left me when I needed you the most! There's no more to discuss!" I roared as the room fell into silence. After I sighed off my anger, I said, "I want money from my inheritance!"

"Why don't you ask your friend Snake?" He finger-quoted Snake. "I thought crooks were all about money. Unless he's taking advantage of you because he knows about your wealth, like most of the folks!"

"He's a good friend. And a lot trustworthy than you." I chuckled.

"You're unbelievable, you know that?" Harris questioned me with frustration rising within him. Obviously, he was ill due to the brash actions I've committed. "We had an agreement that you would stay there until I eventually came back!"

"Which you never did!" I said as I grinned.

"I'm not going to give you money, Kevin. I'm afraid for you and the lives you've potentially put in danger!" Harris said.

"Like I give a shit about their lives! The same lives that spoke down about our legacy or the lives that try to spread this false image that God is a loving God!" I roared. "I'm doing my family a favor!"

"But this isn't how they want their legacy to last." Harris said, now sat down on his chair by the desk on the left side of the room. "You are the son of a holy and wealthy family, Kevin. You come from a line of knighthood. They've done so much good for people and played a role in society. Even if most were against them, they still rose. They fought to be better than what the world expects them to be! You were once a part of it. I hope you remember that."

"I hope you remembered that I didn't come here to reflect on that! I came here to get my money!" I said.

"What are you going to do with the money? Buy more guns? Gamble? Vandalize? Continuously deceiving your family and I? This is completely beneath you! Unlike you!"

"I told you, I don't want to be reminded of who I was! That's over with! Those days are gone! Now give me my money!" I demanded once more. "It's mine!"

He recoiled himself uncomfortably and said with no ease, "I can't do that!"

"The hell you mean you can't do that?" Anger was rising within me.

"Before your parents died, they assured me to donate the money to help advance their campaign. I plan to save lives with this money. Most of it is for your health care! Something your family would've wanted for you! They are gone, yes! But that doesn't mean that we should be inconsiderate of others! Your father and mother didn't raise you to be like that!"

After he said that, silence approached, and it was not to long that my laughter interrupted it. It's my inheritance. I couldn't stand by and let him send it all away just to appear good for public relations; especially for some brainless deity who only granted wishes after we stroked his omnipotent ego.

"And you're laughing... why?" Harris asked confusedly but angrily.

"I'm laughing because it's a joke! Just like how you're a joke! Your career is a joke! You honestly think that you could use my money just so...what...you could give false hope to these children like their sheep! My money! Bloody hell!"

"You're not even old enough to claim your parent's inheritance. Until then, I am holding it!" Harris yelled. "Until you mature and behave, get out from this criminal life, you're not getting an ounce of the money!"

I stumbled across the floor to compose myself. I couldn't bear the thought. But being that they were children, it was fair for them to have good lives and turn out to be good people unlike most. But I personally found it useless to use the money to get them to be brainwashed by this absurd belief.

Sighing from laughter, I said, "Fine...give them that privilege. Lie to them like how you lied to me for all these years!"

"I never lied to you! And I've never forgotten about you! I've always believed that God has a plan for everyone! Especially you! You're just choosing not to come in terms of the things that happened and you're blaming it on God! Your family is gone and yet it gave you an excuse to run away to terrorize the town with criminals instead of being a good example for the world? That's nonsense! I've been looking for you! Everyone has been looking for you after you ran away: only to find out that you've been secretly committing delinquency in the streets this whole time! Only to find that you've killed people in cold blood! And it needs to stop! I'm reporting you to the police and having you put in prison for your own benefit!"

My fist clenched. The thought of me being behind bars for more than 5 years is something I couldn't bear. This fueled me to send it towards Harris' temple, landing him onto the wooden floor. I then send my left foot towards his rib, making him cough and groan in utter pain. I was empty with any care to realize that I've just stricken old friend down.

"It's my inheritance! My money! You don't get to decide what to do with it!" I bellowed so loudly that each corner of the room echoed my voice. I landed my foot onto his chest viciously that he coughed violently.

"So simple...just give me at least six hundred! If not, I could frame you for molesting a child! 'Cause I know that's what you priests are good at. I will do it! I'll pose as someone and frame your arse!" I said as he struggled to get up from the floor.

He placed his hands on the surface of the desk to stand himself up. Completely standing up on both feet, he looked back at me with vulnerability in his eyes.

"You'll...you'll cost my job!" Harris said.

"A job to bull-shite everyone to think that there is a God looking down on us? Guiding us to be good to go to Heaven?! Your job is useless...just like you!"

He looked at me with a brightened bruise on his face. He then turned to the mantelshelf and picked up a silver metallic box from the top shelf. After placing down on his desk, he used a key to unlock it. It revealed large stacks of dosh, all lined up perfectly. After giving me half of the money that was there, he closed the box and positioned it back to where it was.

"Was that so hard, old man?" I asked bitterly. He didn't respond but continued to stay silent. He simply just stared at me with defeat in his eyes.

"Ha...not saying anything now, are ya?" I said. "Oh...and I'll come back for the rest! Trust me on that!"

Just when I was about to leave his room, he said, "Before you take off...remember this. This life you chose...is not going to help you live long. And you're going to have to embrace that someday. You're going to have to get help. You're not well."

"Perhaps...except I don't plan to die! And what does it matter? I already feel like a ghost." I said, finally taking off from his room and closed the door behind me, leaving him defenseless.

As I hurried down the stairs, sliding my hand down the wall, something got me to stop immediately. I palmed my forehead. Those blasted voices came again! These bloody voices always followed me wherever I go. Ever since the tragedy, they worsened. Since I was a child, all I did was prayed. I asked God to remove the curse. To bless the medication my parents would give me to ease. To bless the therapists and psychiatrists to save me. But as I said, he did not care.

He cursed me for whatever sin I committed.

Most times, I feel as if the voices were truly next to me, whispering ill beliefs into my ears. I had a total of sixteen different voices circling and traversing my mind. Eight of them were good, but the other eight were rotten, consuming and battling inside my head. Eight of them wanted me to embrace and accept every burden. The other eight wanted me to move on and do better things in a hopeful future. But all sixteen of them annoyed me. It was as if I wasn't in charge of my own body. And there was this one phrase that has been following me;

"*Audite custodies tui* **Listen to your guardians**"

They gradually got louder and louder to where I cannot even hear my footsteps nor my own breathing. They sounded like a group of people near my personal space, whispering toward my ears nonstop. I couldn't understand them, nor did I care to try. I closed both ears and ran down the steps until I got to the door.

The shadows on the marble walls took form of what appeared to be six silhouettes with long coats, hats, and red eyes. I closed both my eyes, hoping to block them out of my mind. I ran down the stairs as quickly as I could to get away from them.

As I finally got outside, I was welcomed by the same sounds of honking cars and chatty people, being how wide the crossroads were. I ran back toward the other side of the street. Once again, I passed through the crowd, gentling putting my hands onto their cotton made hoodie and suits. I made sure I was concealed within my hoodie. But the people themselves were making me uncomfortable. I couldn't bear to be recognized and placed in jail.

I paced myself quickly and got back into the alleyway right after strolling through the dense sidewalks. Ignoring the distanced complaints from those I pushed out of my way, I made my way through the darkened alleyway with flickering light bulbs on each wall. Compared to the scent of nectar from yellow flowers mother use to plant, the scent in this place was tobacco, piss and used condoms all the time. But Snake advised me to make the best of it. The concrete was riddled with silver cans, soda cans and other residue left of people who apparently don't know how to put away garbage. I paced myself quickly amongst the faint sharp dog barks.

And yes.... I became a criminal for thirteen years. I knew it was wrong, but there was nowhere else to go in New York City. I couldn't trust anyone. I allowed the world to win. And the voices encouraged it. And when I ran away, there was nowhere to turn to. No one to trust. Especially those who call themselves professionals. Thus, I turned to the dirty streets. I knew then how it truly felt to be exiled from luxury. Plus, I joined ever since Snake recognized me when I ran away. He promised to hide me from the public if I joined as his pupil. Also, because I didn't want to be found. And so, sacrificing every chance I had, to prosper according to God, was worth it.

Snake showed me things that I never knew about the city. Taught me about the world. He showed me how to survive by scamming, getting paid, and even killing. He made me stronger and taught me how to stand for myself. To think and learn for myself. To make sure that I take no toxicity from anybody.

Since then, I had more respect for Snake as opposed to Harris. He made me strong, capable of surviving and taking nothing from anyone. And if risking myself by showing up in front of Harris meant to fulfill my duty, then so be it.

I

The Second Life

Exiting the alleyway, I turned to my left and walk down the shadowy neighborhood with dimmed light. After walking through the crowded part of Brooklyn, I was finally faced with the area I knew most.

I stopped midway to pull out a small white box from my jacket pocket. Peeling off the cover, I inserted my fingers as I pulled out a roll-up. I placed the cigarette in my mouth whilst putting the box back inside my jacket.

I then used my lighter to ignite the tip of my cigarette. I watched the smoke bloom as the tip brightened. I sensed the warmth escalating within my bones and vessels. I silently pled for the bitter aroma to wipe away the visions lingering my mind, regardless of the faint barks of dogs, honks of cars, and the chatter of people.

I continued to walk through the dim avenue between the trees on the edge of the sidewalk and the red and brown-bricked apartment buildings on my right. I reflected on things Harris told me about my family by reaching both hands around my neck, nearly forgetting that I still had it on; a silver necklace encrusted with black markings, containing a small capture of my family and I.

Opening it, it displayed a circled black and white photograph of my mother and father holding hands while I was there, sitting with my sister with my arm around her. We were draped regally as I saw my sister and I embracing our dress clothes.

I stopped my pace to glance at it, reflecting of what went wrong; what it could've been. But the good times were most significant. I remembered them more, even in my broken head. I felt more alive with them. They were building me up, only for the world to break me down.

My eyes were focused on the tiny colorless photo and the voice from Kelley emerged within my mind. Everything emerged within my mind. The dark street shifted and slowly seeped with Christmas lights.

Long Island, Winter 1996

I remembered this memory, Christmas day. Obviously, it was my favorite time of the year and my favorite holiday. Not just because of the presents, but it was mostly to truly be with my family. I know that I would always see them, but this holiday was important to me because it gave me a chance to offer my gratitude to two of the greatest people. We were strong together. And that notion has always kept me together, regardless of the voices telling me otherwise.

I had no favorite type of music; most of it ranged from classic rock to music from the 80s. My mother was a fanatic of 80s music, which garnered her to play a guitar for a living. She had an Apple iPod that had an interesting playlist of every song and band from the 80s; listing down from Queen to Dead Can Dance (which I reckon most haven't heard of). My personal favorite to hear, especially during that holiday, was their song *"In Power We Entrusted the Love Advocated"*. Something about that song always got to me. But I never realized it until I was getting order. And plus, I was too young to truly understand it. Growing up, I was fascinated by rock music that had elements of darkwave and ethereal. It made it symbolic to me. Thus, Dead Can Dance became one of my favorite bands.

As for our presents, Kelley would usually get toy sets from the amusement park attraction "*Pirates of the Caribbean*", knowing that she had always been obsessed with pirates. As for myself, however, I would get tabletop games. Contrasting from Kelley's love for pirates, I was always obsessed with the medieval. I used to enjoy board games ranging from Monopoly to Scrabble. But I was craving more tabletop games like Pendragon, a game from 1985 about the legend of King Arthur. I played that during the holidays.

I also had books for Christmas as well. I liked adventure books, so I had books like "*King Arthur and His Knights*", "*Peter Pan*" and "*Lord of the Rings*". The idea of going on these surrealistic and harsh yet epic adventures to become something grander was always something I've fascinated about coming upon these books. I craved for adventure and traveling across the world. I loved to read, and, in some ways, I still did. Except for Kelley. Sometimes, she would pressure herself to do it just to get it over with and make mum and dad proud of her.

My father believed in God traditionally. My mother was more spiritual, but still praised as well. They prayed, fasted, read the Bible, and went to church. It used to be fun and fulfilling. Going to church and seeking God's word from the Bible. I remembered most of its scriptures. Ones that stood out to me. And my parents read the Bible to gain knowledge. They had the traditions of the Christian faith but only to find a way to make it work for them. Even though I would feel burdened, what made me go to church happily was seeing Father Harris; at the time we were actual friends when he left the army. Harris saved my father and made him see God. They became friends when the church we went to essentially treated us like outlaws. With that goodness, I considered him as part of the family. He stood up for us and made us a home at the church despite not being very liked there.

My father was a war veteran. My mother was a singer. When they were alive, my father worked for the United Nations as a humanitarian. He ventured and traveled to other countries, helping, and supporting people, especially to establish a campaign for child abuse prevention called Free Spirits. My mother was a vocalist who sang for a decent audience, as she wasn't singing for fame. She sang neoclassical and neofolk music. But the type of music she was known for dated back from the eighties of England. And today, that type of music is not too popular. At least in America. On occasion, she would be called from several shelter homes to play music to comfort and give at-risk children faith. Because a lot of her songs were about finding hope in any life. Both had wildly different careers. But both had one common goal in mind; to help be the best examples of how good life could be. To perfect it according to God. At least, that's what I was hoping for, based on my ancestor's exploits.

Although I didn't think too deeply about this as a child, I was interested in becoming an art therapist. Specially to help my father advance his campaign by helping other children express themselves artistically. I used to sketch pictures of characters based on my love for knights mostly as an expressive art based on the tales of my ancestor. Even though it was in the arts, I was inspired to help our parents. Kelley was too as she wanted to sing like mother. We once hoped to create a family business somehow. The idea of making the world a better place alongside my family was a life I wanted. I was inspired to do something for the world. Making it better and beautiful. Not for money (we had much of that), but to sorely make our legacy flourish. To strengthen our bloodline for more generations to come soon and continue it.

"Where did you and mum work before, dad?" Kelley asked in interest, seated with her legs crossed on the very vibrant carpet floor, a baroque quilted carpet with colors of orange and green. Our Christmas tree almost reached the ceiling, which was twenty feet from our heads. The halls were bigger as well as the rooms. The living room we celebrated was almost the size of a Broadway stage and decorated with extravagant colored lights.

"Well...before we had you and Kelley, we worked for an organization at a big church in London. Years after I fought in war. Your mother played for the children, and I just did the charity work. She got herself a record deal when Harris and I got her noticed and became a...moderately famous singer." Father said, coddling Mother as she giggled. His lips were patting at the side of her face.

"That must have taken a lot of time." I asked. "When you do good for people, you get more money?"

That made my parents chuckle a bit due to my naïve little mind not grasping real life. But I was so fascinated on how they could afford the home we lived in. I then glanced at my sister, standing up on her two feet, walking over to the tree.

"Son, if you do good in everything you do, you will be more than awarded with money. You'd be blessed." My mother said with a gentle smile. I smiled back to her kind regard.

"But...I'm not sure what I want to be yet when I grow up. But I do want to help you in your work with my art." I admitted.

"I really appreciate it, son! I am very grateful! But you're very young." Father said with a chuckle. "Unlike me, you and your sister have all the time in the world to know what you want to do." He then glanced at a frame picture of a drawing I made on the wall on top of the fireplace. It was a crayoned made picture that depicted Kelley and I as knights and mother and father as king and queen. "I know you like to draw."

"One day, I want to help draw pictures!" I cheered. This garnered a humble chuckle from father. I unintentionally confirmed that I wanted to write when I get older. Perhaps what I would write would hopefully make the world better. It hadn't stopped any influential author before.

"When you get older, you get to draw about anything! Put your mind on anything you want to do. I pray that you enthrall people into your imagination without fear of the world! I know you are afraid of what is out there. But your mother and I believe in you. You and Kelley both! Most of all, God does!" Father smiled.

"How come you are often not around," I asked father. He gave me a sad smile. It was hard to understand what was bothering him at a young age.

Regardless, he said with such an assuring tone, "It's just business, son. Nothing special. But I still have you in my heart."

"Kevin, I almost forgot about this one," Kelley said, approaching to me with a little green box. "This one is for you." The little soft wrapped box landed softly on my hands; my fingers began clawing it smoothly. I looked at my sister with gleaming eyes. Looking down at the gift, I began unwrapping it by loosening the red ribbon, pulling it from the box, opening the box and revealing one of the most precious and greatest things.

Don't get me wrong; I really loved the gifts from my mother and father. But this gift Kelley has made up my day. It was a necklace that had a small picture of my family and I when I opened it. My eyes were watering with tears because of how beautifully charming it was.

"Aww...Kelley..." My mother covered her mouth with happy tears coming down her cheeks.

"I got this when I was shopping with Johnathan. We didn't tell you when we went that day. It is a symbol that shows that we will always remain together, in spirit and mind." Kelley spoke.

When the tears finally came down, I wiped them with my hand, so she wouldn't notice.

"I'm...sorry." Kelley said, noticing my dry tears. "I hope it's nice. I didn't mean to make you cry!"

"No Kelley, these are tears of joy. This gift is beautiful...and I will never give it away or lose it. Thank you, Kelley." I said as I then wrapped her around with my arms. I suddenly felt the arms of mother and father.

My father then said as Dead Can Dance still played in the background, "When we have joy, God is here with us all the time. When he is here with us, we are happy. And it is the greatest gift of all." Soon, they would slow dance with each other by the fireplace.

I was snapped off the reflection as the music faded away and I got back toward the cursed reality, recognizing that I was wandering off without seeing it. I looked down, recognizing myself on the middle of the road. I jolted to the loud honking of a large truck, which was driving down the road I happened to be on. I watched the headlights brighten like the silver gates of the Promise Land opening rather quickly.

It was until that moment when someone behind me wrapped himself around my body as we both launched from the road and onto the other side of the street. I landed on both hands as the fall made the cigarette projected from my mouth and skipped across the concrete. My eyes reviewed the truck quickly driving by as it continued hooting.

"Fuck you, nigga!!" The fellow roared as I turned to realize who it was. He was tanned-skinned, wore a red hoodie, black cargo shorts, blue and black sneakers and had on gold necklaces around his neck. He turned to me and asked, "Yo Kev, you good?"

"Aye, I'm good. Thanks, Snake!" I said.

"No prob, man! But you gotta watch out! This ain't a meadow!" He warned.

"Right. I know." I replied. "I must have trailed off again with another episode."

"You good. C'mon! Let's go." He said as we both got on our feet and trailed off from the scene. After he helped medicated me with water and white pills asenapine, we continued to walk down the streets, only we were pacing more than we should. Snake was a strict one, but he always understood when he had to be. He turned to me and asked, "So...listen, bro; were you able to get the dough?"

"Hell yeah! That old bloke was hard to convince at first! But I managed to get him to give in!" I replied. "I've got six hundred!"

"You shitting me, man? Six hundred?!" He asked. His eyes widened slightly. "Didn't think that much!"

"Yeah, I figured that it'd be enough to pay off the other hood bastards to leave us alone! And given how much evidence we've left a bit after the job at the Dime Community Bank, I figured that we could avoid more eyes from the police by getting money where they least expect. Not likely for a police officer to search a church."

"Right. We rob more banks; we'll be dead for sure. To be fair, what I'm trying do...is to make amends for him, especially before we go! I know I never told you ahead of time. My bad. See, there's a party going on at the Tobacco Warehouse and the Red Puddles are waitin' at this moment! And we ain't givin' 'im an ounce we have from the crib." Snake said.

"Snake, you know how I feel about parties! I get...awkward. I don't feel comfortable with other people!" I complained.

"I know, man! But we ain't got a choice. We gotta be there. You could stick by me to feel comfortable, aight?

"Fine. I suppose it'll be good to avoid bloodshed as well!" I alarmed. We both chuckled as we quickly paced ourselves.

The Red Puddles were a gang that Snake, and I scammed for money. We scammed at least three hundred dollars from when they robbed the Santander Bank. We made the leader of the gang Beelzebub go into his, only for him to gradually realize that we cheated him for his money. Because of this, they hunted us for weeks.

So, it was good on Snake to owe him money, especially learning that the leader was turning to the gang life to get money; only to help his mother get the operation she needed. Snake's sole reason to make money was the reason I also had after my turn of events. It was why I fell with him; to run far away from people. Somewhere truly remote with only two of us. I would've gotten the rest of my inheritance money, but I couldn't risk be found and caught by the police. So, we robbed banks masked. I was under the alias Kelvin Conroy. Escaped before the law could get us. Making as much as possible just to be revived in a new life without humanity.

It felt like a long time, but we finally got there. From there, the Brooklyn Bridge was at sight. We were almost late. As I looked past the brick made arches, a lot of blokes were there, waiting for our arrival. Each corner of the place had rusty barrels, blazing with the scorching infernos. I saw the embers levitating towards the sky.

Snake brought me over to the bloke. I watched him turned towards one of the other gang members. He said to them, "This here my boy, Kevin P! A.k.a....Kelvin Conroy! He the one I told you about!"

"Ain't that so?" The leader, with his red puffy jacket, said. I stood and saw the others looking at me anxiously. I walked towards him, and my eyes met the leader's brown eyes. His head was cocked sideways with a grin. I inserted my hands into my jacket and took out the six hundred dollars.

"I knew you's a rich boy when Snake told me 'bout your fam! You best hope Snake ain't takin' advantage of you!" He warned.

"If he was, I would know. And...possibly slam a bat onto his skull. But luckily, I took that initiative to do it anyway... as opposed to seeing him rejected or killed by your men. So here," I said as I handed him the money.

"Don't bother counting it like a greedy Jew. It's six hundred total. Do what you will with that."

"I'll take your word for it, but Imma do it anyway...in case yo money-bag ass is lyin'!" He said. He looked down at the money as he passed one dollar to another, seeing if the amount was exact. I felt my chest beating in anticipation, waiting for his reaction.

I sincerely hoped that it was accepted because I worked my way to retrieve the money the bastard Harris kept from me. Stillness was present around us while the stereos were playing distantly. My heart stopped once I saw him stop and look towards me.

He then grinned back at Snake and came closer only to give a salute to the man. "Looks like we could call it even, cuz! Bygones be bygones. Hope you stay warm in Iceland! I assume it's cold, hence the name."

"Nice!" Snake said. He smiled at me as I smiled back. We were all walking from the outside to the warehouse, still active and jumping with youthful glee.

"Now why we wastin' time here, man! Let's celebrate this unity...like motherfuckin' animals!!! My mom's gonna be better, y'all!" The red coat wearing leader roared as the crowd cheered after we entered. The bass grew bigger as the music caused the ground to vibrate, shaking the floor as if an earthquake was approaching. It was an orgy of blokes dancing and flaying to the rhythm.

As I reassembled with my group, I was greeted with cheers.

"Yo, you the fuckin' man, Kev! I knew you too good for this!" Snake exclaimed. His buffy arm hung around my shoulder with a drink in the other hand. He patted me with his beer holding hand almost aggressively, in a means for encouragement. "Whoo!!!"

We all strolled across the strobe light covered floors and sat down at an empty wooden table engraved with graffiti. I sat in the middle and watched as bottles were being passed around and the conversations on each of my two ears. I even saw four of Snake's friends who helped us robbed banks; including the Dime Community Bank. An African American women name Laquita, a Hispanic name Jose, and a bloke from Tennessee named Jim.

They all greeted me with smiles of delinquents enjoying being away from a city ran by crooked cops and bastard politicians. As I felt the shattered pieces of ice consuming the glass bottle, I took a great look around to see the people dancing and jumping to the booming stereos.

Others were standing by as all conversations were happening in one area. All the others lounged about, celebrating the non-existence of order, categories, or life's feeble brother. Putting my disdain for people aside, I saw them as equals; knowing that in their own way...they hated the outside world and wanted to escape as well. It was strange for some-one like me, who came from the upper class, attracted the misfortunes of society. Even when they were alive, my family seemed to attract the disenfranchised. Most anyway. There was a shortage of those who called themselves authorities on our side, for we were held to no high regard despite being rich.

A smile curved across my face, knowing that there was no sign of godly motifs or priests ridiculing me for what I've become. There were no traitorous guardians. It was just people living the lives they wanted with no consequence. Something that was important to us. As well as a future where we could live freely and become our own kings and queens.

After I proceeded to open my bottle, the hand of Snake alerted me on my shoulder as I turned to him and asked, "What do you think, man?"

"What do you mean?"

"All...this? This...kind of lifestyle?"

As I pondered, I said to him, "It's...liberating. I feel like I have some part in this shitty world. Thanks to you."

Placing his bottle down, Snake then said, "You're gonna do your fam proud, bruh! You and I, we're outlaws of this world. So why not tell it to go fuck itself? And soon, once we go back to get your inheritance tomorrow, we'll be livin' good in Iceland for sure. I googled and saw a spec of land...somethin' call...Skinnalón...I don't know if that is pronounced. But that is where we'll go for sure. It's an untouched zone for dudes like us to rest in peace! We'll go there, my homie!"

"I...I hope so. I really do," I replied with a quivering smile. It was almost gone just the pure reflection of how my family would see me. But I quickly got it all together. I watched as some folks were discarding from my presence and onto the colored dance floor. Snake turned to me and asked, "But for now.... you wanna go dance?! Music's lit!"

"I'm good. Thanks. I'll just sit here!" I shouted amongst the loud music. I watched as he nodded and turned his back on me along with the others. I sat back and watched the people raved across the floor. It just reminded me of how much I was happy to come across him. I wouldn't say he was likable by most. But he taught me things that I wouldn't have known to begin with. He sheltered me. Fed and took care of me. I learned how to fight for my own free will. I learned how to be my own man and not to let it be threatened. I learned to develop a philosophy of my own without any bloody political or religious influence.

I normally didn't like being surrounded by people. But being with Snake, Laquita, Jose, and Jim were enough to keep me decently sane. Because they were willing and persistent to challenge and condemn civilization's blatant hypocrisy. Unlike the moronic masses who complied to their hypocrisy.

I was glad not to be a part of it. And to think I missed out on this kind of freedom by playing the good Christian boy to better a churlish world behind the lens of the upper class. So, I gave up on bettering it. I chose to exit from it, seeing how it was destined to be destroyed. Knowing that my family was gone and knowing I had no chance in making a mark in the world, there was no point in staying. That was I believed humanity wanted. And it made sense; humanity didn't seem to care about the wellbeing of it anymore. I didn't need to pray to God to abolish it with a flood, hailstones, or some other apocalyptic element in the Bible. The collective of humans was doing that themselves; making me realize how pointless humankind was. Thus, making life pointless.

Minutes have flown by like birds flying across the clouds after I pondered. In my mind, I was very thankful that the shadows weren't seen anywhere near me. There was no sign of them at all. It was just the sound of "Kid Cudi" playing abruptly in the background. I forgot which song, but I think it was revolving around a revolution. Perhaps. I didn't really remember.

As I was to take my second sip of the half full bottle, I got up just to get some air from outside. It was a bit much to take in all the energies happening at once. And I couldn't help but feel like a wallflower. I didn't wish to stand out.

Revealing my box, I unveiled one more cigarette to toke before I went back inside. As soon as I was inhaling the warmth of the tobacco, I felt my mind hammering inside my head. I palmed my temple and closed my eyes, as the migraine was gradually increasing.

"Audite custodes tui Listen to your guardians"

Dammit, I thought! I spoke too soon about those bastards. They came back! Their shadowy figures were all around the party, as if they were taking the people hostage. I looked into their menacing red eyes overshadowed with their hats and surrounded with a misty black haze shaped like fire.

The voices started to come back sooner, but the figures kept staring at me that everything else around me almost stopped moving. I turned around and saw that the party was slowly transforming into what appeared to be a memory of a place I tried extremely hard to repress. I suddenly heard the faint hysterically and blood-coiling sounds of what seemed like children. Men and women also. Authoritative figures roaring in panic, telling all the people to exit the building. Three times, a sudden sound came almost like a cannon going off. Like rapid blood vessels slithering inside of your eye, or a herd of roots cultivating the brittle dirt, these sounds grew louder and were caving in my head.

NO! Please! A young man shouted. Almost a distressed cry for mercy. And it took me a few seconds to realize that it was...me.

"Why are you doing this?" I asked, almost on a verge of breaking down. I clawed and gripped onto my loosen hair. My eyes became black when I closed my lids tightly.

"Because you left them behind! You became irredeemable to change! You left them to suffer by sobering yourself in your own burdens! You choose to escape!"

"No! I didn't leave them!" I exclaimed to the distorted voices. "I didn't!"

"Yes...you...have!!! And you couldn't do what they asked. To do well for the world! Now you will die a pathetic boy! Alone! Delusional! Self-righteous! All you have done will be in vain! As if the ones you love, the family you love, existed for nothing!"

"Leave me alone!!" I shouted on top of my lungs that I realized that I caused the party to come to a brief halt. All eyes were focused on me backed up with confused murmurs from the other people.

I quickly dashed away from the crowd to isolate in the complete darkness. I sat down by the edge of the boardwalk, glancing down at the glistening water flowing under the bridge.

I heard the party then resumed back to its state while I sat away, avoiding the crowd. I felt ashamed to show my face around them. I was getting tired of these figments following me. Even when I was trying to have fun. Or to have a smoke. I sat and hugged my knees. For the most part, the moving cars far out on the Brooklyn Bridge smoothened me. I needed something slow but repetitive to calm my nerves, almost like a symbolic lullaby. But the remains of those memories were still in my head and forced my eyes to well up.

"Yo, Kev." I turned to the voice, which came from Snake. His face was filled with concern.

"Oh, hey mate. I'm fine." I faked my smile. With shame and embarrassment, I turned from him a bit, "Just...another episode."

After he pondered, he said, "Listen, we could all go back to the crib if this is too much for you. Ain't nothin' to be ashamed of. I...I feel bad for bringing you too much company. I just hoped to...cheer you up."

"No...no, I'm fine. Really. I'm grateful...Snake. I...I just need a few more bottles, I think." I requested.

"I got chu, man." He said as he quickly got back to the party. I looked back on him going into the crowd and I faced the trees, making sure that I was mesmerized. I was eased down a notched after my outrageous breakdown.

Snake then approached me once again as I watched him with four bottles wrapped around with his fingers. He then placed them down next to me. After pulling the pill jar from his pocket and placing them with the bottle, he nodded to me and said, "I'll be there if you need anything. Don't let them episodes get you down, aright?"

I nodded back with a smile as I watched him taking off. After popping the pills, I grabbed one of the bottles and began chugging down the poignant taste of pint. I was hoping that if I drank enough, I would repress those shadows. Including the memories. I just wanted them to go away somehow. I mean how else was I supposed to rid of them?

For the next few minutes, I have been shoving down liquefied grains down my supple throat. I gave in to the consumption until most of my shirt was moist with the drops of the beer. Time flew by quicker as I failed to notice due to my mind being on the brink of pure drunkenness. Each sip I take of each bottle, it made the environment around me hazy and smeared like smudges of paint on a painting plate. My mind felt extremely heavy, and all sounds and vibrations became disconnected from their fundamental flows.

Soon enough, I felt my body regurgitating a chunk of fluid, which came bursting from my lips as I bloated it all out that it puddled across the concrete to the water down below. The horrible display was bright yellow with other chunks of what were remains of other food I stuffed into my stomach. I soon accidently slammed my hand on the empty bottles and gradually redden my hands as I tried to lay down. My eyes grew heavy that I could barely keep them open to witness the crimson discharge escaping my hand. I couldn't resist. All I had to do was to let it be, it was a way to rest. Even on dirty concrete as the party was going on. Even the sound of the gathering progressively disappeared until there was no sound in any manifestation.

Despite the pain I endured myself in, I was just glad that these shadows were gone. I just hoped and dreamed that they wouldn't come back.

My eyes opened slowly to the glaring light from the sun, making me realize that hours flew by like wind and it was morning already. The sun was blooming the skies with orange that was warm. There was yelling in the background. Some screams were full of melancholy, as if they were getting kidnapped. Some screams sounded with revolt. Getting myself together, I stood up slowly while keeping my balance. Palming my head, it was filled with boulders that integrated with my brain due to how heavy it felt.

As I watched very closely, I recognized flashing red and blue light flipping in the distance. Some of my fellow mates were held at gun-point, as they lied flat on their stomachs. Suddenly, each officer was placing them in what happened to be a police van colored in white and blue.

I wasn't going to just stand by and let them be forced like that. Regardless of my drunkenness, I stumbled quickly as I tried to sprint to assault the uniformed officers. I watched as two of them noticed me and demanded stoically, "Stop where you are, and let me see those hands!"

"Don't do anything!" The other cop said, aiming his pistol at me. "Just put your hands up this instant!"

I stood and thought of an insult for them. But the best way was just to be basic, just so they got the message. Coincidently, there was an empty beer bottle next to me. They were gaining closer to me very slowly as if I was a wild animal. Picking it up from the cement and slamming it onto the ground, I shouted, "Fuck you!"

I raced towards them, preparing to jab one of them with the broken bottle. One of them swayed right behind me. I was prepared until I felt something sharp piercing onto my back and stirring my bones.

"Ahhh!!" I yelped in pain. It appeared to be a Taser gun that caused me to go down onto the ground. I struggled constantly to escape the grasps of the officers. I felt cuffs being attached to each wrist. One of them roughly grabbed me from the ground by holding my arm tightly. The other aimed his gun as a threat.

"We tried to tell you. Looks like you'll never learn." He said unremorsefully, shoving me in the back of the car and closing it on me. I didn't regret it, as if he might have hoped. I was still keen to find a way to get my comrades and myself a way to escape the situation. I was hopeful, without any thought of faith but pure expectation, that they wouldn't keep us like we're dogs in a pound.

II

"Audi Custodes Tui"

Snake and I were held inside the Attica Correctional Facility, after a drive from the warehouse. I would like to think that Harris was the person who presumably ratted us out. But I didn't have the thought. Otherwise, I would have murdered him before he could ever die from natural causes. I was now a public enemy and no longer favored by some. My reputation was mixed, which resulted to me entering a cold interrogation room.

Draped in white clothing with handcuffs, with my bandaged hands, I sat in front of a wrinkled old white man with a grey suit and a clipboard in his hands. My head was still heavy from the heavy consumption. It was awful to be surrounded by those in uniform. I was being observed and held up like a rare animal. It angered me badly, but I had to keep cool for now. I had to listen to what the man had to say.

"Now, Kevin. The reason why we have you here is because...we believe that we could give you a second chance to do things right. Most of us, at least, were familiar with your parents. Your mother...was such a fabulous singer of this age. I know you probably don't want to be here, but we have no other choice but to keep you in custody. You've committed many felonies and crimes whilst on the run. And it seems clear that you are unstable to function in society. We've been searching for you for thirteen years. All we want from you is to cooperate, so we could find out what to do with you. You think you could do that?" He asked.

After sighing grimly, I replied, "I'm all ears; momentarily."

"Don't be a wise ass. Ain't the time for that!" One of the officers sternly reminded me.

"This is all in the matter of knowing who you are just, so we could find out...well, what have you become and find a somewhat way to help you. We wouldn't want to dismiss you as another child of a celebrity coming down to misfortunes. You're better than that. At least I think so. Now.... to start off." He then licked his lips and read from the clipboard. "Based on this information, you were born in Manchester, England. But you and your sister were both raised in Long Island, New York. We know that your grandfather was the city's mayor in the 80s. After your family's death during a school shooting at the Green Vale School, the private school you and your sister both went to, your guardian was Father Harris of St. Charles Borromeo Cathedral, who got you into the very private Catholic Keeper Home; which you...ran away from. Mind telling us why?"

I looked around the room, briefly disregarding the camera focusing on my face from the right corner. I ignored the bitter faces of the officer. I knew that I had to tell him eventually. There was no other way to lie or runaway. I had to play along until it the right time to get myself out from the room.

I replied, "I felt...betrayed."

"Betrayed? How?" He asked, leaning against the desk while tapping his pen on the table.

"I just felt betrayed. By God. By those who I thought were my friends. I couldn't stay there! So...I chose to be my own God. I was fixated on this life. It felt liberating."

"And it says that you allegedly suffered cases of physical and verbal abuse by some of the staff members at the foster care?" He stated, gazing at my eyes. "Why didn't you call your guardian to file a report?"

"I was prevented from doing so! They would beat me if I did! I couldn't use any form of contact."

"Really? Is that so? Why didn't you go to a phone booth after you escaped? Wouldn't it have been simpler to reach us or your guardian?"

"What...you actually give a damn? C'mon! Everyone knows how your system works! You break your own rules when it's challenged!" I said through chuckles. "Even if I told you, showed you evidence, you wouldn't care! So...I didn't bother! Why do you care? I thought I was being interrogated, not counseled."

The man glanced at the other officers and looked back down at his clipboard. "Kevin, the reason I'm asking this next question is because...conditioned actions are often caused by people with severe mental illness. Nothing to be ashamed of. So, have you been suffering from complex traumatic disorder? Mental breakdowns, violent outbursts, nightmares, panic attacks. They're all written in the report of what you have presented."

I shrugged, though I did wonder about the name for it.

"Symptoms of...psychosis? It's written...in the report that you have...auditory hallucinations. Is this what caused you...to commit those felonies? Was this...also enhanced by the abuse? Without medication?"

Again, I shrugged.

"Is it possible that the abuse has enhanced your condition? Have you...always had this since childhood?"

Without giving him eye contact, I shrugged carelessly again.

"Okay", he said, writing down something on his clipboard. "I'll take that as a yes."

"I didn't say anything. I just shrugged. I know cops are crooked, but not stupid."

"Watch your smart-ass mouth, man," One of the angry cops behind me slammed his fist on the table, expecting me to flinch.

"Or what, you'll beat me? Go ahead! Unless your bollocks are shriveled like horses." When I said that, I felt him tug onto the back of my shirt. When the investigator silently told him not to do anything, I felt him release me.

The investigator continued, "Theft, robberies, conning, pimping prostitutes occasionally, and several killings all within thirteen years.

That's very versatile...all just to get to Iceland, apparently. Knowing Snake, from the many times he was arrested, it was only a matter of time he'd drag someone like you into his career. You robbed the Dime Community Bank. Plenty of banks like it too, most of which we are trying to obtain over $400,000 you've stolen. On top of that, you've committed three to eleven counts of murder. The first are two clergies from the Catholic home: Gerald Gregory and Ann Belford. You and Snake unremorsefully and brutally murdered them, stealing their funds. Those are the people who abused you?"

I sighed, "What do you think? You expect them to run free.... after what they've done? Abuse gets you off, don't it?"

Instead of answering the question, he then continued with the report. "The report also says that you murdered Talia Greyhill, a seventeen-year-old girl and a prostitute in Brooklyn. It was said that her body was found with severe bruises around her neck in the apartment."

"She disrespected me! As if she knows what was best for me! She had it coming!" I yelped. "Sex was all she was good for in this world."

"Right." He said, almost detached from his feelings. What he was doing was not to my liking, but I had to sit through it. I was most curious about who got me in this prison in the first place. And my mind automatically thought about Harris. He did say that he was going to contact them.

"Did he do it?" I asked.

"Who?" He asked.

"Harris, Father Harris. He was the one that called you and got us arrested. And he gave you that information. Am I right?"

Placing his clipboard down, he said, "Normally, I would say that I am the one who asks the questions. But I'll make an exemption for now. Snake also added his two cents to the information. But with that being said...about Harris...even if he did what he did, was he wrong to do that?"

"Oh...so he did snitch."

"He did it for your own good. And plus, you did assault him for your family's inheritance. At least be thankful he didn't leave you to be killed on the streets."

"I rather be dead than to live like a rat in a cage!" I rebelled. I saw the man sighing in agony.

"Hey! Watch your mouth, goddammit!" One black officer, who looked to be in his mid-twenties, demanded, echoing the entire room. "I'm about to kick your self-pityin' ass! You think you're smart with your philosophy lessons! You came from wealth. Don't act like you struggle! You don't get to say that shit! You rich folks always making an excuse for your actions!"

"If you think that I am exempt from suffering because of the status I came from, I feel sorry for you. Status stops us from seeing humanity in one another. But go ahead. I could tell you're a rookie." I said as he sucked on his teeth. I continued with a scoff, "Don't talk to me about status, misbegotten abortion."

Before he could speak, he sighed once more. He then added, "Listen, you don't know how sorry we are about your family. About what you've gone through. It's always hard to repress something you once saw. Especially as a kid. You've had it very rough, no doubt about it. Your father served this country well. And your mother...seemed to be a great singer, even if most of us didn't hear her much. But just because they're gone, it doesn't give you an excuse to commit these serious felonies that hurt your record. I may not be a religious man, but if I were, I wouldn't think that is something God would want. We would've had those clergies arrested and put on trial, had you not played judge, jury, and executioner. Sometimes in life, you just need to...move on. Getting angry, holding it in and taking it out on others isn't gonna make it feel any better. Nor it won't help you. It'll make you no better than the killer who committed that mass murder in your school fourteen years ago."

Before I could let him go on with his dribble, I said, "I suppose that's life. And you like it that way...because it gives you an excuse. Yet, you act as if you care about morals when it's bloody convenient. Law and order, my arse."

"Okay...let's talk *ethically*, sort to speak. Firstly, I wouldn't say that I like how life is, but it is what it is. And yes, as someone obviously in law...I stand for morals. But not everyone here does. I can't change that. You can't change what happened...nor can you change people, Kevin. Can't expect this world to be perfect to you. Only you could be what you want from the world. I think...Gandhi said something in the vein of that. I don't know. All I'm saying is it's always best to accept that it happened and to move on. Understand that not everyone in this world is a monster. Do you understand?"

I sighed heavily, absorbing all of what the officer said. I felt my eyes burning with fumes of Edward Thatch himself. Who would just *accept* what happen? Knowing that you were defenseless and were forced to watch those you love to die right in front of you? And yet, the bastard had the nerve to tell me to *accept it*.

Releasing my breath, I then replied, "I understand. But...you're not sorry. Not really. If you were sorry, I wouldn't be here. My parents would still be dancing with each other in our living room. My sister would still be playing on the backyard we use to have. We could've been the family we set out to be. But you couldn't let us have that. You weren't there in time when they were murdered. And you have the nerve to tell me that you're sorry? I wish it was you and your family. See how it feels. So, who are you to tell me to accept what happened? I bet you never liked my family! I bet you're glad they died! Just like every-one else is! Because all you do is enable evil as a norm! Don't bloody kid yourself. You're just a stupid officer. If I needed coddling, I'd go to a therapist. And they barely do a damn thing to help you! You think you know me based on those files, television, and status, but you don't! Okay? You don't! So, don't act as if you do!"

I then turned my face towards the officers and asked, "Are we done here? I'm ready to go back to my cell."

I glanced at the investigator landing his face on his hand, gesturing the guards to take me back.

I felt the arms of the officers grasping me away from my room and back to the white-lit hallways. I presumed that he was tired of my arrogance and rebellion. But I honestly didn't care about how he felt. But he did have a point. All my life after what happened, I allowed anger to get my way all the time. But the respect that I've earned, and the obedience of others wasn't bothersome. Like how I felt as though Harris only used God to block me from what the world really was, and the idea of God was nothing but to make cope with it. And I assumed that my parents were given false hope and thus met their ends. With that evidence, how was I not allowed to have vein attributes towards God?

I never thought that I would be glad to be back in my cell than to last another minute with a fat bloke asking questions. It was clear that these people wanted me to change; only to comply with their twisted and godless society. It was not about how I felt. It was about how they felt by my actions affecting them and their *precious* civilization.

The adrenaline in me was desperate to break out. I needed to get out from the blasted facility, but it seemed impossible. The least I needed was a rest. I hummed a song with my eyes closed. It was song that my mother used to sing to my sister and I. And all I ever did, when I am alone in my contained cell, was reflect to those days repressing those shadows from my head.

A knock emerged through my door, which alarmed me to open my eyes. It interrupted my comfort, bringing me back to reality. I turned my head, sat up and saw that a guard made that knock. "It's time for lunch! Get up!"

I did as ask, having the guard to open the cell door with his key.

I was later escorted with a couple of guards to the cafeteria. The entire area was filled with other men with white garments that it was barely possible to differentiate which one was Snake and which wasn't.

"Fuck up, and you'll get it. You understand?" One guard warned me sternly into my left ear.

"As you wish," I smirked. But if any other bloke were to put my nerves in stake, then I would have to break that promise.

Since the guards left me alone, the cooks behind the counter gave us the usual kind; dreadfully made macaroni and cheese with meatloaf and fish sticks. I grabbed my aluminum tray, filled with what is likely to kill me and sat down at the corner of the populated room. I had the table all to myself.

As far as I known, Snake was the only friend I ever had. Ever since I've met him, I trusted him. I looked around and saw all the other prisoners cursing and bantering at each other. It would've been a softening day to listen to one of my mother's songs. But of course, the public I was surrounded with wouldn't want to listen to it. Conversations happened all at once. I observed and saw most prisoners shooting darkened glares and looks of disdain at me, only for them to turn their backs and pretend I didn't exist. Not that there was any loss. I was not born in the broken world for them. I just minded my own business as I proceeded to unintendedly kill myself by eating the food.

"Hey rich boy! Not feeling good at all, huh? Now that you don't got that scamming fuck with ya! Now you are just as pathetic as he is!" A random bloke said as he was suddenly coming to my personal space, like the typical dimwit he was. From his ignorant stance, I could tell right away that he was asking to be put down.

He was a tall lanky white man speaking jive. And I swore that I recognized who he was. Upon deep analyzation, I figured out who he was. "I would put your ass to the ground for what you did to my girl Talia! But don't worry; you better off rottin' here! Your ass ain't going nowhere! Serves ya right!"

"Serves me right, huh?" I smirked. "How ironic! We're in the same prison! You bloody bimbo! If anything, you are rotting here with me."

"I'm the bimbo?! I ain't the bimbo with the dead rich family that everyone forgot about. I ain't the bimbo who choked Talia to death!"

"Good to see you again, John Lee," I said to him.

"The fuck is wrong with you, man?" He asked almost in anger. Except, he smiled to hold it in.

I turned to him and said, "I did what I had to do. No one soils my family's name and gets away with it alive. Not even an ill-ridden bitch like her! Plus, she was a fool to think that our relationship actually meant something."

"But she was my girl!"

"She was mine too! And Snake's! C'mon, mate," I scoffed with a grin. "Don't pretend that you gave a damn about her dignity! You're her pimp! We all had her! You know that's all she was worth. I just wish I robbed her soon after." I paused just to let out a chuckle. I continued, "Anyway, what are you even in here for? Let me guess; they caught you driving your Camry with seventy pounds of cocaine, half to make a drug cartel from Guantanamo happy?"

He shied away a bit, knowing that was exactly what he was caught for. I scoffed and said, "Predictable."

"Fuck you! That was none of your business! You think just 'cause you got all the praise and the fame mean that nothin' could go wrong for y'all sorry asses?! Just 'cause you rich?! Well, look at chu now, my boy!"

"If you call the masses playing make believe with your family praise, bully for you. And I'm not even rich anymore! Rich people aren't exempt from suffering, as you would care to know!"

"Bullshit! Once a rich white boy, always a rich white boy!" He busted from his lips. "Don't deny it! You think you're so special! You and your faggot-ass family! Think you above everything! All you rich folks do!"

I scoffed at how pathetic he sounded. I hid my anger as best as I could and said, "Not really. They never said I was *special*. They just taught me how to stand my ground and not give in to moronic rejects like you. Low life miserable pieces of fading flesh who take their burdens onto others because they're scared shitless to amount to anything. You project your insecurities onto those who don't fall into your level because you're either afraid or too dumb to even notice you have a brain. Be thankful that you didn't spend your entire life watching your family being painted wrongfully by a system that you idiots support by simply staring at a stupid box with petty images mocking life. You couldn't leave us alone! So...why don't you redeem yourself ...and bugger off? Or Snake and I will escape this shithole to find...and fuck your mother's little fanny with a crowbar? See it bleed beautifully. Or better yet...how about I have a go, so I can hear her cry louder with sorrowful tears all...day...long?"

"Yo, don't talk about my mom like that, boy! Shut your fucking mouth!" He lashed at me, propelling himself from his seat. "Who the fuck you think you are?!"

"Oh dear. Did I touch a nerve? Here's what you do; fuck...off!" I finally lashed back and proceeded to chuckle that grew into a slight line of laughter at his pathetic nature. I throbbed to stop myself to turn away from his face.

He was then preparing to punch me and beat me to a pulp. "You don't tell me to fuck off! Who are you to tell me...?"

I grasped his upcoming thrash, grabbed my tray, and smacked him across the face with it, having my untouched food splattered all over the place. It was loud enough to catch the attention of the other inmates. I then stood up, over his flaying body, trying to get up. He tried to get me until I got on my knees and beat his face with the tray. Repeatedly I bashed, until his face gradually decayed and shed his blood all over the floor as his face was gradually disfiguring.

Hearing the prison guards trying to tackle me, I turned and threw my blood-covered tray at the face of one upcoming guard. I charged at him and began savagely attacking him as well. The other guard thrashed his baton on my head, several times to get me down! The pain of the baton made me submissive to their stern order. I was grabbed by two other guards and escorted out from the cafeteria. There was nothing but pure hatred and fire within me. All I thought of was blood.

"Out of the way!" Yelled the guards to the other prisoners as they obeyed in desperation. "Move!!"

In the night, I was placed inside a cold windowless room where I was forced to sleep inside a quiet solitary room for punishment. No proper bed other than a flat mattress. A silver toilet at the right corner. The room inside was dim, almost dark. It was quiet, cool, and bleak. I felt the chills piercing through my flesh like cold needles penetrating me. It was weirdly peaceful, yet painful as well. It was quiet and devoid of any sound but my rapid breathing as I sat and shivered my temple.

This sudden peace I had was inevitably destroyed. All the voices were once again cramped in my head. I had no other choice but to listen. To see through their nonsense. They repeated the same phrase over and over. But one of the voices started to sound familiar. Voices I haven't heard for the longest time. But they were hateful and bitter.

"Audite custodes tui Listen to your guardians"
"You're worthless and not a good brother! You betrayed us!"

"Audite custodes tui Listen to your guardians"
"We didn't raise you like this!"

"Audite custodes tui Listen to your guardians"
"Being angry is all he's good for! Hopeless."

"Audite custodes tui Listen to your guardians"
"You're no child of us! You're garbage! Dirt!"

It has gotten that bad to where my own family was ridiculing me! I knew I shouldn't be giving them power, but it felt real. It was as if I was sitting in front of them pathetically, berated and disowned by them. What made it worse what I once again was forced to hear them say that phrase. With nothing else to do, nothing to physically do to take this pain away, I broke down into sudden laughter as I was hugging my knees tightly against a wall dense as skulls. My face was hardened, and my throat was almost parched. I didn't know why I laughed. A laugh that gradually became louder as my heart and lungs were throbbing forward and lines of warm tears were relentlessly coming down my face. I didn't know why I laughed at all. Maybe it was how gratuitous the voices sounded. As if they came from a monster of some dreadful horror B-movie from the 80s. I had no real reason. I just felt the need to let it out since I was alone. I didn't seem to care anymore. I didn't care that my head felt looser than a slacken tooth. Or a balloon. I went with it.

The next morning, I was finally out of that bloody room and back in my cell. But the condition of my entire body was still very callous. At least it was nice of the guards to get me a towel to warm myself before I die. Outside my cell, I saw a familiar face talking with one of the guards. It appeared Harris was here to save my soul. Or so I thought.

"You've got a visitor."

I could see that, I said in mind. Had I said it out loud, I would risk myself getting another baton on my head.

Harris looked sad, still branding the bruise I gave him. I just sat there, looking at him with stone cold eyes. It was as if all remorse has been taken away from me. He sat beside me and took a deep breath.

"Come to offer me more Bible lectures," I asked coldly.

"No, I'm here to bid you...farewell." Harris said sadly. "I'm leaving New York. I'm resigning from the church and moving to Chicago. I have other duties awaiting. And I was called to serve another church."

"Why?" I asked.

"I have to rediscover what path God has made for me. Hopefully, this church will help me. I was in talk with Mr. Blackwater, the butler who retired after...after what happened. He promises to hold your inheritance. After you get help with dropped charges, he'll pick you up so you could go with him to his hometown in Maryland...to start a clean life," He said gloomily. "I feel like...he'll be better for you than me. He was firstly timid since he didn't know how to raise kids, but he wants to take that chance. After hearing that you were abused, I could've known. And I didn't. You have every right to be mad at me. To think I grew up in that place. At least, they told me that you would be given an insanity defense. So...you won't be here for too long. You'll be institutionalized at the Manhattan Psychiatric Center instead. In two weeks."

"Right, because I'm crazy." I scoffed and shrugged. "I'm a loony! Mad! Screwed up! Is that it?"

"No, because they believe that you could still get help despite what you have done. It was either that...or a lethal injection." He said sternly. "Some people know that you are good, Kevin. And that some should be enough for you to be gratified. You've just allowed the burdens of the entire world to inflict on you. And worsen you in many ways imaginable."

He sighed and brought up, "I know why you wanted your parent's inheritance money. They told me that you and Snake...plan to live in Iceland."

When he told me this, I simply asked, "Why did you do this to me? Putting me here?"

"Because I cannot let you hurt others, Kevin. After what happened to that poor girl Talia. You've become...deranged." He said. "And you're wanted. So even if you try to go to Iceland somehow, they will still send every force of the state to get you for what you did. You're young. And you're doing these acts because of your anger. And your *friend* has done nothing but egg in your anger for his own advantage. I understand your pain. I truly do! And it hurts me every day. But you don't know everything about the world yet to hate it. You have yet to know."

I sneered to that nonsense and said, "I know enough! Snake told me everything about people like you! And I will continue running! Anywhere is better than being a part of a failed species that needs to kill itself. To end its pathetic misery fast. Maybe then...life could be good. Not to mention...quiet and peaceful, given how noisy they are too. I want nothing more than to use this planet as a canvas so I could paint it with their blood when they are nothing but sludgy waste. Nuisances! All of them!"

"Kevin, that's enough!" He yelled as his voice echoed in the cell. As he let out a sigh, he said, "Look...I am...I understand that you may never get your faith back because of what happened. And it's my fault. But all I'm asking you...is for your forgiveness. Serving as a chaplain in the army was holding me back from seeing you. I was so tangled in work, tried to do what I did for your father. And I know that I failed. I shouldn't have put you in that place. I know this world has been hard. I just...pray that it will get easier for you...when you get help. I pray that...you learn how to live for yourself. I...I loved you as you were my own, Kevin. I still do. Always will. And I hope you find it in your heart to forgive me for not being there."

Secretly, it scorched my heart the moment his watery eyes began to release tears from his sockets as they poured down his face. I honestly didn't know what I had to say to that. It came to show that he honestly did care. He did risk everything to make me belong somewhere, to make me happy and to make me see the best in people. But he should've known. And my heart was broken to absorb all of what he was trying to do. I was completely devoid to feel any sentiment.

And I responded by saying, "Everything is dead to me, Harris. God is dead. This world...is going to die. I see it now. And honestly, I'll be happy to see it die. And everyone in it. No afterlife, just...a hollow vast ocean of darkness where it belongs. What do I owe this world? What do I owe those within it? My flesh, my blood? I've wanted to grow and help people. I wanted to help my parents. Together, we intended to help the world. And what do we get in return? Bullets, media bullying, a dead god...and now...a padded room." Those words coming from my mouth made his skin flesh out. I continued with no remorse nor hesitation, "I don't forgive you. You were the only one left in this world that I could trust; considered you a part of our family. You betrayed me. Just as God betrayed my family that night. You're just like the others. So...don't call me Kevin. He's dead. He died...along with his faith in...in everything."

"No, he is still alive! He is! He is just lost in a very dark place! And he must be found again!" Harris cried almost tearfully. "No matter where. No matter how. But he needs to be found. He needs to... to be happy and well when I see him again."

After I sighed, I simply replied and stared into his welling eyes, "Then go find him." My lips trembled as my voice did. I swallowed down a lump that was nearly making me choke up.

"Look, I...I ask you not to pity me. I only ask for you to understand."

KEVIN PRINCETON - 31

He then said through sadness after sighing, "But...just know that whatever happens, I promise that you will finally be happy and in peace again. I've never forgotten about you. And I won't. I pray that you won't...forget about me." He then proceeded to hug me. Though I accepted his hug, I chose not to hug him back. He then released me and got up. His eyes were very broken and full of so much regret. At that time, I wanted him to feel that way. I wanted him to suffer with those regrets, so he could feel bad for what he had done.

Before he could ever take off, I had to ask something that needed to be cleared. "I just need to know one thing before you go." I said coldly. He turned to me and asked, "What is it?"

"The voices in my head keep repeating this phrase; Audi custodes tui? What does it mean?"

"It's Latin for... Listen to your guardians. I hope that helps. God bless you and everything you do, Kevin. I wish you well." It was the last time I ever saw him once he walked out of my cell. I was just glad that I was not going to see him again. He was the very last one whom I had faith in. Yet, he failed me.

But I was thankful to finally understand the meaning of that praise; listen to your guardians. I just thought that it was perhaps another way for God to mess with me. It was not like it was going to be pivotal in my endeavors. I just regarded it as just a silly nonsensical phrase. Nothing more.

It was one week later after Harris left. Yet, I was still held here, draped in a white outfit like I'm in a totalitarian film of some sort. But I grew to care less about it. I lied on my bed, contemplating on how I was going to get out. Or how was I going to die. My eyes were closed, and my body was still. All I thought about going to Iceland. Even if I had to die going there. I hoped to find a remote area for both Snake and I not to only be truly happy, but to be far from any contact from everyone else. Including those I thought were friends. I imagined myself at an Icelandic farm or something far wilder for us to be ourselves without the pressures from others.

Even though I was going to be institutionalized in a psychiatric hospital, I knew for sure that I was going to be confined. Just as I was confined in this cell, forced to embrace every burden and filth that was bestowed on me. The world was full of conformity, and it was slowly catching up with me. I was forced to have these memories. To embrace the pain of the past. To embrace the filth of humanity. It was clearly something I couldn't escape from. I was to be mocked for all eternity. The one and only solution I saw was to leave for Iceland. It was either that...or death. Only, I didn't want to die. Not because I was afraid, I just didn't see no point in it anymore. I used to believe that there could be another world out there after my life. A fulfilling place where we could live in a better world of peace. But not anymore. Even so, it didn't matter. My family and I've became ghosts.

Suddenly, the alarm sounded, and the horns touted loudly that it prompted me to get down from the chair. I darted my eyes through the window and looked outside of my cell. Nothing but chaos and savagery were displayed. I saw officers running left and right, shouting all about. I turned to the right and saw a person I was familiar with. I was thankful to realize that it was Snake; he was coming for me.

He was seen carrying a fire extinguisher and he muffled, "Stand back!"

I listened despite barely hearing him through the glass. The cling sounded as the door was being forced opened. After it was forced open, Snake came in and asked whilst panting, "You good, man?" He held onto a black duffle bag, presumably with our things and clothes in it.

"Now I am! What's going on?" I asked, as I got out from the cell.

"There's a riot goin' on! This is our chance to getting out! Now be ready, Kev! We gettin' outta here," Snake said with a smile. "I got one of them keys to the car!"

Afterwards, I left my cell to make our way through what was indeed havoc. There were prisoners and guards fighting one another. It looked like a massive battle. I asked, passing through cell through cell, "But...I don't understand! How did you get to the other building?! We were separate from one another."

"Not really the best time to answer that shit! We gotta..." Snake was interrupted by a group of guards who suddenly spotted us trying to escape.

"STAY WHERE YOU ARE!!!" They shouted with demand.

"Aye, probably the wrong time to ask! Let's go!" I said, proceeding to run through the prison to escape them. Though the guards were approaching as fast as they humanly could, the riot was at least a distraction for them. The carnage was nonstop and continuous as we pass through every stanched kitchen, blocky corridor, and dirt smeared hall to find a way out from the prison. And every interior was occupied by feuds between corrupt guards and anarchic inmates. A flew bullets passed by as well as bloodshed by both inmates and guards. I'd assumed that how this riot started would remain a mystery.

Being that we were rebellious blokes, who were carefree, it allowed us to run acrobatically throughout the prison while disarming the guards to inhabit their pistols. Snake still held onto the bag. We swiftly but sloppily ran past from the cells, entering ghostly bleak hallways. Everything was smeared as we paced ourselves quickly through the dim hallways, avoiding the clutches of the guards. The sound of the police came, hallowing harshly for us to stop. We ran and ran, passing while battling through the pursuing guards from left and right to finally get to the outdoors. Snake managed to close the door, picked up a random rod from the floor and blocked the door handle.

Through the parking lot, we got into the closest cop car we could find. As we entered in, Snake started the car. He looked back to make sure that the cops were chasing us. Thus, he accelerated the car as the police continued shooting. Busting through the gates, we drove away from Attica. On the move, we thought that it would be a good idea to drive on the highway, especially to avoid the workings of the inner city. Though the roads were packed, we used the millions driving cars on the road as an advantage to get the herd of police cars off our tail.

We wooed and cried in victory. I wrapped my arms around his upper body. I was going to be alive after all. Alive and away from mankind.

"Thanks lad! I didn't even know this would happen!" I said.

"You could thank me later, man!"

"Now we need a place to lay low!" I said

"We can go back to our crib!" Snake suggested.

"Yeah! And get shot on the spot! C'mon, mate! They'll catch us then!" I said.

"You got any bright ideas!?" He asked me, with puckered lips.

I thought quickly as I looked right behind the car to see if there were any other cop cars behind us. I thought back quickly, seeing what a place could be where the police couldn't possibly find us or even go to for that matter.

When I was thinking, I was sometimes off by the loud cry of the sirens coming from the police cars. But despite the heavily packed roads populated with cars, buses, and truck, during monumental architectures of glass and stone, Snake would always find a way to outsmart the so-called authorities. I helped by erecting myself from the open window of the front seat next to him. He hastily gave me his pistol, a black .375 Magnum. A decent, but powerful six shooter.

I tried my best to scare them off by firing three at each oncoming car. Some of the bullets plastered onto the hoods, making enough damage to their engines from within. Crashing and colliding their cars onto other vehicles, causing a gradual domino effect and chain reaction of demolition. Screams, shouts, and cries were heard another the wailing sirens. "This is the Police! Stop where you are," the other oncoming police from the car demanded, but we weren't going to give no quarter. Show no mercy. Show no fear. Soon, a thought came into my head.

"Ramapo! We should get to Ramapo!" I said as I got back on my seat.

"The hell is Ramapo?" Snake asked.

"Camping place! We could hide there! They wouldn't think to find us there!" I suggested. But the silence suggested otherwise. Snake was obviously rethinking. He turned to me briefly with uncertainty riddled across his face.

"It's the only place I know! And it's far from the city!" I suggested once again. Snake looked back at the bustling roads and looked back at me through the front mirror. He then asked, "How far is it?"

"Pretty far!" I asked. "Probably just one hour from where we are!"

Still processing the idea of hiding out in a far place in New York, he finally came to say, "Let's get there, then! Ramapo, it is!"

Accelerating, we were passing through the streets, finding a way to get from the big rough city of New York to the calm and very immersive forest.

We were later driving from the city into the woods. It only took us at least one hour and thirty-four minutes to eventually get there and to get away from the surveillance of the city's eyes.

Afterwards, we were then setting a camp for us to lay low from the eyes of the police. After getting rid of the car, we were finally in our clothes and not the wear of prison. I spotted Snake looking towards the open glistening lake with his hands on his hips. The same lake where I comforted Kelley after her nightmare.

I watched and couldn't help but to be seduced by the beauty and wrinkles of the lake which met with the landscapes of the green pines that stood and populated the other side of the mountains.

"Yo Kev, I got chu somethin'," He said as he suddenly got his hand into his pockets and brought out my locket. I devoted my life to that locket. I valued it. Though they were gone, this locket reminded me that they were still there with me.

Wearing it around my neck after he handed it to me, I said to him, "Thank you, Snake! Thank you so much!"

"It ain't easy to get from them at first! Couldn't leave it behind! Too bad I left the medicine, though," He said genuinely. "And, it's a compliment for being a good player for all this time!"

"It's a pleasure, mate! And it's okay. I'll managed without pills." I said, as our fists bumped in salute. We both then face the ocean of the trees as the towers of the city were very far out. I stood next to him, and he said, "My dude, we are so far from the city right now. It's crazy!"

"Well...that's the point, ain't it? To stay alive."

"Yeah, but I didn't expect the fuckin' mountains. Y'know, shit like that. Guess I should expect that in Iceland. What made you want to come here anyway?"

I took a deep breath. I knew where this was heading. "I used to come here with my family for summer. I just thought it would be away from their radar."

"You believed in God then?"

"Aye. My mother told me that going to Heaven would feel like going on top of the mountains, where we could be free from the struggle of what was once surrounding us. It's the inspiration she got for a lullaby she sang for my sister and I."

"That's some metaphorical shit, Kev! All that Houdini bullshit!"

"Oy, please don't call it that, mate!" I said alertly. I felt a bit sensitive about the inspiration that no other vulgarity should be associated with it. I understood it was in our standard language in the ghetto, but it still somehow affected me in a way.

"Damn! Sorry 'bout that bro. Didn't mean it like that! But, y'know what I mean, right?"

"I know. It's just something I hold dear in my heart, y'know." I said. "But...I'm glad you're here to cherish it with me."

"It's all good, Kev. From the years we've been together, you ain't half that bad. And you're all I have in this world! How does it feel, getting what you want for a change?"

"It feels great." Thanks to him.

The day looked nice and a great calling for me to explore the wooden areas of Ramapo. I wanted to feel that same in-depth nostalgia I had with my family when they were there with me.

"You know, I don't think I ever told you that I'm from the Wabanaki tribe." Snake admitted.

"No...you haven't." I confessed. "I mean I figured you obviously came from some tribe, but I was not sure which. I didn't want to seem rude."

"What you went through to find faith reminds me a whole lot of what happened back then. Before all this, my ma and pa always told me about the god Glooscap. He was supposedly considered the kind protector of humanity and all that. All my life, I prayed for him to protect and guide my family. Financially and all that. Especially when I wanted to develop games for a living. It was the moment when my pa fell into alcohol and left my ma because...he felt, useless to the family since he was fired for getting into fights after ...tribulations. I don't think I wanna dive into that...but it was tough for him to be around us. So, I was the only one to support her. Things have gone that bad for us, though. I left her after our fight about this belief. It ain't that long when I realize that this belief was all bullshit. I chose to deny all of it. So...don't think that you're alone. We need each other to prosper and stay alive, not gods. No creeds. Politics. None of that shit. I ain't tryin' to discourage you. I just don't wanna disappoint you. There ain't a purpose for us here no more. Maybe there was, but...this world just keeps making it harder and harder for us to...to see it. This use to be my home. Our home. A land of opportunity, courage, and growth. But...not anymore."

I nodded to his knowledge. I was glad to know that I was not alone in this. At least I was acknowledged for my distaste for God and respected for it. Snake was always wise in that regard, even if it was nihilistic. He was only twenty-five, but he saw the true face of life.

"Sorry, I know it's random as fuck to bring it up. But...what you went through just brought me back to those...times, y'know." He said, almost sad with his hands sunken into his pockets.

"I understand, mate. Sorry you had to go through that. And it's best to...find a calling for both of us." I sympathized as I placed my hand on his shoulder. "I know we will...without this world caving in on us."

"Thanks, man." He smiled as we then both looked out at the foggy vista.

"And Kev, I wanted to let you know that I know this shit was hard. I know I've been hard on ya." He said. "I know that someone like you wouldn't normally hang with me. Considerin' where you came from before. Just know that I did what I did to make you survive. To make you strong. You really came through, man. I remember when I first saw you...you were all young, sad, and broken like a fuckin' stray dog. But now...you're hardened...like a rottweiler. So...I wanted to thank you for havin' my back."

"Sure thing, lad. It means a lot...you are telling me more about humanity than those I once trusted." I said with a smile.

"So...what will we do next to get to Iceland?" I wondered. "And...how do you know about Iceland anyway?"

"Talia told me about it at one point at a party. You weren't there. You were asleep at the crib, I think. She wanted to go there to...escape that life she had. As for what we'll do, once the feds stop lookin', we'll quickly go back to my crib. Get our stuff. Get Rex and the others. We'll go back to that church to get your inheritance money and medicine for you. Finally, we sneak onto a boat that heads to Iceland. Tonight. So, it's best to wait out here until evening."

"That'll be good. Obviously, we cannot simply go to the airport with all the surveillance and security. Sailors wouldn't mind if we stay in some cargo hold. So, we could possibly do it later in the evening. Feds are usually lazy around that time. Most of them anyway. I'm...just not sure why Talia never told me, given how she was always fond of me...for some damn reason."

"Because of that dick! No homo," Snake chuckled as I chuckled along to his jest.

"I just wish she told me before I...did what I did. I never cared to ask."

"Well...what is done is done, I guess. Even then, she was a no-good thot! But hey, she knew how to work that mouth, ass and pussy!"

"Ha ha ha ha...you're right! That's all she was good for. Hell, maybe we could find whores in Iceland." Looking back at the forest behind me, I said, "Think I'm going to look 'round a bit."

"Got 'chu, bro. Or should I say...Kelvin Conroy." He said as I took off chuckling into the trees that were huddled and giving the forest life.

I had the urge to smoke again, but that would have ruined the immersion this place gave. I wouldn't want to do that. New York was an abomination of a city. The whole world was. The only exception to this world was its nature. Animals, trees, forests, mountains, and rivers. Things we took advantage of. I included. And I hated myself for it. Snake taught me how to see absolutely no value in people. He saw value in animals, including his Rottweiler named Rex. He saw value in nature, surprisingly for a gangster.

When I was about to commit my first robbery, that's when he told me when I was very nervous. He reminded me of all the ill-treatment they gave towards my family. Even though they were the same family who wanted to be better versions of themselves. My father worked for the United Nations for that very reason; a way to impact representatives to manifest a just and fair society. Especially for the sake of children. Their actions weren't to seek attention. They made a living to carry the burdens of their fellow man and woman as God intended for them; for they learned from the word of Galatians chapter 6.

A family who wanted to help others become better forms of themselves. With each small step in everything they did, they were making impact after impact on one life, so they could spread genuine goodness. My father was in Africa one time to promote his campaign by improving schools. He told me that he met a young man whose family didn't have enough money to get him to school. He managed to pay off a discount for the young man to intend school. My mother once helped a woman get out of involuntary prostitution to intend a class in Julliard to become a jazz singer by raising money after her tour in Denver. She helped women in terrible circumstances of any kind tap into their potential to be what they truly wanted to be. They were a select people, still they were gratified by their help. Meaning they had a little part in a society that dismissed it.

Despite all that, the minority of devils in human clothing sadly had a voice and cheated their ways to these positions of power to put blood on our name because of the mistakes of someone else. They weren't willing to see any goodness in any of us because we carried a cursed name. We were considered boogeymen. They saw my father as another threat to their precious civilization. And the tales they showed spread as I watched naïvely as a child not knowing what to do nor to say. Sometimes, even growing up, I was a bit annoyed with my parents for showing gratification for a world that didn't care for them. They saw my occasional resentment towards the other kids and called me out for it. they begged me to understand people, but still...I couldn't.

Because if the state of New York didn't see any value in what they did and tried to do, I thought why should I see any value in them? Why should I pity any of them? Why would a world that was ecologically beautiful and unique allow itself to be exploited by such a vexatious species I was ashamed to be a part of?

I hated being human. I hated my cursed mind and heart. And I was immensely sick of people. I hated their imperfections. Their failures. Their biases, stupidity, labels, and haughtiness. Their lack of personal responsibility. Most of all, their fear of doing good. It was clear they didn't see any potential in a better world. And that was why I had to run away. I needed to outrun them. They were a disease with no cure. I wasn't sure about my purpose in it. Our foundation, something we tried to make, would never come to its full existence.

Inside the hovering green leaves of the trees, and the trunks that spread across the field was silent and nothing more than just the sounds of Mother Nature's best birds that she had in store for me. Everywhere was green, sometimes yellow that was reflecting from the sun's rays that danced around the grass I keep wandering on.

Kevvvviiiinnnnn! Keevvvviiiiinnnnn!

My name was called silently. Snake couldn't have called it because this calling sounds more feminine than anything else. It alerted me to stop as I looked around to see if anyone was there with me. But it was just recommenced to a dead silence and most likely just something in my head.

Keeeeevvvvviiiinnnnn! Keeeeevvviiiinnnnn!

It came again.

"Whoever's doing that, you better stop! Or I'll break you! You hear?!" I shouted. It was silent once again. I turned and turned, hoping that no one was there. I was hoping that I was alone. Thankfully, I was. But that voice was getting to me now. I was hoping that it wasn't those shadows.

I resumed to wandering in the woods, submersing myself to the glorious nature that I saw before me. But my ears were secured to hear if the same voice would come again. But it was completely soundless. Nothing but birds. Nothing but the wind blowing into the leaves, hitting one another.

Keeeeevvvviiiinnnn! Kevvvvviiiiiiinnnnn!

Frustrated, I drew my pistol in defense. "Seriously, whoever's doing that, come at me! Yeah? I'm not playing!"

Walking slowly, I stopped and saw someone. I could've sworn it was someone familiar. It was a small girl with brown hair and a white blouse on. She giggled once she saw me for some reason. But my eyes gradually widened as I was slowly recognizing who that was. That sound she made was familiar and something I haven't heard in a long time.

"Kelley?" I asked.

"Come play with me, Kevin! Let's play!" She took off.

"Wait," I called out for Kelley, but she refused to listen and just took off. I passed through the trees chasing her down the narrow grassy slope that was uphill. Her giggle was tempting me, and I was wondering what she was giggling for. I felt the sweat gradually coming down from under my skin.

She took off to the left and so I followed her, only to see that she was no longer there. I looked anxiously for her, trying to discover where she could have gone. But then more sounds emerged from the trees. I no longer heard the birds singing nor the leaves blowing. I heard my name being called once again, almost as if someone afar was calling me.

I quickly placed both of my hands on my ears, trying to block out the noises in which were getting tirelessly louder and louder. I looked around the remote population of trees once again. I didn't see her, but the silhouettes appeared suddenly as I turned around repeatedly, I was trying to understand why Kelley would just show up. Why are these shadows following me? Was God playing a trick on me once again? Or was I having another breakdown? I wasn't quite sure anymore. I wasn't sure of anything anymore.

"LEAVE ME ALONE!! STOP IT!!!" I shouted. I felt every ounce of sharpness when I began socking in my temple. I clawed my fingers around my ears, tearing into my skin. Blood stopped flowing once I gripped.

The noises reserved back to the birds singing and the leaves blowing. I slowly removed my hands from my ears and scanned around the area. I no longer heard my name being called. I had a good glimpse at the sun's ray peeking through the leaves and the birds flying across the forest.

But there was something that suddenly caught my ears.

Distant sounds of sirens whistled and wailed from where I was. There were not fond sounds either. We were caught! It was clear to me that they found us. As soon as I ran back, I was running whilst contemplating on how we would eventually have a chance to escape again. I was thinking if Snake was already caught. A lot of constant thoughts ran through my head, almost to the point where I wanted to stop running. When I reached the campsite, where I left Snake, my eyes widened in great fear and despair.

Four cop cars were parked right in front of where he was taking cover and shooting at the firing police. As soon as I was entranced at the bullets coming from all directions, Snake turned to me with his pistol in his right hand. All the bullets were headings towards him alone. Panic in his eyes, he demanded, "Kev, get the fuck outta here, man!"

"N...No!" I shouted frantically. "I can't just leave you behind!" I attempted to draw my gun. But I saw that his eyes turned from fear into brief fury.

"Man don't worry 'bout me! These feds is ruthless! I got this! I'll be alright! Just get the fuck outta here and hide somewhere! I'll meet..." Snake said before he fell on the ground when his right shoulder caught a bullet. Blood puffed from his wound. "ARGH!! GO, KEVIN! GO! RUN!" He said in pain, holding onto his fresh oozing wound. I heeded his demand and took off. I looked back quickly, only to see him get restrained by one of the policemen.

Shortly after, I was running again. I was running to where I was before. I found myself almost shivering to the fact that I could determine what would happen to me. Behind me, I saw four policemen, some with rifles and pistols in their hands, on my tail. They kept shouting, telling me to surrender so they wouldn't shoot. They even said that they weren't going to kill me, but wanted to take me in. I thought to myself No! I didn't plan to go back to prison nor go to some psychiatric ward. I planned to live and prosper my own way, without anyone telling me what I can and cannot do. I planned to honor my family the way I wanted. And I wasn't going to give the police the satisfaction. It prompted me to run faster, regardless of nearly smashing myself into tree trunks or nearly catching myself in twigs. When I ran, I heard my breath and heart racing along with my feet. I took a quick glance to presume that Snake and the rest got somewhere safe. But from the looks of it, it was sadly clear that he was caught and brought into the car.

"Gah!" I yelped to something piercing into my heart. I felt my entire body collapsing, facing the ground. The gun from my jacket fell and skipped two steps ahead of me. My head felt like it was rapidly decaying. Everything in my body felt as if it was stopping. Everything felt like it was darkening. I sensed a warm wetness drizzling across the inside of my hand. Lifting my hand, it was nothing more than just crimson unsolidified moist that made my eyes widened.

Next came my entire body slamming to the ground. I slowly turned my head and saw a group of people telling me to stay down. My vision was becoming distorted, so I could tell who they were. Gradually, I was trying to stand on both of my feet whilst drawing my pistol from my jacket. As I was mildly on my feet, I was slowly drawing the pistol from the ground towards the shadowy figure. I attempted to shoot at the figure pointing his rifle, but I felt another sharp thrush in my chest.

And another one for good measure. I felt something wet flowing on the side of my torso. I throbbed violently, trying to put pressure on my relentless leakage.

"Gah! Ugh..." I yelped as I trembled down the damp grassy slope.

I felt my entire body getting suddenly cold, my mind began to mold and the green leaves in the forest began to blacken like the sun was somehow getting farther and farther. My heart stopped, and I couldn't move. The noises were becoming low. I was clutched by sudden sharp fingers of the ice cultivating my body.

"What did you do!? What did you do!? You weren't supposed to kill him!" Those faint words were the last I've heard.

I was light and felt as if I was flying very fast. I was captive towards a rapid speed of light, with blue and yellow lights with sounds from all over. The lights were getting brighter and brighter as all the darkness was becoming non-existent. The voices. They got louder and louder. The sounds of crying, laughing, screaming, speaking quickly emerged from nowhere. They felt distorted. Out of complete order. The light overwhelmed all the darkness I was surrounded by, leaving nothing but a blank white sleet.

And I was not sure where will my body go next.

III

❦

A World Where Life Endures

My green eyes shot open to the shining light from the sun that some-how shot its rays upon my face. It was bothering enough to constantly blink at the shining light, but to also realize that I was nearly drowning in water. Going on my knees, I saw that I was still breathing. I was still seeing. But what I saw was unordinary and apparently frightening. I was breathing heavily for air almost drowning, big coughs bursting from my mouth. Afterwards, I slowly stood up and scanned the area I was on.

Stranded I was, on an island in fact. Palm trees surrounded the area and sand is what I was apparently standing on. I found myself lying near the water, apparently. It was no longer grass nor was it the trees from Ramapo Mountains. And I was not in Iceland. Not yet anyway. It was somewhere far. Where? I obviously had no damn idea! Turning my head, I happened to see ruins. Yes, actual ruins of what appeared to be a church as I got out of the tropical forest. The beige tinted rubble scattered across the island, buried halfway down.

"W...Where am I?" I kept turning, starting to panic. "What is this? What is this place?"

The sound was nowhere helpful. Seagulls were passing by crying and the ocean waves slapping against the land was sort of making fun of me. The beautiful clear skies and the wind blew leaves from right, left and center was just scaring me. I recalled vividly being shot from behind by someone, yet I was still standing. I stood normally as if nothing happened. Except I was not standing in a forest.

"SNNNAAAAKKKEEE!! SNNNAAAAKKKKKEEE!!!" I shouted him. Only echoes emerged from the milieu. Nothing more. But I called again, "SNAKE! WHERE ARE YOU??? SNAKE!!!"

I looked all over for him, waited for their reply. I began to feel around my pockets, suddenly realizing that not only my stuff is gone, but so was my gun for defense.

"Oh, come on, mate! You've got to be kidding!" I complained to-wards myself. I checked my jacket pocket for good measure, only to know that it is truly not there. I slapped my hands against my thighs in anger. I kept turning and turning, looking for a sign, but still, nothing more than just beautiful nature.

The panic in me overcame my body to the point I felt massively dizzy, as if I were to faint at any moment. Questions were traversing across my head like bees.

"How is this happening? How is this possible? Am I...still alive? How am I alive? I was shot. I felt cold."

So, I retreated into the forested and bug infested jungle, looking for somewhere to rest before I would faint. Only to find more trees and tall grasses. Upon hours and hours, I strolled and called out for Snake. No proper food to fill my stomach. No clear water to quench my thirst. I was hovered and surrounded with plants and tree leaves blushing. But I became entirely dizzy to notice its intrigue and simplicity.

As I was stumbling across, my left foot happened to hit something. Looking down regardless of the heaviness of my eyes, I stumbled on what looked to be an apple. But it was oddly shaped and looked rather rare. Something I haven't seen before. It was decorated with what looked like glass diamonds. I watched up and saw it fell from a palm tree that had those fruit dangle from them. As I picked it up, my fingers felt warm from holding it. I looked it up to see that it came down from a palm tree.

I couldn't care less of how weird it looked. In hunger, I took a bite of the fruit and chewed it like nobody's business. The diamonds tasted almost like hard candy with cranberry flavor. I sighed with relief as I ate. It was not enough, but at least it was something I could chew on.

I looked around and decided to go back to the beach. It was not a long walk there anyway. But soon, my head felt heavier than before, and my eyes got heavier than before. In fact, the beach looked to be melting like paint oozing down a canvas. I turned back to the jungle, only for it to take the same attitude as the beach. The seagulls' cries began to gradually slow down and shifted into a different pitch.

I looked at both of my hands and saw that they were gradually disintegrating. It looked like sand falling. I was slow and apparently too zoned out to panic, as I saw the world melting right before my eyes.

Then suddenly, I came to an erupted faint.

Long Island, Spring 1997-

"We always have to have faith, Kevin. We've gone through worse before. I know what you were trying to do for Kelley. I am happy for you when you came into her defense. But...no more hitting other children in gym. You're better than that. Remember your breathing practices we went over. Promise?" My loving and ravishing mother advised. After she medicated me. I narrowed my eyes. I remembered I was in a fight after Kelley was bullied in gym class. I had to defend her.

"I promise, Mother. But those kids were just...so mean to Kelley! The...voices... told me to do it! They said that...I didn't love Kelley if I didn't do it," I said. "Am I...am I a monster?"

Mother said, "Oh...sweetheart. Of course not. Please...never say that about yourself again. Listen, we are not in this world for mean people. We live how God wants us to live. You should never go through life worrying about what others say or think about you. Not even those nasty voices in your head. Naysayers will always bring you down. I cannot lie to you. But overcoming them will make you stronger than they are. Just as Jesus's Apostles were ridiculed for their faith."

"The Twelve Apostles." I asked. "Like you told me and Kelley about?"

"Yes. Just like Jesus, they were heroes who dedicated themselves to do his biddings after he died. Sadly, they were killed for what they believed in. Yet, their legacy thrived to this day. We can always learn from them. And I know we will." Mother said. She was always hopeful and kind, regardless of whatever she faced. She saw the light in obscurity. She then looked up at the clock that was above my door, seeing that the time was almost midnight.

"It is getting late, dear. How about we close our eyes for prayer before I let you sleep," The mother asked kindly as I closed both eyes as well as she did.

She then began saying to God, "We thank you for all the goodness you give to this family. I thank you for the lives of our children and our servants, who made this house holy. I ask you to do the same for others who go through tribulations and are suffering in the grasps of the devil. We ask you to protect them, cherish, and accept them, regardless of who they are. Bless us on this night as for all nights. Bless my son and make him see you extracting his dreams. Nurture his head. Make him see the best parts of this world, no matter what. My Lord, thank you for making us see the good things in light and darkness. Thank you for letting us thrive. Amen."

"Amen," I said, absorbing all he had taken from his mother's prayer. She then faced me and kissed my temple, kissing me to sleep.

"Mother...why do we have to believe in God?" I asked her as she began to stare off and pondered at the ceiling. "Is he like Santa Claus?"

"You could say that. I...think of him as a guiding star. A bird that flies through the dark creaky forests to lead you to a castle full of life and love. We believe in God to lead us to a path of good without being trapped by the roots of evil. In life, to get answers, to live, we need that light. We need to live according to what the light wants, not what machines want. You understand, son?"

"I guess. Will...Father come back soon? Will God lead him back to us?"

"He will. Once he is done with his trip." She smiled. "I know you miss him."

"I do. I hate all the mean things people say about him," I said with somberness. She wrapped her arms around me and shuffled my shoulder.

"Your father is a strong man. He is strong with God. He will be okay. I promise. I'll see if I will talk with Michelle to see more of her sessions with you." Releasing me, she adjusted the covered to my chest, kissing my head once more and said, "Sleep tight now, Kevin. I love you very much."

"I love you more, Mother."

IV

The Weird and Strange City

My eye opened rapidly as I discovered that I was no longer on the island, but inside a cell that was moving. I still felt sick as I saw that my skin was paler than usual. I looked through the window and saw that I was now in the middle of the ocean in a cargo hold.

Then it was clear for me to see that I was inside a vessel ship, captured by what is most likely to be pirates. I thought to myself that it was possibly a lucid dream. A good one at that. The sand felt as if it were sand, and the idyllic oceans roared and swooshed before me.

"You!" A voice came about. As I turned, I didn't know if I could laugh or to feel...honestly, anything. A man stood in front of my cell with two other men on his side with long brown muskets. Their outfits seemed to be outdated. The man in the middle had a long cunning face and dark greyish rolled back hair. His eyes seemed to be sunken, and his outfit was light brown.

"Why am I here?" I shouted. "Do you know where I can find my friend Snake?"

"What do you think, you peasant worm? You've trespassed the island of Ghai! And no...we do not know of this Snake." The man said with a very thick Italian accent on his tongue. "Be graceful I haven't used these men to kill you off in your sleep."

"I didn't trespass anything! I just got here! I got shot and I went here! I don't know where I'm supposed to be! I just ate some apple out of hunger and fainted!"

"You ate what is called a *miracle pomme*. We don't eat that. Unless you plan to consider yourself the biggest fool in all of the Promised Land!"

Then I got confused the minute he said promised land; another possibly word for Heaven. "Wait wait...Promised...land?"

"Are you deaf?" He asked.

"No! I'm not deaf! I was just asking!" I was almost panicking. My life couldn't be taken that quickly. I then asked, "By...Promised Land...do you mean.... like Heaven? You don't mean that, right?"

"No; by Promised Land, I meant you are in Venice of Italia with idyllic canals with gondolas floating about. Of course, I mean Heaven, idioti (idiot)! What else would it be?!"

I shuddered. "No. I mean...I'm in this kind of...ship," I stuttered. "No. No...I can't be dead. Not now! Can I?"

"Well, that's for the Chancery to decide. Now, is it?" He said. "Because we're here."

I felt the moving ship stop suddenly. Very sudden. "Where?"

He turned and said to me. "Celestia. The city of Celestia." My face got pale. My mind was at war between the burring facts whether I was dead or not. I looked out at the distance to see that there was indeed a big city at the horizon; mostly consisting of the towers of basilicas, cathedrals, and palaces that looked ageless. Behind the metropolis was an outline of mountains and forests. The vessel I was on made me assume that it was some reenactment of pivotal moments in history. But weirdly enough, it felt as if they were sincerely serious about it. It was almost as if they were taking these roles seriously. Very seriously.

He then faced both his guards and demanded, "Take him."

As they barged into my cell, they both grabbed me by both arms as I felt their grips tighten my poor supple arms. But I was still refusing to believe that I was dead. I just couldn't be! And if I were dead, where was the rest of my family? Surely, God couldn't forget about them. If they were truly here, I knew what I had to say, but was still nervous.

They were leading me to the surface of the large wooden ship with massive white sails that were flapping and smacking one another due to the wind. The guards kept pushing me to go forward with the bitter Italian man. I looked around, astonished, and frightened altogether as I took in the sight of a lighthouse far from the city and large docks on each side.

After passing through the great decorated gates glazed in gold, where we were also greeted by the tall stone statues of angels raising their hands to the skies on each side, we went through a wide courtyard. The floor was tiled with blue marble with a decorated scheme painted onto them. My arm was exhausted as the Italian kept tightening my bicep. We paced and paced across the courtyard until we went through the archways. We were welcomed with an interesting city. It was more of a large city square. The slate-made roads were wide enough for carriages and wagons to go by as the Italian, and I were crossing them. I felt completely small because of the towers that pointed high. Every building had a peculiar fusion of Parisian and Spanish touch to them, in the sense that there are all manifested by grotesque and majestic architecture made of quartzite, limestone and gneiss. The ghostly bells were tolled and traversed from edifice to edifice. Church to church I heard it toll. Blue and yellow striped flags of a cross were flown on each tower.

Most of the horse drawn carriages were not even pulled by horses; but there was a diversity of hybrid stallions. Some of the horses were feathered and winged. Some were a hybrid of different big cats. Some were made of water, mist, or stone. A wolf with the body of a horse and four large talons of a hawk drew one carriage that passed the Italian and me. I looked up and saw various types of birds flying alongside the standard doves and normal birds. Some birds even had dragon-like wings and tails.

Everyone else seemed to be outdated as well; the way they worked the ship as it was preparing to dock, they dressed in very old, aged sailor apparel, and from the look at the city. They were astoundingly massive and monumental in company with stone angels in different poses. It was not New York, but the shear capacity of the buildings reminded me so much of it. The buildings seemed squared and sometimes rectangular with blue grey-pitched rooftops. Some had different color palettes such as brown, red, and orange. The buildings all appeared to be made of stone that was carefully crafted and delicately stylized. It looked remarkable in a way. The aroma felt humid and almost vanilla-flavored as I breathed it into my nose. The aroma was strange compared to the tobacco-ridden New York. Everything was damn antiqued. Washed up at some bits, but still somewhat timeless.

What seemed to be out of the ordinary was seeing men and women, coming, and going with large snow-white wings on their backs. Men had on decorated long coats; some had on tricorn hats, wigs and buckled shoes. Some of their tricorn hats wore feathers to add a rich touch. Women had gowns and quilted underskirts; some had sleeves flared at their elbows. This could also be said to the kids, running back and forth through the misty streets. Everything was noisy to the point that I couldn't even hear myself gradually breathing heavily.

Still, I was limited to have an expression, seeing how I was still being brought to the city hall, in which we finally entered through the silver gates into the surprisingly picturesque city. The roads were crowded with horse drawn carriages, in many kinds. There were soldiers patrolling the streets from every corner, bearing frock coats colored blue, white and yellow with morion helmets. Sometimes, blue feathered helmets.

Although it looked extremely beautiful and historic, I did not like what I saw. It was not New York, and the people were sure as hell not from my time. I was completely out of date compared to the men and women I saw. As the Italian was leading up to the stairs to the marble-made basilica, amid the rest of the buildings, he glared at me, hoping I was able to cooperate.

"Ugh! Where are you taking me?" I asked dizzily as the fruit was still acting up in my system.

He hissed, "You keep quiet! It's off to the authorities to you! Think that you are free to be full of yourself by laying your ass on the land of Ghai, wearing God knows whatever you are dressed in? Why would you eat that anyway? It's forbidden!"

"I just came here! The hell was I supposed to know?" I said for the second time, frustratingly. I was curious to know the man's name. That way, I could possibly report him for kidnapping me.

"Can I at least know your name?"

"You shall not receive it! You will regard me as sir!"

"So, you prefer I call you...I don't know, grumpy shitfaced Italian?!" This remark earned me a sudden slap across my head from his hand. It felt fuzzy and punishing temporarily as my head grinding on my flaking black hair.

"You will regard me as sir! Nothing more! And that's for disrespecting the elders of God!"

"You're not even that old!"

"I said shut it!" He barked. "It's off to the Chancery with you! Considering that you're an astral, no one goes unjudged!"

"But...but I didn't know! I swear! What the hell's an astral anyway?" I cried. "C'mon, mate! I didn't know that place was forbidden!"

"We'll see about that, outcast!" He said. Getting my attention away from the grumpy Italian, I couldn't help but to be in rush for my gang. I couldn't seem to find them, but that didn't mean that I was to give up now.

Without his consent, I shook my arm from his grip and took off down the stairs, leaving him dumbfounded. I heard him shout, "HEY!! YOU PIECE OF...GET BACK HERE!! Figlio di una cagna (Son of a bitch!)"

I watched my back as I saw him coming after me. I sprinted across the streets, slowly causing a hazard for the carriages. I rolled back down to the ground, continued to run on the ground into the shady alleyways until I found some way out of this city, looking for Snake.

I watched as he sent flying winged guards after me, their shadows on the ground and their majestic bodies hovering my head.

"STOP WHERE YOU ARE! WE HAVE YOU SURROUNDED!!"
One of them said as at least three of them attempted to attack me, but I
dived, darted their attacks, picked up a rock from the ground and threw
it at one of them and continued to make a run for it. Nothing was ever
going to get me to stop until I find a way out of this city. I'd go back to
the gate, but I didn't wish to get caught right away. Second, I was not
willing to swim all the way back to the island I just came from.

I was at the city once again, but another part of it, which seemed
opened for ancient marketplaces. I zapped through, using the crowd
to my advantage. By using the crowd, the winged men found it hard
to find me. Even in the skies, they did not find me. I ran surprisingly
fast despite my sickness. Obviously, I had to run from those winged
surprisingly humanistic beasts. And it didn't help with many of them
consuming the city. Soon, I ran through a public space. And although it
was easy for them find me, I used the people to my advantage to avoid
being caught. It felt like Brooklyn. Only it wasn't Brooklyn. My mind
raced as I did as I was still unaware of where I was. And what exactly
was I doing.

Finally losing them, this gave me a chance to finally hide away from
in the back of a house. I came across a bridge and saw a walkway down
there. Between the two walkways was a streaming canal with people
sailing on small rowboats and gondolas. Vaulting over the decorated
bridge, I did it to lose sight of anyone else. But I happened to hit my
face onto the cobblestone ground. The toxicity was overwhelming and
has once again put me to a deep faint.

I don't know whether everything was real, or I was straight up
losing my mind. I didn't know what to think anymore. All I knew was I
couldn't be dead. I had so much to live for, even if I was shot. I couldn't
have my life snuffed out of me. Not now.

V

The Homestead

My eyes opened... again! The environment was different from where I was today. It was no longer a bustling metropolis. I got off from a couch that I was apparently left on when I was knocked out cold. I saw myself surrounded by wood. It seemed like a living room. The fireplace was in front of the couch and the nice velvet rug that lay on the ligneous floor. It felt like a gallery with surprisingly a ton of surreal and abstract portraits plastered on each corner of the living room. Canvases, bookshelves, and canvas stands were near the fireplace.

I rubbed the temple of my head; supercilious of the pain on my face has gone away. Despite the foggy vision, I glanced on my right shoulder and saw that some mushed-up orange substance with other chunks covered it. I came to the front door, opening to what looked like to be something that calmed all the nerves that racked inside me a bit.

It became dim with orange as the sun was setting down. I might have been knocked out for most of the day. The outdoors was all open grass and forested that rested on the other side of the meadow. Young men and women came from right and left, carrying wood, or exchanging baskets upon baskets of what I hope were wheats, reeds, and vegetables. It was as if I was at the Ramapo Mountains again. Only I was not. There were other small houses on the other side, facing the one I was apparently coming out from. Each house I saw was integrated with foliage. It wasn't so small, but it wasn't big either. And of course, it was primitive as I saw primitive living.

My feet clicked on the creaking wood, as I stood dumbfounded on the porch. Despite the little fear I had with this place, I was feeling a little better about being immersed into this lovely ground of rural nature that made me utterly confused and intrigued all at once.

"Lovely place, ain't it," said the same voice that I heard. "It could use some reworking, though. But all in due time."

As I turned, I saw that the voice came from a young man. His hair was sunburned, and his shirt was loose with a brown jerkin. It was tucked into his black trousers and his wrists were impregnated with leather gauntlets as his hands were wrapped around with the sleeves of his shirt. He leaned against the house with his arms crossed and had his left foot on it.

"You're okay?" He asked.

"Uh...yeah, I suppose. Thanks, I guess."

"Good," He said as his eyes suddenly became dark. He glared at me with sudden disdain. "Because as soon as you get healed, I'm gonna send your ass to the Civil Forcers and watch them tear you apart; limb from limb."

"W...What?!" I asked with fear rising in my tone. I felt my heart gradually sink low below my lungs.

But out of nowhere, he suddenly scoffed and chuckled. He slapped his hand against my chest and said, "Dude, I'm kiddin'. You should've seen the look on your face! I'm sorry, I love the sound of Londoners! I couldn't resist!"

Away from his eyes, I sucked on my teeth in frustration.

"You sure as hell caused some traffic jam in the city, though!" He said with a grin.

"I didn't mean too. I...I'm just trying to get back home!" I said, now focused on the village's rural landscape. I turned to the young lad and asked, "How did you find me? Do you know if you've seen my friend Snake? A Native American bloke?"

"I fairly know some Natives, but no one called Snake, I'm afraid. I was just coming from my job, and I checked in the city to see what the whole commotion was about. Everybody's lookin' dumb as hell. I went passed the bridge and saw you down there, vomiting like a divorced father going through depression. I took it upon myself to get you out from there, pretended you were a drunkard friend from Litler's, told the folks to skedaddle. Then I left the city with you nauseated. That about do it for ya?"

I sighed when I looked back at my jacket, realizing what I was. "Sure...I guess." I then asked, "So...what kind of place is this anyway?"

He gestured his open hands and arms right at my face. "Welcome to Joseph's Homestead! Nice place, little community for us men and women to do our own chores, getting around and getting to know one another under the Baron Ryan Cenet. It's like our...haven. But sometimes...we can get a little weird. Or maybe it's just me. Oh, you know we crazies can't make up our minds!"

"R...Right...it's quite... beautiful! But's... scary." I said.

"Scary? What are ya, ten?" He asked.

The way this bloke was talking and moved seemed as if he was full of himself. Even the accent he had was well suited. It sounded Bostonian if I could recall. And I was already not fond of him.

"No! I'm eighteen! I was...it's just I haven't been in a place like this! I feel like...I'm lost."

"Oh.... well, have no fear, whatever your name is! Theodore Jefferson is at your service! In all seriousness, just call me Ted. What's your name?"

Well, I gained his name. That was a first. I introduced mine in return. "I'm...Kevin Princeton."

"Well...Kevin Princeton, cool name, let's show you around." He said, putting his arm around me as we were going down the steps. Aggressively, I shrugged his arm off my shoulder. Yet, he didn't seem to mind.

What he was showing me was surprisingly massive for a place that seemed small. The entire homestead was separated by a large riverbank that flowed across. So, we went to the left side of the commune. There were pubs for us to hang out in leisure; small theatres to perform many kinds of arts, and docks where the young men worked on building boats and exchanging whatever goods they could carry to another part of this scaled village with dirt roads. There were self-funded farms in which they gain animals to use for their advantage. I saw signs on picket fences that forbade outside creatures into entering the village. Every corner and avenue were something different. There were small sacred altars placed outside where they would worship the stone idols of the saints.

He showed me an organized settlement further down the left where they had several games: ranging from gladiator arenas to hippodromes. Various types of jousting and archery games. Canoe races across the streaming river through the outback forests. Poker houses to play poker and other card games. They even host annual endurance horse racing and fox hunting, which was associated with an exclusive hunting job. A lot of the sports seemed fun, but very dangerous of course. I would say it would be good for me, but I had yet to know how all of it would work. I was still staggered by the sheer existence of this place.

Walking over a bridge over a streaming river, we were back at the left but went south to the most cultivated settlements. We saw mostly young women working on an arboretum, filled with interesting, vibrant, and unique plants. Little birds and butterflies flourished and floated all about. The leaves of the trees hovered over the vegetation. One woman plucked an apple from a gradually growing apple tree, placing inside her basket full of other fruits and vegetables, and passed both of us. Those apples reminded me of that bloody fruit that drugged me. It made me had a small disdain for them.

He eventually introduced me to the Baron Ryan who resided in one of the bigger manors on the hill of the homestead. He was a charming fat English fellow in his forties. He had the homestead established to be a community that relied on the youth to trade in goods, creativity, and things of value they manufactured to the city of Celestia. And if necessary, all other kingdoms.

After we made it through the orchard, we were back to the open village. We passed cabin by cabin next to the river.

"So...how did you die?" Ted asked, suddenly.

"Well, first off; I didn't die! I couldn't have! I was just shot. I get shot at millions of times. It happens." I said, justifying my approach.

"Especially when your heart stops?" He asked again.

"Well, my heart is beating now. Isn't it?"

"Oh right. I just recall people...dying from getting shot at *millions of times*. Let alone with clothes like that," He nodded. "So, you're one of them fellas?"

Stopping midway on the path, I turned and asked, "What *fellas*?"

"The kind of fellas that want to deny their fate. They can't cope with it."

He said, raising both hands. "But hey, I get it, man! I felt the same way after I died. Took me years to get used to this habitation. Every spirit who lost a previous life feels this way."

"But I'm not a spirit! You hear? I'm not! And I shouldn't be speaking to you, as a matter of fact!" I yelped.

"Well..." He chuckled. "You're speaking to me now. You're feeling, hearing, thinking, and seeing everything here as you did before. Only...you're a spirit now. An astral, to be specific. This is the afterlife, my friend. Your new reality. All we could ever do, at this point, is start over and take it as a second chance to improve. All we could do is create a better life here. We could always make up after two strikes after all."

"I don't want to start over! I want to go home! Go to Iceland! These people, these monsters, those clothes, these men, and women...with wings on their backs, they don't exist! You don't exist! I mean...this place, if you could call it that, it shouldn't exist! This cannot be real! This can't be bloody real! This is a dream!" I was beginning to sound like a madman. And Ted saw that in my face. He let out a sigh, due to my pathetic nature.

"Except it's not." He expressed nonchalantly. Leaving me in silence.

This seemed unexpected, but I then happened to saw a group of griffin-like creatures emerging from the bushes.

Their paws were flat, and their pelts forested with long and thick-sunburned hair. The back of their feet looked to be sizable falcon feet with sword sharp talons.

Their eyes pitch black and horns, harsh and most likely to easily pierce through flesh and bone. The brutes were the size of dire wolves, and they felt the need to roam the place, as if it were normal. As if it happens every day. I watch some of the women push them off the gardens and orchards by spanking their bottoms with brooms.

"Those are called alvotons. Don't be timid about their size, they're completely harmless. Super friendly. Unless...you piss 'em off. They don't take kindly to disrespect." Ted spoke. "One of them randomly showed up in front of my cabin one night. I was eating...a roasted chicken leg I think it was. It was well seasoned too. Usually. So, I gave him the whole thing and it went back to the woods. With my salivated roasted chicken leg in its mouth."

"Do they often do that?"

"Oh, hell yeah. It's a norm. You could choose to scare 'em off...or to befriend one by feeding or...something respectable. Like a name or something. I don't know. These bastards would accept anything...apart from threats, that is."

Why did this seem normal? Why was I seeing things that shouldn't exist? All these questions ran across my head.

"So...you landed on the land of Ghai, right?" He asked, turning his face towards me.

"Yeah...but I didn't trespass! I just ended up there! I swear I was just drugged by that bloody apple!"

"I know, I know! Calm your liver, crumpets! Guessin' Dante roused you then, huh?"

I asked confusedly, "Who?"

"Dante Alighieri? Y'know! Italian poet? Have you ever read any works of his? *The Divine Comedy*?"

"N...No." I said. I felt a bit bad to be honest. I should know who that was, but the unlawful life took so much of my time that I never had the thought to go back to school. If I were to change myself, I suppose this place would have a sort of educational institution anywhere.

He then spoke, "I'll get you up to speed, moj brat (**brother**)! See, Dante Alighieri was a writer and statesman, well known in fact, back at the early 1200s. One of his famous works, as I mentioned, The Divine Comedy, has gotten a lot of praise and even grew into a phenomenon. A lot of people gained inspiration from his work! Pretty cool, even if the guy's a douche! I personally think he should do himself a favor and get his ass back to writing. Leave the eternal judgment to the right professionals who don't get corrupt easily."

"Then why does he work with..." I tried to ask, before he cut my question.

"He's working as a chancellor... just so he could have relevance as a statesman. See, he's the front for the king's court, known as the Chancery of the Cross; the assholes as I like to call 'em. Led by Leviticus Himlin. These adjudicator folks are rooted to the Catholic traditions and considered everything else that isn't Catholic as deformation of God's word. They expect every spirit to be pure in God's image like before. Basically, to make a Catholic rule of Valestone like before. Are you getting me? Hope I ain't going too fast. I have the tendency to do that a lot."

After he teased me a bit, his smile changed when his faced some sort of cabin that was further down passed two other cabins and looked over the riverbank. Further was a dirt pathway that led into the depths of the woods. He then asked, "Quick question; how badly did that fall hurt you?"

"To the point where I feel like my skull is about to break, why?"

He then sighed, reluctantly and said, "Well...over there is where I wanted to take ya. Especially I noticed your hands." I nearly forgot that I wore bandages, which could be dirty.

"Why did you sigh like that?"

"Well, this is the stationary nursing home I told you about. It's my least favorite place to visit, particularly because of one person. Just one!" He said, leading me up to the place.

"Who's that?" I asked.

"Juliet...Higgins! The head of the nurses in the Homestead. I gotta warn ya...we don't get along that much."

"What do you mean?" I asked again.

"I did some things in the past, something I've redeemed myself for. But she often uses that against me. She judges me for it. And she's not used to having someone like me around her. We're both...in this organization of sorts."

"I'm not sure what to think of that. I'm just concerned about where I'm at now. Can't help you there, mate. Sorry." I said. At that moment, I really wished that he'd stop talking.

"Don't bother! This is something I should handle on my own." He said. Eying at me, he said, "Plus, you are not lookin' too good! You're still affected by the toxicity of that fruit. I'm sure she'll help you out with that."

As Ted and I stopped in front of the nursing hut, I heard him mumbling to himself, "*Gah! I just...really don't wanna do this! But yeah, y'know! Miracle fruit and vomit and crap! I would've gone for pineapples if I were him.*"

He knocked on the door, laid on the side of the door with his arms crossed on his chest. As the door opened, a young woman, in a white dress with an apron and colonial ladies' cap covering her light brown hair, appeared and Ted asked bitterly, "Is she at her office? I got a patient, as you can see"

"Y...Yes she is. What is he needed for?"

"Stomach sickness. He accidently ate miracle fruit."

"Oh...yes, of course. F...Follow me." She said as we did. "Just be mindful. We're full. As you can see."

The sight of the place somewhat disturbed me. Most of the patients were impregnated in dry blood that soaked they clothes, most of them flayed on their beds due to the pain, even though the nurses were only trying to comfort them as best as possible.

The girl knocked on the door that was presumably at the end of the hall and said, "You have a patient, head nurse. He is ill in his stomach."

The door opened, and it was perhaps the most beautiful woman I have ever faced with my own eyes. Her soft freckled skin was pale as mine and her hair was bleach blonde and flowed down to her upper back. Her eyes were sky blue, and I couldn't really take my eyes away from her. She wore a quilted blue dress, which suited her curvy yet decently athletic body, with a white apron hugging her waist. A goddess is what came to my mind when I saw her.

"Oh...I'm sorry, I didn't hear you come in." She said with a cute tone. Her accent sounded as if she came from the north of Ireland. She turned to the nurse and said, "Thank you, Meredith. I'll take it from here."

The nurse nodded and left me with Ted, who then replied, "How the hell did you not hear us come in? Did my badass voice seem pacified to your small ears?"

"Well, obviously I was busy, Theodore. You wouldn't know anything about nursing if you wore a dress yourself. I could imagine you right now, wearing what I'm wearing now. Except you'd look like a pig dressed as an old lady. With Alzheimer's." She said with a surprisingly good sense of humor in her attitude, in which I silently chuckled, making sure Ted didn't see me.

"See. That's another thing; she keeps calling me by my full name. It's annoying!" He faced me, gesturing his hand to her appealing face. "This is what I have to live with!"

"Don't listen to him, he's just being infantile as always. It what he does," She said to me, leading both of us inside her office.

"I do not! Look, his name is Kevin Princeton and I just brought him here, so you could take care of him for a while. He's got a migraine and is feeling ill."

"Gave him one of your *barbaric accommodations*, did you?" She rolled her eyes.

"Not this time!" Ted spoke justly.

"Hmm, what a surprise! But then again, wouldn't be a surprise if you would do it." She then faced me and shook my hand, "My name is Juliet Higgins, in case he hasn't told you."

He sighed, "I have told him! So that's information you don't need to tell us anymore. Look, just take care of him and make sure he doesn't leave and go into the city."

"Why?" She asked. "What did he do?"

"He apparently made a ruckus in the city since that miracle fruit he ate screwed him up! The Civil Forcers are looking for him! I need to talk with Francis, so he could disregard a charge and get him exempt from the Chancery's' judgement somehow! So, could you watch him?" He said, glancing at me. I wondered who the hell Francis was. "I could find anyone else to rely on...and who ain't a cunt."

She groaned to his annoyance, "Alright, fine! But what you say about him better be in truth!"

"Whatever! And you BETTER not let him leave whatsoever until it is safe for him! If he wants air, open the window. If he wants to eat, you know your ways 'round the city. When he wants to piss, show him where the bathroom is! If he's bored, just...I don't know, read him a bedtime story or some shit. You're good at those." He said.

"I know what to do, Theodore! I work here." She said, sternly for him to understand.

He then glanced back at me. "Anyway! It was nice knowing you, Kev! I'll see you around. Don't let her poison ya!"

"Oh, sod off!" She cried at him.

I nodded. He then took off, before giving a glare to Juliet. As he shut the door closed behind him.

"Would you mind sitting on the bed for me, Mr. Princeton?" She asked kindly.

"Uh...sure, yeah." I said, going on the bed and sitting, removing my sneakers, placing them underneath the bed.

She then goes to me, using an antique stethoscope to check all the levels of my body. "My apologies for my attitude. He is just a pain in my arse sometimes. He's okay when he needs to be. But...he's nothing but a bloody court jester...who doesn't take anything seriously."

"It's okay." I said, grinning. "Why do you call him by his full name, by the way?"

"Oh, because I happen to like his full name. It makes him...mature. Like Theodore Roosevelt. Or Theodore Prodromos, the Byzantine poet," She jested. "Don't tell him I said that, though."

She smiled back, removing the stethoscope pads from both of her ears. "Your body is in good health, just stuffed by the toxicity of the fruit. I feel it traversing and circling your stomach. But I should be able to cleanse it." Impossible! How was my body in good health? I was practically filled with coolness after I was shot.

She then checked my head and said, "But your head could use some ice. The coolness can heal, I think. And I need to make an antidote to eradicate the toxin from your body. This could be dealt with very quickly." She then took off to the counter and started grasping and grabbing hold of certain equipment to fix something. God knows what. I didn't get to see what she was making, but I just heard cracking and liquid pouring.

"You should consider yourself lucky; it's rare when I have someone to nurse instead of just keeping track of numbers all day. Keeping track on the other nurses. You're the first...no second patient I've had in recent times. And it's rare to have an astral appear again."

"Well, that's a first," I joked.

"It's true. My first was.....as you saw...lumbers. Specifically, Cal Hanson, the most reckless. They keep hurting themselves supplying wood for architects in the city. I can't be too harsh; they are hardworking. I'll give them that," She said, walking towards me with a glass cup of what I hoped wasn't poisonous. As I held it, it had the scent of mint, licorice, and a bit of aloe, creating a strange green substance. I looked up at her.

"Well, go on then" She said sweetly, but pushy. She had a peculiar cuteness to her. "It won't kill you. Trust me."

I hesitated a bit. But I had no other choice in the matter. So, I gradually let the substance enter my throat. I nearly gagged, but I swallowed quickly so it didn't have to come to that. Afterwards, the cup was fully empty with crummy residue. I then handed the cup to her as she grabbed it.

"Excellent, that wasn't bad! Was it?" She smiled.

"Except when I nearly vomited! What is this stuff?" I asked.

"Gilly Juice. Peppermint, aloe, and licorice. It's too rid of any toxin. It's important for any spirit to have it. Our bones are made with clear quartz. So, we wouldn't want any toxicity to weigh down our anatomy. Especially miracle fruit." She said, taking off to the counter to wash the cup. I grew paler when she said that. Are my bones really made of crystal now? But before I jumped to frightening conclusions, I had to keep my composure.

"That's good to hear." I then got up from the bed to scan around her office. Observing every aspect of her room, I recognized that half of her shelves were packed with various glass jars of what appeared to be several bodily organs. Next to the several books she had, there were brains, intestines, eyeballs, and kidneys all concealed in water filled jars that had scrapped with parts of the organs floating inside the jar. Including a heart with a crystal embedded in its ventricle. On each level of the shelves, she had different types of green, red, yellow, and purple herbs hanging like foliage over her desk. On top of each shelf were different types of toxins and potions concealed in vials. Some vials were big, small, fat, and skinny. But I was more fixated on the presumably surgically removed organs in a bizarre collection of jars. I gazed at the paper diagrams of skeletons that looked to be colored with light blue highlights.

"So...I'm taking that you're more than just a nurse and herbalist, huh?" I asked.

"I'm a surgeon as well. Most of the time," She said as she stood next to me to observe the shelves facing us. "I know it's...unusual. I collect and use them to analyze. It's my job to make sure that I know the anatomy of spirits. For astrals, our bodies are advanced and unique in this world as oppose to the physical one. We want to make sure that we are loose and free from material bondage. Now let me get you that towel."

She then took off to get the wet towel from the little bucket that was against the wall. I looked around just to understand my current but accidental environment. I would ask myself if it was happening right now.

"Here, I got the ice for your head." She said, soon coming towards me with the pack in her hand. She then placed in slowly and gently on the temple of my head. I winced to the stinging pain that was being pressed against the ice.

"How does that feel?" She asked.

"Argh! A bit painful! But pretty good!" I replied.

"Great." She said, smiling. She then glanced around my body, to check for any more wounds. She saw my bandaged hands. She gazed at my eyes and asked me, "If I may..." I nodded.

When she unveiled and removed the white bloodied bandages, she gasped a bit and asked, "Goodness!"

"Oh...just accidently crushed some beer bottles. Stupid mistake. But...it's no big deal. Really," I said. She took off to her drawers and shelves. I glanced at both of my hands and saw how deepened and nearly dried the lacerations looked. Soon, her footsteps came in haste as she came to me with two bandages that looked moist and were dipped in yellowish gooey substance. She then said to me, "It may not be to you. But...it could give bad results, Mr. Princeton. Swollenness...for instance. Infection. It's quite a thing. Now...let me see your hands please."

Sighing off, I allowed her to tie the bandage around. She was doing my right hand first as I felt the cool wet sensation of the goo. Next, she walked around to get my left hand. "What exactly is that substance your putting on me, if I may ask?"

"It's yellowdock roots mixed with water and honey. It should heal those nasty lacerations," She said.

Her glossy eyes glanced at my neck as she then saw my locket. "That's very lovely," she said. I looked down, forgetting that I was still wearing it. Thankfully I kept my word for my little sister.

"Th...thank you." I said.

"I don't...mean to pry, but who was it from?"

"I...I had...have a little sister. She got it for me...for Christmas." I gulped afterwards.

"That's very nice." She said kindly. "She must have been proud to have such a lovely brother."

"Aye...she was." I said in a gleeful but sad tone.

Yet I smiled back at her and said, "Listen...thank you very much. And I'm sorry about...Ted."

"Oh, it's my pleasure. It's no problem. And don't worry about Theodore. He just has an ego I can't sustain, that's all." She said, almost motherly. "Now why don't you lay here while I fetch something for you to eat? I can't have a dead boy on my bed, obviously!"

I laughed at her humor. And I said, "You wouldn't want one! Especially with bloody maggots!"

We both laughed. Although at that moment, I sensed myself losing my head again. So, I was laughing to play along with her joke. In addition, the woman was being genuinely kind for her age. So, I couldn't really bring myself to disrespect nor rob her. Like I did to most women. But I still had to bring my guard up in case she blindsided me like a fool.

So then, I asked her, "Listen love...you don't happen to know someone called Snake, do you? He's a friend."

"I'm very sorry. I do not see him nor know him. But I'll let you know if I do." When she left and closed the door behind her, that was when I was beginning to feel the insides of my stomach being played and twisted in all shapes.

I really hoped that she would find Snake. No matter what it took, we had to get to Iceland. We had to. So, I'd like to think that this world was my equivalent of Wonderland to cope with the pain I endured by those bullets. I could only hope.

Long Island, Summer 1997

Another fragmented dream I had. As if God was seeping these memories to make fun of me. But I remembered when I was generally happy to be alive and grateful in a home.

A big house surrounded by trees and isolated from all other houses. A rich home in Long Island, New York with an English butler named Johnathan Blackwater, nine interiors with antiques and flags of the Hospitaller Knights hung on walls, a backyard taking space behind the lake behind our house and a family of four. I was in a heavenly home. A home God blessed. Away from hell caving the world out there. And I was always happy too. It was the closest thing to make me whole on Earth. I felt like I had a place with them in it.

I was sitting on my bed, scratching, and scattering colors on the white paper I had on a sketchpad. It was more than an hour now. I was trying to replicate a picture of my family standing with Jesus with stars in the background; a life I longed for our family. I was so concentrated on making it perfect and vibrant as I possibly can. I remembered everything about it. Blue walls riddled with my drawings of knights. A dresser by my right bedside. A toybox in the left corner that I didn't use much anymore. A rectangular window between my shelf and wardrobe behind me.

The door slammed against the wall, and I was instantly taken out from my drawing. I saw my sister, with her pink and blue shirt, jeans, and a big smile on her face. She rapidly came toward me.

"Kevin, the play set is here! It came! Mommy and daddy brought it!" She cheered.

"That's nice, Kelley. But I'm busy drawing..." I tried to speak.

"Come on! Play with me! Let's play 'Captain P. Knuckle'!" She pulled me by my arm from his room, making me drop my sketchpad and drawing on the floor. They instantly ran through the long gold, white and brown ornamented halls with John greeting us as he was polishing the mirrors on the walls.

"Good day, Mr. and Ms. Princeton." He said with a smile.

"Good morning," We both replied in haste.

"Do be careful, Ms. Princeton. It's quite delicate," Mr. Blackwater advised with a smile. Kelley nodded.

In a sense, at the time I had, it felt heavenly. That was why I was so comfortable at home than I was with others. I was safe from the naysayers who ridiculed our family. Johnathan, Harris, and Michelle Yolanda were the closest to having friends. It was a good environment that prevented me from acknowledging, or even indulging myself, in the most toxic bits of the world that some fetishize. That was how I felt anyway.

Kelley and I were comfortable around adults than we were with children our age. Most of them anyway. There was no wisdom in children our age, as they were conditioned to be complicit into living willingly in an illusion of what we called the real world. Which was why we saw wisdom in our parents to tell us subtly of how the world was and how we could navigate it with faith. Kelley and I faced envy, bullying and judgment by other students despite trying our best to show kindness as our parents did for others. But I digress.

We then went down the flight of stairs, through the white clear kitchen and finally out to the blooming perennial backyard. She had an entire display of a pirate playground. We saw our parents there, waving wooden swords. Being a big fan of pirates, this was all she could ever ask for.

"Come on! Come on! Let's play Captain Knuckle!" She jumped up and down, full of energy.

"Alright, Kelley! Alright!" I said chuckling. "But we have to be careful before you hurt yourself again. Like what Mr. Blackwater said."

"I know. I know. Hey, let's go over there! To the ship! There be urchins comin' to get to Yesteryear!" She spoke, mocking the pirate language, running off to the pirate display as I gleefully followed.

"Argh! Let me find you your map to do it!" I said.

"ARGH, Matey! Bring me the map! We're sailing to Yesteryear!" She said with courage as we were both running towards our little playground. Mother and Father played a part in their imagination as well, pretending to be crewmen as I pretended to be Kelley's quartermaster.

"Yo ho ho! And a bottle of rum! Here she is! Here she comes! Yo ho ho! And a bottle of rum! Captain Knuckle's treasure, here we come!" My parents and I sang. They danced silly like pirates did as Kelley steered the wooden helm, fantasizing about sailing down the raging seas.

That is often what she would do. Kelley was always confident, happy, and full of so much joy. And the best thing is how our mother and father went along. The smiles on their faces showed genuine happiness that God gave them.

"Is that a happy family I see there?" I heard the sound. A familiar sound. As my sister and I turned to the backyard entrance gate, we saw a kind-hearted friend of ours. He was an old man, dressed in all black with a white collar wrapped around his neck. His grey hair was circled around his bald spot. He was an actual angel sent from God. He helped my parents move in after spending months in England when I was born. He suggested my father to live in Long Island to buy a mansion after the money mother made as a singer.

"Father Harris!" Kelley and I joyfully shouted, getting down from the display, onto the ground to run towards Harris. We both wrapped their arms around him. I felt his torso pounding from laughter.

"Kevin and Kelley Princeton!" He said through chuckles. He got down to our level and said to both of us, "Look at how big you've gotten! Especially you, Kelley!"

Tipping his finger on her nose, she giggled. He then rose and saw our parents approaching from the playground. He then glanced back on us, a smile across his face. "You were the size as the small briefcase I use to carry to work before. Now look at you! You've grown passed it! Little pirate!"

"It's good to see you, Harris." Father said with a smile, shaking his hand. Mother smiled and shook his hand.

"It's a blessing to see you all together!" Harris said. "I see that you got them a pirate playground. Very nice."

"Thank you so much! Kelley was begging us forever to get this one after her birthday. And the sale for this was surprisingly low. But how was your Saturday mass?" My mother asked.

"Oh, it was a joy. You should all come next weekend. We were celebrating Rosh Hashanah in St. Charles Borromeo Cathedral today. It would've been more of a joy if you were there." Harris said. "But there's no harm if you can't."

"Oh! That's right! Next time, we'll definitely come!" My father spoke generously. "We were busy for the past few weeks donating to shelters last week. Next Friday, we're intending to see Kelley perform in her school. It's a production of "Hamlet". So...we have a lot on our shoulders now."

"Oh, of course! The play." Harris exclaimed.

"It's supposedly mandatory. I'd say mandatory because I know that I would definitely want to see whether or not Kelley's behaving!" Father said, tickling Kelley's neck as she giggled heavily.

"Dad! It tickles!" She exclaimed.

"Exactly," Jone chuckled with laughter.

Suddenly, Harris made a frown. He didn't seem so fond as I watched his smile come to a stiff mope. He gave Jone the newspaper from his suitcase after he opened it.

"What's the matter, my friend?" Father asked in concern. He took a glance at the first page. I didn't know what it read, but my father's face came from sheer joy to disappointment when he read it.

"I mean...I just pray that you will always be the bright family that you are because you have potential to be the pinnacle of what this world needs today. Especially with the campaign you're building. The family foundation is what America needs." Harris stated. "This country...has such a tendency to misguide folks. Lead them astray. They hate the idea of people being people. That just came about yesterday. I just wanted to come by and tell you not to pay any mind

Putting the paper down, he said gloomily, "Yes, I'm aware. That's America for you. And to think I fought for a country inhabited by those who only care for validating their self-worth than they do for...helping others. Amelia and I...have been aware about naysayers in the media making false accusations. Now I'm reading that I have claimed to use my campaign as an advantage to become mayor like my father. Saying that I carry the sins of the father. They're paranoid about losing New York's integrity again. It's as if they take pleasure in fabricating stories. And they won't take our solitude seriously. I really hate getting into this media circus. But all we can do is pray and ask God to lead us through it."

"That's all we could ever do at this point. In times where logic and integrity are sadly becoming futile. He will lead us through. It really hurts to put the kids through this, but I know God is in control." Amelia said as Jone placed his arm around her shoulder. "It brings us closer to him, if anything."

"That's why I have to sacrifice a bit of my time with these two lovely children.... all to remove this stigma and run this campaign. Removing this...falsehood...about our family that plagued us for years," Jone said, gradually releasing angry breaths. "I don't want to have to think about that. The kids get unnerved when I leave. Especially Kevin. But what kind of people would do something this awful? Digging into a family's history just to condemn who we are? Relying on past mistakes of someone else for a narrative? I mean....is it that hard to leave us to serve this damn world in peace?!" He paused and took deep breaths and added, "F...Forgive me. I nearly lost my temper." Mother soothed his shoulder. At the time, I was very confused about what he was so mad about. But I felt hopeless because whatever he was upset about, I wanted to desperately help him.

"Not necessary. You have every right. Unfortunately, given your status and your positions, everyone is going to have all eyes on you. Some want to see you prosper. Some don't. It's an ill thing to do to someone, but it's just how life works unfortunately. They see what you are, not who you are. Just do what you must do for yourselves and your children. They will understand. Right now, they just need to be children...knowing that this world will take that away from them. You must continue to help Kevin as well. No child deserves to see their father wronged like this." After my father nodded, Harris then said, "Why don't we pray now, for blessings? He, alone, can make a breakthrough for you and this family that came from knighthood."

I grabbed my sister's hand and she attached hers to Mum. Our mother and father had theirs together and each hand they had was holding Harris'. All our eyes were closed, but our ears were left opened.

There was darkness all over, but Harris's words were sounded. "Oh Lord, we thank you! We bless you, glorify you, and most importantly-thank you for this blessed family, oh Lord! I pray that you protect them, to always look after them. To make sure that they are always happy and one with nature. One with the divinity. Because you create miracles, and we are thankful for those miracles! Bless Jone, his wife Amelia, and the children Kevin and Kelley Princeton. Bless them eternally and always give them honor! Give them love! Give them joy! And abolish anything that is sinful that tends to get into their way of gracefulness, righteousness, and faith. Let them become embodiments of your grace to shine in the darkness caving the world. In Jesus's name, Amen."

"Amen." We all said.

VI

A Melachonic Discovery

I was happy to wake up from that dream. Not because it was a bad dream. Not at all. It's just that it made me grim to realize what would eventually happen that week when Kelley performed.

I sat on the bed, trying to regain my energy, trying my best to forget about it. And thankfully, the same woman came in with a hay basket that had a piece of cloth over it. She closed the door behind her saying, "Sorry I came so late. It was quite a bother at Davidson Borough. And I looked for more herbs in Eastbound and sent some money to my mother. I didn't mean to leave you alone. And...I couldn't find that friend of yours. I'm very sorry, Mr. Princeton."

"It's okay. You know...just call me Kevin." I said, low-spirited. She came next to me and placed the basket and removed the cloth. It was a banquet of grapes with two loaves of wheat bread and hot steamy potatoes.

"A...Alright. If that is what you want, Kevin. I hope that should be enough to satisfy your stomach. If it's better, that is." She said kindly.

"Aye, thanks for that. My stomach is fine." I said gloomily.

My downs unfortunately got her attention and she asked, sitting by me. "What's the matter? Is it bad? I could go back and get something else..."

"No, no...it's not the food. It's just...I had a bit of a...sad dream. Well, it becomes sad to me. That's all."

"Sad dream, huh? That's always not a good way to start off sleeping. What was it about? If you don't mind me asking."

"I...I don't really want to talk about it. I'm sorry." I said, as I suddenly watched her hand, holding mine. Somehow at that moment, I felt kind of better. Her lax tone even lightened me up a bit.

"Listen, I know we've just met, but if there is anything that you have in mind, don't hesitate to tell me. Don't feel the need to hide it. Even if it's as stupid as Theodore's excuses. I'm a head nurse for a reason. Whatever is bothering you...even personally...you could tell me. I love getting to know my patients."

She said very motherly. After chuckling a bit, I felt lifted to suddenly have my hand to touch hers and I said grinning, "Thanks." I sensed something in her that I liked a bit. Better and less annoying than Ted.

Although, she swiftly removed her hand and looked at me awkwardly, almost as if she regretted what she did. But she gave me a humble smile.

"You're very welcome." She spoke. The door was then opened, with another nurse who spoke. Freckled, slim and red-headed.

"Ms. Higgins, forgive me, I was given note a little late. But it's time to go to the Main Chapel. It's a memorial for those who passed from the rebellion."

"Of course, I'll come shortly. Thank you for the message, Paula." Juliet said as the nurse nodded and left the door closed.

As she looked back at me, I asked, "Memorial?"

"It's a Saturday night that is important. Today's the annual anniversary of the spirits who passed during the old-age rebellion."

"Oh...right. What?" I wondered. What rebellion was the other nurse referring to?

She then got up to the door, with her keys and said, "Please do me a favor and just stay here until I come back."

"But why? I could come."

"There's still a chance that Civil Forcers will be on you for what you did. It's for the best. Trust me."

"Well...okay then. I suppose."

"Promise me you'll stay. Promise. I can't risk you being caught." She begged desperately.

"Okay...I promise." I said as she then wrapped her arms around me and she then said, "Thank you. Thank you very much. I promise to return shortly."

She then left and closed the door right behind her. And I was not sure how to say this, but Juliet seemed motherly to me. Not because she a nurse of course, but I was not sure if she felt the same way with any other patient. She might have, but unlike other nurses, at least from where I came from, she was more compassionate and caring than other nurses who only want a paycheck. And I was growing attached each minute I saw her.

After Juliet left, another nurse apparently entered the room. The woman was essentially half naked. Her dress had two splits for her stocking legs to walk free. Her broad shoulders were explicit, and her tanned face was impregnated with powder and red lipstick. The crevice of her bosoms was exposed underneath her dress. She then asked, closing the door, "So you're the new boy, then."

I scaled my eyes left and right. "Uh...yes."

"How are you liking Heaven?" She asked. Yet, I still stood by on my opinion.

"Um...well, it's a little weird and...historic. It's surprising to see good people like her. But this cannot be Heaven! I still refuse to believe! It's probably some lucid dream! Fever dream! A damn good one...I must say!" I claimed. "I'm just gonna stay here until I find a way to wake up, find my friend and we could get to Iceland."

Sucking on her teeth, she then asked, "I reckon you've met...Ms. Higgins?"

"You mean Juliet. Aye, she just left."

"What do you think 'bout her?" She asked, coming closer, laying her back against the wall next to the window and her arms crossed.

"Well…she's fine, I suppose. Quite quick to welcome someone. I'll admit."

"Well…I warn you not to get too attached to her. See, she is using that tactic to seduce you." She spoke.

"But…she doesn't seem that way. She's…she's quite different, actually."

"That's because she is just using a mask to appeal to you. Around here, she's a bit of a skank. That's the thing about heathens like her! She's a pagan, you see. I hate pagans. You know how they are. She comes off as being a daisy, only to become a filthy orchid soon after she spreads her legs and justifies her hormones with some blind horned god! She's a bad image for women in the afterlife. And these nurses." She finished a rant she suddenly conjured.

"Well, how would you know that? Coming from someone who fancies her tits, apparently?" I asked her.

"I don't have to seduce someone with my tits, baby." She defended. "Unlike her, I happen to have principles. You should know better as a man."

"Fucking hell, lass! Just get to the point! What do you want?" I snapped.

"I'm saying that you shouldn't let her control you. Telling you to stay here would only prevent you from discovering where you are truly. I know you are an astral based on your attire. And bewildered expressions. If you just sit here, you'll never know, and your mind will slowly dry. If I were you, I'd go right ahead to where she is. Mark my words. I will be sure to pray for her to leave. I'll be a true image for women here. That's why I'm here as a nurse…to get the message across."

She had a bit of a point, apart from all that other rubbish about Juliet. I was nodding slightly. If I was truly in Heaven, if I was truly dead, I had to get more proof. How was I still seeing things, breathing air, and even moving? And none of the people I have met today had any sort of proof. Angel wings, alvotons and some crucifixes around the city were the only sources I could find to prove me wrong. I needed more.

"Go on, through here. Make a discovery." She said, opening the window. "This way would be easier than the front door. No one will suspect you here."

With no hesitation, I got up from the bed and took off, after saying to her, "I'd follow you to hell for this. Good luck with that...crusade...if that is what you call it."

I jumped out from the stationary nursing room to the outside, which was dark, and the skies were glistening with stars over us. As I was heading towards the exit of the homestead, to enter one of the parked carriages, which were all in a straight line on a dirt road, I happened to cross over to something odd. I was overhearing a conversation from afar with certain grains of wheat being traded off to a castle.

Panting his tongue, it was one of the alvotons that apparently appeared right in front of me. His tongue was greyish as ash and the in-side of his mouth was stretched by long streaks of saliva. His hot breath kept pounding as he pants.

"Oh...hi there. Uh...not sure how you got out here at this time of night, but see, I'm in a bit of a rush to the Chapel, so...I'm going to leave now, if that's okay with you..." I said, now leaving him slowly as his pitch-black eyes would leave mine.

As I turned forward, I couldn't help but to hear more steps cracking the twigs and grass on the ground. Turning my head, the brute was still there, panting happily.

I sighed exasperatedly. "Look, please just piss off! I'm in a rush!" I then watched as most of the carriages were leaving. The creature suddenly began whining.

I turned back to the beast and back at the carriage, which gave me somewhat of an idea.

I then said to the beast, "You want to come with me, do you?"

The beast joyfully bounced around on his two front paws and back talons. He barked a bit loudly, making me to shush him.

"Okay listen, you could be my little...diversion. I don't...really have any food to offer you. But, if you help me do this successfully, I'll...give you a name. How does that sound?"

The beast panted happily.

Soon, we were both entering the back of the carriage silently to avoid conflict. We felt the vehicle vibrate as it began to move swiftly across the ground. From outside, I heard the loud galloping from the horses, meaning that we were now going back from the homestead towards the city. The lights were all off and it was nothing but silence that filled the entire aroma. And it took a long while, almost two hours, to get to the place.

Heading towards a bridge over the crossing ocean, getting away from the metropolitan once again to another part of the land, what I happened to saw from a little distant, without being seen, along with the beast laying on me, was a large grand structure of grotesque architecture. Surrounded by foggy mountains in the distance, the castle was tall and humongous from the distance, surrounded by stonewalls. From the distant, the castle had four other towers point towards the sky. Two parallel towers were grotesque and the other two were spiky with large spikes pointing up. In the middle of it all was a largely scaled cathedral backed with harmonious bell tolls. The entire castle stood high on a mountain and was worshipped around by pine trees.

The trotting was slowing down, meaning that we have reached the front of the gates, which was sterling gray. As it was opening, we passed two large gardens that were parallel from each other and a fountain right in the middle of it the entire wide courtyard. As we were going around to get to the stables, the turn was long, given the size of the structures.

Apparently, we were going towards the back to find the stables to have the wagon parked. And as the driver did, the alvoton accidently sneezed, making the driver suddenly suspect us. I dearly hoped we were not during getting caught. As I heard locks getting unlocked, the alvoton successfully roared at the driver.

"What the ..." He said, before I kicked him cold at his face. I turned back to the alvoton and said, "Nice job!"

He barked thankfully. I proceeded to hop over from the wagon and crouched to sneak.

We passed from the stables through the entire outer ward, which was a long way to get to the chapel. I made sure that me and the alvoton were quiet. We were slowly and steadily passing every part of the castle, including blooming water and flower gardens that contained flowers and other plants are impregnated with a silver color, fountains and pretty much everything rounded by the marble barbican that was left. We swift through the castle like ghosts by not making a sound to alarm the gold and white-cloaked guards. Soon, we reached the corner tower on the left. Unfortunately, two men with long pole axes guarded it.

I had to formulate another plan to get me inside, which I presumed was locked. I then faced the brute, as an idea came and said, "Remember when I said you're gonna be my diversion? Well, this is your chance now."

I recall a moment when I said that the things, I had with me been gone, including my gun. Thanks to my resourcefulness, I nearly forgot that I had lock picks with me. I thanked Snake for helping me achieve that skill, being that we robbed banks several times.

I use the sharp part of the pin to make myself a slit on the wrist, making the beast look at me weirdly. I winced at my wrist as blood began to emerge from the crevice. It was fine, though. I was used to mutilating my wrists, especially to doze slowly from living. My plan was to pretend that the alvoton was wounded. "Hold still now," I said, placing blood marks around many areas of his long, furry, and fluffy body. "Wash yourself at some pond, afterwards. Yeah?" He responded with a bark.

I send him off in front of the guards, giving him the cue to whine. Luckily, he does, and it gave him the attention from the guards.

"Look lad, that poor alvoton is wounded." He said.

"I reckon that it got into another brawl, evidently. How did it get up here," The other guard said.

As both began to get and examine the poor creature, I went around the fence to go around to sneak behind the guards. I then got behind them and clicked both temples right against each other, knocking them cold. Their limp bodies fell flat in front of me as I began to pet and rub at the brute's fur, congratulating him.

"Well done, lad! You remind me of Rex." I said as he closed his eyes in glee.

I said, after rubbing him, "I promised you a name, I remember. Okay then! Being that you're an alvoton, I think I'll name you...*Algor*. That's right! How does that sound?"

He pants happily. "I think that suits you. Now I need you to stay here until I come back, okay?"

He nodded, which earned him a petting on his horned head, and I took off.

After I picked the lock inside the door, after I commandeered one of the guards' keys, I was finally inside the tower. I went up the spiral stairs, which was leading me to another part of the castle, in a way of finding out that these towers are extremely connected and integrated with each other, making behemoth than I thought.

After going up the spiral stairs, I went down a hall with light lining up against a wall. And from what I saw on the right side of me was ritual going on before me. A lot of people were surprisingly inside, sitting on the benches, facing a large altar. Probably one of the most profound, the most decorated and tallest altars I have ever seen. And the choir singing rang through my ears, the Latin stanzas lifted my feet, and I was slightly immersed. The choir of women and men, dressed in white, sang beautifully like they came from a higher good. Beautiful but full of melancholy, it was still strangely intriguing to hear.

It was a beautiful sight and one I believe to never seen in a very long time. Maybe isolation from spiritual goodness was what happened in my life. This gave me a bit of hope that I stopped to watch. And yes, I remembered that Juliet told me it was a dedication to the soldiers and spirits out there, sacrificing them to war to serve something and to protect their own. Especially the rebellion. I saw their portraits, floating across the entire church like ghosts. There were men in dark brown and black cloaks flaying incense burners left and right and I watched the paper-thin smoke dancing in midair. It made me miss going to church...only those days were gone now.

So then, I took off, focusing back on my purpose of breaking inside a gorgeous place such as this, leaving the choir to sing as I kept hearing it from the distance.

After exiting the hall, I went up another fleet of stairs, going into another room, using my lockpicks to get inside, all in desperation.

As I got inside the pitch-black room, I grabbed a lantern that was hung on the wall next to me and flicked it on, in which it lighted the room. This was a library. A circular place filled with books. Countless of books were all around. And this was a tower I was supposedly in.

I looked around, holding the lantern to light up my way of finding out if I was truly dead or not. Until I came across one particularly book that was on a pedestal, right between tow bookshelf on four steps up.

I went up the steps, going at the book, gaining my attention by its golden lace design serving as borders, which was disturbingly read at the cover; *The Lives and Deaths of God's Children: A Book of Astrals.* It was the size of a large atlas book.

I had to skim through this to find out what this was. It was as if this was a dictionary of all the people who had a life and who passed. All the years they were born were listed, as well as the date that they have died. Not only that, but it illustrated how each person died. It was sickening to look at. Suddenly after skimming through the H section, I first came across Juliet's name, day of birth and day of death. It was written that she was born on November 23rd, 1992. She died from a chokehold on December 20th, 2002. She died earlier from me, which was making me more curious. After I continued to skim, I stopped at the letter J and came across Ted's name, day of birth and day of death. It was written that he was born on July 19th, 1993, and he died from suicide on January 25th, 2004, when he was 11 years old. He was only a kid. He died before me, which began to slowly frighten me. My stomach began to twist, and my nerves were racked. So curiously, I began to skim through the pages until I found the letter P section to find the letter to my last name.

Finally, I stopped at the page, I was too nervous if my family was listed. My eyes began to gradually water to what I happen to saw. It was not only showing the death of each member, but something else stood out. It was listed as it showed.

Kevin Edward Princeton
October 12, 1992 – May 18, 2010
Ascended to Heaven
Cause of Death: Fatal Gunshot Wound

I stumbled and trembled down the steps, feeling my head filling with air and my eyes welling up with tears. It was not possible! It was just a hallucination! It had to be! But somehow, it was convincing. Very scarily convincing.

"No! No! N...N...No! NO! NO! NO! I can't be dead! I can't be gone! I can't...! I just can't! I CAN'T! This can't be happening! This isn't happening! This isn't happening!" I belled out from my heavy chest that my cries echoed the room.

I broke down and got down to my knees, exhausted from this bitter discovery I have come across. Whatever I have just witness cannot be true, it cannot be real! The angels, the crosses, all this talk about the higher good came to me to realize that fact.

"Found what you needed, outcast?" That familiar Italian tone came, making my devastation disappear, as I then turned towards him, and it was who I thought it was. Alighieri.

He gestured one of his men, who he stood between, to knock me out once again, at the same spot on my head. I felt to the ground, cold and out of insanity. Whatever waits for me, cannot be a comfort zone, but another hell I must face. I disobeyed Juliet and broke into a castle. I shouldn't expect something happy go lucky.

VII

⤜✦⤛

Embrace the Truth

The roar of beasts immediately woke me up from my slumber. I presumed that I might need that ice pack that Juliet offered me because the musket got me at the exact same spot. And I felt a hot wetness moist on my head, realizing that I bled. So, the lions, yes lions, in a den that I was apparently impressed in, smelled the blood and were slowly walking towards me.

Shaking my suspended hands, which had the bandages removed since they were finally healed, I spanned to see that chains attached to the wall suspended me. On top of that, I noticed that my clothes were completely different. I felt restrained and tightened. I was wearing the same shirt that bloke Ted wore and grey trousers with black boots. Only I had on a grey jerkin over the shirt. I shook and shook while I was unintentionally focused at the hungry and growling man lions.

The drooling and hot breath of weird lions with humanoid faces caught my attention. I was surely done for.

"Away with you both! Go!" A deep voice emerged as the lions then backed away from me, lying by where they slept. "Forgive the manticores. They are always in rush for meat. Especially fresh ones."

As I turned, it was coming from a man. He had black greasy hair accumulated with a white lock dangling over his forehead, a white robe with a dark navy and white cape down his back, two leather shoulder plates with white feathers underneath both. His white mage robe with a navy sash accumulated feathers and other charms. on his left side. He walked down towards me with his walking cane and got on my level with me.

He then said with this very odd drawl one would hear when watching films from the 1940s, "Welcome to Heaven, Mr. Princeton." It sounded like a strange fusion of British and American.

"What is this place and why am I here?" I asked, furiously shaking my chains. "Why am I wearing different clothes?"

"Well...to answer your first two questions; this is the manticore's den, or simply a dungeon; a place for maniacs such as yourself who brought it upon themselves to break into castles during a memorial...with an alvoton. As for your third question, I had the maidens of the castle to change you. Your original clothing was...well a bit outdated." He said with a regal and deep tone.

"Outdated? You look like you came out of A Christmas Carol or some shite! It's like I'm in a midst of a damn renaissance fair! And you call me outdated?" I spat.

I continued shaking, hoping to escape in time to shove my fist against this man's face for judging my clothing. But it appeared that he read my mind and assisted, "Allow me. These chains are too rusty for a temptation to leave."

He picked out a key from his coat pocket and unlocked my chains, letting me be free. I comforted the pain on both of my wrists. When the man looked away to place the key back in his pocket, it gave me a chance to attack him.

Throwing my left fist, he immediately clawed his hand on my fist without looking, and I felt the back of my head slam against the wall with his cane on my throat. He glared at me with disdain. Suddenly, my head was jam-packed with a series of blood coiling screeches and loud devastated crying, almost like a group of men and women are being tortured to the core. It was bothersome to hear, and I needed it to stop.

"I am here to help you. I wouldn't be bailing you out otherwise."

He said almost darkly. The sterling figurine of an eagle from his cane was held against my throat bone. "You have the aggression of a warrior. I like that, only if you have it centered. So...I'm asking you...to calm down. You think you could do that?"

"Okay...ugh! Fine! Argh! I'm sorry! I'm sorry!" I cried until the screeches stopped. His cane was released from my throat and sighed. "Did...did you do that?" I asked.

"Iticom; the power to cause horrors within the mind...to the brink of driving any man towards insanity. I even use it to overhear conversations. My apologies." He stated. "Those reports were not kidding. You are one to get hostile."

"Well, that's the consequence of finding out you're dead! Isn't it?! How...How could I be dead? How could I die?" I asked aguishly. "How could I die?"

"You've met your fate at an unfortunate time. But sadly, it was inevitable based on what I've seen from you." He said, somehow calmly. However, I was livid and devastated on every level.

"This is Heaven, right? Where is my family? My mum? My dad? My sister? Where are they...?" I asked again, feeling warm moist watering my eyes and my heart dropping low below my chest. "Do they not want me anymore?"

"Of course, they do. They've been on a run from certain terrors that have been summoned." He said. "But they're safe. They've been traveling the Promised Land with the Civil Force Detective Agency to find a spec of land to be safe somewhere."

"How can I trust you?! Why couldn't they just stay in this city? I want to see them! I want to be with them!"

"They are safe. Do not worry. Trust me. All they need is a settlement to live in. And once we know where, I'll lead you to them. They long to see you. What's the matter?"

"I'm just...I just feel so scared! What am I gonna do? I...I feel so lost...." I said panicking, "How the hell could you be so calm when I'm the one trying to get back home? I feel so lost...! I feel..."

I felt his hands placing on my shoulders and said to me softly, "It is okay to be in fear. People who have died and resurrected have encountered this feeling. It happens very often and should not be sheltered. And you are going to be saved, Kevin."

"Saved?! What do you mean saved?! W...What do you want from me?" I asked, still trembling words.

"Your faith." He said calmly, almost reminding me of Harris. "That's all of what is required. I know it is hard now, but you're going to have to trust me."

I was confused. He knew my name without asking. I then asked him, "Who are you...? What are you?"

"My name is Francis Bailey, the Holy Spirit of the Promised Land. At your service. Come, we have much to discuss. Or would you prefer to get stalked by the beasts again?" He said.

And with no hesitation, I stood up, curious about my destination to the Promise Land.

We surprisingly went back into the castle I happened to break into the other night. After going through the spiral steps, we were out of the stone-built stairs and now walking through a decorated yet very rounded hallway. The man was leading me through the halls, which were brighter and decorated with unusual shapes painted with gold, mercury, purple and blue on the gemstone walls. Each window we passed was letting the lights of the sun come down like projectors.

"Where exactly are you taking me," I asked.

"I can't tell you just yet." He replied.

"Why not?" I asked as he then stopped and stood near a large and wide brown door.

He then turned to me and said, "Because it would be pointless to tell you without showing you."

I squinted my eyes in question.

"I mean that we are already here." He made it clear for me.

I then widened my eyes and said, "Oh, right."

After pulling a key from his pocket, he inserted it into the keyhole, twisted it and finally pushed the right door open. It exposed a room much larger than I expected. My eyes were widened when I witness what looked to be a massive dome over our heads. In front of us was a rail surrounding a behemoth roundtable surfaced with a black glistening and wavy substance. I was in utter awe with each piece of large glass forming a coned dome. I watched as Francis went towards a wall and pulled down a lever that was near him.

Unexpectedly, several dark pieces of matter erected as they were both consuming every ray of the sun. Eventually, we were shrouded in mild darkness. I then faced the table to see that it began glowing with various colors.

"Don't be shy, go have a look," The man said. After I glanced at him for a bit, I went near the table and placed both hands on the rail. I saw that the water was in fact forming what looked to be a galaxy of stars and planets. My mouth dropped in amazement.

"W...What is this place?" I asked.

"Welcome to the Kaleidoscope Room. This is where we observe the universe. Spiritual and physical." The man said.

"Like...an observatory?" I turned to him. He walked and stood next to me.

"If you wish to call it as such." He said. He then faced the liquefied display of the universe. "As spirits, we traverse from world to world. This allows us to observe everything from each world. Every universe. Every planet. Every star. Nothing goes hidden. Jesus Christ helms this."

"Huh. And...what about you? What do you do for work?" I asked.

"Being the Holy Spirit, I happen to be a royal representative for our government called the C.R.O.S.S., an acronym for the *Congress Row of Spiritual Society*. Although, sometimes called the House of God. I observe, manage, and uphold well-being of all spirits on behalf of the king and the kingdom."

"Okay, well...why did you bring me to this place anyway?"

"I wanted to show where your body is located at this very moment; proving that you are dead in your previous world," He said, swiping the water with his hand as the entire cultivation of sparkled stars and smeared cosmos dissolved into extremely optical and rather mind-altering images. As if I weren't numb already. The water stopped dissolving and located us to what appeared to be a cemetery. It was a familiar cemetery.

We then focused on a grave that was decorated with jewelry. And there was one person there who was extremely familiar. I recognized the reckless use of clothing and Native American descent. My eyes widened, and I exclaimed, "T...That's my friend! My friend Snake! That must be in New York! Is he...?"

"He's mourning near your grave, Kevin. They placed you right next to your family." The man stated, as I looked deeper and deeper to finally realize that it was indeed my own tombstone. I just wish I didn't know that quickly. The truth throbbed like a cruel knife piercing harshly and gladly deep into my beating heart.

"You're not the only astral who attempted to coat himself with flesh; nor to hold himself still with bones. As much as I wish that would be possible, it's not." The man concluded.

This resolved everything I had questioned, but not in a gleeful sense. I was not happy. From all the outlandish and otherworldly things, I've seen thus far, it was clear that I was indeed dead. Essentially a ghost. A ghost trying to live again. Every hope I had to prosper on Earth was gone. I felt truly forgotten. And it was because of all my doing. Because I was so consumed by the world that it led me to die. There was no excuse to fatally fail my family, our bloodline and foundation. But I was surprised for them for giving me a decent burial, despite my behavior. Presumably, it was Harris who may have founded out. Bless him, I suppose.

"It's over. Every chance I had...gone. I...I ruined it. It's gone." I said gloomily. I hung my head down and shielded away from the glistening furrows of the waters. "I'm...dead."

"I wouldn't say that just yet, Mr. Princeton. This is exactly why I came for you."

I turned to the man and asked angrily, "Why, mate!? I'm done for! Don't you understand? I've done nothing! I have nothing left! I lost my home, my family, my friend! Now my life is gone! What else is there to do?"

"Perhaps hearing my proposal?" He suggested casually. He sighed and said, "Listen, I'll explain more of it. There's a place where I often go. I shall tell you more once we reach there."

I grew curious about this proposal he brought up. He lifted the lever to bring back sunlight and we then left the room.

He took me back to one of the busy boroughs, scattering with people continuing to work, exchange, yelling out their products, everything else. Stands where bread and other pastries were pounded, wielded, and made. We were walking by the open buildings, passing through conversation through conversation, heading to a saloon he later told me about. Some folks had strange resent looks towards Francis for some reason. But some we very glad to see him, offering him flowers which he kept in his pocket. Fair to say that he had a polarizing reception.

"Are they okay?" I asked. "Especially Juliet?"

"I wouldn't get my hopes up, unfortunately. She felt...a bit disobeyed, as she said. Ted was not very pleased with how she took care of you, which made it worse for her. So, I wouldn't expect much or put my guard down." He said as I nodded slowly. I already felt guilty and couldn't help but to blame that cunt nurse I saw.

"And Algor? The...alvoton?" I wandered next.

"Scattered back at the forest of which he came. I'm honestly surprised that you've given it a name. No man nor women of Heaven has ever the thought." He said. "It was genuine."

Nothing was making sense. I still felt lost. Curious about this entirety of this supposed city of Heaven, with people somehow struggling to relive history, seeing how all of it was no reenactment, a question came to me. "So...I don't understand. Why is Heaven so...urban?"

"Urban? What do you mean?" He asked as he turned.

"I mean...I've always thought of Heaven as a.... well... you know..."

"A utopia? A paradise? Streets of gold? A place of eternal sanctuary and...relaxation?" He said with a grin. After he chuckled, he proceeded to say, "In some ways, it is. There are some things that are distinctly different from your world. The forty-nine kingdoms here rule with their own beliefs and values. The seven-two boroughs in this city are decently ran by most competent nobles. Every shop, establishment, even the architectural ones are created by even the most average spirits alive, self-funded jobs in other words. Schools are open minded and very focused on helping students learn and think for themselves. High-rate military forces. Apart from the working class, poverty is low. But...it's not entirely heavenly as you were taught to believe. We live differently according to how we see a heaven. I would say it's...a fair society. One with order, of course, but one that truly tries to acknowledge discrete humankinds. The sore goal for all monarchs is to make this world a different and in ways better world for all spirits. We're very far from making it that way, but we'll try in God's grace."

"What...you don't want peace? Well...why is it even called the Promised Land? Or Heaven?"

"The promise was for your kind, astrals, to live again. The heaven is to be blessed with eternity. And to use that eternity to do as you please; mostly to reconcile with the universe and truly discover your true self. And of course, we value universal peace. But is simply not possible in practice, Kevin." Francis said. "This life...is just like earthly life itself. Besides, the idea of a utopia is even destructive itself. Would you want to live in a civilization where everybody ultimately lives, thinks, or acts the same way all the time? All in the name of wanting perfection or harmony?"

"Well...no. But I expect to be perfect." I admitted.

"You're not the only spirit to wish that. But no one can ever be completely perfect, Kevin. But we could always strive for excellence. Challenges exist to build us. And if we don't acknowledge our flaws, accept, and learn from them, what's the point of growth? That's the core beauty of living. It's the journey, not the completion. Sure, it feels good to be fulfilled. But it feels even better when you are always seeking, evolving, and elevating on that path. It is why stories are created. A world of pure perfection would be artificial living in the name of safety and harmony. Any life isn't about being safe all the time. It's about eventually growing up and learning to craft not just a happy life, but one with meaning. It's not always good. But it's better than one made of a cruel delusion of a perfect life. And we wouldn't want that. Would we?"

"I...suppose not." I said. To get straight to this proposal, I asked, "So what is this proposal you speak of?"

"It's a special one. But...it could also explain why Heaven is in devastation lately."

"Devastation? What could be possibly devastating than to be away from a planet riddled with an abominable species?"

After letting out a sigh, he finally spoke, "The afterlife...has lost its mind. Most folks believe it's dying. The monarchs and their armies are doing their best to reclaim its sanity; trying to get back on our feet. A time where we did our best to come together and intended to make this world evolve. A place where buildings grew high as mountain peaks and flowers weren't outlawed by frontlines. But it's not easy. There's been an epidemic in which it has been about sorely living up to the standards of the monarchies, especially the Chancery, as they are disregarding their humanity. It's become a foreign concept to spirits. And it has been a long fight to get it back. Resulting to war, hysteria, division, corruption, madness. And factions."

"Factions? In Heaven?" I asked with my mouth wide open. "What...like angels and demons? That kind of stuff?"

"Yes. But it is more than just them. They are just the outlier. Here's what it is. I...I also happen to lead... this society of guardian angels. They aren't the same as the angels you've seen here. The Apostles are what we are called by; an order of guardian angels called knights of the afterlife. We not only protect it but help guide it in a way that feels closer to the universe."

"Wh...Who are you going against?" I asked. Confusion was stepping into my head.

"We had...plenty. Me and the Chancery don't see eye to eye for one. Assassins, paid mercenaries, gangs and monsters occasionally, artificial beings or pseudo knights who wish to drag us into competition to take glory. But our primary enemies...were the Satanists, Lucifer's militant unit of dark assassins and spies who work for his empire. I assume you know who he is? Lucifer?"

"Of course, I do. Satan." I answered. I know it's his real name as opposed to just the Devil. I then asked, "But I don't understand. So what? He has a knightly order too?"

"Compared to our Order, his is...more like a cult; a deadly legionary force of militants that has been trying to stop us from protecting the afterlife. As Apostles, we do – or rather did – everything we can to protect and maintain safety and sacred freedom for every soul. As the gods who created it intended. He's been silent since then. But we are preparing...in case he attacks again. He hasn't attacked in a long while since Jesus has enforced a...peace treaty. But...I have an etching feeling they may return, especially with these curses that plagued the villages. It could be a deadly act of their return."

How could that be? If I were correct, I thought that there were only twelve apostles. I didn't think that it would be a generational society.

"But...I thought that there were done with after Jesus resurrected." I asked. "Why does this still continue?"

"Well...it's not what you may think. I was inspired by their deeds and named the Order after them. Instead of just sending a message towards those who dare stand against us, we...illustrate, so to speak."

"By fighting? By having actual weapons and ending their lives?"

"Yes. Afterlives to be exact. When spirits pass away; we reincarnate into stars and go into a place what we call...the Void. Or the Abyss. Sometimes, they reincarnate into paintings or statues. Acting as silent guardians."

That blew my mind. I've always known about a war between angels and demons. But I didn't think that it would be an actual thing. Everything was beginning to make sense somewhat and it got me curious. Specially to understand why I was really called upon here. And perhaps the stars my mother referred to at the time were these people roaming this place as I spoke. It was mind boggling!

"So...I suppose Lucifer conducted that...rebellion some blokes were talking about?"

"Yes. It's one of the most tragic events in the history of the afterlife. It cost the lives of at least eighty million spirits in the beginning of the tenth century in the eighteenth of May. Astrals, purities, shifters, from all over Heaven and the other spirit realms. Including monarchs like Queen Mary, Jesus's earthly mother who was one of Valestone. A lot of them were purities; native spirits in the afterlife," He said. "But that ten million...is whom we were mourning for. Even though we bested Lucifer, it was no virtuous victory to be celebrated. All of us nearly survived, but a lot of lives were lost. Do you...usually break in into sacred places? Specifically, during memorials?"

"Well...no. But I...I'm sorry about that. I didn't mean to do it. I was just eager to find out about...my fate. But now, I wish I didn't." After I released a sigh, I then asked. "Why was I called here then?"

"Meaning?"

"Well, I've caused so much pain towards people. I robbed, beat women, and killed so many. I mean I might as well be in Hell."

"But you're not. When all humans die, regardless of what they are, they come here to Heaven to be judged by the Chancery as they determine your earthly life and your spiritual system to see which realm you best fit, unlike the other governors. Despite Jesus being the monarch and having control over the kingdom, most astrals often fear them because they have records of their personal lives as humans. And they could use that against those who disobey the law of their...branding of being awake spiritually. Now...they were in favor of sending you to Hell after reviewing your earthly life and for what you did last night. They still see you as a criminal. So, I made sure that it was disclosed, especially since I saw that you have an eternal soul in you. Though, it wasn't easy. They are wrongfully doubting you, which is why I am offering you a chance to prove your worth so you could find your place here."

"How lovely. Thanks, I suppose." I replied grimly. In hopes to see my family, I must *prove* myself if I wish to be in the same world as them.

"Oh, believe me, I'm not quite fond of them either. Not anymore anyway. Dante is somewhat okay if you get on his good side that is. But we have no other choice. They do uphold the laws to keep the values of Valestone reinforced. And they're in charge of maintaining law and order since Jesus and Mary do not take part of any decisions on politics openly. They weren't always that condescending, I was told. They did, at one point, care about dealing with foreign affairs of other kingdoms and realms to prosper in alliance. With a decent sum of money and soul, they allow common spirits to create jobs and opportunities themselves, only if it benefits the kingdom that is. They do care for the spirits, but only if they serve God. They basically have an intent in making an empire of Valestone. It used to be one of the most powerful Catholic kingdoms of the Promised Land before it became diverse. It's a lawful monarchy, but they don't have complete power as they may think. Maybe the Civil Force and its constable branches, but nothing else. They are simply officials on behalf of Jesus, just as other governors in the other kingdoms. Jesus has no intention of becoming emperor...even if the court insists."

"R...Right. So, how do these...spiritual systems work anyway? You said that I have an...eternal soul. How is that possible?"

"The Gods pick randomly. And the three realms, heaven, purgatory, and hell are named after crystals. Same as other realms. Spirits hone core gems that allow them to stimulate spiritual growth. For example, every spirit here in Heaven has petalite; allowing them to have eternal lives. Hellish spirits possess brimstone, short lives. Purgatorial souls have turquoise, the same lifespans as humankind. Other spirits possess different gems in the afterlife. Most here are seeking to develop their connection to the stars. And you have all eternity to figure what kind of spirit you want to be in this life."

He then looked to his right at a brick fashioned building. "Ah...here we are."

"What is this?" I asked.

"A saloon in the name of Bo Peeps Litlers. It's where we drink, eat, stay in, and formulate current events. At least when sober." He said as we took off inside.

Inside the building were men and women, some plastered and some clearheaded, passing around conversation. It was not a rough tavern, but it was full of an alcoholic stanch and fried meat, was all. One young man at a corner tapped and scaled his fingers across a piano, surrounding the place with a scaled and melodic nature.

"Oy...well if it ain't the Holy Spirit makin' bad choices." The bartender joked and chuckled, wiping the counter back and forth with a white cloth.

"You made bad choices when you built this saloon." Bailey joked back as we sat in front of the bartender, near the counter. "How are the kids?"

"Fine. Bo is there at the piano." He said pointing at the same young fellow playing the piano. I could already tell that it was Bo. "Peep is with her friends. So...me boy and I are being versatile if you catch me drift?" He then eyed at me and asked, "Who's the fella?"

"This here is Kevin Princeton. Just serve us something subtle, would you? Whisky, perhaps." He said. "Kevin, this here is the best man running here in Celestia. Family business. He makes this place alive...when there isn't another fight or spark of blood, that is."

Franklin came with his elbow on the counter and said, "Any time you want to settle for a...drunken escapism, you come here, eh?" I nodded.

He then took off to serve other customers, leaving me with Bailey once again.

"Forgive me, I understand if this environment is not to your liking." Bailey said.

"That's okay, not my first time at a pub." I said. "So...I still wanted to ask. Aside of killing, how does this all pay to God's honor? Not that I give a good gobshite about God anymore. But I'm just...mildly curious to a degree where I might willingly forget."

After sighing a bit, he spoke, "There was fifty of us back then. The Apostles were once among them. Lucifer was one common enemy of ours. But the Demonic rebelled again and...abolished all of them. So, in a sense...we're the last of our kind, especially with the kingdoms paying to keep military growing; meaning that knights are no longer needed. Our chivalry has been defeated time and time again over the years. We need elements of courtliness. Otherwise, in all things...religion, politics, ...all of them would tremble. And it has from what I saw in the natural world. Most warriors fight not for honor anymore, but for money or material accolades that make them into shallow noblemen. Most leaders are classless and godless bullies who would rather seek power for their own fragile egos and instead of using their laws to protect lives, they intend to reestablish those lives by keeping them dumbed down and ignorant. What I'm saying is...is that there is no sense of civility as it used to be. No honor. No independence. No love. All of it seems as if it they are no longer needed. No longer necessary. Outdated for the sake of garnering a life of competitivity for some.... imaginary food chain. I was a young man, but I admired men who fight with honor. Sovereigns who strive for fairness over their lands and protect their people's rights and freedoms. What I could hope for is for the Apostles to inspire others to act upon their own chivalric deeds and make a difference without being held back. The afterlife needs more than just crowns and labels to protect it, they need a...a resurgence. To be revived for something greater that allows the souls to have some semblance of humanity again."

This gave me some idea that he was only persuading me into this society. Still, I was mostly intrigued about his ideas of knights. I knew about knights. I fancied them. But his vision for them was something else. Something rather unique. Beyond anything I was made to believe.

"There is more to becoming an Apostle than just to fight. Let alone to be a knight. It's about breaking from the molten clay that shelled us so we wouldn't see our true potential. Breaking that belief that we are the possessions of man. It's more than just serving a king, a kingdom, or its god. It meant serving life itself. Life's hidden knowledges that cannot be trusted by the corrupt, reckless, or evil. My ancestors who fought in a decade's war, those who came before, who studied and read beyond inks, reflected on what is knightly. Some knights were scholars, artists or even teachers. No matter how long that takes, what the afterlife is known for...is revivals. Second chances to revive what was truly missing and to...to make it better."

The bartender placed the drinks in front of us, but I didn't think to sip once. The man saluted his drink to me and the bartender before he drank it. I just briefly glared at the darkened ripples of the orange ale.

"And you honestly think...someone like me would be qualified for your...little band of knights," I asked with a skeptic tone. "Because you're really selling this right now. Plus...I don't see myself as such nonsense. I mean...I couldn't find a purpose in the world I knew anymore. I was already forgotten in a way. What makes you think that I could possibly find one here?"

"Well...of course, it's up to you. You could be a baker, a potter or simply a playwright. You could always pursue in the arts, which is quite a popular profession in the afterlife; not surprising at all. I'm just showing options. There are prospects left and right to pick here. But...you tell me. Who knows? It's not about being qualified, but a matter of being helped. I intend to help you. And this is the only way I know how. I see you redeemed, remembered, empathetic enough to help anyone rise above their molten clays. To make them see the betterment and intrigue in themselves. Regardless of any danger, each step you take, each blood you leave will make you wiser. Each obstacle you overcome will only build your soul to be stronger than it was before. Heroes don't let themselves succumb to those who worship broken creeds. They are folks who do what is right without shortcuts. Internally blemished, but willing to be an example. To be a beacon. A monument to flourish more monuments. This is a way to honor God."

Before he sipped, he said, "Again, it is up to you. Whatever choice you make will not affect me negatively or anyone else. It is only a suggestion. So...what do you think?"

"I...I'll think about it, I suppose. For sure. Just not now." I said.

"There's no rush. It's simply a proposal." He said. "I'll make sure to charter a carriage for you once we're done here." This decision making called for a rest and most likely a lecture from Juliet on the way back to the homestead

VIII

⚜

The Act of Thought

"Why? Why did you have to utterly disobey me like that?" Juliet questioned, pacing across her nursing room in anger. I was back at the commune, after the long ride back. Only to be condemned. Obviously.

"Look, it's not like I wanted to disobey. I just wanted to know if I was really dead or not." I said, with my arms crossed and sitting on the bed.

"What made you think that you weren't dead?! I specifically told you to stay! Yet, you left!" She shouted. "Now Theodore had to shame me in front of everyone! Even the nurses!"

"But it was that nurse..." I said.

"I mean how could...wait, which nurse?" She stopped pacing and turned towards my face.

"Just a nurse, I don't know. She was a brunette. Provocative as hell. She's the one who convinced me to leave. She talked shite about you. And other things." I said, watching her suddenly becoming fumed with redness.

"Lustina Wiscoli! That...Greek.... BITCH!" She yelled, pacing once again. At least, I knew the name of her. Her nationality. And the kind of woman she was. "I'm going to have a word with her! Give her a piece of me bloody mind!"

She then faced me and told me, "Do me a favor and never give in to whatever she says. She's nothing but a tramp who cheated her way to get this job! When she moved looking for work in this kingdom, she seduced and slept with noblemen to give good word to the baron, hence her bloody name! I was given evidence by the other girls, which I am sure are true. This is the last straw I've had with her!"

"Right. You've been working with her for a long time?" I asked.

"Unfortunately, but she has always been getting under my bloody skin!" She spoke. "She's too full of herself...all just because she has envy of me being in charge. She only used her platform to be this vindictive, promiscuous, and spoiled girl hiding behind socialism to justify her behavior. She treats the patients with no respect, especially men and those who are not of her kind! I wish she could just sod off back to Elysium already!"

"Well...why don't you just fire her?"

"Obviously! She has no real reason to be here apart from promoting her...message about womanhood, which I've never cared for generally. But it's all a poor way of finding her place in Valestone!" She replied. But she pondered and continued, "Although, I've never fired anyone before."

"There's a first for everything, isn't it? Seeing how you're the boss." I suggested.

"The Queen, Mary Magdalene, is a patron for the nurses and priestesses. There are other huts under Baron Ryan. I'm just in charge of this hut alone, as there are others. But...I don't technically own this place. Not yet, but hopefully. So, before I could do anything, I had to make it known to the queen first by giving notice to the baron. Even she doesn't trust her!" She spoke. I was not aware of who that was. Being in this life, I guess it was fair to say that I was to learn about her sometime.

"Right," I said, simply. I was still puzzled over Francis' offer. I figured that Juliet might have known about this group and I wanted to know if she did. So, I asked, "Juliet, I meant this man; Francis."

She turned to me with curiosity and said, "Oh? You've meant Francis Bailey! Nice. What about him?"

"Well, he got me out of a dungeon and offered me...a position. It was an offer to join this society...the Apostle Order. I was wondering...if you know anything about it."

She grew concerned, as she indeed knew about this group as well. She puzzled herself and looked conflicted. She then asked, looking defeated, "Did he tell you about Theodore and me?"

"No, but Ted did say that you were both in an organization. Are you and him apart of it?"

She pondered quietly and sighed. "Y.... Yes." She replied reluctantly as her blue eyes looked at me. "I didn't wish to tell because I didn't want everyone else to know. It's sacred. It's an identity I swore to keep so I could keep everyone else safe from these conflicts. I'd wish for you not to know."

"So, you more than just a nurse and a surgeon. Fascinating sets of interests." I said, getting the impression of this superhero motif.

"In all honestly, I have these professions as a living since I died. As an Apostle, it's a hybrid of both. And given how knights in general here are not well liked anymore, I didn't want to make it known. That's why I didn't tell you sooner. I never tell anyone," She admitted, as she grabbed a chair to sit right in front of me. "May I ask why you brought this up?"

"I was given a choice. And I thought that perhaps you could help me. I want help, but I just feel like I can't. I don't see myself doing it." I spoke.

"That is for you to decide, Kevin. I cannot make that choice for you. There really isn't a consequence if you choose not to. Especially since you just came here. I wish Francis didn't have to put that sort of pressure." She spoke. "But it's your decision."

"You're right. Thanks. And...sorry again." I spoke.

"It's no problem. But just stay next time until I come back. And ask me." She suggested as I then nodded.

I rested in the nursing hut until the night. For the past few hours, I thought and thought about what I have experienced so far as the dark caved into the sky.

I was wide-awake, thinking. I was thinking about a lot of things, such as how I encountered Ted and Juliet, how I died and ascended to Heaven, how I was given a choice to redeem myself or to live here and regret for the rest of eternity. I was also thinking about what the man Francis Bailey was saying to me at the pub. The perception of joining the Apostles seemed promising.

After resting, I decided to go out for a breath of fresh air. To taste authentic air. Surprisingly, no one was in sight aside of the crickets chirping like birds. Algor was nowhere to be seen, meaning that he retreated into the forests. I looked around and saw how beautiful it was; how the stars glimmered with the flowing river and how the fireflies waltzed gently across the air. I just walked around, still considering what should I do. Most importantly, what or who will I do this for. During my rest, I managed to craft myself a cigarette that was made of white paper and some of the jarred lemon grass from Juliet's jars. I hoped she wouldn't mind. Everything I've witnessed thus far warranted a smoke. That way, I would be sane.

As I inhaled the warm but weird smolder, my family came first in mind. Everything I've done was nothing but for them, nothing and no one else. Mainly due to how doubtful I still was about honoring God and helping others. I still felt betrayed by him. I still didn't feel the need to help others who don't even care for themselves. But if I were to join and if they can help me personally, then perhaps I could have hope once more. And perhaps I could make a true impact on others who did want to be saved. But I have yet to know because I still wished to believe in that. I still wanted to believe in being an example. But it seemed impossible after everything that happened. Maybe I didn't have to join sorely to help others. Maybe I didn't have to join to reconcile with God. Maybe I could join to help myself from these curses.

A faint cracking of the grass caught my attention. I slowly turned and saw a man staring down at me. He was cloaked by darkness. Yet he didn't move. It was as if he were a mannequin. "Hello...you need something, mate," I shouted. But no response. No other movements. I shrugged it off, assumed that he would go away eventually and began to inhale my cigarette. Besides, I thought. It could be a fellow homesteader going out for a night walk.

However, I was taken out of thought from a sudden grim sound. It sounded distorted and unpleasant. I turned around and widened my eyes as I was caught off guard by the same man. Only this time, he wasn't shrouded by the dark. It was an odd fellow with pale skin. Paler than mine. In fact, he looked sick. Sick in an unfortunate way. He wore a dark light breastplate, gauntlets and shoulder armor, black trousers and was branding a scarf mask over his skeletal face. With a black hood over, his eyes were red like rubies and his figure was smothered with a black aura. His shattered cape draped his back.

His ivory blade was unsheathed and ready to charge towards me.... apparently.

"Kevin, watch out!!" I turned to realize it was Juliet, along with Ted. Each of them carried weapons and wearing them as well as their attire.

I turned back to the man, only to meet his gloved claws, which took me into the grass. I fell and trembled as I felt my face loosened and moist.

But my ears grasp screeches of the man. I took a glimpse at the man, who was literally blinded by light. I was picked up by Ted, who was then told by Juliet, "Take him back into the hut!" She unsheathed and summoned a floral wand that somehow became a sword. I even saw that she somehow summoned that light. What exactly kind of knight was she? And what was Ted?

He nodded as he then placed my arm around my shoulder. "Stay with me, buddy!"

For the little glimpse I saw of Juliet battling the bastard was extraordinary. It was impossible to keep my eyes open. Surprisingly, I felt very weak and couldn't move a single ounce of my muscles. Blackness took over and caused me to fall right by the floor after we entered the hut.

"Kevin!" I heard a shout.

IX

In Tragedy or Triumph

The next day, the sound of faint commotion woke me up, thankfully from a dream that changed me. My entire face felt as if it was tightened up and aching more than ever. My vision grew clear, and I kept wincing to the scorching pain that scanned throughout my body.

"Kevin, you're, okay?" The man asked me. He wore a white and red tonic while he wore a sword around his waist. He wore shoulder plates colored silver. His short loose hair was the same color as Bailey's and me. It was weird to come across people with the same hair color as me. His eyes were hazel with the hint of brown.

"How are you feeling?" Ted asked.

"I...I feel very different. Physically. Uh...thanks for saving me." I then asked. "What happened? Who the hell was that bastard?!"

"You were attacked by a Satanist. Ted and Juliet saved your afterlife. She had your face stitched before she left for Eastbound, since you were badly scarred. I'm sorry you had to experience that. The homestead is usually safer than the city." The man said. "My name is Saint Michael, Archangel of the Promised Land, at your service. Again, my apologies. I shall increase more soldiers here."

I reckon he was offering a handshake. So naturally, I shook despite a little bit of hesitation. "I never thought I say this, but thanks. That man...the Satanist...what did he want from me?"

"It beats me, man. I'm not sure why was that Satanist working alone. I guess he was summoned." Ted said. "Seems like they're after something in the Promised Land. This is...the first time I've seen one of them. They're.... creepier and animalistic than I thought."

"Really?" I asked, curiously. "Well, the army should be after them, right? I'm sorry, I don't know anything about warfare."

"It's no issue, Kevin." Francis said. "We just need to protect the other spirits as well. To make sure that they won't meet the same fate."

I was genuinely confused about what happened. I expected to revolve my thoughts around it throughout the day. It was silently awkward.

"I'll give you a moment. You'll get better, Kev. Maybe I could take you to my workplace later." Ted said as he stepped out from the room, leaving Bailey, Michael, and I to discuss more.

"Is there something you need me to do, Kevin?" Michael asked.

I wanted to hide my decision. I still wasn't sure about this knightly society. I must rethink everything over to make sure that I was truly ready.

"Uh.... no! I...I just want to be left alone. That's all." I lied. "I just need to rest."

"No problem, Kevin. Whatever you need, I'm around." He smiled and placed his hand on my shoulder. He then said, "We're thankful that you're okay."

"Thanks." I spoke. He nodded.

"Take all the time you need," he said as he then left the room with St. Michael.

Later in the afternoon, Ted unfortunately led me to where he worked through the carriage and wagon filled cobblestones. I did remember he said that he worked as a painter, so I expected to head to a paint shop. I looked around as I walked, seeing how colorful it looked regardless of the sophistication that still hovered the city. It reminded me so much of the artistic side of New York and how glamorous and creative it looked. I was in awe of what I have witnessed. The borough was known as Great Nails. We were headed to 41 Covenant Street; it bloomed with artistic integrity and value compared to the other bustling districts in the city. It's where jesters and clowns performed the most surrealistic tricks. Musicians of all kinds played and sounded throughout the streets. Mummers, illuminators, sculptors, and painters made home in the place. I just wandered if they were ready to be deceived by institutions.

From the children painting the signs of their stores with vibrant designs to young lads displaying their pulsating crafts for others to see, and most likely buy, I was astonished. Even in such an old environment in the spiritual world, some might have gotten inspired by the culture astrals carried from the world they once lived on. And they looked passionate, on top of that. Something I wish I still had. One could have passion but could see the obvious falseness of that passion being fulfilled.

"Look around you! Look at everyone! They're fighting their battles, yet they're winning. What about you? Cowering in self-pity as usual. Nothing new." The voice came back. Again. I shook my head in all places to remove them.

The shop was called *"Potter and Clay"* as I viewed the swinging green sign outside of the store between several other colonial buildings on the street across the colorful city square. It was written with such delicate care.

"There isn't actual pottery or clay. Just so you'd know." Ted warned me, opening the door as the bell rang. I went inside and saw the staked-up room. It was a decorated with highlighted canvases and several tools staked on every shelf behind a counter. I've witnessed all types of art in just one room; astonishing, it was. Oil paintings, watercolor, ink wash, frescos, and portraits. Some canvases were amid being painted by floating brushes. Next to the counter, I saw painted canvases on a platform, displayed behind the window for show. The paintings came off as unique and provocative, for it seemed to represent internal turmoil that struck into the hearts of open-minded viewers.

While I was still amazed by the environment, Ted came to a person behind a counter on my left and tapped his shoulder. He was a strange fellow when I first saw him. He removed his leather goggles and wiped the sweat from his darkened face. He had on a green jerkin on and a yellowish chemise. He looked up at Ted and said, "Oh, Ted. I figured you'd come a little later. It's nearly 2:30 pm."

"Really, Frask? You know I gotta make a living as well." Ted clowned as usual.

"Obviously! Luckily, we don't have as much work as we usually do. But we still gotta get these paintings out of here at some point," The man said as he was gathering crates from his counter and placing them against the back window along with other crates. He then took noticed of me as he stopped.

"Kev, I want you to meet my business partner, fellow painter, and aspiring inventor...Frask Douglas. Frask, this is Kevin Princeton." Ted introduced me appropriately as the man approached with his right hand ready for me to shake it after he quickly wiped the sweat from it.

As we shook, he said, "It's such a pleasure to meeting you. I hope you didn't take the name literally; we don't actually make pottery."

"Yeah, Ted here told me," I informed him.

"It's still a growing shop. But...I could've sworn that I've taken noticed of you before." Frask said, fixated at me.

"Oh really?" I asked in curiosity.

"Oops! Sorry, I must've confused you for the latest consumer we had before. Had the same hair color as you did as well." He said under his breath. "Forgive me for this messiness in me. I've been so busy lately that I couldn't keep track of names. Or how to clean, apparently. You must've known what that's like, right?"

"I wouldn't know." I admitted. "I've never had a job, to be honest."

"Well, that's fine. It's hard nowadays from what I've heard from the humans. But whatever you can come by, that's always a benefit." He then looked back and saw that his room was completely stored with crates in every corner. "You paint at all?"

"No. Well, normally, I do sketches. At least...I used to. A friend of mine from Earth told me that businesses take advantage of artists for their gain. So, I gave all that up," I said a bit depressingly.

"That's unfortunate, Kevin. I'd love to see what you've sketched. Any world could use more artists."

"I doubt that." Then I asked, "So, what are you in a rush for, if I may ask?"

"You see, I made a promise for Jesus to do a painting for Saint Sarah, Lady of Valestone. Now normally, we paint for a selected few. But Jesus is one of those leaders I respect for his genuine care for all kingdoms here. And for his people. So, we make exceptions in favor for this honor. It's rare, since this is a small shop. And we barely sell or get noticed because of the misleading name. His daughter's birthday is coming soon. And I want to make it perfect as I humanly can. Or *spiritually* can. I just have to get this place cleaned up." Frask said. "This may seem inappropriate. But seeing how Ted and I must get down to business today, I was wondering if you were open to help somehow. You can consider it as a.... *hands-on audit* for today. Just to test the waters. I'll pay you rolics...even if you're not an employee. Ted told me that you'd help."

I kept my guard up for a bit. But the man seemed very honest and not harmful. And I learned a jest about who this Sarah fellow was. Though I was still sore right after being attacked yesterday, I said to him after angrily staring at Ted, "Sure. It'll be good just to get it over with."

"Spectacular! Thank you very much. You could just take those crates from the corners and put them right there in the basement. Careful, they're fragile." He said as he then turned to Ted, "Ted, think you know what to do?"

"I'm gonna help you finish the paintings. Later, I stay to clean up and count the cash we have! But you ladies have fun!" Ted said, taking off to the other side of the room beside the counter. Possibly to start painting his latest creation.

"We will," Frask said as we were both going over to one of the beige crates. As I lifted one of them, my arms automatically felt like straws. They weighed a ton and were already straining my muscles. Going down the stairs of the basement, we were away from the light rays of the sun to the dark and barely lit underground of the gallery. After placing down the crate, I took a breath and saw Frask lighting up the lamps on the walls.

"Damn! These are bloody heavy! What's in these crates?" I asked. "And...what are rolics?"

"Oh, just some...potions, runes and herbs I need for my project. It's...confidential. Now the rolics.... they're the currency here in the afterlife. Bennies are bills. And these items costed a lot of it. Nearly flushed my wallet!" He replied. "Don't take offense. It's not that I wouldn't tell you about my project. I don't tell anyone."

"Why?" I asked as he sighed. "You're going to have to, eventually."

"Well...it's from the alchemists who reside in Jeremiah, where I was ascended to after I died. I was once a member of a group of painters, poets and alchemists called the Neo-Romantic Society. They were a group in one of the last schools of alchemy I attended called School of Jezkel Hermes. They're secretive about most of their stuff since most items are made for arcanists. We specialized in modernizing the Romantic arts by diverting through a variety of different ideas and arts, but in the heart and essence is the innocence of Romanticism. And we had blessed items to produce and experiment to push the boundaries of ordinary alchemic magic."

"That's...very interesting," I replied with a bit of confusion in my tone.

"Oh yes. It's neither to condemn nor forget all these values and beliefs, but in a universe, and civilization, that is bound to change...no matter how much most of us tend to stop it...or to deny its presence, this movement is a way to never forget our veracity," Frask explained. "As a human, I was always fascinated with romanticism and how it could traverse through many genres. Especially if they are experimented correctly. Things can never stay the same, as much as I would like. But we can never fight change...apart from being that change we want from the world. Or this one. That is why they are renewed to adjust. Given how we all must. Wouldn't you agree?"

I nodded as I was gradually digesting what he was telling me. I said back, "That's an interesting way of looking at it. Do you...still practice in alchemy at all?"

As he sighed, he then said, "Not as much. I felt like it was taking a toll in what I truly wanted to do, y'know. It's part of why I intend to invent. Maybe...these tools would be a start...once I sell these paintings to generate more cash to help build this project. If I can market better. I've always been a poor marketer. I guess I have anxiety of being rejected."

"I hear you, lad. But...what would you need them for," I asked.

"I need them for a secret project that I'm developing on the side. I mean...we may have access to advanced technology in the next couple of years or so in the afterlife. Especially with the kind of magic we have. Doesn't have to be man-made as it often is on Earth. So...I had this idea that I wanted to show to the House of God specifically. It's just a simple idea. I believe we've been brought here to flourish new ideas, values, and opportunities, even if they aren't different from what was done on Earth. But...maybe the afterlife could be better. I could only hope when this world reaches enlightenment at some point, establishments would be in the hands of passionate visionaries. Not extreme investors justifying their means for a buck." Frask said generously. He seemed extremely bright, especially when he just had good eye contact with me.

"That why every painting you see is different, but still has heart. Some very abstract more than others. It's complex and hard to comprehend at first. But you've come to accept it for what it is soon enough. I think it's always about embracing change. Especially when it's for the greater good. As opposed to always doing things formulaically and being...y'know, stuck in one aspect of life all the time. I mean...that's how I look at it anyway."

"You're right." I said as I absorbed every word he said. This man honestly had ambition and it honestly would be a bit of a shame if he didn't share it. Reflecting on what I had developed to at least encourage him, I said to him, "Why don't you share it with Jesus? I'm not fond of the bloke anymore, but...he might be open to your ideas. You don't have to make it a secret."

"Y...you think so?" He asked with his burnt eyes very bright. "Someone like that Chancellor Dante is easily unimpressed. That Chancery he's from is not fond of anything that derives from their standard of holiness. I don't know if he acts like this to show his arrogance...or just for desperate validation. Especially with the position he has. I mean what if he's right? It seems like a lousy idea, but at least it could sustain modesty in this realm. Because technically, I'm not supposed to receive these since they are stingy about spirits of Valestone making trade with other spirits from other countries, states, and realms. Jesus allowed me though, since he has my shop protected, even though the Chancery technically allowed me to establish this little shop."

"I mean...yeah...sure I do. Look just ignore that Italian bastard. You seem to have a lot to offer other than just paintings." I said genuinely. I figured someone like Alighieri would be a burden on the government and would dismiss ideas he disapproves of. I then said, "Why don't you go for it without the fear of not appeasing to them? Because... that's what they want you to feel. In the name of some...bloody harmonic world, I suppose."

"That's...very kind of you to say. Thank you, Kevin. I appreciate that. Perhaps in due time, I could show you the ideas that I'm developing. Just not now until I know when it's ready." He said joyfully. "Sound good?"

"Aye. Why not?" I said smile. He then looked up at the open door of the surface.

He then said, "Come, we should continue bringing those crates here."

"Definitely," I said as we both strolled upstairs to get the crates back to where we once were. He then stopped and turned to me.

"But in all honesty, I need to change the name of this shop. Makes no sense in the slightest. I think I was trying to make a poor reference to the Bible."

"Right." I replied, heading up with him.

It was truly a long day and I've never thought that I had this feeling of pure tiredness from working. And yet, the sun was still present regardless of setting itself behind the mountains far out from this city. The sky was nothing but the sight of mellow blues and dense oranges, bourgeoning a unique picturesque view Frask or Ted would like to capture.

After we came out of the shop, Frask had the wrapped-up canvas underneath his left arm with a briefcase in another. After he gave me a medium brown leather sack of what were obviously coins, he was approaching to his carriage whilst facing us with a big smile. "Sixty rolics, all in the bag."

"Thanks, mate!" I said, astonished but genuinely graceful. I placed the bag into my right pocket. It felt like flattened coins all cultivated in a smooth leather bag.

"Ted, you did such a fantastic job with this one. It's your best one yet." He spoke.

"I'm sure he'll like it." Ted replied. Frask did face me.

"Thank you very much for the help, Kevin. And for the idea. I hope to see you again sometime."

"It's no problem. And thank you too for the pay." I replied gladly. As he placed the wrapped canvas on the back of the horse drawn vehicle, he then sat on top and was prepared to leave. The red shire horses moved and snorted almost impatiently.

"It's getting late. I gotta get home so I can catch some sleep for tomorrow...and to think of a better name for the shop. I'll give you guys a dove. Until then...Ted. Kevin." He said as he saluted us as we saluted back. Yanking the reins on his beige spotted horse, he took off and had the horse trot his way onto the road into the midst of the active cobblestone streets.

I felt a tap on the shoulder. As I turned, Ted said, "You wanna hang for a bit? I need to talk to you before we head back to the homestead."

"Um...sure," I said a bit irritated. Suddenly, he was grabbing each crack of the shop's wall and scaling himself on the side until he was gradually getting himself to the top of the building. He then stood and just stared, expecting me to come over.

"You're gonna come or what?" He asked. I turned around as I decided, regardless of my aching arms, to gage myself on the side of the shop. I winced silently to myself, "Goddammit!" As I pushed myself onto the red-scaled roof, I looked down on the road and felt the breeze of the cool wind.

"Any idea why we're up here?" I asked as I saw him looking over the entire metropolis. It wasn't a tall building, but it was decently big enough for us to enjoy the view. I didn't even care to ask about his parkour skills.

He gestured me to come over next to him. I strolled across to meet with him, confused but concerned about what he wanted to discuss. Possibly to discuss my departure to this world, the Apostle Order, and perhaps the attack that happened to me. But I needed to put my guard down. I had to be open for once. I stood next to him and looked out at the rain-mist ridden rooftops with him. He then said, "I already know what you're gonna bring up. *Ted, you asshole! I'm still recovering! Why did you do this to me? Et cetera, et cetera.* Forgive me for not telling you about you helping. But I did need extra hands. I reckon that nothing else in your body is broken...apart from your face, which should be healing. So, I figured. But now ...tell me, what do you see out there?"

"Like what exactly?" I asked confusingly.

"Whatever comes to your mind; but just look out there," he said, gesturing to the buildings that were high landing like cloudy mountains behind them. The bells of the churches and the Main Chapel were once again tolling. But they were more eerie at the hour than they were harmonious before.

"I see...uh...buildings...and more buildings. And occasionally towers. Mountains. Angel statues. Some buildings. Churches." I answered. I then asked, "Yeah, what's the point of all this sightseeing?"

He chuckled a bit while straining his knuckles. "Do you know what I see? Life."

"L...Life?" I repeated strangely as he nodded. I watched him going close to the edge of the roof. His hands were holding each hip. "By life, you mean...a bunch of ghosts living like human beings. Like it's somehow normal. Whatever."

"You got jokes; I like that. You know what I see? I see a life that is not afraid of being honest anymore. It embraces its dualities. I see a life that is fair and...realistic with its fairness. It seems like everything here is old age. But...honestly, it's a good thing in my opinion. Despite its faults, this age's aesthetics take me back to a time when humanity was serious about revisiting arts that once made an impact on civilization. Helping it find itself. Most of these so-called ghosts don't see themselves as such. They don't see this place as a plane where dead people go to rest. They see themselves as... people, like any other world. Walking human consciousnesses who have expressive lives. Maybe that's why it's called the Promised Land. Maybe this realm of Heaven is...not the ideal heaven we were led to believe. But the very idea of living through a world that is given to us to cherish every part of it, make the most of it, become what we want to be and conjure from within.... that is what heaven is to me. People think they know how the moon looks like, not knowing that it has mountains like any other planet. And life has mountain peaks. It's a world of peaks. A world of rebirths. A world to grow up. Something that elevated our humanity and revived its most professional, pivotal, and creative moments. It's a world...of timelessness. The resurrection of it. The poetry of it all."

"Yes. That's very nice and all. But...what does it have to do with anything?" I asked, unsure of where it was going.

"You seem like someone longing to know of life's hidden laws. At the same time, escaping it. I reckon you are someone who would fancy...deep conversations like this. You seem like someone who's in thought all the time, which I respect because...there really ain't a lot like that these days. Even here, there's spirits who deny their indigo shadows."

"So, you're saying I'm special? I assume for your own means?"

"Hear me out, partner. I just wanted to know...what did you think about the life you once had? It'll make sense soon, I promise."

"I doubt that. I mean...it was once a good life. With my parents and sister. Family is something that meant a lot to me. I treasured it; knowing that they understand, appreciate, and know you more than others. And they build you. A community committed to stay and go through hell together to create a heaven out of it. But ever since...your God took them away; I couldn't thrive anymore. Because I couldn't...survive it. I brought it on myself." It was hard to admit my wrongs. I swallowed my regrets and refocused my attention to Ted. "What about it?"

"I wanted to know hypothetically; if you did join the Apostles, what would be a patronage for you?"

"I...I don't know! Maybe, to do what they wanted; do something for the world? But I don't care for life anymore. I don't care about people and their systems anymore! What's the point of all this, dammit?!"

"The point, my friend, is that some spirits here are still shelled by the laws of man. Community, tribes, kingdoms, they ain't bad at all. They're there to keep us civilized and safe. But most of them often hold us back from truly making a life of our own. It makes us feel useless about ourselves. That is the only thing missing, a true humanity. The world we came from made that difficult. That's why the afterlife has more potential to be a chance for folks here to remember their inner selves, to live according to their own accord, not the accord of others above them. Nor the world around them. These folks here, I'm sure most of them mean well. Anybody can be whatever profession is out there in any world. But there's more to life than a profession or community. It's about how we ourselves thrive through it."

I was not sure why would Ted tell me that, but I was suspecting that it was their goal. One of them at least.

"If you were to join, would you be open...to build and stay true to yourself? Because we all have the urge to fall to lose ourselves when we appease to things like religion. Or what used to be religion. They break and belittle our virtue of making an impact on the world. The Apostles are in the business of protecting the free thoughts, faiths, and values of every spirit alive. In any life, instead of depending on machines to make the world a good place to live, it's on us to make it so. And to give the people here to realize that...or not. Communities need to respect that. I know some do, but not all."

I glanced down at one of the tiles of the roof, thinking hard about what he asked me. I had to be sure with my answer because the question almost didn't sound hypothetical at the slightest. Taking a deep breath, I said, "I would be open, I guess. Only if it's necessary. Only if I could trust it."

"Right. I figured."

"But...if I do join this... Order of yours, and pursuit on this cause, what's in it for me?" I asked.

As he gave it a decent amount of thought, he spilled, "Well...anything that you manifested in your head. Those who are opened minded and modest manifest this entire world, this entire land, this metropolitan. If you were to fight with us, you would be different. Not only different, but it gives you a chance to become something better. You wouldn't have to walk through hell alone. Oh, and you get to have cool powers too!"

I nodded, still absorbing everything. I then replied after sighing, "Fair enough. Just as long as I'm not dragged...into any conflict."

"I can't promise you that. But I could promise that you'll overcome it somehow." Ted informed.

"Right. I...I hope she's okay. You know, Juliet. I felt bad for...leaving the hut for a smoke." I said, overthinking as if I have disobeyed her once again.

"You have nothing to be sorry about, dude! A Satanist came and attacked you."

"Well, I wish I did something about it!"

"You couldn't have. But...if you ever do think about getting back at him, and fuckers like him, you'll know when to find the Order. It's always there and open." Ted said with a grin.

I sighed off the bitterness from my breath and said, "Like I said, I'll think about it. I need some time...to digest all this."

"That's understanding." Ted said, continuing to look out to the horizon of the city becoming lit with bright lights through the windows. The buildings were shrouded in dimness. I watched the sun taking its time to sleep beyond the horizon.

"It's just unreal, y'know? This entire world, I mean." I said, still in disbelief. "It's like I'm in a bloody fairy tale. Here I was, thinking that the stories in the Bible were simply just allegories or just that...stories, especially in the vein of this place! Now I must live in this bloody fantasy! But then again...the life I had already felt like a fantasy."

"It's still true though," Ted said after he pondered, looking back at me. "It's still a book of allegories, or stories. But everyone always strives to fulfill themselves in ways they never thought of. I know I had. Maybe this world could be my chance to reach that true potential. To be a better person. And it could happen for you too. Whether you like it or not..." He then faced the horizon. "...This fairy tale... is your reality now. But here.... think of this new life as a book. You're the main character on the journey. The author of your allegory. Your Bible. And you can choose to finish it in tragedy.... or in triumph. So...don't think of this state as death. Think of it as writing in process that is either eternal...or infernal."

Something to think about, I suppose. I then said, "I guess. I'll try."

X

Love and Praise

It was quite a beautiful day on the Homestead. The sun was perkier, and the grass was so green that it didn't even hide its entire olive splendor. Aside of the alvotons, there were other various creatures. Some were familiar to me, and some were out of the norm, such as these white doves that had the wings of a moth. Or even these iguana shaped reptiles that had falcon beaks, eight arms, blue eyes and four tails, crawling about the bridge Francis and I were walking on. He stopped by just to check upon me before he asked me out for a stroll through the Homestead. And it was a perfect time to talk to him.

We both stopped to look over the glistening river and the rest of the camp area.

Francis glanced at the iguana looking creatures. "Ruthers! Not my favorite critters in the afterlife. One came into my bedroom and bit me on my leg when I was a child. It got me temporarily infected. Worst day of my life! They're like STDs from insects. That's very immature of me, I apologize."

I chuckled. "At least they don't seem as bad as crows."

"What's wrong with crows?"

"They just...scare me. I'm not exactly sure why though. I know that they attack. They tried to attack our campsite. It was the time I was camping with my family. I remember I saw a carcass of a deer. It had its insides completely deserted. It had its dangling eye plucked from its socket. It was mad how they devoured every flesh and bone of that poor creature. Worse than vultures. Ever since I died, most in my dreams I've always wondered whether they are circling around my corpse."

"Eh...I could see that. Surely, they aren't circling my father's." Bailey smirked.

"That's because he's always been dead." I replied as we then both laughed hysterically.

"You damn bastard!" He laughed. "We were always purities. Just ones from Bordham. He...he wasn't a good man, though. But that's another tale."

He then asked me, "How is your face feeling?"

"Could be better. But it's fine."

"I know. I'm sorry about this again. We didn't know they would attack." He spoke. "It's been quite a while since they appeared. But he seemed like a loner Satanist. Word is he was sent to do a bit of reconnaissance on the Promised Land for something we don't know of yet."

Despite feeling exceptionally sore from helping Frask, and sore from that attack, I felt ready to say what I had to say to Francis.

"Can I ask you something, Mr. Bailey?" I asked.

"Why of course, Kevin. Anything." He replied.

"I was thinking a lot...about the Apostles. Ted and Juliet just told me about it too. And I'm not sure if what you said was true. Would I honestly make a good Apostle? After everything...I did?"

"Not good. A great one. I was surrounded by a select view that appreciated knighthood. Knights and dames did what they did to perceive justice by their codes. It is what intrigued me. And from what I have seen from you here in Heaven, I just feel something within you that could truly help the afterlife and make a difference. Why did you feel to ask?"

I sighed and looked back at him. "Because...I can't help but to feel afraid. After everything's that happened, I'm just afraid of making the same mistakes again. I just hope that if I do join...it could help me...on a personal matter."

He turned to me. "Of course, it will."

"I'm...I'm such a failure! To myself! And to my family. Everything we fought for, what we wanted to do for the Earth...I squandered it. I'm irredeemable."

"No! You're not!" He then placed both of his hands on my sunken shoulders. "I need you to listen carefully. You are imperfect, Kevin. You must accept that you are. It doesn't mean that you are bad. Not at all. To have faith, you must come to terms with your limitation. You will be accepted and whatever you are looking for in this life...will come. But it has to begin with you." He smirked at me. "There's a phrase that is a part of our sacred code that fully explains that; Love the dark, praise the light."

I was stunned by that phrase. So, I asked, "What is that supposed to mean? Some bloody haiku?" His hands were removed from my shoulders as he explained.

He chuckled a bit, "No...it is one of our primary guidelines. To love the dark means to embrace the notion that we are flawed. It's not an affection with the darkness, but an affection for wisdom that is within it. To understand the light is to accept its dark side. It requires us to be mindful and aware of not only ourselves, but of others and what they do. Within and outwardly of life. To praise the light means to have faith in divinity. Its essence. An eternal strength that allows our conscious-ness to keep moving forward. The light is our guidance. To manifest a guide from within, get attached to it and to seek its wisdom. To do what is just and wise."

It was odd at first to know exactly what those words meant. But at least the man was nice enough to let me know. It wasn't as if I was going to take that to heart anyway. That is if it does occur again.

"So...we must embrace our faults, but always seek out for second chances? The darkness is for knowledge and the light is for guidance?" I asked. "Something like that?"

"This is everything that the Apostles always stood for. It is the balance. None of us are flawless, but we seek to uphold the idea of finding faith and wisdom. We need a modicum of guidance. A life without it would make us into mindless monkeys." Francis said, looking out at the running sublime river. "Every Apostle has his – or her – own hopes too. Every Apostle has something to indorse. And they use the Order as an advantage to fulfill it. Ted wants to uphold self-realization and integrity. Juliet wants to uphold faith and bravery. So, you're not alone. If it is renovation you seek, God will make it so. To maintain a bright soul, we must go through darkness."

After I grasped what he said, a thought came to my head, and I felt the need to express it. "I guess you don't give a shit about humans." I spoke. "Not that I blame you. I hated being one. I hate having these faults."

"Those flaws are what make you who you are, Kevin. You cannot berate yourself for it. And of course, we care for humans. But that's the priority for the Gods." Francis said. "To be frank, mankind must help itself be better. They're still given guidance by the universe. But when the world is in complete devastation, we'll be ready...just if they are truly in need of us. But...they have their own world. We have ours. We don't wish to expose our kind. They have to discover it themselves."

That world used to be my home. At least before it all went to hell. Regardless, I felt satisfied from what I heard. I couldn't really see myself trusting any other profession. And I somewhat owed the man for not only breaking me out of prison but exempting me from being damned to Hell itself. So, after contemplating myself, rethinking every possibility in my head, I finally said to Francis, "I want in."

"Hm?"

"I want...I want to join the Apostles. I want to do everything I can...to be saved."

His eyes widened with surprise, but with pleasantness at the same time. "Are you sure about your choice, Kevin?"

"I am. But...just in two conditions. Promise me that you will keep my family safe. You'll lead me to them when they are found. That way...once I know that they are safe, I'll...eventually leave this behind to live with them. The other is not to mention my past to Ted and Juliet. Keep it between us. I can't afford to let them know who I am. Who I truly am. Deal?"

"If that is what you require, then it shall be." Francis said. His lips curved into a smile. "I'm...honored that you would join us."

He then placed his hands on my shoulder. He then heard a ticking noise from his pocket. He pulled out an item from his pocket, which was a pocket watch glazed in gold. "I have to attend a meeting with the so-called Chancery. But I will be sure to meet with you, so we can officially initiate you. I'll be sure to have Michael lead you to our headquarters."

"Of course." I replied. "And...Francis?"

"Yes, Kevin?" He turned to me.

"If...If I...choose to be in the Order, I assume...that there's no turning back?"

"That's up to you, Kevin. I can't make that choice for you." He spoke. "Whatever choice you make, nothing will be held against you. Do what you think it's best. For your sake. Walk out from a world of constraints...into one with chains off. Either way, it's your life. Take care, Kevin."

He said to me as his cape materialized into cloudy white wings and he took off to the sky. The leaves and grass blew and swirled like little tornadoes when he took off right in front of me. I looked up at him in some form of admiration. He seemed like another breed of angels. I'm just not sure which.

It seemed like a bit of a rush to automatically vow to join the order. But if becoming a knight was a way to be different from whom I was, then so be it. Whatever it would take to at least do something useful for the world and prove that I could find a place here. I was still questioning my actions. But I have yet to know what will happen. So, I would have to soon open my mind to unpredictability. It was the only way not to be disappointed or regretful with my choices. I knew that I was far from reaching Iceland with Snake. It was hopeless. But I would take the chance to make amends with my family. I still believed in building what my father wanted for us. If joining the Order would be a way to get our title noticed and respected, I might as well go for it. It's all that mattered to me now.

XI

The Order of Knights

Finally coming out from the nursing hut after resting, I stepped outside along with Algor only to see Ted and Juliet waiting for me. They were alongside the archangel Michael; only he was in a white, yellow, and blue attire with broad shoulder plates. And I was welcomed by the evening lights of the sun peeking through the leaves of the trees.

Stepping down the stairs, I said, "Morning all. Sorry for coming out a little late."

"You're not late. You're on time. Nice alvoton." Michael spotted Algor panting with his long tongue out.

"His name is Algor. He just simply came to be my pet." I spoke.

"I see that you've managed to befriend with one. Nice! I told so," Ted said, petting his longhaired pelt.

"Juliet has something to say, by the way." Michael said as he then gestured his head towards her to speak.

She looked a lot lighter and brighter than she was before. This was a good sign. She looked at me and said, "After I came back from a village for supplies, Theodore confirmed that he told you about the Apostles. I'm glad you've come to your decision. But are you sure this is what you truly want?"

Inside my mind, I was still a bit hesitant. But knowing that there will be no turning back for me, I replied, "I mean...it's worth a try. Oh, and thank you for the stitches, by the way. It helps."

"Of course. Forgive me if they seem amateurish. I'm still working on it. So...Kevin, we came here to tell you this; Theodore and I decided to...try and settle our differences, so we will be able to train you to become an Apostle."

"Let bygones be bygones kinda thing. And we have you to thank for, Kev." Ted said with a smile, done petting Algor. "Sure, we banter, argue and stuff like that. But as naggy as she is sometimes, she ain't half bad."

"I could say the same for you, Theodore." She said to him. "And I'm not that naggy."

"Just a bit naggy," Ted joked.

"I'm not!"

"Teeny tiny bit!" Ted clarified as Juliet let out a sigh.

It placed a smile on my face. A few days here in Heaven and I have managed to make them both come together somehow. At least for the time being.

"So why are you guys really here for?" I asked.

"Francis asked me to take you the Apostle hideout. I don't know if you are familiar with riding horseback?"

"No, I am not." I admitted. "But it should be a start."

"Excellent. You could just follow our lead. But uh...they're not really horses. We call them...pegs. Horses in the afterlife related to the Greek creature, the Pegasus, in which they could not only summon wings but could be summoned at will by the owner. Especially when you've bonded with them." Michael said, now leading us to where the pegs are were located. Four of them were obviously not mounted, saddled, and had their reins tied onto a fence. We were making our way and crossing a bridge, making our way to another part of the homestead.

When we reached the horses that were in a stable, they all got mounted their horses with no problem. As for me, I was taking a bit of time climbing upon the stirrups. I saw Michael chuckling and getting down from his horse, obviously to help me up.

He grasped me by my waist and got me on top of the saddle. The horse was a simple brown stallion with a black mane.

"Oh...thanks." I said to Michael. "And...I'll just refer to them as horses...for my sanity's sake."

"No worries. You're not the first to have that issue. Now, make sure you grab the reins as good as you can." He said, getting back on his steed, which was a white horse with black spotted riddled all over its pelt.

"What reins? What are reins?" I asked, fresh off my mind. Ted, on his red chestnut Turkoman stallion, gestured his head towards the neck of the horse. I looked down and saw a curved rope dangling from the horse's bit. Grabbing them both, I got a bit nervous as the mount began flaying its head all about. But it suddenly got settled.

"Don't worry, this will grow to you." Juliet chuckled. I looked back at her for reassurance. She simply curved her lips upwards as her hands were griped onto the reins. And thus, we swayed and trotted.

We finally left the homestead to a very enormous, mildly foggy, and surprisingly open country. From there, it was nothing but trees, meadows, great gold valleys and bulky mountains that were reaching the sky. Even abandoned battlefields and fortresses, only rarely. From there, we were walking down a very long, narrow dusty pathway. All were consumed with evening fog. From there, it really showed how strangely and ghostly nice of a place Heaven was. I noticed how foggier it was compared to Earth. I saw more of the wildlife as well. Bizarre creatures inhabited some parts of the countryside, and even the woods. I witnessed a herd of lion-like beasts with ram horns, longhaired tanned oxen and tons of doves flocking in the sky. Algor went ahead of us, only to run around playfully across the field and chasing other animals.

"Algor! Get back here!" I demanded. I was worried that he'd be lost.

"Alvotons have a strong sense of smell, sight and sound. He knows you to where he could recognize you instantly. Even your allies. So, don't worry." Michael said, which calmed my nerves. I was praying that he was right. Regardless of being an absurd creature, Algor did behave like a dog from the days that he was with me.

Michael was then leading us into the woods up a steep slope. Though the journey was long, it was not a painful wait. I felt calm when I saw the trees dancing with the breezing wind. The beams of the sun shined through the hazy fog. I couldn't help but reminisce back to the Ramapo campsite.

Nonetheless, it was still a beautiful place to be. I turned to the right and saw another herd of beasts. Only there were large brown stags with extravagant antlers, five tails, eight black pitch eyes, and an absurd design on their pelts that glowed with white light. They were fascinating to look at, yet it was unreal to comprehend.

"Those are called Luxen. They grant charm in the forests of Valestone." Michael said.

"Right." I said. "So...how close are we supposedly to the headquarters?"

"Oh, we're here actually. Just out of these woods and we are already set." Michael said. I then saw a big gleam of light bursting through the trunks of the trees. It indicated that we were truly there at the base.

"Here we are. Welcome to the Khalservan, Mr. Princeton. The Apostle Base of Operations." Michael gestured his hand with Ted and Juliet beside him. I faced another castle. Except it was a lot different from the Main Chapel.

It had many towers, very grotesque towers. Each white winged man was circling the castle, supposedly guarding the place. I saw trees that were integrated with fog so thick that no sign of ground was seen surrounded it. It was high on top of the hill that it was possible to see the mountains. At least it was a hill up towards the gates, which were also guarded by men with white and yellow cloaks.

"Who goes there?" One of them asked in such as strict fashion.

"St. Michael with Theodore Jefferson and Juliet Higgins. This other young man is with us." He placed his hand on my back.

"Open the gates!" The men ordered. And they were opening, revealing the courtyard. As we entered with the horses, the place was extremely guarded than I imagined. The courtyard alone was inhabited with men who looked extremely persistent and not to be played around with.

"Don't take it personally. They're not up to having their base infiltrated." Ted warned. "Think of it like when a kid doesn't want to share with a bully he's forced to befriend with."

"That doesn't make sense at all," Juliet said.

"It made sense to me. That's what matters." Ted replied. We then had our horses' reins tied in a stable and we soon dismounted from them.

Once we took a good sight around the heavily guarded courtyard, we went inside the castle. The place seemed benighted and wasn't something that I'd see. The pavement-built walls were draped with various portraits, armor, deadly weapons, and the coat of arms of vibrant designs of the Order. The main symbol of the Apostle seemed to be the typical red crucifix, only it had a celestial swirly white star in the middle and several doves on each side.

The portraits had paintings of armies fighting one another, varying from what appeared to be different eras in time. The weapons, unique but strange aged masks (usually ranging from regular antique masks to scarf masks) and pieces of armor were placed and displayed inside these glass cabinets.

From broadswords, short swords, and spears, to crossbows, longbows, rifles, and firearms, I was surprised by how many varieties there were. Including staves and axes. By the number of different armors, masks, panama hats (yes, even those) wares, helmets, and weaponry, it really came to show how committed they were to take afterlives to serve the gods and those worthy of protection. Only in their own clandestine way. The walls were also covered with portraits, displaying feudal style artwork of what looked like a group of knights fighting or journeying on their quests of any kind. A rescue. Quests. Whatever the case may be, it showed. The knights were surprisingly diverse with men and women. Some of the men were old aged. But the majority were younger.

I just wandered how many members they were now. Four, six, eight, ten? I was curious to know.

When someone is in the afterlife, one would think that the castle was a museum. Or the city of Heaven was just an old, aged amusement park. Discovering more and more of it would make them realize that everything that was happening and everyone that was acting upon those environments are legitimate. The feeling of complete disbelief is unimaginable that it's nearly untamable. Feasting my eyes on these antiques in an actual castle was the last thing I never thought I'd see.

"As you may have guessed, we're killers. Warrior monks. The good ones." Ted said casually.

"That's good to know." I said to that response. I then asked, "I somewhat get the masks, but...the fancy hats?"

"Not all knights or dames go to war in armor. Most of us rely on skill and agility, not always blunt action. The tantamount of witch-hunting hats. So, when one goes to battle with elegance, it makes our adversaries mad," Juliet added.

"I...I see," I said after digesting the information.

We then went through an outlandish hallway, architected with gothic motifs. I saw open rooms of what appeared to be a small group of elderly men and women praying in these misty rooms. They were surrounding by a monumental ivory structure with candles extracting their wispy smoke, polluting the dark interior.

"Virtue Elderlies. Most of them came from the monasteries of the Main Chapel to share the same pantheistic ideals with us. They are teachers, messengers, and almsgivers. They pray for protection of the afterlife. They've provided for the village caravan and all others with possessions. The Order is funded by a bank sorely for knights in Celestia called Bridget Bank. So, they had enough to give to the poor and all others in need." Juliet said.

My eye then caught one of the elderlies in the room, but she didn't look old at all. She looked young. Very, very young. Her pale white face was concealed with a blue hood and her eyes closed as she meditated with the elders.

"That's St. Emily of Germany; the youngest saint. Well...she is considered a saint...after she died as a human for her faith. She was tortured and burnt by her grandmother...after she was seduced to a satanic cult she ran. Truly upsetting. She's usually not supposed to be here, but she always assists as an almsgiver of the society. Francis has a room for her," Michael stated.

"So...what is she supposed to do then?" I asked, especially weirdly due to not having any knowledge of this saint.

"She goes to a school of high priestesses, mages, maidens and angels. Forgot the name of it, though." Ted added.

"La Divinum Estelle. I was taught there once when I was new to the afterlife." Juliet said.

"Yeah, didn't ask for your backstory." Ted joked as Juliet sucked on her teeth.

As we passed the rooms, we finally made it up a flight of stairs up to where we then entered a room that had more paintings, coat of arms and portraits. Perhaps it was the portrait room as the entire walls were covered with them. Only there were paintings of what looked like representations of Jesus and his Twelve Apostles from his time. There were more various weapons concealed in these glass cases bordered with mahogany wood displayed at each corner.

"Hello beautiful!" Ted raced passed us to get to one of the glasses displays. He took out a key from his right pocket, opened and took out what happened to be two sterling pistols in holsters, two black leather gauntlets and a frankly usable scepter made of what looked like green mahogany. Thumping it on the ground, it immediately shape shifted into a green with brown spotted python, which was slithering around Ted.

Instantly, I caught the fact that the serpent was his pet.

"Did you miss me? Huh? Did she miss me?! Oh, yes, she does! Yes, you do!" Ted said, mimicking a baby child, as his python licked his face with its tongue. Algor growled.

"Oh brother!" Juliet rolled her eyes, but with a smile.

"What's that supposed to mean?!" Ted spoke back as he wore his serpent as a scarf. "I miss this girl!" He yelped. He then said to his python, "Don't listen to her! She don't mean it!"

"Girl?" I asked, turning my head towards Michael.

"His scepter has the ability to take form, quite like Saint Moses when he freed the slaves of Egypt and split the Red Sea apart. In this case, this is a female python whom he named...what was it again," Michael asked Ted.

"Penelope! I can never make it out alive without this beauty of a serpent! Fought by me ever since I joined this Order." Ted said.

"Basically, every Apostle has unique and diverse artilleries." Michael said.

"Even when we overvalue them to a reach," Juliet piggybacked from Michael, clearing referring to Ted.

I then glanced at the portraits, which really got more of my interest. The wall was plastered with golden frames of images of what looked like other chivalric orders. All of them were surrounding one specific portrait. The portrait took space of the entire wall I was facing. Every painting that surrounded this one came to this romantically painted portrait. The Twelve Apostles stood there with Christ. The biblical ones. They posed as if they were scholars, philosophers, and idealists. They hands did not carry weapons, but books and scrolls. Their weapons were words and modesty, above all things that we used at our time. My eyes were widened by the sheer loveliness that went into making this portrait.

On top of that, it was joined alongside another group of portraits that showed more of the same knights I saw. They weren't dressed as knights, but they seemed to be qualified as such. The tiled, stained, and organized mosaic patterns made sure to capsulate it. Michael then came and said, "I see that you've read of them."

"Aye...I know those Apostles, but I don't recall them." I said, pointing at the portrait above the biblical ones.

"Those were the twelve spiritual apostles that came before. Michael Cadogan, Timothy Gregory II, Abraham Darius, Selena Guinevere, The

Knights Templar ex-leaders Hugues de Payens and Jacques de Molay, Greg Percival, John Lancelot, Jacob Tristian, Philip Galahad, Reginald Redford and of course...Henry Finland. After the afterlife came to a collapse, Francis founded them here in Heaven, befriended them, trained them, and they lived on for as long as they could. They were sometimes considered by few as the reincarnation of the original Apostles." Michael said. "I fought alongside them, only to witness them go. They signified what the afterlife should be." He then eyed at me.

"Not only do we gather as equals, but we train for what will eventually come. Knights were a special breed. They reflected on what the afterlife could be in a deeper sense. They made me see it beyond my own ideals." Michael said, getting my attention from the portrait. "I am not much the ideal Apostle, of course. But it has my support of the Angelic Paladins. I admire them for doing the deeds that others couldn't finish. My kind...the Archangels...most have passed away. But I am humbled to at least see this group live on. They remind me of what...we used to be. And no matter what kind, angels must stick together. Now more than ever."

"So...if you're not the first in...in this millennium?" I asked. "Then...who could've possibly come after the twelfth one?"

The room was silent. Confusion rose high within me. It was clear to me after Michael and Ted both glanced at Juliet. My eyes widened, as my mouth was slightly open.

"So...Juliet, you're the..."

"Yes. I'm the first Apostle of our generation. Technically, the Thirteenth. Theodore here...is the Fourteenth. It's only us so...we've served as senior enforcers."

"We've done this for a long while after the past twelve. Protected the spirits of humanity. In times like these, we need to revive things that embodies greatness." He said, clearly talking about me. "We need someone to help up give a sense of hope to the spirits beyond the illusion of common peace."

It really amazed me. "Huh. So...there's only...two of you. How come you never..." I was going to ask Juliet.

"We thought that it'd be best for you to discover that for yourself. I couldn't just explain everything, otherwise it'd ruin the mystery of it." Juliet grinned. I grinned back at her generosity.

"It's getting late. I should lead you to your chambers. You should stay for the night." Michael suggested.

"Why?"

"What do you mean why? You sleep here now. And you're gonna get anointed as soon as Francis comes back later." Ted said.

"Oy...I didn't agree to some...bloody cultic ritual!" I said, defending myself.

"It's not what you might be thinking...in a way. Don't listen to Theodore. It's to see if you qualify for the Order by connecting to the divinity. If you are truly ready to join us, it's best that you stay. It'll be a big honor for you to be with us. But it's only by your free will, which won't be taken away from you." Juliet said.

After hesitating for a bit, I remembered to be fully committed. I volunteered to join after all. I knew then that there was no turning back; at least for now. I was about to change everything. I was tired as well after galloping six miles to get to a hidden base of operations. So, a sleep was all I could use for the time being. "Show me to my chambers."

Michael nodded. As we were leaving, I looked back at the portraits. I wondered how the previous Apostles felt when they had to commit themselves to one ideal.

Whatever would happen the moment I sleep, I had to keep my head high. I had to have thick skin. If it were even possible.

The moon was on the horizon of the mellow skies. Michael had the nuns lead me to a nice bedroom to stay for the night in a small chamber room. But I didn't feel the light shining before me. Instead, I felt my body shaken. I felt my ears receiving several words.

"Wake up. Wake up." A hidden voice told me as my eyes were quickly widened. Turning my head, I saw what appeared to be two men with dark brown cloaks and hoods over their heads. I only saw their grey short beards and crystalized grey eyes.

"It is time for your initiation." One of them said to me.

Getting down from the bed, I placed my feet inside my brown boots and followed alongside the friars. They closed the door behind me.

"You could've just knocked." I suggested, obviously to be then ignored.

After going through the halls of the castle, I was led to a large, decorated ritual room, masked with wispy smoke. A circular room with large stained-glass windows hovering over us. The voices came from cloaked fellows, reciting a prayer in Latin. I hope to distance them from being some bloody cult. I tried my best to remember that this was an official knightly order. An order who shrouded in secrecy just because they had a different way of serving the afterlife and seeing God. Juliet, you liar, I thought.

The large room was fulfilled with people in cloaks with the inside of hoods darkening their faces. It was glazed with smoke from the incense burners that were hanging from the ceiling.

Six people with cloaks stood in the center, behind a table. I assumed that four of them were Bailey, Ted, Juliet, and Michael. The other two, I was not familiar with. The two monks descended away from me. Each monk was lined up on two sides, making a path for me.

"Mr. Princeton, please approach." He spoke.

After a bit of hesitation, I approached to the front of the cloaked individuals. I get down on my knees and faced my saviors.

Francis spoke, "Kevin Edward Princeton, you have made the chose to become a crusader of the night and a master of the day. You have made a choice to defend freedom for the celestial world. And most importantly, you chose to join to stride down a path towards salvation. For that, you shall be awarded with an awakening. As you may know, an Apostle must remember and go by the sacred code of which we, as the past twelve, as Jesus' disciples, have embraced."

Juliet then spoke, "This is the sacred code of the Apostle Order; Wrestle against the wicked to defend the flesh and blood."

"Wrestle against the fallen angels to defend all souls of the divines." A young, cloaked girl said.

"Defy false prophets and creations, listen to your curators and guardians." Spoke an elderly.

"Make the darkness your discretion. Make the light your guidance." Ted emerged.

"Embrace the pain. Embrace the fear." Michael then said.

"Love the dark, praise the light," a hooded elderly said, mimicking what Francis told me back at the homestead.

"We are crusaders of the night. Masters of the day." Another hooded elderly said.

Francis stepped forward and finished the code by saying, "And never disgrace the fellowship."

I simply nodded to the code. I mentally had to study these cyphers if I wanted to belong to the guild.

"These are the codes in which a true Apostle should accomplish to save the afterlife. It tells of our duty. Just as knights were chosen by God to protect king or queen and country, our sole obligation is to protect and guide all souls of humanity to angelic divinity. We use the wisdoms of Jesus Christ to make sure that every spirit is lifted to find their own values to prosper to create a life with full connotation and higher consciousness. We use our ideals to be mindful of those we intend to protect. We uphold our integrity and honesty, not just our image. No one shall surpass one another, for we are all leaders in our own right. We work together as one. We use violence, not for pure amusement, but in the means to defend the innocence. We don't allow emotions to cloud our minds from our task at hand. It is our task to preserve freedom and salvation for all souls; no matter whom they are. No matter what belief, ideal, or principle. So, are you ready to become anew? Are you ready to walk down a path of righteousness? Are you ready to walk the path of the dove?" Francis said sternly.

Without any hesitation but determination, I responded, "I accept. And I'm ready."

"Then prepare yourself to journey through faith. Prepare to become a renaissance." Bailey said. He then glanced at Ted, tilted his head at the table, which had a goblet lay on top. Ted went up to fetch the goblet. I moved my head, curious to see what was in store for me.

Ted then came down, right in front of me. I stood up on both feet. I glanced at Francis and asked in confusion, "What is that?" I then glanced in disgust at what looked like blood. But it didn't smell like blood.

Bailey then said, "It is an anointment. It is oil that will grant you great abilities to enrich your grounded knowledge and skills. A meditation that helps you connect to the stars. Tap into your Blessed Eye. Be warned, what you are about to experience is a journey through your inner mind. It is a trial of three elements to see if you are willing to have the universe, in its entirety, in your complete favor. To find, face and rebuke one sinful memory of all memories that prevents you from growing in angelic divinity. Or you could also choose to meditate on your own time."

I glanced at the rippling plasma colored oil, glistening with silver from the goblet. "Well...whatever it takes, I bite."

I held the cup to my lips, letting the musky fluid fall down the interior of my throat. It was difficult to swallow because it was like drinking cranberry juice mixed with mercury.

The goblet was empty, and I was relieved to finish it. I looked up at the hooded crowd, obviously observing me and some of them stepped back for some apparent reason. My eyes were suddenly getting weighted, and my vision became blurry and distorted. Everything in the environment were oddly proportioned and weirdly sounded.

I felt lighter. I couldn't stand as I did before. A cough burst from my mouth. As I coughed hysterically, I felt my nose leaking with a hot wetness. My head felt like a boulder was concealed within my head. And it didn't help as I was violently coughing.

My entire body collapsed as energy was drained away from me. Everything else around me turned pitch black. This feeling I had took me back when I was shot. I had to embrace it, but I was still afraid.

I was awoken by the sound of voices. I stood and turned around, realizing that I was standing on grass. But there was something different about the place. Everything was outlandish than ever before. The entire sky was enflamed in with the color of blood. The grass was the same color as my hair. The field I stood on was concealed in a murky cover of mist. Therefore, there was nothing in sight. A sound grew louder.

There are many ways of cleansing
The devils within you are dancing
To stop them is to hold the light
For God calls for the grasp to be powered with might

I didn't know where it came from. I didn't know what it meant. There was no one in sight to tell me. Nothing else but a person. Except it wasn't a person. It was a figment concealed in my mind. There was an absence of light and an obscure haze of smolder consumed it. Dressed in a black suit. It stared straight at me with its fire-colored eyes. It began running towards me after I made eye contact. Suddenly, I felt the droplets of what seemed to be something beyond rain. I saw the sight of crimson blood on my hand, prompting me to look up quickly to find myself in a storm of raining blood. Then the voice came once again.

The rain hails from the dead
The drops of beads colored red
But it falls for the love of what is true
That the blood of God reigns and is within you.

Fear was strong in me, instructing me to run away as I was soaked in blood. I ran and ran through a lifeless field, not knowing exactly where I was going. When I was running, I noticed how I never had the thought to stop. The fear I had for that creature made adrenaline flow through my body. Running through the black colored trees, I finally stopped, catching every breath that escaped me. I stood and looked around anxiously, seeing if the monster was there. Everything fell to silence. No song sung by birds; no sound of wind passed. Just pure silence. Stillness circling around me.

The silence vanquished by the sound of footsteps approaching. My head darted around, only to find a mysterious group of individuals, cloaked. All of them were masked in shadows. They had no shame as they were all surrounding my presence. What got me down to my knees were the voices coming from their mouths. Familiar voices that made me suddenly mirror a series of memories from my time on Earth.

Suddenly, the scene swiftly shifted like wet colors of red, yellow, and green smeared across the canvas. I saw the dirty apartment room, found myself surrounded by it. Why was it there? And what did I have to learn from it?

Outside the building was raining heavily to the point where the city lights were shattered by the rain droplets plastered on the window.

Before anything happened, the last interaction I had with Talia Greyhill was finding myself at my final moments of flexing my hips forward, thrusting between her legs under the navy covers of a cheaply made bed. My face mounted right next to her head as I felt her brown hair tickle my face. With my left arm gripping hardly around her supple waist, my right clamed and clutched onto her hair. When I finally climaxed inside of her, tightening her, I let out an exhausted breath next to her neck. I rolled off from her and laid catching lasting sniffs of air for a few minutes.

My body soaked with sweat. Removing the sticky condom from my member, I turned to her asking with hot breath, *"So...how much do I owe you this time?"* She said nothing. She just gave me a blank expression that descended into sudden bitterness with her hazel eyes.

Aggressively, she just roughly removed herself from the sheets and proceeded to walk across the beige quilted carpet to change.

I sat up and asked almost angrily, *"Oy, what's wrong with you?"* I just watched her cover her plumped bum and bosoms with her black bra and undergarments. She was saying nothing.

But she then said, *"So after the years we've been together..."*

Knowing where the conversation was headed, I just said, *"No! Not this again!"* I then sat up and grabbed my boxers and jeans from the carpet. Then my grey tank top.

"After we've been together, this is still how you treat me?" Talia complained as she was finally changed to her white jeans and yellow tank top. She had on pink worn-out Nike shoes with a brown purse only her slender shoulder.

"Treat you? How many times do I have to say it? You treat me, I don't treat you! I don't owe you anything!" I spoke.

"You have to owe me something...after I've helped you!"

"Help me? You got some bloody nerve. I think you'd say anything to get this nonsense notion of affection!"

"I don't get it at home! So that could be it! Ever thought of that?!"

"I give you the bloody money I earned. Isn't that good enough?"

"It's not about the fucking money! It's about us!" She said with her hands on her hips.

"I'll say this once more for you to get it! There's no fucking us! There's no we! It's about the money you want from me! You date Snake and John! Don't act as if you have dignity. Whores like you never do. We pay you to fuck you! That's it! Quit making it into something it's not, Talia! I mean...what were you expecting when you got into this life?" I said before I proceeded to chuckle.

I then asked, *"Is this about you wanting to come with us to Iceland?"*

After she pondered with her arms crossed, and tears welling up in her eyes, she asked almost tearfully, *"Is that a problem now? In case Snake didn't tell you, that was my idea! I didn't want this job, but I had no choice! There's no point in being here! I can't even take care of myself! I can't love what I've become! I gotta have enough to get out of here with Kim! You know that, Kevin! You fucking know that!"*

"Aye, I do! And I couldn't give a shit about you nor your sister! We're wanted men! I'm trying to hide! You think bringing you along wouldn't garner

more attention from the government's liabilities? How bloody daft are you women?"

I questioned her as I rose from the bed after being dressed. "*You could go...but not with us! You and your sister would be nothing but nuisances! Like everybody else! Unless I have to brain you for you to finally get it!*"

"*Because that's what I am to all of you, isn't it? A toy that you could throw away after you're done playing with it, even though I have a heart and a sister who needs me! I don't know if you realize, but not every problem revolves around you! Food for thought!*" I saw her quickly wipe the tears from her tanned face.

"*Well... be with your poor Kimberly. She needs you. I don't! And certainly not Snake! Maybe the pilock John, but not us! You have no use anymore, Talia. You could be someone else's fuck toy! That's all you'll ever be! Disposable!*" After saying that, I proceeded to pull a crumbled twenty-dollar bill from my pocket. I went to her and looked into her eyes and shoved the dollar to her chest.

I then said, "*I mean...I don't know why you victimize yourself. You've sustained all sorts of pain before. I thought women in this country fancied getting abused. Especially by their fathers.*" I chuckled darkly to how true it seemed.

I snickered, "*I mean who the hell do you think I am, really? Prince Charming? What, you expect me to rescue you from being locked away in a tower? Is that it? Hmph! You women are all the same.*"

Talia was someone who believed that having a deep love consisted of having frequent sex until we were both weak on our feet. Or sending me nude photos of herself. Yet, she always felt sentimental to me. But I didn't care for how she felt. Obviously, we were both trying to escape our burdens. Our own voices. The only difference was that I was mentally cursed with them. She wasn't.

If I'm honest with you, apart from my mother and sister, I saw no true worth in women. I've never cared for them, for they could never be up to par of what my sister and mother were. I never thought about dating, knowing how vindictive, promiscuous, and materialistic they were. Always living in their fantasies, lacking discipline, and seeking to be coddled. I only cared for what they provided, which was sex, food, or entertainment.

But I wanted no part of their souls. I didn't care to show love, for they didn't have it. Let alone from Talia or any other sow trying to have a personality.

As I was proceeding to wear my jacket to take my leave, I swore I heard her mumble, *"Real charmer...like your dad."* My mind loosened again. At that point, I watched myself not caring. I watched myself off a leash.

"I'm sorry? What was that?"

"You heard me! You rich people are all the same! You don't give a shit about anybody but yourselves! Makes you wonder why he's dead!"

I saw myself chasing after her as she was proceeding to open the door. The minute she opened it, I slammed it shut and clawed her brown hair as she yelped.

"Look at me! Look at me, you...," With her teary eyes focused at me, I rose my right hand and swung at her supple face, slamming her to the carpet. I then launched my left foot onto her temple five times.

Despite her sorrowful, cries, I picked her by her hair and pinned her against the wall next to the door. Clawing her locks tightly, I often bashed her brow against the door. She squealed and flayed as I roared to her face, *"Take! That! Back! You stupid cunt! Take that BACK! Right now! You stupid bitch! Take that back!"*

"Fuck you!" She cried. When she would send her hand onto my face, I would slap her back. Twice as hard.

Soon, I saw myself, my hands agitatedly gripping Talia's neck after what she said. The rain was still drizzling outside the window. Giving her neck a nice squeeze as her eyes slowly dilated, pupils shrunk, and pulse stopped. I still saw my face, with no semblance of regret or pity.

I saw how I shivered after doing what I just did.

"You made me do it," I said. After, I saw myself sigh and echoed quietly, *"You did."* With that, I descended out from the room, leaving her static decolored body.

But soon, everything else washed-out to blackness. I found my eyes closed. I thought that was over. I wanted it to be. Yet, the voices never stopped. And the shadow people were still taunting me. Each voice coming from their mouth was familiar to me. I recognized that these voices were from the foster caretakers, Pastor Gerald, and Sister Ann. They were responsible for the pain they inflicted on me. Making me lose trust in humanity, my humanity and God. People like them weren't aware of the monsters they created in society. And often, the monsters are in dark places they refuse to escape. Like Stockholm syndrome. That dark box was now their haven. And what I did to Talia and others were mine. Only now, I wished to escape it.

"Devil! Monster! Killer!"

"STTTTOOOOOOPPPPPPP!!!!!!!" I yelled on top of my lungs until my throat felt tarnished. Then the entire woods vanished in thin air. My feet felt an extremely heated and moist. I opened my eyes, seeing myself in on the black grass again, only this time I was suddenly surrounded by broken pieces of grotesque architecture and stained glass. Broken pieces of my head, which I was forced to look at. And the glasses were broken to millions of pieces that I couldn't make out of what they were depicting.

The broken gargoyles of angels were circulating around and through the deconstructed pieces. Even the sounds of wind were chopped and distorted. It was like I was in space and amid a meteor plane. Something felt as if it were growing in my hand. It grew faster as a flower given every ounce of water. The mysterious item grew into a broad sword. I grabbed it by the handle. I glanced at the tall steel that was almost reaching the red clouds. I then faced the misty curtains, watching to see if anyone shall get on my way. The voice came back for the last time.

Listen to what you fear
Listen to what urges you to shed tears
The shadows lurk to make its due

For the one who controls the shadows is you

The shadow appeared once again. I had to face the monster. I began to charge, holding up my blade to destruct the shadow that reflected my mistakes.

We clashed our swords and began to fight once again. This time, no one is going to run away from one another. Striking my sword towards its torso, it blocked my thrust. I bounced off from my balance. I stood and held myself together, keeping my stance.

Clashing once again, it dodged my strike. It swung it sword, trying to slice my leg. Luckily, I had the instinct to hop. My foot connected to the torso of the shadowy bastard and began to tremble down the black hill.

Picking itself up, it began to charge at me. It grabbed me around my torso, punching me several times in my gut. I hammered its back with both hands. The bastard fell on its face into the grass. I tried to strike once again, but it moved out of my range.

It rolled again. I heard it getting back on its feet, I felt one of its feet kick me from behind. I fell to the ground, but quickly stood back up once again. We both lashed out our swords, gluing them to one another.

The wind grew angrier, and every particle of leaves and fluff flew past us. My hands were almost sore by the force I made with the shadow's blade. Meanwhile, it was staring at me with its eyes of disdain. My eyes widened as voices suddenly appeared within my head. I watched as the shadow transformed its face to many different faces. Faces I quickly recognized. Pastor Gerald's face was wrinkly, and his hair was white. Ann was brown haired and typically bitter and old. When I saw them, I was hesitant to fight them.

"You are weak. You shall never succeed. You will always fail. You are worthless. Filth to the core of mankind. You need to stop trying. You need to STOP NOW!!"

I shut both of my eyes, not letting any word get into my heart. This sudden light of hope within me encouraged me to push off the rebellious shadow. It then faced me once again, lashing out and attempting to strike. I twirled around it, making his strike disastrous. Grabbing it around, I held it by its chest, held my blade against its throat and slid the blade around his neck until I felt a warm wetness leaking from his gash and onto my hands. It was dark waters and it drizzled onto my arm. I pushed off the bastard onto the ground, leaving it to succumb to death. I looked around and saw that the wind had stopped blowing and the particles were still in the air. The sky was coloring itself to become redder. I looked back at the body, only to see it quickly decaying into red doves.

The broken structures quickly materialized into a roundtable. I suddenly found myself standing on the table surrounded by stained glass windows. It turned out to be colorful windows displaying the saints; some of which I recognized like Joan of Arc, who I was facing. The shadows that were surrounding me came back as well. As I was preparing to take them out, I watched them bow in front of me. They bowed.

I glanced and got down from the table when I saw a being. One made of light. It was not a man nor woman. Just a personification of brightness. It held a sword. It stood looking at me, as if it were waiting. I was unsure, had all questions swirling in my head. But it was alluring. I glanced and saw its shimmering aura. I walked slowly and was a few inches away. After I stopped and observed the large windows of saints looking down, as if they were encouraging me. I knew I had no other choice. I had to see it through. As soon as I came in front of it, getting closer to its bright essence, it said to me, *"Kneel on one. As I am with you."* It sounded like the voice that guided me through the strange odyssey. So, I listened.

I kneeled on one knee, as instructed. The light gradually placed the sunny blade upon my head, which suddenly cleared everything around me. Nothing was black or red anymore. Everything felt warm when it all seemed cold. My heart and mind felt lighter when they were once heavy. And my body was lifted when it was once grounded. From there, I truly made my choice.

My eyes were slowly peeling open and two people lifted my body up. My apparition was gradually becoming clearer. Juliet gave me a napkin and it became clear to me that my eyes were dry with blood that was apparently drizzling from my eyes while I was having that vision in my head. It felt real. After I wiped my face, I saw that the rest of the cloaked lads stood there, watching me. And I have noticed the stunningly darkness that surrounded the room, except for the little illuminations of candles, which were held by the friars.

"How do you feel, Kevin?" Bailey asked generously.

"I...I feel...I feel clear." I said, trying hard to find words. "I mean...I feel as if I've learned everything, except I haven't yet."

I felt my heart slowly sinking. The voices that came from each aspect of my life, ones I tried to repress, almost brought me down. If I were to be initiated to this group, this was the time to be honest with myself. Although not too honest. I took a deep breath, "All I want...is to be saved. To forget my past. To forget these burdens. Forget where I came from...to transcend. Leave it all behind...to...to save myself, my heritage, my family everything that once made me whole. It's all I care about. More than ever."

After I felt he pondered on my words, Bailey then asked, "Please kneel for me, Kevin."

Kneeling on one knee, I bowed my head. I closed both of my eyes. I felt his hand rubbing across my hair with the warm ashes falling from my head to my body.

"Kevin Princeton is dead from the earthly grounds. But he is alive on our grounds. God, bless him and give him strength. Let him come to you and make him see you that you are not evil. Let him see that you are his, so he could come to terms with you. Bloom your kingdom within his heart without the bondage of man. He was once fueled with hate, but now he is fueled by love. He was trapped, but now he is free. He is now the head and not the tail. He was a loner, now he belongs. Rise,

Apostle." As I rose on both feet, I opened my eyes. I looked around, only to find the hooded fellows surrounding me.

Michael approached me with a thirteen-inch wand-like rod with three gems. As he flicked it, mist and wispy smolder began to appear and slowly take form of what looked like a longsword. It was a beautiful one. Strands of hazy mist rose high from the thirty-eight-inch blade. It had a bronze grip, cross-guard, and pommel. The pommel was a diamond shaped crystal piece. The guard was decorated with two short-ened purple crystals on each side. Next to the blade and on the guard were two ninety-degree crystal shards with purple gems plastered on each one. The blade was strong and almost had the color of glass.

Michael then said, "The Redeemer. A blade made with quartz that could absorb any element of magic from star angels. A true arcane weapon made by God. I used to fight Lucifer himself with this sword. Wounded him even. It's in your hands now. But be mindful, this is a sacred weapon. Don't be foolish. It is meant to slay the wickedness, never the innocence."

"I...I will." I said, fully committed.

Ted came down from the steps of the altar, grinning at me and chuckling in joy. I grinned back at him. He placed his arm around me and said proudly, "Welcome to the Apostles, brother!" I nodded.

"May the Lord Reign victory to the Apostles! May he Reign victory to all of the Afterlife!" Bailey said, both arms and hands held up.

"MAY THE LORD BLESS US ALL," Everyone else shouted. I stared down at the metallic blade of the Redeemer, which was now my responsibility. I held it high to see its height and observe its meaning. I felt mighty holding it in my hands. And I anticipated for the days to come.

XII

❦

The Dismantle of Modernity

My remaining months has been nothing but intense training since May. I don't think that I have even trained this excessively before. Even if I had accomplished these skills, I was warned several times that it was just a way for me to get an idea of how the methods are done. I was simply a novice. But I felt different than the times I was alive. My acrobatic physics were increased, combat skills were increased, and my brain capacity was more expanded than before. Apostles had to be versatile in all things, combat, stealth, range shooting, horseback, magic, and knowledge. So clearly, the training was expected to be intense. I had to be mentally prepared.

For instance, every Monday to Wednesday, in a large Hellenistic circular room surrounded by foliage and elegant arches, with an opening revealing the superb skies, I was faced with a challenged to become a fighter for a just cause. The circular ground was also riddled with illuminated candles that gave off the wispy smoke that filled the discreetly darkened room. So, I had to put my skills I was given as a criminal to good use.

Garbed with only white loose shirt (though, I was mostly shirtless throughout a lot of my training, given the hot weather), brown trousers and leather boots, I always must watch Ted on the other side. His eyes would morph into black and white color pallets, his right hand was lit with blackness as he lifted it up, which meant that he was using his powers to summon blue dreary and misty figments from his mind. It was the first time I 've seen his powers. I held the position I was taught by Michael, who was one of the people observing me. I had my sword guarded up.

Along with Michael were Francis himself, that girl I once saw and several other cloaked elderlies. But their hoods were down so they could witness my progression. Never liked being the center of attention, but I suppose it was the point; to never get distracted and to focus. Each bloody week, Ted's eerily lively figments would get gradually stronger. The waves of wispy fabrications would increase in numbers to test my skills. Hence, it made it very challenging. They wielded swords, metal shields, axes and spears and even had muskets at some point. He would also duplicate himself and used his illusionary clones to test me. They were frustrating weeks to go through, but I was appreciating it for making me stronger than before. If anything, at least in terms of combat, it enhanced all my skills I was given as a criminal. Whenever I would fail, Ted told me that he liked those who fail and have the strength to get up and keep going. Those who succeed right away and get everything right for them were considered boring to him. I've kept that in mind with every lesson. For several weeks as the winter was gradually approaching, I learned how to hold the Redeemer. I learned how to wield it and to keep my stance. I had to treat this blade as if it were my own despite having no training with a sword. But over the weeks, I was coming in terms with it. Though, I had to practice my pirouettes. Being it was an arcanist weapon, I had yet to see the type of magic it was said to absorb. But as a weapon on its own, I was growing to it.

Every Thursday to Saturday, in the bewildered wetlands three miles away and northwest from the Khalsevan, Juliet taught me how to become quiet and cautious when it came to assassination.

My wrists were concealed with red leather gauntlets integrated with two blades on each side that were attachable. I had a reflex deflex longbow and a quiver of arrows around me and action pistols holstered on each side of my waist. This was to help me enhance my ability of stealth and shooting. It was just Juliet and I in the middle of the wetlands. The more I saw her as she trained me, the more radiant she looked. It was not but a motivation for me to get better. Her strict but genuine matter was for me to be aware of everything that attends to hunt me. I had to become a predator, as my enemies were the prey, she told me. Whether it's silently pulling my bowstring and releasing numerous arrows at each dummy to unleashing the two blades (almost the size of bayonets) from my gauntlets, like claws, and swiftly penetrating the dummies as if they were real, I constantly grew to grasp these skills. I was once loud when it came to my sneaking skills, but I was soon so quiet that I would hope that no enemy would find me.

What happened next was she would have three dummies in front of me. I learned how to deal with such a big recoil. I was dealing with antiqued unique firearms. Including rifles. The chambers of the pistols were loaded with pieces of Herkimer diamond crystals. With each hammer cocked back, I pulled the triggers of both guns. My hands would kick back with intense force as sharp explosive light beamed from the barrels. Firearms worked differently in the afterlife. The crystals would generate ammunition in a form of hardened pieces of light. Not only was this helpful, but it was also a good way not to rely on reloading. Although, I had to make sure that they wouldn't overheat. Each day, I would master the recoil. The decorative floral engravings on the pistol barrels would bloom and spark with each shot. Even when they were cocked and prepared to fire. And because they were made from arcane magic, whenever I pull out the gun's grip, the rest of the pistol materializes.

Next, I learned how to ride a horse, which felt like learning how to ride a bike. Or to drive a car. Juliet would be on her silver coated and white spotted thoroughbred named Violet and had me follow every move she did on horseback. From saddling to washing, she taught me the essentials that were making me slowly seep into the adjustments of being ancient.

The hardest part of training was to summon my powers. From light-keepers to alchemists, shamans to psionics, spell casters to elemental practitioners, there was a diverse variety of magic in the afterlife. The original Apostles were lightkeepers and psionics, the primal forms of magic. Some were considered as tri-lightkeepers, which meant we had three sets of mystical powers that integrated with our biological system. One of which tapped into who we truly were. Lightkeepers had powers given by star angels; personifications of the stars that integrated with our bodies through prayer, dreams, or meditation. Psionics had star angels too, only within their minds. And the more we develop a balanced relationship with them, the more our powers would expand.

Every Sunday, Francis would give me private lessons revolving around the Order's ideals. Specifically, the concept of "angelic divinity"; their cause. He did those in the past to understand and help each member individually. We'd mindfully meditate for at least five hours before I was given a lesson to practice magic. We were at a library different from the Literature Room. The windows had floral curved ends and happened to be large as well as the shelves. Aesthetically, it was more than a holy place. Apart from the bible, there were many glossy hardcovered books. Books that were not in all libraries in Heaven because of the subjects that was considered "New Age" or "sacrilegious" to the public. During the days though, I was seeing that they were the opposite of those assumptions. Although Francis was not too fond of the Bible, he did respect its previous intent, in which it was full of wisdom for readers to adapt and live a holy life. The issue he had is that it was often used to scare people into believing it is fundamental to live their entire life according to the text, which holds them back from being truly spiritual.

He also taught me that there was no such thing as one reality and that we can ratify a perception of our own reality. Just as there is more than one deity people worship. Sort of like spirit animals, wise ancestors or even gods or goddesses of any kind. Even the past Apostles had different beliefs. The idea was that God was everywhere. All the gods were. Comforting idea, I thought. I never really thought of it that way, for I always thought that to find God meant to serve a specific dogma. I always thought that he was above. I always believed that he was even a man. And maybe I still believed that. My entire family did. But not Francis.

He believed that notion killed the nature of being spiritual since it conforms people into limiting beliefs; making them feel unworthy of themselves and need earthly systems to validate their worth. He saw how the afterlife considered it a sin to think that all spirits were gods because of how it took away our humility and strive to serve a higher being. But it was also because of Lucifer. His actions have caused spirits to fear being truly divine. The solution was to live according to our own spirit guides and for lawmakers of society to acknowledge and respect that.

With this idea of angelic divinity, Francis advised that we could seek deep guidance and have our humanity at the same time. We could stand by our personal beliefs, but also tolerate others. We could have freedom, but also be mature enough to be responsible so we wouldn't let that privilege be used to excuse degeneracy. We could do good, but not judge those who didn't live how we lived. We were all capable of angelic divinity, whether it served good or evil. Even Francis was aware of how it was hard to maintain these ideals.

Apostles seemed to see God as not a man, but the universe itself. They see him in an astrological way. Overall, the teachings came down to reaching our high divine selves by being one with divinity. Only he was using Jesus's teachings as a pillar to support it. Jesus once said that there will be signs in the sun, moon, and the stars. And if we take a deep look at them, it was then we could see the true face of God. So, seeing God as only a man was a foreign concept in the Order.

Soon, we would then practice using my new powers. The first time

I held my hand at the open area of the tapestried room, I felt my eyes tearing apart. My vessels would burst. The voices made it worse when they feel discouraged. I would stop and scream on top of my lungs, due to the pain. I would close my eyes, only to see my hands soaked with my own blood. We have those days when we are discouraged. But when you are criticized by your own mind twenty-four seven, it makes you feel grim. Normally, a lightkeeper would be able to use the Blessed Eye the minute they get it. But because I limited myself, I spent months with Francis as he was training me to slowly open my chakras to use my abilities and to be in control of my heart and mind. The ritual I did was a test in a way; a meditation to determine if I was willing to reconcile with light. To trust in it with patience, which was the key. Perhaps this was how Ted and Juliet could use their powers effortlessly. They had to face what hurt them or made them regret to trust in the light.

Today on the month of August, the test was to levitate objects. The objects were a chair, stakes of books, and a large golden four-foot-long crucifix in the middle of the room. My first power supposedly consisted of having control of the atoms of any kind. I turned to Francis, and he would tell me, "The key is to have a strong heart and mind. You must breathe. Make sure that everything flows. Don't focus on the outcomes, don't linger on your regrets. Just focus as you're in the moment; right here and now."

When I began to breathe slowly, he then said, "Close your eyes as well. Block out anything that burdens you. Internally...and externally." I was letting in everything he taught me. "Focus on your breathing. Like we practiced. It eases the heart, revitalizes the mind. Let it flow from you. Reckless society has prone you to rush. Even if you are in control, do not force it. Forcing it out will hurt you. Allow it to come naturally. Stop if you feel like you're ready."

As soon as I took a couple of more, I finally stopped. I made sure that my heart was guarded. I made sure that everything inside me was flowing. It was like I was physically feeling every cell rushing through my body. But it was surrealistically much slower since I was calm.

"Good. See if you can unravel your first power." He said. "Remember one of the odes from the trials. Once you've engraved it into the core of your mind, you will be able to use it. Express who you are and let your powers...become a front for those expressions. Tap in tune with your light...and allow it to flow."

I would nod and focus on the items. Keep in mind, this was one of the three powers I was capable of condoning. I lifted my hand once more, erecting all my fingers into the objects. I placed them all in a clawed gesture and held my stance tight. My eyes were so focused to the extent where I felt my brain throbbing. I felt my eyes letting go once again with streaks of warm plasma going down my face. It was hurting like hell. I wanted to desperately retreat. Until the voices came back to me and said, "Embrace the pain. Embrace the fear."

One of the tenets of the rule was repeated in my mind over and over until it was soon engraved in my brain. The pain was inexcusable, but I had to come in terms of it. Francis told me over and over, almost strictly at times, "Focus, Kevin. I know it hurts. But you will feel less pain when you let it flow. Don't force it. Never force it. Have...patience. Be balanced. Allow the light you reconciled to flow through you."

So, I listened. I just simply held out my hand. I did nothing. And before I knew it, my hand had the same effect as Ted's. Black veins were rapidly growing within the tip of my fingers as smoke was smoldering from them. Francis explained that every Apostle had a unique perception as they used their Blessed Eyes. And they will grow further as we honed them. So, my vision was a dreary blood red atmosphere with every object in the room blazing with darkened black haze that grew like fire. And once I knew it, as I exited from that reddish state, I saw the objects ascending. Floating as if they floated in the bottom of the sea. My hand was gradually getting worn-out from lifting them.

"Excellent, Kevin! Well done!" Francis would cheer with a chuckle.

I shut both of my eyes and released the object from the midair. I dropped to the ground along with them, exhausted and already feeling my head pounding. I opened my eyes, and the fuzziness was calming down as well as my breathing. Yes, my eyes were soaked, and I felt my nose bleed. But I was satisfied. I never thought that I would die and achieve these powers; almost godlike. I looked once more at my fingers, watching as the black veins vibrated within them.

If there was one thing, I really appreciated about this training is that it gave me knowledge, skills, and powers. It was an unusual feeling, but at least it made me different than what I was. Everything Francis taught me also seemed too ideal and almost unattainable.

The Apostles just had to be that example by spreading the knowledge I suppose. I'd like to hope for others to learn from it. But something told me that they won't. They never do. So, all I had to worry about was to be saved. Thus, pressuring myself to aid those who wouldn't even dare do the same for you was the last thing I wanted to attain.

I've had it with serving others anyway, even if I had to according to the tenets. I knew that it isn't what my ancestor would've want me to say, but I'm not him. And I could never be him.

And at that extent, I came to accept the fact that I would fail to live up to his glory. I cared about doing right by my family. Thus, I couldn't care for what happens to the afterlife. I didn't care for life's hidden laws or its beauty. Not anymore. What did I owe it?

XIII

A Wanderer in the Spirit Lands

Four Months Later...

After all the excessive training, it was about time for my first test. Well, it's technically a first mission. But I considered it a test to see what I could do with my newly found skills and powers. Eight months of training felt worthy because though I was still new to the Order, I felt like I'm experienced. And because of my ghostly mechanisms in my body, I felt as if I can absorb very quickly than I could when I was a human. It was the month of December, which meant that the weather was getting colder and colder. But the night never looked this bright. And I was now nineteen years old, which meant that I was trained at the right time.

With Jesus's permission, Francis invited Ted, Juliet and me to the congregation known as the Annual Gathering of the Spirits, which essentially meant to celebrate the existence of the afterlife. It was a way to honor the spirits of all kinds and to extract total change of pace for each course of action. Say a mix between the Royal Ball and a State of the Union. Every corridor was decorated with blue, gold, orange and silver confetti and drapes printed with various exotic designs and colors. My fellow Apostles and I strolled through the halls of The Palace of Jehovah. It's usually where kings and queen will conduct their practices. So naturally, it was normal to conduct an entire festival. Francis only instructed us to come to protect the monarchs. Francis was always one to give us tasks to fulfill as Apostles. And this mission was the first, given how Apostles weren't allowed to festive occasions because it attracted "trouble".

Sometimes, we would be assisted with the Angels themselves. But in this case, Michael was with us. The Civil Force Principalities of the city were guarding the palace for the night. And given how that one Satanist summoned and attacked me, it was safe to assume the grim possibilities of expecting more of them. Now I've been to big parties when I was alive. My family held parties in the same vein as this, but not to this extent. And I've always felt awkward in them. I was never a fan of gathering with folks who were all wrapped up in their pseudo goodness just to put up an impression.

My father would host gatherings with a decent amount of people who were his true friends to celebrate certain occasions. Private investors, lawyers and promoters who were all trying to help flourish his campaign. I remembered they had private meetings in our living room afterwards in which Kelley and I weren't allowed to attend. Our mother was there too. These were the few who were there for us, but I didn't know them personally. And I assumed they've forgotten about us as well.

As we passed the large mahogany doors, it didn't take long to know that it was indeed a large palace with very large halls made with marble, alabaster, and colorful crystals. They were lit with a quartz white tint hitting against the golden accents of the interiors. Pillars were starry-eyed and integrated with the white marble walls.

The entire interiors busted with accents colored with bronze gold, crystal whites and blues. Outside, as I gazed into the windows, had dark blue skies riddled with stars, which were livelier than ever. My fellow mates and I were obviously dressed properly. Ted had on a very elegant brown coat with black boots dark brown trousers while Juliet wore this very regal and radiant light blue shoulder less dress, which matched her eyes. I wore a black coat decorated with white ornate accents, which it should be expected anyway.

Despite mostly being there to guard the king, we spent half of our night acting, as we were part of the crowd. A crowd of folks posing and prancing in these lavish, sophisticated, and most likely expensive dresses, jewels, and suits. From getting our portraits painted to exploring all the rich halls of the palace, I felt like I was truly lost. All this time, I had to stick with Ted and Juliet. At one point, Juliet engaged in a brief conversation with this dashing and rather dapper looking fellow with rolled up brown hair, a white coat with navy accents, black breeches, and sharp chin.

Though, she didn't look very happy to see him. I was too overwhelmed by everything else to ask her of the man she was speaking to. Soon, during our walks through the great galleries, I complimented Juliet, in which she heeded and appreciated. Even blushing.

Her blue ballroom dress really caught me off guard because of how much of a fighter she was. And as an Apostle, it was always important to be versatile in everything, including in style. Obviously, being the first Apostles in my generation, Ted and Juliet clearly did their homework.

As we exited from the grand halls, we entered the ballroom. The entire room was crowded and had a table surrounding another table, which held roasted pig, cow beef, boiled fish on lavish plates and other beverages like moonshine, ale, and various ciders served with prestige glasses. It was filled with priests, priestesses, aristocrats, clergies, and other citizens of the Promised Land.

The Chancellors Francis and Ted told me about where there as well with their decorated gold and white religious robes with miter hats. And I figured that it was them as soon as I recognized the Italian bastard Dante dressed amongst them. Marquises, maidens, barons, bishops, duchesses, lords, ladies, noblemen, noblewomen and dukes of the city stood about with shiny wine glasses in their hands, laughing and spewing God knows what. The vocals of bright angels and a choir of little lasses filled the room, cohesive with the number of conversations going on at once with a few dancing regally. The priestesses were holding and softly swinging chained braziers as lines of smoke were escaping the pinholes of each pot.

I turned to a royally dressed Michael and he warned, "There are bound to be something wrong. It's fine to enjoy this fine ceremony. But...be vigilant as well."

"Be nice as a dove, wise as a serpent." Juliet revised. "Understood."

"Best of luck. It's best you find a seat to wait for the king's arrival." Michael said before he nodded and took off, disappeared into the crowd.

I then turned to Juliet as she spoke, "Here how it goes; one of our eyes will eventually bleed out. That's our signal to be ready and leave immediately."

"I'm sorry...bleed out?" I asked, hoping that wasn't true. I know that were tri-lightkeepers, but that seemed deadly.

"Most often, your eyes will bleed when the star angel in your body senses danger in your environment. It could happen at any time. When something is not right. So, be aware." Juliet warned as she then turned to see Francis alongside Jesus and a few other well-dressed people.

"Okay...well...that's just both interesting and disgusting, isn't it?" I questioned.

"It's a matter of perspective," Ted said.

"Nothing has ever happened in these events. Ever. So, when it does come, one of us must leave and find out what, or whom, dares to intervene. Before the celebration, Francis managed to reserve a room on the third floor for your clothes and companion Algor, Kevin."

"Juliet and I will use the first floor. Our stuff is held in the other interiors." Ted added.

"So...why am I all the way at the third floor?" I asked.

"Obviously, we aren't supposed to have creatures in this place. But Al is our best chance of sniffing anything suspicious, just so we don't abuse too much of our powers. And since you and Al are close, we thought it'd be best for you to see if anything comes from there. This palace is easy enough for these bastards to make a target out of. We must keep a close eye on each interior. You got it?" Ted asked.

"Understood. I guess." I agreed, though I was still a bit distracted by the number of spirits they were. I jested, "Just as long as we get endorsed somehow or.... you get killed, I'm happy."

"Very funny, friend," Ted said with sarcasm.

I then observed until my eye caught two young gentlemen sounding the horn of the trumpets: a symphonic but almost demanding melody. This made the entire room silent.

"That's our cue to split. Good luck, mon frère," Ted said as Juliet and he strolled away from my space.

Despite the colored draped spirits nearly covering my way, I managed to see the Lord and Savior Jesus Christ himself rising from his own table, which he shared with other interesting fellows. During my training, I've read how Jesus claimed the throne after he went back to Heaven and eventually married Mary Magdalene when she died, one of his fellow Apostles. They had a daughter Sarah La-Kali, who was called the Lady of Heaven. I read that they gave birth to her after they were married in the afterlife. Mary Magdalene joined Jesus' side after she passed. And it was quite frightening yet astonishing to see them all before me. They all stood to burst their chests with regal profession, as well as Francis. They dressed in drapes that were riddled with jewels, sapphires, and pearls.

Jesus looked a bit superior. More than I expected. I would assume that he was an everyday bloke, like all of us. At least that what I was told. But from my eyes, he made himself an actual king. And he looked much elderly as well. He had bits of strained white hair conjoined with his burnt brown long hair. He had on a silver crown with Jewish accents on it. Kings have the tendency to abuse their positions when they allow it to get into their minds. Even as a kid, I failed to trust those who call themselves kings or presidents. It was never about the wellbeing. Only their royalties and reputes. Nevertheless, I was interested to see what the orange and purple robed king had to say. When he spoke, I was surprised to hear his accent. From the world that I've known, every form of media has made Jesus clear spoken and down to our time. But it was clear that the Jesus I see and hear at that very moment was the opposite of what I was raised to believe. So, I was stunned to truly hear him with my own ears. He looked to be hiding a cautious feeling on his face. Perhaps he had an intuition. But not to worry his audience, he swallowed it and flashed a smile across his face as he began to speak.

"My dear sons and daughters of God, I welcome you all to this gathering that we have here today. My father, God, only knows how I am overwhelmed by your presence. Before we feast, I was in hopes to give a few words just, so I wouldn't leave you standing anticipating consuming the delicious food our chefs have thrived for us today. Firstly, we all must know by now that we are all of God's children, regardless of who we are. What we believe in," he said as the crowd applauded amid his speech.

"That is what we strive for. This is the purpose of the Promise Land; to live once again. It hasn't always been easy to do so, especially with the likes of Lucifer in our midst. But with the great influence of our hands that will make the souls of humankind see a revival we will have a fair world. I would love to give credit to our students of La Divinum Estelle and for the saints and professors who continue their work. They have done the afterlife justice," he said, this time gesturing to the hierarch of women and young girls who were dressed in virginal dresses with floral patterns as the crowd applauds greatly. "I also want to give much credit to the Holy Spirit of Heaven and best friend, Francis Bailey, my dear wife Mary Magdalene, my lovely daughter Sarah, my fellow guardian Saint Michael the Archangel, Chancellor Dante Alighieri, and the leader of the Principalities' Civil Force Detective Agency...Ms. Bertha June."

The given names rose from their seats and smile as they received the applause from many that it filled the entire room. Afterwards, it went back to silence.

"With their help, and yours, with proper guidance, we will make the afterlife a holy place. As some of you may know, I was a carpenter at some point in time when I was sent to the natural world. I was prompted to create furniture. Soon, I was called by God to give my life on the cross. And when I was welcomed back to Heaven, I had to create this place different. That is my priority. I believe that we are all carpenters in our own right. We all intend to create something for ourselves with personal responsibility and improvement. This world grants you the chance to become something better. That's why the Gods created this universe, so we could continue to exist. So, we can have a second chance. Do not think of me as your king, but as an equal. Just as all of you. And with the eventual unity of other divinities with codes of honor, love, and nobility, we will brighten the afterlives of all spirits. I believe that everyone deserves a second chance to become better; no matter how much darkness there is to sustain, it takes strong commitment to see and bring the light. Things in life starts from you. God bless you all," He then turned to his daughter. "Sarah, my dear, if you would please finish with prayer?"

I personally didn't bother to close my eyes for prayer. I just observed, which I was surprised that Jesus didn't seem to mind. I saw that a few didn't as well, including Ted and Juliet. I watched as the Lady's eyes glowed like rubies as she got up and spoke, "We thank you, God. We thank you for your holy land of souls. This kingdom, this land, this life, was made in your accord and we vow to do what we can to continue to let it flourish. Let us dine and do it in you glory as we dine with you on the throne. In God's name, Amen."

"Amen." He repeated.

After the applause, and that bloody lengthy speech, we all proceeded to our seats where we were all serve roast beef with Caesar salad and a loaf of bread by waitresses. I sat down and all I have done was observed. But I mostly observed how happy these spirits were to see one another. My eyes widened at the thought of being in an actual palace with people who have a sense of modesty and faith. It was strong in the room.

Never on earth have I thought of myself being surrounded by spirits. It was like I was pushed to discover a new species. But they were just like me. Like all of us. Except that they were celestial from their physical bodies and are forced to live spiritually in this new strange life. I witness Jesus swiftly whispering something to Michael as the Archangel suddenly stood up from the table to disperse alongside few other guards. But I remained focus on my food.

I dug my teeth onto the beef, eating it as properly as I can. I had to remember that this was the new me now. The renaissance me. So, I had to disown my savage behavior. Especially in a diplomatic place. I reflected a bit back when I had a party like this in what was once home, Kelley and I would run around and unintentionally disrupt the guests out of boredom. So, I smiled as soon as I saw several children wandering around. They wandered around like they are discovering a new land to inhabit. I guess we are all discovering someplace.

My enjoyment for meat was suddenly interrupted by a voice, "Fancying fresh beef, I see. No worries, everything from the spirits of Valhalla is delicious. For war-obsessed spirits, they're pretty good cooks too. But what else can you get from Vikings anyway?"

As I turned, I was stunned to see the red head woman Bertha June standing next to me with a great stance posture as her hands were placed behind her back. Out of all women, she was the only one dressed as if she were in an army. Her tunic was button from her neck to the belly button with her sword worn on the side around her waist. Her bright red hair shined with the lights of the chandeliers.

I then asked nonchalantly, "Can I help you?"

"Oh right," She scoffed. "Where are my matters? My name is Bertha June. Though, obviously Jesus already brought my name up anyway. It's a pleasure to meet with you, Mr. Princeton."

We greet by handshake, but it was a diplomatic handshake a best. She then pulled up a chair and hastily sat down. I was intrigued by her odd enthusiasm to see me. "It's good to see that you're keen to meet me"

"Why wouldn't I be? I'm looking forward into working with you as well as Francis. You could see how much of a great community he has manifested. It's almost...paradise. Momentarily, at least," she said with a chuckle, possibly anticipating for a response from me. "But we're getting there."

"Right. So, what do you do as a Civil Force Detective?" I asked.

"I investigate and solve crimes independent from the regular Civil Forcers who patrol the streets in the city. We're private security. Agents of the Chancery. Sometimes, crimes are a lot bigger than they need to be. My overall job is to keep the spirits from harm's way, like what you do as knights."

"Right." I agreed. "So, you have free range of going about your methods when saving the city."

"Truth be told, we've been lately...investigating in many villages, most of them north of Valestone. It's an almost desolate space. The residents...suffered from attacks from unknown folks and are forced to move from place to place. I've been helping to move them often. Perhaps, the Satanists are at large than I thought." She answered.

"R...Right. What do you suppose we can do to go after them? You know...the Satanists?"

"That's what we're trying to figure out. It's not that simple, I'm afraid. They keep coming and going like parasites. They caused these arsons and curses before we could ever reach to them. Word says that they are going after something hidden within the villages, but we don't know what. It's been happening for two years now. But we'll continue to help them find a place that is safe. Rest assured. But to the matter at hand. You're probably wondering why I came to you."

"I am, actually. Out of...what, a behemoth of spirits roving here tonight. And my fellow allies. What could you possibly want from a delinquent like me?"

She then waggled her finger and said, "Never entitle yourself as one. That's the first rule." She then placed her hand down at the clothed table. "Also, the real reason is because I came across something interesting as I was doing my job. When I was helping the folks find a village. Someone you, specifically, may be familiar with."

"Such as?" I raised an eyebrow.

"Well... there's people within the pilgrimage since I've been helping them move to somewhere safe. When I was there, they wanted me to give this to you...whenever you ascended here." As she inserted her left hand into her coat pocket, she pulled out a beige envelope with a red wax seal.

After giving her a sincere and suspicious glance, I stared down at the envelope and eagerly intended to open it.

"Wouldn't recommend opening it here." She urged me.

"Why not," I asked almost in hostility.

"It's not the right time. You must be rational when it comes to these things, Mr. Princeton. You can't trust anybody here. Anyone could be a spy for Lucifer," she said, engaging beside my face. "Truth be told, it's from your family. Particularly...your father."

I then emphasized in question, "My father? You got this from my *father*?"

"I know it's hard to believe..." Bertha admitted.

Her seemingly cunning posture got me hostile and made me question, "Who are you playing at? How could you possibly know my family is truly out there?"

"They gave this to me. Why would I lie about it?" She asked in a passive way.

I was not convinced by her shortsighted answer, which made me truly believe that she was lying. So, as I was ready to descend, I told her, "Lovely to meet you, but I'm not willing to make a deal with a fraud. No offense. So why don't you enjoy the steak, assuming you could..."

"Jone, Amelia and Kelley Princeton. Family of four, meaning you included; once a rich family from Long Island, New York on Earth; a good family who met their unfortunate and unexpected fate in a school shooting. That about, does it?"

My eyes widened to what came from her mouth. Perhaps it was stalking, I was curious to know more. I assumed it was a way to get my attention. "How do you...?"

"They gave me enough to lead me to you. I often see them. Not always, but enough. They've been praying for you to come here since forever. They're worried about you, truth be told. And I can't blame them. The way you led yourself to be here is devastating; the intense bring up. And I know you feel some sort of guilt, I can tell. You want to find a way to bring something great to the world and to settle with your family again. To get to my point, I could help your parents and fulfill your goal...if we work together. You could still work within your Order's bounds. But in time, I would need your assistance to find these Satanists wreaking havoc. And because of these recent attacks, your family will be in danger when they are dragged into hellfire. And only you and I, with my fellow team, can help them." She recommended. "Just something to keep in mind. You don't have to be tangled in all this. You could be free from all this. From life's conflict to be in the peace you've never gotten. What do you think?"

As I was going to think deeply about the situation, my thought processing was interrupted by something leaking from my eyes. I wiped my face with my hand and saw that crimson blood was tearing in my eyes.

"Are you alright? Should I get you to a doctor?" She asked with concern.

"Er...no, it's fine." I stood up from my chair. "Listen, we can discuss more of this another time, but I have to go."

"Okay, well...it's a pleasure to meet you, Mr. Princeton." June said optimistically. "You take care of that, would ya? And think about my offer."

"For sure." I nodded as I walked hastily away from the crowded ballroom. Juliet warned me about this; something was wrong. Something was sure to happen. I remembered Juliet said that she had a room reserved for me on the third floor. I made sure to head up there.

I made it through the hallways and made my way to the third floor since I felt something creeping through from there. Once I reached the upper floor, it was quieter than expected. The music and crowd were faintly heard when I entered one of the rooms left for me. But then the voices came up, *"You're going to mess this up! You know it!"* I just continued to proceed.

As I ensued into the unlocked room, it was masked with complete darkness with shards of the sad moonlight shining through the revealing windows. I changed from my formal and classy suit to my traditional Apostle clothing I was given fright after the initiation; think of it as my superhero outfit.

I wore a black decently long frock coat with a red sash around my waist. High leather boots. Behind my lower back was a rectangular satchel attached to the black strap around my sash. I also wore a black buckled satchel over my shoulder. Underneath, I had on a grey jerkin and red cravat with my locket worn around it. Two pistol holsters over my chest. To top it all off, I had on a black panama hat with a red band around it. After I took a brief glance at my locket, I placed it around my neck. I then placed my hat nicely on my head. I received the attire for my birthday. And it made for a competent gift to cherish.

I felt a nudge on the leg. Looking down, I saw a big familiar bloke I haven't seen in a while. Seeing Algor panting happily in the spotlight alongside me, it made me grin a bit. It may sound cliché and obvious, but he was very much like a dog, a large monstrous dog, but still like a dog. And I always did want a dog as a child. But my mother was unfortunately allergic to them. Especially hairy dogs.

Kneeling to his level, he looked at me with his black bean-colored eyes and let out an almost loud bark.

"Oy," I said silently, rubbing both sides of his pelt. "I'm glad to see you too. But I need you to be silent, alright? Some bad guys are coming after the king and I need you to be near me, okay?"

By his enthusiastic panting, I assumed he got the message. I then stood up and gathered all my weapons, including my concealed blades that were almost the size of bayonets. I held my sword on my right hand as Algor and I were nearing the slightly open door. I leaned against the wall and suddenly spotted a group of gentlemen walking down the hallways. All of them were masked. But they seemed shadowy, especially since they seemed to move hastily.

Reminding Algor to stay silent, I moved away from the dark study to the bright halls once again. My steps were easy and steady to avoid their detection. My senses detected their fast-beating hearts, which meant that they were in a rush for something. I went through the halls in silence, making sure that I used the empty halls to my advantage. I stopped briefly on the way when I spotted something odd about one of the white vases painted with purple roses. Once I stepped and dug into the abyss, I unveiled something plastic and hardened. I looked and saw that I unveiled a volton mask designed with Baroque accents.

"Seems like our friends fancy a masquerade ball. Let's give them a ball to remember." I said to Algor, who looked at me with those blinking bright black eyes.

I made my way to another entrance as I tailed them. It appeared that they were heading towards the fourth floor of the palace. Algor's panting gave me a clear instance that he was still with me. As the stairs turned, we were already at the end of the hall.

As they both stopped, one of them gestured the others to get into positions of each room. It was very clear that they were entering the rooms in an illegal matter. I was so concentrated to ignore the faint cheers from outside, as well as the fireworks that projected, thundered, and roared in the mellow skies.

I pinned each enemy with my eyes, making sure every count was correct. I placed the fear I had aside to see it through. When I was done, I lifted my hand in the air and tapped into my powers. My fingers darkened while my eyes were lit with complete and brief whiteness. Once I felt weightiness's from my fingertips, I was convinced that my power was used. Everything in the hall began to levitate, floating as if there was no gravity in the room. Floating as if we were underwater. The blokes stood still. Very still. They struggled to move as if they were stunned. I still felt my head weighted and yarned, but it was worth that risk. The truth was.... they were in my control as well. Including their eyes. Every nerve ending and atom was in my favor.

"What the...what is this!?"

"Someone's here! Find him!" One of them said.

I scoffed under my breath as they were grasping to move slowly and slowly, trying to turn to see me; battling the force I placed. They stood dumbfounded, unaware of my presence and everything mysteriously hovering in the room. It was time I'd be my own shadow. For a fair fight, I released them. Plus, thanks to my cantation, I weakened their nerve fibers. And they were straddled. It was destructive, which was good enough for me.

I whistled for Algor to go and charge at one of the blokes. As he zapped through the levitated halls, I watch him charge at one of the figures. The person yelped in pain as Algor's mouth was barely tearing off his leg.

This gave me an opportunity to summon my Penobscot bow out of nothing. It was a fancy bow made of the wood of an oak tree engraved with crosses and dazzled in red beads. The white smoke dissolved as my bow was summoned. Pulling back the string, a smoking white arrow was summoned between my fingers and at the end of my firing arm. As I let the arrow fly, leaving a wispy trail, it flew towards one of the opponents as he plummeted down on the ground.

I saw the main guy trying to swing his short blade at Algor. He then commanded his men, "Don't just stand there! Attack whoever is doing this!"

"But we can't! We're weak! It'll kill us!" One of them pleaded.

"Do it or I'll kill you!" He said, and they listened. He managed to kick Algor in the face several times. This made him more aggressive to where he sunk his teeth all the way down his flesh. The man let out an agonizing screech. I blew the rest of them a far with a strong push of my power, along with everything in the hall. Unfortunately giving the maids and servants more work. I summoned my bow once again.

As the armed men were charging at me, I manage to shoot another arrow at the closest one while I leaped from the ground. Bringing out the blades from my wrists, I integrated them both at the other approaching enemy. Both enemies were down simultaneously, leaving one of them alive. As I stood up with my blade rejected back into my sleeve and the bow dissolving, I whistled for Algor to let go of his oozing loose leg.

Once I reached to him, I lifted him by his neck and lifted my hand to release every ornament and item from the hall. All of them plummeted on the pictured-clothed carpet. I saw that I might have left a trail of blood from the fight.

I looked back at the masked man and removed it from his face. He was bearded and scarred across his face. I looked down at his medallion; a pendant shaped like the sun. What caught me were his eyes. They were bright red, the same as the one who attacked me that night. His expression didn't show any fear, apparently.

"You better speak about your damn intentions, you ghoul!" I demanded, as I heard Algor growl next to me.

"You think you've won, haven't you?" He asked with a sinister smile followed by a cryptic chuckle.

"I want to know why you brought your men." I asked sharply.

"To fulfill the deeds of our Bright Star. Not a fool like Christ. So, you're too late!" He grinned.

I slammed him against the wall, which echoed in the empty beautiful halls, with my hand still around his neck. "What do you mean too late? Answer me!"

Suddenly, he spoke in a very lurid voice as his eyes glowed; "Ka-les-mada!"

I instantly saw another one of his minions conjure out of nowhere. I supposed that it was a call to summon. In his hands looked to be a glowing object, in which he slammed onto the ground, creating a blacked environment. The entire palace went completely dark, without the use of my powers. Shrieks of what seemed like horror came about and were heard from the bottom of the building. I turned back to the man and saw that the lights quickly came up. He then pushed me away from his space as he unsheathed his blade. From my shoulder holster integrated by my right pistol, I summoned and unsheathed mine into a wand, positioning myself to engage. The wand I had already formed after it was flicked.

"You want them to be safe, you surrender!"

As he charged toward me, he leaped and ejected his sword towards me until I deflected his attack; giving me a chance to frantically swing my sword down his chest. As he struggled to stand, it didn't take long for him to attempt to swing at me as well. I took hold of his arm and connected my fist onto his jaw. My sword then injected into his neck as blood was streaming down his mouth. Light quickly bloomed from his eyes until his eyes became vacant and dense. I pulled it out and he fell to his death, struggling to breath.

I looked down at his fresh corpse, realizing that I've just had a new awakening. I've killed a spirit. I've killed several of them; nearly forgetting that I was no longer human. It was true about what I read.

Soon after, I was caught by more of them appearing in the hall. This time, it was five of them. And it would be a waste of time taking out one of them at the time.

"Stay behind me, Algor!" I demanded. With my sword erected, I ran towards the five of them and rapidly engaged. My plan was to succeed by slaying them all at once. Luckily, the coat I wore was very light. So were my trousers. It made me move with angelic versatility and devilish speed.

Leaping from the ground, I jousted my blade to one of the Satanists' blade, making him unbalanced. While he stumbled, I turned to the other and engaged my blade onto his. Upwards and downwards our blades elegantly went, until I twisted in the air and rounded my right foot onto his head. With his head locked down, I grabbed my sword with both hands, making the blade come down the side of his neck. I sheathed the Redeemer back into my shoulder holster on its side, giving it time to rest by the pistol.

I heard the heavy stomping of one Satanists coming from behind me. Quickly, I erected my hands and triggered my Blessed Eye. I held his neurons with my power of cantation. I quickly came to him and unsheathed his hunting knife from his leather waist holster. At the corner of my right eye, I saw one Satanist preparing to fire his arrow at me.

Shortly, I relentlessly threw the knife from my hand and had it imbedded into his skull. Reaching out my left hand, I had the knife pull out and flew back into my hand. I then flung the knife onto my right hand and locked it backwards. With it gripped in my hand, I impaled the frozen Satanist in his neck. Soon after, one more Satanist, who was raging towards me with dual swords, presented me. Wielding them monstrously.

I quickly and scarcely dodged and swayed from every strike and swing he was trying to achieve. Once he swung both swords on his right, I swayed on his right and sliced his waist. Bellowing in pain, he intended to swing both blades once again. I countered one of his hands and disarmed his right hand, snatching one of his swords. It felt a bit lighter compared to the Redeemer. Thus, it was easier to flow around and simultaneously block every attack.

Finally, I sliced and wounded both of his arms, making his powerless. Especially without his swords. I took the pleasure of levitating his body from the ground and ejecting his own blade into his chest. His eyes flashed before me like a quick camera shot. Soon, I released him from my grasp, and he plummeted to the carpet. I stood and panted heavily. Straddled but somewhat amused, I looked down at the knife I realized that I was still carrying. I pondered on everything that happened. But there was clearly no time to ponder for long.

"Come, Algor!" I said before I whistled for him as he soon came on my side. With Algor's help, I raced, shot, and swung my blade at the summoned Satanists furiously down back to the first floor; only to come across a hallway bloomed with chaos. The cloaked guards were engaged with other figures like those whom I attacked. Vaulting over a knocked over table, I launched my foot onto an up-and-coming Satanist to the floor. I continued to sprint to the ballroom. The other spirits fled in fear, bloating their incoherent yells. I rushed through the warring factions to get back into the ballroom. What once looked magnificent became chaotic.

I saw Jesus and the rest being escorted by Michael while the others were fighting. I studied the room, seeing most engaged in a fight with these figures. I also happened to briefly witness Ted and Juliet, dressed differently from what they previous wore for the occasion. They danced and twirled whilst wielding their favored long weapons, leaving blood to spill onto the polished wooden ballroom floors. Ted bashed onto one enemy and the next with his scepter in great speed. Juliet, using her sterling ring broadsword danced as she sliced and decked every Satanist until they were dismembered. She soon performed a tornado kick towards one of them.

Suddenly, I felt a grasp on my shoulder. I turned to see that it was Francis, wielding his longsword against a Satanist. For his age, it was quite impressive to swiftly wield a blade of that size. After ejected it from the bastard's chest and slaying his neck with his retractable wrist blades from his right, he said, "Kevin, thank God you're here!" He quickly rejected his blades into his sleeve and sheathed his blade into his cane.

"What's going on?" I asked.

He ignored my question and pointed towards the open doors, "You have to get the princess back! The rest of us will fight them off and escort the spirits out of here! Quickly now! Go!"

I groaned, knowing that saving a princess who couldn't help herself was one of the last things I wanted to do. Regardless, I took off and ran from the ballroom with Algor. We both hurried through the crowd of fighters and the innocence fleeing in mad fear. We both exited the palace and I studied carefully of where Lady Sarah could've gone. It was too long as I saw four men holding and grasping poor Sarah against her will. I saw her amongst the running crowd, struggling to escape.

As I ran down to get to them, they spotted me and dissolved into ashy smoke. They suddenly vanished into midair.

"Damn it!" I yelped in frustration.

With Algor, I rushed down the large, crowded steps and into the open gates of the palace, making my way to the courtyard. At that point, I almost felt hopeless. I wasn't sure how I was to ever find her. Let alone putting my companion in danger. My eyes instantly caught one of the guards on the mixed breed horse. The closest one was inevitable for me to get. So, I ran towards the guard and yelled, "I need your horse for a bit!"

"You mean peg," He corrected as he got off and placed the reins in my hand.

"Whatever," I said as I soared from the ground and had myself seated on the horse.

I then glanced at Algor, knowing he has a great sense of smell and told him, "Algor, lead me to where they took her!"

Barking loudly, he ran in front of me. As I saw him exiting the courtyard and out at the streets of Celestia, I saw him turn left. I galloped the horse hastily to exit and get out from the palace. As we exited, we were back at the streets. I galloped my way through the crowded and huddled civilians, passing by the building as I followed Algor. Hey, I might have not learned how to drive, but at least a horse was useful for transportation.

The sweat drizzled from my head and flew pass me as I ran through the populated avenues. I felt the wind blowing passed me as I was racing down the streets to see where Algor was leading me. I wasn't sure how a night like this ended up bonkers. Was it meant to happen, perhaps? Or was it a coincidence? These questions ran through my brain as I made different turns on each large corner. The more I rode, the more I realized how massive the city was. Almost larger as New York. Which made me sentimental in a way. But I digress.

As I continued galloping, I suddenly saw a carriage rushing through the crowded road, causing havoc in the street. Whatever was in my way, I made sure that I pressured the horse to jump over several obstacles. From crossing large bridges to passing underneath large arches, it felt like drag racing at this point. My hat nearly fell off due to the rushing pace. It came to my mind to realize that these were the bastards to hunt down. Everything was in a rush that the entire area became hazy and dizzy. I spotted one of them preparing his rifle to shoot me down. Luckily, I swayed the horse to move us out of the way. At times, they would try to stop me by blowing up random moving carriages to throw me off. The horse I was mounted on would thrash and wail, but I managed to calm it down so I could continue to ride it.

I nearly lost course again as soon as sudden creatures were coming towards my face. Scaled and grey furry winged creatures with pike shaped teeth raging at me. I swayed and suppressed fire at them. I turned and maneuvered through the narrow streets until I was slowly approaching to the seaside.

The more we ran, the more far off we were from the city. As we were gradually descending away from the rustling metropolitan roads, we suddenly were making our way to an intersection that was leading us to the coast of the city. We raced down the moist sands with the water pushing through the rocks as well as the shore. Hooves of the horse were scratching against the sand and letting it fly.

The blokes were firing all sorts of projectiles at me; from bullets to arrows as I felt my heart ruthlessly throbbing. Whooshing past my face were warm iron metal bullets and hot fiery arrows. Algor came and suddenly jumped onto the moving carriage and pushed one of them off. The other attempted to stab Algor. So, I drew my pistol and shot him in the head as he fell off his horse, making the steed retreat. When I shot my pistol, I noticed that the bullets weren't the same as the Satanists'. As I shot, it looked to be glazed with white light and shined like quartz. The bullets from the Satanists' guns were molted magma.

This helped me gain closer and closer to the carriage. I peeked through the window and saw Sarah struggling to get out.

"I'm gonna get you out of here, lass!" I guaranteed her, looking for other opportunities. I was almost shot once again as it then pushed me to use my gun and aim it at his head. Blood sprayed for the back of his wound as he fell off the horse as his eyes shot light as well. Turning around, one Satanist was moving his hands symmetrically as it was creating a picturesque vortex several miles away from where we were. I looked closely and saw how the red and grey liquid particles were spiraling.

I was then hesitantly standing on the black leather saddle and made a great leap from the horse to the top of the carriage. I saw that the driver was attempting to shoot me down. Thus, I kicked his hand as he made the gun fly from his hand.

I felt someone's arm around my neck, strangling me excessively. I let out my blades from my gauntlets and inserted them both onto his eyes.

I turned to the enemy and connected my foot onto his torso, kicking him off the moving carriage. I turned to see that we were nearly approaching to the whirling vortex.

I then came to the driver and pierced deeply into his jugular before he could attack me. I felt the crimson liquid running down my wrist and soaking my sleeve. It felt warm and very wet. But I was careless of that. Wasn't the first time I felt blood on me. When I attempted to stop the carriage, it was clear that the horses weren't going to stop. Not even with my cantation.

I climbed down on the side of the running carriage and saw the devastated Lady. Knowing that I was blessed with powers, it enhanced my strength. I then alerted Sarah, "Move your face from the window!"

As she did, I pulled my hand and hastily kept punching as the cracks were gradually coming and weakening the glass. One final punch made it combust. This got me to open the door from the inside. As the door flipped open, I took hold of the princess by the waist.

I made sure that I held her tight as we both jumped off the unstable vehicle. Once it reached the vortex, it shrunk and combusted into tiny particles of smoke. I saw Algor running past us. He then stopped by barking and growling towards the disappearance of the vortex.

Picking up my hat, I let out some air by panting heavily. I turned to the petite princess, her blue eyes dazzling at me, and asked her, "Are you alright?"

"Y...yes." She replied. Regardless of her confusion, she said with a smile. I picked her by the small hand to get her off from the sand. Wiping the sandy debris from her dress, she said, "Thank you very much. You don't know how much this means. Is there anything I could do to repay you for your kindness?"

Before I could answer her question, I stood up from the sand and premeditated the entire coast. We were far from the city and to top it all off; the horse I rode on took off. Perhaps it got frightened. I was too tired and already pessimistic to be pissed off. I replied, "A way back, for starters. We're pretty damn far!"

She suddenly took it upon herself to grasp hold of the white sand.

Curious, I engaged my eyes to what she was intending to do. Holding her clamped hand to her mouth as the bits of sand were slithering through her fingers, she whispered something. Somehow, it caused to show a white light that shined through the crevices of her fingers. When she unveiled her hand, a flock of glowing doves came out from her hand and descended into the air. Obviously, I winded my eyes. Never would I have guessed that the Son of God's daughter would perform such sorcery. But it worked. The doves traversed and flew in a flock in the east above us.

"This should be a signal for the guards to come and get us." She spoke.

Amazed, I asked, "How...when did you learn that?"

She turned to my face with a smirk and replied, "When you are the daughter of a messiah, nature could work to your favor. Though to be honest, I learned it recently from my angel friends. I've been mastering with it. It's a unique spell. And it works!"

"That's quite impressive." I spoke. At least she had a sense of humor. And I knew what was going to happen. So, I asked to make sure, "So...of course we have to wait."

"Yes." She sat on the sand with her knees high. I looked out the outline of the ocean under the mellow blue sky.

"Oh joy," I said with pseudo-excitement as I sat next to her with Algor. To which the woman replied, "Do not worry. They shall send help soon."

"I hope so". I replied as I then turned my face to the soft roaring seas. But seeing what I saw as I saved her made me contemplate a bit. So, I was in my own thoughts for the next fifteen minutes we had to wait by being voluntarily mesmerized by the bluing sky watching over the somberly windy ocean. And it was an excuse to avoid conversation. But I had to understand and get another two cents on what I saw. "Are we going to ignore that vortex we just saw back there," I asked after I turned to Sarah.

"It seems like they summoned a passageway to Hell. I wondered what they would want with me." She said, finally relieved from the near abduction. She turned to me with a smile and said, "I thank you once again."

I replied, "It's nothing, love. Really. I was just doing my job."

"True. But I know it was more than a job."

"How you can be sure? You're reading my mind?"

"No. But I can sense something wearying you. Your heart is full of doubt. I can feel it."

"Well, I ask kindly for you to stop!" I asked in a polite but aggressive tone, directly towards her. I sighed as I saw her smile temporarily disappear. Turning away from her, I said, "I'm sorry. I just don't feel too trusting with people reading into my thoughts. I have sixteen that do it for me."

"It is...fine. I'm very sorry. It was not my intention to pry. I'm an empath...and I gain certain energy from others. I know that you are cynical about everything. I pray that you will feel truly at home here. We aren't what you may think. Especially my father." She looked at the right and saw four paladins on armored horses cantering in a line. It looked as though they have already seen the signal.

I turned to her and said, "I doubt that, but sure." I watched as her face turned pale when I said what I didn't mean to say. My guard was up as I was determined not to be deceived again. Especially someone supposedly of God.

She and I stood, as it was clear that they were coming to fetch us from waiting too long. Quite quickly if I may add. I said to Sarah, "They grasped that rather quickly."

"They're probably city guards. In an event such as this, you would want nothing more than for your city to be plagued with soldiers." Sarah stated. She smiled at me once again and said, "I thank you again, Mr. Princeton."

"Just...call me, Kevin." I said as I saw the mounted horsemen approaching.

"Oh. O...Okay then, Kevin." After she said that, the soldiers came, and we were mounted on each of their horses. I whistled for Algor in hopes to make sure that he followed us. Thus, the front guard swung his horse to retreat to the city. We galloped along the sandy trail.

As soon as we traveled with the soldiers, we were right back in the palace. We dismounted from the horses. I turned to the entrance of the palace and saw the invitees being helped by the angels. Comforted and counseled, it was clear that there was a state of fear after what happened. Tears were present on most of their faces as the angels gladdened them. What was once cheery and festive became devastated and sorrowful. Whimpers, sobbing, and mumbling were circling their air whilst I saw Jesus talk with Francis and Ted and Juliet.

As we walked towards them, he spotted me with his daughter. "Sarah!"

"Father!" She cried, wrapping her arms around him after he approached us. He then looked right at me, with humility in his warm tan eyes and a smile.

He then spoke to me, "God will bless you for this, Mr. Princeton."

I never imagined that the Son of God himself would thank me. Let alone speak to me face to face. I would be ecstatic, but given everything, I felt nothing but a bit of bitterness towards him for abandoning me. Abandoning those he supposedly loved and died for. But I swallowed and bowed, "Of course. Um...you're welcome."

"I imagine the hasty air was not in your favor. Do forgive me, I was fearing it would turn out like this." He said. "I did not envision this to come up. Especially the attempted assassination. Mostly, nothing ever happens in these events. But...I fear that Lucifer's wrath could return. So, forgive me."

"No worries...I guess," I said.

"You are in our debts. That and much more blessings." He said, petting Algor. He turned back to a very puzzled Francis discussing with Ted, Juliet, and Michael. Ted and Juliet were in their Apostle appearances. Ted had on a gold jerkin with bronze curved droplets and had one a long tailcoat piece behind him. He had on purple trousers with shin high boots. He wore a gray fingerless glove in his left hand. Juliet wore a blue jacket with a white scarf around her neck. With a blue flowy skirt wrapped around her waist with a tailing fabric, she also wore light blue trousers with snow-white opaque tights with classy Chelsea boots that wrapped around her ankles.

"It's likely that Francis needs you. I shall not keep you. I hope to meet you again soon. Thank you once again for bringing back Sarah, Mr. Princeton. You are blessed."

I sighed. "If you say so, sir." I replied as I watch him coddling his child. A guard was escorting him into a carriage where his wife was awaiting him. Sarah turned to me with a smile at the same time as the carriage she was in descended from the palace's courtyard.

I turned back to my group and walk towards them with Algor, suddenly ending their conversation. Face filled with fragility, Francis said, "I can't thank you enough for what you've done, Kevin. And Algor, of course."

"No problem." I said. "I'm just trying to figure out what happened."

"I'm guessin' that Lucifer got butthurt and sent out his henchmen after the Lady for some particular reason. And to assassinate the king. Which is why...we managed to catch two of them. They won't be vanishing now." Ted said.

"Clearly, they have a narrative." Juliet added. "Then again, why else would they disrupt a fine evening?"

"Are they inside?" I asked.

Michael then tilted his head to his left. Francis then said, "You go with Michael and check with the Satanists. I'll see to these spirits. I'll see you all at the Khalservan." He turned to me before he took off. "Once again, thank you Kevin."

"You're welcome." I replied as I watched him take off, his cape flying across the flagstones.

I then took off with the Apostles and Michael as we went back into the Palace. There, the Satanists were on their knees, unhooded and cuffed behind their backs. One of them in the middle even gave me a smile; a strange smile consisted with distorted teeth and an almost dislocated jaw. Bertha was there as well, having her silver pistol pointed at one of them. All held at gunpoint by the guards, one of the winged guards turned to Michael, "What should we do with them, sir?"

Michael's face showed skepticism. He then took a breath and said, "I don't wish to discredit any of my comrades work to get them in custody. But if we want them to talk, we must be thorough and strict. Even at the point of terror. These are Satanists we're dealing with."

"Just as long as it does not involve violence. You don't have to beat the information out from them." Bertha added as she stepped away from the masked fiends. "We could just give them a fair warning and let them be. Making sure they never return."

"What? They deserved to be bulged! They nearly kidnapped the princess!" I reasoned. "These bastards clearly have a reason for what they did. We can't let them get away with that!"

"Kevin is right, Ms. June. It seems easy-going for something that has caused distress. You can't just simply have the Civil Forcers let them go." Michael added. "This is more than a Civil Force situation. It's an act of war."

"I know. I don't mean to let them be free. But I feel it is best to keep them...in fear at least. Imprisoned. They work for the devil, so the light of the angels could fear him. That way, we could probably get answers from them."

"What are you saying, Ms. June?" Michael enquired.

"I'm saying that it would be best for you to let the Civil Force to have them in our custody. Because it is a Civil Force situation...not another case for a specialized unit to solve on their own. Especially one without proper guidance from law enforcement." Bertha argued. "It's the matter of making sure that we have some strong clarity of knowing about this attack. They will soon become our problem. I was pardoned by the Chancery to handle the Satanists case as well."

"Are you serious! That's unfair," Juliet said with angered eyes.

"Yeah! And...*specialized unit*? You're questioning our methods, lady?" Ted enquired. "We're ain't just... killer magicians, y'know!"

"What? No! Of course not." She said, alarmed at Ted's questioning.

She then continued, "Just want to make sure it's only fair. I am in no way disrespecting the Apostles. But we cannot have...any act of unwarranted vigilance to act as judge, jury, and executioner. The Civil Force had a history of dealing with monsters and rapidly getting answers with a more mental and regular method that is useful in getting information to piece in puzzles to something potentially bigger. You could never give a knight a case such as this. They need to answer to the law of the Chancery. Answer for their assault."

Michael yearned and said to a sweated Bertha, "Listen Ms. June, I have no doubt that you have mastered at enforcing your duties and accomplishing them to the best of your ability. Doing everything you can to protect the good spirits. But with all due respect, The Satanists are the sole enemies of the Apostles, not just the Civil Forcers nor the Chancery. They will never answer to the law nor God, only to lightkeepers because this is whom they fear the most, even if they don't admit it. And even if they do answer to you, it will not lead you anywhere. Believe me on that account. You could just focus on getting the village caravan to somewhere safe because there could be more of them out there. But leave these two to the Apostles. They've earned this. And we can't risk you being in danger. You saw what they could do."

He then turned to the guards and ordered, "Have them in the stagecoach and send it off to the west of the Homestead. We'll take it from there."

"Yes, sir." They complied as they took the criminals outside from the palace. I saw disappointment in Bertha's face. I honestly nearly felt bad for taking away her opportunity, but they didn't deserve a merciful interrogation. And given what has been lost, I couldn't exactly blame Michael for being a bit hardened. It would seem too sugar coated to create a plan such as that. And it was too soon to talk to them about the vortex I saw.

I was feeling exhausted from today but relived that I did something good for once. It's been interesting how things turned out. So, I wasn't sure how it would turn out for what was next. I looked at the Satanists, now entering and being locked up in the carriage equivalent of a

SWAT truck. They drove off from the courtyard of the palace under the moonlight.

XIV

A Point of No Return

We were soon in a dungeon of the Khalservan, interrogating with our methods. I stood and watched as Ted threw both of his blooded fists onto the crooks responsible for the attack. Bailey and Michael both had their arms crossed while Juliet's hands were in her skirt pockets. Dimly lit and dense, the dungeon smell with the toxicity of the blood splattered on the floor. After flinching twice to the sound of skulls getting snapped and cracked, Ted sighed off and walked away from them. Juliet handed him a towel to wipe the blood from his knuckles.

"Thank you, Ted." Bailey spoke as he turned back to the cuffed Satanists, "Now, are you ready to give us a mature reason for your attack? Or do you want...barbaric accommodations from Ted?"

"We answer to Lucifer! Never to a coward devoted to a useless god!" The brown moist-haired Satanist spat as blood drizzled from his nose and mouth. He spat at Francis, which he wiped his face in response.

Bailey glanced at Ted and nodded at him. As soon as Ted was nearing one of them, the other retreated. As his eyes suddenly became white and black, he took out his hand and hovered it over their heads. It took a while for something to happen. The dungeon unexpectedly shifted and materialized into an endless room of buzzing white noise with grotesque eyes riddled all around us. Words couldn't describe how nearly frightful and confused I was to be surrounded by nothing but wide white eyes eerily moving and staring down on us.

The weird sight made the cuffed Satanists to squirm. They constantly twisted their heads in pure agony. They began to screech and moved frantically as the room was becoming more and more hallucinated as the eyes began to cry the crimson sight of blood mixed with yellowish-white discharge. Suddenly, it rained what happened to be atrocious bloodied fetuses that began to crawl at the screaming Satanists. Oh, not to mention how they were vomiting large amounts of maggots, making Juliet squirm and cringe. I squirmed as several of them were rapidly surpassing me. Their eyes bugged out and widened sporadically. They were handcuffed onto the wall, so it made it even difficult for them to escape.

"You see those horrors.... those are what good folk go through when scum like you attack. This is what we face. You're lucky they aren't real. But let's say you won't be unseeing them. By the way, if he wanted to, he could have you trapped in this nightmare." Francis said followed by a chuckle. "If it were me, the infliction would have been far worse. You would be dead internally. As well as...physically. Now...do you care to give us a reason? Or does Ted here need to make you deaf as well? It's your call."

"Wait! Please! We'll tell you everything you need to know!" One Satanist shouted. "Please stop!! STOP!!" Ted left them alone to finally breathe. Soon, we shifted and materialized back into the dungeon. All I thought was...*goddamn Ted*. When he saw me staring at him, he simply shrugged.

"You coward! You actually..." The other bellowed at the cowering Satanist.

"Shut it!" Juliet yelled, ejecting herself off the cement wall. She looked genuinely interested to listen, as she then said sternly, "Talk!"

"We...we...we were instructed to intrude into your gathering by our leader! He told us to do it!"

"Lucifer?" I asked.

"No, Sathanus! Our leader of our guild! Lucifer is our Lord!" When that name was said, I glanced at Juliet. Apparently, that name was enough to make her cross her arms in an insecure manner. And Francis' face grew pale when the name spoke. So did Michael.

"What!? You swore not to tell them, you fu-," The other shouted as Ted, out of nowhere, bulged the man's head with the butt of his pistol. It caught my attention. He finally fell flat as Ted then said, "Now that's that, tell us; what would Sathanus want from Lady Sarah La Kali?"

My mind was interested to understand who Sathanus was. But I was still presuming Lucifer to be the soul suspect. But I was open to the idea.

"He doesn't want her. Lucifer does!"

"What would he want with her?!" Michael asked aggressively, almost reaching the hilt of his sword.

"Because she's the daughter of Christ. We assume that she shared the same abilities as her father. All I know is that he wants the noble mystic spirits from each kingdom of your realm. He even has priestesses and mystics from Arcadia! What he wants to do with them is beyond us! That's all I know! I swear!" He begged.

Puzzling expressions were thrown around the dense room. "I guess some Satanists do have a mind of their own! Heh, who would've thought!" Francis said with a scoff. He then spoke strictly, "Very well. You will remain there until we decide your fate. But thank you kindly for the information. Just don't stanch the floor with your shit! That's what the bucket's for."

He then nodded to the cloaked guard to unlock the door. As it was left open, we all left the dark room and were out at the shimmered night-lit halls of the castle. We all began walking towards the door to head upstairs. All I thought to myself was what have I've gotten myself into? Perhaps it was a conspiracy. Or worse...a war. I really prayed that it didn't result to that.

"Something's wrong. These are not ordinary kidnappings." Ted spoke. "I mean it's one thing to attack someone at the Homestead for information. But...the kidnappings are gonna make things complicated, I guarantee."

"Why would Lucifer want with mystics? Out of all spirit civilians?" Juliet asked. "It just seems odd. Let alone from Arcadia."

"What is that? Arcadia?" I asked.

"Another monumental city of the Promised Land. It's a Pagan city in the kingdom of The Summerland." Michael said. "Queen Arianna serves the kingdom, and she did send warning to us after they suffered the same disaster just few weeks ago."

"We can just...simply go to Hell and rescue them all, right?" I asked.

"Oh, we would...but it's not that simple. We go there...and it's an instant death sentence." Michael stated.

"What do you mean?"

"Lucifer has manifested a lethal force field in the realm after the rebellion. Those who enter...will evaporate into oblivion. So, the victims in Hell, they're essentially stuck there! Held prisoners! Building a force like that here in Heaven would be the equivalent of forcing out other spirits because they aren't us. We can't afford that." Francis said. "My theory is that he could be using them for ransom. He probably wants us to surrender our power to get them back."

"Yes...but why these people in particular? That's what I don't quite understand." Juliet said.

"I wish we knew, my dear." Michael said.

"What about...that bloke Sathanus? Who's he?" I asked.

"Lucifer's most trusted lieutenant. Last of the Seven Princes. A violent destructive savage. He's a demonic warlord that follows the orders of Lucifer and leads the Satanist Order. His group were simply militants up until he collided forces with Lucifer's legionaries. Thus, he serves him. Nothing but a ruthless raider, heartless rapist and godless brute." Michael said grimly. "I did not have the fondest memory when he attacked the villages up of the north of the Promised Land. The good Lord knows what he may possibly do to those people. It was not easy comforting those poor victims. I...I just hope that he is not truly returning."

"He will not." Francis said, placing a hand on Michael's shoulder. "It's obvious that Lucifer hasn't stopped pursuing his crusade. This is the first time in forever since he attacked this realm. Seems like he didn't take the treaty well. This is his way of provoking a war with us. To prevent it, we must find out more intel to weaken them. There must be more to this. But if he insists on one, we have no other choice if we want it to end. One thing to understand ...is that it's never a fair declaration of war they make. It's annihilation. An inquisition on the hunt. Still...we could beat them. Just like last time. I just pray the losses aren't high as they were before. We've had enough of those. And we've had enough of being dragged into conflict."

"And we will help stop it. Theodore, Kevin, and I," Juliet spoke up. My heart sunk when she spoke out my name. I was not sure how to feel. I'm not one to get involved in a war that would potentially span for thousands of decades. I only hoped to at least do regular knightly duties. But not get into a war. I didn't ask for it.

"If we're going to go to Hell and reclaim those nobles, we have to gather many herbalists to develop gallons of the Fahrenheit tonic. Especially for the entire army of angels." Michael said. I was clearly unsure of what that was. "Which any luck, we might as well establish a lab for them."

"How long do you suppose it'll take," Ted asked.

"That's for them to tell." Michael answered.

After Francis nodded, he said, "At least we can work with what we have. Perhaps...we could think this through with some sound sleep. Tonight, was definitely tiresome." Bailey suggested. "I shall let you flee for now."

Soon, I was relieved to be in bed, resting in a chamber bed next to the large window shining with moonlight that stood in the dark cold sky. Few hours in and I was already having these images going through my head; especially everything that happened not so long ago.

Mostly, I was confused about this world of Heaven itself. At times, I thought that it might not even be Heaven at all. If I were truly in Heaven, I would instantly meet with my family. I would be in peace by now. Instead, I'm working with a secret order of assassins that act as knightly angels as we fight against a satanic cult larger than it had to be. All this just to see my family. And to protect them from this war. Even though I knew damn well that I wasn't mentally, physically, nor spiritually cut out for it.

But before I could go to sleep, something inside motivated me to get up from the bed and take off to the cabinet in front of me. There, I pulled out my coat and picked up the letter from my "father". The letter Bertha gave to me at the gathering.

I then unveiled the letter and began to read.

Kevin,

This is your father. We are okay. It hasn't been easy. There are curses coming about and destroying settlements. But your mother, sister and I are safe, though we have yet to find a place to live. All thanks to Mrs. June's accomplice. We are ready for you to join us once we settle somewhere. And regardless of the mistakes you've committed on Earth, we still accept you. You are my son, and we are waiting for you to start over in this new life. Back to what it could be.

I love you very much. And may God bless you.
Your father, Jone Princeton

I almost felt my eyes watering a bit. Not because of the tiredness, but for the honesty in his writing. And it was something he would write. All I knew was that I had to see my family again. I needed to be with them.

Soon I was leaving my room and garbed with my gear, I went back to the dungeon. I investigated the sleazy bastards, seeing how exhausted they were. I took this time to lock pick the cell to make sure that the

Satanists were still okay for me to bring to Bertha. I drew and cocked my pistol to make them comply. I said strictly and silently, "Make a sound and I'll end you both! Got it?" They nodded hurriedly.

We soon managed to pass through the hooded monks roaming, fogging, and guarding the castle's darkened halls. The darkness really worked in my favored. I traveled back to the city alone on horseback with the two captives. I went down the hill. It was a good thing that I grasped the muscle memory of horseback riding. It took me a while to finally reach the city of Celestia. I saw that it was completely guarded than usual nights. The nights that I've been here, the number of guards was modestly decent. But it was large. And I could only assume that it was due to the attack. I sensed what I could assume was hostility, especially with the Civil Force.

And not knowing where the exact location of the Civil Force Department is, I had no choice but to talk to one of them in the now chilly streets. As I stepped from the stallion, I warned the captives. "Stay here."

I made my way and turned on each corner of the streets. Obviously, it was early for people to get up. The moon was still on the horizon. I could see the angel gargoyles looking down from some of the higher buildings.

As I was trying to alert one of the guards, without leaving the area of the captives, I saw someone familiar; perhaps too familiar. It was Bertha, working alongside two of the guards. She still held up her opposing stance with her hands behind her back. Just as she did back at the dining hall.

As soon as I picked off the captives from the horse, I approached her and was alerted as one of the guards turned toward me. He narrowed his eyes underneath his hood and said, "Oy, you're not supposed to be out here! This is the Civil Force Watch! Now clear off, fake angel!" He sounded as if I was a creature of the night. I would have lied if I didn't say that it made me a bit discouraged. He talked to me as if I were still a criminal. He looked into my eyes with this unnecessary dislike.

"I know who you are! I've seen you! You caused havoc amongst the city, break into the castle, and now you decide that it was time to play *boy scout.* Huh?"

I then stated my authority with a shaky voice, "I...I'm an Apostle, bringing attention to Ms. Ju–"

"Aye...I know exactly what you are and who you got your orders from! Go back and tell that king's pity pet that he..." The Civil Forcer nearly shouted.

"That's enough, officer. Let him exceed," Bertha demanded. She turned to me with delight as soon as I had the Satanists with me.

"You heeded my advice after all. What made you change your mind...since you seemed assured about your methods?"

"Just anything to make you fulfill your promise. I just want my damn family." I said firmly.

"Fair enough." She said smoothly, gesturing me to hand over the two captives. God only knew what she was to do with them. She looked at me with glee in her eyes, "This truly means a lot, Kevin. Don't let the Civil Force's aggression engrave you. If you keep this up, we could be sure that we can find out more about this conspiracy. We will meet again soon...with more intel about your family's whereabouts and wellbeing."

I nodded as I watched her take off with the two captives. The hooded guards held each Satanist aggressively; making sure that no one would even attempt to get out from their grasp. And I just stood, hoping that I would evidently make the right move.

You shouldn't have done that. You shouldn't! You rush too much! Now you'll make things complicated for yourself, you idiot!

The voices in the back of my mind criticized me. Perhaps rightfully so. I defied Francis by removing the Satanists from the cellar. At the same time, it had to be done just to make sure I get closer to where my family was. It came to two things; helping the Apostles to bring back the priestesses to prevent a war or to make sure that I work closely with Bertha for information. I couldn't help but worry because Bertha warned me about my family being in potential danger. I was a fool to think that I wouldn't suddenly get involved in a war. This was what I hoped didn't happen. What the hell was I thinking? What did I get myself into? Aggressively, I took my right foot several times against a crate that was against the brick wall. Anything to extract the turmoil I held.

Afterwards, I mounted back on the horse's saddle and galloped on my way back to the Khalservan. Still puzzled and confused. But as of now, all what was left to do was to see this conflict through until an opportunity erects to help Bertha so I could join my family. As of now, I stupidly got into a cave I couldn't escape from. Getting myself into a hell I made for myself.

XV

❦

Fire of the Past

The next morning, as soon as I freshened myself and prepared my garb, I came down to the Apostle Common Room. The room's amber aesthetics were like how a college dorm would look like. And this is coming from someone that hasn't gone to college. But I did remember how my father described his college experience, even showing me one of his photos. The Apostle Common Room is a squared parlor room where the knights were gathered and would come together to discuss terms, pray, and plot. It was also a place to comply to leisure after battle. The fireplace was on the left side of the room and two large bookshelves on the right. With more coat of arms on each corner of the room. Including large statues of angelic looking knights in silver armor.

I came down hoping that some of the friars and elderlies wouldn't suspect me of letting go of the Satanists. But I did see Ted, Juliet, Michael huddled all around Francis' desk in front of a large glass-stained window which consisted of doves dancing around the Twelve Apostles. Francis was in his black vest with a smoking ivory pipe in his right hand. He blew out a corn of smoke after taking a toke. I was quite surprised.

As I approached to them, Francis's face lit up as soon as he saw me. The others turned to me as well.

"Ah Kevin, your sleep went well?" He asked.

"Aye, but it could be better." I replied. "What's going on?"

Francis that he held then gave Michael a large paper. He then said, "As I was planning to meet with Queen Arianna of Summerland, apparently, our suite guests have escaped. But they've dropped something unusual. It appears to be a page from a manuscript of some kind, but it's written in satanic language. Looks like it was written weeks ago."

When he handed me the yellowish rusted paper, I skimmed through it. I've come to see a very absurd written language that I couldn't even read or translate. It seemed to be written as a poem or prose. It was difficult to analyze, let alone trying to make out what its intent was. I then looked around and asked, "Do you know if anyone here can translate."

"Obviously, a lot of us don't speak satanic language. But I can assure you that it can be difficult to find someone who does. Never have we had to seek for someone to decode something cruel as this." Michael admitted.

"No to mention, we rarely hear them speak this language. It's certainly not any language I know of." Juliet joined.

"What about the numerous of books in the library? I mean, at the very least, it could lead to something." I suggested.

"Yeah, maybe if we were Satanists. But we're not so...nice try, though." Ted jested as I reacted with a sarcastic grin. He suddenly snatched the paper from my hands and analyzed it carefully. He investigated the shapes and symbols, getting suddenly entranced. "Wait...some of these are familiar. That's why it's good to have a second glance. I don't know if any of you heard of occultism?"

"Everyone's heard of occultism. What about it?" Juliet asked. She took a glimpse at the paper once more.

"I noticed that Satanists have a fascination with occultism. Usually, ritualistic sacrifices of any kind are the name of the game. They're

198 - KENNETH VIVOR

usually hidden knowledge of the universe, and this is no different." Ted stumbled across his words, as if he lost them. "An alchemist can definitely decode this. Alchemy shares a relation with occultism. They're both ancient practices. This makes sense. Their written language look to be runes in which an alchemist could read and understand. Looks like old runes, though."

We all puzzled, dependent on what Ted would say, even Francis. He then snapped both of his fingers. "I think I may know someone who could translate this."

"Who do you have in mind?" Michael asked. "A lot of the alchemists are in Jeremiah, and little are in Heaven. Herbalists wouldn't know this either. Let alone shamans. If this were in angelic dialects, I'd understand it."

"You guys know Frask Douglas at all?" Ted asked.

"The...painter from 41 Covenant Street? Who owns the store Potter and Clay? Sure, I'm quite familiar with him. I'm quite a fan of his works." Francis admitted. "But I can't see how your business partner would...." He paused, and his grey eyes brightened. "You think he could possibly give his second thoughts to it, do you?"

"Working with him for years now, I know he's more than what meets the eye. He was an alchemist in his days in Jeremiah. Just trust me on this one, Francis! It's perfect!" Ted sounded sure. So, it was safe to go by his words for now.

"Very well, I just don't wish for him to get involved. Something is bound to happen, and I wouldn't wish for him to cross the hellfire. We cannot drag any other spirit into this." Francis warned.

"I know. But it's worth a try." Ted suggested. "At least we will have something. This could be based on some other runes that served as an inspiration for their twisted language. It's what they do anyway. You've prepared Juliet and I...even Kevin here for a moment like this, Francis. We gotta extract what you taught us. It's about time. Besides, none of us are alchemists."

After puzzling a bit, Francis said, "It's settled then. See if he can decipher the language. Come back any time if you have any information. Find out what he could do. You're dismissed, for now."

I watched as Ted, Juliet and Michael all bowed their heads slightly. They then trailed off from his desk. I felt the urge to leave just to avoid being potentially persecuted for disobeying his order yesterday.

But as soon as I was about to join the Apostles, I froze when Francis called for me. "Kevin? Is it okay if could have a quick word with you?"

I turned to him with my stomach sinking and my heart pounding almost rapidly. But I knew I couldn't escape nor use my powers in any way to go by. I faced him and swallowed my breath.

"You know, I was contacted by one of our guards here about the Satanists earlier this morning. And they told me that they saw you breaking them out to give them to the Civil Force." He said, his grey eyes locked at me.

Letting out a defeated sigh, I said, "Yes, I did. I...gave them to Bertha. But I only did it because...I think she knows where they are. My family. And the only way I could find them is if I work with her too. She told me that they were in potential danger...because of those attacks! She promised me intel if I help her get the caravan to safety."

He sighed. "I understand. I could sense that. But in the future, consider asking me first. Do I make myself clear?" He asked very strictly, expecting a straight answer from me.

I replied grimly, "Yes, sir."

I watched him stand and face the window with his hands behind his back. He let out a sigh before he said, "These are very troubled times now. And you must know that you're still new to all this. The love you have for your family is beautiful. It truly is. You will see them again."

"I hope so. Because...it seems like you're getting my hopes up. I just hope you're not...holding me prisoner. Or something." I admitted.

"Of course not. Where did you come to that silly result? I promise that as soon as your family resides somewhere safe, you will leave. Please, don't feel like you must stay. I'm just a bit protective since the Satanists are returning. Lucifer has a large network of spies, even here in Heaven. After you kill one, it could attract others thanks to an aroma that spreads like a plague. Unfortunately, they could find out about any of us. And worse, hurt those we love. You saw how they were yourself," he said.

"So, you're saying that I can't help the caravan?"

"I'm saying that we don't want one scenario dragged into another. Especially given what is on that page with satanic runic letters, which could in theory lead into something worse, which it often does. If it happens, it will get messy and your family, along with the others, will get dragged into more fire than they already are. I'm not trying to stop you, but I want you safe for their sake."

As I was pondering on it, he did have a point. They were going through enough problems with the village attacks. Whatever that piece of paper was going to lead to, I didn't want it to explode and make it a lot worse.

Francis then said, "I will do what I can to provide for your family and get them protected."

I gaged my eyes with his. He then sighed heavily and scoffed a bit.

He continued, "My apologies. It's just that...the Civil Force and the Apostles are not in best of terms, I'm afraid. They think we're vigilantes, fake angels, who do their jobs illegally. Which is not the case. So, if you ever intend to stop by the Civil Force Department, expect harsh judgement. That's all I'm saying. Plus, we can't risk putting them in danger. They aren't exactly no match for the Satanists. That is why I intend to have information like this within the Order until it is safe to tell others."

"Isn't it our job, though? They make themselves into casualties." I asked in jest. "Plus, I had a run with one of them last night."

"The Chancery possibly had the C.F.D. to intervene just so we couldn't do anything. They knew what they're doing. It's been years since the passing of the knights, and they have yet to still have confidence in us. I digress. All I'm saying is don't get swayed too easily by Ms. June. Not sure what the Chancery or the Civil Force see in her. Something just...seems off. Especially how she has some fascination for

KEVIN PRINCETON ~ 201

you. I just...I hope that she won't take advantage of you. Just...always keep your guard up. And just ask me."

"I understand. I do." I said to him. "I get it. I just want them to be safe. That's all."

"I understand truly. They will be. And you will see them again. You have my word. You may make yourself scarce for now. I'm going to write a complaint to the king addressing this interference and a way to get the herbs for the toxins. Perhaps you could meet with Ted and Juliet if you aren't busy. Thank you for heeding my advice. I'll keep this conversation between us." He said as I nodded and took off from the common room. I did what I can to note everything Francis told me in my head. When he talked about how I would see my family again, I was indeed hopeful. But I was caught off guard when he essentially told me to 'expect the unexpected'.

Nonetheless, I knew that I had possible people to find and take down. And he was right. Lucifer's spies could be anywhere. Thus, the Satanists could be summoned, and I could lead them to the caravan. So, I'd have to remain with the Apostles for now. I just prayed that my family weren't surrounded by spies and the C.F.D knew what they were doing.

Later, I was back at Celestia. I was a bit enthused to see Frask again. And I would think that Ted was there with Juliet. Great Nails seemed to progress like a regular city with barely any artists to brighten up the street as I saw before. Occupied by soldiers, I felt misery, fear and grudgeful energy from the walking common folk of all ages. To avoid it, I faced the store and saw that he was on the verge of changing his sign. The sign he had was in the process of being changed. He wasn't joking about changing it.

After crossing the road, I went into the store and happened to see Ted with Juliet sitting by the window. They both turned to me, stunned to see me.

"Hey Kev, didn't think you'd show up." Ted said.

"We're just waiting for Theodore's partner to come back." Juliet said. "You can join us if you want."

"Uh...sure," I said, hoping they wouldn't ask about my conversation with Francis. I would want to stir up suspicion with my association with Bertha. I sat right next to Juliet on the bench with the window behind us. I took a glance over, seeing that Frask was still gathering up new paintings.

While we waited, I thought it would be a good idea to start small talk between the three of us. And see if I could avoid any question regarding my disappearance.

Letting out a small cough, I asked Ted, "So...were you and Juliet discussing something?"

"Oh, we were just discussing about our next match." He replied.

"Match? Match for what?" I asked, leaning a bit forward for curiosity.

Juliet turned to me and added, "Theodore and I happen to play this board game during our spare time. It's called 'Traveler's Progress'. The plot to the game is to help the Traveler to go to either Heaven or Hell. The obstacles are sometimes metaphorical and represent the inner conflicts of what is preventing the Traveler to make his choice. He either listens to good custodians to rise up and leave the burdens behind or to succumb to bad custodians and get held back."

I puzzled at the thought of the concept of the game. I never thought that actual games would exist in the afterlife, let alone board games. And being someone fascinated with board games, especially role-playing games, I was a bit interested. "So, what do you have to do for the Traveler to make it to Heaven or...Hell?"

"There are two different entities the Traveler is in monopoly with: The Good Voice and the Bad Voice. Juliet plays the Good... since she thinks I'm a piece of shit obviously." Ted kidded.

"Oy, we agreed on a rock-paper-scissor challenge!" Juliet resisted, pointing at his face. "Don't make me to be the villain here, now! You should know it's just a game."

"Of course, I do! It's just that...no one really wants to be the bad guy in this type of scenario. You're leading a dude to Heaven; a place of complete bliss and stifling solitude." Ted reasoned. It was ironic since the Heaven I was in had a bit of bliss and aspects that weren't so different from the world I came from.

"Well, you should've been quicker. You usually are. Don't know what to tell you." Juliet said shrugging as a jest. Ending their brief bantering, she faced me and finished what Ted would've said.

"The thing is you have to see which entity with reach to the Traveler and help him go to Heaven; either the good or the bad. When the Good reaches the Traveler, for instance, it's on me to lead him by avoiding the obstacles of the Bad."

"I'm not a big fan of anarchy, but when I need to be." Ted added. "I do have a soft heart for seeing shit go down like the Romans! Or the reputation of losers who call themselves politicians. Or religious folks. Or boastful celebrities. Award shows. Or...hive minded uncreative jackasses who blindly enable the overconsumption of cultures being exploited by acquisitive establishments that result to societal decay and disorder. You know...shit like that."

Goodness! Ted really knew his knowledge. I found it rather admirable. Even for someone who seemed crazy.

"See, there's something to be happy about being the Bad. Just don't...pull that off like last time, yeah?" Juliet joked. I wondered what happened last time.

"Hey, I'm not that psychotic." Ted retorted. "I mean...I am...in a way. But I'm psychotic in a...noble, loving, and good-natured...not at all evil nor disturbed kind of way. Does that make sense? I think it does. Hm."

"Whatever works with you, Theodore." Juliet shrugged. "I don't know how to answer that."

"That sounds brilliant. Simple, but brilliant." I replied enthusiastically. It sounded like a fun role-playing game to try out. "I ought to try it out sometime."

"We were thinking about starting sometime if you care to join us. Especially when this entire Satanist conspiracy dies down a bit and has more leads. And if Francis doesn't call us."

"I will definitely." I said feeling compelled to join. "But I'll be the

204 - KENNETH VIVOR

Good. I have a fascination of being on the morally high ground. At least when I'm not killing anybody out of spite, that is." So bloody ironic, I know.

We all caught ourselves chuckling. I felt the need to find my sense of humor. It's been a while since I laughed. I've been puzzled and skeptical about how I was to adjust to this place. But the days I have been here, I was beginning to at least see a sense of humanity from this place. At least from Ted and Juliet.

"You can read off the descriptions, like a narrator. Michael usually does. So, I'll make an acceptation for you since he's in Arcadia." Juliet said after he chuckled.

"True. That's good enough." I said, smiling at her.

The bell rang as we faced the door and saw that a panting and sweat-faced Frask finally came into the store. Holding his beige leather briefcase while wiping the sweat from his forehead, his eyes clocked towards us as he took notice of us, waiting for him.

"Oh Ted, Kevin, what a surprise!" He said humbly, but confusedly. "I didn't think you'd come this day."

He then took notice of Juliet and asked, "I'm very sorry. I don't think we've met at all."

"My name is Juliet Higgins, Mr. Douglas." She responded while Frask shook hands with her.

"Oh…just call me Frask. Everyone does anyway. At least, I think they do." He said politely while trying to grasp for his breath. He then faced all of us; specifically, Ted and me. "I haven't seen the two of you in a while. I don't know if you happen to see what has happened at the Gathering yesterday. I couldn't make it."

Clearly, we had to cover the fact that we were in the Order. I bet Ted never told him anyways. So just to be safe, we lied. So, I said, "Oy, very bloody tragic. And unfair!"

"I know. I heard that folks of Heaven have disappeared, including Pagan priestesses from Arcadia. I hope they come back safe. I can't imagine what's going through their heads at this moment. I hope Lady Sarah is okay as well. Her kidnapping is big on the *Daily Testimonies*.

It's gotten folks scared," He expressed. His voice rang with a bit of distress. Letting out a sigh, he then asked, "So what is your reason of coming here?"

Juliet pulled the page from her bag and handed to Frask. As he was given the yellow paper, he took a good glance at it.

"Theodore tells us that you were an alchemist at some point in time. We were wondering if you can possibly decipher it's meaning," Juliet asked.

He took a good look into the paper, puzzled, and stunned with the language. "Hmm...I've done alchemy, for sure. In Jeremiah. But if I'm wrong, learning this kind of language is illegal. At least as far as I know. You mind me asking what this is for and...where did you find it?"

The three of us glanced at one another, anticipating for one of us to come up with a convincing excuse for him to not to get suspicious about our Order. Mainly since we vowed to Francis that someone like Frask shouldn't get involved for his safety.

Ted then spat, "It's for a game. Yeah, just some stupid game. We stumbled across the woods and found it. It seemed like a game."

Frask looked confusedly at Ted and glanced back at Juliet and me. She and I looked at one another hoping that he was convinced.

He then shrugged with the paper in his hands and said, "Sure, I could see if I can get a crack at it. Just hope I don't suffer from writer's block. Or...alchemist's block...if that makes sense. But I sincerely hope that it's not legitimate. You guys are too good to mess with this kind of stuff. Satanic language is very dangerous in heavenly standards."

"No doubt," I said, agreeing with his statement.

"We offer our thanks to you, Frask." Juliet said as she slightly bowed as a sign of thanks.

"Of course." He smiled. As soon as we were all intending to leave the shop, he then called, "Hey guys."

Turning out heads, Ted replied, "What is it, Frask?"

"I don't know if you saw it, but I'm currently trying to change the name of the shop." Frask said, pointing at the swinging sign outside of the store. "I don't suppose any of you have any suggestions. I cannot think of a thing! My mind is still fixed upon what happened yesterday. The whole of Celestia and the kingdom became jacked up with unease!"

We all glanced at one another. I reflected on my conversation with Ted that night. The idea about Frask painting these different styles of painting would inspire others to do the same. Calculating all of that thought, I then spoke, "How about...Frask and Ted's...Shop...of Divine Worlds? Or something of the sort?"

Ted and Juliet looked back at me, stunned about the name, and finally faced Frask. His faced backed up with a very stunned facial expression. His hand was scratching underneath his chin. I watched his head slightly nodding and his finger snapping (almost seemed like he was going to break into a musical number or something). He suddenly began to chuckle, "Ha, that actually sounds...amazing! Ha! That's brilliant!"

Ted said after scanning his eyes left and right. He grinned, "Thought you were gonna have a stroke on us, Frask!"

"If I did, I'd be drooling like a bloodhound." He stated. "But that name would definitely bring in more customers and people urging to engage in these paintings and their meanings. It has potential!"

Suddenly, he ran and grasped all three of us in a cuddle. I felt close, perhaps too close to Ted and Juliet to where I felt my hand nearly clipped onto her hand. It was unintentional, but her hand did feel good to hold; as well as my shoulder touching hers. But then again, I was holding onto Ted as well, feeling Frask's arms around us.

As he released us, he then said with glee, "Thank you. Thank you very much! I had to intend to this and get busy. As soon as I change my sign completely, I will get started at deciphering that paper thingy!"

"That's brilliant, Frask!" Juliet said, encouraging his enthusiasm. She then questioned, "In terms of the paper, do you know when it will be done?"

"By a week, I guarantee. Like I said, satanic language is not for me. So, I'm going to have to search far and wide in the rarity of things so I can get the correct translation," he said.

"That's good. We'll have enough time to catch up on things!" Ted said. "Take care, Frask. See you in a while!"

"Definitely." He said, with joy. "And very nice to meet you, Juliet. Come back anytime, especially when I get a better shop name."

"Of course." Juliet smiled. Afterwards, we all left the store. The sun was still bright on the horizon of the buildings.

I then faced the Apostles and asked Ted, "So, are you *truly* sure about this?"

"Like I said, the guy is a professional at this." Ted assured. "It's just gonna take time to find out what the Satanists are intending. These are runes far cryptic for any ordinary alchemist to decipher. But I believe in Frask."

"I hope so," I stated. "What of Michael?"

"Michael is already investigating from Arcadia to get clues about the disappearance of the priestesses." Juliet added. "Francis often urges us to go on these missions alongside the Paladins, even though they are conventional. But for the sake of our safety, he's only keeping us away. Especially from Demonic Legionaries who could also summon out of nowhere."

"So...in other words, we have to wait." I summed up the idea of where they were going for. If that were the case, it would at least give me time to know a bit about the world and its wonders, perhaps.

"Essentially. Plus, we should have room for you to play Traveler's Progress. When we can." Ted said. "We just have to be open to when Francis will summon us."

"It's the only way. And not to make any mistakes," Juliet added.

"Right." I said.

The next three days, we rest while the week was gradually passing by, anticipating seeing if Francis will soon call for us and to see if Frask will eventually decipher the paper. And I spent most of my time, training and meditating by myself outside. When I was done, I took time to explore the castle; pondering on how I was going to adjust as a spirit. Let alone adjust to becoming a knight. Or to escape the Order's conflict to live peacefully.

From the large gothic halls with armored statues of angels, folk-like paintings, I looked around each inch of the place. Each room, hall, and even the common room had very fascinating and outlandish crystal chandeliers dangling from the ceilings. A lot of the walls had tapestries that displayed other mythologies. It showed what looked like other knights working with one another to defeat some common evil. I slid my fingers as the rough quilts scratched underneath. I often wondered how these warriors were different from regular spirits and why Francis would boast about them so much. Most importantly, what was it about me that truly stood out to him.

As I continued to explore the hall, I stumbled across a slightly open door, which revealed the same girl I saw when I first came here to become an Apostle. St. Emily, if I was correct. The door she sat on the floor in her bedroom and by her arm moving back and forth, I would imagine that she was drawing something. I was fixated into what she was drawing.

So naturally, I decided to see just for curiosity. I knocked on the door just to get her attention.

"I figured you were outside," She spoke through her German tongue. "You can come in, Mr. Princeton."

After some hesitation, I decided to come into her room. Her room was decorated with linen that draped on stonewalls and her large bed. The arched window displayed the cloudy weather and showed the mountains cloaked behind the mist. The floor had a carpet, styled almost like a painting of siren dancing in the meadow. Her floor was riddled with various porcelain toys and dolls. Even though she was not supposed to be in the castle, it was dear for the maids to make her own room.

I took a little glance at what she was doodling. It looked to be as if she was trying to recreate the angels descending the demons back into the fiery pits of Hell. The disjointed figures almost put a smile on my face. It took me back to the time when I saw my sister Kelley drawing in the similar style too. Except it was all in colors, whilst Emily was using only charcoals. It made me miss sketching.

She slightly turned her draped hooded head and asked me, "Could you close the door, please?"

"Uh...sure. I'm sorry," I said, doing as tasked. After I shut the door, I decided to sit right by her. I crossed both legs just to be comfortable.

The room was full of silence. I waited, expecting her to speak about her drawing. But of course, I had to be the man in the room. Usually, it was politer for a man to ask first. Especially just to start a conversation and get it across.

"You're Emily. Right," I asked as I watched her head nod. She was too focused. Concealing a cough inside my mouth, I then asked, "So...uh...what is it?"

She fixed her pearly grey eyes towards me and responded, "What is what?"

"The drawing you made. It's...it's fascinating. Very deep...for someone your age."

"It shocks you?" She asked somberly. "I'm glad. I expected it."

"Well...I wouldn't say it shocks me. But it's good. Avant-garde, I'd say." I said awkwardly with a chuckle. Not sure why I brought up a term she wouldn't know. Her voice sounded almost mundane. I can sit through dreary conversations if it didn't lead to anything sinister or weird. Mostly just weird. "I...I used to do these too. Only when I feel a certain mood or...had a fascination with knights. That sort of thing."

"What happened?" She asked me.

"I...I stopped. But that doesn't mean you should," I said. After she gave me a small smile with her violet eyes, she expressed, "I hope you continue. As for what I draw...it's from a dream. A scary dream. So...I draw them out to remember. And eventually forget. I take my...sorrows...and draw them...so I could put away somewhere. Like removing a tumor."

I fixed my eyes to her face, regardless of her still engrossed to her artwork. I then asked, "Do you...know what the dream was about? If you can tell me, that is."

She did respond. I still sat and patiently waited. I wanted to see if she would bold enough to tell me, since she was bold enough to make such a profound drawing. "It's okay if you don't want to tell me. I was just curious, that's all." I said.

"It was about...my death." She said, pointing at the drawing. The men did really look devastated as the crudely drawn raging fire was consuming them.

I then asked her, "Why are you drawing that?"

"Because I eventually want to ask God...to burn it. I...want to forget my past. To forget that nightmare." She spoke. "This dream...when I close my eyes...I felt like I was back in the Liberation Hall defiled, being beaten to death and having the fiery embers and flames tearing onto my flesh. Roasting my bones. And that dream..."

Suddenly, she started shuttering. Her body was quivering, and tears came down her face. This alarmed and saddened me. I saw how it really affected her. She was just a little girl. Gradually, she was quietly sobbing. The tear droplets fell onto the picture and soaked into the paper. I decided to soothe her shoulders.

"Hey. It's okay. It's fine." I said, quietly. "Don't cry. Everything will be fine."

"I want to move on!" She cried. "Knowing what has happened! I want to be strong...for God! And yet, I can't..."

To assure her and lift her soul, I fixed my eyes on her wet face. She looked up at me. "It's going to be a matter of time that we're next. I've heard of Hell, and I dread every time I hear of it; how it is and how it works. I hate having this human essence. It makes me endure pain I do not want. It holds me back, even though I hope to have faith in it."

After I exhaled, I said to her, "I know how it feels. I hate the human condition as well. It's a disease. But I promise that things will get better. And you have a lot of time...to do that. With your age and all." I said to her smiling. She smiled back and sniffed away the tears.

"So...you had a troubled past too?" She asked.

"I did. But...I prefer not to tell. I'm sorry." I said, hoping that she would grasp what I had to say. I then asked her, "I've been meaning to ask. How come you're always here? Aren't you supposed to be in that school? La Divi...something other?"

"La Divinum Estelle." She said before letting out a sigh. "I'm always here...because I don't really feel welcomed in...the school. I try to fit in, but it is impossible to be yourself in school. Because I'm not like them, the pure spirits. They mock me for my past. Here, I feel...much appreciated. I find myself contributing more as an almsgiver of the Order. Out there...no one cares to welcome you...yet they call themselves heavenly."

"Well...that's an innocent child-like way of calling them hypocrites, my dear," I said in jest to lift her spirits. I glanced back at her drawing. "From what I could tell, and from seeing and hearing from you, you're a bright humble girl. And a lot of chaps and misses with so much negativity despises that. They want to think they know you...so they could find some excuse to break you. When you hide out in here, you're...only giving them the satisfaction by not being there to face them. It's good that you want to help, but...it's dangerous. And getting you into this war is deadly. You're special just as you are. And because of that, it's what makes any life unique. Don't go to school just to be accepted. Go...because you want to learn and excel in your passions with those who do adore you for who you are. Understand?"

She nodded and said to me with a smile, "Thank you...Mr. Princeton."

I smiled back at her, "Anytime, miss. I mean...I didn't survive much in school as a human. Bullied because of what...well... I'm not sure if I could...even look at a school the same way. But...I know you could. You're lucky if anything."

She smiled and nodded. I got up from the floor and decided to take off. Emily then said, "I understand. I know how it feels, by the way. The feeling you sense when you are taken away from those you love. You are not alone."

After I nodded, I turned to her. "What was your family like?"

"My family was...confused. Confused about my faith. About what I wanted from life. I loved them, but I wish they loved me. I've always felt like the black sheep. And I thought that I would find solace with my grandmother. But I was wrong. She was like every devil who call themselves human. The world wanted to make me sell myself. And I was killed when I refused to serve man. But it made me learn that I can never be what man wants me to be. I can only be what I want to be. I felt like I didn't exist in the world anymore. But here, I do. I know now to serve God. Not devils who play him."

I was entranced to Emily's strong faith and her devotion to do well in God's name despite what she went through. Regardless of how I approach to any of this madness that storms in front of me, I still had to save myself. Luckily for Emily, she had nothing to redeem herself for; figures because she's a saint. Especially compared to me.

"Well, just know you're still a person with feelings. Even if it's hard to cope with it. I'll see you, Emily. Thanks...for telling me this." I grinned.

"You're welcome, Mr. Princeton."

As I nodded, I checked out from her room and resumed back to the halls. I knew I had a lot to think about, for sure. I thought a lot that the voices were quite absent than usual, probably due to the frequent meditation I've made. The conspiracy was getting in the way of getting back to my family.

I finally retreated to my room and laid on my bed.

XVI

❦

The Angel

The days of dilly-dallying in the Khalsevan were done for now. Ted and Juliet, who informed me of Frask deciphering the paper, soon alarmed me. It was now only a manner of time before we can possibly find Francis and tell him about our discovery.

On horseback, we went back to 41 Covenant Street and straight into Frask's shop, passing the sign that was still in the process of being changed. We stood shaking and slowly swaying our frames as we tried to catch our breaths. Frask stood optimistically, as usual, and greeted us before he could show us the paper. I saw that his left hand was grasping both the paper and another piece of paper.

"I believe that I have decoded the paper! With a lack of sleep and some candy, I think I may have done it!" He said as he then went around to his desk, placing down the papers. We simply followed and huddled around him like vultures. As we looked down, we saw that he made markings on the paper and circles around each stanza. As I glanced underneath his desk, he had a stack of three books that were colored.

"I went to the Great Library of David at Bartholomew Drive and discovered something about it. Obviously, we don't have books from the demonic school of thought. Let alone from Hell itself. But...I studied the paper...and saw that it's inspired by a set of ancient runes specifically from the Germanics of the Anglo-Saxons. I was able to decipher the accurate formations to come to this. It seems to be...a poem, or some aspects of a message, from someone called The Angel." He said, his face locked at us.

The three of us glanced at one another, perplexing on what to think of it.

"The Angel?" Juliet echoed in question. "Is that's the only name he or she left, Mr. Douglas?"

"Afraid so. But...whoever wrote this was kind enough to leave a somewhat poem that I managed to translate from the original. Listen to this;"

> Our sun will rise again when lighting strikes
> Soon the false prophet will meet its might
> If you need me, my brothers, and sisters,
> I reside in the land where nonexistence withers
> My science will vanquish the falsehood of God
> He and his angels will soon be gone
> Come forth and we shall meet in darkness in two weeks

> -The Angel

That seemed very cryptic and very vague. But whoever wrote it was probably intending to make it that way so we wouldn't discover its meaning. I grabbed both the paper and the translation to compare the two. Usually, something written in a Satanic language (or any language) would be much longer and written in-depth. I was impressed that Frask went out of his way to painstakingly decrypt a complicated and sinister language consisted of symbols and shapes. And I saw that it was written three weeks before the attack.

He pulled out one of the books from underneath his slightly messy desk and opened it to a specific page he had folded. He pointed at a picture of the sun and saw the names affiliated with the word. I was stunned when Lucifer's name was there.

"Obviously, Lucifer is supposed to be the sun. Because think about it; what is another name for the sun?" Frask asked. I knew that it might have been referring to Lucifer, since he was the 'morning star', which was the sun. But Ted already beat me to it before I can answer.

"Isn't it the morning star?" Ted asked. "I mean, that is what he is often referred too."

"Exactly! What the poem, or the message, is saying that he will put his wrath upon something. Like lighting. Calling Jesus..."

"False prophet." I recited what was written.

"I think it's pretty clear that he wants to destroy Christ, Mr. Douglas...I mean Frask!" Juliet said. "The line that talked about the land where nonexistence withers are what it's interesting."

"That I am not sure. I just assumed that they were extra words just to sound artsy," Frask shrugged. "And maybe I haven't been out much, but I don't know of many lands in the Promised Land that are non-existent."

"Hold on. Juliet can be leading up to something." Ted said. He then looked at the book Frask had and took a glance at the passage once more.

"What are you grasping?" I asked.

"It mentioned sciences. I think this person is residing at some kind of...alchemist laboratory. Maybe not in Celestia or the whole of Valestone, but somewhere in the Promised Land." Ted stated. "I'm just not sure where it is."

Snapped both of her fingers, Juliet stated, "We should look more in the Literature Room."

Quietness came, as we were all puzzling; possibly to find out where we could locate Francis to tell him what Frask discovered. We were a bit oblivious to Frask staring very awkwardly at the three of us, obvious trying to find his place in all this.

Juliet walked over to the desk and looked at Frask. "May we take the translation along with the paper, Frask?"

"Well, of course. That's why it's there for." Frask said as Juliet took both papers and began to trail off.

Before she does, she turned and smiled at Frask. "Thank you once again, Frask. You're a genius!"

Frask smiled back and threw his hand, "Of course! I hope it helps."

"It does. You've done well, Frask." I added, trailing off with the others. I briefly witness Ted gesturing a thumb up at him.

"Sign's lookin' good, Frask!" Ted said before we walked out. "See you soon! And drink coffee! Lots of it!"

Once we were outside, we walked away from the shop and were trailing the hall crowded sidewalks. I noticed that it was drizzling from the greying skies. We got back onto our mounts that we had tied near the hitching posts in the alleyway. Once we were mounted, we galloped on our way. We galloped alongside the on-going carriages. I followed behind Ted and Juliet as the hooves pounded against the cobblestones.

"Where do you suppose we go from here?" I asked in curiosity. "Knowing that we've got our clue?"

"We're going back to the Main Chapel to get to the Literature Room. We won't find much in the Khalservan since it's mostly about lightkeeper magic and guardians. We need an atlas book. With any luck, we can find Francis there too." Juliet said as her face was focused on the road. She turned to Ted and said, "You have our thanks, Theodore. For getting Frask to help."

"Hey, anything to get somethin' done!" Ted said. "And it'll be good since it's been two weeks."

"Yeah, those were actual good ideas. First time you've ever had one," Juliet mocked. "You should have more of them often."

"Oh, shut up!" Ted yelp jokingly. "Like you thought it was a good idea to let Kev run off knowing damn well the C.F. was looking for him."

"Give it a rest, already! You glop! I said I was sorry. So was Kevin," Juliet said as she turned to me. "Aren't you, Kevin?"

"Yes, I am." I said grimly. "Let's just get to the bloody castle already. We can sulk about my mistakes later."

So, our next destination was the Main Chapel. That same place I broke into the past few months I was here. It's been quite a while since I've been there. I was caught up at becoming an Apostle that I felt as though I've grown past things that I've known.

Once we were nearing the bridge to the castle, it still stood with its pointed towers. We raced down the bridge that was rowed with statues of angelic guards in diverse poses. I wasn't quite sure why I haven't caught that before. Then I quickly realized that it was during nighttime when I broke in. So, on that record, I didn't see the point of luring onto that little mistake. Nor did I see the point on writing this paragraph.

Afterwards, we dismounted from our horses and the three of us ran into the castle. I removed my hat to wipe the rain that drizzled on my face. Once we dismounted from our horses, we hurried into the castle. Storming in like raging Vikings, we rushed up the spiral stairs that were leading to the marble-walled hallway where I was at last time. We were so focused that we were naïve to the scholars and other civilized spirits passing by through the same hall as us. There, we came across the Literature Room. Luckily, a sign stated that it was open until 11 o'clock at dark. Thus, we had time.

Once we opened the door, although it was raining, it was good to see how different it looked during the day. The room was big and circular, stuffed with many shelves of books and tables between them. The ceiling was decorated with astronomic ornaments that were dangling. The glass dome window shined down strobe lights from the fog-covered sun, giving the room an interesting atmosphere. My eyes fixated at the book on the podium in the middle of the wide room now concealed in silvery aurora lights, which I came to remember that night; a frightful night that I discovered the truth. I turned away from it to avoid contemplating.

Distracted by my tiredness, I was catching my breath after we ran and watched Juliet and Ted pacing around like chickens, looking for something specific. I walk around, hoping that I can be of any help at all; especially hearing Juliet complain under breath. She sounded completely frustrated as she struggled and skimmed desperately to find the book. As much as I was still iffy about the Order and my involvement in this conspiracy, I wanted to repay them for the help they gave me. After trying their very best to make me feel at home, the least I can do is to repay the favor.

I turned to each shelf, skimming through every colored book.

"So...what are we looking for? A book on alchemy?" I asked. Perhaps it was a stupid question to ask, but...whatever.

Juliet replied as she was raiding into the shelves along with Ted, "Not just alchemy, Kevin. A book about the various labs in the Promised Land. It's a geological book, so we should find it here. Shouldn't be long."

"Alright then," I said. "It's not here though."

She turned to me and said, "That's the children section. Usually nursery and fables, somewhere of that sort."

I turned to pull out one yellow book from the shelf, only to see that it was indeed a book intended for children. The yellow cover had cartooned versions of what appeared to be the Norse gods and their history; obviously it was family-friendly from the looks of the cover. Placing the book back, it sparked my chances of being useful. That is what I hated about being in groups; they make you feel useless and pathetic.

I was soon alarmed by Ted called, "Hey. I think I found it."

We both hurried to the nearest table as Ted brought a large green and blue book. Once he approached, he placed it down.

"Excellent Theodore!" Juliet said, pulling out the two papers from her bag. She placed the papers on the right side of the book. Slightly licking both her index finger and thumb, she flipped the book and skimmed through the pages to find one page about any labs in Heaven. She first stopped at a page called *The Laboratories of Heaven*.

It consisted of a large list of laboratories that were there. Some were in Valestone, some were in other cities, towns, and villages. Some were in faraway lands, which was what we were looking for. Juliet then spotted the alchemy category of the same page and scrolled her finger to find a name. Surprisingly, it was only one alchemy lab.

"It seems that there's one in the coast of the Jury Cove, far right from the Isles of Ghai." Ted concluded.

"But it's been deserted for decades now. They cannot possibly be there." Juliet said.

"Why not?" I asked, leaning in to look more into the white page plastered with names. I then looked back at a confounded Juliet.

"At the time, even before Theodore and I were ascended here, I heard that the mystics before alchemists here were burned during Lucifer's first rebellion. Before alchemy, it was ceremonial magic, ceremonialists. They were locked inside that laboratory... being burnt alive. They placed a lethal energy force around to prevent the angels from saving them." Juliet informed. "They could be in there. A ceremonialist lab."

"Back to the document and the translation, do you think this can be the land that the paper was referring to?" Ted asked. "I mean it has to be *A land where nonexistence withers*. That place is a dead zone. As far as I know. We need precautions...since it seems like the only plausible place they could be at. Or where they are going to be at."

"You're right." Juliet said. "Well...that concludes our destination. But I'm still lingering on what would they want with Pagan priestesses."

"Do you think...perhaps he's trying to train them into becoming his...like his priestesses?" I asked.

"They can be undertaking the spirits...illegally. Some brainwashing shit!" Ted said. "Maybe the priestesses can be here...in the Promised Land. And this Angel...is expecting some invitees for a gathering."

"We need to tell Francis." Juliet suggested. "We must get back to the Khalservan as soon as we can."

"Good idea." I said.

As soon as we placed the book back into the shelf, we took off from the room and went back to the hall. And once again, I was not sure if it was just a miracle or some mere coincidence, but we happened to come across Francis down the hallway on our right. He appeared to be with Jesus and Mary Magdalene, who still stood just and regal with their crowns on their heads. The other spirits in the hall greeted them as well.

We were not one to intervene or to interrupt a confidential conversation. But since we basically had the answers to what they sought to find, we needed to warn them before it was too late. There was no time to waste. The three of us nodded towards one another, signaling to approach to the Francis. Only Francis.

When we were nearing their lane and gaging eyes with them, (perhaps it was another miracle from God) Francis turned and took notice of us. Jesus and his queen went along and greeted us with smiles. Francis then spoke, "Ah, Kevin, Ted, Juliet...very good to see you once again!"

"Yes, um...I'm sorry! We're sorry!" Juliet said, nearly stuttering. "We didn't mean to intrude. Especially with you, our king and queen."

As she and Ted bowed, I decided to go along just to appease. I then looked up to Mary, who fixated her blue crystal eyes on three of us. Her jeweled and layered necklace and dress nearly made me took notice of her complex beauty. She bowed her head softly and humbly. She said graciously, "I want to take this chance to thank you three kindly for what you did. We didn't mean for you to be captured in stress by what those villains has caused."

"Of course, Your Majesty," Ted said.

She then glanced at Juliet and slowly stroked her bleach hair. "It's so honorable to see you take your talents to new heights, Ms. Higgins. You were always so strong in heart and mind when you were my maiden. You have the thanks from all priestesses. And I included...for looking for the Pagan girls."

"I...I'm honored, Your Majesty," Juliet replied, smiling. "And I shall. We're awfully sorry...again. It wasn't our attention to interrupt."

"No worries, my dears." She spoke calmly, gesturing her hand to Francis. "Jesus and I were simply discussing the safety of the other girls with Mr. Bailey. We were at a close anyway. Whatever you have to discuss with him is now accepted."

We nodded as I then faced Jesus. I then asked, "How is your daughter?"

"She is well, all thanks to you, Kevin." Jesus smiled. "It's just troubling for her to get over the traumatization. But she is blessed. And we shall continue looking after her. She's a great importance to the afterlife, like all others."

I nodded in agreement.

"Well, I believe we must be going before the rain grows far worst. You all have a blessed day." Jesus said, taking hold of his wife's hand and leaving us with Francis.

"You too, your Majesty." We all said.

"Francis, we shall discuss elsewhere. You take care now." Jesus regarded him as he nodded in reply. As soon as the royal couple were leaving, Francis faced us.

"Forgive my lateness, guys." Francis said. "I had to tend to the Lady for a while. Jesus and I discussed my departure to gain aid from Chief Achek of the Happy Hunting Grounds to cultivate sage and lavender to trade with the herbalists to make the toxins. So, I plan to take my leave tomorrow to see it through. I might do it often, just so you know. But I'm not leaving you behind. I assumed you've updates on finding the person responsible?"

"Frask helped us decoded the paper. It turned out to be a letter from someone called The Angel." I said as Juliet hastily passed on the translated paper with the letter. I then handed them both to Francis as he took a good look into the decrypted paper.

"Our instincts tell us that whoever wrote this is intending to perform rites at a deserted alchemy lab on the Jury Horizon. We've done some investigation at the Literature Room not so long ago. With any luck, the priestesses should be there...recently returned from Hell; possibly held against their will, though." Juliet said.

We studied carefully to his reaction to the translation. His face seemed to be stunned and possibly thought to himself on how he might have underestimated Frask's abilities. Subsequently, he viewed us and grinned.

"I am...thrilled." He grinned. "The only laboratory would be at Jury Horizon. That was burnt down during the rebellion. I am impressed that you've managed to do this with each other. You should be proud of yourselves. I mean it."

"Thank you, Francis." Juliet bowed her head silently.

"Yeah, thanks for heeding my advice, Francs!" Ted added.

He then glimpsed at me and patted me on my right shoulder. "Keep this up and you will soon become an Official."

The thought of it made me genuinely grateful. Even though I was dead, even though I wanted no part of the conflict, I at least knew I might be doing something good for once. Even in a different world.

He then said, removing his hand, "I shall make sure to reserve a ship. And perhaps...get Jesus to get Michael to gather up the Angel Paladins; in case if any hell breaks loose. I hope for good news the day after tomorrow. I wish you good luck and blessings from God. Especially you, Kevin." I nodded.

In the evening, the rain got heavier and poured down like salt. They fell like a mass of fallen angels. We were garbed and prepared. Ted and Juliet also wore hats. Only Ted wore a light grey fedora. Juliet a dark blue panama hat. As requested, Francis managed to get us a sailing vessel. I felt the wave tossing the ship through an angry squall. It signified that we were getting close. I sat underneath the ship with Ted, Juliet and eleven angels led by Michael while the crew had to suffer just to get the ship to shore.

Each face of Michael's men had expressions ranging from determined to frighten. You wouldn't think angels like this would be sent to war. The angels in the ship were completely different from the angel guards I usually came across. Their suits still had the white, grey, and blue scheme. But it seemed like they were flexible as opposed to the heavily armored angels I came across. Perhaps they were the more tactical looking angels.

The ship held everything you would expect, including a ton of loot presumably collected by the people who used this ship, loot from golden crowns or ancient treasures. Perhaps they were used to exchange for benefits and not to hoard. I respected that.

I decided to turn to face the celled window and saw that we were very far from Valestone. I didn't see any site of a city. Or anything for that matter. Just moving mountains of water going in diverse directions. I turned to the right and saw that we were gaining ahead to the island. It fitted the description of the paper for the most part; lighting did strike down across the sky, but there was no sun. I had to admit that I was a bit tensed because of the mission. I hoped to find the priestesses. I hoped to be right. We didn't go through all these investigations just to be wrong. I was desperate for a toke of a cigarette, knowing that it usually calmed my nerves. So, my right leg began to shudder.

After I sat back down, I faced Michael. He then took noticed of my tense face and shaking leg. "Scared, Kevin?"

I was alarmed by his sudden conversation-starting question. Obviously, I decided to reply and be honest, "A bit. Never thought that I would be involved in a mission like this. I just hope I don't muck up."

"You will perform fine. Trust me. You've impressed the Order thus far with your actions. And don't worry...we will be right behind you. You have the two best Apostles with you as well." Michael encouraged, which got Ted and Juliet to grin at me. I grinned back. He then said, "Now...according to the Queen of The Summerland, not only the priestesses disappeared. But she didn't have time to say which. With any luck, we could recover both."

I then said, "I don't mean to seem rude or arrogant, but I wanted to know the purpose of the priestesses? I mean I've known about priests, but I never knew a woman could be a priest also. All my life, before this, I just know more male priests." I then added in regret, "Sorry, I know it's a dumb question."

"It's not stupid! It's an honest curious question." Ted corrected. "A stupid question would be if people are still eating chowder in Boston. Or if people still believe that hoarding amounts of money or accolades would make them spiritually happy. Or if...planking was still a thing."

"What...does...that have to do with anything?" I needed an answer.

"Exactly, I think that's the point."

"What point?"

Ted shrugged and scoffed. "I don't know."

Juliet rolled her eyes. At that point, I must learn how to accept randomness from Ted. It's a part of his charm, I supposed.

"The priestesses are essential and very well-respected women in the afterlife, just as the priests." Michael said. "They had great involvement in arts, ethics and overall cultural constructs. And they benefit everything that is great about being a spirit and to embrace spirituality in all things; ranging from self-discovery to humility with their sacred rites and ceremonies that serves what the monarchy represents. They are precious and important to this place as they serve the kingdoms with divinity. Their existence was established by Haniel, one of the Archangels who made the school...before she died. Her soul rests in her statues."

He then glanced at Juliet. "Juliet would know more...since she had experience before she was an Apostle. She served the queen when she was just a girl after she ascended here. Performed beautiful rites."

"It's a matter of sisterhood. We're all the same." Juliet stated. "And even if I am obviously no longer a priestess, I technically still consider them...as my sisters. They have power within them that elevates what it truly means to live as a spirit. I remembered how we would be at these festivals and celebrate life with music, arts, and stories with rites in the Main Chapel. These women worship a religion consisting of spirits coming together to enhance and celebrate the natures of the Gods. I wish for those days to return sometimes. And I've been a spirit for only a few years now. Still, it was a fun experience."

Ted nodded as he began to play with his revolver, spinning the chamber. I nodded along.

"In fact, one archangel I admired, who had the qualifications of a priestess...was Ariel." Michael said, his eyes becoming sorrowful. "I miss her dearly."

"They had a thing...together." Ted teased as Michael glared at him in annoyance.

"No, we did not!" Michael retorted. "But she was a dear friend. You...do realize that us pure angels are infertile, don't you Ted?"

"I know. Just being dumb! You know what I am!"

I looked back and asked, "Where is she now?"

"In the Void...with the others," He said gloomily as his head bowed his head in shame. "I miss fighting by her side. It's not the same, y'know; Gabriel and I being the only Archangels left in this world. It used to be simple when we fought and stand together. We had it all before. Our own fellowship. Our own roundtable. But ever since...Lucifer turned on us, we got lost through the ages. Seeing our fellow men and women being slaughtered by someone I once considered...a brother...it's something that could never leave your mind." Michael said after he sighed. "My apologies; didn't mean to stray away from our task. I just...trailed off."

I wished I did meet the other archangels since I was told about them as well. Especially from what Michael explained to us. "I'm sorry about what happened to them," I expressed.

"I appreciate it, Kevin. But all we can do is honor them in name. That's all we can do for those we had in our lives pass. Usually, we angels weren't made to engage in the likes of war. Only to guide, enlighten and protect spirits and humans to find their inner peace. Still, on that same token, we were also made to push out evil forces in all forms. So, if we must engage in war to make that so, we will. But it...it comes with a prize. Like everything in life."

"*Land ho!!!*" We overheard the crew's muted cry from under the deck.

Michael then fixated his eyes on us and said to us, "Looks like we're already here."

I felt the ship lowering its movements, indicating that we have stopped sailing. I watched as the angels were getting themselves prepared. They placed on their helmets and sheathed their weapons. Unrolling my sleeves, I readjusted my retractable blades just to see if they were sharp enough and polished enough to draw blood. I then placed back my sleeves.

I then stood up and gathered around with others to see what else Michael had to say.

"Remember Apostles, you are to find this Angel, kill or stop him, and then get out with the priestesses. I'll be sure to be right behind you with the men." Glancing at the soldiers, he said, "While the Apostles are scouting within the laboratory, we will search outside around the settlement to obtain possible evidence of Lucifer. Sixteen will head out to find high points in the land to prepare an ambush for any Demonic Legionaries. Sixteen will follow behind and do a reconnaissance around the lab's exteriors." Then he turned to us, "Should there be any problems, disregard our target and bring the women out safe." He then faced all of us and finished by saying,

"There's a chance that we may come across the Satanists if summoned, but getting those women out is our one priority. If we're lucky, we'll find this Angel and bring him to justice. He's expecting his fellow men to come, so we'll be the guests. Keep your guard up, vigilance strong and mindfulness intact. Any questions?" Michael finished with a question as an expression of concern. He then said, "Alright then, let's go. Good luck and God bless you all."

As soon as he led the way up from the poop deck, the armed warriors followed him. Sixteen soldiers rushed past us to set up an ambush. The rain was coming down like a shower once the door of the ship was opened. I prayed that it would go well.

I fled off with my fellow Apostles. I watched as Ted then placed on a very interesting prop. A mask. It wasn't the same scarf mask I was given. It was an actual mask; an eerie one like it. One of the eyes had a star draw around it. The lower part of the mask was a wavy pattern with blue and orange stripes. As weird as it was, it did match his unorthodox personality and outfit. It nearly resembled a jester.

After tightening the strands, he then asked through his muffled voice, "How do I look?"

Studying and sinking in his design choice, I replied, "Like a bloody wild card."

"Aw...Kevin, so sweet!" He said in a mockingly cheery way. Clapping his hands in excitement, he then yelped, "That is what I am going for! Come, let's kill me some Satanists!"

He paced past me as I then heard Juliet say to me, "When it comes to bloodshed, he always gets excited. And really enjoys it. Eerily enjoys it."

"Definitely a wild card." I repeated, taking off from under the deck to the pouring and dazzling surface of the ship.

My eyes were not deceived when I saw the size of the land with my sterling spyglass. It was abandoned and consumed with dark foliage. It looked to be a castle consisted of not only extremely high rectangular towers, but with broken glass domes. But the entrance itself was hard to find due to a decent number of trees, deconstructed buildings, and other structural forms were cloaking the place. Thus, I was satisfied and placed away the spyglass in my satchel.

I studied every inch of the wide moody portrait of the forsaken place. I stood on the moving ship along with a masked Ted and a now masked Juliet. She had a scarf mask as well as me. I turned to Michael, awaiting his signal to go forward. As soon as he nodded, the three of us came down from the ship to the shore.

As soon as we reached the sands, we raced towards the deconstructed village on our way to the laboratory. To get a much better view at where the entrance (or any entrance to avoid detection) can possibly be, we all managed to reach the rugged rooftops. Leaping and jumping from roof to roof, we were flowing and moving like leaves in the wind, but we were cautious to the pounding drops of the rain and the stability of the rooftops.

My feet felt heavy as they pounded and scrapped particles and water the roof palettes. While running, I was astonished by how Ted and Juliet ran. Both had different ways of performing as if they are dancing in midair. Ted moved almost like his pet python; flexible and seamless. Juliet moved as if she was flying; her arms would always spread apart as she ran. Each step and leap were making my vision jumpy but gaining closer and closer to the lab. My heart was racing, and my arms swayed up and down when I leaped from roof to roof. My coat was moist with the water plastered on it. It was hard to keep the pace with them.

I looked above to see Michael's men right behind us, holding up their rifles, swords, bows, spears, and shields. Their wings were spread as they flew behind us. I quickly remained my focus onto the buildings, in which I saw were occupied by the paladins as they prepared.

The three of us were approaching to the edge of the roof and simultaneously dived from one roof to dive roll to another. I felt my leg nearly slipping into the dark abyss of the broken roof. Thankfully, my masked allies snatched my arms and picked me up. Once I gained back my steadiness, I resumed to running. It made me reflect on Snake and I; how we used to take it to the rooftops to make our escape from the law.

We eventually reached the laboratory. While desperately struggling for air, I was obsessed over the architecture of the building. It looked like a ludicrous capital, but very massive in size. I didn't even care about the showering rain. I was too concentrated to try. I looked back to see if Michael was still behind us. And indeed, he was.

A masked Juliet came to me, forcing myself to focus on her, and asked, "You're ready, Kevin?"

I nodded. My eyes were then fixed on what Ted was constructing with his magic. His fingers were dark and had strands of black smoke. Suddenly, a flowy rippling effect was displayed right in front of him, indicating that he summoned it to appear. He placed both hands to his side as his fingertips resumed to its original color. I assumed that this was his way of teleportation.

I then followed through the ripple, which turned out to be a vortex from where we stood to the roof of the lab itself. I looked back to see the vortex close in an instant. We faced a tower window of the lab, which was a good and secretive entry to the inside. I walked towards the edge of the roof, and I really couldn't make out on what was going on down at the ground, since we were very high up. I hoped that Michael and the angels were there, doing what they planned to do. I turned back to the Apostles, to see that they've already gotten inside. Ted then asked, "You're comin'?"

I raced down and jumped into the window. From the pounding rain to the shadowy industry, we were sure that we were quiet. It turned out that we were at the end of a two-way staircase of the building. Every corner was scattered and plastered with broken glass, ash, murky water, and dirt. We looked around, wandering curiously and cautiously. The entire place seemed surprisingly quiet from where we were so far.

"Theodore, why don't you see if you could find anything that moves? Kevin and I will explore to see what we can find." Juliet suggested. I watched Ted as he drew out both of his pistols with ease.

"You got it." He said as he suddenly shifted away from us at a heart-beat. When he ran, there were blurred blue duplicates of him running coming from his movements. Dirt and dust flew by as he took off. I was fascinated with the abilities Ted had. And they seemed to fit with who he was.

Distorted, fast-paced, and quick to get things done. As far as myself, I seemed to be shadowy and want to get things done my way; given how I was able to use psychic abilities. I have yet to see what else Juliet can do aside of healing. And summoning, of course. We're capable of doing that anyway.

A ball of white light emerged in Juliet's hands and slowly lifted above our heads. It held still and steady. It seemed imitate, just being with someone undeniably beautiful yet potential dangerous as Juliet. Her short blue dress swayed as I nodded and followed with her to sightsee more of the dark and decaying corridors, broken laboratories, disenfranchised libraries, and dissolving hallways with wind hollowing through them like wolves. We looked and search for where the priest-esses can be held, hoping to death that we weren't wrong. From the top to the bottom floor, we looked around. We searched around the build-ing, only to find ourselves suddenly coming back to where we started. It felt like being stuck in a condensed level in a video game; especially open-world video games. It was sort of burdening my heart of how much damage Lucifer's rebellion has apparently done. I imagined that this was once a beautiful lab that manifested charms of all kinds.

I was still hoping that we weren't wrong about our conclusion and realizing that we dragged Michael, his men, and a ship all for nothing. We knew that we had to be right, seeing how Frask decrypted the message, and it was easy to understand. And it seemed like a place where existence was futile. Hell, not even necessary.

Soon, we found ourselves, stumbling across a library. The room was large and forested with many shelves with lost texts that took up the entire room. But instead of books, the shelves were filled with ales. Whatever concoctions or other contagious alchemistic liquids they had been beyond us. And being that this place was left to decay, it wouldn't be a good idea to taste any of them. So, we paced ourselves through the ledges, though it felt like going through a labyrinth of shelved collections. The light Juliet held helped us lead the way through the darkness. It almost took us at least half an hour to find the girls. Ted was nowhere to be found. And Juliet was soon getting frustrated. I even sensed her frustration.

"Dammit!" She yelped. "Where can they be!? I know they're here! I know it! The letter has to be true!"

"We'll find them." I said, trying what I can to give her encouragement.

"That's vague, seeing how we haven't stumbled to any living spirit yet." She said. Suddenly, Ted quickly reappeared and made wind and dust blow onto our faces.

"There's nobody here!" Ted exclaimed. "I've been running around like a headless chicken here."

"They can be here. We're just missing something." I stated.

"They have to be hidden. But I just don't know where!" Juliet said with irritation in her voice. "I don't want to rely on Alwyn too much."

"Who's Alwyn?" I asked.

"A spirit eagle she summons." Ted answered. "She's often used him as a scouting and aerial viewfinder."

"I haven't been using him for a while because I don't wish to take him for granted. But I suppose I have no choice now." Juliet said nearly gloomy.

"Hey, I used Algor to help me get Lady Sarah back." I said to her, nearing her face, not in an aggressive way. "Just because you're using them for assistance, doesn't mean that you're taking advantage of them. They're more than just measly pets. They're companions for a reason."

Sighing through her mask, she gave it a thought and said, "You're probably right. Thank you, Kevin." I nodded in response.

"Well...here we go, then." She then held her up her right hand, holding and curling her two fingers. A big chunk of smoke was appearing and was gradually building up a large bird. I witness wings spreading as smoke strands flowed towards the dark ceiling. A head with a beak emerged from the smoke. The eagle was soon formed and rested on Juliet's fingers. She then petted its head as it made a happy squeal. It was a gorgeous bird with burnt feathers mixed with palettes of ashen white and rusted gold feathers. His narrowed eyes were bright yellow, striking into the hearts of its prey.

"Kevin, meet Alwyn." Juliet introduced.

"Very lovely bird." I complimented.

"Eh...I've seen better." Ted jested, receiving knuckles to his shoulders from Juliet. He winced and rubbed at his pain.

"Since I'm connected to him, I could sense with his eyes." She said. "Perhaps then we can find where the girls are being held."

Turning to Alwyn, she said, "Do what you do best, sweetie. I'll see you soon." The bird squealed. Juliet then propelled the bird, launching from her fingers. The bird spread its wings with strands of smoke attached to its wings. I saw him exit from the shelves and through the ceiling.

Juliet triggered her Blessed Eye state and closed her eyes. Sitting down, she sat in a meditating pose with her kneecaps pointed and her legs crossed. Ted and I sat to join her, studying her figure to know what she was seeing through Alwyn. The room was in much silence than it needed to be. But at the same time, it was necessary for Juliet to concentrate. With her eyelids twitched, it was obvious that she was much focused. Suddenly, her eyes drew lines of blood. It came down from underneath her eyelids. It could only indicate that she sensed danger.

"Argh!!" She gasped with her eyes busted open. Blood was growing dry on her face. I quickly wiped it off, so she could see.

"What happened?" Ted asked. "What did you sense?"

"The priestesses! They're...underneath the laboratory!" She cried, getting up from the floor. "Alwyn will make his way around."

"Well...we have to see if there's any way to get down there!" I said, probably obvious of our next move. She, Ted, and I rushed out from the library to the main hall of the building. We wandered, anxiously to find our way further down the bottom.

I wandered and investigated the ridged area. I couldn't let the frustration slow me down; otherwise, those priestesses would be done for. The investigating stopped as I then came across very peculiar smears underneath the broken glass and dirt. As I swept the wooden floor, I feasted my eyes on what looked to be the smears getting larger and larger the more I swept. It looked to be a line, possibly ten inches in length. It connected to another line, which looked to be six inches width. Getting on my knees, I dug my gloved fingers into the sharpened crack. I saw I was trying to lift what looked to be a block to an underground passageway.

"Oy, I think I've found something!" I alerted the Apostles as they raced to my position.

"Help me lift this up! I think it's a passageway." I implored. The three of us lifted the large piece of pavement, which then revealed a dirty wooden door attached to concrete. Of course, it had a lock that looked to be combusted but quickly fixed. Glancing at the Apostles, they nodded; suggesting me to break the lock.

I then drew out my pistol, cocked the hammer back and fired at the lock as the lock zapped and jumped across the room. Ted opened the floor door. I got up to my feet and witness a pitch-black abyss, leading to wherever it led. Juliet controlled the ball of light into the entrance, which was giving light to the underground. We all focused down there to see a floor masked with scraps and other debris.

"Lady's first." Ted jested once again to Juliet. She jumped into the small passageway. Then Ted. And lastly was me. As I landed on both feet, I saw that the only big light we had was the surface we came from. Other than that, the entire room was a complete black and hallow hall with mangled dry bones on the ground with water.

"Delightful." I said sarcastically. We were suddenly alerted by loud wailing sound coming from the left side of us. I summoned my sword as well as Juliet. Ted summoned his scepter.

"Come! It's coming from there!" Juliet said, leading the two of us. We raced down the pathway through the hall riddled with more broken bones, shattered glasses, and deconstructed cement. The walls were covered in obscurity, but with Juliet's light we at least know that concrete walls surrounded us. I often question myself silently on how a place like this would exist in a supposed paradise like Heaven. But I had to put that to rest.

The agonized wailing continued as we then heard it coming from the right side of the halls. It got louder and louder. The wailing was hurting and bone crushingly haunting more than a banshee's screech. It meant that we were getting close. But close to the abyss of some hell.

"Wait...someone is crying! Something is wrong!" Juliet yelped quietly and frightened. My heart was sinking. For the first time, I was afraid. I was mostly afraid for Juliet, knowing that she might have been close to women like them. Seeing them hurt, or even killed, would devastate her.

Eventually, we got to where the sound was coming from. We stumbled and stealthy moved to what appeared to be a room. We crouched and took cover behind a structure that was convenient for us to hide behind. It looked almost like a theatre, except there was no audience. There were no actors on stage. Perhaps, it used to be a room for alchemists to perform experiments. But it looked to be five devastated women standing alongside with two skull horned soldiers pointing their muskets at their heads. The four guards were nearly bigger (probably eight feet) and more protected by armor than the three Satanists. One Satanist wearing a strange Jesus mask with a crown of thorns carried a red violin. For what reason was beyond me. And there was one other bloke with no shirt on him, a long black woolly scarf, grey trousers, darkened boots, and an eerie looking mask made of porcelain. Something out of a Greek play. He looked to be observing away. On his bare back was an obscure tattoo of a celestial drawn sun just like on his mask. He had a sickly slim figure.

Observing the surrounding dispassionately, the captain looked to be ten-feet tall. His outfit was war-driven, fitting well with his muscular frame. An interesting, darkened pelt of some creature surrounded his neck. He had a silver shoulder-plate on his left shoulder that was strapped from the plate and across his chest. A black worn out cape draped on his right shoulder and dropped by the back of his ankles. He donned a skull of a bull with his dark vacant eyes. He wore a worn-out kilt with boots. He wore a sword with a large hilt on his hip. The lad was the stuff of nightmares. His helmet had horns tall as towers and sharp like talons.

But the horrific screeches snapped me back to the reality I faced. My eyes widened to what I saw.

And for the first time, something has awakened. I felt my heart pounding, punching inside to escape my chest. I didn't see something I resented. I saw someone who seemed innocent and in need of help. We were disgusted and saddened to see the bruised and malnourished priestesses forced to witness one of their own being soiled in front of them. Their beautiful virginal dresses were covered with black smears and stanched with urine (perhaps due to their immense fear). The priestess getting assaulted looked to be at least fifteen years old. Her virginal white dress was torn and thrown far right across the floor. Stripped, bruised, helpless and humiliated, she was pinned down on the hollow concrete floor, with legs forcibly spread open, while one of the skull-worn Satanists grunted and howled as he constantly lunged himself into her.

The other guards barely stood, laughing like crazed drugged up hyenas as the young priestess continued to wail in blood-coiling agony. They were encouraging this, telling the guard to flounder every part of her. Tears were uncontrollably damping from her eyes as she was continuously soiled and pounded onto the dusty floor. I was completely frozen. My eyes watered because she could be someone's daughter, lover, or sister. Those other girls could have been also. And yet, their lives were being toyed with in the vilest way. I really wasn't made to see this. And I felt as if it were too late.

I turned to Juliet, only to see tears rolling down her face, soaking the tip of her mask scarf. Her teary eyes widened with intense petrification that slowly turned into rage. Ted's eyes were the same through his mask. Fueled with anger, Juliet was ready to come out from the cover to stop the scene from continuing. But Ted quickly reached out for her arm. She turned to him as he shook his head in warning.

"What do you mean?" Juliet cried angrily but quietly as she wiped her tears away. "You expect me to accept this!?"

Ted placed his index finger to his mouth and pointed at their armor. I then took noticed of glowing red lines traversing through their crossbows and bayonets, including the captain's pistol made from some dirty gold colorized crystal. I saw genuine pity in Ted's eyes through that mask. "Their weapons are enhanced with cinnabar and arsenopyrite. If we try to fight them off, we'll be dead. So will the girls!"

"We...we can't just sit here!" Juliet retorted on the verge of angry tears.

"I know! I know!" Ted spoke back almost in frustration.

"Who is that?" I asked in whisper.

"Sathanus. The other guy with the mask...it has to be Lucifer." Ted answered. It did not sound like a good sign from his silent voice. I was awed at his appearance. I knew this was someone I couldn't take on; at least not if it was necessary. The man was the size of a titan!

We all then faced back to see that the guard was done soiling the poor girl. After he got up to pull up his trousers, the naked girl curled up hugging her knees and started whimpering. Her broken whimpers were joined along with the other girls who were kneeling, watching hopelessly with gun barrels pointed at their heads. One of the girls was attempting to cover her, but had her hair pulled away by a skulled soldier. She was thrown across the floor. They had no choice but to simple leave her there wailing on the floor. "Any of you try to help 'er, I'll break your knees! You understand?! Stupid girls," One of the guards barked as his voice echoed.

The porcelain-masked man came to the girls. He eyed at them very closely and carefully. His black woolly cloak dragged across the room as he stood next to Sathanus.

"I know you're in pain." He said in a surprisingly soft-spoken tone. And he sounded middle aged. "It hurts dearly. I understand. I am truly sorry for this. Don't cry. It's okay." He got down and carried the molested girl. He got her on her knees and made sure she leveled her teary eyes to his sunken vacant eyes. She shook uncontrollably, trying hard to control her tears. Her teeth were gritted. Suddenly, he stroked his fingers on her face to wipe away her lines of tears. "But I cannot forgive heinous acts. We cannot have that in our new heaven. You know this, don't you darling? Hm?"

The girl continued to whimper and sob quietly. But the cloaked man was softly comforting her. He brought her into his arms. "I am willing to forgive you. All it takes...is compliance. Understand that I will save you. I will save all of you. From your nature. From your defiance. It just takes time to embrace pain. Learn from it and you wouldn't have to resist anymore. Only then...you will be destined for greater things. Only then...you will be delivered. I have a saying, my dear; My words will flourish. My reign will thrive. And when my legends are heeded, our new heaven will survive. Help me make that so...that way I shall help you."

Before he stood on his boots, he placed his forehead onto hers for a good two seconds. He then turned to his soldiers, including Sathanus and spoke with sudden loud pride in his tongue, "No more will we succumb to imperfections or anything that makes us grow away from divinity! No more will we normalize sin of man nor the filth of whores! We will become true angels, true gods, of the New Heaven! We have become too comfortable with our natures within this afterlife being a pathetic shadow of its former self of what it used to be! It is about time to come to accept the radical eradication of our natures! Only then, we will control the future! We will be free! And when we are free, our afterlife will survive! We will not coexist with false gods and kings anymore."

The soldiers cheered and howled like wolves to his sudden speech, throwing their spears in the air as he opened his arms briefly. Placing them down, he then gazed at Sathanus and gently placed his hand on his shoulder plate. The captain looked closely into his master. Lucifer then said to him, "Crucify whatever bit of mortality they have left. But...show some semblance of mercy, my friend." The captain nodded. But given who he was thus far, I presumed that he was not going to heed that.

Shortly after he said that he soon vanished into a smoky oblivion. The captain was left satisfied. Perhaps he had a grin across his presumably hideous face. He then faced the frightened priestesses.

"You see, I never wished for the situation to come this way." The captain said in a very demented and dark voice, faking his empathy. He walked around them, fixating his dark eyes on them. It was like looking at a beast taunting its prey. "But the thing with you priestesses, you...you have the leaning to wire man's feelings. Using it. This is what happens...when you decide to defy orders. If it were up to me, you'd be crucified right now. But luckily, Lucifer has shown you pity. So, I would be grateful. We saved you from death. Especially knowing that the greatest fear women and girls have more than death...is having their dignity... stolen by hardened cocks."

The monstrous guards laughed gleefully and wooed to his sick joke. I strongly gripped my sword's hilt, readying myself to slash them. One of the Satanists spoke with laughter, "Oy...that's one way of gettin' rid of one! Let me tell ya! They really know how to tighten up 'em crevices!"

The captain inserted his hidden eyes at the curled-up hyperventilating girl, scoffing behind his mask as he stared down at her. He said as he hoped every word would strike into her shaken heart, "This is how a Pagan priestess looks without purity; naked, flowerless and weak. Covered with soot and piss. Stewed with cum. Like the heathenistic whore you are. But that's okay, you know better now than to call upon your horned god or queen's blessing to protect you. You're a tool anyway. And you're not as special as you make think. Now... let's try this again..."

He turned to one of his guards and gestured for him to come forward with what looked to be a bedazzled long chest in his glove hands. Once he opened it, it revealed something once he pulled it out; it shined like lighting. The scepter was medium sized compared to Ted's. It was decorated with interesting floral designs. The crystal glowed very agile blue light on top of the scepter. The short staff was glowing through his fingers. Everyone was charmed by it, even the three of us. My eyes widened, silently urging to know what it held.

Presenting the staff to the priestesses, he asked, "Will you pledge to the force of the Morning Star? Will you defy your Gods and the rulers you serve?"

One of the priestesses, who had dark brown hair, cried through sobs, "We can't!" But then she had surprisingly sounded angry afterwards, "We are servants of the great Selene and loyal to Queen Arianna! We will never go against her!" I was inspired and warmed by her bravery. I figured it was tough in the literal face of evil.

Angered, Sathanus grabbed her by her supple throat and lifted her from the ground. "You dare defy the name of the Morning Star", he roared, making the girl jolt.

"You're a pig!" She cried as she then spat through his helmet, which earned her a smack across the face. Hitting her body and temple to the ground, she suddenly panicked and panted heavily. Blood was damp down her lip and on her temple. I was ready to attack to prevent more of this pain from happening to these women. But I had to stay hidden for their sake.

The captain ordered one guard to point a ready crossbow at the humiliated girl, preparing to suppress fire. He then faced the other priestess and asked, "Are you going to pledge to renounce your faith...renounce your nature...or do I have to break my promise and kill this filthy girl of yours on the spot?! Do we need to go back to your new home as we celebrate her corpse with ale in our tummies? As we did for one of you? Proceed to act brave...and we will make it so."

She didn't answer, but only responded with sobs. Those sobs were begging to be heeded when her sisters were being threatened. They wailed almost like howling wolves. They were full of desperation. But being heartless as he was, he ordered the guard to fire. He rejected her sobs.

"Wait...please! Okay! We'll pledge! Please! Just leave my friends alone!" She cried.

"Very well," he said, sparing the girl's afterlife. "Just as you were willing to defy Lucifer, we'll willingly use your emotions against you. We need strength, not weakness from you!" The guard pulled away his crossbow from the girl. But he then plunged his foot towards another priestess' face when she attempted to help her molested sister. She cried out with very shaking high sobs.

"This is the will of the Morning Star."

What really saddened and disgusted me was how the girl looked to almost resemble my sister. I couldn't imagine if she went through what the poor lass went through. I would never imagine it. One of the guards, who was a shirtless bloodied soldier with only dark trousers and donning a murky goat skull over his head, asked, "Shouldn't we wait, captain? Before we do the ceremony?"

"The Angel will go elsewhere, knows what to do." Sathanus replied. Again, I was trying to figure out who were they talking about. "We have the tools we need, broken and shameful whores! They should conform nicely that way. And if not, well...I suppose we'll give the Trill Sonata another run. Eh?" The women shuddered and whimpered to those words. All the girls circled around the shining scepter and grabbed each of their hands. She was given a book that I assumed had satanic language in it. The leader of the priestesses looked up to the captain in fear.

He eyed at the scepter and glared back at the girls. "As I reflect the words of the pledge, I expect it to be repeated."

As he concentrated at the scepter, he said, *"Pain creates discipline."* The girls repeated frenetically in unison.

"Blood quenches thirst." Once again, the girls repeated.

"We are possessions of the Bright Star." the scepter was gradually turning from a light blue color to a dark amber color.

Juliet signaled us to move closer to the next cover that was near the girls. As we were gaining a little closer, making sure that the Satanists, and their captain, were completely in trance to the girls. Once we reach into the room without making a solitary sound, we stood behind another decayed structure. I made sure to hold my breath to avoid being detected. Pow! A large barge was heard from the upstairs, which alerted Sathanus.

"Wait." The captain said, unsheathing his cruelly designed sword. "We're definitely not alone."

"You think it's them Apostles? The Son of God's prized puppies? I heard that they were coming for us again," One soldier spat, which made me cringe with sweat conjuring down my face.

"No, that's impossible. They've been dead for five centuries. But...if they are, we could always put them down again...like the mongrels they are." He then turned to the soldiers and demanded, "You four, be at the ready. You three keep an eye on them. Any disobedience from them..." He gestured with his thumb sliding across his neck, indicating an order for execution.

"But Lucifer said...," one of the Satanists spoke.

"I know what he said! I'm not deaf, you fool! But it wouldn't matter anyway, would it," Sathanus questioned with a very threatening voice. "Once we get the bigger game, they won't be that useful anymore. I hate to compromise his wishes, but these spirits...let alone these women...don't deserve kindness. It'll only be a burden on us. He should understand. I'll just tell him...that they couldn't handle it anymore. You know how women are. Let alone them." He scoffed at the sight of the priestesses.

He turned to the guard with the violin and nodded. Preparing the violin, He had to bow placed on the strings and began to softly skid it across to conjure a harmonic noise. The girls tried to cower, but the Jesus masked Satanist began to play the instrument. I was confused as macabre music suddenly filled the cold room. The cords sounded contrasted with what the girls were going through. My attention was on them. I watched as they suddenly fell back and gradually began to thrash their arms and legs violently. Their veins were very visible and looked to almost blacken. I didn't even try to move, for I was just genuinely petrified by what I was seeing.

"Perhaps this should correct you. Remind you of who you serve now." Sathanus said.

As we finally saw him leave the room with the four soldiers, turning to the right side of the hall, it gave us an advantage to take down the three Satanists. The three of us nodded at one another, making it clear for us to take them down. I killed the other Satanists back at the Gathering, so to me, this shouldn't be too different. And whatever they were playing, I knew it wasn't good. So, I had to kill him too to make the music stop.

Quietly, we crouched and snuck behind each Satanist from the side and injected our retractable blades into them. Blood bloomed through their tunics. Lights blooming from their eyes, they had dived to the ground. I unsheathed the dead Satanist's knife and threw it at the violinist's neck until he trembled and dropped the violin. The girls looked happy, but at the same time very frightened to see us. I didn't think they even noticed that we were there due to how petrified they were to defy their orders. They looked as though they haven't eaten for days. And I noticed how the veins were calmed and not turning. Still, their bodies sulked and weakened.

The girls came to Juliet, each of them hugging and hysterically crying on her shoulder. Especially the one priestess who was assaulted. She cried her eyes out on Juliet's shoulder.

"I'm so sorry, dear! We're so sorry!" Juliet said, quietly as she stroked the girl's ragged dark raven hair, calming her nerves. "Shh...it's going to be okay. You're safe now! You hear? You are safe!" She then released her.

I glanced at the violin and carefully analyzed it. I saw how it was also glowing with red lines; concluding that the instrument was made of some blood reddish crystal.

After removing the contraptions that were bestowed all over my coat, I managed to remove my wet coat, turned, and quickly placed it around the girl to cover her nakedness. I was only in my jerkin. She looked at me with her wet crystal blue eyes. "T...Thank you, sir." I nodded with a small grin.

"I'm sorry! I understand you girls are scared. But we gotta get out of here before it gets worse. You'll be safe once we get back to Celestia," Ted alerted as he carried the poor girl, knowing my coat was too long for her to run in. "Don't forget the scepter."

I quickly held the rod from the ground –which felt very warm, glossy, and smooth – and inserted back into the chest. I took noticed on how it was blue once again. I didn't get a chance to engross myself into it since were in a hurry. We soon left the room with no hesitation, going back to the dark halls. We went left this time around, obviously to avoid Sathanus. We made sure that the girls were with us, so we can escape and regroup with Michael. Juliet led the way with the light in her hand and a sword in the other. One of the priestesses held the strongbox towards her, keeping it close to her chest.

I panicked, and we wandered for a way out from the place. I really didn't want to be there anymore. My heart continued pounding and sweat was gradually emerging from certain corners of my body. I felt the sweat moist my hair. I could feel the fear within the group. The halls were bad and dusty enough to go through, but my heart stopped as soon as I heard a roar.

"Hey! Who goes there?" I presumed that it was Sathanus demanding for an answer. His cold sharp roar crept into my skin. Turning around, we were fixated at the bull-horned captain standing alongside his men. Each of them held torches alongside their swords and guns.

We all froze in place as the whimpering of the priestesses was heard as soon as he spoke. I knew that I couldn't take him. Neither Ted nor Juliet couldn't take him. The goal was to assassinate a target, but the main priority was to get the girls back to Celestia safe and sound. If I wanted to fight him, I would have, but the girls had to live.

"What do you think you're doing with my maidens?" He said in a demented tone. He then ordered. "Get them."

Run! Don't worry about the beast! Just run, you fool!!

The good voice motivated me. I knew it was only right. "Run!" I shouted.

I then heard Sathanus call out, "Ka-les-mada!"

As soon as he chanted, three Satanists materialized in front of us. I drew my pistol from my shoulder holster and suppressed bright warm rounds at the raging Satanists as we were on the hasty move. They fell and plummeted as soon as I constantly pulled the trigger back repeatedly. Each shot made the poor priestesses either whence, gasp, or whisper. I felt bad for scaring them further, but I had no other choice.

After I placed back my gun in the holster, we continued to take off through the hallway. We paced ourselves quicker and quicker, making sure that we were still breathing. We ran around like it was never ending maze, hoping that there was someplace to escape. Each corner we would turn too was blocked by stonewalls. We avoided the dirty gold projectiles shot from the soldiers and Sathanus himself. My heart would sink each time a projectile would pass by our faces. I wanted to desperately urge Ted to use his teleportation powers, but I knew that it would drag down too much of his energy. We hurried and turned left and right each hall, which felt endless and hopeless.

Every chance I had from escaping the monster fled from me. Facing a large and hallow wall, we were trapped and only had to reply on our weapons. It appeared we had no other choice but to use our powers. At that point, it felt necessary. My fear was if he used it as an advantage to kill the priestesses. But it excelled when I saw one of the priestesses screeched exceedingly. When Juliet carried her arm over her shoulder, I briefly glanced at her leg, which a bullet flew into. Blood was leaking from her wounded leg and was regrettably leaving a trail, giving Sathanus and his men the advantage. Juliet tried to slow them down by summoning a ghostly flock of birds. But it didn't slow them down at all.

When they were catching up, I conjured two metallic bombshells from my satchel. Once I threw it right in front of them, bursts of smoke came out like a Jack-in-the-Box. With that, the tunnel was masked with this cloak of grey fog, giving us the advantage to move quickly. When we turned to the other path, I looked back, hoping not to see the three armored soldiers. The wounded priestess cried and whined about since she was losing blood. When I turned back, I watched in revulsion when the two soldiers and their captain managed to make it through the fog. It was he blood that was leading them to us.

We faced the bull horned man, twirling and twisting his sword as some act of intimidation. I couldn't tell how he was feeling behind that mask he wore, but I can tell by his voice that he seemed gleeful. He was nearing us like we were prey. He gestured his soldiers to prepare to fire their guns. Pointing with no hesitation, the soldiers pulled the triggers, letting the projectiles fly towards us. I instantly closed my eyes whilst shielding the priestesses. Juliet did the same. I thought my afterlife was over; everything I planned to do, especially finding my family, would've been done for.

That was until I opened my eyes and saw that the arrows were not flying but...floating towards us. I faced Sathanus and his soldiers, who stood in action for some reason. There was no sign of movement from them. And the entire room felt quiet and light. I turned to my friends to see that they weren't frozen. The priestesses were in awe. I then saw Ted with his arm out, realizing that somehow, he might have frozen time. Through his mask, I saw that his eyes were getting weak with bloodshot eyes.

He turned and advised, "Let's get outta here before it stops!"

With no hesitation, the group and I moved away from the shots and moved away from the soldiers, making sure that they stood in place. We continued to run before time will eventually reset back to its original pace. We made good use of it. Although, I felt terrible for Ted as I witnessed him running sloppily while holding the girl due to how much the use of power took effect to his health. Regardless for how long we ran from Sathanus' sight, we were sure that we were officially far away from him and his men.

Upon reaching to the open surface, we jumped from, we saw that Michael and several of his men were finally there. It was clear that they are trying to come and save us. Thankfully, they weren't affected and were stunned to see us.

"Forgive us! We were looking around for all of you! It's like a labyrinth!" He spoke. "We were lost after fighting off the Satanists. We tried to follow your voice, but we were overwhelmed. Our ambush was half-baked!"

"It's fine! We just have to get the girls out to safety!" Juliet said, catching her breath.

"Of course," he said, gesturing the soldiers to secure the girls in their arms as their smoke made wings summoned behind their backs. Each jetted from the underground and back to the lab. Michael and I then grasped Juliet's foot, propelling her body to the surface. Luckily, she grasped the edge to push herself off. The same thing happened to Ted after he let the girl go up with them. I was the last to go. Michael held my waist as we both jetted quickly from the dark halls towards the light.

We were soon heading back to Valestone on the ship, away from the crippled laboratory. Michael sent out a dove with a scroll attached to its leg, apparently to Francis.

The rain was still coming down profoundly. I could stop concentrating on Juliet consoling the molested girl by holding her close to her and soothing her shoulder. The other priestesses were shuddering and whimpering under their breaths. They were given bread to eat, water to drink. The wounded priestess was having her bloodied calf wrapped with a long brown Band-Aid after it was treated with green mushed up herbs. Ted was given water to regain his energy right after he saved us. In fact, everyone was eating. At least we had something to fill our stomachs on the way back. Even if it would be hard to take a single bite after what we saw.

Though what I saw will be forever imprinted in my everlasting conscious, I was still happy that we came out alive. I was glad we saved the priestesses, even though they will be frightened forever after going through that horror. I couldn't imagine what else they were going through. I didn't know what else would have happened if we hadn't escaped. It felt like a hell house in Heaven.

"What in God's name happened back there?" Michael asked.

"Sathanus was there. And Lucifer too, I think." I answered. "He was forcing them to do some bloody ritual. With this." I pointed at the crystal-covered chest that contained the scepter; or the Imperial Scepter of Selene as one of the priestesses previously stated. I handed it to him as he opened it slightly to witness its purist form.

"It's the Scepter of Selene from Queen Arianna. This was stolen." Michael claimed, almost in anger.

"Do you think we've been betrayed?" Ted asked as his eyes were gradually getting healed.

"I hope not." Michael replied. "I don't think he's the Angel we were looking for. Francis nor Jesus will not be happy with him returning."

"I think we may have let our guard down a bit," Ted added. He suddenly ranted in whisper, "Can't believe we were late to save them! Goddammit!"

"And...one of the guards...was playing music. With a violin. The girls began to shake as if they had a seizure!" I spoke. "It...It was bloody frightening."

"That bastard! That's his way of *training* his victims. He first poisons you with liquefied cinnabar. It's meant to cripple and break your soul, especially if you are vulnerable. Afterwards, the violin plays. Once it plays, it fully consumes your mind. If played for a long period of time, it gradually destroys your consciousness, your sensations, your eternal independence, just so you can become a brainless instrument for them." Michael said. "They use arsenopyrite to kill lightkeepers and psionics. They're immune to their magic. They use sunstone to eradicate all spirits. They advance them each time. Ever since he became the emperor of Hell, Lucifer experimented with all sorts of toxic minerals in favor of wiping off those who do not share his views nor conform to his rule."

"How do you know this?" I asked, almost horrified.

Before he can speak, he glanced at his concerned-ridden men in arms and sighed, "One of our men was under their control of the cinnabar. Constantly tortured and lost all senses until he became a vessel for them, he did. His consciousness was there...in an infernal trap he couldn't escape from. Suicide...was his solution."

"I'm so sorry about that, Michael." Juliet said.

"I appreciate it, Juliet." He replied. "But at least he rests in the Void. We have to care for those who are still with us...so they wouldn't have to meet the same fate."

Suddenly, the girl comforted by Juliet, wearing my coat, began to sob. It caught our attention. Juliet pacified her, chafing her shoulder. Soothing her. She coddled her to ease her nerves. The girl laid her head on Juliet's shoulder.

"It's okay, dear. It's over. It's over." Juliet promised. "Once we reach the homestead, I'll look after you. All of you." She referred to the other girls who simply starred at her with broken eyes as if every fiber of their being was ripped from them. Rose blood was nearly flushed from their bodies.

"I...I...." The girl stuttered. She couldn't get the words out since she was held back from her sobs.

"What's the matter?" Michael came to her, leveling himself to her height by kneeling in front of her. "What's your name, child?"

"B...Bella." She spoke after some hesitation. From her intonation, I caught the fact that she was Norwegian.

"Bella. Very lovely name, that is." Michael complimented to calm her. "Now, tell us what wrong."

"I.... I...I.... I stole the chest. I stole the scepter." She said as all our eyes were widened. "But...please understand that it was not my intention! He threatened to kill all of us if we didn't do what he asked. He poisoned us. He had us, under his...control, steal from the Sacred

248 ~ KENNETH VIVOR

Altar of The Queen. We spent weeks in that...that place. He tortured us. He killed...Sally...one of...us. Right in front of us after...." She trailed off sobbing for a bit as Juliet coddled her. Afterwards, she continued choked up, "He starved us until we participated in the ceremony. When we misbehave, as he says it, he used the violin since our souls...are broken."

"I'm...very sorry for your loss. We will honor her. But...what was the ceremony for? If it's okay for you to explain." Michael asked again.

"He...He wishes to alter the power of Selene, our goddess. He wants to give it to The Angel. To exploit it." She said through tears. "When we refused, he...he had all of us... soiled. Each one."

I felt everyone contemplating over what she said. Juliet placed her head down, her eyes looking at the floor in shame and anger. Her right leg was shaking a bit. Ted palmed his face with his left hand and shook. And I felt my blood rushing in fury after hearing that. After a brief silent breeze, Michael asked, "And have you ever seen The Angel at all? Do you know of its intentions with the Scepter of Selene?"

"No." The other priestess spoke for Bella next to her, garnering Michael's attention. "He was...said to be looking for something else."

"Okay. Another man. And...that is all you know?" Michael asked again.

"That's all we know! I swear it! All we knew was that they were pushing us to channel the Queen's scepter. But I swear... we didn't use it, for we knew what it held! I'm...so sorry! Sorry!"

She resumed back to crying whilst Juliet pacified her tenderly. Every hyperventilation somehow pained me deeply. And here I was thinking that ever woman wanted that pain.

"You have absolutely nothing to be sorry for." Michael said with a sad smile. He had his hand on her shoulder before he stood up. "We're just happy that you are all okay. Do not cry."

He then faced Ted, Juliet, and me. "We give you our thanks for this, Apostles. We're content with getting these women out, even if it did come with a heap of trouble and leaving us on a weak spot."

"I think it was a set up. Knowing that they could just summon the

Satanists, they didn't need for them legionaries to keep watch outside the lab," Ted suggested as he was still healing. "I mean we knew what we were up for. At least, apart from Kev here. But...not this. We weren't ready. I'd like to think the Angel possibly planned all this before we came."

"Maybe. Someone must've summoned them from afar. Forgive us again for our short lateness. We should've known there was an underground passage." Michael said.

We nodded. Juliet then added, "Kevin founded the passage first. If it weren't for him, we would've lost them."

I was thankful for Juliet to give me credit, but I was still traumatized to what I have witnessed. I gave her a sad smile, but still a smile, nonetheless. Michael patted me on the shoulder and said, "You have done greatly to the Order, Kevin. I will make sure to tell Francis to move your rank; nearly close to be where Ted and Juliet are. Very well done. We owe you."

Feeling a bit warm in my heart, I said, "Thanks." I thought it was only fair to give her and Ted credit as well. "But Ted got us out from there with his powers. And Juliet used her spirit eagle to find where they were located. I can't have all the glory. I...I have never seen that before."

"This is what it is often done in war." Michael said. "It's...a vile thing to think that they could do no wrong by committing these disgusting acts on others...as an excuse to feel superior."

"I mean...why would there be evil in the afterlife? I thought people came here to rest in this... *paradise*, supposedly, after suffering on Earth. I always thought the Earth was meant to be imperfect." I question, feeling my skepticism coming back to me.

Taking a deep breath whilst sitting back on the bench, Michael then answered, "The natural world you had, the Earth itself, was never imperfect. Just those within it. This world promised that you would have a second chance to live; to live how you wish to live eternally. Unfortunately, spirits with no light could use those privileges as well. It always happens. This universe is just like yours. As pure, eternal, and endless it could be, the afterlife is a harsh life as well. Every spirit has a way of living or looking at this world; most of them evil. No matter where you are, you cannot escape it. Even Heaven is guilty of it. It's a constant unwelcome guest. But it all depends on how you take it and how you become better than it by counter."

"But it'll be over, especially with the Apostles, right?" I asked, trying to be hopeful.

"There's always more to come in any shape or form. It's inevitable. Angels and Demons have fought each other for a long time. And we keep fighting. I've fought evil before the Legionaries even existed. I continue to do so because it won't stop. Even in a paradise like this. It's the idea of freedom. But it's both a gift...and a curse. Nature itself is double edged. We were all given free will. Lucifer even. The problem with people like him...is that they misinterpret it. Sometimes intentionally. We champion for freedom to be utilized wisely, not in ignorance. The freedom to make a difference and doing what is rightful on our own accord. The freedom to follow the true guidance of God, not by man's imitation of his word. To fear God means to fear evil. But that isn't always the case. Most folks never learn from their mistakes, mainly to avoid accountability and self-improvement. They think it makes them less of a man or a woman."

I then scoffed, "I guess everything will always be taken to extremes. No matter how much we try to deny it. Each to their own, I suppose. I mean what's the point if we'll...never get better. You would think that this place would be away from sin."

"We are fundamentally prone to fail sometimes, even as spirits. Nothing new. It goes with everything, crumpets, money, religion, politics. All those things are a necessity to live to a degree, but people get too extreme with them to where they forget themselves. Even freedom can bring out the worst. But people will do anything to get what they want in life," Ted added. "It is what it is, sadly. But it is up to fellers like us or anybody to promote being centered, which has been lost for a long while now. In this world and the one we had."

Something struck me about Lucifer too. He didn't sound as demonic or evil I was taught to believe. His actions and demands were despicable. But the way he was when we saw him for a bit, he seemed different. He seemed as though he believed in everything he said.

So, I told Michael, "You know...when we saw Lucifer, he spoke of a...new heaven. It was odd. I never thought that this was something he was apparently longing for. I was always taught of how much evil he wanted to have in the world. But...not out of...ideology."

"The New Heaven. That's what he calls it. Hell is meant to be a prison realm for irredeemable spirits. A place where they are supervised by colossuses. But he intends to make it more than that. He wants dominance over the afterlife to craft a paradise in his vision. He's strangely obsessed with the Old Testament in the Book of the Saints. But I feel as if he wants to demoralize it." Michael stated. "We have yet to know what he plans to do with those words. But this is not of our concern now. The girls are important."

I began to ponder on everything as I wait to get back to Valestone.

Our heads are yet to be cleared off from what happened last night. We technically slept in right after we were dropped off. Even though it took me a long while to sleep, for the cries of Bella were still overriding my head. I was very sure that Ted and Juliet felt the same.

XVII

❦

Madness in Stoicism

The next day, we prepared ourselves to meet with the King and Queen of Celestia at the Main Chapel to bring the news. The day was still moody and greying. Perhaps it was implying that winter was coming soon. But I didn't pay much mind to it. I was nervous about how Jesus would feel; knowing that the Promised Land was intruded in an unwelcome fashion.

When we passed through the gates and maneuvered through the courtyard, we went up the steps as we met with the two hooded guards justly holding their halberds. They let us through, leaving the four of us to make our way to see the King. The altar looked a lot different than what I saw that night I broke in.

In the daylight, it was much lighter. Not only there were two columns of benches, but also the room was wide enough for three thrones to be placed where the altar was. The concealed bridges were held up by marble Roman made columns. Besides each bridge were larger than life stain glass windows, depicting how the Jesus I knew was different from the one I was taught. It depicted the cross patty that was surrounded by the peculiar symbols of the other beliefs; Egyptian, Greek, Norse, Pagan, Buddha, all others. Astonishing my perks, it seemed to be a reminder of who Jesus really was and all he wanted from all of humanity. Though it was sad that his message didn't seem clear to most. Including someone like Lucifer. And maybe I was a bit harsh when I first met him.

My eyes were fixated on the King, Queen, and Princess anticipating for us. Dante was there, which seemed weird to me. But I remembered that he was the front for the Chancellors, but also served as advisor for the king and queen. So, I expected him to be very bias. Jesus's hands displaying his lacerated caved-in wrists were hardly placed on the cathedra throne's arms, his fingers almost clawing its engraved extravagant hands.

Shortly approaching to them, Michael, his right arm holding the chest containing the crystal and left hand holding his sword, bowed right in front of the three of us. "Your Majesty, Highness, Majesty, we have come to give you word."

"Good morning to you all." Jesus greeted. "Are the priestesses ascending from ailing?"

"They are taken care of by Lustina Wiscoli and the other nurses momentarily." Michael addressed. I almost heard a scoff coming from Juliet. I knew that she was cautious of the scarred priestesses being in Lustina's hands. I also saw how distraught it made the princess, knowing how much she practically became a patron for them.

"Something unnerving you, Juliet?" Jesus took noticed of her hidden scoff.

Juliet grinned with her arms folded. "No concerns, Your Majesty. My worries are not at all relevant in this matter." Her tone was convincing enough not to unease Jesus. But I knew that she wasn't okay.

"Well...whatever is in your mind...do not hesitate to tell us." Jesus assured.

"Your Majesty, upon discovering the location of where the priestesses were held captive, we discovered that this was stolen." Michael held the chest on the floor, placing it down to open it. When it was revealed, the staff combusted with light. It caught our eyes.

Dante stared bitterly, almost as if he seemed to have a resentment for even the littlest thing that didn't seem to fit his dogma. He asked, "Why is that here? In Valestone?!"

Jesus's coffee-scheme brows drenched as well as his lips. Leaning forward with a gasp, he stated, "The Holy Scepter of Selene from The Summerland! What in Heaven would Lucifer want with this?"

"It's one of his accomplices...The Angel. She intends to use her power to utilize into it for whatever reason." Michael said. "But the person responsible for leading Sathanus to steal it is not to blame. They were under influence."

"Who may that be?" The queen asked as she joined in.

Hesitating a bit, especially with Dante looming over, he had no choice but to answer just to get it out of the way, "One of the Pagan priestesses...Bella."

The castle interior fell to silence and skepticism. I wouldn't blame them. You wouldn't think someone very young would be capable of having that strength. But you would expect someone of that age to be manipulated; having her innocence turned against her by vile people.

Dante then roared suddenly, "Goddamn witch! She's seduced herself to his silver tongue!! Nearly, destroying half of the monarchy and endangering the spirits! I say that she should get exiled back to Hell for good, if not worse! This is exactly why we need to expand Valestone! We cannot let people like this foil Heaven! Either force them out to other deserted realms or to make them see the error of their ways! They tarnished the old ways that granted us peace in this Catholic kingdom!"

Ted stepped up before Juliet can verbally attack him. Even before I can do the same, though I was going to do worse. "The fuck's wrong with you!? She was coerced! She didn't want to do it! So, calm down!"

"You don't decide to make orders, Jefferson! Neither your outlaw mentor! Don't tell me to calm down!" Dante shouted, wagging his index finger at a fearless Ted. I clutched my right fingers into a fist when he blatantly called Francis an outlaw. Bloody prick!

"Neither do you, Dante!" Jesus roared at Dante. "Have you forgotten about keeping the peace of all kingdoms to broaden and strengthen the afterlife? Have you forgotten that we will rule as equals? Why would you urge me to make such a cruel penance for an honest mistake? Let alone...towards an innocent girl who was soiled?"

"Honest mistake!?" Dante stepped near Jesus in an agitated fashion. "Your Majesty, she is old enough to know that her actions have drawn Lucifer and his legion to our kingdom again! And I do not plan to see Valestone fall to a third rebellion! I couldn't care less for her well-being! That is the thing about spirits like Pagans; nothing but witches who curse us! Filthy...sinful...witches! All of them! Including the Queen herself!"

"Enough from you, Dante! I am the Son of God! Therefore, I shall decide the fates of my fellow spirits. Not the Chancery! Nor you! So, know your place!" Jesus shouted as his risen voice echoed the entire inside of the cathedral. "Have some civility, for once! Because it sounds as if this is more about what you want for this land than what God wants! And there's more to the afterlife than your principles. Let alone Leviticus Himlin's! You are positioned to uphold the laws of the kingdom to reinforce the core virtues of our land, not to use them to conform lives to mindless programming! We are spirits, not machines! Am I understood now?"

I grinned knowing that the Italian bastard finally got what he deserved for once. He stepped down and bowed to Jesus as a form of an apology.

"Y...Yes, sir. F...Forgive me, la sua Maestà (**Your Majesty**). I...went out of line." He spoke with his voice shaking. Jesus nodded, but a smile was absent.

"Clearly." I scoffed. I ignored his dirty reaction towards my statement.

Taking a deep breath, Jesus then spoke once again, "Evidently...those poor girls were controlled against their will to take the scepter. I shall have this sent back to The Summerland so that Queen Arianna Moon of Selene can have it. And since she is one of the more understanding monarchs, apart from her people..., I think it is...about time I make peace with her and her kingdom. I plan to go to Arcadia." He eyed at

Michael and said, "Michael, I think I would need you with me. I also need to exchange goods to show my peace."

"Of course," Michael consented. He then added, "I know Gabriel serves her. So, it'll be good to see how he is."

"I put my trust in Francis to look over my wife and daughter when he returns. If my voyage must expand, my wife would be a big blessing among the spirits of Valestone. The last thing we want is for more common spirits to fall victim. As for you three, you are free until we meet again. I know this affected you very terribly. And I do apologize. Truly. Take some time to rest. You are free to go."

"Thank you, Your Majesty." We all said, bowing before we took off from the inside of the castle.

Once we were outside of the Chapel, as the sunlight bloomed in our eyes, we sat down on one of the steps, hoping that we can somehow resolve all this and come up with a plan to defeat Sathanus and find Lucifer.

"So...if Sathanus is not The Angel, then who is?" I wondered.

"That's what we want to know. Sathanus can lead an entire army of Satanists and Legionaries, but he can't write an entire letter. He's too much of a brute to even spell the word brute." Juliet said. "So, he couldn't have come up with this message. Even if he tried."

"Maybe it can be another accomplice working for Lucifer. But the message was clear; it was in the alchemist lab." I replied.

"Maybe it's another piece to a puzzle. I have no clue why Lucifer was even there. Just to fuck with those girls or somethin', I guess." Ted stated scratching underneath his stubbed chin. Juliet suddenly groaned in annoyance and stood up from the steps, taking a two-step pace down from us. She twisted her head towards us, looking at us with a narrowed expression.

"We cannot just rest on this! We need more results! Evidence! More about what Lucifer is getting out of this!" She barked.

"There's nothing we can do now!" Ted reasoned. "This is somethin' we just...we can't rush! We gotta give it time!"

"I cannot just give it time, Theodore! How else would I get the priestesses healed!? And I can't think of them being safe with Lustina! Especially Bella! This is a bunch of bollocks!!" Juliet nearly roared. "I can't stand this! And the others are imprisoned in Hell, and I feel useless!"

Standing up, I took it upon myself to step in front of Juliet and took hold of both of her shoulders. I didn't want her beautiful face to be ruined with anxiety. "Juliet.... calm down! We will solve this! The girls are still alive. Just be glad we got them out of there, okay? You told me that spirits shouldn't let toxin weigh down their anatomy. We will get the others back. Trust me."

She looked aside, grinning a bit. Perhaps it was when I probably used her words against her. Feeling her tense muscles soften underneath her woolen shirt felt good. Almost intimate. As she sighed, I removed my hands. I felt her soothing the side of my arm, which almost made me blush.

"Thank you, Kevin," she said, fixating her sky-blue eyes at me. "I'm sorry."

"I was gonna say she should pray to! But that works to! Good thinkin' Kev," Ted said. I nodded in response. I then resumed back to Juliet's glowing face, not realizing that I was looking at her. Looking into her ocean scheming eyes. As if I was staring into her soul. When I caught myself doing that, I quickly released her before it would get awkward.

"We...just need a better approach to this situation." I spoke. "But Ted is right. We shouldn't rush it. Besides, you heard what Michael said; if we just go there in Hell, chances are we will die ourselves. As of now, we just need to deal with this Angel."

"Ha...never thought you would buy into this very quickly, given the months you've been here." Juliet smirked.

"Aye...what other choice do I have, lass?" I asked shrugging. "I have to accept this world for what it is. At this point, I'll accept anything. My mind is already prone to insanity."

I then thought a bit longer than I must as if all time froze for me. And I realized that I nearly forgot about Bertha. Perhaps she was still helping the villagers move, but I grew very paranoid for my family. Knowing that these bastards could be summoned anywhere, I had to make sure that they do not get them as well. I knew that the Civil Force had resentment towards us, but maybe I could trust Bertha alone. So far, she has proved it with my family's safety and the well-being of the other villagers. It'd be an advantage to outrun the conflict to be in peace with them.

I have decided to bring it up to the Apostles, waiting for opinions, "Oy, I was thinking. What if we were to go to Bertha?"

They winced at my question and glanced at one another. Ted asked, "Bertha June, Leader of the Civil Force Detectives?"

"What if she helped us get down to who the Angel was?" I reasoned. "I mean...we have to remember that she is going after Lucifer as well. Regardless of what her methods can be, perhaps we can use her as an asset to at least bring The Angel to justice. I mean that letter couldn't have been made up. It was intended for a group of Satanists. With the girls. But the Angel somehow dismissed it, as if she changed her mind on something. So, she had Sathanus instead."

"Hmm...I don't know...I'll feel awful for working behind Francis's back. Besides, Civil Forcers hate knights." Juliet said in skepticism. "Plus...guardians never worked well with most authorities of law enforcement. Let alone with the Chancery. Unless we are requested like we're mercenaries."

"We don't need them. We just need Bertha specifically. The point is to get Bertha's help somehow, just this once, to get to Lucifer. Yes, she's technically still a Civil Forcer, but she might know things that we don't know. Maybe things Francis himself doesn't know. Or Jesus. She's seen evidence of what they left after cursing those villages as they are raiding for something. The problem is that they disappear before she could question them. It would be at least a step in the right direction. For all we know, she's made some sort of dealing with someone who knows of Hell to find another way to get past that force. All it would take...is to ask her." I concluded, thankfully. "I know we may put her in risk, but it's the only way. That scepter, the kidnappings and those village burnings are all connected somehow."

"You're sure about this?" Juliet asked.

"It's a theory." I said. "A stupid theory. But still a theory."

"Stupid theories usually turn out as a smart course of action. I know myself," Ted said.

"Most of those courses were just dumb luck anyway, Theodore!" Juliet snared.

"Eh...same thing." He said.

"Well...we just have to tell Francis. This can go to two or more ways than one, Kevin." Juliet warned. "So...I pray that you know what you're doing. You've helped us get this far. I'm sorry. I don't want to seem..."

"Hey, all I want is to see this through to get this batshit war over with. We need to get those people out. This is one of the ways we can do it." I assured, hoping myself that I knew what I was doing. And I needed to be sure my family was safe from Sathanus. I was glad that Juliet was relying on me. But at the same time, it felt overwhelming.

Shortly, we all decided to descend from the Main Chapel's courtyard and brought ourselves a coach carriage back to the Khalservan. I never said this but sitting inside of the carriage felt like sitting in a much cleaner and old-fashioned cab. I sat on the left cushion next to Juliet while Ted sat at the right. While the driver moved and swayed the coach to move away from the castle and face the bridge, the three of us discussed and concluded our new plan before we take off to our next plan.

"It's important for Apostles to rest and meditate. Lightkeepers need to let the light regain. The good thing about Francis is that he doesn't neglect our humanity. He doesn't demand our presence all the time." Juliet admitted. "It's just that this entire thing has me on edge. I never thought our first encounter with Sathanus and Lucifer would...escalate."

"No kiddin'!" Ted claimed. "Think it's gotten everybody on edge. I just hope it won't lead to something big. But...I have a feeling it might."

"It's funny! Nearly forgot...it's almost Christmas." I spoke. "The King's birthday."

"Of course. Though, I'm not sure how Jesus would want to celebrate. I feel very sorry for him. All this chaos is burring, just because he strives for unity. Maintaining freedom and equality of all spirits, just as it seemed before we came here. It sounded great...like how I expected it to be. When I first met him once I ascended here, he's different from what most churches would say. He's everything we knew from the Bible. It's sad that not everyone sees his true humanity as they claim to do. And he's being pressured."

"These dogmas are made to not serve God nor Jesus, but to serve themselves. Because they are caught up living up to a label they can't reach. They call it a sacrifice. But it sounds like...intensive suicide to me." I answered. And I believed this.

My parents were loyal to Jesus, but they didn't let their beliefs deteriorate the fact that they were still complex beings. Unlike these radical devotees, they didn't allow that fact to shame them. And at the time, it made me embrace what Christian doctrine could have been. The only reason why I want to make this sacrifice is to rid this illness that has burdened me. Clearly, that didn't help.

While we rested in the Khalservan, Ted and I played Traveler's Progress while Juliet went back to the Homestead to check on the nurses, including Bella. She decided this on the way back to the Khalservan because she still had a bad feeling about Lustina keeping watch of them. So, Ted and I decided to play Traveler's Progress as we waited for her. Although I knew I had to still be aware of what we witness, it was a decent idea to play it just to soothe our nerves for a while.

Playing the game by the large fireplace, it took me back to a time when my family and I played Nephilim and Pendragon, two of my favorite tabletop games. I took Juliet's place as the Good Voice while Ted remained as the Bad Voice. Still, I had to multitask as the narrator as well and read out on what were to happen to one of us. The board consisted of two pathways (east and west) for each voice to go on to reach the Traveler. The other two pathways (north and south) were for the Traveler to either get to the gates of Heaven or to the gates of Hell. Ted was on the lead while I was nowhere near where he was. I had to be as good as he was. I had to play this game more often. Rolling the dice got me a seven, which meant I had to move seven steps towards the Traveler. But I moved several steps back because I was blocked by the Traveler's doubts, which read Wall of Doubt. Ted rolled for a three and it landed on a three. This meant that he moved three steps closer to the Traveler and being the Bad Voice, he was to lead him to Hell.

So, I did a lousy job trying to get the Traveler to Heaven. But I didn't take it too seriously. Although unlike Nephilim and Pendragon, this was difficult since the game worked almost like a psychosocial test. It consisted of doubts and psychological rebellions as pushbacks towards your progression. It acts as a brain traversing thought. And playing the game got me to reflect on myself; almost seeing myself as the Traveler. The voices reminded me of my actual voices. There were good voices and bad voices in my head, warring against one another to see who can claim my mind; taking command on every action I made. Perhaps the Traveler was going through the same fate as I was. He must have two different voices to lead him to either the righteous or the sinful path.

I leaned back against the chair, faced the board. My heart weighted almost a ton. Something hit me, which I never thought about nor asked about. And I had every opportunity to do so. I would ask Francis and the others, but they were busy protecting the city and the Chapel itself. And I wondered if I could ask Jesus Christ himself this question as well. Perhaps even Ted can answer since he was the only one in the room and the one, I came to know in the afterlife. Ever since I met him that day at the Homestead, I somehow founded myself developing a connection with him; despite his unpredictable behavior that I was personally not fond off. He could somewhat be just as wise as he was beating me at Traveler's Progress.

"Somethin' wrong, man? Am I too good!?" He teased.

"No..." I spoke. "This game...it hits home."

"What do you mean?" He leaned forward, curious to hear what I had to say.

"The Traveler...I know what he's going through." I expressed. "I know how it feels to constantly have to listen to your consciousness harping at you or controlling the sum of your actions."

"I guess that's kind of the point. It's a test on your mind to see if you are comfortable in trusting your instincts and embracing your choices at the end of the day. We can never go back to how things were. Let alone try to go back and make things right."

He then asked, "Something in your mind? Somethin' about...last night?" He then added while looking down regretfully. "I don't blame ya if that's the case. Those broken eyes of innocence tainted could never leave your head. And Bella's scream...the tears on her face. It broke my heart."

"It...it did affect me. I don't even know how we're still playing this game. But it's not just that. You see, I have these voices...in my head constantly bickering at me for my actions and thoughts. Some of them good. Some are bad. But they're all annoying. The bad ones have been frequent. And this phrase that keeps repeating in my head.... *audi custedos tui*, it's been on my mind. All my life. It means to *listen to your guardians* in Latin."

"So...have you *listened*?"

"I don't know. Sometimes I wished, but at the same time...I feel like it's up to me to determine my own actions. It's my mind after all. Having these voices, it makes me feel like I'm not in control of myself anymore. Or if I was ever in control of myself at all. Hell, I'd once thought about blowing my skull off with a gun to get rid of them. You know?"

"I know the feeling." Ted agreed. But then said, "You know, it ain't just people or the world that wrong us. Sometimes, it's ourselves. Our minds." He said. "As we could be our own best friend, we can also be our worst enemy. I know it's no walk in the park to repress mind attacks. Or just get rid of 'em altogether. I personally try not to focus on pain...as best as I could. Especially by the mind. So, I only dismiss them as just thoughts. But then again, I don't have voices. I can't really know what it's like. Sorry, if I seem insensitive to that."

"That's fine. I know it's not that simple to help someone with it. So...do you suppose it means anything?" I asked.

"That's for you to make up. You can choose to make it legitimate or not. It sounds like something left to your interpretation. But still. That doesn't change the fact that it can either mean somethin'...or nothing at all."

Perhaps he was right. It's just as I suspected: it meant nothing. It was just my condition playing tricks on me. If it were truly legitimate, it would truly mean something.

"I wish I had it removed. Just so I could be truly pure, you know?"

"By doing that, it also removes your humanity. Francis dealt with folks who were in his Order who might've suffered what you may have. They all wanted the same thing. Instead of removing what we thought made us sick, it was always about endurance. Removing who you are...is lobotomy. He knows how messed up some spirits could be. But he knows deeply how capable they are for good. And betterment. I respect him for that wholeheartedly."

"You're maybe right. Have you...ever regretted making choices?" I asked Ted afterwards.

"You kiddin' me? It's like...a human function to regret somethin'!" He scoffed. "Of course, I have. I'm sure you have regrets!"

"Aye." I said. "I wasn't always...like this, y'know."

"I guess your come-up has been hard on ya, I could tell."

I said nothing. I just shied away from his slight. I felt ashamed for hiding who I was. But it was for the best.

"It's fine, man." I felt Ted's hand on my shoulder. I took a glance at his blue eyes.

"You know.... when I came to the afterlife, before I became an Apostle, did you know...I was in a gang? Only momentarily." He said. My eyes widened.

"Ha. Really? No way. Gangs in Heaven? Are you serious?!"

"Yep, apparently. Remember when I told you how I did some bad things in the past? Well, I was in a gang. The Astral Ghoul Boys is what it was called; just a gang of Polish highwaymen committing robbery and scamming here and there; stealing expensive portraits to sell to fencers in exchange for cash. But with the growth of the Civil Force, they've been rarely loud. Not much gangs left these days. But they were back then. Hell, I was once entranced to a black girl name Eliza Harlock, who only fell in love with me to get with the gang leader Bush Papienne. Don't ask why he has an Ethiopian name. I don't know either. But anyway, Eliza...she ignored me for my...weirdness. I didn't stand out to her, I guess. So, I let her be. Most girls only like me for how I look, but not for who I am. I realized soon that the gang was a bunch of assholes stealing from colored folk to prove their loyalty to God. As soon as I met Francis, and eventually met Frask to become a painter, I decided to get out. I committed a mutiny by selling back those portraits, returning the money to those fencers. Although, I've kept some for myself. Specially to help Frask establish his shop." He sighed. "Only Bel knows where they are now; either planning on how they will kill me and take the money or...or sucking each other's dicks. But I don't care."

"Wow! You...told Juliet about this?"

"That's kind of why we didn't get along that much." He said. "Because of the gang I rode with. She held that against me, worried that I would somehow mess things up for the Order. But it seemed like she grew out of that now. I feel like...she had a bad experience with dudes like me, which would make sense."

"Well...at least I'm definitely not the only one who makes regretful choices." I said.

"Course you're not. It all depends on how you look back at what you did. And what you learn from them. I guess I took aspects from my dad, trying to be a man. I don't have the purist of goody kumbaya Christian heart. But...I...I try what I can to do what's right on my terms. I'm just made that way, I guess. I mean...my ancestors believed in Belobog, whom I was told was a god of light and sun. A light for those who believed in him...to make them into conquerors...and not slaves," He admitted. Eying at me, he then said, "Though at least we both know better now; never join shitty gangs. Especially since the Satanists are now the problem. And at least you had a better life as a human. Especially with your family. Bet you miss them."

"I truly do." I admitted from the bottom of my heart. Still, my hopes in finding them were still awry. I then asked Ted, "What about you? I bet when you died, you miss your family."

Ted sighed almost in genuine distress. And his eyes narrowed. I almost regretted immediately for asking.

"I'm sorry, you don't have..."

"No, it's fine man."

I knew internally that he committed suicide. So, I didn't want to bring it up to him. I just hoped he would tell me how he led to making that decision.

"Nah, it's alright. It's just that...I don't really like to talk about it. It's not good for the spectrum I suffer with."

"What do you mean?" I asked, moving my chair next to him.

"I mean it's something that still affects me. Something I realize when I was ascended here is that you could die; but your consciousness, the memories, the turmoil, they still follow you. They haunt you even more than you haunt others." He said. "And that is what I've been dealing with. It's something I'm still dealing with."

"But you always seem confident all the time. Which isn't a bad thing at all, anyway."

He leaned forward and took a deep breath. "I don't like talking about myself because I don't want to seem like I'm callin' for a...pity party, if you get what I'm saying."

"Aye. I do." I nodded.

"Good."

He sighed once again and said to me, "The only reason why I seem like I'm confident all the time is only because I don't want to show my weaknesses. I hate being a self-pityin' victim. I hate showing people my flaws. And yet, I ain't so good at hiding them! You may think I didn't share Juliet's empathy when we saw that priestess Bella get violated. But...I truly knew how she felt. I felt bad for seeing her get hurt. And it's not like I wanted to see her suffer. It's just that I didn't want her or us killed when we showed up. They knew what they were doing with those crystals, Kev. I guess.... I just don't want to show that I was weak; quick to let my guard down. And those pieces of shit hurting the priestesses made me feel weak. Like I couldn't do anythin'! I'm done with that shit. Giving power to assholes."

I was getting curious now. I asked, "You're not one to share your vulnerability a lot, are you?

"Fuck no. But that don't mean that I don't have empathy. I just don't show it much. And even though I do, I...try to lighten it...y'know...to make it seem like it ain't too bad. I was raised back in Dorchester, Boston.... when I was alive. I wanted to be a painter and wanted to paint what was unusual. Basically, Surrealistic styles. There was something so fulfilling, like you're in a world of your own crazy mind. I always saw potential to bring something new to the world. My daddy...on the other hand, just held me back from tapping into what I could do. He was an immigrant on a boat from Poland. It wasn't long for him to be Americanized...just because he hated the country he came from. He was fake. He used a church for Mormons as a front to run an arms business to sell to the Irish mob. They paid good cash. So of course, he wasn't willing to spend it on helping me get into an art school. Or help my mom. She was a prostitute. She sure as hell didn't like the job, but my dad was kind of like her...well...I'm too ashamed to say. Still, despite her circumstance, she wanted a good life for me. She did everything she could. The thing is...I was technically considered...an accident to him. He didn't want to raise kids. So...to prove my loyalty to him, just to earn his love, to prove I was a man, I left painting to help his arms business. It felt good at first, aligning with dad. But ...painting was all I wanted to do. It freaked my dad out because I truthfully didn't want any part of his crimes. I had to have a life and he couldn't stand it. He resorted to violence towards me. Beat me for speaking his language, scorn me for my talents, drug me with pills to be as dull as he was since I'm very hyperactive at times. I have this tendency to flip flop my emotions so...that's what he couldn't stand. When I was tormented by kids in my neighborhood or school, he didn't care. *Because you're a weirdo that shouldn't have been born...he says. Art is for losers who think they could change the world with a paint brush.... he says. It won't make you a man.... he says. You should be grateful that you're even alive because I would've had you aborted."*

He then sighed and his face became gloomier than it did before. Perhaps what we saw really brought him back in thought of what he went through.

"He didn't see me as his kid with dreams. He saw me as a business partner to advance his life as he gladly destroyed mine. And whenever my mom would encourage me to be myself and get me out of that line of crime, he would stop her. Give her a piece of his mind; beating her or force himself on her out of frustration. And I was forced to watch. She feared him, but she always had faith in me to be a better dad than him. That's why she named me Ted...because I was a gift to her. a gift to the world. There was...one night. A night that pushed me. I was just by myself, a damn wallflower in the comfort of my own home. Most of my relatives were former mobsters from the Boston criminal underground. Some were immigrants from Poland. And there were whores my dad had unapologetic affairs with. French. They all noticed me but shrugged it off as if I was another sack of flesh. Either way, I just stood there, helpless. Bored as hell, but hopeless. However, my mom's sister was drunk that night, noticed me in a weird way. She...dragged me to my room upstairs, locked the door, and...and...and..."

He was trying very hard to hold back tears with a sudden laugh. It was obviously a very sad laugh. And it etched into my heart.

"...She forced herself on me. How 'bout that? But since I'm a dude, guess I can't say that I was. Right?" He joked with pain in his heart. "All she told me was to hold still while I fuck you hard! I was shouting for help with my face wet with hot tears. I cried *Tatus* (**Daddy**)! *Tatus* (**Daddy**)! *Mi pomoc* (**Help me**)! *Mi pomoc* (**Help me**)! But...the damage was done. He told me that...it was a lesson for...not being a man...or focusing on pain. My mom couldn't take it anymore. She distanced herself from her sister since then. She and I moved out from our house to live with her mother several days later, especially knowing how violent my dad gets...when he's disobeyed."

I felt very disgusted when he was telling me this. Disturbed. Intoxicated or not, what father would allow that to happen to their child? I felt guilty and very sorry for Ted. I couldn't imagine what he went through; being forced to give up who he was just to be like his father. After spending a year with him, I never expected him to be this open. Yet, he wasn't this vulnerable with anyone else. Not even Juliet.

Deeply, I felt guilty for how I preserved him when we first met. I believed I was more envious than annoyed because I really wished to be that strong hearted, stoic, and free-spirited as he was. But it was unexpected to see him in such a state. And I could guess that what happened to Bella deeply affected him. Especially this unwelcome feeling of being too late to prevent that kind of pain to happen to someone so young.

"You know, when you're a kid, it's easier for some grown-ups to take advantage of you because they use your innocence against you., I realize then that they're no different from kids. They care more for petty things, things that don't matter, than to think deeply about their lives. All what I went through literally made me isolate my entire sanity from reality. Because I refused to believe any of it. Like it was some messed up dream. I mean...I was only a kid! I was a kid!" He said, nearly tearfully. He suddenly bellowed out a rageful cry and hammered his right hand on the table, causing the boardgame to tremble. "Why do I do this? It's not all about me." Ted asked himself.

I would be lying if I said that I didn't flinch as soon as he began bashing his head with his hardened fist. Something I used to do to myself as well. He suddenly let out a silent chuckle. I looked back at him sadly.

"Ted, I'm...I'm so sorry. I'm sorry, mate. I had no idea." What he went through made me not miss the world at all. It only made me hate it than before.

"The world I thought I knew wasn't meant for me, no matter how much my mom did to make it otherwise. It all made sense that night. I was nothing. I wasn't good enough. And despite living in a much decent environment soon after, my mother...she felt shame for being afraid of...trying to give me a good life. She wanted to please two people; me and my dad who pimped her out and forced her to sacrifice her dignity. She only wanted him to change, for my sake. I still carried that pain, realizing I'm much empathic than I thought. I saw no point in living...and I gave exactly what he wanted."

"Wha...What would that be?" I struggled to ask.

He turned to me with sorrowful eyes and said, "Not existing at all. I thought at the time that I wished they did abort me. So, I got to the bathroom, locking it. I carried a razor blade with me from the shelf...to drown my arms. I saw no point, seeing how I saw no chance in being Van Gogh's spiritual successor or to freely express myself without having to feel threatened. But I felt useless to the world. Useless to my mom. Useless to...everybody." I glanced and saw his healed lacerations on both arms. "It's like I had no true place. Not at all."

Soon, tears welled in his eyes and came down his face, but he quickly wiped them off. I watched him with narrowed eyes, sad that he had to say that.

"But it felt weird afterwards, I was suddenly pulled into a bright light, almost like I'm traversing. Everything was so bright. I didn't know what it was at the time. But when I saw Jesus Christ himself, I realized that I was surprisingly in Heaven, which was weird at first since I'm mostly a pagan of Slavs, even though my so-called dad did not have any regard for his heritage. I had to get in touch with it. I felt like I belonged to it. Jesus told me that the most vulnerable, including those who accepts their openness, are accepted. To be accepted, you must accept yourself. Even though I personally don't follow him as a messiah, I respect him for that. He accepted my imperfections. My essence. I guess it shows that I mean something to at least one person."

"You mean a lot to those who truly loved you. Ted, you shouldn't have thought that way about yourself. You're...you're funny, kind, amazing and wiser than you think." I said with a smile on my face and my hand of his shoulder. "I...I just wish I was strong as you," I said in regret, knowing that I've allowed the world of criminals get to me.

He smiled back. "Your ass is wise, all of a sudden!" We both laughed.

"Nah, but I really appreciate it, Kev. I really do. Sorry you had to see me cry like a bitch."

I shook my head. "Come on, now. There's nothing wrong with crying. It releases distress. There's nothing wrong with showing your vulnerability sometimes. It doesn't make you less of a man. In fact, it makes you a real man. And no matter what, you are loved."

We smiled at one another. He then said, "I guess it's about time I understood that. I'll try."

"No doubt. There's no rush. So....do you think you'll tell Juliet about this? What you told me?"

He looked down at the game board. "No. Not yet. I prefer to keep to myself. I don't bother getting soppy like this. My mistake was to live for everyone. My so-called father. The Astral Ghoul Boys. Eliza. They didn't care about my happiness nor my freedom. Yet, even here, I was trying to find my place. So...I had to do that on my own. Like I'm doin' now. At least now you know. And...I'm thankful for you for understandin'."

"Of course. And...Ted, I'm...I'm sorry...for how I came off when I first met you. I just get very hostile sometimes when I'm with people." I spoke.

He smiled back, "No worries, my friend. I understand that I give a very random impression. But it's who I am. Trying my best to make life a bit better. I'm not like other people. This world is not perfect, but at least I'm making an actual life compared to the one I came from. Hopefully, you find your place here too." I nodded with a smile.

I hoped so as well.

XVIII

The Heart of the Afterlife

I took my time to think over everything. Everything that has happened recently was on my mind; from discovering the afterlife to joining the Apostles and getting myself into a scheme. It congested my mind, so I needed to meditate. Juliet also seemed very busy.

Today, all of them made me want to smoke again. It hit me. Hilariously. I haven't had the thought to smoke in a long while. I would inhale the smolders of the cigarette to think to myself. I never made much of an effort to try and find a store in Celestia. I could have use the money Frask gave me. But I wanted to save for something valuable. So, I was outside of the Khalservan, twirling and twisting the hilt of my sword, conducting an orchestra of winds.

My eyes closed to be in solitude with darkness. Perhaps, I was unintentionally making myself healthier. In all honesty, all the practice I have been doing on the side has made me relapse. Which felt both good and awful at once. It made me in tune with the light being within me. Made me forget about everything. I bopped, swung my sword in circular pirouettes, surrounded by the fog waterfalling through the highlands. The light would move every part of me in ways I would never think of. It was my prayer. It was meditative. A silent one as my hands and feet swayed with the claws of the wind. Instead of the comforts of the cigarette, I inhaled the air of the god supposedly around me and not above. My falling locks would brush across my damp face. Francis taught me that to control my thoughts was the equivalent of having control of a sword, which was why I wanted to extract.

After my practice on an isolated battlefield manifested with dying crucifixes and decolored flag spears of Valestone, I played catch with Algor far away from it. I wanted test how far he can truly go soon as I threw a broken tree branch, flogging it into the open mountainous fields that was masked with afternoon miasma. Luckily, he would quickly retrieve it and bring it back. He was mildly fast, but perhaps not as fast as Ted. I felt that it was nice to give him attention since I haven't done it for a while.

I then sit down on the grassy slope afterwards, taking my time to look out at the mountains cloaked by the morning mists. My hand would stroke across Algor's pelt, feeling every clogged strain of his brown hair. My entire hair was moist from not only the sweat from my brows, but also the drizzling rain that charged from the greying clouds. I thought about how I was to approach to Francis about affiliating myself with Bertha to find out more of the conspiracy just so I could help get it over with. I wondered if it was possibly the wrong time to ask. I contemplated with this plan for half and an hour, waiting for an idea to spark. It was just as tedious as trying to get rid of writer's block. Or overcoming addiction.

My eventual solution was to get on my mount and gallop my way to the Main Chapel once again. Specially to see Francis who was said to have returned. After going there several times, I practically knew how to get there independently, even if it was a long-distance ride there.

I needed answers about everything, including Lucifer's need with the scepters. I understood that he wanted to essentially become a better than Jesus, but it still didn't answer my question on why he would need it since he, himself, is also a deity. It was weird how I was already getting engaged into what was at stake. It was weird how I was being accustomed to this knightly life despite trying to find how to live normally again with my family.

As I was nearing the gates, the four hooded guards halted me. I dismounted from my horse and walked with it on foot.

"Please, I wish to speak to Francis Bailey." I asked in a diplomatic matter.

"The Holy Spirit is in a midst of other council duties." The guard spoke. "He is not seeing anyone at this time."

"But I'm one of his students...an Apostle." I stated, hoping that stating my profession would grant me to enter the castle. It wasn't easy seeing how I wasn't with Michael.

"It's not up for discussion, regardless of who you are." The other guard commanded. "We'll see you go."

I felt discouraged a bit. Even if I was professed in a knightly position, I still felt I had no power. But as soon as I was already ready to take off and go back contemplating back at the Khalservan, I heard galloping descending into a halt as if someone was riding on a horse.

"It's okay. You could let him in."

"Y...Yes, sir." One of the guards obeyed.

I turned to see that it was indeed Francis who made that command. He dismounted from his nimble and graceful coated grey Friesian horse. I was pacing myself towards him with no hesitation as I ignored some of the nasty looks the hooded men gave me. Francis gave one of them the reins of his horse to lead it away from the sight.

I saw Francis, seeing that his shadow black hair looked nowhere near as clean as it did before. It was almost wet and greasy. His eyes sockets looked to be heavy. I could only tell that he wasn't physically looking good. Yet, he still stood elegantly and was still his stately self. Both of us holding our horses' reins.

"Kevin. How are you?" He asked.

"Fine. I just came to..." I wanted to ask him so I could get it out of the way. But knowing that he was stressing over something, by the look at his face, I decided to leave out the request for now. "I wanted to know how you were doing?"

"I'm doing fine. I'm just...preoccupied. That's all. Just getting ridiculed by the Chancery once again. A nice welcome back from the Hunting Grounds. With everything that's happened, it's impossible to rest on this." He said, sighing off his frustration. "And I'm glad you came to. Because I wanted to take this time to apologize. Especially for my absence."

"It's fine, sir." I assured.

"Well...no, it's not fine, Kevin. I was foolish to send you to that lab! I didn't think you and the others would come across Sathanus! Out of everything returning, I didn't think he would. And yet, I had no regard for your safety. I'm very sorry. I hope you understand." Francis expressed.

I was shocked to his vulnerability. Though I appreciated his apology, it wasn't warranted. It was unneeded. We were still strong enough to take down the Satanists if we wanted to. It was just that Sathanus seemed too powerful for us. It would've been impossible to defeat him; let alone trying to get him to get to Lucifer. The important part was to get the priestesses out. And that's what we did.

Suddenly, we saw Dante along with the other members of what looked like the Chancery exiting from the left dome of the castle. I recognized them from the Gathering, including Mr. Himlin. They were making a left turn to one of the buildings on the right side. Francis and I were met with their bitter glares.

"Hey, the important thing is that we got those girls out of there." I said as Francis and I ignored them.

"Thank you for understanding, Kevin. And...I'm proud of you too for helping. I'm truly humbled." He smiled. "Michael even suggested that I move you to a different rank. And I gladly took that to heart. So, you're an Advanced Apostle now. You've grasped very quickly. How do you feel about that? I'm sorry...it's not a proper knighting. Usually, it's a ceremony in the castle. But...I'm not sure if I'll be around in it much."

"No worries. I really am grateful. Thank you." I said, feeling a warm air inside my body. It honestly felt good to move up a rank. I felt like I did something worthy and noble for once despite my fear.

"So...where is Michael?" I asked.

"He's currently traveling with Jesus with the Angelic Paladins to The Summerland to make peace with Queen Arianna. He's offering her back the scepter. Heard that she's been ill. So, he'll be gone for a few days to aid her. So, I'm protecting the queen and the princess. Just hope he could make it in time for the holidays. Especially for his birthday." He said. "Anything to stir us away from this madness. At least for a while. I swear, Kevin. It's as if history intends to repeat itself."

"History always repeats itself, sir. You should know that. But anything from the Happy Hunting Grounds trade?"

"There are already getting started on cultivating them in preparation for trade. Time to time, I will travel to check its progress." He replied. "So...it's a chance that's it's going to take a while to grow. I just pray that those people in Hell...will stay strong. To continue praying. Knowing that we're doing all we can to get them out of there!"

After digesting what he said, I then said to him, "You probably will disregard this, but..." I stopped a bit. I was hesitant, but I wanted to know more about the scepter. What it does and why were the Satanists (or at least Lucifer, Sathanus, or The Angel) were keen to get it. So, I asked, "...What does that scepter do exactly? It seems important. More than just a mere ornament, I assume?"

"Sure. Why do you ask?"

"Well, I've been thinking about how they connect to everything that's been happening, the kidnappings, the village attacks. It's as if they are trying to gain something from doing these acts. Provoking a war."

Francis looked exhausted to say anything. I gave him no choice but to explain. It could be bigger than anything. He explained after taking a regretful breath, "My meeting with the Chancery was more than just another *lecture*. Thanks to some evidence gathered kindly by the Civil Force Detectives, they've connected the Queen's scepter with kidnappings and the attacks of the villages too. They're going after them, it seems. I know it sounds ridiculous, warring over scepters now. But they're truly important. The scepters.... are created by the gods themselves. They were passed down to the monarchs to rule the kingdoms on their behalf. They're blessed, having their own attributes awakening chakras, reincarnating souls, and practicing divinity. If they were fully corrupted for a prolonged timeframe, the powers would work against their rightful owners. And...they are keys to something...more vital to the afterlife."

"Vital? What is vital?" I asked in curiosity.

Gazing at each side once again, he then said to me, "The Axis Mundi. It grants access to your previous world. It makes the afterlife connected to it. It's a place concealed with cosmic energy from the gods in all things that are in the temple. Inside...conceals the staff once created by God after Adam and Eve descended after their deaths as humans...called the Holy Insignia. It's often called...the heart of the afterlife because it keeps everything alive. It originally had the ability to manipulate the minds of spirits, humans, and the whole of nature intended to create an ideal paradise for both worlds to live in common harmony. Resurrect all things in the user's vision. But because of its... destructive power, Jesus decided to turn its power into a shard and hid it somewhere. It was impossible to break it, for it was godly made. He hopes to, though. He channeled the staff to connect to the natural world's celestial plane. And if necessary, to cleanse it when it's on the brink of collapse. The scepters of the monarchs are keys to the Axis Mundi. And if a deadly force channeled them means that it would affect the Holy Insignia as well. Only Jesus himself can channel it properly. God waited for him in Heaven to utilize its power."

"Oh...alright. Do you think that's what he wants to do with the staff? Lucifer? You think that half of the Satanists are looking for the shard?"

"That is what I'm thinking. While they seek for the shard, the others are seeking for the scepters. Their guerilla tactics are caving in. At this point, I'm convinced that Lucifer would do anything to have the afterlife. These scepters are not just for beautification, but they serve as vessels for the gods to truly exist. To revert the power to evil, this would mean that Lucifer would have all the afterlife and the spirits in his hands. There are those who attempted to create an Axis Mundi many times, but they failed. If the Insignia is not only removed but corrupted...everything will die out. Whatever means necessary, we cannot have him mangle with it. No one should. That's why Jesus is timid to speak of it...knowing that when others hear of it, they will go after it. We'll focus on the scepter snatchers. Leave the villages to the C.F.D. for now. We can't juggle two war crimes at a time. Plus, the shard is well hidden. So, I doubt that the Satanists will find it."

That would make sense. And I was seeing more of why Francis warned me about getting too close with the C.F.D. I guess even the most powerful messiah wouldn't want to dwell with that kind of power, especially if it was the cause of deadly things when poorly dealt with. Even though I still felt that Francis was crowding the scepters in mystery; at least it answered my question.

"How do you think he does it?" I then asked. "From what we saw, he seemed to be posing himself as some kind of...messiah."

"That's his intention." He said. "He couldn't accept his place as an Archangel. It wasn't enough for him. And it's quite a shame. I didn't know him well. But I was told that he was full of prosperity and greatness once. He seemed like a good man from what Jesus kept telling me. But his bitterness and resentment for the souls of humanity got into his head. And his pride with him. He fights for complete righteousness so he himself could create a paradise he envisioned. And he has followers sacrificing themselves for his bleeding crusade. Like I said, he would do anything."

Then he said something that really shocked me. "By the way, I have been preoccupied...trying to contact your family on my travels."

Eyes widening, I repeated, "My family?"

"Yes, I still haven't forgotten our deal. I wrote to them, telling them that you are okay and are longing to see them. And I want to know exactly where Ms. June's group is leading them, given how she just...disappeared. She didn't bother to send us any notice. Nothing."

Now I got worried. How did she just disappear like that? I pondered and thought that this could be an opportunity for me to see if they were okay. I was having unwelcome thoughts erupting in my head. Especially by what was happening. I asked Francis, "Do you think you can send another dove under my name? I just want...to know if they're okay, at least. I...I need to know too."

"Certainly. I could even show you if you wish. But if I do it, promise me that you will tell me everything in the future. Even if it is personal. Don't think of yourself as merely an asset for the Order. You're still a man."

"I will. I promise." I said, looking down on the ground. "I just.... didn't want you to think I was joining the Order for my own personal needs. I mean...it was at first. But..."

"It's fine, Kevin. A promise is a promise." He said surprisingly calmly. Half of me expected him to get angry.

He soon led me to a place in the castle where doves were being exchanged. In one of the towers, it was a large room of caged doves. Some flew from open windows while some were coming back from the outside. In the middle of the room was a board decorated with small pieces of paper with a table that contained quills inside ink jars. I proceeded to remove one of the papers and wrote a note to my father with the white quill. Surprisingly, I was good a writing with a quill as I was with any other writing utensil. With the little room I had, I had to make sure that it was effective enough for them to know that I was here looking for them. I proceeded to write;

Dear father,

So much has happened here. I'm so sorry I haven't made much of an effort to come and check on you. I wanted to write this to know if you are doing okay; if you, mother, and little Kelley, are all okay. Please respond if you can. Once I found you soon, we'll be together again. I promise.

I love you. Tell Kelley and mother that I love them very much. I miss you all.

My regards,
Kevin Princeton

Francis carried one of the doves and counseled its milky white feathers to calm its nerves. It gave me a chance to roll up the note for the dove to carry by its leg. Francis tied the note around with a little rope and let it fly from the tower and out to the cloudy skies. I watched it go, hoping that it will reach them somehow.

And based on the information Francis gave me, I was beginning to feel skeptical of Bertha. It's been a while since I heard from her. It's been a while since everyone has heard from her. And it was weird that she suddenly disappeared right after the priestesses were rescued. The only time I even saw her was when I handed her the two Satanists. Something just wasn't sitting right with me. Especially given how she was prolonging only me to help her with the village caravan.

"I should wait for their arrival. If I don't hear of them soon, I'll shall go down there myself depending on where they will be settled." Francis said as he then turned to me. "I'll notify you, Ted, and Juliet if I ever need you. That is, if you are still affected by what happened?"

"We'll...get over it soon. Thank you again for sending the dove."

"You're welcome."

Feeling conflicted about the deal, I then asked him, "So...do you truly mind if I left the Order at some point? For good to see my family?"

"Of course not. It's your family, Kevin. And like I said, you wouldn't hurt me if you do. I want you to be happy. That's what matters to me the most." He smiled.

XIX

Untouched Maidens

As soon as I rode back from the Main Chapel, I made a mental change of plan. Instead of going back to the Khalservan, I wanted to check on Juliet and the priestesses. With Lustina taking care of them, I was cautious. So, it was a good, and somewhat wistful, feeling to be back at the Homestead. From what I saw as soon as I arrived, aside of the moody weather, it hasn't changed. But there were some tweaks that caught my eyes as soon as I came. Not only I noticed the increase of guards patrolling the place, but I also noticed more alvotons were freely roaming around the place.

Small alvotons were playing around in the mud pools while some were even playing with some of the Homestead villagers. Perhaps after I made Algor my companion, I might have sparked a new movement. Whether it was unintentional or not, it was good to see other alvotons freely running and being themselves as the homesteaders shared the grounds with them.

But I had to focus. My concern was to find the nursing hut and check on the priestesses.

As I was going to the hut, I suddenly came across Ted out of no-where. I would assume that he was going to visit the hut to meet with Juliet as well. As soon as I was nearing when I was reaching the entrance, I called out for him. "Ted!"

Noticing my voice, he responded, "Hey Kev. You're checking on the priestesses too?"

"Aye. Where were you?"

"I was at work." Ted said. I nearly forgot that he also worked. "Frask's business is growin' and growin'!"

"That's brilliant! I'm happy for him!" I said genuinely. I was glad that Frask was doing well; and he didn't get hurt or captured. That was one of the last things we wanted.

"I told him that I won't be working for him for a while. Just so he knows. But I didn't speak of the Order. Anyway, we should probably go inside." Ted said as he proceeded to knock on the door. I wasn't sure if he was going to bring up the fact that he brought me here when I was sick. I couldn't help but to be a bit nostalgic about that. It's how the three of us met eight months ago.

At the door, Juliet was there to open it. She was dressed in her nursing garb this time. "Kevin, Theodore!"

"Juliet." I recalled. "Is everything alright?"

"You should see this." She said, leading the two of us inside the hut after she closed the door behind us. On each bed laid the priestesses. Bella was seen screaming uncontrollably but was muffled due to her mouth being covered by the nurses. Some were still crying quietly underneath them. Some were bursting out loud coughs as they were crying. They were being comforted and questioned by the nurses; something was going on. The other girls were calmed by alprazolam injections the nurses gave them; getting them to gradually going to sleep. The entire cabin was consumed with screeches and loud sobs of Bella who kept thrashing up until one of the nurses injected her with a cold syringe of alprazolam.

When she was gradually becoming calm, she was up and alerted by our appearances. Remember those black veins they had? Well, they suddenly were growing back.

"What the hell is going on here?" Ted asked.

KEVIN PRINCETON ~ 283

"They're suffering with the affections the Satanists inflicted on them. Bella the most. They're panicking, vomiting occasionally, from potential growth of fetuses within them. And the cinnabar with them. The injections aren't helping much. It's worst." She informed. It caught my interest.

"What do you mean," I asked.

"I discovered that they held...seeds. Those perverted bastards ejaculated into them. This means that they are effected and could get pregnant soon." Juliet said uncomfortably. "I'd have to make Bella here undergo a surgical procedure to remove it. The problem is...I can't get her to calm down. She woke up from a panic attack. Poor dear's been having that all day. The nurses did all they could. Including amputation for Daisy who was shot in the leg, and she's scared. They're gradually calming down, but...not Bella."

Juliet sat down by Bella on the bedside, stroking her back to calm her. I felt pitiful watching these girls suffering at a very young age. Especially Bella. Her eyes looked puffy and bright red, possibly from all the crying and rapid breathing she did.

"Bella, darling. My friends are here to comfort you. Is there anything we can do to help relieve you from this pain?" Juliet asked smoothly. The girl's eyes were jumping around. She was completely unfocused. Juliet constantly counseled her to make her steady.

"It's alright, baby doll." Ted said, putting his hand on her shoulder before removing it. "Take your time."

"Aye." I said, adding to Ted. "What's happening?"

She was fighting back tears; I saw that in her constant shifting expressions. She said before sobbing, "Every time I close my eyes...I still hear the violin's screech! I still see...that monster...inside me! I still see...Sally. I can't sleep nor eat! Everything's just not the same!" Juliet continued to comfort her. It was clear that she was not going to stop crying. To ensure that she was safe with us, I took the initiative to place my hand on both of her confined hands. She looked into my eyes as I looked back at hers. Tears stopped rolling down her face.

"If...I may ask briefly, how did it feel? Being in Hell?" I asked before I proceeded to an idea I was having.

Through warm shaky tears, she replied, "The world...is a prison. Full of such evil. They say they want to redeem us, but only in their eyes. They stole us from our home and branded us as their vessels. They sedate us...into seeing a paradise. A heaven they made. They're animals. They act...as if they're not...but they are." She drifted and began crying again. I felt bad for asking her. But I had to know so we could find a way to help them. Her voice choked, "It's my fault! It's my fault he had control of that power and...killed Sally!"

"Oh no! Of course not, dear! It's over now!" Juliet wrapped her arms around her from the side. She shuffled her shoulder. "Don't ever think that. That monster wants you to feel that way. But you are okay now. You are okay."

After I contemplated, I told her, "Hey...Hey...Bella. I know you're scared. But if you want, I...I have a song that should make you feel better. It's a very good song. Would you...like to hear it?"

After she sniffed a couple of times, she nodded. I nodded at Juliet and Ted to ensure them that I had an idea to make sure that she was calm. When Juliet let her go, I inhaled and exhaled slowly to gain air. I began to sing;

"On the Mountains high – the birds pass by
To find a path that is – just nearby
The sky is blue and the wind – is nice
The air is still and solid – like ice
My dear dove – don't flow those tears
For I have seen your beauty for many years
On the Mountains high – the birds all sing
To see the good – our light – will bring"

Eventually when she was easing down, the lullaby worked like a charm as I saw that she was humbly entranced by the lyrics of the song.

I saw how stunned Juliet and Ted were. I figured that they did expect to hear me sing in front of them. I turned slowly to see that it affected the other priestesses too, including the nurses themselves. I overheard quiet murmuring across the entire room but couldn't make out some of the words. Some even awed in amazement. I was almost embarrassed and shy because I usually don't sing in public. It was safe to say that she loved the song.

"Wow...Kevin." Juliet awed.

"I...I just thought that it was a way to calm her." I admitted. I then faced the girl. "I know it must have been scary to reflect back on what happened. But we need you to be calm. You're back in Heaven now, safe from that evil world. Juliet is going to do everything she can to help you. But you must be calm. Think of something happy and hopeful. Just try. And we'll bring you justice for what that monster did to you and your fellow priestesses. Including Sally. I promise. You think you could be strong?"

She said nothing. But she gave us several nods, implying that she indeed understood. She took a deep exhausted breath and said, "Thank...thank you."

"You're very welcome, Bella." I said smiling softly.

As Juliet got up from the bedside, she said to the girls, "Now I'll be back for a bit, so we can begin the procedures. I'll need to discuss something with my friends. It shouldn't take long." With that, she left the hut alongside us. And once she rejoined with us outside of the hut, we were making our way down to the homestead. Once again, the sky was still cloudy as usual.

Ted then said, "On one note, that song you sang back there...that was nice."

"Yes...it was," Juliet said, glancing at me, almost taken by my charm. "Where did you learn that?"

"My mother wrote that song and sang it to my sister and I...when we were afraid, sad, or upset about certain things in our past lives."

"I had no idea that you can sing," Juliet said. "But it was really thoughtful of you. Comforting Bella like that with that song. Thank you." She smiled at me. It wasn't a typical smile, but a very enchanting smile. She was impressed with what I offered.

I said to her, "It's no problem. I'm just glad that we were able to get to what is happening. Do you think it's true?"

"What do you mean?" She asked.

"Was Sathanus really forcing them to...produce children against their will?" I asked.

"It's...quite worse than that. Francis told us about it. And I nearly forgot this...because I was...it's rather distressing," Juliet expressed miserably.

"Tell me." I asked as she then pondered.

Finally, she said, "Sathanus is known to have...eighty to one hundred wives, whom he called maidens. So, half of them were young, sometimes very young, girls from Heaven who were kidnapped against their will during the rebellions. He would have his male Satanists force them to be *bedded* to test their fertility; if they were worthy to bare...his children to become his legacy. When they grope and infuse them, he would...beat them, then force them to...to...kill the unborn and...and...eat them. For fun." She recoiled and tried not to break down.

I sunk all of that. Bloody disgusting degenerate! But then again, he was a demon. He lived off being one. So, I wasn't too surprised. I was sickened. But not surprised.

"And the asshole tried to make these poor girls apart of his demented collection!" Ted then asked, "But what does Lucifer want with the scepter of Queen Arianna?"

"He probably wants to consume it, so it could revert back to him." I said. "Perhaps he wants to manipulate so he can somehow...control their minds to submit to his sick wishes."

"Funny you said that. You know about...behavior modification, right?" She asked.

"Aye, we do." I said.

"Maybe when he uses the violin, he constantly plays the music so that the victim can be complied. Remember when Michael said how they use this method to forcibly erase their consciousness; especially those who are damaged? That would mean that the musical fugue, or any dark energy, would evoke what they don't want to become. The music was the stimulus that caused the girls to respond in a submissive way. And possibly taking out any awareness of who they really are...so they can be exploited by Lucifer." Juliet said gloomily.

"So...brainwashing?" Ted answered. I was thinking the same thing.

"Maybe something more. We must see it past that logic, Theodore. It's as if they want to completely mold nature itself...to how they see fit. They want to reestablish the natural ways of living and thinking to their vision. Breaking souls in exchange of a new one they made for them. Like building a robot whose solitary purpose is to serve the master who created them. Bella said that they are...being sedated...possibly by some darkworker magic...into seeing Hell as some idyllic paradise of peace." Juliet answered. "That's probably what they're doing to the other mystics there in Hell. And those villages that were burnt, maybe Lucifer has another group of Satanists doing those things for some reason. There has to be a reason behind any action."

"We have to make sure that we find those who are utilizing this kind of energy to their bidding. By some miracle, we can invent something. If only we were technologically advanced." Ted suggested.

"Does this change your mind on finding Bertha?" Juliet asked me. I was skeptical now, knowing that she basically left Celestia without a word. A possibility could be that she was still moving them, but she would've told any of us, especially Francis. So, Bertha would have to wait for now, wherever she was.

"Let's deal with one problem at a time." I said. "Bertha would just add more issues. Maybe...we must wait for her return. Francis told me that she suddenly left her team to look after the village caravan. Without a word."

"That would be a problem. I have a feeling towards her. Not an okay one. As far as this progress is concerned, we might as well wait until

Jesus returns...or if Francis will call us again through telepathy. Waiting is tedious as hell, but I think it's best not to make it into something that is already tiresome. We don't wanna make any mistakes."

"Theodore is right. I'll see you both after I perform the surgery." Juliet said as we both nodded at her. She then went back inside the nursing hut.

XX

~

The Dame of Eastbound

We rested once again in the Khalservan. I was hoping that this wasn't going to be a constant routine. I just felt as if we continue waiting, the Satanists could turn up elsewhere without our notice. We're supposed to be knights.

I felt a bit underused as an Apostle. I reckoned that Ted and Juliet would be too. But I understood that Francis and the rest of the House of God were holding us back in the name of protection, especially after coming across Sathanus. And I did appreciate that. But at the same time, we weren't given these powers for nothing. So, I hoped at some point in time, we would be given an opportunity to fight back. I understood that there was more to be an Apostle than just to fight. But I just hope to act when it was right and necessary. It just seemed as if what we did, what Francis and Jesus were doing for Heaven, weren't making a difference as I thought. Even though I still anticipated to find a moment to get out from this feud, I at least wanted to see it come to good terms. Especially given how it was integral to the afterlife.

In the Khalservan, I took it upon myself to go back to the library. As I strolled a bit inside the empty room, I saw through the windows that it was starting to shower with frosted flakes of cultivated ice. Winter was nigh. But I trailed off to find myself surrounded by many books.

It was strange that I was finally getting back into reading again. Ever since I was a criminal, I stopped reading. I had no care for it. But now, it seemed as if I was getting back my drive for reading. And to at least learn about how this world worked.

I picked up a hardened cotton blue book from the shelf and exited from between the two shelves. I sat down and lay back on a pile of slightly soft cushions to read it. It was called *"Rebirth of a Ghost"* by Brenden Redden, a philosopher and musician. When I took a glance and skimmed through some parts of it, I read that it was a book about reincarnation; hints the title *"Rebirth of a* Ghost".

In the afterlife, some spirits have the tendency to reincarnate themselves into anyone, or anything, they want. Especially since death was foreign to spirits. It meant that as a spirit, you could transform into anything you please every end of each century. Even some of the most notable superstars, historical figures, and influencers of our time – when I read – were said to be in the afterlife; only they are physically someone else. Or something else. Or much younger again. They were called shifters in afterlife terminology. Some spirits believed in a continued existence, not a static death. Because consciousness needed to expand.

After reading the book, I got up and went back to the shelf. Putting it back, another book caught my eyes below the shelf behind me. When I removed it from the shadowy bottom shelf, I wiped the bit of dust from the cover. Exiting the shelves, I sat back down at the cushions. This book was called *"The History of the Apostles and the Knights."* It was written by Andrew Lockhart, a member of the Cavaliers of the Mind, one of the second knightly societies. This really caught my interest as soon as I saw the bleak red Roman text. I assumed that he knew that he was going to die. Thus, took it upon himself to recollect and write down the events though legends and documents. Based on each chapter I skimmed through, the battle between the Apostles and Satanists went on for five centuries, right after Lucifer apparently rebelled against every single realm in the afterlife. It was an ancient war that has traversed through time. Only the knights were dragged.

I've read one page where it was said that Lucifer and Sathanus met after he was banished from Heaven. Sathanus was the leader of a group of dark assassins who worshipped Satan, the deity that eventually merged with Lucifer's soul after profaning humanity. Sathanus served him. When Jesus was becoming King of the Promised Land, the Apostles had to protect him from the Satanists who intended to assassinate him for Lucifer to take his place. His cult grew from simple fanatics to one of the seven branches of the Demon Legion Army. The bigger the numbers, the more threatening they were. They were made by darkworker magic, the hellish counterpart of lightkeepers who hone the beings of light, only to shift them into darkness.

As a young man at eighteen, Francis met Jesus and told him about the Order. He gave Jesus the idea of having an order of knights as another group of protectors of the afterlife and to solely bring the idea of higher selves into light. Jesus was skeptical at first because it was abnormal and even illegal for any spirit, especially astrals, to become an angel. It was sacrilege to worship anything that affiliated with astronomy because it made us stray away from the gods. But he accepted it soon after further research and saw potential in spirits becoming angels at will.

The Cavaliers of the Mind, a knightly society of psionics, was the second order to be established. The third was called The Sovereignty of the Virgin Mary, an order dedicated to the Virgin Queen. Thus, the likes of knights became a movement from the eleventh to twelfth century after the Apostles were made on April 15th, 1052. Despite their differences, they often founded a way to forge alliances at times. Some knights were even for hire. Francis's unique heroic actions and astrological philosophy surely garnered inspiration.

Unlike military forces, who waged war in battlefields, most knights waged outside battlefields. Endurance missions for things of value, counter terrorism, espionage for valuable intel that regular militaries didn't know about, private, or public assassination of targets of importance, using political or religious movements to their advantage, reconnaissance, scouting, you name it. They professed in all of it. Once they did, they were accepted by most of the afterlife's society. Especially the House of God. It was no wonder the Angelic Paladins took a sort of liking to them. They were a compliment to the Archangels who died. Some, however, saw them as a mockery and disgrace to their legacy. Especially the Chancery.

From Angel Paladins to Spartans, Vikings to Samurais, alchemic and element magic soldiers, armed forces from kingdoms across the afterlife bared energy given by the actual gods to protect and serve their kings, queens, lords, ladies, countries, and empires according to their will called *blesswork*. They have always fortified the afterlife from all evils that waged massive wars just to determine its fate in an everlasting period. All just to determine which would reign supreme; making it no different from the world I came from. Each mass army extracted powers of their gods in these everlasting defensive wars that deteriorated the afterlife's purity. Defensive because it was always about warring against invasive forces. Mostly from Lucifer's untired empire. And all the kingdoms had to come together to fight them off, knowing how unified – and vast – Heaven was.

But what made the guardians stand out was lightkeeper and psionic magic, something that was considered abnormal to other spirits. They extracted sorcery of the angels who had yet to be a part of the hierarchy. They were trying to find their place in it. They were pitchers for star angels, mysterious angels personified as stars that was seeking to find a place after the unknown destruction of their realm in the nebula. The age of guardians was theirs to shine. A wild west to help all spirits to become close to divinity as possible. To become that fragment of life and uphold it.

They were either unpredictable or direct. Some were harsh and cruel on the job; some were pure hearted and kind. Often, they were feared. Mainly because they weren't (and still aren't) fully understood yet. They were a new breed of angels. Very human angels. Guardians were once dismissed as a myth for humans and spirits. But their exploits have inspired a good bit of spirits to call upon them as well. Regardless of their different codes, their teachings revolve around helping spirits to be in control of themselves without earthly orderly things trying to control them. With angelic divinity, their aim was to help spirits embrace divinity and live by it. Not fear it nor to let dishonest leaders tell them how to find it.

But...it wasn't long when Lucifer conjured more and more powerful armies from every kingdom of Hell. They weren't just warring against the kingdoms. Three centuries later, their sole goal was to specifically hunt the knights. They were discovered. Thus, to serve the Legion, the Satanists were molded sorely to find and kill all knights and dames, especially the Apostles. Another massacred rebellion...worse than the first. Thus, becoming a battle within another; making the afterlife slowly seep away from the flourishing divine heart and beauty it presumably had before.

Despite their best efforts to survive, guardians were completely wiped off in the late nineteenth century. They've gone extinct. Their knowledge was left as neglected fossils. And sadly, they have since been forgotten. Star angels were disclosed as spirits refused to trust in them; especially in fear of being hunted by the Satanists. Thus, making the afterlife short of guardian angels. However, despite getting exiled for it, I saw that those losses didn't stop Francis, for he has been trying all he can to revive the Order. He still looked decent and not too old after decades.

He seemed to find a way to bolden and broaden the Order's ideology as well as accumulate the lost knowledge that fell. The Khalservan was rebuilt as well to pay tribute to all knights who passed away. Regarding Jesus, he had to worry about harvesting the afterlife as the new king before Lucifer expended his rule from Hell. To that extent, he still had a chance to make things right. After sending a peace treaty to Lucifer, Jesus focused on maintaining that unity he had with the other monarchs after Sarah was born. He focused on trying to help spirits to discover life beyond what they were told by earthly leaders or elites who were content on leading them astray. Just as it was written in the Bible. In fact, he hoped to shine a light for all monarchs to be better than earthly leaders.

Soon, I skimmed through another page where it talked about the

Apostle Gauntlet. Specifically, how it was constructed. Knights had a variety of different small blades like karambit knives, trench daggers and push daggers. Even hooks. The retractable blades I wore were once created and developed by one of the Apostles named Timothy Gregory II. Inspired by the push daggers, the idea of the tactic was supposed to swiftly take down the target, whether in combat or in stealth. The blades were made from pyrite; crafted to remove negative energy. Thus, eradicating evil and negative spirits quickly. It was exclusive to the Apostles.

Surprisingly, afterwards, I browsed through other pages and learned that several saints inspired Francis's vision for the Apostle Order. I assumed Francis gave Mr. Lockhart enough to tell the tale. Saint Peter Damian, who was a Benediction monk, was a patron from free running and parkour - a skill that is later learned today by knights (although I've already learned it when I was human). It emphasized on what it meant to be flow like leaves as it winds in nature. It made up for the fact that knights don't have wings (apart from Francis). Some knights did have it by choice.

The idea of knights came from Saint George of Rome, who was a patron for knights. Francis's personal hero. Pope Gregory I also inspired him. He was a patron for teachers. Essentially, they were Francis's mentors. And a lot of sacred books he saved from Bordham that were more speculative with morals beyond the general basics of living life according to God. It was no wonder why they were content on half texts of other beliefs removed from institutions. Whilst skimming, I came into Mr. Lockhart's final wish written. His wish on the book's last page was for someone who came across his words to rejuvenate that golden age of angels again. Only it didn't need to sorely be knights. It could be anyone.

It was just fascinating on how they have gotten Francis to create and experiment with the Order of what it was now. And we were the next to resurrect what the past members fought for in an age where it apparently wasn't needed anymore. I wondered if these unique angels built knightly codes around their orders to disregard the fact that they were just vigilantes or common spirits playing gods, which was obviously blasphemous. Or perhaps they were full of shite. Still, I learned that I've gotten into something that was somehow hated by most of the afterlife as if being hated as a human weren't bad enough. However, I had to admire them for committing to a prolonging fight for something they strongly believed in. I was reminded of Edward and what he stood for. And I was reminded of how much it meant to him.

Afterwards, I closed the book for a moment and placed it on the red cushion. I then stood on my feet, facing the window, which displayed more of the snow slowly falling. I wanted to see if it were still possible to allow the light in me to flow and extract my next power. If I were confident enough to practice.

I took a deep breath, preparing to dive into the Blessed Eye. I closed both eyelids, seeing only darkness. I held out two of my hands and proceeded to let the quartz work the energy inside me. My blood streams moved hastily through me, which meant that I felt my powers being used. Though my eyes were closed, I felt the vessels in my eye harden and expand rapidly. Perhaps, I was rushing to know.

When I opened my eyes, what I saw really astonished and horrified me. Eight strange-cloaked shadowy figures stood before me. The weird thing was they looked awfully like the shadows I had been running from as a human. The shadows that were haunting me when I was alive appeared. There they were, standing before me as they stared blankly at me with their glowing white eyes. Their outfits were like my Apostle wear; only they were completely pitch black and consumed with misty but choppy dark smoke. I was amazed that it was I that summoned them. But it was horrifying to look at.

They even carried a variety of weapons. One shadow carried a shadowy version of the same sword I had. The second one had a sword and a heater shield. The third one had a poleaxe. The fourth had dual swords. The fifth had a spear. The sixth had a halberd. The seventh; a battle-axe. The eighth and last one had a war hammer.

Suddenly, my mind felt very light. My entire body felt as if it drowned. I barely kept my eyes open. I saw that everything around me was becoming dark and blurry. I couldn't even stand. Next thing I knew, I found myself falling onto the ground. The last glimpse I saw was the shadows still staring at me. And I swore that these were the last words I have heard from them.

"He has found us!"

Later, I soon woke up. As soon as the blur was gradually going awry, I saw that I was lying on a couch in front of a fire. I glanced on my left to see Ted and the girl Emily looming down at me. His arms were crossed on top of the couch and his brown eyes were locked at mine, a sense of concern.

"You're alright man?"

"We found you unconscious in the library...with those shadows disfiguring." Emily said. I sat up and placed my hand on my temple. My head felt very heavy as if it carried eight rocks.

"Thanks," I said, rubbing my forehead. "Uh...so you saw my powers?"

"You summoned figments of yourself. I think that's why you fainted; they're apart of you. It's known as a *Macer*." Ted informed.

"A...*Macer*?"

"It's one of your more definitive powers. Because it really correlates to whom you are. The heart and mind are gifts. But often, they are curses because we feel that we aren't in control of them. Specially the mind. A Macer works with your system to make sure that you have control. Mine is the Psychomacer." Ted said, as he trailed away from me to pace around. He looked at me. "Yours... is known, in this case, as the Shadowmacer."

"The Shadowmacer, huh? That's...completely bonkers."

"You'll adjust to it. It takes a while."

"Right. What about Juliet's?"

"The Avesmacer. You can use these powers to your advantage. You can control illusions, like me, or summon your illusions, shadows, anything that defines who you are. And have them help you at will." Ted said.

"How come I felt as though...I couldn't control them?" I asked.

"It seems that you have to still come in terms of it. It does not come from illness, but something within your soul." Emily primed. "How did you feel when you saw them?"

Gulping, I said from the bottom of my heart, "I felt...astonished. But mostly afraid. These shadows followed me all my human life. I've been trying to escape from them. And the voices too. But...it seems like I can't! And I've yet to know what they want from me! Summoning them felt like I was ripping another part of my soul."

"Perhaps that is why you can't control them; you have yet to accept them. You must work with it. Accept that essence and it will bow to your will. Don't let them control you. Control them through meditation and prayer."

"I agree," Ted said. He stood by the table that was inches away from the couch. The table consisted of the same Traveler's Progress tabletop game I played before. I assumed that he was playing with Emily.

Perhaps, I thought, maybe Juliet could give a good insight to this. Perhaps she can give me more insight of how to control this power. As of now, I've learned how to use telekinesis. I have yet to discover what else I was capable of. Learning this power could potentially help me find and defeat the Angel for good. Although, I felt like she was stressed enough about everything that's happened. As much as I would want to ask her, it had to wait. So, I asked Ted instead, "So how do I control them?"

"Having that feeling of your soul being torn always happens the first time. It's premature. The key is to let the star angel within you infuse with your nature without rushing it. Even one that scares you." Ted said. "Like what Emily said, when you embrace it inside you, you can control it. Not for it to control you. It's a lot like...like eating pineapples. They're sour...depending on the readiness...but they become sweet when you eat them, swallow them, and move on with your life. I know that's a weird as fuck analogy, but that's basically how it works. For some reason, I crave for pineapples whenever I make analogies involving pineapples. It's weird."

After digesting that weird but somewhat helpful advice, I then asked whilst standing up from the couch to approach him. "Any idea where Juliet is?"

"Oh, she's at Eastbound." He said as his eyes locked at the game board. "She's done with the surgery."

"Where is that anyway?" I asked, finally gaining his attention. "It sounds far."

"Why, you wanna show off your Macer?" He joked. I turned to him in shock. He continued, "Chasing tail?"

"Wh....what are you – no! I just want to see her! Where did you come to that conclusion!?" I said, avoiding eye contact. "I'm no good at romance."

"Oh please, the way you calmed her a week ago after our mission. The way you often gaze at her when you trained with her. I saw how tenderly you looked into those washed-out blue eyes. You commented on her dress at the Gathering."

I looked away and prayed that Ted would stop talking. But I just felt him smiling at me, which he was with all teeth.

"You got a thing for her, don't ya? Ain't nothin' wrong with that." He teased.

"I could see him blushing," Emily tagged along. She giggled slightly. Ted snickered along.

"No, I'm not! I mean...she's indeed beautiful. And quite...lovely." I admitted. "I mean even if I did...what if she rejected me? Especially since I'm not that much of a romantic. I'm not that good with women apart from my sister and mother."

"You don't need to be. Romantics are fools who pretend to be someone they ain't based on some soppy young adult book they read. Or Nicholas Spark. I don't know. But, I believe in...your God's how-to book, it said Do *not be conformed to this world, but be transformed by the renewal of your mind, that by testing you may discern what is the will of God, what is good and acceptable and perfect.* See that? I did my homework. And I'm pagan!"

"Lovely. You know Romans. Do you have any useful advice?"

"I'm saying to be yourself, crumpets," He replied with his tone full of jest. "Talk to her as you would talk to...your mom or sister."

Scoffing, I asked, "So what? You're a love guru suddenly?"

"I'm just sayin'. In case you do someway find a connection to her, I don't want you to make the mistake I made when I dated Eliza. I was a victim of identity crisis. I still am, in some days. I don't want you to make the same mistake I did. But before you could love her, you could only love yourself first. That's what I'm doing...until I found the right one for me. I have yet to know love beyond...ardor. But...you have that chance. Unless you wanna still discover yourself."

But that was the problem. I hated being myself. I hate what I've become. So, I dismissed by saying, "She is just a friend. Honestly. Plus, I just want to know about the surgery."

"Okay," He scoffed. "Whatever you say!" He then pointed at the window that was behind Francis's desk. It appeared that he was pointing at where I could find her. "Eastbound is just below where we came. You'll find a path and eventually see a sign that says Eastbound. You can't miss it."

"Sure, as hell won't." I said.

"Yeah...'Cause you got that tail to catch!" He jested.

"Shut it!" I replied jokingly, walking away from the common room to make my way to the stables.

I was soon outside of the castle. Knowing that I might have passed out for a long while, the sky was already darkening. But the blue aurora was shimmering across the sky and the moon shined. I saw that the snow was covering everything for the most part. Mounted on my horse, I looked back at the castle. It looked nice with the snow on top of the towers and the roof. I saw that the monks were still patrolling outside and the winged guards patrolling the gates.

When I left the castle through the gates, I was making my way down the path I would take to get to the hideout. I made a mental note regarding Ted's directions. I was hoping that I wouldn't end up getting confused. I soon got into the forest after galloping away from the castle, losing myself in the beauty of the trees. After trying my very best, I eventually spotted the right path to get to the forest. It was just like what Ted said. As I galloped across the snowy pathway, I couldn't stop thinking about what Ted jested about. I was in my thoughts once again, ignoring the various creatures roaming in front of me.

Though I did lie to Ted and Emily, they were right about one thing; I was suddenly finding myself falling for Juliet. And it was weird, considering how I didn't consider myself a romantic. I still don't. And as I said, I had little faith in women. But she seemed different. I was entranced of her strong spirit and her bizarre beauty. I would reflect on these medieval fantasy movies and stories where the knight would fall in love with a woman and would consider her as a fair maiden. I know that it's cliché to think that way about a woman, but it's how I felt. And never in my previous life have I've founded a woman like that around my age. She seemed very rare. And so far, in terms of her being a woman, someone I could trust.

I was intrigued in her kind nature. But I knew behind that iron-clad exterior was a down-to-earth, compassionate, and loving woman. The way she comforted the priestesses reminded me of my mother. It reminded how she comforted me when we met. Though it made sense for her since she was a priestess at some point. To top it off, her bleach hair always made me awe at how angelic she looked. And although I would consider it somewhat invasive, she was very eager to know me and to help me find my way in the afterlife. Just as Ted and Francis.

Soon, I finally saw the shaky picket sign that read Eastbound – after tirelessly trying to find it. The path became a two-way street. The sign was pointing on right, so I went to the right and followed down the path. Upon following down the path to Eastbound, I saw something strange but arousing about the forest. I was beginning to see why Juliet would often reside there.

The leaves on the trees were coated and smeared with vast bright colors, ranging from blue, yellow, purple, tortoise, and white. The leaves on the branches made a beautiful collage of colors mashed together. The tree steams were striking with a mix of blue and green lights, streaming down the barks like veins. The grass was much taller and was also colored with red, pink, and amber. The entire area was cloaked with blue mist, as if someone had a smoke bomb.

The firefly-looking creatures that flew and floated across the forest enlightened it. Their lights were brightening in the mist. I looked up in the sky to see hazy covered birds (like Alwyn) flying through the mist as thin strips of smoke was flapping and rolling. Including a diversity of lovely peacocks and owls. In the distance, there was a herd of one-horned horses with colorful highlights on their pelts running through the rosy woods.

As stunning as this was, I couldn't be distracted. I was still looking for Juliet. I galloped my horse forward to flow the path. I rode, trying my best to not be blinded by the fog until I made my way to a brightly lit area.

It looked to be a temple of some sorts that was circulated by torches that lit hazel colored fire.

I dismounted from my horse to observe the area. Still surrounded by the enchanting forest, I was slowly walking towards the entrance, taking in the cosmic tranquilized nature of this region. It was an unusual spot, and I wouldn't think someone like Juliet would reside here. But I saw that her horse Violet was hitched by a post. So, I brought my horse to the post and decided to tie up the strains. Next, I went to face the doors.

I opened the doors, only to reveal a magnificently decorated room. The inside almost looked like a Japanese temple, especially since with the number of illumined candles there were against each corner of the wall. The walls were decorated with art that depicted what looked like Celtic mythology. It was starting to make sense. I observed, taking every inch, art, and culture that was bestowed right in front of me. I removed my hat and just glanced at everything. The floor was decorated with white marble that was smeared with green, white, and orange colors. The hazel lit candles were giving the room a hypnotizing smell too, almonds and vanilla. In front, there was a ritual made by offerings, flower pedals and candles recently used. It seemed as if Juliet was in the temple, extracting her prayer through a somewhat precious rite surrounded by virginal women statues made of stone.

My ears then caught a sound. It was that time I caught it at the last minute. It sounded lovely like a siren when it isn't trying to kill you after its seduction. But it was softly sung on the other side of the room. Perhaps it was Juliet singing or humming. I followed it to see where it was coming from, avoiding the trance of being in this sacred temple. I then saw that the sound was coming from a closed door.

I opened the door slightly to see that it led to another interior in the building. The room was nearly dark but was lit with aurora colored water. I managed to figure out that it was a rather circular room with a dome over my head. The ceiling was draped with tapestries, silk drapes, and chandeliers. It looked almost like a bathhouse when the circular tubs that were grounded on the floor hinted me. I sneaked into the room by slithering my frame through the door. I took in the area and glanced at the water. It's water blue, but much lighter and brighter than the usual waters I see. It glowed as big as the forest outside.

Upon strolling about and wandering around, with a brief sense of bliss and wanderlust, my eyes caught something I thought I would never see. It wasn't horrifying and not damn near creepy this time – thankfully. No. It was outstanding. I finally saw Juliet, but she was completely different in terms of her – ahem – frame. I wouldn't think that someone with a fighting and merciless heart would look this damned gorgeous.

My eyes widened, and I felt my skin almost turning red like rubies when I saw her nearby. I watched her bare wet figure brooding herself among the wrinkles of the water. In my heart, I felt bad for looking at her with such arousal because it seemed stalkish. Who was I kidding – it was stalkish! I turned quickly to avoid peeping at her like a bloody pervert. At the same time, something about seeing the body of an angelic woman made me entranced. It felt like being harmonically seduced by the blissful endearing hymns of a siren. Or a Greek nymph moistening by the enchanted waterfalls near a gleaming forest. She was humming softly as she was stroking her slender arms. Her body was of an undermined goddess or a neglected handmaiden.

I turned around and was about to take off. I felt a little ashamed of doing this. It was a weird feeling to me because I didn't have courtesy for others when I was alive. Let alone for women. With Talia, I would pressure her to hurry with her makeup so that I could engage with her. But it was different this time. I wanted Juliet to have her peace. And I was feeling a stream of weight taking a toll for trying to intrude that peace.

As soon as I was about to take off to give Juliet privacy, my name was called. "Kevin?" With that, my heart sank, and my nerves tangled. *Oh shit*, I thought in my head. I turned to see Juliet was focused on me.

"What...what are you doing here?" She asked embarrassingly.

"Uh...I just...I just wanted to see you. I thought about talking with you a bit." I said, struggling to find a proper way to speak without showing her my weakness. "But I see that you're busy. So... I'm just going to go. I'll...see you back at the Khalservan. This was a bad idea. I'm very, very sorry."

"Y...You don't have to." She said, nearly blushing while her arms were crossed over her breasts. "Normally, I would say that it is rude to enter when I'm like this. But I...I could use some company right now, before I could forget. I need to express myself to someone. That is...if you're okay with it?"

I tried my very best not to let my testosterones overwhelm me. I wanted to show that I was not taking excitement to seeing her naked frame. So, I just replied genuinely, "S...Sure. Okay, I guess. I'm sorry again."

I closed the door and approached her. When I sat down by her with my legs crossed, she leaned her upper frame against the edge of the tub with her arms crossed. Her bleach hair was shined by the moistness of the water.

"Interesting place for a bath." I said.

"Aye...I often come here to meditate, after I collect some herbs.

It's a place made from the spirits of *Tir Na Nog*. It's supposed to be a temple for blessings in the form of a bathhouse. After I pray, contemplate, I wash myself. Because the water is holy, blessed by the gods and goddesses. So, I just come here; mostly to clear my head and ask for Anu to guide me. Wash away the burdens. And ask for forgiveness. It's a way for me to get closer to her. A prayer...in a way." She replied. "Forgive me. I didn't expect you to see me like this." I recalled about the *Tir Na Nog*, which was an Irish place here in the Promised Land called Otherworld.

"No...it's fine." I said, hoping she didn't take notice of me blushing. I gulped. "Honestly."

But she did take notice and briefly showed red flash across her face. She then cleared her throat and asked, "So...uh...what did you want to talk to me about?"

I sighed and said, "Everything, I guess. The priestesses. The scepters. The villages. The Satanists. This Order. Everything that's happened. It just feels like it's all over the place and...I just don't know how we can end it altogether."

"I know what you mean. I'm still not sure why are they longing for mystic spirits. I don't even know why they must begin this war crime now. Why are they turning up just when this world was starting to get back on its feet?" She said. "Just dunno anymore. Even if I think I do."

"Soon we will know." I said, taking a good glance at her eyes. Her eyes were captivating when they became concern suddenly. I then asked her, "How did the operation go, by the way? It's why I came here. Just to ask."

"It went well. Thank you for asking. We managed to rid the semen from Bella and the girls. But they're still...not cured of the cinnabar. It's etching in their souls. They're really affected from what they experienced. It's horrible."

"Right." I said. "Hopefully, it ends soon. No one deserves that."

She then said after she pondered, "I wanted to apologize, about my behavior last time. It's just that I'm on edge with everything that's happened. I couldn't stop thinking about it...seeing Bella like that. Seeing those girls in such distress. Their screams still linger in my head. I can't imagine anyone else going through that." She spoke. "I just needed to get away from it for a while; think of a better way to encourage them. Seeing whatever I can find. I just.... I can't believe how failed that mission was. I felt like an idiot. We've could've...I'm sorry. I just..."

"Don't worry about it. It's completely justified how you're feeling." I said. "I want to stop this lunacy as much as you do. Especially if it reaches my family. We must be strong together. What matters is that those girls are still alive," I said, garnering a smile from her.

"So...how do you feel so far; being a spirit in the afterlife, I mean?" She asked casually.

"Heh...well...it's been alright; y'know, being...dead and all. It's no Iceland. But it's okay." I jested a bit. She chuckled. "All I can say is...it feels different. It's not the kind of place I expected to go after dying. I just expected to be in...I don't know.... a still plane. Not one that...sort of...evolves."

"Like being invited to the golden city. The kingdom of God...an unchanging state?"

"Something like that. Yes." I answered. "The thing is I was always told about Heaven; how it's a paradise that is awarded to you when you live a just life on Earth. A place to rest, simply for being of codes that pleases God. My parents told me that the reason why the Earth was at the state of where it was...was because it was a way for us to seek Heaven after we left it. We weren't meant for it. All of us. As if our lives, our bodies, didn't belong to us."

"Same here. I thought at the time that...you have to be a pure soul to be accepted to Heaven." She said. "But, it's no different. At the same time, however, I believe there's a purpose to all of this."

"What do you mean?"

"There's still semblance of evil and corruption in this world. Even here in Valestone, the entire Promised Land or any realm. But I learned something. Something I wish that I knew when I was a human."

I asked, "What's that?"

"I learned that...that Heaven could be a place of your own creation.

Your manifestation of what you want to do, what you want to be, what you want to see happen." She explained. "It could be a place of your own and to keep it to yourself. You don't have to be a certain level of goodness. Heaven can be something you form. Just as Hell. Whether in this life...or the lives we once had. What makes us happy, what makes us sad, it would create a state that we indulge ourselves in. Whether that state is heavenly...or hellish."

That seemed very true. I wished someone like Harris told me that as well. Even my parents. But then again, I wasn't raised how Juliet or Ted were raised. I was meant to be different. But turned out that I was no better than anyone else.

"You can find tranquility, friendship, love, adventure and prosperity in the Heaven you created for yourself. Learn about the hidden trues of having those qualities. This world...is to wake us up from what we were told by men playing gods." She stated. "I don't think of this place for the dead to rest, but another life that continues to exist. I'd like to believe that we're all capable of being creative in that factor, but...I know not all of us are. And it's okay. It's what matters to me. It always will. We lived in a world where they intended to hide that truth. Just to play make-believe with our lives."

"That's...a rather...unique way of putting it. I never thought of it that way before." I said. I briefly observed her get out from the tub. I made sure to turn to give her privacy to get herself dry with a towel.

"I wish I was taught that. That way I would have lived longer."

"Then you wouldn't have met us." She said in jest. "Especially me."

I chuckled. "Aye. I guess it's easier to make friends in strange places...than it is in a place you know. Or thought you knew."

"Well, I'm flattered to be that *strange friend* for you." She said as I chuckled to myself. I briefly saw her bare body trail behind a room divider on the right side of where I was. I watched the towel fly onto the rim. I heard shifting and a bag dropping. I sat in a bit of silence as I waited for her to get dressed. I just stared at the water, having my thoughts to myself. Just as she has.

"I still...can't believe that it's only the three of us in the Order. When

Francis first told me about it, I expected...I don't know... more of us. It makes the Khalservan feel quite... empty. Wouldn't you say?"

"Well...some spirits are afraid of becoming angels. It's very hard right now. Especially with Lucifer coming back. We are there to give them a reason not to be," she said. "Sure, we don't hold up to the Archangels or any in the hierarchy. But we could be angels in our own right. No matter what anyone says. No fear of systems that feels the urge to define us. We pay tribute to what they did for this world. I pray that there will come a time where they see value in the Order. But it's up to them."

"Aye." After I pondered, I asked, "How about you?"

"How about me?"

"How did you feel when you died, and you were ascended here?" I asked.

"I dunno. It seems like...I managed to have a much better life here than the one I had before. Despite everything." She admitted behind the divider. That seemed very bold of her to say that; to consider a world of spirits and ghosts a lot better than our very own planet.

"That's bloody bold!" I exclaimed.

"Well, that's how I felt!" She said through a short-tempered tone. I saw her leave from the divider, fully dressed in a navy dress that reached her ankles with a satchel strapped across her torso. Underneath her dress with a sash around her waist, she wore a smart brown wooly jacket. "Is that a problem?"

"No..." I said lost for words. Christ! I didn't think I would make her upset suddenly. I stood on my feet and spoke to stop her. "I didn't mean to. I'm sorry. I was just a bit shocked, that's all. I didn't know it would upset you."

She gave a regretful sigh and turned to me. She then said, "I'm sorry. It's not you. I just get a bit...offended when people say things like that. I guess...I hold this world of spirits in high regard than...than where I came from."

"It's alright. I just assumed it came out of left field." I said. "I take that you didn't like the life you had before?"

She then glanced down at the floor as if all her happiness was taken right out from her. Letting out a depressed sigh, she said, "Not really. At least...how it turned out." She then passes by me, across the room, and sat down on the bench. She looked down at the wrinkled bright water as the blue lights plastered her face. I went to sit right next to her.

"Have you ever wished that... you can try to find light within yourself before you could ever be that light for someone else? You try to find it within your heart, but your mind tries to tell you otherwise." She asked grimly.

I wasn't sure how to answer that. But I tried what I can to start a conversation. "Sometimes, I guess. Usually, I try...or tried...to love myself before I could love anyone else. It's...it's been hard. It still is. It's easy to hate yourself. But the world we came from preferred it that way. They live off it."

"I could say the same. I have yet to have faith in those who claim to be civil. I have yet to have faith in life." She said, scoffing under her breath. She then said with her eyes still fixated at the water. "That song you might have heard me hum...when I sang it, it made me remember that song you sang to Bella. I was wondering...do you know the meaning?"

I was unsure myself of its meaning, but I tried my best to interpret as best as I can. "It's mostly about finding faith. Regardless of any burden or hardship, there is always a chance to chase for good things. My mother...never really had the time to explain its meaning. But that is how I see it, I suppose."

She stared at me and grinned. "That's very nice. It's hopeful. I think I heard your mother sing before in the lesser-known radio stations. She had a lovely voice. And it runs well in the family. Francis told Theodore and I about her...after learning of your family. And it made me remember it."

"I see. Thank you. I didn't think her music would reach that much. I know what you were humming was obviously Irish, but what was it called?"

"'*The Quiet Land of Erin*'...by Joan O'Hara. In Gaelic, it's pronounced *Ard Ti Cuarin*."

It sounded familiar. Being raised by a singer, I would assume that my mother would know about the song as well. But it was very rare to hear it again. Even in the spirit world. "Do you know the meaning?"

"To me, it's about being away from it all; pain, suffering, guilt. It's about being in a place of bliss, tranquillized and beautiful. A place that you could call home." She spoke. "I loved that song when I was a child. I would often sing that song to the other nurses. Even the patients. As a priestess, I sang it in front of a bunch of girls for choir practice. And I blushed instantly when I was applauded."

"That's beautiful. Do you know who sang you that song?" I asked. When I asked her, she suddenly stood up from the bench and crossed her arms. She sighed once again. Something was holding her back to answer.

"My mother...she sang it." She finally said. I guess we had a lot in common.

"Your mother?"

"When I was always afraid of the dark, or sad after being bullied by other girls or men, my mother would hold me and take me out to the highest meadows at the cloudy dusk, the peeking morning star, the birds always flying, and she would sing it to me in a voice that even the angels themselves would be raised. I loved her very much for that. I miss her voice. I miss her smile. I...miss having her by my side. I've always felt safe with her in Wales."

I then stood to check on her. Her face seemed to almost quiver. But she took a deep breath, restraining herself from breaking down. I was curious to see what she had to say. "You were in Wales at the time you were alive?"

"At the time, we were poor, and it was only the two of us, living together in the slums of Wales. My father left us for that...just because he never wanted to admit his wrong doings. And it was upsetting, considering that he used to be a good man. He wasted money, including my mother's, for gambling, drinking, sleeping with whores. When the authorities took our home, since he didn't pay for the taxes, he gave up on us as soon as we were useless to him. Plus, he never cared much for our beliefs. And mother's previous job didn't give her enough to pay off the debts, enough to at least keep a roof over our heads. We worked as bakers and herbalists when we were in debt. We lived in a shack. We would bake bread, make herbs, different kinds of pastries, and sell them in our community. As best as we could to be afloat."

"What did she plan to be before?"

She then continued, "My mother worked hard to be a teacher, so she can teach students, making a chain reaction of children becoming better people in the world. She didn't earn much to become one, so she would homeschool me. My mother was the closest friend I had. We would spend time out in the meadows. She would tell me stories...about knights rescuing damsels from tribulating devastations, which gave me something to dream about...as I hoped a prince would rescue us. And if we were made decent money, we would visit Ulster for the most beautiful herbs, where she came from and...where I was born. Open Irish country. A quiet old country where I hoped to live on one day. Words couldn't describe how much I wanted her in my life and did not want anything to break us apart. Despite our living conditions, it was... heavenly. Because being with her and thriving together was heavenly to me. However, it all...descended into hell soon after."

She then looked up at the tapestries and then glanced back at me.

"When I was eleven, I remember hearing arguing in the night. It frightened me and bewildered me because it was always the two of us. So, it was strange to hear another voice. I soon came to realize that it was my father. He came for...me, from what I heard. I realized that my mother was protecting me from him. I didn't know what he wanted. Whatever was happening, I wanted to do what I could to save her from him. Despite my fears, I tried to fight for her, to fight him back, but he knocked me out cold before I could even reach to her. But as soon as I woke up...I saw that...."

She sighed heavily, trying to stay calm. "She was...murdered, wasn't she?" I asked. I saw her nod as I then saw her sky-blue eyes were filled with water.

"Her...lifeless body laid in front of me after he stabbed her to death.

It was the very last time I saw her before I was dragged away by my father. I hated myself for not doing anything to save her. As if that wasn't bad enough, knowing that I was too weak and too late to save her, I realized that my father tried to make me an altar server, for this...rich church in Dublin, since he was Catholic. He promised that it was a way to help us get out of debt, claimed that he loved me, but he never came back for me. His way of helping was to submit me to a collective of vile cowards hiding behind a cross, whose only motive was to use their rule to hurt me. Beating me into repressing myself and how mother raised me. Shaming me for where I came from, for what I believed in and telling me that I will go to Hell. I was eleven and they told me I was going to Hell while they would proceed to hurt me into their twisted vision of being spiritual. How can a place of sanctuary and holiness be perverted by criminals dressed as priests and nuns? How?"

She then trailed off and sighed very frantically, which seemed as if she was on the brink of crying. My heart sank very low towards my diagram when her shoulders were drowned. I went to her and wrapped my arm around her shoulder and stroked above her right shoulder. Her hand covered her face, which was turning red from fighting her sobs. "I'm sorry," she muffled with an almost tearful tone.

"It's fine." I took her back to the bench to sit down. I stroked her back in a slow manner to calm her. "I'm so sorry, Juliet. You...went through a lot. It's unfair." I shared her my sympathy, even as a victim of that kind of abuse. I was internally bashing myself for thinking all women seek to get hurt and battered. Especially after Bella and those priestesses.

"The worst part is...I didn't care. I felt so hopeless and unsafe without my mother. Without a father. I felt like I couldn't trust myself. I felt like I couldn't trust life anymore. I was just afraid of it when I saw it for what it was. One night, a pastor...tried to force himself on me in his office. But...he suddenly died from a heart attack. Two clergies caught what happened and...accused me of...murdering him. I ran away. When I was running away from the church, I was caught by father who was called by the church. He was told about what happened and he tried to hit me. It resulted to him...to him.... choking me to death. Everything turned black... and once I knew it...I was dead." She said in a calmer, but very dejected way. It wasn't any better. "I was ascended here to Heaven, which I never thought would happen. Yet, Jesus saw something in me that I have yet to realize, given how I lost all hope in making a good life for myself as a human. I reunited with her when I traveled and saw her with a group of traveling nomadic gypsies called Women of Revenants in Otherworld not far from here. Words couldn't describe how happy I was to see her, feeling her in my arms again as we both wept happily. And she looked much younger and beautiful." She sighed and looked up once again. Her face was brightly lit.

"I later became a priestess in La Divinum Estelle. After graduating from there, I became a nurse, to give the same care to patients as my mother did for me. and I am thankful for the lives of the nurses I work with. Soon, Francis saw potential in me and made me become an Apostle when I was eighteen. I wasn't sure at first. But...he treated me as if I were his own and got me through it. He always did as he provided safety and needs for my mother. He taught me how to fight, read better, to see the best in people and to trust in the universe. Even if it was hard...and still is. And if I could have faith and honesty in myself, I could have faith in others. Even if I'm not always around my mother, I feel her presence in my heart. It keeps me alive and ready to craft life on my terms without being afraid to thrive through it."

It really amazed me. What both Ted and Juliet went through has made me feel guilty. Sure, I had my fair share of bleakness in my life, but they had it far worse. These two people were struggling to make the best of their situations, creating a better and heavenly world for themselves. Yet, out of three, I had the potential to make myself a better person and to do what I wanted to benefit the life I had, even if my family was gone. Even if I was abused. But I squandered it because I chose to victimize myself. But Ted and Juliet were humbled and stronger because of it. So obviously, they were fit to be guardian angels. More than I could say about myself.

"Do you support your mother...in any way?" I asked in curiosity.

She nodded and replied, "I just did it again today. I went to see her today. She needs my help, Kevin. Even though I'm not there a lot. I'm happy that she's not in one of the villages...knowing that y'know, the Satanists are apparently attacking them as well. But...I hope your family is safe somewhere...since they are also traveling to find somewhere to live. I pray to Anu to protect them."

"That's a good thing. And...thank you. I really appreciate that."

"When my mother was murdered as a human, I...I never sang that song again. It felt pointless." She said, turning to me with dried tears on her pale face whilst wiping them off. "But...you got me to hum it today in this empty bathhouse at a wellness center deserted in Eastbound. I want to thank you, Kevin."

Shocked and surprised, I asked, "R...Really? What could I have done? I simply sang just to calm her nerves. It's.... not really a big deal, honestly."

"Of course, it's a big deal, silly boy! You must recognize the kind of impact it has beyond words. You made me sing this song. A song I was not able to sing in a very long time because of everything that's happened; with this everlasting war and spirits living off the depressed. But because of that song you sang, Kevin, it...it was a reminder. To remember why I loved my mother after all she did. To remember...why I love life's quiet beauty. I remember why I take value in becoming an Apostle; to protect that beauty." She suddenly wrapped her arms around me. I hugged her back. It really felt good to hug her slender frame. My chin was on top of her shoulder passed her head. She felt warm. Her hair was still a little moist. "Thank you very much."

And we truly had a lot in common; except that I had yet to find my own family while she – on the other hand – found her mother. Even though she died a tragic death, I was glad that she found something to be happy with the afterlife. "It's no problem, Juliet. I'm... glad it resonated with you," I said.

I quickly remembered what I just said to her not so long ago; about how she can find trust within herself. Perhaps that was my answer. It's perhaps what I had to learn before I can love Juliet. It seemed very clear that I loved her. And maybe she sensed that in me too.

I released her from my arms and asked her, "What about your father? What would happen if you saw him again?"

"I hope that I don't ever cross him in the afterlife; let alone having him near mother. I'd cut him down if I had to!" She yelped. Then she said in a calmer manner, "But that would make me no better than him. I forgive him, but only for myself. As I said, he was a good man at one point, but he allowed the world's evils to corrupt him. It's just...every time I see Sathanus, or think of him, I think about my father. Both are the same to me. And...I don't know...I get afraid."

"Afraid? You never seem afraid...apart from that mission we did."

"Well, I am. Every fight I do, I'm afraid. Afraid of losing myself or...what I face. Especially when Francis told stories...about how Sathanus single-handily slaughtered the Apostles who came before us with that pistol of his. How he killed all those other knights and dames...like cornered animals," Juliet said with uncertainty. "When I saw him, for the first time in that lab, I was...frozen. I felt hopeless. Like the night I tried to fight my father. You must understand, Kevin. We are living in a time where monsters are being championed and leading every facet of civilization. And they want you to succumb to that. All my life as a human, I felt that way. I felt like I had to be pure in man's eyes. And my father used my fear against me when he left me with those monsters. Mother always told me to be the byword of hope, bravery, and freedom I wanted to see in the world. I hope to be that. But lately, I feel like I'm not a good Apostle. I try to be, but...I don't know. I mean...look at how I treated Theodore before you came. Putting my burdens on him with no regard for his own issues."

"C'mon. Cut yourself some slack. It's your first time fighting the Satanists, which you seem to do naturally," I said as I had my hand on her shoulder. "Even an attempt to stand up for yourself and others shows your bravery. And you dying...doesn't take away the fact that you're the best Apostle I know. And Ted...he realizes what you've been through.

He's there for you...specially to make you laugh. Because...you deserve to be happy...after all you endured."

Her lips grew a soft smile and she said to me, "T...Thank you very much, Kevin. And you're probably right. Theodore...despite his randomness...he does make me laugh. Maybe he is helping me to be open, which I've shamefully neglected. And it helps him heal as he helps us heal."

"Of course. Hopefully, this life will be better for you. You're too kind for cruel people." I watched as she blushed a bit with a smile. She then faced away from me. After I pondered a bit, I then asked her, "Hey, do you think...after all of this is over.... after we'll get the people back from Hell I mean, do you want to take in sometime with me? A...get together?"

She chuckled a bit, "What makes you ask that?" I assumed at the point that she founded it laughable.

"I don't know. I mean...I just thought about it. Especially just to be there for you. And to get to know each other more." I admitted.

Out of fear, I said, "I wouldn't want to pry if it means you won't."

With a bit of silence, she then said after she smiled, "I'll see what I can rearrange. But I'll consider it. And...I'll let you know. Sound good?"

"Definitely."

From there, it was just the two of us finding ourselves staring at one another without realizing it. It was almost as if we were two different types studying one another. Her sky-blue eyes were glistened by the light of the amber torches. Her smile was still curved across her pale face. I was nearly sweating, not because of my coat. But it was because she made it hard for me to be restrained from kissing her. I couldn't resist looking at her. Her beauty was undeniably beautiful. I couldn't stress that enough. We looked away a bit after.

"You know, it's...pretty grand to...meet someone with pagan ideals. I didn't see much of it from where I came from. I know I came from the school of thought that...condemns it and potentially stole aspects from it," I admitted to her. And it made her smile at me. "But...that's what makes it...adventurous. Special and...free. It's a shame that it's seen as...evil."

"You don't know how much it means to hear you say that, especially for someone faithful to God. Pagans are not that cherished by most here. Let alone other spirits of different beliefs. You heard what Dante said about Bella and the priestesses. What he said really hurt my feelings. He put me in tears. It brought...unwanted memories, as if I should feel ashamed in something that makes me hopeful."

"Because people like him cannot fathom someone who doesn't share their views and forces them on you in the name of peace. Some people are just unaware of the harm they do to others. But my parents always told me and my sister...to see everyone as an equal to God. No matter what they believed in. So... you believe in this goddess...Anu. Who is she? She sounds lovely."

"The mother goddess of prosperity, comfort and fertility. Sometimes she is called Danu. I had to rediscover her after I served the House of God. My mother told me of her. Lately, I felt as if I have been profaning her presence. But I know she will forgive me. Although, I keep it to myself, given how it may seem unusual to others. I know that...our doctrines could bring out the worst, but...her divinity...reminds me of what life, light and...love could be again. I just want her presence to be proven and to fulfill me, guide me to light. Something that is meant to fulfill us always gets stained by people who twist it. I can't associate with that. Especially.... if it serves themselves and not her."

"Me either. But...if there's one thing, I've learned from being Christian...is that every creed brings out the best and the worst. So, if this is something that makes you happy, strong, and alive, that makes you do good, you shouldn't feel any shame for that at all, Juliet. It's what you believe. It's something to live by. You don't need to cry for them anymore, alright?" I said as she smiled. I stopped looking into her eyes so she wouldn't get any ideas and asked, "So...uh...do you want to get back? I could keep you company?"

"Of course, it's getting very late. But...thank you very much, Kevin. It means a lot." I smiled back at her as she smiled back.

When we rode back from Eastbound, we went back to the Khalser-van. We saw that the corridors and interiors were dark with the presence of dimming lights from the torches on the walls. I could assume that everyone else went to sleep, meaning that we were extremely late. Regardless, I couldn't stop thinking about our talk. It was so personal, specifically from her side. I reflected on everything once I was back in my chambers with Algor resting and snoring. I looked up while lying down on my bed, look up at the painted ceiling of the chamber bed depicted two gothic mirrors. The left mirror had an arm reaching out from the shattering cracks. The other had another reaching out downwards.

Still, my mind was engrossed by Juliet and what I talked with her. Even though it takes much for me to gain my faith, I was gradually seeing a match; both of us were ill-treated by zealots. Except she was overcoming her pain. Everything she went through to become a good spirit and Apostle was inspiring. In a way, although I still wanted to run, it almost motivated me to remain; especially since I wanted to be with her.

XXI

 ⟨⧓⟩

An Unexpected Reunion

The following snowy morning, after fantasizing about Juliet a bit, I was awoken by one of the friars again. I looked outside to see that it was still dark outside. I was quite unsure why would they wake me up that bloody early. But they just simply told me, "Get dressed and make sure you are at the courtyard. We shall wait until you are fully prepared."

I got up from my bed and proceeded to brush my teeth behind a mahogany room divider. Then after I cleansed myself and dressed myself – with a charcoal cloak over my shoulders – I proceeded to get Algor with me. It was almost a while since I had tagged him along on my duties, but the monks then stopped me.

"He cannot come. He must remain here."

I turned to Algor reluctantly and said, "I'm sorry, lad. But I'll come back." He wailed and went back to his sleeping mat that was by the window. I then took off with my cloak over me.

Once I finally reached the snow-covered courtyard, Ted and Juliet were there. They wore cloaks as well. Ted wore his long cotton brown cloak while Juliet wore a red rose cotton cloak. But this time, Emily was with them. It was a first, but very odd. Usually, she was much concealed with herself. She would always seclude herself in the Khalservan. But there she was mounted on her Kladruber horse preparing to leave with us. As I mounted my own horse, I galloped a bit to meet up with them until we were away from the castle and into the winter woods.

"What happened?" I asked.

"We're going back to the city." Ted informed. "Apparently, Jesus has an announcement."

That was interesting, seeing how he wasn't in Celestia. So, I wondered if there was a way he was going to pass on his message. I saw how silent Juliet was. Especially after our talk yesterday.

"Oh...and Emily said that she wanted to come." Ted said, gesturing at her.

"I feel like I'm confident to go back to La Divinum Estelle soon." She said.

"Really?" I asked her.

"I wasn't talkative about going back." She admitted.

"Oh, of course," I said. Facing Ted and Juliet, I then explained, "Emily told me that she was being bullied by other girls in the school. She felt left out. That's why she retreats in the Khalservan."

"I'm so sorry to hear that, Emily," Juliet said, finally speaking. "Why didn't you say anything? To any of us or Francis. Even Michael?"

"Because I felt scared to tell. I assumed that any of you would simply just brush it off as if it was nothing. I've avoided it for a while. I feared that I had no chance of becoming a priestess like those girls. I don't feel valued or wanted there." She said, almost gloomily.

"C'mon, you don't have to feel that way. You're valued! You really are!" Ted said. "You were considered a saint for staying true to your faith. Even in the face of unwarranted death! Makes you badass!"

"And Emily, you don't need to be like other girls. You're bright, loving, and kind just as you are. You don't have to be valued by everyone. Just be yourself. Trust me, being valued by everyone would be frightening." Juliet added. She received a smile from the young girl. "We'll always value you."

"And listen, if anything or anyone is bothering you, you can tell us." Ted said grinning. "I wouldn't mind giving the little shits a piece of my mind." He winked, which made Emily chuckle.

"Oh...uh...by the way, Juliet, I wanted to apologize again for...being a dick for the past few years being in the Order." Ted spoke. He was genuine about it too. "I know we had our differences, but I'm glad we could settle this together. Specially to help Kev here."

"T...Thank you very much, Theodore." She replied humbly. "That's one of the nicest things you ever said. And I'm sorry too. I feel I was no better, especially passing unfair judgment towards you. It was selfish and egotistical of me. It's just...people...life."

"Hey, no worries! Safe to say that this entire bullshit conspiracy with the Satanists has brought us together." Ted said.

"Looks like it has. So...no hard feelings, I hope?" She asked.

"Not at all." He replied with a smile.

"I assume a group hug is out of the question?" I kidded. We all chuckled among us whilst on snow trotting horseback, nearing out from the woods and out to the snowy meadows. The hooves were hammering through the snow. It shoveled within itself as we galloped. On the way, I was taken by surprise by the fog that concealed all over. I was a bit nervous on the way; hoping that no bad news would happen. I was hoping that something went right with Jesus and Michael. I did not know what to expect since I decided to keep my expectations lower and lower. I had to be open to something, even if I would most likely not be fond of it.

As soon as we arrived at the big city square, which I came to know that it was called the Plaza of Hope, it was very crowded with dozens and dozens of common spirits huddled around a large square of large fire bowls lined up. They blazed with purple flames. The blazing torches were in front of the city capital building. I realized that I was back at the place where Dante took me when I first arrived in Heaven.

The only difference was that every roof on every building was completely covered in white snow and Christmas decorations; obviously anticipating Jesus' arrival. After we waited for the people to disbursed away from our exit, once we dismounted from our horses and tightened our reins to the post that was in front of one of the buildings, we made our way across the road to meet with the event.

We dug our hands into everyone to get a view of what they were surrounding. Some were responding with quiet complaints, scoffs, and murmuring. A lot of conversations happened all at once. By the event, we happened to see Francis who was joined alongside the Queen, Dante, and the Lady herself. At the front of every single spirit, including us, were angels guarding the squared torches. Two angels were on each side.

Suddenly, two herald angels appeared as bright white smoke evolved and dissolved. They weren't in armor, nor did they have weapons. They wore white waistcoats with yellow baroque design along with breeches and white tights. Two of them then placed each trumpet on their lips and sounded them. This silenced the people we were surrounded by. The only present sound was the wind whisking with the flames.

"We call upon all of you today for a message from the king!" One of the heralds cried.

Eventually, they both bowed and walked off for us to witness the event. Each flame of the torches was gradually growing and hazing out large gulfs of smoke that hovered over the torches. Every single one of us fixated our eyes to the forming smolder until it was forming into a face: a bearded face. It was Jesus, who was now in smoke form. The haze completely captured every inch and aesthetic of his face. Murmurs and quiet gasps were all heard around us. But I was too focused and astonished for what was displayed right before us.

He then spoke with a slightly distorted voice; "Greetings, my fellow spirits. I have come forth upon you today to make an announcement of my disappearance. I do not wish for any of you to be at stake regardless of the past events that have occurred as of late. And I am aware of my day of birth approaching. But because of the circumstance that I am in alongside Saint Michael and the Angel Paladins, unfortunately I will not make it on time to celebrate. This mission requires my attention. I prefer that you celebrate without me."

Everyone gasped and sighed gloomily. It was weird to see his facial movements as a misty-holographic projection. It was clear that the torches were the equivalent of that.

"As of now, my wife – Queen Mary – shall look after all of you until my return to Valestone. So do not fear, my fellow spirits, I am getting to the bottom of this and want for this unknown treachery that bestowed on our great land to end. But that shouldn't block your chances of celebrating the holidays. And I ask all of you...to have faith and do not worry. Everyone who is in Lucifer's grasp will be soon recovered. And you will all get to live happily once again. I wish you all a Merry Christmas and God bless everyone."

His face dissolved from the squared torches. The angels commanded us to disperse from the area. I watched as the Queen and Lady were escorted to their carriage. I saw them being joined with Francis, who I could tell that he didn't recognize the four of us in the crowd.

What Jesus said, I knew that I had to keep that in mind. And in addition, it was not only lovely, but also brave for Jesus Christ himself to fight off this conspiracy in his own way. As if sacrificing himself on the cross wasn't enough, the man had to sacrifice his own birthday celebration just to protect his people. Now that is what I call nobility.

Afterwards, my friends and I decided to hang out at *Bo Peeps Litlers*, which was two blocks away from the Chancery's almighty basilica around another city square. It's been a while since I went there with Francis. We all agreed to take Emily back to La Divinum Estelle afterwards. But being that Emily was with us, it was going to be hard for us to see where else she would stay since she was underage. I was uncertain about what would happen. When we arrived, it was still the same bustling place where I left it. The music was still the same where I left it. Everything was in its right place. Only it was a guitar played by some random bloke. It sounded like something my mother would play.

Frank then greeted us, the bartender I first met. He said whilst wiping a glass mug with a white cloth, "Kevin! It's good to see you again, my boy!"

"It's good to see you too!" I saw as I shook his hand. I then gestured to my friends, "These are my friends, Ted, Juliet, and Saint Emily of Germany."

"Oh, you've met Ted...it's lovely to see that you have friends now. It's good to meet you." He said as the three nodded and shook Ted's hand, "Good seein' you again, lad."

"Likewise, buddy. Place is still lookin' awesome!" Ted grinned with teeth.

"Um...I know that Emily is underage to drink..." Juliet said. "So...we can just..."

"Nonsense, she can have our more...subtle beverages. And food." He said. "Any friend of Francis is always welcome."

He then called for one of his children, his youngest daughter Bo, to lead us to an open table. Frank's son Peep was helping his father. Bo was a kind, quiet and very young girl with red hair. And she looked to be shorter and a couple of years younger than Emily.

Disregarding how crowded it was, we were escorted to the second floor of the bar. Next, we were given a table that was near the balcony, giving us a good view of the first floor. It was good to see that despite the hell that they went through, it was nice to see them have everyone rejoice. At least until the hell is put down completely. I saw that Bo gave us drinks and steaks with potatoes, placed them on our table, bowed and left us to go back downstairs. Everyone, including Ted, was slumped back on his or her chairs.

"To... honor amongst scholars, leaders, fighters, monarchs, and creators. Thieves of idiots and morons. For we pray that they continue to prosper in a new heaven!" Ted said, raising his glass high.

"Cheers!" We all said, raising and clinging our drinks together and gulping them down our beverages, which tasted very natural and not artificial. I almost tasted its residue. Soon, I cut up and ate a piece of the juicy steak.

"Hm...never thought that I would drink in this kind of place." Emily said twiddling her mug full of what looked like fruit punch. "I assume children are invited to taverns now."

"It's only for today, lass. This place gets very adult." I said to her.

Ted and Juliet snickered. Ted then said, "This fuckin' girl's already a riot!"

He then faced me and continued, "Anyway, I didn't know you even know about Litler's! It's where the old folks of the Order use to pursuit leisure with Francis. It goes way back."

"I remembered you mentioned it when I was poisoned."

"Oh yeah, right!"

"But Francis took me here once. When we first met." I said. "After I discovered that I..." It brought back thoughts. Thoughts I wanted to remove. I remembered how unhappy I was to realize that I was now a spirit. That feeling of underachieving made me slightly depressed.

"Discovered what?" Juliet asked.

"It was the time I came to realize that I was dead on Earth. I left my body." I replied disheartened. "That night when I came here – when I broke into the castle – I discovered that book. It was a bloody big book with a list of names of astrals who were ascended here. Including yours."

"And you saw your name?" Emily asked. I only replied with a sigh and nod. It would be too painful to answer. I was a bit depressed to realize that I was ruining my quench to drink the ale Frank offered. In my thought, what hurt the most was that it didn't have to be that way.

I felt a hand touch my shoulder. I looked up to see Ted with his hand on my shoulder. He then said, "We've all been there. It's only a matter of time to come to terms with it. And it seems like you're doing a great job." He then removed his hand.

"You've been such a good help for us for the past few months." Juliet said. "And...I know that it's hard. And it still is. But you have to be strong."

"I know. It's just...it's just that I wish I'd done different things when I was alive. But it seems like it's too late now."

"It's too late?! Dude, you're an Apostle now! You gotta realize the opportunity you have here." Ted cried. "And you've done great things. Had it not been for you, those priestesses would've been gone. And it would've been our faults. And the night of the gathering, you saved the Lady. And you made Juliet and I settle our differences. Now...if those don't show nobility, I don't know what the fuck does! We've got your back, Kev!"

I smiled. Especially because what Ted said was true. For all the bad I have done on Earth, I was satisfied to know that I have done great things. I had to keep that in mind, so it can also lift my spirits. I then said to Ted, "Thanks Ted. And I'm sorry again."

"For what?"

"For saying that you don't exist. When I first meant you, I mean." I said, recalling that moment from the Homestead. "It was uncalled for. I was just...afraid."

"Hey, I understand." He said, shrugging it off. "I didn't take it to heart. And I know because it was new to you. That kind of shit messes with your mind."

"Thanks for understanding." I said, smiling towards him.

My eyes then caught the attention of a couple of blokes looking out the window right in front of us.

Standing up from the chair, I got up to see what was gaining the people attention. When I got closer, I was enclosed by constant gasps, murmurs, and even laughs of what was going on. Talk about blissful ignorance. There wasn't enough room for me to know what was truly going on. But when I got a decent view, crushed a bit by two coated blokes, I saw what looked like a fight on the street. Three bastards were tossing with another. The bullied man looked familiar. Perhaps too familiar. He was a black fellow, which I came to realize that it was Frask.

I raced away from the crowd and made my way downstairs as Ted, Juliet, and Emily followed me. I was fumed to why would someone like Frask was being tossed around like a ragdoll. His bag was snatched from his side and tossed aside of the road. And I always distasted how certain people would not take initiation to at least offer some aspect of help.

"Kev, what happened?" Ted asked.

"It's Frask!" I said as I saw that we finally got to the commotion. A decent amount of people was huddled around and surrounding the fight. Some were cheering on for the bullying to continue. Some were trying to stop the fight. When we were nearing them, another person went into the circle, commanding the people to leave. It was a woman who looked strangely familiar. My eyes widened when I came to know who it was: Bertha! It was really her! She returned after weeks since everything that has happened.

She was still the same with her red hair and regal posture. The only difference was the scar conferred on her face.

With her voice, she raised, "Everyone disperse this instant! Right now! Move along! Move! Let's be civil for once!"

Her words were loud and clear. The people began to gradually dissolve the circle. I then saw her go towards the three large blokes as she then threatened, "Astral Ghoul Boys, I never thought I see your band of idiots again! Crawl back to your holes at St. Johns! If I ever catch any of you pulling off this circus again, it will be off to the manticore dungeons for all three of you! Your clique and leader included! Your time of thugs has vanished. Am I understood!?"

"Yes...ma'am." Three of them said, leaving in sorrow and embarrassment. Each of them passed Frask with disdain looks. With that Bertha was going back into her carriage. I saw the blokes stare back, specifically at Ted as they recognized him from afar. "Don't think we've forgotten about your arse, Jefferson! We'll come for you! You owe Bush! You and your nigger friend 'ere!"

"*Whatever, Clay. Dupek (Asshole)!*" Ted mumbled to himself as he erected his middle finger at them.

We all then rushed to Frask, who was still down on the concrete and picked him up. I was ignoring Bertha for a bit; even for the fact that I was a bit angry with her. How could she disappear without any word and suddenly come back when things have settled as of now? I knew that she was busy. But it still seemed strange to me to leave by the time chaos bloomed.

I then asked Frask, "Frask, are you okay mate?!"

"Kevin! Uh...yes, I'm fine now!" He replied with a frenetic voice.

"Why the hell were they messin' with you like that?!" Ted asked, angrily. "I outta fuck them up if I ever see them again! Piece of shits!"

"Thanks, Ted. But it's fine! I've seen them before. They're just a bunch of bullies who rely on petty name-calling. They vandalized my shop sign numerous of times before." He said. "At least it shows that not every eternal soul here is good. In fact, they usually use it as an excuse to think they are greater...by projecting their insecurities because their self-esteem is about as high as a teenage girl. They're just lucky I don't have my Winchester with me. That's for sure."

"Wait, you have a gun?" Ted asked with widened eyes.

Frask replied, "Yeah. I got a permit; in case I want to defend myself. Nothing more."

"N...nice." Ted complimented cockily. He then said, "To think I was in that gang. Nothing more than a fan club of cowards!"

"I'm so sorry, Frask!" Juliet said, wiping off the dirt and snow from his bag and handing it to him.

"It's no problem at all," Frask said. "It's good to see you three again, that's all."

"Anyone who does that again, let us know!" I recommended him. I was starting to feel my temper decreasing slowly.

"I am Emily of Germany," Emily greeted him. "Pleasure to meet you, Mr...."

"Frask Douglas. And I might have seen you before. At La Divinum Estelle, if I'm correct?" He asked.

"Yes. We planned to bring her there today." Juliet said, rubbing off the snow from Frask's coat. "Why don't you come with us to the school for a bit."

"I was going to see the queen. I had an idea that I wanted to discuss with her. Something that could revolutionize Valestone. But I suppose it won't hurt to see how the school looks like in person," he said excitingly. I was amazed on how he didn't let the bullying get to him. He was still his quirky, upbeat, and incorruptible self.

I then sunk my shoulders when I heard my name called from afar. "Kevin!" I turned to see that Bertha was still there inside of her carriage, patiently waiting for me. Out of all people.

I approached her after glancing at the others. I then replied to her, looking into her glistened grey eyes. "It's been a while."

"I know, which is why I wanted to discuss it with you." She said directly. I then turned to my friends (yes, they were technically my friends now). They all stared at me, anticipating my next action. I then turned to her, almost giving her an irritated reaction.

"Would it be possible to bring my friends?" I asked, trying to hide the anger.

"That wouldn't be necessary. You'll see them soon enough." Bertha said. "This is urgent. I'll need a word. So, I would need you only. Unless you had other plans to intend."

As much I was irritated with her not notifying any of us – or me – about her sudden disappearance, I still couldn't forget about the plan I had. From whom she was, she seemed very mysterious and secretive. It was ironic, seeing how she sort of criticized our methods during the attack. Perhaps, she would give us good insight of the conspiracy. Perhaps, I wondered, that was why she disappeared. She wanted it to end as well.

I turned to my group and said, "I'll see you guys soon."

"No prob, Kev." Ted said. "See you at La Divinum!"

With that, I went inside of the carriage. I sat at the opposite of her, closing the door as soon as I went in. She called out for the driver, instructing him to lead us to La Divinum Estelle. We took off from downtown and were riding on the road.

On the way, all I thought about how I was going to explain everything that I have just witnessed this month. And I know that she didn't intentionally invite me for the ride just for sightseeing all the monumental landmarks of all Celestia. But still, it was frustrating to know that she suddenly left the city. I understood that she was a Civil Force Detective. But the last time I literally saw her was when I took the two Satanists, offering them to her. I was unsure of what did she do to them.

I heard her inhaling and began the conversation during the ride to the school. "I know...you must be unsure and are questioning my departure. And I do have an explanation."

"Where the HELL have you been?" I busted, feeling agitated. "Everything has happened since you left without saying anything! You just left the caravan without a word. It felt longer than that!"

"I could tell." She responded surprisingly calmly.

"And...that doesn't bother you at all?"

"I have a good explanation. But for me to tell you, I would recommend you...to take it easy. If it is too much to ask." She said.

I let out a sigh and then said to her, "Fine. So... where were you?"

"I was in Hell." My eyes slightly widened when she said that. Especially in a nonchalant way. What she was doing in there, I wondered. But then she further explained, "I was infiltrating one of their council meetings. Their rituals. Lucifer was there. Especially with the other monarchs and the hierarchs who help him. I didn't want to endanger the Civil Force, the monarchy nor your Order. Telling the common spirits would be far too distressing."

"How...How did you manage to get there? The toxins aren't even finished yet."

"I posed as one of them. Remember those Satanists you gave me? I got them to give me a toxin that allowed me to pass through a force field surrounding the damned place! Turns out...any other spirit that entered would evaporate into the Void. And it was in a small vial, so I couldn't risk my team force. Nor the monarch. Nor you."

That made a little sense now that she told me. I was right about one thing; since she infiltrated their world, which would mean that she would give us more details that could help us find The Angel and get to Lucifer.

"So...what's your side of the story?" She asked.

"We discovered who kidnapped the priestesses. Someone called The

Angel. Sathanus was there too...torturing them with this violin into conducting a scepter to their control. The Angel was in control of them while Sathanus committed all the actions. We were under trained to fight him. And his guards."

"It must've been horrible. Did you manage to get them out? The priestesses?"

"Yes". But I then asked, "I don't suppose you know about what Lucifer's planning? Seeing how you got into their domain."

"Well, I don't know for sure. But I know one thing though; these victims weren't kidnapped." She then engaged to my face. "They were sold by some noblemen and women here in Heaven. They were sold for a purpose."

"What?" I widened my eyes in disbelief.

"Yes. Turns out Lucifer has selected several fallen spirits of Heaven to sell their fellow mystics to him. In exchange, it's rumored that they were rewarded with the powers of a Satanist, even promising them to become more than mere spirits. Gods. They're called Watchers. He was planning more in the rituals."

"So...it's...a betrayal. So, someone from Arcadia's monarchy must have sold the priestesses. Fucking bellends." I said, trying to hide my frustration. "They essentially sold their souls to the devil. So...is The Angel one of them?"

"Yes. And there's two more working with this Watcher."

"What? Who are they?"

"Someone called The Unicorn and another one called The Phoenix. Each of them residing in this realm."

Those were very ironic names for very devious people, an angel, a unicorn, and a phoenix. But at least I understood that these turncoats are supporting Lucifer and are conspiring against Jesus and the other imperators.

"Did he speak of what he plans to do with the scepters if they're stolen?"

"He wants to use one of them to get to a place called the Axis Mundi. Apparently, they are keys to the place. He has the sold nobles building something for that kind of power. And apparently, he has established a network of spirits from other realms to go against those combatting the New Heaven. Threatening wars, crimes, and havoc to further his cause. He's just getting started. Now...if Francis wouldn't mind, you and I can work together to find these bastards, even with my forces," She suggested.

This seemed a lot bigger than I previously thought before. This was something I couldn't handle by myself – let alone work with someone whom I mildly trusted with my family. But I wasn't sure why she was so obsessive with working with me alone. So, I said to her with an imploring tone in my voice, "Alright, I'll see about that. But...I want to bring my friends too. They're just as skilled as I am."

She seemed skeptical when I asked her. I was a little nervous, expecting her to reject my request. But she then said, "Of course. But...you must be careful of being too close to comfort with what you think it's right. You wouldn't want anybody hurt, would you? You want to have nothing, no one, to lose. Besides, there is something in you that has more value in what we must do as a recent astral. Specially for your family's sake. We don't want them dragged into this conspiracy."

"You're right, I suppose." She did have a point. I watched as she turned her head to the window on the right side of her face.

"Let me ask you something, Kevin," She said. "What makes a good soul?"

"What do you mean?" I asked her.

"I mean...what does it take for a soul to truly be redeemed?" She asked as she then eyed at me. "I'm only asking because...have you really thought that we were given so much when we were alive? Most of us anyway. I mean...we were given so much. The gods gave us the world. Our God."

"So, what's your point?" I asked.

"As much as I disagree with everything Lucifer has done, what I took away from the time I was there...is that he does somewhat have a point."

I raised my left eyebrow. I wondered what was there to agree on from a fallen angel.

"Have you ever thought that humanity was given too much? Things like free will, or even these moral codes they choose to dismiss? Because if you think about it, the humans had done a great job building themselves up...only to destroy themselves again in the end. It's an endless cycle."

"That's an odd way of looking at it. I mean...I know humanity has had its problems. No doubt about it. And...I was no better. But that's what this universe is for, right? To have a second chance to be better." I said.

"That would be true...if people weren't so irredeemable." She said. "Lucifer intends to be a god, but not just that. He wants to somehow be a better God. He sees himself as a savior. The kind of savior some apologists would see him. Not as a force of evil – which he is commonly known for, but a liberator, a guardian. With all his harsh and dangerous methods, he's somehow helping them get better. He wants to make them perfect as gods. That's what he promised the Watchers. He's saving them from making any mistakes. Or the same ones. It's his way of giving them a second chance."

"How? By breaking their souls?"

"He sees that as the only way...to be saved." Bertha said. *"To live is to suffer. To survive is to find some meaning...in the suffering."*

"So, he quoted Friedrich Nietzche! Bloody good for him! What does he want? A cookie? An expensive harlot?" I said. "Anyone with an iota can quote from something they've read! Hell, I could quote from *Harry Potter*, if I wanted to! The point is...it doesn't make him in the right for what he has done!"

"But what if it was true?" Bertha asked. "Did Jesus ever stop to think about that? To ask why he was crucified? Why was he rejected by humanity when he only came to save them?"

"That's for him to think about. Not me." I asked. "You can't honestly buy into what he says."

"Dear God, of course not! What kind of person do you take me for, Kevin?"

"The kind of person that does things...in the shadows." I said, almost heated.

"I'm a Civil Force Detective, Kevin! Not a Paladin or an Apostle. I'm doing what I can to solve this. Occasionally leading the village folks, your family included, from those cursed villages are enough of a burden on my shoulders! And be thankful that despite my position, I'm out of the only Civil Forcers who stands up for your Order!" She then sighed, regaining her composure. "Forgive me. I digress. The reason I ask about Jesus is...sometimes I don't think he himself has figured out why he did it. Not yet anyway. Or anymore."

"Of course, he did. He... died for our sins, I suppose. He sacrificed himself to save us from eternal damnation. Although, I'm not so sure about what exactly he died for anymore...knowing that it made no damn difference in the world. Sometimes, I don't think he cared much for it anymore as well. And chose to escape it."

"But you forget, he rose on the third day. No matter how much wrong he was given, he gave love and forgiveness. He inspired all of us to be better people. He does cares. And yet...for some reason, we still haven't learned from his sacrifice. We didn't learn from his suffering. We have yet to put any meaning to it, just as we did for ours." She then engaged to my face. "Do you know Ecclesiastes 3:1-8?"

"*A time to break down...and a time to build up*? Aye. What about it? He fancies the Old Testament."

"He fancies the Bible. It's use. This is something he believed in. This is what inspired one of his methods. Especially the Legion. The only way we can be redeemed...is to be broken within. To break those tired morals holding us back from achieving true paradise. That way, he can build us up. Truthfully, we need to be imposed to pain, even if we don't deserve it. Even if it feels wrong. Suffering is what molded us, just as religion. It's a religion that is necessary. A tradition that is beneficial to our system. To avoid it...means that we are destroying the principle that created us to begin with. We seem to have the tendency to do that."

After digesting that, I didn't know what to think. From what I gathered; Lucifer is somehow trying to become a wrathful God. The kind of God some people would assume that is vengeful and wants nothing but ugliness for those who don't worship him. But I had a problem with that. Because it was a god that 99% was worshipped by a doctrine that lost its meaning. A god I once believed in.

I asked Bertha, "So... if I'm getting you right...you're telling me that the only way to be redeemed...is to completely be ashamed of our nature. To have our spirits break down completely...only for him to fix us? He only wants to redeem the spirits so that he can use us for his own rights! His ideals would be noble hadn't been for his own benefits! He doesn't care about them! He cares about what they would do for him alone! He's exploiting their faiths so they could be used to be mindless slaves! Tearing us down so we can go his ways! He wants us to suffer for his benefits! Just as those...bastards who hurt me...wanted me to suffer so that they can prosper! They claimed that they wanted to help me, but they only coddled me so that I can comply with every infliction of pain they gave me! They forced me to break my faith, so I can comply with their twisted one! So...if that wannabe god thinks that this is his way of building us up, then he's no better than those bastards who ruined me and those other kids! And he's naïve to recognize that!"

By her face, she was extremely stunned to hear something like this coming from a nineteen-year-old. She then sighed and said to me, "Forgive me. I intend to get very insightful when it comes to hearing from the opposite side. I'm sorry about what happened to you."

After letting out a sigh, I said, "It's fine."

"Perhaps...I've been a spirit for so long that I haven't gotten in touch with my own humanity. But me personally, I did find meaning in the suffering. And for that, I feel...free." She then looked out at the window again. "Attack therapy is what they call it. I was always accustomed in fighting. Whether it's fighting for what's right or just for an exchange of some remedy. But...I came to realize how hard the afterlife could be. Especially being...you know...being a lady in such a feudal system. I didn't become a C.F.D. overnight. You must go through trials to determine how strong your soul is to be in any battle. I had to be broken down at times. Here and in the natural world. I've accepted that. Because when you learn from a pain, you get to finally know what it means to truly be free. My soul has been rebuilt with a new one. No man or woman goes through life kind as a dove. I understand that now when I didn't before. Because every flock of vultures in life will take great advantage of doves. It's just how it is. Only it must be combatted someday. Somehow."

She then looked out of the window and said, "I know it's not clear. But it comes down to this; there's meaning in pain, Kevin. Agony has its purpose. Learning that...means that we're truly free. But that does not mean that I am justifying Lucifer's actions. You know that I hope. I just thought I explain."

"I know. I mean...Francis taught us about being open to...thoughts that aren't our own. But...I don't know. Is there a line when those views are...destructive not just to us...but to everyone?"

"Of course. In an ideological war like this, you find destructive opinions being justified all the time. Just because our enemies often have noble intentions, doesn't mean that they are excused. Sometimes, it's just an excuse to justify their cruel actions. Those Satanists think they have an ideal, but they are literally pieces of dark magic who were prone to think that they do. Lucifer makes us want to believe they do. But they don't. Still...what he strives for is interesting. And his way of going about it." I looked outside to see that we were now exiting the city and riding down a path to a more open area where it would be possible to spot a scholarly estate.

XXII

⬮

The Divine Lavender

Soon enough, we were on the way to the school. It was much further than expected, which made me question how Emily was able to get herself from there to the Khalservan. We passed under a gate that read La Divinum Estelle, which meant that we were technically here. The entire school was surrounded with a limestone fortress, surrounded by snow-covered mountains. And I was incorrect about it being an estate. It looked more than that. It almost looked like the Homestead, but it shined a lot more. If anything, it was like entering another city. Each building on the side of the road looked like Greek-inspired pantheons. The palaces were built on these snowy hills that was decorated with diverse plants and exotic flowers. The snow-covered flowers were mostly purple lavenders, alstroemerias, daisies, dandelions, and sunflowers. All of them were spread across the hills and were scattered like Mother Nature left a mess and chose not to clean it up.

Finally, we've reached the main building. From the front, it was inspired by Greek construction, particularly the Hellenistic timeframe. It was such a breath of fresh air when I feasted my eyes on its complexity and exotic aesthetic. It looked like a big pantheon with dark red pillars and orange tiled roofs. It was surrounded with pine trees, statues and from the look of it – enchanting gardens. When I stepped out, the aroma was somewhere between caramel and iced tea when I sniffed it into my nose. While it looked beautiful in the snow, I could only imagine how it would look like during the spring or summer. The songs of the natures were present, calling for one another.

I saw those two male angels guarding the entrance. I found it funny since it was an all-girls school; a bloody massive school, if I must say. I stood by the concrete, and I turned to Bertha.

"Beautiful. I know. It hasn't changed since I left."

"You were a priestess too?" I asked, mesmerized.

"Momentarily." She said. "I left for more...physical needs." It reminded me of Juliet when she said that. "Though I doubt that the saints would recognize me."

"Anyway, thank you for the ride. And for the information." I said.

"No worries." She said, smiling. "I'm going back to get the village caravan led. Perhaps, you could tell Francis for me to see if he's okay joining me. Or to at least use the C.F. on my behalf to find these Watchers. Sound good?"

As I nodded, she called for me once again before I can take off, "And Kevin?"

I turned to her. She then said, erecting her index finger, "Remember what I told you. It's for your own good. Whether you know it or not, I'm only looking out for you. And your family, of course."

"I...appreciate it." I said, trying to show my decency. "Thank you."

When she left with the carriage, I faced the gates. As an Apostle, I had to explain myself before I've gained access to the school. Which made sense because of everything that has happened. Afterwards, the floral engraved ivory gates were opened, and I was presented La Divinum Estelle for the first time. In the middle of the circular courtyard was a large marble fountain of a cloaked young woman raising her hands to the sun. She looked to resemble the Lady. But only she sprang big wings from her back. I assumed that it was Haniel, the Archangel who founded the school.

I began passing by the young women and girls who were all in very long silk dresses. Some of the older women were in white gown with cloaks, which I can only wonder if they were the professors and faculty of the school. Some were hanging out together. Some walked alone. Some sat by the fountain and read. Some leaned and lazed about. I swore that I even heard some of them giggle when they passed. Whether it was towards me or amongst their conversation was beyond me. To top it off, I was nearly in trance by the harps played by some of the girls on these Roman pedestals. I then passed the courtyard to get up the stairs. Each stair has sculptured angels columned from up the stairs to down. When I reached to the ornamented door, I was then stopped by one of the girls. She was a young light-skinned black woman with facial tattoos that looked to be inspired by Ethiopian culture.

"What are you doing?" She asked, giving off her accent. "Are you lost?"

"Um...I'm just trying to look for...Lady Sarah. I heard she was here." I said, seeing how getting to Sarah was a way to get to my friends. "Happen to know where she is?"

"She is by the Gardens of Arcana." She was pointing through the door I was clearly going through. "Just exit at the end of the class hall. You should be able to find her with these other fellows."

I then saluted her with my panama and grinned. "Thank you, love." I caught a brief glance at her face blushing.

Once I opened the door, I saw that it was crowded with other students. Some of these students happened to be angels flying above my head. I thought back to the name of the garden; the name arcana came from the Major Arcana Tarot Cards. Though I did not know too much of them, all I knew were that they were a suit of twenty-two cards in a seventy-eight-tarot deck. The ceiling was painted with Hellenistic influence and depicted a large gathering of women who I assume were priestesses of our lifetime. Glass chandeliers were dangling from above and glittered the ceiling with shined light. Each wall was plastered with large luxurious mirrors. How was it that a place that suffered two massacres managed to still have its beauty remain, I thought to myself in awe.

Even a lot of the students wore prudent loose-fitting dresses, ranging from Greek to Egyptian influenced. They were some Pagan inspired priestesses as well, which took me back to Bella and the other girls. Obviously, they wore cloaks due to the cold weather. I was fascinated with what I saw. I didn't even care if some of the girls found it strange that a young man dressed in all black was passing through the hallway. Through one of the classroom doors, I saw the inside of the room. It looked very much circular. I saw that the students didn't sit on desk but sat on these white limestone stairs that left a triangular space for the professor to lecture. The floor was just as the same as the hall; it was painted with colorful and diverse flowers in an almost surrealistic way. I saw that Emily was there, paying attention to the lecture. She was writing in her brown book with a blue quill. All the girls had the same. In fact, two other girls were sat on each side of her. I didn't even bother to get her attention. I was glad that she was brave to get back to her education. Having Frask involved in our apostolic duties was risky enough; I wouldn't want Emily – a young girl – to get involved. I suddenly saw her turn to me with a smile that grew across her face. As she gave me a wave, I waved back with a grin.

Afterwards, I decided to walk past the class and stride my way to the exit. When I finally got there, it revealed what looked like an outlandish parterre garden covered in snow. Consisting of two fountains, the place was surrounded by bushes, pine trees, and statues of angels playing harps. What took me for surprise (as well as briefly scaring the shite out of me) was that these statues were truly alive. I mean alive. I caught every motion of them playing the harps and making music to embrace the ambiance.

Once I was stepping from the steps, after I exited the building, I finally saw Lady Sarah again. She looked to be doing a lot better ever since the attack. She was dressed very differently as well. There were many beads and other fragments of jewelry around her neck. She had a blue sleeveless dress with a white cloak over her exposed shoulders. She still had the facial tattoos as before, but wore a unique headpiece that had purple, yellow, and white feathers crowning over her head. She was exotic.

I came down and saw that she was with Ted, Juliet and Frask. He seemed to be talking to her about something. He was showing them presumably from his bag. It didn't take long for any of them to recognize me.

"Yo Kev," Ted said, raising his arms.

"You're here," Juliet said as the rest turned to me.

"Hey guys." I greeted. I focused on the princess and said, "It's good to see you well, Your Highness."

"It is good to see you too, Mr. Princeton." She bowed her head.

"I see...that Emily is getting things done for once in classes." I said.

"Emily told me of the issues she was having with other students." Sarah said. "I promised to work it out with her. She is doing fine now. Thank you very much for looking out for her."

"It's no problem at all. It was more of her need to be surrounded by self-righteous maniacs that did her." I said with jest. "So, what is all this?"

"Mr. Douglas is presenting something very extraordinary. Something he is currently developing." Sarah said, gesturing to Frask. He then presented me with large prints of paper that depicted illustrations of something he was making. It looked almost like a robotic drone, but in an abstract form of a dragonfly.

Juliet stated. "We explained about everything that happened." She then said with her lips trembling, "And...about our Order."

"What?!" I asked in shock, fixating my eyes at hers.

"Oy, we had no choice! It was inevitable at this point." Juliet defended with a shrug. "I know we must keep him away from our turmoil, but at least make this an exception."

"It's okay, Kevin." Frask said modestly. "I took it well. In fact, I think it's extraordinary you, Ted, and Juliet are these chivalrous knights. It's like the equivalent of working with King Arthur. It's pretty messed up to think that you're not wanted anymore."

"Sorry we couldn't tell you sooner," I said. "We just didn't want to put you in danger."

"Hey, no worries!" He said smiling. "In this world, adventure is vital.

And what's living without a little risk? Right? And I'm glad to be at your service, especially hearing how all of you went through a lot. I may be merely a painter, but I am much more than what others would think of me. So please, don't hesitate to ask for my help. I want to add my support in saving this world too."

"Thanks a lot, Frask. It...it means a lot. So...what was your idea?"

"Remember when I told you that I was working on a side project? What if I were to tell you of magic so advanced that you would think that the future was just around the corner? In the case of this world, I mean. Well...I feel like this could be a baby step to innovate the after-life. And after what Ted and Juliet told me, I feel like this could be my opportunity. So...it bolstered me to take the ingredients I was given from Jeremiah. My old friends from the Neo-Romantic Movement spent years looking for certain herbs and runes blessed the goddess Cerridwen to create some form of advanced magic. I took the initiative to create something that can become a beacon of a new dawn for the entire Promised Land! Maybe the entire afterlife."

Taking a good glance at the diagram, I saw that it resembled a dragonfly. It had four wings. But it looked to be drawn from a different perspective. I said to him, "It...looks like a dragonfly."

"*Prototype Dragonfly* is what it's being called for now." He said. "I grew very concern about the recent kidnappings, and I wanted to help. I know that...I'm not the kind of person to get into a war or battle, but this world is full of chances to be something better. Especially as thanks for...booming my business. It means a lot."

"It no problem, Frask." I smiled. "Thank you very much, mate."

"I'm glad you approve. Plus, it gives me a good excuse to play with the new toys. So basically, I am inventing this to decipher signs of dark energy. Adding a compass. Maybe it could be a way to detect those who are using satanic magic."

Feeling genuinely impressed, I said, "This...This is brilliant! When do you think you could have it done by?"

"At least in two weeks' time. I'll need time to tweak some things and coat the codes properly. But...I'm making test prototypes to see if it would work once, I use the real version. In addition, I'm trying to make it compatible to lightkeepers, since their magic triggers and utilizes them. So...seeing how you three are...it could help. But don't worry, I'll make sure that I utilize in a way that it wouldn't be too dependent on your powers."

"How would we know if the persecutor is near?" Juliet asked.

"I'm integrating two enchanted crystals; red and green. Simple right?" He asked. "If the green light stays still, that will mean that it's definitely spotting item. But if it twitches from color to color, then that means that these sources of energy could be utilized.... well, from anywhere, which means that it wouldn't be a definitive one. The device would get confused. The Promised Land is a massive country. Heaven is bloated with many land masses. So, we have to be sure that what we find is true."

I glanced at Ted, who then said, "What did I tell ya; more than a painter, this guy is."

"This could change the course of history for the afterlife. At least in Heaven anyway." Sarah cheered. "Very well thought out, Mr. Douglas."

Frask playfully bowed. "Why thank you, Your Highness. The only thing I can do is to ask the permission of your mother the Queen to see it done. Seeing how the King won't be here for a while."

"Of course." Sarah said. "I shall make sure to tell her of this. Now I have more of a reason to speak highly of you, Mr. Douglas."

"As if having an amazing art shop wasn't good enough!" I said as a compliment. Although I couldn't risk Frask, it was good that he wanted to get involved as well.

"So, Kevin, what did Bertha wanted to talk to you about?" Juliet asked me. "Did you learn anything?"

"Learned a lot, actually. A little too much if I may add." I admitted. Looking frantically to see if any of the students were still around, which they weren't thankfully, I said to them "She was infiltrating in Hell."

They all gasped and widened their eyes.

"What?! Really?" Juliet asked, hoping it was true. "Are you sure?"

"That's what she told me." I told them. "She took that toxin that allowed her to go through the field that prevents outside spirits from entering."

"How...was she able to get it early?" She asked. "The herbalists from Goliath's Bay are far apart from finishing based on what we were told!"

"Turned out one Satanist had it, it seems. The ones we tortured after the gathering."

"Huh...well. She's certainly one to do things at first hand. So...what else did she gain from there?" Ted asked, getting right next to me to get a good sense of what I was saying.

"The victims imprisoned in Hell. They weren't kidnapped. They were sold somehow." I said. "Sold by fellow nobles who got out from Hell scot free." I saw the princess cover her mouth with her left hand. In distress, she looked away and faced the wrinkles of the water in the fountain.

"Seriously?" Frask asked.

"Kevin? Are you sure about this? This sounds too outlandish!" Juliet asked as she began pacing back and forth.

"I'm sure. This is what Bertha saw apparently. They're called Watchers, this gang of pseudo heavenly goons who are loyalists to Lucifer's New Heaven." I admitted. "The victims have been slaved. The mystics are used for something."

"What about the scepters?" Ted asked.

"Lucifer's relying on one of these Watchers to use them to get access to the Axis Mundi. Turns out that he wants the staff that is concealed in the temple." I said.

"So, this Angel you speak of is not alone in this pursuit." Sarah asked in desperation.

"No. There's two more: The Unicorn and The Phoenix."

"The hell is with these ironical names? The Unicorn? The Phoenix?" Ted asked.

"They sound like pennames to hide their identities. They could have anything to do with the plot as well. They're probably working away from the public eye so they can do Lucifer's deeds. Or God knows what." I said.

"So that means Sathanus and the rest were summoned by The Angel."

Juliet said. "Remember when we were there? He was supposed to come. But he delayed his arrival. Probably off to get some other scepter."

"Maybe he's plotting to get the scepter from Jesus only to get to the Axis Mundi. And maybe he had a mark on Sarah, for her to be sold to Lucifer." Ted added. "He has to be within this kingdom. And the only way we can find them is to detect the demonic energy."

"It seems like before we can go save the victims from Hell, we have to deal with these people first." Juliet said.

"It sounds...as if they want to get to what is in the Axis Mundi. Good job, Kevin. We might be getting closer to decreasing the mist from this plot."

I grinned slightly and nodded. I then asked Frask, "How fast do you think you can get that machine to work?"

"Hopefully, after the second prototype. I was too caught up on selling these portraits that I found it hard to multitask. But I'll see what I can do. Now that you've told me, I've got to get this made and completed."

"Who do you think we're going after first?" Juliet asked. "The Angel, The Unicorn or The Phoenix?"

"Francis will tell us. At least it'll give us something to do for once." I said. My eyes then caught Sarah in distress. She suddenly sat down on the snow-covered fountain and her eyes were locked at the ground.

"Your Highness? Are you alright?" Juliet asked.

She said nothing at first as she contemplated on what was discussed. But she then spoke, "It truly ills me to think that...Lucifer would do this. He's...lost. It's like being deceived by those you entrusted and cared for. Those people looked up to my father for blessings and for a will to live again. And the thought of them being tortured like this is..." She struggled to finish. Her gray crystal eyes began to form water.

She was then slightly sobbing. I placed my hand on her shoulder whilst sitting next to her. Wiping the tears from her face, she then gazed at me. I said to her, "I can greatly assure you that we won't let that happen. Not a chance. You have my word, Your Highness."

Her mouth curved into a smile. She next said, "Thank you so much, Kevin."

XXIII

The Sudden Inclination
for War

As soon as we got back from the school, Frask dropped us off at the Main Chapel before he could get into his house, so he can finish his project. He left the princess with one of his illustrations to present to the queen.

When we were getting towards the castle, I was skeptical. Though it was satisfying to know that we were finally having our possible leads, I felt nervous to recognize how I agreed to work with Bertha to get to Lucifer. I was thinking of many possible ways to make him understand. But at the same time, Francis always came to me as a man with a calm demeaner. Sure, he could be strict. And he didn't shy away from that when he lectured me weeks ago. But he was calm and levelheaded compared to someone like Dante.

As we passed the gates, we were already in the courtyard. It had better times during the summer and the fall. But regardless, it was still blissful to see it in the winter. As we entered the throne room/altar, it was different with the queen sitting on her husband's throne; though it made sense since she was taking his place and claiming it for a short period of time. She was still worthy of worship just as her husband. I saw Francis standing by her, playing Michael's role. It must be different from him, but not too different. And of course, the Italian bastard Dante himself was there as well. I hid my disgust within me in hopes to avoid his gaze and his urge to stir up another tantrum.

We stopped in front of the Queen and kneeled in front of her. Our heads bowed along with our stances. My eyes briefly glanced at Sarah meeting and reuniting with her mother, Dante, and Francis as well.

"You may rise, my fellow Apostles." Mary ordered. As we rose on our feet, she then asked, "What news have you brought forth?"

"Your Majesty...Kevin here was in discussion with the Civil Forcer Bertha June, who has returned to Valestone. She was infiltrating...Hell, acting as an informant." Juliet spoke. "She warned him of Lucifer's Watchers; a group of fallen spirits of Heaven that have been selected by him. They're somewhere within *this* world."

Francis eyed away from us and focused on Mary, anticipating for her further words. Mary faced narrowed with shock and eyed at me. "Is this true, Mr. Princeton?"

I sighed, not knowing how to respond diligently. But nonetheless I responded, "It is true, Your Majesty."

She leaned her back against the bronze throne, reflecting on her thoughts. She then asked, "So what of the victims in Hell?"

"They were sold into slavery by these people. They're working for him against their will." I said. "In exchange, they are plotting to take your scepter and enter the Axis Mundi to steal that Holy Insignia. Perhaps for Lucifer to get his hands on it."

"There's three of Lucifer's Watchers; The Angel. The Unicorn and The Phoenix." Ted said.

"So that means one of our own was trying to sell Sarah." Francis assured the queen. "They intend to be puppets for Lucifer. He wants to exercise his power through them. Destroying our monarchies."

"This invasive conspiracy is growing consecutively. They intend to release the beast we've repressed for decades. Each time, it appears every event seems to get worst. All of this just to pursue this new heaven plot!" Mary claimed unhopefully. She gazed at her daughter for comfort. "Sarah needs her father. This land needs their king, not some puppet ruler of Lucifer. Whatever he's formulating, we must arrange as well. This world should be a place of hope, not of war zones or war crimes."

She then turned to Francis and asked him, "Francis, would it be possible to talk with the Chief in the Happy Hunting Grounds? To see if they've grown enough to trade to the herbalists at the Isles of Ghai? We have to be sure to have enough for the entire Angel Paladins."

"Of course, milady." Francis said.

"I have to raise all guards to secure the shrines. On top of that, I want to have each noble of the monarchy questioned by Bertha. I know that the common spirit folk are...skeptical of the Civil Forcers now. But we have no other choice. We must be sure that Sarah was not placed on some...hit list by one of our own. Whoever is conjuring these invasions is here! We cannot allow it to go further!"

"Yes, milady. I'll also have the guards secure the shrine."

I then asked the queen, "Your Majesty, would it be possible if we can have a word with Mr. Bailey."

"Certainly." She said. "I thank you three for bringing news and continuing assisting my daughter's safety. You are dismissed."

"For once, you three didn't endanger us! Continue doing that if you please! Especially you, Francis," Dante said sarcastically before he scoffed, urging me to get up there and deck him in the face. But I composed myself. In my mind, I sincerely wanted to say out loud, *"Go choke on a salami, you crooked nose bastard!"* I knew I had to get on his good side. But the bastard's constant negativity towards us and Francis, specifically Francis, made it difficult.

As we bowed, we walked to the back of the throne room, reassuring, and settling ourselves outside of the castle's doors.

"What else you have to tell me, Kevin?" Francis asked. I felt my stomach being tossed around. Not because of hunger, but because of total nervousness. I didn't know how to tell him about my agreement with Bertha. And I certainly didn't want to speak of Frask's assistance, though I believed that he would be impressed as well of what Frask would offer. So, I had to at least tell him one thing at a time and expect another harsh lecture from him. I was hoping Bertha asked him as she assured.

After sighing, I told him, "Ms. June has asked of me to work with her to get to them. And...I agreed to work with her forces on her behalf." Here we go, I thought. I expected another oncoming harshness from him.

But it was a big relief when he said, "At this point, I approve of this. It'll be a first to work with the Civil Force. But...we'll stick to this issue. Let her group finally get the caravan to a safe place. I haven't been the best mentor." I sighed in relief.

He then said, "I know that you three have felt left behind. And I'm sincerely sorry for this. It's just...after what happened at that lab, when you crossed Sathanus and nearly getting killed by him, I couldn't help but have guilt. I don't want you to be killed."

"You're still thinking about that bloody lab?! It's done, Francis! We've got bigger problems at hand!" I nearly shouted out of frustration. Ted was holding me back.

"It's never done, Kevin!" He yelped in frustration, making me, Ted, and Juliet jolt back. Even though, it was mostly towards me. "When you're in my place, you'll understand! But as of now, you are not!" Afterwards, he let out a sigh and said, "I'm sorry. But I can't risk any of you three until we know what is capable for you. Lucifer's empire does not play nice."

"But we have powers beyond our limits! We could change things! We won't play nice either! Empire or not!" I assured with an aggressive voice.

"But they have consequences too. Just because you have them, doesn't mean you are not above the whole of nature. It empowers as well as kills when all is used excessively. You're using all your mind and heart. And they'll use that against you." Francis said, suddenly pointing at Ted. "Look what almost happened to Ted."

Ted and I both eyed at one another before we faced Francis again.

I assumed he remembered when he was told about Ted using his time bending power to stop us, nearly draining a lot of his energy. His fingers stroked both of his closed eyelids. Juliet placed her hand on his shoulder, stroking him in a calm matter.

"Four of us are the last of our kind now. And I won't allow you to break yourselves, only for him to play with you. I saw it happened before. On many occasions. Never again," Francis said.

"We dearly appreciate everything you've done for us, Francis. And we're very thankful. It's just a tough time now." She said, speaking on behalf of us.

"Thank you, Juliet." He said as he stopped stroking his face. He then faced the three of us. "I've lost far too many people truly dear to me... to that monster who has the temerity to call himself a man. And the thought of you three, and the priestesses, losing your souls to him, it made me ill. It made me very ill, to be honest. With or without your powers or skills, Lucifer and Sathanus are unforgiving. Nor their large network. They would want nothing more than to use your integrity to serve their will. The last thing you want to be is too prideful. They'll use that against you and your soul. Because that is what they expect. The more prideful we become, the powerful they become. And when we lose our powers, it'll weaken the wellbeing."

He then faced me. "So, Kevin, I want you to understand that I'm not trying to hold you back. I just want to assure that you don't get killed. Like I said, he's watching us from where he is. Because of his need to be God himself. The Chancellors are already thrashing on my back to prove that the legacy of the Apostles, and other knights, are not just mere child's play of vigilantes. And if I let you die; I'll never forgive myself. I won't."

He then glanced up at the sun that was hiding behind a curtain of grey clouds. He then said to Ted and Juliet, "And that applies to the both of you as well." I recognized how much he was sounding a lot like my father. And I didn't mean it in a bad way. From him shaken voice, I saw how genuine he was about what he was talking.

Inserting both hands into his pockets, he said, "With that being said, I shall inform Her Majesty of Bertha's alliance, so we could also look into this issue. I'll see you three soon. And again...I thank you for understanding."

"You're welcome, Francis." Juliet said as we all then walked away from the castle. I was reflecting into my thoughts about what Francis lectured me. I had to remember my reading. I retained how he lost the Apostles. So, I understood why he would obviously want us from harm's way regardless of our powers.

Ted and Juliet needed that information more than I did, so they would be able to do what I could possibly fail to do. I was eager to save those people from Hell so that I could finally be in peace. I seemed suddenly tending to the battle.

I was surprised at myself. Perhaps it came down to several things. Firstly, it was to get it over with so I could leave after getting myself into the mess. Secondly, to bring justice to the priestesses. I really hoped there wasn't more to it than that.

The week has past, and Christmas was around the corner. It was too bad Jesus wasn't in the city to celebrate his own birthday. Juliet went back to the nursing home and decided to stay there for the remaining days to take care of the priestesses. Ted was still working with Frask as a painter and presumably showing little bit of his project to him. Emily was back at her school, staying there. And I was still at the Khalservan with Algor. It felt almost too lonely with the three of us temporarily splitting up, having our thoughts to ourselves about everything.

Though I was still unsure about almost everything, I recognized how I've essentially gotten very attached to this world. And my interest in the Order has been decent. But I couldn't help but look back on what I've went through for the past few months.

One day, I was a child of a rich family. The next, I was a criminal. Finally, I was not only dead, but a knight. Sometimes, I felt as if I was losing track on whether I am honoring my parents or not. Or if I am close to my salvation. Or if I had yet to find my true calling in this world. There were moments when I was regretting joining the Order. Not that I was against Ted, Juliet, or Francis. Not even Jesus to a degree.

But it was more so the war I've gotten myself into. A war over stupid scepters, no less. A war over the afterlife. A war praying to eventually erupt. And I felt like there was no way out as I would've hoped. I felt more trapped than I did before. I would seek far ahead and saw how disheartened and unattainable it seemed. It was like I was doomed to be tangled in humanity's difficulties, opinions, and conflicts. Things I couldn't do anything about. Things that stop me from living the life of which I want to have, solitude from life's illness. I couldn't get to it on Earth; thus, I could find it in the afterlife.

Three days has gone by, and it was during the silent night of Christmas Eve. For the entire day, I played *Traveler's Progress* again, but with Juliet, Emily, and Ted when they were finished with their duties. The more I was beginning to understand the game, the more I was getting very good at it. I was the Good Voice while Ted was the Bad Voice. Juliet was narrating the story and Emily was playing the Traveler. Coming back to the game freshly made me recognize several things I didn't learn before I played it.

When I played it for the second time, I realized that you could play the game in two different ways. Emily could choose to play the game alone as the Traveler and make his way to either Heaven or Hell. In each path, there are various obstacles that would be preventing you to getting to your path. For Heaven, there would be various demons, evil dragons, and cultists trying to stop you. For Hell, there would be angels, knights, and sorceresses trying to stop you. The Traveler was equipped with several weapons such as a wand, sword, and a shield to help him on his journey.

In terms of the Good and Bad Voice, it was a different game. While the Traveler remained on the middle of the board, it's only up to the

Good or the Bad to reach to the Traveler. Whoever won will automatically drag the Traveler to a preferred location. And so far, I was doing far well than what Theodore did. The Voices would have their own obstacles as well. It would range from the Traveler's doubts or by some unfortunate fate. When I played last time, the doubts of the Traveler would constantly block me by rolling a less number between four or two. But since I was feeling lucky, I would roll much bigger numbers ranging from five to seven.

Once I have rolled a dice to seven, I finally reach the Traveler's path, meaning that I had a chance to lead him to Heaven. This resulted to me winning the game. It took me time to understand how the game worked. But it was starting to get to me.

During the night of Christmas Eve, I saw Juliet looking out the window of the dormitory behind Francis' desk. She leaned her shoulder against the column of the window. She looked even more enchanting in her white chemise that was dropped below her knees. I saw that her feathered eagle pet Alwyn has returned and was on her left shoulder.

Walking towards her, I complimented her by saying, "Good to see Alwyn again on a lovely shoulder."

She turned and blushed a bit. She began stroking underneath Alwyn's beak. She then said, "Thanks. Al and I were just hanging out here."

"Ha. That's what I call Algor by also..." I said.

"I reckon it would be short for his name." She said. Eying at me, she asked, "How is Algor by the way?"

"He's being his loyal and...goofy self as always, the brute." I said as I then stood next to her by standing on another column, looking out of the window. I then took a gazed at her, noticing something odd about her hands.

Something I haven't noticed before. She apparently had darkened red smears across her knuckles. I eyed back at her and asked, "How did that happened?"

"Oh...this?" Juliet asked, pointing out her knuckles. "Well, let's just say that I had a lovely chat with our friend...Lustina."

"No bloody way!" I said, amazed. I figured out what she did. "You mean you..."

"Aye." She said, which answered my question.

"Damn!" I said with a chuckle.

"You got that right." She said. "I had to set her straight some-how. Unruly witch! So...this was the result. She couldn't stop crying afterwards, the Greek boman (**the Greek idiot**)!" She then waggled her finger towards me. "Sorry, but no one should ever have to get away with bullying! I was told that she called the priestesses *witches* and deserved what they got. So, she got what she deserved for once! I even wrote her up, so I can have the baron remove her from the hut for good."

"Excellent!" I exclaimed. The bitch was going to finally leave. That truly lifted my spirits up. "You did the right thing."

"Heh...thank you. I hope so." She smiled. But her smile quickly curved to an upside-down moon as her head was locked downward.

"You seemed to be contemplating about something else?" I asked her.

"Aye. It's...it's about Francis." She admitted. "Last week, I thought that I would never see him like that. Seeing how...much stress he was under. Most of the time, he'd always keep it together. He's not perfect, but he always tries his best for the spirits. Despite their churlishness."

"You know, I didn't mean to raise my voice at him that day."

"I know." She said. "It's just that it almost saddened me to see him that way. It's Lucifer's toxicity that has spread across Heaven. It's been affecting everyone. Though, I try my best not to let it affect me."

"Me too." I said. "I feel bad for what I said to him. I feel awful. I...I just feel like I need to do something before...I don't know."

"I know. But you didn't mean it, Kevin. Give yourself some credit." Juliet said, now releasing Alwyn from her presence. The eagle flew, and shape shifted into smoke. She then said, leaning her back against the window curtain. "You're eager to stop this madness like all of us. And you want to do everything to help. To bring your own virtues to this world. You wouldn't have joined the Order if that wasn't the case. I mean I know you joined to be...saved. Aren't we all?"

She was right. I joined the Order to promote my family's name. But as much as I truly missed them, and was very eager to see them again, something was making me realize that my reasoning for joining the Order was becoming much bigger than just my own needs. I was seeing myself identifying with those I came across despite how differently they lived. I was tempted to tell her the truth. But if I did, I was afraid that she would lose respect for me for something that trivial. And perhaps I would lose the love she possibly had for me too. And it would scorch me internally to leave her for good.

So, I hid the truth by saying, "That's true. And I just want to do what I think is right for everyone, that's all."

She gave me a soft smile and looked down at her rose-colored feet briefly. I briefly glanced at her pale shoulder erecting from her gown collar.

"Sometimes, I often forget how much Francis went through. Re-inventing an order everyone thought was dead. Or a failed attempt. Or an act of self-righteous vigilance," Juliet said, which made me focus back on her. "Maybe it's because of how hopeful he usually is. That's what I admire about him so much."

"That's excellent." I said almost sadly, guilt blooming within my heart.

"When I joined the Order after becoming a priestess, he...was like a father. A father I wished I had. I never forgot the day he founded me stranded in Burgundy after I ascended here. He saved me." Juliet said, nearly tearful. "He never claimed to have all the answers, but.... his sole goal is to have us to see any life as more than just to worship the prettily words of man. To unravel something about ourselves we never got a chance to know. He himself is learning...which is what he wants for us. To grow. He taught me how to be strong. I would be devastated if anything would happen to him."

"You're right." I said. I sighed and said, "Me too."

I realized that I never gave Francis the credit he deserved, especially of what he dealt with the ungrateful Chancery. He was the one that got me out from that manticore dungeon. The man who proposed this opportunity when I felt lost. The man who took me in and saw me as an equal unlike the Chancery. The man who was making an actual effort to get me to see my family. The man who gave me a second chance to better myself. I had to give him that much credit.

And because of this, I felt like I had to leave the villages to Bertha.

For better or worse, the Apostles had accomplished helping me to be better. To be saved, in a way. And for some reason, I felt like I was beginning to have a purpose. I had to thank Francis for that.

XXIV

The Christmas Gift

On the morning of Christmas, I had more of a reason to thank Francis. And it was unexpected. Despite everything that's happened, it was good to wake up again and digest the same wistful feeling I had since I was five years old. After prepping up to get ready to celebrate with my friends, Francis was there in the Khalservan. I saw that I was still alone in the castle, assuming my friends were off exchanging gifts to one another. He stood next to his desk smiling at me.

"Merry Christmas, Francis." I said smile.

"Merry Christmas, Kevin." Francis said. "You won't believe what I've gotten from the dove today." He then reached into his coat pocket and pulling out a beige envelope. It had a red seal with a cross-marked on it. He then said holding it up, "Bertha got your family to a safe place. They're currently located in Corinthian County. One of the northern villages that is developing, but still stable to live. All those other villagers reside there as well. They're finally settling in. Never thought I say this, but I have to thank her for this."

I widen my eyes and they were nearly flooding with water. My heart was rapidly beating in my chest. It couldn't be true. "You're bloody joking?!"

"You don't believe me? They even went as far as to sending you a letter attached to it. Ms. June told me to give this to you." He handed me the envelope. "Here. See for yourself."

I took the letter with no hesitation. It felt like opening an acceptance letter for college. I gazed back and forth at the letter and Francis, hoping what he was saying was true. It was impossible to hold my breath and fight my tears. The letter read;

Kevin,

Words cannot describe how excited we were to see that you have responded. And I dearly hoped this letter went through. We are finally residing at a settlement known as Corinthian County. And we were hoping that, perhaps if you weren't overwhelmed by your duties, you could possibly stop by and spend time with us this holiday. We have been longing to see you ever since that day we had our human lives taken. And when we told that you were in Celestia, we were blessed and thanked God. I'm sorry that you couldn't live on Earth that long, but if we are together again, that is all what matters at the end of it all.

We love you and miss you dearly. It has been far too long. May God bless you and shine the light in the darkness.
My dearest regards,
Mom
Corinthian County, 1397 Byre Street

I was on the verge of breaking down without realizing it. I have been waiting so long for this since I first came to the afterlife. I looked up to Francis, smiling and chuckling to my overwhelming joy.

"Now you believe me?" He asked. All I did in response was wrap my arms around him and holding him very tightly. I stroked his cape, and I felt his hands stroking my back and my head. I showed my full appreciation as I embraced him, and he embraced me. I finally felt strokes of warm tears coming down my face. I got to see my family again after fourteen years. I was finally going home.

"Thank you so much, Francis!" I said tearfully. "Thank you! Thank you!"

"Consider this a Christmas gift." He said modestly. He then released me from my arms, giving me a chance to wipe my tears. Gaining my vision, I saw him put his hand on my shoulder.

"I feel bad that I...."

"No. Don't even apologize, Kevin." Francis stopped me. "Seeing you becoming much better as an Apostle, as a spirit, is the greatest gift I can ever have. You have done nothing but impress us. This was the least I can do; Ms. June included. If I were you, I'd pack. Don't want to delay now." He smiled at me.

He was right. I needed to take this opportunity. I raced from the common room and went straight back to my chambers. On the way, I've received making Christmas greetings from the monks and the other shamans in the castle. I busted my door open, excitingly grabbing my bags and other accessories to be with my family again. I greeted Algor with a Christmas greeting and stroked his head between his horns. Stroking it excitingly, all I was thinking in my head of how much I was ready, but nervous.

I packed my weapons, just in case of any danger on the way. I grabbed my bathroom toiletries and extra clothes. I hurriedly stuffed them all into my traveling luggage I was once given by Saint Michael. Once I was ready and prepped in my everyday clothing, I was intending to walk out. But before I left, I turned to Algor and saw him with his eyes narrowed. He began whining, implying that he was assuming that I was going to leave him behind forever.

A female monk suddenly showed up behind me and said, "We will be sure to take care of him while you are away. Don't worry. Spend this Christmas wisely. Your things will be moved to a new cabin at the Homestead."

"Thanks a lot, lass." I said as I then eyed at Algor. I kneeled in front of him to be on his level. I stroked on the side of his head, consciously knowing that stroking him would let him know that I wasn't going to be gone. I looked at him in the dark eyes of his and said, "Don't worry, buddy. I'll come back. Ted and Juliet will look after you. I must go. Plus, my mother is allergic to hairy animals. You understand, right?"

He whined, deliberately putting his head down on the curtain, with his snout facing the bowl of deer meat and water in the other. I was a little discouraged when he did that. But I had no choice. I vowed mentally to take him with me sooner or later to meet my family. But I figured that it'd be better if they saw me alone. It was far too personal. The friar reassured that they'd continue feeding him regularly when I'm away. Once I finally took off from my room, the friars were leading me to see where Francis was. When I went outside of the castle, I saw him waiting by a white carriage with blue accents on it. I looked back at the castle, hoping that Algor and the rest of my friends would benefit regardless of my late disappearance. After sighing under my breath, I stepped into the carriage and sat right next to Francis.

Eventually, we were on the way to the village. The terrains, valleys and meadows of the Promised Land were looking very beautiful in the snow. The sun was smeared with colors of blue, pink and orange surrounding it. We rode from the Khalservan through the terrains that were far behind it. I could stop thinking about it. When I was seated with Francis, I would often reach into my pocket and re-read the letter, hoping that every etching of ink was true. As excited as I was to see them again, I was exceptionally feeling a lot of weight within me. It has been fourteen years ever since that massacre. And I couldn't resist acknowledging all the wicked things I've done soon after. I figured right away that it was a red flag and would heavily impact them. I've committed a negligence, which I've soon – after being in the afterlife for six months – came to regret. At the very least, all I hoped for was for them to find it in their hearts to forgive me.

On the way, the snowy terrains and the various creatures that roamed mesmerized me. The shadows of what looked to be dragons, or

KEVIN PRINCETON - 361

some other breed of winged monsters, would circle around the mountaintops. On the snow-covered meadows, there were white crystalized horses running from once place to another in a herd. I was pretty sure that some of the other animals were hibernating until the spring, so that was to be expected. For the most part, at least it stopped me from being too nervous. I saw that Francis leaned his head against the window with his eyes closed shut. I saw how he was taken in by the smoothness of the ride. And he deserved that rest.

Later, as daylight was gradually approaching, he alerted me when he spoke. "Kevin, I wanted to...apologize for nearly shouting at you last week. It wasn't your fault...it's just that...I needed some way to vent my frustrations I had with this plot."

"It's fine, Francis. I might have jumpstarted that in the first place." I said. "I just wanted to find some way to help. I didn't...want to show my...fear for him."

"It's okay...to admit that, Kevin. Everyone fears him. But I'm thankful truly." Francis said. "It's the stress of doing this job. Especially being a leader."

"I could tell. I mean...at some point in time, you'll come to a point when you have to admit that you're overwhelmed."

"Humph...isn't that the truth?" He said in agreement. "Between looking out for the House of God and the Apostle Order, it feels like I'm taking care of kids." He turned and eyed at me. "And it seems as if all of this is happening because Lucifer is arrogant. He's sly and strategic, but still full of too much pride. That's both his strength and weakness."

"And it's no better with that bastard Sathanus serving him. The chap is nothing but a kiss arse." I added. "Any results from the herbalists?"

"Not now. It's a frustrating wait, but they're going to need more time to craft whatever they must wait for the herbs. Only then, will those people be safe. I just feel terrible about all this."

"Lucifer placed us in a dilemma on purpose." I said. "We can't hold that against ourselves."

"You're probably right. He knows exactly what he's doing with that...damn force field! God willing, we'll be blessed to take it down!

I feel terrible for celebrating currently. It feels...tasteless. Knowing that these people are still suffering there." He looked out through the window. "At least...I should feel better when I go to mass at the Main Chapel. Sometimes, I don't realize how idealistic I get time to time. Not realizing the reality that seeps into it. I've been too assured in seeing things go back to exactly how they were. The afterlife, Heaven, the Order...I don't know. I guess I have been caught up on the whole *renaissance* ideal of the afterlife as its promoted, not knowing the consequences of it."

Because I felt like I could trust Francis, I wanted to tell him something I've read about him in the Apostles book. I took a deep breath and said, "You know, I've read a book in the library...about the war. By Andrew Lockhart."

"Did you now?" He asked, his eyes turning from the window to face me. "I nearly forgot that it was there. I miss Andrew. I miss him dearly. I thank him for doing this. You must have read a lot."

"Well, I've read a good chunk of it. I've read when I can." I said as the carriage interior fell to brief silence.

"You know...the Khalservan was once intended to be a school for knights. It...kinda is, in a way." He informed while chuckling a bit. "This may come off as wishful thinking. But...I hope that there'll be a time when they'll be resurrected again."

I assumed that he was referring to either the conspiracy or the war between the Apostles and Satanists. That would be a smart idea when I thought about it. As someone who didn't get to go to high school or college, I found being an Apostle to be not only essential, but also somehow educational. "It already feels like school, but less indoctrination hungry. It seems like all schools here are. At least what I saw from La Divinum."

"That is what we want for Heaven. I'm glad you agree. I know most wouldn't agree. But that shouldn't matter." He said after a chuckle. He then asked, "So...what exactly did you read? Which part, I mean?"

"I've read that the Apostles that came before us died during the war. And how you were exiled from the House of God because of it." I recalled from my reading. "I could see why it affected you."

"I didn't think he would write those parts. But I suppose it was inevitable." He said. "Lucifer always claimed that it was his righteousness that made his group stronger than us. But he was motivated by hatred. And hatred is stronger when dwelled with. Not to mention that it seems that hatred is more appealing to the majority. Not knowing that it kills us. And it was all my fault that the Apostles died out." He then looked out the window and said, "I lost everyone I loved and befriended to Lucifer, as if causing two bloody mutinies against us was not enough. I lost my friends. My foundation. My home. My...my...my wife."

"Y...you had a wife?" My eyes widened.

"Catori Songbird was her name. She was everything that made me whole. My daughter too. Her name is Johanna." He said. "After the Apostles died, I was lost. I never told you this, but I was once a Chancellor. They allowed me to build the Order under the condition of doing tasks by their rule and making Valestone a Catholic rule as it was before, meaning that I had no choice but to disregard the other kingdoms and the realms that were in need. I soon decided to take the Order in my terms to help others, but they considered it as a failed experiment when the Satanists discovered us in Heaven after our exploits; something they were preventing. So, they had me exiled from the kingdom...until Jesus came to me in warning before he intended to vouch for me. It turned out that Lucifer placed a contract...on my family to get to me, since he discovered that I made the Apostles. Jesus had the angels sent to save them but were killed by the forcefield. Sathanus came to my home at the country of Burgundy where I used to live after moving from my realm at fifteen years old. He was trying to get an answer from my wife. When she refused, he summoned vampires. He had her tortured and violated. When I came to fight them off, it was too late. I was stabbed, nearly mutilated and left for the Void, but managed to survive."

He then swayed his hair back to expose the three dried blemishes on his neck. Afterwards, he then said choking up, "But my wife...my beautiful, graceful wife... she was gutted right in front of me, right in front of my little Johanna. It was too late for me to do anything."

He was holding back the tears he had in his eyes. Sniffing heavily, he said steadily, "I never intend to create martyrs. It's just that every evil I tried to eradicate...ends up catching up with me and those I loved. Despite what others said, I had to give myself a chance to rebuild the Order...because no matter how hard it was to get rid of this guilt, this grief, I couldn't let it stop me from honoring her in name. I owe it to her."

"I'm...I'm so sorry, Francis." I said with empathy. "But where is your daughter now?"

"She currently lives in a community of shamans in the Happy Hunting Grounds. They were kind enough to accept her. And it's much safer than Valestone. I am a good friend with Catori's father Chief Achak in charge of the Abenaki tribe. He's looking after her and helping to build the toxins. She preferred to stay there...since she wants to be like her mother. She taught Juliet herbology and nursing when they were both girls. I made a promise to always keep her in contact. I might see her this holiday." Francis said gloomily with his hand covering half of his face.

"She's the only family I have in this life, Kevin. And I don't ever wish for her to come across someone devious like Sathanus. Or for anyone to come across him. And I'm very proud that she intends to be like her mother. But I pray that she could become...what her heart wants her to be. And if I may seem like I am chasing something...too idealistic for the afterlife...it is not for my sake. It's for her. I want nothing more than a bright future for her in this world."

I was breathing a bit heavily with blood steaming inside me, raging at what Lucifer has done. But I didn't want to show Francis. So, I cooled down. "I understand. I'm sorry for what he did. But you know it wasn't your fault, you realize?"

"No, it was! I had no excuse, Kevin. To this day, it...hurts me." He said. "But by becoming the Holy Spirit and recreating this Order on my own right, I'm making up for all the mistakes I've made that day. I learned that to be a specimen for others means to outlive the evils that try them damnedest to get rid of you. The afterlife was destroyed for too long. It's caused division and fear across the realms. It made us forget how to live as spirits. It made us forget how to serve the gods. I pray that what we do...what Jesus does...will remind them. Maybe it won't be the same as before, but...it could be better. It could be better than this. I pray...no matter what it takes."

"It will. And...listen...if I do happen to come back, I'll help you kill Sathanus," I reassured, patting his shoulder. "You have my word, Francis. I owe you that."

He grinned and said, "I appreciate the thought thoroughly, Kevin. But please, I don't want my sorrows to bestow on your excitement to see your family. Forgive me. At least you have people you care about."

"I know." I said. I then eyed at him and said, "But when you daughter knows everything you've done, especially getting a rich kid turned delinquent like me into this so-called *dying* Order, she'll be proud of you."

He grinned. "Thank you, Kevin."

I nodded. But then another question came to my head. "I was wondering...what did you see in me to join the Order? I never got to ask you that. Out of all spirits presumably my age, you picked me."

He chuckled, "Well, you could say I'm a very picky man, Kevin. No, but the thing is...I'm an empath and since I am a psionic, I could tell who is one to think deeply. To speak and live mindfully." He eyed back at me. "Ten of the past Apostles were my close friends from the schools in Heaven we went to. We formed a clique of scholar students who were eager to know more about life's laws beyond books. It was after my home was...well..."

"Right. I'm sorry again." He nodded after I spoke.

"But I had a member...who was almost like you. Abraham Darius, Third in the Apostle Order. He was one of my most gifted but very troubled friends. He had a condition, almost like yours. Despite his profession, he often thought I was a fool for trying to extract this fantasy of knights. The idea of higher perception was new in the afterlife.

Everyone didn't think it was...possible for spirits to become angels. Some thought it was blasphemous. So did Abraham. But...he was also seeking recovery for his past mistakes. He wanted to...escape life's imperfections itself. He had a woman he loved and wanted to live far from civilization. Become an ordinary farmhand and occasional philosopher. He allowed his enemies to break him, furthering his condition. His soul was very broken to the extent when he began to believe those lies. He was inflicted with so much pain that all he did was fight himself. He considered himself a burden to everyone. He felt irredeemable. Like it was too late for him to change. He asked me to let him go...to leave our Order...when the time was right and...if Lucifer was defeated once and for all. But one night, he disappeared from the castle after I made that promise. We tried searching for him. Only for...."

"What happened to him?"

"He...he became a Satanist. He felt accepted by Lucifer, who promised him a perfected soul. He wanted the battle to end for good. We all tried to get him. But he declined our trust and disregarded our deal. Lucifer fed lies into his head, promising him a chance to live peacefully in the New Heaven, causing him to sell his soul. But it came with a price, his own humanity. He didn't see him as a man, but simply a vessel to pass Satan to in case he dies...just to continue his crusade. I was angry towards myself. I was trying all I can to help him. I tried to guide him into freeing himself from burdens. To make him understand that he didn't need to run from life but thrive through it and make the best of it on his accord. I could've stopped him from fighting himself. But it was too late. He...ended up...killing himself, to rid the body he was in. The procedures of Lucifer put him in so much pain that he couldn't take it anymore. I sent him to his death...like the others. He was just a man seeking change to find a good life...for the sake of his love. And I felt like I didn't do anything to help."

"I'm so sorry. I'm sorry for Abraham."

"You have nothing to be sorry for. Obviously, you weren't there." He said with a gloomy chuckle. "The fault was mine. I'm not as holy as I make myself to seem sometimes. Even I have my fair share of sins. And

I acknowledge the fault in what I created. That's when the Chancery doubted me. And there was a moment when I thought that ...they were right. Because I felt like I've put far too many knights, who were only common spirits, to death for an idea I thought I believed in. Something I thought that could make them strong and faithful in their own way. So, when I saw you for the first time, Kevin, I was on the edge of seeing you as a reminder of my past mistakes. Prior to that moment, I thought about giving up. But...as God spoke to me, I saw you...not as a reminder...but...as a second chance. A second chance to do what I couldn't do for Abraham or the others. And I know it wasn't easy. But...you gave me that chance, Kevin. You, Ted, and Juliet. You made me believe...that I can change things for good again. Prove the Chancery wrong! All I can say...is thank you."

"Wow...uh...you're welcome. I didn't think I...would make an impact on someone. Let alone you. I didn't realize I had it in me. But...for what it's worth, I'm glad I did." I smiled. I then said, "If I'm honest...you don't need to prove anything to the Chancery. Despite my mistakes, if there was anything I've learned from Earth, is that you could never give in to elites who claim to be for good, civility and nobility but are just as guilty for crimes they say to be against. Just because they are lawmakers and builders of society does not excuse them from breaking their own rules when it's fitting for them. They deemed my family as cursed. I was to be sent to an asylum before I died, for Christ's sake! They didn't even try to help me! The way I see it, the only difference between the House of God and them...is that you have the longing to be mindful and honest. Do what you must do for yourself and those you care for. You don't owe anyone else anything. Besides, what have they truly done for you...apart from trying to use your creation for themselves? You gave those knights, who were just common spirits, a voice...a chance to become something better from...within themselves. And they stood by those values. Even in death."

He nodded with a grin and said, "You're absolutely right, Kevin. And that's very thoughtful and wise of you. I hope I could do so. I'll say the same for you. And for what it was worth, you...served the Order well.

And it means a lot to me. I thank you from the bottom of my heart. And the Order is always open whenever you wish to return. Your rank progression is placed on hold until you return."

After I nodded and smiled, I pondered about everything I felt. Despite the excitement, I was battling myself. I wanted to truly be with my family again. The life I never got a chance to have, especially one without conniving people speaking ill of us behind our backs. But at the same time, I felt like I was having a purpose as an Apostle. I felt ill for having to leave Ted and Juliet behind, knowing that they were very fond of me. And I felt even bad for Francis since I was a light in his life. Despite everything I've gained, I was never meant to be an angel. Let alone a guardian. I just didn't see myself as such. All I wanted was to pretend what happened prior to the afterlife was just a bad dream. I wanted a simple life without any burdens. Having eleven voices was enough for me to feel that way. I didn't want any more from life. I gave up on it. Hopefully after I settle in in Corinthian County, I could rest. Once and for all. I still didn't find myself trusting in life anymore, whether as a human or spirit. Life wasn't going to accept me. *Why should I accept it?* I thought.

Soon after the ride, we were approaching to a gate that was cloaking the numerous small houses. When we were granted access to go through, we passed it and found ourselves amid a guarded village populated with small white and grey houses. The mountains were in the foreground, pushing the settlement. I was getting a very comforting fragrance when I stepped out from the carriage, holding onto my bag, eying at every house, church, small bank, market stand with fruits, vegetables, and naked hanging chickens. I was greeted by some of the folks; some were working the food carts whilst some were children playing and running through the streets. Most of them even eyed Francis and greet him too. I was slightly shaking as I was walking on the sidewalks, both excited and nervous. I really couldn't help myself. Crossing from one street to another, I saw that the street was accurate to the letter: 1397 Byre

Street. This was it. I had to go as far as to think about many possible ways to tell them that I was sorry. I also had to know how to accept sudden rejection.

I saw that it was a small house just in the corner of the avenue with other houses. It was facing the other corner of the crossroad. I glanced back at Francis, who reassured me by winking, implying that I was going to be fine. I turned away and got across the road. When I approached to the front door, right after I passed through the picket fence and past the lawn, I took a jumpy breath and knocked on the door. I really didn't know what to expect when I anticipated for the door to be opened. I removed my hat from my head to show modesty. I looked back at Francis for another reassurance from him.

But as soon as the door open, my heart was going down and down. It nearly stopped once it opened. After thirteen years, I didn't think that I would ever see them again in person. The first to open the door was my dearest sister. She was inched shorter than me and looked more beautiful as I had pictured. Her black hair was tied into pigtails, and she had on a woolen dress with a black belt around her waist. Her green eyes widened, and tears were flowing like rivers. Covering her mouth from gasping with her little hand, she was holding back from nearly crying when she saw me. Seeing her like this overwhelmed me that I almost felt my heart toggling further and further down, prompting me to let lines of tears come down my face. I couldn't believe that it was really my sister. My little pirate was all grown up to a fine young woman.

Coming from behind her, I knew right away that it was my father and mother. And both looked relatively younger, which was a bit strange. But I didn't care. I was very happy to see them all again. That's all what mattered. They smiled, and their eyes were also full of tears.

"Mum? Dad? Kelley?"

"It's good to see you again, Kevin." Mother said, which really hit my heart.

"You came! You came back!" She said whilst jumping on me with her open arms. We both embraced one another. It was a very long time since I felt her hug and heard her laugh.

She then took a good eye on me, analyzing me none stop. "This can't be really you, can it!? Am I dreaming?"

"You're not dreaming, little pirate. I'm here." I said to her. We embraced each other again and I said tearfully, "I...I missed you so much." I then got up to face my parents.

I tried to contain myself from shaking and frantically moving. Next, I poured from my mouth, "I'm so...so sorry. For everything! For what I did on Earth! I...I've failed you! I failed our legacy! I felt so lost, confused, and weak! But I'm trying my best to be good! All I want is for you to find it in your hearts...to forgive me! Please! I don't want you to give up on me!"

I suddenly found myself shaking and crying softly. Without giving an answer, both my mother and father pulled me in and embraced me in their arms. I felt Kelley embracing me as well. With all my energy, I held them tight.

"Don't be silly, son!" My mother said cheerfully through tears. "We would never give up on you! We were just sad when you lost your way. But we knew in our hearts that you would eventually come back to us, wherever place in the universe. We understood that you were just lost and angry, even though what you extracted was immoral and unjust. But we understood."

"It makes us happy to know that you've realized that. And we just wanted to see you again. That's all that matters." My father added. And he was right.

My father got up and went to Francis, who I almost forgot that he was with me. "Thank you so much, Mr. Bailey. You don't know how much this means so much to us. Are you up to have lunch with us? We offer it as a token of gratitude."

"Much obliged. And please, have the supper amongst yourselves. You have a wonderful son, Mr. Princeton. And he's going to do great things for this place." Francis said. "I shall leave you be in peace in your new home. I hope you find peace here this time. I just wanted to drop Kevin off and wish you all a very Merry Christmas."

"Thank you so much. We wish you a very Merry Christmas." My mother said.

Francis then eyed at me and said, "I...I hope we meet again, Kevin. I'll miss you. Hopefully we'll cross paths. Have a wonderful holiday."

"I'll...I'll miss you too, Francis. Thank you again." I said as he nodded and eventually strolled away from the house. It scorched my heart to see him go. I wouldn't think that he would truly take my word. And it showed how understanding he was.

I turned to my father who then said, "How about we get you settled? Your mother, sister and I were just cooking lunch, just in time for your arrival. You must be hungry by now!"

"That would be brilliant." I complimented.

XXV

◦✸◦

It's A Wonderful Afterlife

When I got into the house, it was very comforting and smelled like it was truly a good home. Of course, the living room was decorated with Christmas materials and goods. The wooden table was sat in front of a fifty-inch natural made fireplace that was plastered on the brick wall. They had a rectangular silver framed portrait that contained a moving romantic painting of what happened to be a blue dressed ballet dancer. On the left side was a big sofa with the Christmas tree. It reminded me of our own living room; only it was much smaller and fashionably old aged. I turned to the left and saw that the kitchen was there. On the stove, it appeared that they prepared a medium-sized turkey, cranberry juice, pumpkin pie, cheesecake, gravy, and salad. The oven was a circular stone chamber with fire blazing inside. Kelley was instructed by my mother to lead me to a spare room on the second floor.

When Kelley was leading me up the stairs, she was leading me to where they have prepared a room for me. It was a decent sized room surrounded by oak walls. There was a relatively decent sized bed on the right corner, facing the window. On the left was a big wooden cabinet. I went inside and placed my belongings on the chair of the desk that was on the left side of the bed. The desk consisted of two candles. I turned to Kelley, who was smiling whilst leaning against the side of the door with her arms crossed.

"I hope you like what you see." She said. "It's not as...you know...big as we had on Earth. But it's at least a nice change of pace. It's slow, but...in a good way. I like it."

"No...it's brilliant! Honestly!" I said eying her. She gave me a smile. "Just can't believe it's been that long. Fourteen years. And you've gotten so big! You were so small before!"

"I could say the same for you too, big brother." She teased. She smiled when she spotted me wearing the locket around my neck, "It's so cool that you still have that around you!"

"Of course, what kind of brother would I be to leave it behind?"

"Right. Of course. I was told by Ms. June that earthly charms with personal value go with you after your human life."

"That's good to hear that the world of spirits is not too harsh on materialistic things," I said as we then chuckled.

After studying me in a hybrid of shock and awe, she expressed, "And you look very...intense; with the whole...black coat, hat, scars, and all." She then looked closely and analyzed my lacerations. "How did you get those anyway?"

"I...I was attacked. By some demonic being." I told her without exploiting what I had in mind.

"No need to sugarcoat it; it's from those...Satanists, right?" She asked, which got me surprised. I didn't think they would know of that. "They've been plaguing the other villages we've ran from. Ms. June told us about them. Mum, Dad, and I were worried if you were killed by them. Especially what happened at that Gathering a while back."

"Luckily not. But I've seen better days. A friend of mine in Celestia helped stitch me up." I jested. Then I said, "That's why I'm going to protect you from them."

After she smiled, something prompted me to think about all the questions I wanted to ask her. Questions like if she was going to school? Or if mum and dad found jobs? Or how did they even get to the village after they were on an extensive pilgrimage to find a better one. But I had to go one at a time. I just got here, and I couldn't afford to mess it up again. At the same time, it would at least be good to know how Bertha treated them.

So, I asked, "So...how did she treat you? Bertha June?"

"She's been very good to us."

"You like her, do you?"

"Yeah, I do. I...It's been hard, Kevin. After we ascended here, we got to one village down the southern terrains called Malach Haven. It was peaceful at first, but there were sudden curses that befell like burnings, unknown deaths, and other plagues like myiases. So, we met Bertha and her group of Civil Force Detectives, who are studying the sites for evidence of the cause time to time. But she was the only one to help us travel with a caravan. She provided for us while we were traveling towards north of Valestone. She brought us food and supplies from Celestia to survive when we were on this journey. Those accidents would happen whenever we went from village to village once or three times a year. From the south to the west valleys. She wasn't always there, but she helped us through and kept us safe. She even considered me as her little sister. We would often have tea parties or read stories. She would call me *Sissy Kelley!*" She said with a chuckle as she then went to sit on the bed. I shook my head with jest, sensing Bertha's vague but charming humor. Kelley added, "It's weird to say this, but...even if she's older, she's one of the closest things...to a friend. No one would've done what she did. We got very close."

"That's very good to hear that. I owe her a lot. I was a bit ungrateful to her when she disappeared for a long while. It's everything that's been happening. It's been weighing me down. It made me a bit mad. I was worried immensely about you. Because all I thought about...in that city...was to escape it to find you...so we could start over. My way of making amends...for the shit I did on Earth."

"It's fine, Kevin. Really. She told us that you were in Celestia."

Letting out my breath, I said, "It's a long story. A long bloody story."

"I could tell you went through a lot." She said. I nodded in response.

"I hope you didn't feel like we didn't want you anymore, especially from what you did. Like I said, it's been difficult to keep you in contact since we've been constantly moving here for fourteen years now. But...I feel like here...this settlement...I think we'll be okay. We'll be okay. Finally."

I nodded and pondered. "But how are you adjusting to this...kind of lifestyle, if you could call it that?" I asked. "Better than I did, I hope."

"Yeah, I mean...it feels very...simplistic, ancient and...pretty practical. It's just that I never thought that I would be happy having less after having so much. Apart from wearing a corset for church. Those crush your lungs," she said as I chuckled. I continued to unpack.

"So...are you warrior of some kind or something? Bertha told me that you were in an order of knights." She then gasped as a thought suddenly came to her head. "Do you know if you've met pirates? Bertha said that there were pirates in the afterlife, but I haven't met one yet! My mind will BLOW if I ever see one! You know how I feel about pirates! Bertha read me this story about a pirate called Captain McKriddle, an old afterlife fable!"

I chuckled. Good to see things haven't changed. But I told her, "I haven't really met a pirate. But to answer the first question; let's just say that it's more of a knight's role. We're called the Apostles. I joined to...to save myself."

"Wait...like the Twelve Apostles? There's more?"

"I thought the same thing at first. But no. It's more of a society of guardian angels called knights that was named after them. Sworn to protect spirits. In the afterlife, there were twelve members before us."

"Oh..." She said, innocently curious. "Wow! So...you kill demons, monsters, and stuff? Including those Satanists?"

"Something around that range; mostly men who were once men. But they've become monsters. Like the Satanists." I said. "God, I'm sorry! I didn't mean to sound bleak there."

"It's fine! I'm just amazed! These only happen in fantasy movies or books!" Kelley said. "But now, it's a reality! And my own brother is an angel now!" I chuckled.

"I don't exactly have wings, but you could say that," I said with a grin showing all teeth.

"Kevin! Kelley! Lunch's ready!" Dad's call from downstairs alerted the both of us.

We eyed at one another and smiled. I failed to describe the unconditional feeling of being with my sister again. My own sister was seen by my own eyes again.

We got downstairs to the living room, only for our mother and father to gesture to the table, which was well organized with plates, forks, spoons, and knives. I could already smell the burnt flesh of the turkey from where I was. And by coincidence, my stomach growled as I felt it twisting and turning inside me. Seeing the table warmth my heart and took me back to a time where we would eat during the holiday.

I went to the table and sat down on the right end of the table. Mother sat on the right side of the table while Kelley sat on the left. Father sat at the other end of the table, his back facing the sofa and Christmas tree.

Father was holding out his hands and attached his right hand to Mother's and his left to Kelley's. I held each hand and bowed, knowing that they wanted to get into prayer.

My Father, with his eyes closed, and then prayed, "Lord Jesus, we thank you and glorify you for this special gift. A gift shown to us on the day of your birth. Getting us into this settlement was enough of a breakthrough...after these thirteen years of travelling across to live a simple and small life. But this is like a birth of our unity, our reunion. We thank you for bringing Kevin back to us, making us see him, seeing how grown, handsome, and different he is. My Lord, we wouldn't know what would've happened if we were to never see him again. And yet, here he is, sitting at this table. And we are thankful for bringing him into the light. And once again, thank you for the meal that you have made us work through with you on our side. We dedicate this supper to you and the reunion of our son. We also...pray that you look over those who are imprisoned in the Inferno, for we know that you will bring them back to the light. Just as you have brought our son...and a home to finally live. Finally, being in peace as we've longed for. In your name, Amen."

"Amen." We all said.

We began to eat. As soon as we filled our plates with food, we had every inch of it inside our mouths. But I began thinking as well. About everything Francis taught me about finding my own faith to God. I was quite unsure on how to explain it to them. I've always lived traditionally and it's what made sense for me at the time. But after everything that has happened, I was not sure how to reveal it. And I wouldn't want to make my father or mother, or Kelley discouraged by coming out of the "faith-oriented" closet. Plus, I didn't want to ruin the moment. The bad voices tried doing so, saying that I hated them. Or they hated me. Just like last time. *"You will not last long. They won't. You hate them! You do! They hate you more!"* I clutched my left hand to block them out, turning it into stone and prayed silently to God for them to go away. I desperately wanted to slam my left fist on the table, but I couldn't bring myself to do it. I didn't even realize that my mother took notice.

During our supper, with most of the food being eaten and stuffed, my father stood up from his seat and went underneath the tree. He picked up two different presents; one was small, and one was almost big. Mum and Kelley both gasped, pretending to be shocked as a joke, and they both gazed at me. I turned my frame to face what Dad had in store.

"I know it was your birthday two months ago too." He said. "The big one was for your birthday. The other one is for today. Which one would you open first?"

I was overwhelmed to the point that I let out my breath. I then said, "I feel bad that I didn't get you guys anything. If I've known where you were, I would've gotten you something. Plus, I had little money to get you something nice. I was quite busy these days."

"Son, seeing you again is the best gift I could ever had. Your sister

and mother feel the same. Plus, we're satisfied with what we've gotten."
He said, regarding the two women who nodded and smiled. He then
eyed at me, "So...pick what you're going to open first."

"I ...I suppose I should pick the big one first." I said, as I began to unravel the green sleek wrapping paper. When I gradually unveiled it, my
eyes grew big, and my mouth widened. My mother and father giggled
at my reaction. It was a guitar, made with dark oak and five courses of
gut strings and gut frets that were easy to move. I've seen these types of
guitars in the afterlife, especially in Litler's. I saw that there were note
between the strings of the instrument. When I took a glance at it, there
were musical notes I was able to learn. I recognized the lyrics from the
songs from Dead Can Dance.

"Well...what do you think? Your mother thought that you'd be a good
guitar player in your spare time. She copied every note from every song
Dead Can Dance sang. You could learn to play them." Father said.

"It's known as a Baroque guitar; I believe with my musical knowledge. What do you think, son?" Mother asked.

"I love it! I truly do! T...Thank you." I said hugging my mother,
who also embraced me. When I was done, I opened the other present,
unveiling it from the red wrapping paper. It was a journal with a cover
made of hard and tanned leather, with a customizable quill.

"Kelley got you those, knowing your love with sketching. You could
also use it as a journal or anything you desire." Mother said, as I had no
hesitation to hug Kelley.

"I haven't done this in a while since I've been here. I've been skeptical
of pursuing my craft. Thank you so much, sis!" I told her humbly.

"You're very welcome, Kevin! I'm glad you like it!" She said cheerfully.

As I let her go, I eyed at the entire family and said, "Honestly, I
didn't expect this. I mean...how is it that...after all I've done on Earth,
soiling everything we fought for, how could you still award me with
gifts? I...I really do appreciate these, but I don't deserve them. You
deserve...way more than me. I mean it."

Kelley's face went from being lightened to slowly becoming gloomy.
I felt bad for what I said, but I really felt like I didn't deserve this

kindness. I felt like I was only patronizing them like I was some bloody charity case.

"Listen carefully, Kevin." Father gazed at me with his hands clutched onto my shoulders. "You've already apologized. You've already shown how much you have changed for the betterment. You have no idea at all about how much we missed you! You have nothing else to be sorry for...because you have already been forgiven. We would never hold what happened against you. No matter what happens, we will always love you. Because we knew that you would always come around. If there's anyone to be sorry...it's...it's me. I wish I'd got us all out of that...chaos together. Things would've been different."

"We all wished that night turned out differently. Truly. I cry about it almost every day as it pains my heart to talk about Kelley's performance. All because of what it led to. But all what matters is that we are together again. And nothing will break us apart ever again." Mother said with her hand on his back. "You mean everything to us, Kevin. We will never leave you. Never. You understand?"

I nodded after digesting those words. Water was gradually growing in my eyes, but I tried my best to hold them back. I didn't want to see myself weep again. I embraced my family once again, huddling in the living room with the fire crackling.

Later, it turned out that my father had another surprise for me. After I took it upon myself to help my mother and sister clean the living room table after lunch, Father took me to the backyard, which was big. It had a small garden up in front of me. On the left side happened to be a small stable. It contained a horse, free from a carriage, eating from the barrel of hay. On the right side was a shed. It had a laundry yarn attached from the edge of the roof to the branch of the tree that was in the middle of the field.

Father turned to me and asked me to close my eyes. When I shut my eyes, I waited in darkness. But from the sound of the horses wailing, it would seem like he was getting something from the stable. I could only find out what it was. All I could make out were sounds. With my ears, I heard sudden trotting and hooves scratching through the snow. Big huffs, nickers, and snorts were made.

I could only assume that it was a horse. My father said excitedly, "Okay son, you can open now!" Once I opened it, of course I was in completely disbelief. I thought that 'No way, that's impossible'. It was perhaps the most beautiful thing I have ever seen displayed over me.

"I know it's not exactly like a car, but...it sorta is!" He said, presenting me a horse. But it seemed like a much special horse. It was a size of a regular horse, but it had a strong and big built. It had a beautiful black coat with a dark grey shaggy mane. Underneath its head was a hairy black pelt around its neck. Two of his back hooves were crystalized white. The saddle was grey leather with red accents, full of saddlebags and accessories. It was safe to say that Algor will have a new friend. Now that I have taught about, perhaps I should've introduced Algor to them.

"What...kind of horse is this?" When I asked, he also offered me a tiny wooden cylinder. Possibly a whistle to call upon the stallion.

"An Icelandic warmblood peg breed called a pertlow. It's a race and war peg. It is one of the three breeds. This one is a boy. A feller who sold me this told me that this breed could help riders travel through space and time in the afterlife depending on how fast it could run. If necessary, he could travel from, place to place three times. You can even call him at will with that whistle...and it'll appear. It's a very smart animal, so name any place you wish to go, and it'll lead you to it in a flash if he's well fed and not tired." Dad informed. "His name's Aventurine, named after a spiritual crystal. Who would've thought that you would come across this...in a place like this?"

"Aventurine. Lovely name. So...you're saying..."

"Think of him like a car since we weren't able to get you one. Or Harris. Especially because of what happened." He said gloomily. But he then said cheerfully, "But hopefully, this still counts. I hope you like it!"

"I bloody love him! It's awesome! Thanks father! Thank you!" I hugged him and looked back on the beautiful steed once more, endured by its beauty. After I hugged my father, he encouraged me to pet the creature, but I was hesitant. I would want to aggravate it. But little by little, each foot would gain closer and closer to its snout. Once I eventually got to his personal space, I felt his smooth and pillow like pelt. It snorted happily, knowing that it could trust its new owner now. I looked into its misty eyes as they brightened when he saw me.

Eventually, we sat together on the table and watched a beautiful performance from a colored ballet dancer displayed on the fascinating swirling portrait. When I saw it, it was weird at first; simply seeing scenes change very gradual and smoothly. The dialogue would shift and change depending on the scene. But it felt mesmerizing as if it were like watching an actual movie. Of course, eventually television would be built. We all sat side by side, facing the large, decorated portrait together. It felt like I was back in Long Island again.

Four weeks after Christmas, after settling in my new home, Kelley and I played a boardgame about Cthulu surprisingly. It was one of her Christmas gifts. It reminded me of *Candyland*, but only with Cthulu. It was called *The Balled of Cthulu*. You had to play as two colonial archeologists who must escape Cthulu's temple after deliberately disturbing him. Why would we play as two complete idiots – who shouldn't have thought of that in the first place – was beyond us. Cthulu was an entity created by H.P. Lovecraft, who happened to be one of my father's favorite American authors. I remembered on Earth, he introduced me to some of his books such as *"At the Mountain of Madness"* and *"The Shadows Out of Time"*. These were books he read when he was at the battlefield. I never considered him as my favorite, but he was a fascinating artist to study.

After I played, Kelley would go out and help wash the clothes with father. Meanwhile, my mother was teaching me how to play the guitar with a few chords. I positioned the guitar as she did. Knowing how much younger she looked compared to her human form, she looked like she came straight out of her album covers. She told me that stroking the chords with each finger on the string would give it a mesmerizing and unreal effect. We were playing the cords to Mesmerism; another favorite song from Dead Can Dance. I gazed carefully at the musical notes placed nicely on each triple lined section. I plucked each chord carefully, feeling the vibrating sensation of each string, as my mother was helping me by walking through with it. Eventually through the hours, I was starting to get a grasp of it. I was a bit sloppy, but I was beginning to get it little by little. All it required was much practice. And thanks to my Apostle skills, I was sure that the process wasn't going to take long.

Further throughout the lesson, when I was gradually starting to make my way around the instrument, I've managed to ask her about the meaning of the lullaby she sang to Kelley and I when we were children. And to my surprise, I turned out to be right. She told me that when she grew up in an abusive household, her father wrote the song to help her escape her harsh reality. She dreamt of a way to find hope in a world where it bombards you with trials and tribulations. A song called "Suddenly, There's A Valley" inspired her. She loved the version by French singer Edith Piaf.

When she listened to that on her father's radio (who was the only one who cared and supported her dreams of being a musician), she was entranced. It was a well-known song, but she told me that something about Edith Piaf gave her a sense of hope that was enhanced by heavenly light. Not because it was a French version. Piaf's version of the song was ethereal and made it feel as though that you can truly find this wonderful place far from our own. It motivated my mother to write her own original song, which helped her get through the harsh instants in her life in England.

After we were done, she then said to me as she held her guitar graciously, looking at the notes, "Madame Edith Piaf...did you know she inspired me to find my passion in singing? It's how your father and I first met...when I sang this in a club in Manchester, where you were born. I was seeking to establish a career. I swear...meeting your father felt as if...I were rescued by a cavalier after being locked in a tower. Along my departure, my father's blessing."

"That's beautiful." I said back to her, holding my guitar by the neck. "And as for Ms. Piaf, she suffered greatly, I remember."

"Her story sometimes feels like it aligns with mine, not to sound conceded. I'm sure she had to deal with cowards hiding behind newsrooms as well. Only, she managed to...die peacefully," Mother said almost in gloom. Holding onto the guitar neck, she continued, "I knew that at one point I wasn't going to live long. But...I've had dreams of that night. Especially on the way here. Because of how...unreal it was. I could only pray that it doesn't repeat; in one form or another."

"Me too," I agreed wholeheartedly. "Despite her suffering, she seemed lucky."

"She went through so much in her life. Yet, she managed to have spirit in her vocals." Mother said, glancing back at me. "Every time I was in a constant state of conflict with my mother...you and Kelley's grandmother...I would go to my father in his room. He'd wipe the tears from my face. He would pick up his acoustic guitar, open these notes, and sing this song to me as I rested on his lap, drifting. He told me that there was a reason behind every song ever written. From the lyrics, reflecting on idyllic journeys to paradise and happiness, it was clear why Edith adapted it," She trailed off to harmonically humming the words with her eyes slowly closed: *When you think there's no bright tomorrow, and you feel you can't try again, suddenly there is a valley, where hope and love began.*

She then opened her eyes and said in the most very softest voice, "This is how I came to write that lullaby...for you and your sister. Think of being in a mountain by yourself. A lovely form of solitude to be in tune and peace with yourself. I need to see you both...in peace. After the bullies, the shooting, I want nothing more than to see you happy...as you were before. That is the meaning behind the song."

It saddened me as I noticed that it was a while since I was very happy. As I looked down in contemplation, I soon asked, "Do you think...that I will find hope and love again? Out there in life as I do here, I mean."

"Of course, you will. And you can. This world is what it is for, my son. It could be scary as well, but I know enough to see light in you. One that will thrive into the dark, like thriving into the woods of camp." She said with a smile. I chuckled as she referred to our camping trip in Ramapo.

She continued, "Life is very big, my son. My father told me that there are two types of broken men. There are broken men who prefer to be broken and wish to see life broken like them. And there are men who are broken but don't stop fixing themselves to help life. No matter what they are up against. Everything that you thought you've lost...you can find them again. After I died and came here...all I ever wanted was for us to be together again. As a family. All I wanted was to see you again." She then softly stroked the left side of my face. It prompted me to embrace her hand on me. "And here you are. And your sister is not alone anymore. She's always looked up to you."

I smiled, choking, and holding back a stimulation of sentiments. I softly closed my eyes to thank my God in silence. But then she struggled to keep her smile as if something else crept into her head. As she released the guitar next to her chair, she then said, almost choked up with her hand clammed together on her lap, "I only wish that...I was a better mother. That world was vile, not allowing me to give you and your sister a future in it. I...I failed to make that world your home. I'm so sorry. Please forgive me."

I then said to her as I reached my left hand to conceal her hands, "It's not your fault. It's the world down there. The world is to blame, not you. You still can make a home, Mother. I still can. Kelley too. Being with you is home. And nothing will destroy us ever again. Not now. Not ever."

Gripping onto my hand, she replied, "You're right, my son. Now I can be in peace, knowing you are in the same world as us. We will always be together."

She then embraced me in her arms. I hugged her back. "I promise you that. We could finish what we started. You'll get to go to a better school, a good job, help us around and to pursue a career in the arts like before. Bertha told us of the *Grand Arts Academy* just east of here. It's a start. For you and Kelley to take classes to help you. Sound good?"

"It's all I could ask for. More than anything. I...I love you, mum." I said.

"I love you too, son. I always will." She said as she wrapped me around with her arms.

Later, it was my turn to feed my newly owned mount. Father would teach me how to do so. I would stake the hay in front of Aventurine after removing the snow from it. He would eat and snort all at one. I stroked his soft neck underneath his white pointed beard. It was a way to calm it down. According from what I've learned from my father, Aventurine would have to be fed regularly to gain strength to travel. And to be fit to ride overall. By the large whirly light blue veins that shined across his body, that is when I would know that it was being fed.

It reminded me of Eastbound. His large explicit veins would glow and traverse across his pelt. I was told that if he wasn't fed enough, it would stop glowing, meaning that he would soon evaporate. He even introduced me to their horses. His horse was a red colored turkoman; like Ted's Newman. Mother's was a brown mustang. And Kelley's was a beige Andalusian horse named Lucy. All of them were unique as well. And we fed them too. Aventurine had got along with them, despite him standing out.

Soon after we also helped a few other neighbors in the village who turned out to be amazingly kinder compared to Earth, even attending a local church for the first time in a long time, I washed up and went to bed.

I tucked myself underneath the covers. The inching creek of the door, only to unveil father, alerted me. I fixated my eyes on him, wandering if he was going to check on me, which he essentially was doing.

"How are you doing, kiddo?" He asked, leaning against the door.

"I'm doing fine." I said. "These days have been very satisfying. I feel like I'm sane again. I'm just thankful for being with you guys again."

"I'm glad you think so." Father said as he entered. Before he sat on the chair, he eyed at me gestured his hand to the chair; implying that he wanted my consent to sit. When I nodded, he sat down and placed his left leg on top of his right with both hands folded.

"So...Kelley told me that you were a part of some kind of... society of knights."

"Yes...but it's a good society." I poised, a bit nervously. "Of...guardian angels."

"Don't be nervous, son. I just find it interesting, that's all. Were you fond with this group?"

"I...I was. I felt like it's helped me to be better than who I was." I disclosed. "It made me into an angel, despite not having wings. But...it hasn't been easy."

"What about the Holy Spirit? Mr. Bailey? I thank him a lot for providing furniture and supplies for the house. I owe him as much as Ms. June."

"I know. He's the leader. He got me into it to help me." I answered. "But...I made a deal with him...to leave so that I could be with you again and start a new life with you. Start by going to that school you and mum had planned for me and Kelley."

After staying quiet, he nodded in satisfaction. "I'm very proud of you. Bertha told me how you rescued those Pagan priestesses. It must have been uneasy, but I am very proud of you for saving them. I guess now this would mean that we have two fighters in the family. Although obviously I'm a veteran of that life."

I chuckled, "You could say that. I...I joined...to perhaps...get our name out there. Our foundation to find a home...and to be respected in this world. Plus, I had to prove myself."

Grinning at me, he said, "After all these years, your loyalty to it still hasn't changed. I'm so grateful to have a son like you." I shied away with a smile.

"I assumed that your step-uncle...John...he didn't want you around?" Father soon asked. "When you were a human."

I gazed down and said, "Aye. He just...turned on me. As if I was nothing. Only our step cousin Victoria wanted me around. How come...he hated me so much?"

After he sighed, Father said, "He hates me. He saw me in you. And he couldn't stand it." He leaned forward and continued, "You see, your grandfather...he had an affair with another woman by the name of Claire Edwins. When John was born, he...just neglected her as if she was nothing. He didn't even bother to raise John. So, Claire raised him on her own. It figures why I never saw my mother. Your grandmother Henriette Princeton. She was devastated, filed a divorce at a heartbeat. But she never had full custody of me. He was violently against her."

It finally made sense to me when he said this. So, I let out a gloom filled sigh and said, "Family is complicated, huh?"

"Can't argue with that, kiddo. A blessing and a curse. I'm sorry that you and your sister don't have the nicest ...family history. This is all because of your grandfather's criminalistic days before he was mayor. He crippled our reputation as a humble family that came from Hospitaller Knights who served the people. Of course, we raised you both to be good and better than he was, but we wanted you to have good childhoods and lives. Something your mother and I never got a chance to have. But...the world didn't want that."

"Guess they didn't want much of anything with us. Or anyone like us," I added. "All thanks to our...I don't wish to consider him as a grandfather. He cursed us."

"I understand, son." He then left out a breath. "Before I met your mother, I joined the army when I was twenty-one in the Lebanese Civil War. My father was dependent on me to fight as he did. He claimed to be devoted to God. Yet, showed no evidence of it. He was discriminative of others because of how they demoralized America. He was always a very patriotic man and the New York City government... the entire state.... saw his bias towards others. From financial crisis to residential issues, he caused some damage. Still, I always wanted to honor him, so he could be proud of me. So, he wouldn't have to think that I was a mistake to him. So, I took it upon myself to enroll in the army after leaving my home in Woodbridge, New Jersey. But along the way, I lost my friends. Those oppressors killed the people I've managed to bond with during the war. So, I was full of hatred and vengeance. All I thought about was to rein hell upon those who killed. But then it hit me when I was nearly forced to execute one of the Syrian soldiers. I saw that...he had a family; a wife with two sons and a daughter. Do you know what else happened?"

"I assume...that you didn't kill him." I replied.

"Absolutely correct. I don't expect you to adapt this action. I just want to show the kind of person my father wanted me to be. War often makes you forget who you are...because it changes you. That's probably what he wanted for me. So, when I was twenty-two, I met Harris...who served as a military chaplain. He gave me two paths to choose; to do things to make my father happy...or to find my own purpose and servitude to God. Thus, I chose to leave the army behind when the war slowly ended. But it was a struggle to find my calling soon after. All because my father expected me to be a vessel for what he valued for his country since he fought. He's not a good man and I try so hard not to be like him and raised you not to be like him. No matter how much you completely dislike those who oppress you, did you wrong in many ways – you can never lose yourself. Never allow that hatred you have dictate your actions, your soul, or your life. Those things deteriorate who you are like a cancer that must be removed to be whole again. It almost removed me. I don't want the same for you."

I pondered. This was why I had to leave the Order. I then asked, "Did you have...resentment for your father after he...disowned you?"

"I did. A bit. But it was his choice. He chose to be angry at everything. And it's his choice. I forgave him to save myself from the burden of hating him," He said. "My biggest mistake was trying to be like him. To live for him. And I failed to be myself at the time because of my desire for his approval and the country's approval. I wanted a father to love and learn from. But that moment in Lebanon showed me that I didn't need to live in his shadow. He even called your mother a whore when I intended to marry her. He made a lot of damage in the city...only for me to fix, despite the media outlets making me out to be as bad as him based on pure resentment for what he did. I know I should've told you this sooner, but how could I tell this to two young kids?" He let out steam from his mouth; a sigh that sounded hardened and almost saddened. "So...whatever enemy you are fighting, whether it is external or internal, don't let them make you into their image. Be led by God, son. Not men. Society will deceive you like your grandfather did to me. God could never do that to you. My father imprisoned me...only for him to free me that day. Remember from Matthew 7:15 and Psalms 27."

"I will." I made a promise after I pondered. I hoped that I did, knowing I had no control of myself sometimes. "It's hard to forgive...after all they've done. I wish I could have the same love for others as I do for you, Mum and Kelley. But...I just can't. How do you make the world do good?"

"You don't. Do what *you* think is good for it. But never do it for pride or validation from anyone. Despite being held back, over trivial rumors and political decisions, I was establishing that campaign to see what I could do to make sure that no child would suffer the way I did. I'm not sure how would I start that again here, but...I will figure out something as soon as I find work. Still, it mattered to me. It was right to your mother and I to help those who wanted it. It was about helping the world, not to forsake it. Especially according... to God. If God appreciates and loves you, it's more than enough to ratify what you want to see in life. It's bigger than what we can offer you. When we are not always around, he is. Remember, son." He said in a firm manner. I nodded.

"When you were a criminal, I was just...sad. It was what I feared. It made me feel like I failed as a parent. It reminded me of your grandfather. But in your case...it was understanding. I wouldn't go as far as saying that they were justified. Especially committing robbery. But...we understand." He said before he sighed once again. "We heard what happened...at that foster home. How you were mistreated. And you've developed the condition because of it."

"I did." I said as I felt the sadness bloom within me. I never wanted to remember that. "And it destroyed my faith. It destroyed who I was. And the voices won't leave me alone. I truly wanted to be better. I wanted to be normal. I wanted God...to help me. But...I was broken. I'm just so bitter at the world...at him...for not letting me be a byword of good...for Kelley or...anyone. It's the reason why I truly wanted to believe in God. But...I felt like...he failed me. Or I failed him. I don't know. Sometimes, I believe them; the voices." When I said this, I gawked at my father's eyes, which began to water. My heart felt sharp and squeezed when I saw him look away as he began to shudder and break. I heard him softly whimpering behind his hands. My nerves felt loose and trembled.

"I'm...I'm so sorry, Kevin!" He said, choking back tears. He looked back at me. "When Ms. June told me of this, I...felt so ashamed and hurt. I wasn't there to stop it! I wished I were there! I shouldn't have helped their business for relevancy! It didn't need to be this way!" He covered his mouth quickly, holding in a sob that came out. I wrapped my arms around him, giving him a sign that I was okay. I felt him hug back. "I was such an idiot! I've hurt you! I'm so...so sorry, Kevin! Could you forgive me?"

"There's nothing to forgive, father!" I said, almost tearing up myself. I held onto his hand. "It's not your fault. Please don't cry. Please?" Doing as I asked, he wiped the tears with his sleeves and took a good look at me.

"Kevin, I swear. Even if you are far from us, I promise, in God's name, that I will never let anyone hurt you like that again. I couldn't imagine if Kelley went through that! Don't let anyone hurt you!" He said in a gradual normal tone now.

"No one is ever going to hurt me again. Not with what I've learned. Not with what I have."

"That's my kiddo!" He spoke. "It's those extremists that give God fearers a bad name. They claim to be holy, only to mask their corruption. Those people who took care of you, they were full of greed and hatred. They only wanted to break you. And it's my fault for naively feeding into their habit, thinking they were fair and good. Just like how

I wasn't always around for you and your sister because of the...damn media circus!"

"It's okay dad! Really." I said, as I noticed how he was starting to sound like Francis. "I still love you. I love you very much."

"I know. I love you too. That's why I, myself, am making amends. Every damage your grandfather has made on this family will be fixed. I promise." He then sighed, "And this isn't Harris's fault either. So...please find it in your heart to forgive him too, son. Even just for a bit. Can you do that?"

"I...I'll try." I said, digesting everything that was said. I hoped I still found it in my heart to truly forgive Harris. I hoped I still found it in my heart to forgive the world. But something was telling me that I shouldn't. The world I came from got us to the afterlife in the first place. So, there was nothing to forgive in that. I'm sorry, but there wasn't. And this was something I decide to keep to myself.

"We all have to make amends anyway by learning from horrors. That's how we'll know we're redeemed." He said. I nodded and digested it in my mind. I tried to have it engraved. He also added, "I didn't mean to shelter you...from all of life's problems. I just didn't want it to hurt you as it did for your mother and I. But...I know not to stop you from growing. Especially to God. Because we eventually all have to face life; in its brightest and darkest moments."

My eyes gloomed and I asked, "But...what if I muck up? I don't trust myself...in life. Maybe I'm too inclined to the foundation we intended to build because...because I'm not sure about my own path. Maybe because I'm a coward with no purpose."

"Everyone has a purpose, son. And God always has a plan for someone; often one we don't expect nor ask for. And he has planned yours, son. And you are not a coward. You are not cursed. You're a fighter. And you didn't let me down!" He placed his hand on my right shoulder.

He continued, "You want to know the truth? My biggest fear...was seeing you and your sister...grow up, given what that world was...and what people are. And what they could do to bright souls like you. But God tells me to pray for you, but to never fear for you. Because he himself knew that both of you would eventually become what the world truly needed. That you will seek for his Word in your own lives. I know…. that outside of our home…life could be scary. Unfair, cruel, even strange, or intense. It makes you depressed, fear uncertainty. You want nothing more than to…see it stop. But…that doesn't mean that it's not possible to find what is good and meaningful out there. There are those willing to welcome you. I'm sure you've made good friends in this world…like Mr. Bailey for instance. It's possible to still be better than what everyone expects you to be. Because your heart still carries that undying core. You must trust in it. You can't keep neglecting your self-worth like this, Kevin."

After I wiped the tears from my face, I then said admittedly with a sigh, "I know. It's just hard. How did you…deal with such madness? How do you…go out there in a life filled with battle and…pain…but still have your humanity? Is it even possible? Because it seems like it gets more and more complicated."

He pondered deeply. Thus spoke, "Life will always be that way. But what I do is…I focus on being a light. I can't tell you how much fear I saw once we stormed through the rubbles of Lebanon, fending off tanks and salvaging what we had. I can't tell you how some men, most of them younger than me were frozen, fighting with themselves as they were internally determining whether they were going to live or die. I had to be there. I moved forward. I placed my bias aside to help them. I chose not to be afraid of people nor to condemn them. Do I still have some issues with them? Of course. Who doesn't? But I came to know that in their lives…they are in battle. Plato once said *to be kind, for everyone you meet is fighting a hard battle.* I learned that you can't run away from battle. You can't run from life. It can't live without you. Be the knight you've always fantasized as a kid. We believe in you. But you gotta believe in yourself too, Kevin. Believe in your humanity. And no matter how dark or complicated it gets sometimes, believe in life again. Don't run away from it."

He then gazed at his pocket watch. "I don't wanna keep you awake. So…I'll let you sleep."

He got up from his chair to roll up the covers to my chin. He then kissed my forehead. He then said rubbing and scattering locks of my hair, "I love you very much, son."

"I love you too, father. Thank you for the advice too." I said as he then took off after extinguishing the candle lights on the desk with his blows. "If you need anything, just call me or your mother." He then took off with a smile and closed the door behind him. I prayed that I would extract what he advised me.

As I was ready to shut my eyes, I felt my eyes shriveling back into the Blessed Eye for some reason. My mind felt gradually stuffed and weighted. I inserted four fingers on each hand to reassure and rub off the pain. Was it my voices once again? Well, a voice appeared, but it wasn't from any of the shadows. Neither were the sixteen.

"Hello? Hello? Hello! Cześć (Hello)!" It was a familiar voice too. Especially with the jest.

"Hang on?" I wondered quietly. "Ted?"

"Oh hey, Kev! Whew, what a relief!" His voice echoed in my head.

"Ted...hi!" I said, very shocked that he responded. "But...er...how are you communicating in my mind?"

"We have telepathy, remember? Sometimes, it could also work as a sense creeping into your intuition."

"Oh right, nearly forgot. Lightkeeper magic."

"That's alright. Also... sorry I got to you late. I had to help Juliet collect herbs for the herbalists. I just wanted to check up on ya. Francis told me that you're with your family now. That's awesome. You must be happy." He said. *"Bet there were tears involved."*

"Of course, I am, Ted. It feels great! It feels...great! My family is here and finally allowed to live! Sorry I took off without saying anything to you or Juliet. It was just...unexpected."

"That's fine. I knew you were probably off somewhere. So that's why I didn't bother. I'm happy that you're with your family. So...with everything that's happened, I can't blame you for wanting out from the Order. I saw that a lot of your stuff is being removed. We're gonna miss you, but...we understand.

The door's always open if you wish to come back. It was awesome having you around for the ride when it lasted."

Saddened and somewhat overwhelmed with guilt, I replied, "Thanks. But...that doesn't mean that we can't be friends anymore. Right?"

"Yeah...of course we could still be friends, crumpets. You could also visit us if you like. At least you're a lightkeeper now. It feels good, don't it? So, I hope some good came when you were with us, despite...you know."

"Aye, it did. And thank you for that. Thanks for understanding, Ted. So...So how is Juliet?"

"She's fine, though she was saddened to know that you'll leave the Order. She and I were just hanging out at the Homestead with the priestesses. Especially with Lustina out of the picture for good, the bitch."

"How are they? The priestesses," I asked humbly, hiding the sadness I felt when I was told of Juliet. "Well, I hope."

"They're doing good. They're doing better. Bella told me to wish you Happy Holidays. And she's singing that song you sang to her weeks ago. Along with the other priestesses." He said before he jested, *"Seems like you started a cult. Naughty. Naughty."*

"That's bloody awesome." I said feeling inspired. "What about Frask, Emily, and the others?"

"Jesus and Michael just returned from their trip. So, he's back on the throne. Frask traveled to the Cholla Springs in the east after finishing those dragonfly thingies. And Emily is with us as well."

I took a breath of relief after hearing that Frask was done with the inventions. "That's good. I'm glad everyone else is doing okay there."

"Thanks, man. Right now, I'm just trying to figure out how to place this portrait of Paul Newman and Robert Redford from "Butch Cassidy and the Sundance Kid". Frask knows it's one of my favorite films, let alone westerns. My mom got me into westerns as a kid. Turns out Frask made it for me for Christmas. Let me tell ya, despite my shitty human life, watching that film with my mom was off the chain! Took me back when movies actually gave a shit!"

"Ha. I see where the old west outlaw mood came from when you perform as a knight. That's awesome."

"*Ha! Yeah, that is what I go for. But it was more so...to pay tribute to her. Especially for all she did for me to...live through that hell.*"

"That's very thoughtful. Lovely. I'm glad that you did that," I said. After I yawned, I continued, "I'm about to sleep, but I'll contact you again. Whenever I can. Okay?"

"*Sure. Just wanted to keep you on the loop. That's all. Tell your peeps Ted says hi. Happy Holidays. I'll...I'll see you around.*"

"Sure will. I'll...see you around, Ted."

After that, my head was cleared, and I exited from the Blessed Eye state. It was just the chirping of crickets outside my window in the looming moon watching over. I went underneath the covers and slowly drifted to sleep. I was once again concealed in darkness. During my sleep, I was suddenly losing all feeling I felt in my body. Every stream and vein within my body stopped. It felt like I was being pinned down on the bed; forced to be still.

XXVI

✱

Lucid Dream

When I woke up, I looked back down and saw that the bed has vanished. I appeared to be standing on a surface filled with water that was pitch black and obscured. Standing on two feet, I was slowly walking around, slipping my feet into the waters. I was taking in the obscure surrounding me. It was completely silence and very tough to make out of what exactly was happening. I began walking around and around, wandering tirelessly of where I was supposed to go. I had no sword or any weapon to defend myself. I felt very powerless, even to wake up from this dream.

The more I walked and walked forward; I was beginning to hear a sound. It was a song. It sounded angelic, but very distant and distorted.

It kept repeating and repeating the more I kept walking. But I wasn't sure why it was done in such an eerily demented and distorted way. And it was getting louder and louder, the further I was walking. Several sketchy characters began to appear right before my eyes. They were walking right passed me, wearing what looked like masquerade masks. It was as if there was a festival or ball going on, but I wasn't invited. Or perhaps their senses were fixated on the same song. Except, again, it was going backwards. I stopped to observe them, questioning their destination.

After moments of hesitation, I was curious. I began to follow them.
I kept repeating the last lyrics of the song. Maybe not as a means of
comfort, but perhaps this was a way to help decipher what the message
this dream entails. But after thinking about it, I was sure that it was The
Angel. I was sure that she had something to do with this. The thought
of who she could be, what she wanted, it was clear that the image of
her was to drive me towards the realm of pure madness.

But when I followed the masked individuals, it looked like all of
them were huddled and facing what appeared to be a behemoth screen
of gold and orange fog. It felt like I was at a music concert; though I
wish it was a concert. Preferably a Dead Can Dance concert. Instead,
it was an event that was yet to display. It was completely silent as the
individuals around me were very muted. I was curious, but I was unease
by the pure silence and hollow wind passing through the obscure sky.
There were no stars, or any shed of light. But I was not sure how was I
able to see the people right in front of me.

That was until stars did appear in the sky. And too my surprise, a
giant moon, colored in blood red, appeared right in front of all of us.
It nearly took up the entirety of the room, shedding stems of blood red
light. In fact, it made the entire place suddenly come from an obscure
black to this sinister red color. The music in the background suddenly
stopped. It quickly reminded me of the Trials of the Spirit's Mind. It
was as if my mind constructed another test for me. But when I faced
the moon, it unexpectedly turned black.

All around me, the masked individuals began to cheer louder. I was
confused and nearly held back from their intense chants. It got to the
point where I covered both of my ears, hoping that it would stop. But
even with them closed, I still heard them shouting. I was intending to
leave but was blocked by the cloaked individuals. I wrestled with them,
trying all I can to shove my way through and escape. I recognized how
big of a mistake it was to follow them.

One minute I was standing, but one of them pushed me onto the
ground until I fell the bits of water hit my face and moistening my hair.

When I rose whilst kneeling, I looked up and saw that the individuals were making way for me to face a man on top of a platform. The room was suddenly black again but was illuminated with fire lined across the stage. The man wore a familiar mask.

An ancient porcelain mask with flowery gold accents striking down it. With only black trousers and bare feet, he was shirtless. Embracing his slim built with his arms raised.

Suddenly, during this unreal place, all the vacant marble masked individuals faced me. They stared at me, faintly breathing, and looking into my heart with their hollow and empty eyes. The room was in complete silence, and I just felt very estranged and confused on what was I supposed to do at this very moment. I glanced around and saw how surrounded I was.

"Your soul must be broken!" One of them said. As I turned, I saw that one of the individuals came to me. The tone was masculine, which I concluded that a man was behind the mask. He faced me and looked deep into my green eyes. The golden masked bloke unveiled himself...only to be myself. He smiled eerily.

Suddenly, his right hand was palmed on my forehead. I eyed at his hand and eyed back at him, wondering where this was going.

"Face your nature. Face your life and you will be free." He said. He then told me to close my eyes. I kept them closed, as all I saw was obscure darkness. I kept them closed for a good three minutes, waiting for my next task. This felt like I was trying the Trials of the Spirits once again.

Finally, he told me to open my eyes. When I opened them, I saw that I was suddenly in the middle of the ocean. By that, I mean that I was standing on actual moving water. I didn't know what it was supposed to reflect. I didn't know what it was supposed to mean. I was completely left confused, but I did remember the words from that man; I will break you rotten soul. And you will be free. What did he mean by that? I wondered.

But then I thought about it very carefully. It was something in the realms of what Bertha told me. Maybe I have been really thinking about what she said. And in addition, it was clearer when this happened afterwards.

"Kevin." My name was called from afar. When I turned to my left, someone else was standing on water. Someone very familiar. As I gained closer and closer to him, I recognized the white robe and bearded face. It was Jesus. I know this was he was commonly known for, but I didn't know what he was doing in my dream.

"Kevin, come over here. It's okay." He said. When I got close, I was suddenly facing him. We looked into each other's eyes. He just looked at me smiling at me. His hands were suddenly on my shoulders.

"I appreciate your thoughts. Everyone does in the afterlife." He said with a smile. He wondered off to the ocean, zoning out. "We appreciate your efforts and actions on bettering the souls you want to protect. But...there is something else you can do."

"Like what?"

He said nothing. For at least a good two minutes. I looked at what he was staring at. But he suddenly looked back at me, getting me to re-focus at him. His smile slowly went away. "Break them. Let them burn in his name."

"Wait...whose name, Your Majesty? Whose name?!"

"His name! His name! Suffer in his name! That's what he wants! Suffer and he will grant you salvation!" When he said that, something was wrong. Suddenly, his eyes became hollow and dark. When he opened his mouth, blood and murky white fluids pour like a waterfall from his mouth. It became an unpleasant smear of colors draining from all his orifices.

I stood back from him, releasing myself from his hands. I saw how the water was becoming darker. The sky became red. It felt as though I was on another planet. When I looked back at Jesus, suddenly...I saw him in a very common state and pose. The crucifix.

He was stripped from his clothes and only wore a loincloth. He bared scars and lacerations on his body whilst wearing the crown made of thorns. His mouth was still bleeding out and his eyes were dull and black.

Suddenly, four more crucifixes arose on each side of him. My eyes enlarged in horror. I covered my mouth to what was seen before me. My mother, father, sister, Mr. Blackwater, and Father Harris were nailed on each crucifix. They cried in agony and mourned as blood was draining from their wounds. Suddenly, seven more crucifixes were rising from the ocean; this time, everyone I knew were victims; Ted, Juliet, Emily, Sarah, Frask, Michael, Francis and even Mary. I was confused and frightened. I stood frozen by what I was seeing. I couldn't understand what was happening.

And for some reason, I saw a group of individuals summoning right in front of me. Shadowy, dark, and mystified, they all happened to be the reflections of myself. The shadows I have summoned were right in front of me. They carried spears and lances above their heads. My heart sank lower and lower, seeing something unreal and surrealistic.

They swiftly turned to me and stared at me strangely. They were festering their red eyes into my soul. But I was too distracted by the cries and wails of my family and friends. Especially seeing Jesus like that. It was much horrific as I was taught to believe.

"You did this! You have allowed them to suffer! You ran away from your destiny!" One of the shadows said. Two of them began to engage to my personal space. I felt their misty hands grasping my arms.

"No, I didn't!" I shouted in panic. "I didn't!"

"And now...you will suffer with them. You will learn its meaning! You will be...redeemed. Just like the rest of them!" One of them said, gesturing his hand to show me something that was apparently behind me. Once I turned my head over my shoulder, I enlarged my eyes and covered my mouth with both hands. I stood back and saw a crucifix behind me. I was stumbling back, but the two shadows strained me from escaping. I looked back at the leader of the pack, begging him to reconsider. It was at this moment I nearly forgot I was dreaming. Being dragged and placed on the cross, I closed my eyes to fight the paralysis. I had to wake up! You bastard wake up! I cried in my mind.

But I had yet to wake up. Because as soon as I opened my eyes, I saw burning trees hovering over my face. The dusky night skies were fogged by dark smolders and flaky bright embers. I slowly stood up on two feet and began to see my surroundings. All around me were feuds after feuds. Crucifixes were planted all over the woods as they blazed relentlessly through the darkened night. Some stood behind the fires. I studied the armors of each soldier. A group of men sporting blue, gold, and white uniforms. Another group donning horned skulls in their head as they sported black and gold armor. Men were being slain left and right as their blood-coiling shrieks and agonizing screams summoned across and all around me. Pleads for help were chartered, yet I was not seen. And I swore I heard very faint cries. The faint but unbearable cry of a very young girl. I was just not sure who.

I was intrigued, yet frightened, by the amount of torn flesh and snapped bones I witnessed. The endless skin crawling squeals from the blue and gold donned soldiers as they had their arms, legs, and head severely severed by heavy ivory blades of the skull-wearing soldiers. I watched around every corner as every soldier was plummeting to the blood-soaked grass. I was yet to be noticed by either army. I saw more soldiers getting cut down by a dark man donning a sharp-horned skull helmet. Eerily like Sathanus. The captain made his final strike upon a solider in front of a wall of fire. He stood with his back turned on me. But slowly and steadily, his head was turning. His eyes were hollow black as the black hole. The look was a pure invitation to death. And I just...froze and stared into his eyes.

When the fire began to spread throughout the woods, I took the moment to run nonstop. Was this how the infamous rebellions acted or just my own perception? Whatever was happening, I didn't want any part of it. I had to wake up. I closed my eyes to block the flames from my mind. Then a voice came. *"You did this! This is all your fault!"*

After trying to fight this paralysis with my mind, I finally opened my eyes. I stood up and saw, between the red windows curtains, which it was dusk. The dark blue sky began to gradually light up to a softer shade. For some reason, I saw it as a sign. Almost a calling for me to...to leave. I briefly contemplated on whether to leave without notifying any of my family. But the voices in my head were not making it easier for me to make my decision. Some wanted me to tell them. Some didn't. I yelped silently in frustration, scaring away the voices. "Quiet, dammit," I said in an aggressive whisper.

Something told me that my work was not done. It told me to get back to where we started. I had to go back. Father had to sacrifice his longing with us to protect us from adversary. That is what men do to protect those they love. To protect them, I had to leave. Father depended on me to be a light the world needed. So did my mother and Kelley. My Apostle friends. Francis. Jesus. Those priestesses. And not that they wouldn't care, but the prisoners in Hell. With that notion in mind, I had to not fail. I had to prove that I was saved. All I had to do was push what I struggled with aside and to trust in the laws of the afterlife as best as I can. I owed that to Francis for all he did. And to Bertha.

After I washed up and packed my stuff, whilst having the dream imprinted in my mind, I exited my room. But before I went downstairs, I walked silently to check on mother and father. Slightly and quietly opening the door, I watched them sleeping peacefully with my father's arm around mother. The inside looked almost identical to the room they once had on Long Island; a chandelier, two dressers on each side of the bed, and a king-sized bed. A smile summoned on my face

As soon as I moved away and closed the door silently, I turned back. My heart stopped briefly when I realized that Kelley was standing in the middle of the hall. It made me jump a bit. Her room was next to mine, which I nearly forgot for the four weeks I have been there. Her hands were rubbing both of her sunken eyes. She wore a long white linen nightgown reaching her feet. "Oh, Kelley. You...You're up early." I said nervously.

"I was just going to the bathroom." She said through yawning.

When she adjusted her eyes, she asked, "Are you...going somewhere at this hour?"

I took a breath before I said, "Uh...yes, actually. I...I have to leave, Kelley."

"What...why?" Kelley asked after her face adjusted. She then walked a bit closer to me. "Don't you want to stay? We were having so much fun together. Especially being with you again."

"I know. I would want to stay. Trust me, I want nothing more." I said before sighing in regret. "But...I felt something in my head when I was dreaming. But I don't know if I could tell you."

"Kevin, I'm your sister. You can tell me anything. My heart is never closed. You know that. Is it your Apostle business?" She asked, curling her right fingers around my arm.

I finally told her, "It was a nightmare of some kind. I just didn't know what it was." Her eyes widened and contracted down to brief horror. "I saw you, mum and dad...crucified. Along with my friends. Then there was...a battle. One in tireless flames with...a demon... killing everyone. A voice telling me...that the battle...was somehow...my fault."

"I'm...so sorry, Kevin." She said. "It's probably the voices again as well. Is there anything I can do?"

After I pondered a bit heavily, I said after I sighed, "You have to be safe. I'm only doing this...for you. For all of us. I know it's scary out there, but I must help the Apostles. I owe them that...for helping me. And I owe it to Ms. June for helping you find a home here. But once I do, once the people are free from Hell, once I end this battle, I will return. To live with you again as we did before...what happened. Before all this. I promise." I then assured her with my hands on both sides of her soft face. "Just look after yourself, Mum and Dad for me, yeah?"

"Of course, I will. But...it was amazing to be with you after so long. I hope to see each other again."

"God willing, we will," I said as I then wrapped my arms around her as I felt her arms around my waist. I took a bit time to endure her touch before I could take off. After we hugged, she nodded with her lips tucked in. The lips curved into a smile.

"I'll tell mum and dad that you said goodbye." She said as I nodded in satisfaction.

After using the bathroom, she was leading me down the steps into getting to the dusk filled backyard, so I can release Aventurine. When I coddled and tendered the steed, I managed to grab hold of his reins and led him out from the stable. Kelley and I got Aventurine out from the stable after I placed my luggage on the back of the saddle and attached it down with harnesses. We then moved the creature into the open but silent stone road, with the only presence of crickets chirping, leaves dancing to the winds, and unknown wildlife crying. I climbed onto the stir up, grabbed both reins and looked back at Kelley, who stood smiling with her hands grabbing one another.

"By the way, a friend of mine from Celestia told me to say hi to you."

"That's nice. Tell him thank you." She smiled. "Go forth, my fair cavalier," she joked as I chuckled.

"I will, my fair lady." I replied whilst tipping my hat to her as I then face the parallel houses and avenues. I then released a breath from the bottom of the inside whilst my eyes were briefly closed. I then opened them and lashed the reins, alerting Aventurine to go forward. Snorting and neighing, he moves forward. And I had the advantage because the roads were wide enough for me to ride. And he felt smooth to ride on.

I wanted to test out on how far we can exactly travel back in an instant. I knew that I must tell the others of what I saw when I arrive. And I remembered what my dad told me. It reminded me so much of the science fiction film trilogy *Back to the Future*. To test if the same method would work, I lashed the reins gradually, getting Aventurine to go faster and faster. It was no car. And no DeLorean. I had to make sure that I rode him regularly.

As soon as I was yanking it a couple of times and gave out the name Celestia, I felt the steed vibrating with the movement. He began galloping throughout the street. Going through the straightened road, passing the parked horseless carriages, everything around me looked to be in motion as I moved fast.

As soon as we were rapidly going fast down the road, I saw bright blue eyes shining from Aventurine's eyes. I briefly looked around and saw large blue strips of smoke conjuring from Aventurine himself. We were instantly evaporated from the village road through a spiraling and mind-bending gold and white vortex.

When I left, there was nothing left but pride. In the sense that for the first time in a long time, everything was set to go my way. Knowing that my family was with me in the afterlife, knowing that they were safe and alive, it was enough for me to truly feel content. It made me confident to help the Apostles end this long war. For the first time, I felt contented. Maybe the afterlife can revive what I have lost after all. Maybe God was still alive too.

XXVII

The Watchers Among Us

Escaping through the spiraling atmosphere, we arrived at the front of the Khalservan's gatehouse. I yanked the reins, which calmed Aventurine as he stopped before going any further. The smoke circulated and slowly escaped from us. I sat a moment, sitting and reflecting at what just happened. It was like everything just rushed past us and happened all at once. When I unmounted from him, after I briefly meditated, the guards who gave me stares at amazement welcomed me. As I was approaching them, I stopped and grinned. I could tell that they were very amazed by the pertlow.

"Morning lads," I said.

"Is that...a...a pertlow?!" One asked.

"I mean...what else could it be? A donkey?" I asked with a jest, as I gestured my hand to Aventurine. I then asked, "Anyway, do you know if I can find Jesus Christ?"

"Um...yes, he is currently at the Main Chapel, addressing to the people. And he is with the other Apostles." The other guard said, still dumbfounded by the look of Aventurine.

"Thanks. You could tell the monks to get my things back to the Khalservan if that is alright. I've come back to stay," I said as I raced back to the horse and mounted on the saddle. I yanked the reins around and made my way out to exit from the courtyard. For the remaining hours, I began galloping across the grasslands as the orange colors met with the dark mellow blues in the sky.

When I soon arrived at the castle's bridge, I saw that it was completely over by what were the citizens of Celestia. There were throwing their hands into the air, shouting not only in anger, but what happened to be in intense fear. Some were whimpering during all the murmuring happening all at once. Some were perhaps begging to see what Jesus was saying. Some were even angrily cursing or condemning him under their breaths for leaving them just to make peace with The Summerland kingdom. They seemed to distaste the other kingdoms, presumably for leading the Satanists towards Valestone.

I also remembered what else dad told me about Aventurine's powers. It was like Algor, but quite different by how it worked. According to others, pegs can be summoned at will when you whistle.

I decided to test it out by telling Aventurine to make himself scarce, especially away from the people. I didn't expect anyone else to take notice of the creature. After I stroked the creature's snout tenderly, I watched as he ran and disappeared into thin air. I slowly faced the castle, which I could quickly tell that it was crowded as well. I understood everyone's desperation and happiness to see the king once again. But then again, he only came back.

I was making my way through the crowd, pushing, and tucking my way into the men and women completely in trance to the gates of the castle. When I got to the gates, I was hoping that the guards would recognize me, so they could let me through. At this point, they'd had to know the Apostles' authorization to be with the king. When I got into the courtyard, it was as I expected; crowded and huddled with desperate, entitled, tired or happy people.

I saw that Jesus was there, on top of the stair as he stood behind the door with a beige podium in front of him. He had six armored guards with halberds all in front of him, as it was clear that they were blocking the people. Jesus's hands were raised, obviously to calm and silence the civilians.

"My dear people, I have received a vision from God, warning me of Lucifer's pending return. About what he will do to lot of us to take on me." He roared to his people, who began to gasp among their mouths after hearing the news. I guess he was still amid his speech when I arrived.

"But rest assured, my great people, for I intend to look into this matter further. Your afterlives are precious for you to get in the way of harm. Which is why I urge all of you, for your own safety, to not go into the depths of the lands of Valestone. Lucifer's Satanists and Legionaries are bound to appear at any time. Be sure to protect your friends, families, and yourselves importantly. And I will use my position to have you protected to the best of my ability. As the Son of God, King of Valestone and of The Promised Land, I guarantee that the monarchy of all the heavens will put an end to this monstrosity so that Lucifer will not do any harm to any of you. Through me, you are safe. And together, Heaven, and all the afterlife, will forever triumph."

The sudden cheers and loud claps of applause have taken over the wideranging air around me. The people began disbursing from the courtyard and the bridge, giving me room to finally breathe. As I escaped from the clutches of the crowd, I was granted access to meet with Jesus by the guards. I took notice of how Jesus' cyan eyes gazed at me. He smiled with all teeth showing when I approached him up the stairs. He greeted me with his hands shaking mine.

"It's a blessing to see you, Kevin." He said. "I was told by Francis that you were with your family."

"Y...Yes I was, Your Majesty," I replied, gaining a smile from him.

"I am pleased that you were able to see them again."

"Thank you, Your Majesty. It's nice to see you too again." I said.

"Come, I could only tell you are already urging to see your friends." He said leading me inside of the castle through the doors.

After getting into the throne room, he led me into the side of the castle, which led me to another room. But I learned that this big room was a component of the castle. The chandelier was hovering over a stretched out rectangular table with forty chairs underneath. Surrounding the room were portraits portraying the monumental moments of every spiritual leader's life; including Jesus himself of course.

In addition, everyone else was there, Ted, Juliet, the Queen, the Princess, Francis, Bertha, Dante, and Michael.

But there was another fellow who I wasn't too familiar with. His robe looked quite like Michael's garbs, but the colors were distinctly different. They were three variations of blue and yellow. And his decent-colored brown hair nearly reached his shoulders.

"Kevin...welcome back, man." Ted said cheerfully with his arms raised. He got up from his seat as he greeted me with a handshake that came to a hug. I was very overwhelmed and content for the first time to see and feel him.

Soon, Juliet came to me and hugged me. I embraced her in my arms. She said, "Welcome back. I thought you wanted out to be with your family."

"I thought so too. But I promised them that I'll come back. But I need to finish this first. I owe you that...for helping me." I said. I then took notice of her pendant, which Ted told me of. It was a beautiful one as well. It was a bright silver ornament with Celtic design behind an eagle engraved on it. "Nice pendant."

"Thanks. My mother gave it to me." Juliet said, looking down at her ornament around her neck.

I then addressed the Queen and Lady and kneeled for them before I stood up. I watched them nodded and smile at me. The Lady waved at me with enthusiasm. I was then hugged and welcomed by Francis and Michael. I nodded at Dante, who grinned briefly. I even greeted Bertha and thanked her for what she has done. It made me acknowledged that I really did have good people with me.

"I owe you, Ms. June. I owe you a lot," I said after I shook her hand heavily. "I'm sorry if I gave you a hard time of not always being here."

"No worries. But just rest assured, I'm doing what I can to help. And I'm content that your family is doing well too. You all deserved to be happy," She smiled. I then turned to Michael.

"How is everything, my dear friend?" Michael asked me, with his hand grasping my forearm in greeting. "Your family too?"

"Brilliant. Thank you. How was your trip?"

"A bit interesting if I must say. Speaking of which; Kevin, I would like to introduce you to Saint Gabriel." Michael said, bringing me forth to the archangel.

"Pleasure to meet you, Kevin Princeton." He said to me.

"A pleasure to meet you too, sir."

"Gabriel has just arrived from Arcadia after hearing upon the news." Francis said. "And to check on the priestesses. At some point, they would have to leave and be at peace of where they once came."

"I thank you so much of what you have done with those girls. Arianna was ill, confused of what happened." Gabriel said humbly. "We tried searching for them, but they were nowhere to be found. But Michael told me when he arrived. You have our thanks."

"So...what's going to happen now?" I asked, sitting in a chair as I faced him.

"Jesus and the rest have spoken highly of you three, especially when you located our priestesses. We discussed in hopes to find a solution to our problem. Someone addressed as...the Unicorn." Gabriel said.

"That's one of the accomplices of Lucifer." Juliet said. "The thing is...we have no idea what any of them do. But we do know that they are after the scepters to get to the Axis Mundi. We saw Sathanus in Jury Cove, along with the priestesses."

"I know. Michael told me of that too." Gabriel said. "I'll tell you more on that in a bit." I could already tell that something wasn't good.

"I was told that the Lady was almost sold to the devil!" Dante said bitterly. "I was even interrogated few days ago! As if I could commit such treachery! I'm a damn Chancellor!"

"Forgive me, Sir Alighieri." The Queen said. "But we had to make sure that no one is a suspect. It's difficult to tell sometimes. So, calm down...for God's sake. I just don't understand why they would do this."

"Maybe..." I said while thinking hard about what to say. I then concluded, "Maybe...these Watchers were given another side to Lucifer's story. I mean Bertha here told me that after they sold the other nobles to him, they were allegedly rewarded with the powers of Satanists somehow. All what is left for them is to do his deeds; like getting the scepters."

"And once they get their hands on the queen's scepter, they could find all others in the afterlife and the Insignia." Jesus added. "But I don't understand. Why is he sending out his Watchers to do his bidding?"

"It's quite simple. He doesn't want blood on his hands." Bertha stated. "He's using them. You'd know how that works. He knows that these are spirits of Heaven. That way, he managed to control them into doing what he wants them to do, promising them lies to a false paradise. They're nothing but eyes and ears for him. Whether we'd like to admit it or not, it's simply the fact that we have turncoats in our midst."

"Good outlook, Ms. June." Jesus said. She nodded at the respond. He then added, "A sad one in fact."

"And so, he has The Unicorn, The Phoenix, and lastly...The Angel working to get them. Purposely putting all of us in a predicament." Bertha said. "Now the question is...who should we go after first?"

"I suggest we should get to The Unicorn first." Gabriel suggested. He then walked and looked through the window with his arms behind his back. "Until those herbalists are finished with the potions, the victims of Hell would...unfortunately have to hold on. I think it's clear that Lucifer's accomplices are operating within our bounds to overthrow the monarchs as an excuse to get to the Axis Mundi. Unfortunately, despite our best and experienced guards, they were found dead, and the staff has been stolen...again."

"How?" Mary asked.

"Before dying, one of the guards stated that the Satanists were summoned, but where very strong compared to the others. Along the way, several peers were found slaughtered as well: including...a child. As for the scepter, it's lost somewhere within the city. We can't seem to find the conspirer! Not even our best detectives."

"When did this happen?"

"Just...yesterday. That is why I came for your help." Gabriel replied.

The room was silent to digest everything that was discussed. We all contemplated on how we would approach this plan. And maybe it was clear that they were using rituals to do their biddings. And perhaps Lucifer is staying behind to continue building something he has in store for us. What was it? An idea? A new order? It was beyond me. I remembered how I was confused on why he would want the scepters to himself.

But by his message, it was clear to me. And his goal was ambitious. To become the only god of the afterlife, the only creator of the universe, would take great lengths to eradicate every other god and religion from this very existence. And the accomplices were clearly complying.

"I don't understand, Your Majesty?" Gabriel asked Jesus. "I mean I understand he wants dominance. That's obvious. But why the Insignia? What could he possibly see in it to have millions of spirits murdered? Including our...archangelic comrades?"

Before Jesus spoke, he gloomily sighed. He then said, "The Insignia was to be the supposed key to paradise. But if you saw what I saw, you would astray away from it. When it was first created, the gods called me into testing it. The Tiennes de Gracia is a lonely spec of land where I tested it, gathered as many spirits as we could to make a garden like the domain of Adam and Eve. The Insignia's power was...destructive. The staff's cosmic glow crept into their hearts and minds, tightening their biological brain and heart neurons, crippling who they were personally to become mindless conformed beings doing tasks by command without question. They acted like sheep who obeyed easily. Their neurons would crush, damaging their muscles, if they didn't act according to its power. They would get sick, have constant seizures, vomit blood, and lose their minds. So, they were in great fear and chose not to think for themselves. To want a perfect world meant to risk everything in favor of it. Your integrity, the lack of those caused the land to eventually collapse as...the poor souls collapse. The garden was completed, beautiful. But its beauty concealed the broken people behind it. Lunacy, depressions, anorexia, and cold hallowing death were seen those days. The intense desperation for a perfect world is what ruined them. The plagues came true those days."

His eyes were closed as his shoulders sunk. His face grew very grim with regret. "Those shrieks and cries of debilitating agony...calling out within a shallow darkness...are forever in my mind. That land is forbidden and cursed with their screams. I can't let Lucifer take it. I can't. And yet, he does not understand. I try to do what my mother did. I try everything to save these souls by giving them a different world. A better one where they do not have to be deceived or used by godless leaders ever again. But...I fail. I somehow succeed as a messenger of God, but...I fail as a king." His eyes closed in dejection.

"My dear husband." Mary said, soothing his arm. "You only did...what you thought was right, but it turned out wrong. God had no intention of making such a dangerous item. You haven't failed. There are no such thing as good or bad kings. You know this more than anybody. Creating a world of universal peace is no simple task for any king to accomplish. But the clear difference between you and Lucifer...is that you are not afraid of seeing men and women waking up from the matrix they were burdened with. Unlike Lucifer, you don't cheat. I followed you when we were humans because you taught us how to live according to God, knowing truly that the universe could give us truth and expand our minds and souls to possibilities we've never thought of. You encouraged spirits to seek for the cosmos in their lives so they could be with them. Connected to the Gods. Some refuse to wake up. But you've touched those who do. I love you, my husband, my king, because you do not seek for a perfect world, you seek for one that grows as creation itself."

"And yet, Lucifer plans to take that away. Just so we could live in a delusion of a peaceful world." Juliet stated.

"We won't let him. That kind of power shouldn't be controlled by any-one!" Francis said in a strong-minded tone. He planted both hands on the table, looking at every single one of us. "This is just a plot rising from the darkness. Whether this was a test or not, we won't let him, nor his accomplices, get the best of us so he can win. He's the emperor of Hell. And like most emperors, they tend to take and control. We won't let it come to that. Besides, logically.... this supposed paradise of his is utterly superficial. It's all an excuse to have spirits suffer eternal damnation for going against his principles."

"You could be right, Francis," Jesus sat down in relief. He then said, "There are things in this land that I promise. But a world without the entirety of sin is one I cannot keep. And I cannot afford to make promises that are impossible to keep. I do not enjoy taking part of this war; neither putting much into it. I'm truly saddened about this state in the afterlife. But Lucifer left me with no choice. It's for the afterlife's own good. And the souls within it," We all nodded silently.

"So now what...we all agree to go after the Unicorn first and the others will soon follow?" Ted asked.

"Yes." Gabriel said. "And we are also in need of the shepherd's purse herbs, so we can heal the Queen. You three can help us track and assassinate the bastard!"

"Certainly." Juliet said. She then asked with her arms raised. "But will we still need assistance?"

"I have contemplated on what was said, especially by Kevin here," Francis said, gesturing his hand at me. I eyed at him with a stunned look. "You three are still undertrained to take on the legionaries. Keep that in mind. But...I believe that you could be powerful enough to take on The Unicorn and The Phoenix."

"But...I do have a device that should help you summon us and my soldiers." Michael said as he removed something from his bag. He handed Juliet an ivory blowing horn decorated with angels painted with black ink. "I rarely let others use it. Let alone knights. But just in case, blow into this in any circumstance and it should help summon me and the Angel Paladins."

"I should contact the Civil Forcers at Arcadia and tell them about your arrival in case of any circumstances as well," Bertha said. "Being that we are all connected, to a degree since I am in a different branch, they should be easy to come by if necessary. Things could get hazy. You could use them on my behalf, now that I've help the villagers find a home."

"If I may add to something," Mary asked as we all faced her. "Our daughter Sarah has told me about Mr. Douglas, the painter of Covenant Avenue, about a device he is creating to locate the Watchers. And I have granted him the position to finish the project, so you can use it. Anything would work at this point."

Everyone started murmuring, stunned at what a single painter can do with the magic he had amongst the rest of the civilization.

"Upon the city, you should find Virgil Maro. A friend of mine when we used to write. He was once a Chancellor. I remembered that I often got letters from him." Dante added. "He wrote to me that he was released from Lucifer's confinement, which I was surprised. He became quite the socialite for the Queen's amusement. But he is very useful, though often secretive. He should have intel of Hell now and what goes there so we can find a way to get everyone else out. Find him...if you can. He should be able to help." I was honestly shocked that Dante decided to help us.

"You three have all these options." Francis said. "It's on you to choose and go with one of these approaches. So, I'll leave it up to you. You have the entire House of God at your disposal."

"Thank you, Francis." I said smiling to him.

"While we're at that...I believe I should contact Arianna and tell her of your arrival. I made a promise to be in peace by helping her," Jesus said. He eyed at Francis. "Francis, if you please?"

"Certainly." He said as he eyed at us before he went with Jesus. "You three know what to do. So, you are dismissed. Take the time to prepare to get to Arcadia."

"Pleasure to meet you once again, Mr. Princeton." Gabriel said as I nodded.

We also nodded to Francis before he left the room as well as the other monarchs. Before Dante could leave with his hands behind his back, I said to him in a very generous way, "Oy Dante." He turned to me with a fatalist face. "Thank you for the suggestion."

"Don't take my assistance for imprudence, Mr. Princeton." He said strictly. "It's the last thing you'd want to do. I want this madness dealt with as much as anyone, even if it means to put the afterlife's fate in your hands. We usually accomplish without the likes of a...special unit. So, to speak. But with Lucifer's power growing more and more...I don't see any other choice than to have guardian angels. For the time being anyway. Just know that you are still not up to par with what the Archangels were. You will never be! Don't try to be. So, do me a favor, on behalf of the House of God and the Chancery; Do. Not. Mess. It. Up!"

"Right...sir." I said as he closed the door behind him. The entire room felt empty without the rest of them.

Ted laid back on the chair, like an old man or grumpy guy rocking on his rocking chair. "Wow...he helps us whilst simultaneously continues to be an asshole. Who knew? Hell, his friend sounds a lot more fun than he does. He's just butthurt since the Order is not the Chancery's toy anymore."

"All of it sounds well and good. Momentarily." Juliet said as she stood up from her chair. "But how will we get to Arcadia in a matter of time? We cannot delay any further. Time is of the essence as it is. And the Unicorn could be at large. I don't plan for what happened at the lab to repeat."

This triggered an idea I had in my head. I grinned to myself while scratching underneath my chin. I then eyed at the two of them and asked, "I've gotten an idea. But are you lads up to see something awesome?"

I asked as I was given uncertain reactions. Of course, I was clearly ready to introduce Aventurine. Especially knowing that I could use him to my advantage. And he was indeed going to be my advantage.

The dusk was soon becoming drowned into the day. When we got back to the Khalservan on a carriage, I led Ted and Juliet to the stables on the side of the castle, hoping to find Aventurine there. To my surprise as I was leading the Apostles to the stables, a familiar companion came out of the blue, swaying himself away from the other side of the castle.

It was clearly Algor, who was obviously happy to see me again. I only assumed that the monks let him out for fresh air. I also assumed that he was introduced to Aventurine by the monks right after he traversed back to the Khalservan without me. I watched the hairy brute jump onto my torso, almost making me jolt back on my heels. My hands were feeling moist and sticky from his slobbering. Ted and Juliet also greeted him by patting and stroking his head. He jumped back down to suddenly lead me to the stables, as we soon followed.

Underneath the shadowy stables, I saw the glowing beast chugging his snout into a wooden bucket of water. As soon as he recognized me, he sorted and neighed gleefully. I stroked his snout as he closed his eyes in amusement. Ted and Juliet's eyes widened as their mouths dropped. I introduced Aventurine formally, telling them of what he can do and how he can help us traverse the afterlife, if lucky.

Ted got closer and stared with complete awe. When he turned to me, he asked, "That's a pertlow! They're usually ain't one to show in Valestone. How did you get this!?"

"Christmas gift." I said.

"This is a beautiful Icelandic creature." Juliet said as she stroked Aventurine's grey mane. "You're very lucky, Kevin."

It made me grin.

"Thanks. We just have to let him rest and eat for now, so he'll be able to help us." I said. "Let's ride properly for now. We gotta get the device from Frask."

We rode on horseback. I rode on a regular horse for my steed to rest. We stopped by to Frask's shop to get the device, which was evolving every time I was coming back. I remembered when I first saw it; it looked like a progressing store. But now, it was flourishing like a five-star gallery. Four paintings, inspired by neoclassical arts, were displayed outside on these easels planted into the snow. Inside was cleaner and organized than what I previously saw in months and weeks. The store was filled with shelves, each containing painting products and extra utensils for aspiring painters in the afterlife. Every wall was scattered with paintings encrusted with gold decorated frames.

When the three of us met Frask again, he was still his bubbly self. And he was excited more than ever to show us what he has created. I was anticipated to see what he had in store for us. When he took us into the back of his desk, he led the three of us to the basement, where I recalled the time when I first met him and helped him rearrange. But that wasn't what he wanted to show us. The basement that was deserted was completely different than when I first came. It was unreal to think that something this secretive was underneath a simple painting gallery.

We were surrounded with grey walls that he painted. It welcomed us. Shelves on each wall that contained vials, jars, bottles, flasks, and beakers of various colored chemicals. Including several jars of different herbs such as yellowdock roots and rosemary. In the middle was a large rectangular wooden with glass tubes, microscopes, and organic glassware to experiment with several types of chemicals. On every wall, it had diagrams of what was in Frask's mind. I saw nothing but ambition from him. There were diagrams of cars, trains, airships, telephones, and other forms of ideas for what he wanted to build. All of them were drawn on these clear white pieces of paper with eraser smudges scattered at some parts.

On the side of the table, where he was leading us were the three dragonfly prototypes he was building from scratch. One of them was rusty and colored in copper. The other one in the middle was made completely out of chrome. The last and final one was colored with schemes of jet black, which cover the entire base. The dragonfly-like eyes were pure bronze. And the wings were chrome colored and made of dried leaves.

Frask explained while being his bubbly self, "What do you think?"

"You never seize to stop amazing me, Frask," I said, still fixating around the underground lab. "It's extraordinary."

"Thanks. I've been prepping this place for six months on the side of advancing my painting business." Frask said, gesturing his open hands at the entire environment. He then eyed his focus on the dragonfly drone. He removed the completed version of it as he then displayed it right in front of us.

He went on and explained about how the compass worked, which was placed onto the head of the dragonfly, and how the eyes will detect anything that is working. As he was explaining in great lengths, he made sure that his finger was pointed at each feature of the machine. He pointed at the wings, explaining that they can reach no more that twenty-two feet from the ground. Inside the back of the machine, he stored inside a crystal that can be manipulated with lightkeeper magic, which we luckily had. When he unlocked the contraption that held the battery cover, he unveiled two small white quartzes that were comfortably stored inside the appliance.

He explained that the mechanism worked like controlling an aerial vehicle. It reminded me of how an RC would work with a controller. And this was almost the same idea. He activated it with a book of alchemic runes. With the opened book, he said, "Great might of Cerridwen! Extract your great lights of divine prestige!"

Thus, its eyes glowed for at least nine seconds. Thus, he had the book closed and glanced at us with playful smugness.

"That seems plausible." Juliet said. "But how would it work?"

"Someone has to use the power of telekinesis to control the crystal, powering it to move. It would react like a controllable convertible," He instructed.

The three of us eyed at one another, exchanging eyes. I studied each Apostle and re-identified their abilities. And knowing that Juliet could easily use Alwyn to rediscover the sound, chances of him locating them was slim. But I identified myself and recalled to how I used telekinesis before. And I thought about how it can truly work in our favor. Thus, I volunteered to levitate and power up the device if this was the means to truly help us find The Unicorn. And chances were that it could detect what source of powerful relics she could be using to attempting to enhance the Promised Land to their will.

Frask assisted that we tried it out to test it. When he placed the device carefully on the dirty-colored concrete floor, we all stood back. I turned to Frask; whose fingers were crossed until the tip of his fingers was brightening red.

I triggered back into the Blessed Eye and closed both of my eyes, remembering what Francis told me: above all else, guard your heart, for everything you do flows from it. What I had to do was let it flow from my body. What I held inside was something I must let go.

Once I peeled my eyes back open, I saw myself lifting the moving machine from the ground. I watched in awe at the device flapping its wings in great speed, almost like a real dragonfly. Each eye bloomed with bright white light, which looked like I was staring at two headlights. Before I desynchronized myself from the Blessed Eye, I carefully swayed the dragonfly in midair.

With the eyes of my friends looking at me, I gently placed it back on the table. I saw the lights quickly disbursed from its eyes, implying that it was switched off. Cheers and applauds came from Ted and Juliet, but mostly Frask. He cheered and sighed in great relief. Placing two hands on his hips, he scoffed with pride. I was huddled with brotherly slaps on the back from Ted and Frask. I felt being bumped forward in a friendly gesture. When Frask thanked us, he warned us to try it when weather conditions are harsh, which could potentially weaken it. That means the sky had to be clear for the device to be accessible.

After we rode back from the city, we were at the Khalservan's keep, preparing ourselves in the Common Room. We packed up Aventurine's saddle was placed in the trunk on it. I even brought along my guitar, in case of boredom. I even brought the journal and book Kelley gave me during Christmas. Aside of my personal things, we prepared and packed our weapons. We wore it proudly.

Juliet and I were polishing our swords on an old-fashioned grinding wheel and cleaning them with holy water, including our firearms in the Khalservan's blacksmith workshop. We adjusted our holsters when our swords were in wand formation right by our pistols. Ted was polishing and cleaning his scepter Penelope, who was not in snake form just yet. When we removed our coats, we harnessed ourselves with holsters to place our pistols. All three of us had holsters to carry two pistols. In addition, with our powers, we can conjure additional weapons such as our bows. And bombs in our satchels. It took us a little while for us to prepare ourselves in case any Satanist was to come across our path.

The monks prayed over us for our safety, asking God to protect us along the journey and to bring good news. I asked God to help me put an end to this chaos, no matter the cost.

I closed my eyes, consuming every word of mouth from the monks. As for the two Apostles, and myself we prayed in pure silence as the monks spoke. For the first time in a long while, I asked God to give us strength. I asked him to give us the energy to accomplish this task and to avoid, as Dante put it before, messing it up. And I asked him to keep my family safe this time. Just as Francis gave me a chance, I decided to do the same for him. And I did not plan to be let down again. Ever again.

In case we had to camp out, especially if our horses got tired, we brought an enchanted satchel on the saddles for supplies and accessories for tents and matches to make fire.

As we were done, we were all outside of the castle. It was as if we were going into battle. But it was in a metaphorical and physical sense. Only the battle seemed small and meant to be awry from the common spirits. While I was of course mounted on the saddle, Ted and Juliet sat on their horses. I had ropes attached to their saddles just, so we would traverse all together. And yes, I decided to bring Algor for the ride, just so he didn't get mad at me again. I also saw that the two Apostles wore hats as well. Juliet's own panama hat and Ted's fedora. When I turned to the front, Francis was there before we were able to take off. He walked up to me, his eyes admiring Aventurine. "See you got yourself a pertlow. These are sacred creatures, Kevin. Cherish him as you cherish Algor."

"Of course." I said with a grin. "I could be sure to traverse in an instant to Arcadia."

"Certainly. And...I'm glad you came back." Francis said stroking the creature's mane. After he smiled at me, he then faced the three of us. "Remember, you do not have to do this alone. You should meet several allies to aid you into finding the targets. Arcadia has got quite a lot of nice folks who show respect to God fearing folks like us."

"What are you going to do, Francis," Ted asked.

"We have to protect the kingdom and detect for more demonic energy. We'll be in contact with the herbalists of Goliath's Bay." Francis said. "You just have to worry about The Unicorn and The Phoenix. Get any information from them and see if they have taken anything that belonged to us."

"Right." I complied. "We will."

"May the Lord be with you three." He said smiling.

"And also, with you, Francis." We all said. I watched as he stood back from the horse.

Afterwards, I faced the front and exhaled a breath I held unknowingly. Whipping the reins, I felt Aventurine danced a bit as he began to gallop. I did the same routine as I did before. When I was getting faster and faster, I watched and grinned as Ted and Juliet were holding on tightly to their horses. Their heads turned confusedly, not knowing my reasoning for my speed. We rode further and further away from the knight's keep.

"Uh...why are we going fast, Kevin?" Juliet asked, almost frightened.

"You'll see." I watched Aventurine's eyes bloom with light once again and the smoke was revolving around us when we suddenly felt very light. The vapors of blue smoke surrounded us once again whilst we were finally getting led towards the spiral.

XXVIII

Arcadia, The City of Nature and Charms

Once we were out of the spiral, we found ourselves galloping towards another path that was between two mountains. All around us, the trees were decorated with ornaments painted with Pagan design. It was telling me that we were already in The Summerland. I heard Algor panting right behind me, next to my ear as he was also entranced by what we were seeing.

Once we were heading towards the peaks of the mountains, the sun began to bloom in our eyes. And I knew that it was indeed morning already.

Once we were on the other side, I saw a floral designed gate that read *Welcome to Arcadia.*

Through the open gates displayed a massive ocean of orange and brown rooftops, grey towers, basilicas, pine trees and mosques. We were finally welcomed by the city. Further from the city was a large castle integrated on a mountain with waterfalls pouring down at some presumed river or canal. It smelled of mint chocolate this time around, since I guess we were in Summerland. Beyond were pointed mountains and seas cloaked with white sunny mist.

"Arcadia." Juliet recalled the name. We were then heading down to the city, taking in its wonder. We were going down a swirly path that had rows of pink, blue and yellow gypsum statues of what looked like the various Pagan gods ranging from the luxurious Selene or the wild forest god Pan. The snow was gradually melting, which made it easier for me to feast my eyes on the meadows completely overflown with sunflowers. Dragonflies (hah, funny!) were hovering over the sunflowers while some were flying from place to place. Some were even flying around us.

The look of the city alone made me appreciate the attention to detail everyone has built for this city. After we passed the gates, we were on the main street of Arcadia. It looked like Celestia, only the art nouveau buildings were diverse with many different colors and were even painted with fluorescent and swirling designs. In the middle of the city center was a silver fountain with dancing virginal women statues. The people were dressed almost the same, but the women and little girls were dressed in these loose-fitting flowery, almost ceremonial, dresses. The men were garbed in robes with three to four layers of various fabrics. But every single person donned these flower and leaf crowns on their heads. To me, it felt like traversing through a true medieval city with its secular houses made of stone and wood. I sometimes wondered if the cities in the afterlife looked this flourished and elegant before.

"They call this city the *City of Nature and Charms*." Ted stated. "That's what it's famous for."

"I could see why." I agreed and adjusted on the saddle. There was more to Heaven than I realized. Five large land masses within the heavenly realm. But of course, cultures there were different. There were different gods praised obviously.

I was riding Aventurine to the right. When we about to leave the city square, we were suddenly stopped by two guards. While on the subject on guards; they were different from the angels. Most of them were women who had white wispy butterfly wings on their backs. Their halberds had an extravagant look to them. The blades were curved and almost shaped like roses. The women even had pointed ears.

The first one, wearing pink and green colors leaf armor, asked, "Are you the Apostles?"

"Yes, we are." Juliet answered. The two guards glanced at one another. They then looked back at me. She then said, "My name is Clemency Stardust, leader of the Fairy Army Force. I would kindly like for you three to come with us. We received the dove from Jesus Christ regarding your arrival."

I looked back and eyed at the Apostles, then eyed at Algor. I looked back at the guards and asked, "Can I bring my pertlow?"

"Yes, just not the alvoton." The other guard, with blue and red armor, said. "The Queen has a fear for alvotons, I'm afraid."

I looked back at Algor. He looked sad, knowing what I was going to tell him. He was a smart lad. And very loyal. Always strived to join along my adventures. I stroked the side of his big face, reassuring him. "Don't worry, lad. I'll call upon you too."

He barked happily, which made me grin. I saw Juliet smile at him and stroked between his horns. The other fairy was then leading Algor to follow her with a small wand with a fuzzy smiley face on it. His black eyes were widened in amusement, which made the Apostles and I chuckle. I watched him disperse into the crowds to find somewhere sacred and secret to hide.

"You could see him again after you meet the Queen. We'll have him entertained at the stables. The Queen is awaiting you." The other guard said.

Upon going through the city, we finally reached the castle's entrance. I could barely hear any sound of conversation due to the waterfalls pounding down the mountains next to the castle. It was a hybrid of a basilica on top of the cliff. A large dam was place right in front of the cliff beneath the basilica. There were other gatehouses on each side of the door. We were walking on a bridge with four white marble effigies on each side of the bridge. I briefly looked down to see a streaming moat between the castle's cliff and a plateau in which the city was on.

As we were walking, the other guards stood parallel of us and bowed as soon as we arrived.

When we reach the massive green doors, they opened in front of us after we dismounted from our mounts. The opening alone made me feel slight vibrations underneath. Upon reaching the inside of the room was the main compound of the castle. The guards told us since Queen Arianna Moon was not feeling too well; she was resting in her chambers. So, after passing through the weapon and armored ornamented room, they led us to an elevator that was located inside another room passed the main one. It was a decently medium-sized room made of brick. In the middle was a dark wooden platform attached to four strings on each corner. It was underneath an open orifice that shot down rays of white light.

Shortly after we stepped on, we were instantly being pulled up from the room. It gave us an opportunity to look over the city's horizon as well as the warm misty mountains surrounding it. We were getting no higher than sixty feet from the ground. The three of us looked out in amazement, almost like we are seeing the entire spirit world with new eyes. I looked in front to see the elevator pulling us up against the front of the dam. Once we reached the top of the cliff, the basilica welcomed us. And I assumed that this is where the queen would be resting in. Beyond the cliff was a forest of pine trees, leading to whatever part of land.

When we were led inside, after taking in the natural aroma, we were inside the main room. Another one, I mean. The ceiling has a chandelier made of purple and white quartz. White clear cloths were looped and draped across the doming ceiling. The basilica was being taken care of by these women in loose fitting-colored dresses. There were other guards who patrolled and protected every corner of the place. The guards then led us to the right stairwell, leading us to the right side of the building. After going through the hallway, in front of us was looked to be the entrance to her bedroom. Once the maids opened the door, after getting Arianna to acknowledge our presence, she called for us to come inside.

When we were invited inside, the color of the room brightened and shined like I was in the chamber of God. White and gold drapes were hanging and dangling from the ceiling. The maidens were spreading green leaves across the marble tiled floors. Each side of her king-sized bed, which had a gold headboard with a white floral frame, she had two dressers that contained candles, iris pedals, and bowls with incense smoke floating up. Her headboard draped with white cloth.

We were finally introduced to Queen Arianna, who was in her blue celestial nightgown and her red braided hair was poured down to her shoulders. Her face shine like the sun and was riddle with little freckles beneath her purple eyes. Underneath her eyes were dark sunken bags. Two other women were dressed in floral dresses, like the priestesses. One was wiping the queen's forehead with a moist towel while the other was praying over her with her hands clammed together. The three of us bowed in her service.

"These are the Apostles of Valestone, Your Majesty." Clemency stated.

"How nice of you to come. It is an honor," She spoke smiling, but with a sickly tone. She glanced at the two women and said, "Thank you, Clemency and girls."

"You're welcome, Your Majesty." They both addressed, disbursing from the room. The guards nodded and left the three of us with her alone. After the door closed behind us, I faced the Queen.

"I take it that you are pleased with Arcadia so far?" She asked.

I then said to her, "It's very unreal. In a great way, I mean. Something out of a fairy tale book."

"I'm glad you approve. My apologies for my state." She said, following a sequence of coughs. "I don't mean for any of this to happen."

"It's not your fault, Your Majesty." Juliet said. "That's why we're here."

"Yes. At least I know I'm a taken care of by Selene's blessings. I should feel better eventually. But to the matter at hand...I know you simply didn't come to visit. It's about Lucifer's co-conspirator; The Unicorn." She said as she coughed once again. This time, she coughed into a tissue, which showed smears of blood on it.

Widening my eyes, I asked her, "Should I get the nurse?"

"That wouldn't be necessary." She said humbly. "But thank you, Mr. Princeton." I looked back and saw Juliet raised her eyebrow at me. I figured it was her way of saying *I'm right here.* Nearly forgotten.

"Jesus sent me a dove's note about you three. And from what I hear, you three are experts in this line of work. Seems like you're the semblance of what's left of Francis' band of knights," She said grinning.

"Well, we're still learning, Your Majesty." I said. "And quite frankly, killing the Unicorn is a start. And then The Phoenix. Soon...The Angel."

As I stated this, her eyes were widening. "You mean there's more of them in the Promised Land?"

"Well...only two, Your Majesty." Juliet said, stepping further to the queen. "But we are keen to lift Arcadia off the curse first. And to get the scepter back. Gabriel had us come here for that."

"Thank you." She said. "I called to let you know that you have the Civil Force of Fairies at your assistance. I know they have connections to Ms. June of Celestia. Whatever I could do to help, it's on you to summon my soldiers."

"Thanks, Your Majesty." Ted complimented. She looked down at her floral comforter. Her eyes were suddenly filled with guilt.

"I know it must be odd, assisting the queen at this state. I understand it's your duty to protect spirits, not just kings or queens. I don't wish for us monarchs to be the blockade of that purpose."

"We protect every form of innocence, Your Majesty." Ted said. "We don't discriminate."

"That's good to hear. To defend the spirits, the monarchs need to be in good health themselves. I guess I was so reduced in looking out for myself as oppose to looking out for my fellow people. Their well-being is as important as my health."

"We understand. The monarchs are just as important." Juliet said. "We won't let the sickness get to you. You have our word." The queen gave a gentle smile through her wrinkled face.

"And I thank you, from the bottom of my heart, for taking great care of the priestesses of Edenstone. Including little Bella. My heart ached, and my eyes watered after I was told about what happened to them.

Especially to poor little Sally. It was very disheartening to tell the news of her death...to her parents. Lucifer will perish for what he has done!" She said in a softly bitter tone in the mention of Lucifer.

She then continued with gloom, "Those girls were full of light and joy. Especially Bella. We Pagans are grand lovers of life. Those girls showed it once. And those soulless harbingers of the Devil took that away from them. I feel very ashamed for not knowing sooner. But nonetheless, I am utterly grateful, on behalf of the Pagan spirits, for your aid."

"You're very welcome, Your Majesty." I said.

"Where do you suppose you would start when you are searching for the Unicorn?"

"We could figure that out for ourselves." I said. "You just worry about healing in the name of the goddesses Selene."

"Amen." She said. "You three are blessed. And blessings from Jesus Christ. I hope that your actions will also reconcile with my people...given how they went...quite anarchic when he arrived to meet me. I know you will." She then tried to turn to her left dresser. By the struggle of her hand and body movement, she was trying to reach over for a jar of honey that was next to the incense bowl. Juliet grasped it and handed it to her.

"No, it is meant for you." She said following her coughs. "I already have mine. This is what I have been using for a while now to heal. The gods and goddesses enchant it. If you can, you can give this to the girls, as a token of my gratitude. I ache to see them again. I know it may not do much, but I'd do anything to see them happy and bright as they were before. I might as well get a chakra specialist. But...still, I bid you to have this."

"We will. Thank you." I said.

Soon after we were led off from the castle by the queen's guards, we were back at the city once again. We rested on the fountain, briefly sightseeing every building, and taking in the Pagan and forest-like atmosphere the kingdom of The Summerland was inspired by. We saw other people and children pass by us, creating moving smears of figures bringing life into a world of the deceased. Horse drawn carriages were being driven as well.

Though instead of horses, there were mountable, almost large elks, reindeers, milus, does and stags. Large rainbow butterflies flew across the sky, flapped, and looped like birds in Celestia. Like I said to the Queen, I felt like I was in a Grimm tale. And the buildings were giving that away with their Romanesque and Gothic motifs and style. But the task was on hand. And I had to recall one of the easier options out of all three, Dante's. As much as I had an immense problem with him, he did give us a potentially better option.

"I was thinking." I said. "Perhaps we should try...Dante's idea."

"Are you sure?" Juliet said.

"Yes." I stated. "If we want to do this without dragging the Civil Force yet, we have to do it subtly. We should find Virgil if he's even in this city. Or if Dante was just being an arse and lied to us. Which I doubt, given his profession."

"I suppose we can ask somebody." Ted implied. "Doesn't hurt to do so, anyway." We all stood up, wandering amongst the crowd.

"Oy." A voice rang. As we turned, we realized that it came from a chap, who looked to be a young adult. Obviously way older than us. "You lads are talkin' 'bout Virgil, the poet?"

"Aye," I said. "I can only assume that you know where he is?"

"Course I do. Ain't he friends with that cocker Chancellor Aligheri? Not much of a fan of any bloke from Valestone, I'm afraid. None of us are." He said.

"Yes. He was a Chancellor before," Juliet added. "At least that is what Dante tells us."

"Well...he's apparently a star among this city. Serves the queen as a nobleman. But he's very mysterious." He said as he gazed upon the area. Facing us, he said, "But from what I've heard...he's been at a place called *Cupids of Clionadh* lately. You should find 'im there."

"Cupids of Clionadh? Is it like a...theater or something?" I asked.

"No, it's a love hotel, mate. But most of us go there for those massages from 'em hostesses. Especially rich folk from the Summerland monarchy." He said, pointing at the left side of the narrow avenue. "Just straight over there. He usually charms the people with everything he recites from his works. He could woe an audience. Got to advice you though, it's best to travel on the canals. Trust me. Really fun being in one of 'em gondola tents. I've been there meself. A couple of times. For...reasons."

"We'll take note of that...I suppose." I said, estranged to hear about a love hotel. In Heaven no less. "Thank you, mate. Cheers."

"Cheers lads." The man took off. The three of us exchanged weird looks at once another. Nevertheless, we had a mission to do. Thus, we took off.

XXIX

❦

The Unicorn

From the city center to the canals, it almost reminded me of Venice, where my mother did her music tour. It was a place I know of, but I never got a chance to go. But I digress. When we got onto the canals, a good rower took it upon himself to sail us down the streaming path. We passed underneath bridges and past other houses and buildings...on the way to a love hotel. Words fail to describe how strange it was for a world like Heaven to have a place like that. I had to remember that this was no different from the natural world I came from. But at the same time, I was curious on how it was like. Maybe it's not the kind I was thinking about. But then, I've never went to a love hotel. So, I wouldn't know.

"I'm curious, guys. Are there any other brothels or...exotic places in Celestia? Or somewhere in Valestone? In Heaven?" I asked.

"Well... yeah. Listen, any world would have places for loose women to indulge with, for free or a good price. There are sacred prostitution temples, often commercial for me. When I was in the gang, I went to this place called Birds of Paradise with the boys in Eranson. In fact, I went not so long ago to do portraits of the girls...and dudes. So...yeah." Ted said. "But these harlots are different. They view their nudity and sex as a work of art. And it's a chance to revive its sacred nature by being vulnerable to the gods. At least that's what I was told."

"I believe they're called...Neotantras." Juliet stated. "Hostesses and lasses who adopted the practice from the Tantric tradition. They help spirits free themselves after intense and extensive repression that manifested guilt and shame. They practice it order to see the act as a sacred act that could elevate us into becoming truly one with divinity. They use these love hotels as places to help practice that in private with sessions. I think I've met several of them as a priestess."

"Dear lord! That young, eh? And I suppose...you're against that. Works revolving mating?" I asked out of curiosity.

"Not really. It seems institutionalized, but they seem to do it for a good cause anyway. Most anyway. They deserve to follow whatever path pleases them. Hope they chose that life...and weren't forced by others. And if they are, of course, protected from diseases. But it's been difficult to discuss or practice these days because, like most things in life, we tend to be reckless. It's very sad because...it's such a beautiful act of love that's been either shamed or tarnished, which is why I respect these women for trying to revive what made it great." Juliet admitted.

She continued, "It's...not just for me personally, that's all. I'm very timid and preferred to do it with...someone I truly loved and valued. Private, of course. Not sporadic like Lustina."

"That's obvious. Whatever floats your boat, it seems. No pun intended." Ted said, referring to the moving gondola. "Just as long as we don't have the entire afterlife manifested with orgies. We've had enough revolutions led by perverted collectivist assholes who take it too far."

"Truly. But I'm just...astonished by the mere fact that an accomplice of Dante would reside there." Juliet said. "Let alone to woe the girls. And we know what kind of person Dante is."

"I guess he became a libertine." Ted added. "Dante did say that he was somewhat of a socialite. Maybe these girls are easily wet by pretentious foreign poets."

"Well, love hotel or not, if we must ask Virgil for any information on

The Unicorn in there, we have to take the chance. Even if it means to be seduced to a bunch of nymphs." I jested, which made Juliet scoffed playfully.

"Oh, and Kev, as part of your training.... once we find the Unicorn, I want you to do the honors of killing or stopping him. We'll save our blades." Ted suggested humbly.

"I appreciate that, lad." I said, focusing back on the canals.

After a good while, we made it to the entrance of the hotel. When we stepped off from the gondola, we were presented with two marble statues of Hindu women offering themselves to the gods. It looked like a relatively big palace amid other buildings in the avenue. Other gondolas surrounded us. But they were relatively large compared to ours. They even had tents integrated into them accompanied by muffled and rhythmic moans and grunts of pleasure. They were just adrift across the large canal and floated in front of the hotel.

When we approached to the gatekeepers of the hotel, they asked us for our purpose. As soon as we stated our occupations, they let us inside. An elderly Celtic woman, who wore a flamboyant festival headdress, led us. She was the building's owner. Her white dress was decorated with blue, amber, and purple gems. She clarified a bit about the place, saying that it was a place that was to help spirits bring sex with divinity; just as Juliet modestly explained before. According to her, she believed that the natural world has commercialized intimate sensuality for the sake of making a profit. With the Cupids of Clionadh, one of the most famous and richest love hotels in the Promised Land, she claims that it was different because they want to show genuine help for their clients. She hoped for people to practice their sexuality and to connect to spirit and themselves. And she wanted to prove that. She proved that as she banned pedophiles, polygamists, incest doers, necrophiles and other forms of crazed degenerates from entering the hotel. Still, they accepted choices that were harmless. We told her that we didn't need to rent a room when she asked us.

We reached the main hall that led to the stairs. I was almost distracted by the voluptuous, breasts-barring, and exotic women and etching covered nymphs lounging about on the upper level of the stairs. As arousing as the place was, we had to keep our eyes peeled. I reckoned that they were the hostesses the bloke was talking about.

Every chandelier shined with a white-pink tint color. To point out, mosaic walls were decorated with these eerily stirring pagan and neo-classical paintings of men and women going at it in various positions. I was taken back to how I was with Talia. I remembered having constant sex with her in a broken-down apartment. In a way, I knew what to expect. I wouldn't be surprised to see slightly opened doors with a man and woman fully undressed going at one another. It was what I saw in the apartment.

But that wasn't the case. I could only assume from some of the muted cries of achieved orgasms were the signs of love being rediscovered, re-signed, and elevated through many planes. Sensual, not fake. Each room had various types of experiments to enhance a spirit's sensual sensation. The madam told us of the attractions on our way. Massage rooms, where even the massager was stripped of her clothes to be vulnerable to nature. But I saw it as some sort of endurance test for the clients, especially since they couldn't engage in any intercourse with them.

There were private rooms where they practiced rites, including something called a *skyclad*. There were massage rooms in which the hostesses help clients to practice balanced self-pleasure as a procedure to release strain, ease the mood, and improves sleeping. It's one of the most popular attractions; for obvious reasons. Somehow, a thought crept into my head when I was grasping everything around me. It made me feel rather disgusting for how I treated Talia, despite what she was. I wished that I saw her as I was seeing Juliet, instead of someone to sorely have unmindful sex with. I disregarded her tears and her essence as a person. I felt nothing but shame as I heard the moans of love that I wished I had with myself and one whom I treasured. I wished Talia would have seen herself as a woman, not a piece of meat for dogs such was I.

Pagans, and other ancient beliefs I've learned about in the afterlife, seemed broader when it came to accepting life, whether as a spirit or human, for what it was. Yet, they knew how to make it beautiful, free, and unique to live through. They weren't seeking for Heaven, for they felt it all around them. They made heavens for themselves. They didn't see the body as a sin or prison for the soul, but sacred temples for them. I truly admired that. I truly hoped to grasp that. Some rooms contained poets publicly reading erotic works in which they wanted to share to a decent group. One of them had to be Virgil. Perhaps he was a charmer and wanted to seduce these women to his words. The woman told us that he had been a frequent attendee for the inn as of late.

The man wore a loose white shirt and had dark blue breeches. Each wrist was bedazzled with several bracelets consisted of many types of gems, limestones, and minerals. His hair was ashy grey, and a bit of his hair bang covered a notch of his green eyes. He had stubs across the bottom of his face. The women in the room were entranced and aroused by what sounded like an epic poetry, something he might have written from the days when he was alive.

The Madame cleared her throat to catch the man's attention, which I was coming to figure that it was indeed Virgil. "Mr. Maro! You have three enchanted guests who are urged to see you." He raised his head and swiped the hair from his eyes.

"How could I trust you?" He asked, as he spoke with this odd voice of sophistication.

"We're...friends of Dante Alighieri, Chancellor of Celestia in Valestone." I stated, but I knew well that Dante and I weren't friends. To be truthful, I was trying my best to avoid eye contact with the big eyed and half naked hostesses sitting lavishly on the red and pink carpet. I saw why some clients, who were single, went there. Some laid on their bosoms with their bums erected and feet waving back and forth.

A smile curved across his face, "Ah! Dante! In this case, any friend of Dante...is welcome to join the circle." He then gazed at the Madame. "Thank you, Charlotte. I'll take it from here." The woman nodded with a smile.

Once we went inside the drape-covered room, the Madame left us with a smile, wishing us a good time. When we all turned to the man, he said, "Come, join us. I was just reciting one of my greatest works, The Aeneid. Not the most romantic nor arousing title, I recognize."

"Um...actually, Mr. Maro, we were hoping if we could talk..." Juliet was asking as she too was trying her damnedest to avoid the women. "....in private."

"Of course. Of course," He said as he placed down his brown covered book and regarded to his female audience. "Ladies please, you're making the guests uncomfortable with your awe-inspiring looks of desire. Do your jobs of welcoming folks. Please give us a moment. This sounds serious." He charmed. He was right. This was serious.

All the women got up from the ground, picked up their dresses and began to disburse from the room. With a quick glance, I swore I thought I saw Ted briefly gazing at each half-undressed lady as they were disbursing. Once they all left the room, I closed the door behind us. Virgil gestured his hands for us to sit on the circular bed masked with a pink bed sheet. I tried not to imagine what his work might have made those women do to themselves or to him to make him sound as if he was in ecstasy.

"No offense. But knighthood is a bit outdated, from what I've heard around here. Is it not?" He asked.

"Well so is charming women with pretentious poetry, but we don't complain about that apparently," I said.

He glanced at Juliet and said, "I love this one already. So fierce!" Clearly, he fancied my hardened demeanor. Bully for him, I suppose.

He then went off to the cabinet to make drinks for us. "So...what are three fine friends of my dearest Dante doing in Arcadia? I wasn't aware that he would send...apprentices. Unless you are aspiring poets?"

"Well...no." Ted said. "I couldn't creatively write shit."

"You see, sir...Dante told us to come to you." Juliet said, getting us back on track. "He apparently believes you might know a thing or two about the secrets of Hell. Being that you were imprisoned there...along with the others. You were recently released. Yes?"

"Yes. And I've been residing here ever since...just to be surrounded by love. Dante and I truly bonded ever since he put me in that ambitious poem of his... The Divine Comedy. Since we were working for the Chancery," he said as he offered us three glasses of white wine. "Ever since I died and ascended here, I was thankful for the nobility the Queen gave me. But because I've gotten bored in diving into politics...I retreated here. As for these secrets of Hell, as he puts it..." He then sat down on his rocking chair with his legs crossed. "...I don't know much. Although I do know they have...interesting tactics. They made us do the most fascinating things." He sipped his drink. "I hear it from victims all the time. Most of them true. But a lot of them...complete balderdash. I urge that you take these with a grain of salt."

"So, you do know most? You know how?" I asked.

"Credit to the victims, they say that the Devil himself plans to... let something else die for another to live." He said. "He's willing to stop the afterlife from having an identity crisis. Even the most drunk would admit that it's become quite twisted than it was before. He even had me, and the others write their pledge in black ink to remember his cursed code. It seemed like it made sense to have one. Civilizations have always been conditioned by leaders to follow a specific agenda for universal peace. But he wants to do what others couldn't. Rumor has it he plans to make the afterlife one universe only."

"Interesting...I suppose. But...how?" Juliet said confusedly.

"I can't tell you that." He said with a chuckle. "I'd be caught and dead on the spot. And you would be too if he knows. Like I said, take it with a grain of salt." He elegantly took a sip of his wine.

"I'm not sure how much energy you've drained from your brain, after you've supposedly fucked those women we saw, to realize how much of that does not make any sense," I said. "The afterlife...one universe only?"

"Whatever do you mean? It could happen. And no, I haven't done those women in. I'm practically old enough to be their midlife crisis honing grandfather." Virgil defended.

"And what do you mean take it with a grain of salt? What salt is there to take, man? Seems like it's his way of trying to get more folks into his flock," Ted said. "I get spirits. But...the entire afterlife being just one universe? That's just being too ambitious! Everyone knows that the afterlife wouldn't survive without the natural world. It's a goddamn bridge that holds both worlds together. Balance, for Christ's sake! How come nobody gets that?"

"You would have to be Anu herself to do that," Juliet added. "I resent humanity sometimes...but I wouldn't go out of my way to destroy the only place they live and prosper on. It's...where we came from before. And humans need to excel to a new life after their old ones. You should know that surely."

"Maybe, but like anyone else...he has reasons. Either good or bad. And some would go far to verify them," Virgil stated. "We forget that no one is good or bad in life. Or the one we had."

"Obviously we know that, but what I'm saying that he's no different from any other zealot or revolutionary trying to rectify world peace and harmony. I could name them all if I have too! And need I remind you of how badly those turned out? It's the same song and dance. There's always some guy whose butthurt about how life works, preaches about a pure world until he slowly becomes a tyrant. Utopias are unachievable because of nature," Ted stated firmly. "It doesn't matter since...y'know, we ain't exactly squeaky clean as we'd like to believe."

"They're really not, dear boy. And they do matter. The truth is that we could reach standards we thought impossible; building a flying machine or...develop a large cathedral big as a mountain. All it takes are the eradications of distractions and full attention to perseverance and a helluva lot of sacrifices. Even if it kills you."

"Either way, it's no excuse for doing what he does," Juliet added her two cents. "If Lucifer really wanted change, he himself should have changed. Changed his perception and not to become some...relentless tyrant intending to create an empire out of this place. In his vision, no less. Even Jesus knows better."

After sipping his white wine, he said, "That's always been the game, dear. It just depends on those who play their cards right. There are two teams, love; those who welcome all to it...and those...who want it for themselves. Regardless of how you see it, it's the ultimate heist for power. No different from our old world, isn't it? One big heist for dominance since time began. But still...I understand why you truly value Jesus as king. He's humble. He puts his folks over his own needs. Therefore, he doesn't take part in any silly games conjured by men on top of the food chain. He's like one of those...individuals who...act upon the generous food for thought. But eventually...that is going to kill him in the end."

"Why would it kill him? Because he'd be stopped by folks who hate goodness?" Ted asked.

"No. We tend to deny it because we fight an oppression of our own making. But all kings need power. They need to extract power. That's what they represent. But the throne needs the right power. Every good stallion or mare needs a good rider. Every infant would need that perfect nurture of a mother's tit. Every universe needs that perfect force. I could only hope that Jesus...is that force," He explained. "And the afterlife is a place for proper...professional authority. One who takes his or her role seriously. Some would see their crusade fulfilled by seeing their people as liabilities...tools. And it often works. I mean...it works for Lucifer anyway."

After I scoffed, I asked, "I...suppose. But what does this conversation have to do with anything?"

"A lot, dear boy. This is everything I grasped when I was held prisoner in the Inferno. Don't ask me how nor where. To live in the afterlife, you must know how it came to existence. You must understand what others would do for it. Otherwise, you'll be arrogant to things around you passing by. They can never be ignored."

"I could surely ignore those who only validate their existence with threats or...aspects of the madness of their nature. And that's coming from someone like me." I said.

"Ha...of course, you can. Praise be for free thought." His eyes caught on how we didn't sip the wine. Not once. The information he was giving us was very new. He then asked, "Now...is that all you came to ask me?"

"No. We wanted to know if you happened to know...anything at all about one of Lucifer's accomplices; The Unicorn?" I asked. His grin gradually turned to a frown, showing a bit of concern. But he was still masking himself with this flamboyant character.

"The Unicorn. That's interesting." Oh, now he's concerned as he echoed with sudden certainty in his voice.

"Aye...that's why we need to find him before he hurts others. Before he hurts those, we love." I said.

"Of course, definitely..." He said as he then got up from his chair. "And I shall tell you...right after you hear a bit of my latest works...about a man who went to Heaven and found faith again."

"I'm sorry, but I don't think we have much time for that." Juliet said.

"Oh nonsense...we have all the time in the world!" He said with his arms raised. For some reason, he began gazing at our boots, including Juliet's. We eyed at one another, estranged to what was he on about. Clamping his hands together, he then said, "Your feet must be strained from the miles on end. How about...I get two hostesses for you three."

"I think we're fine. Thank you." Ted said. His tone sounded unease, which made me unease as well as Juliet.

"Oh, come on. You don't want to be crippled with strained feet. It's the worst kind of pain. Let me fetch them for you. They're fantastic! Trust me. Stay here. Enjoy the white wine. I'll be right back." He said, staggering from the room.

He left us three, feeling almost dumbfounded. We meditated a bit, finding a way to see how we can approach this. I wondered if Virgil really knew anything about The Unicorn, given his reaction. The conversation felt very quick, and it zigzagged the three of us. But one thing was for sure, we were at least granted to more information about Lucifer's ideal ways of pursuing to make his ideals of a new heaven a reality. A haunting reality. But we had yet to figure out how he was doing it.

I slumped myself onto the bed. Just the mere subtly of everything happening all at once was exhausting to me. I felt my hat escaping from my head. As I glanced over to the left, I saw that something fell from Virgil's book of poems. With curiosity, I grabbed it and sat up.

"I don't even like white wine." Ted murmured to himself as he got up and placed the glass cup on the cabinet. Juliet then said, "Me neither. It's like vodka, but more bitter." She got up and did the same.

"My mother would kill for this type of wine all the bloody time. Every other party we had to celebrate her debut albums, she'd be the first to ask father," I jested after a chuckle, taking a glance at the folded note, which I proceeded to unfold.

The writing was strikingly like the paper from The Angel. It even had the same satanic language. So, I grew curious to know why exactly Virgil had a page of satanic language in his book of poems. I felt a bit helpless since I couldn't read the language. I was wishing Frask were there to translate it, even if it took a week or two for him to finish. But to my surprise, on the other side of the page was the language translated to English. My eyes were closer to the yellow page, trying my hardest to read cursive writing. Even I didn't write this over-exaggeratingly elegant. The poem was written:

> *Pain creates discipline*
> *Blood quenches thirst*
> *We are possessions of the Bright Star*
> *We are architects of the New Heaven*
> *We are the godly over the godless*
> *Earn faith through power*
> *Earn freedom through chain*
> *Earn thought through conformity*
> *Dispose inner disappointments*

And just as I thought, it was another cryptic writing. At least it was in English this time around. But it was obviously a poem about worshipping Lucifer. But then something came to my mind, the first few lines sounded very familiar. It was as if I heard them before. And so, it was. It was when Sathanus forced the priestesses to chant something to enhance the queen's scepter to his will. I wondered if this was what he was revising. I was curious to know why Virgil would write it. Because it sounded like an oath than poetry.

Shortly I showed the poem to Ted and Juliet. They were just as staggered as I was when I read the two pages. Ted first denounced it, saying that it could've been anything. But Juliet and I recalled that the victims wrote the same pledge many times in black ink. Whereas this was written in red ink. And the ink somehow glistened with the sun light. It was something I shouldn't have been reading. Just out of sheer curiosity, Juliet pulled out the dragonfly device from her bag, which I was thankful that we brought. I used my telekinesis once again to power it. Once the lights beamed in its eyes, it levitated across the room. All our eyes were glued to the device. Suddenly, the eyes became green, and the dragonfly flew across the room and towards a trunk that was on the right side of the room. Eying at one another, we all went towards the chest. Juliet kept watch of the door, seeing if Virgil or anyone was coming. Ted and I stopped and gazed at the iron trunk with a lock binding it.

"Juliet, see if you can find me small tools in the cabinet." I told her.

"Tools like what exactly," She asked, heading towards the cabinet. I then told her, "A paper clip and hairpin if you can. I need to unlock this. Before you ask, a friend taught me it as a human."

"Lockpicking. Aren't you just full of surprises?" She said with small bewilderment. Shortly after she raided the shelf, she gave me the hairpin and a paper clip. I was able to use my teeth to extend each end. Carefully, I inserted two of the pieces inside the lock's keyhole. Luckily, I still had my lock picking skills with me. Once I was able to trigger the mechanism, the shackle of the lock jolted from the lock. After I removed it, Ted and I opened the cover of the trunk that turned out to be extremely heavy. Each of our mouths and eyes were opened to what we witnessed. It looked to be very familiar, the violin. It was the same one we saw before, shining with crystalized reds. I wondered how he acquired it. Why did he have it inside his wardrobe? But it was clear to me that he was one of Lucifer's accomplices. It seemed to me that he was hiding to practice in the shadows of those poor women. That was why he was spending every rolic and bennie to be there.

Then something else caught my eyes on the right side of the

wardrobe. Something was glowing blue. As I dug my hands underneath the clogged clothes, he had piled on whatever item it was, my eyes widened to that familiar touch. Smooth, sleek, cylinder and warm. When I pulled it out from the sheets, passing the violin, my eyes felt as if they were deceived. It was the same scepter we saw Sathaus tried to channel. When I presented it to my friends, they expressed in shock. And our eyes bled once again. Something was very wrong in the place.

"Jesus!" Ted yelped. Juliet took a glanced and gasped with her mouth covered. We wiped our eyes.

"Virgil...he's The Unicorn!" I concluded to the Apostles, who were rightfully shocked. It was sickening. All I had to think about now was how will we tell Dante? How would we tell him that his friend, someone he trusted, was an accomplice of Lucifer? We wiped our faces to think without feeling wet.

Afterwards, Juliet collected the dragonfly and placed it inside her strapped bag. I threw the scepter to her, only for her to quickly place it inside her enchanted bag. Once we heard the door clicking to open, we quickly closed the wardrobe, locked it, and sat back down on the bed. I tossed the note to Ted. We opened to see that the two women, who were dressed in virginal pink and purple dresses holding a large bowl of warm water and a towel. The bastard Virgil was with them, adjusting his collar with his hooked finger. He smiled and asked, "Everything okay?"

"Oh yes, we're fine. For sure." I said, grabbing and placing my hat on my head. He then gazed at me. He scoffed and smirked. He noticed our sudden aroused postures.

"You look like you saw something." His eyes seemed very phased by our sudden upbeat moods.

"Oh no...we're fine," I said as I saw the two women approaching to us with the bowl. Placing it down in front of our feet, the African American maiden asked us to remove our boots. Before we did, I asked him, "Oy, my friends and I were reconsidering that perhaps you can read a bit of The Great Odyssey? Before we can take the massage. We talked about it and thought...why not? We're admirers of all forms of creative writing. We have time. Plenty of it, as a matter of fact."

"Of course, certainly! I'm glad you approve."

After he went back to fetch his book he had placed on the cabinet, he opened it. The two women sat on their knees as they were already enchanted just by how he stood. He had a majestic stance, with one hand behind and another hand holding on to his book. I eyed at Ted, who gazed back at me. His eyes were down to his hands inserted into his pocket. Inside, he had the crumbled pages of the satanic language. I looked back at him as he nodded. On my left, Juliet saw that too and gave Ted a thumb up. Afterwards, we all glanced back at Virgil – or The Unicorn – as he was preparing to read.

After he cleared his throat, he then asked before he read, "Actually, I could truly go for some wine. How about..."

"No thank you!" We said altogether.

"I'm on a diet," Ted said. Juliet silently sneered at him for that comment. He shrugged.

"Um...right! Okay. But I, for one, am going for one. If you don't mind, that is." He said, proceeding to go to the cabinet. My eyes took glance at him placing the book down as he was filling his wine cup with a red bottle of wine. We caught him turning the book, almost to the final pages of it. We saw him skimming through the book in gradual panic. Little breathing was heard from under his nose. He knew that it was over for him.

"Something wrong, my gallant poet?" One of the hostesses asked. He then said, struggling to find words, "Oh no, my dearies. It's uh...it's fine and well. Just making sure I have everything written properly. Gotta check for errors."

I then tapped at one of the hostesses' shoulders, asking her to get closer to me. I whispered into her small ear, warning her about Virgil and everything he has done. I asked her to contact the Civil Force of Fairies. I did this while I kept an eye on him, seeing that he was pouring in his cup. Ted gave me the pages as I then passed them to her. When she took a good glance at it, she nodded to us.

Ted, Juliet, the hostesses and I remained our focus on him as he then took a sip of his wine.

"You're good?" Ted asked with his hands in his pockets, acting as if he was concerned.

"Yes, most definitely." He said nervously, twirling his cup of left-over wine that he proceeded to drink. He took a good glance at his opened book. Ted then said, "Let's hear it then, my gallant... poet."

"Definitely," He said, clearing his throat and adjusting his chemise once more. "You know...it's never easy, entertaining, or charming. You even have to go in lengths of wooing your reader to keep them engaged."

"Aye, I bet." I said, pretending to agree as I stared into his eyes. I was almost caught off guard when he caught that. I then said, "Seems like you have a fascination with music too. Very versatile."

"Well...it's enchanting. It's very important in the afterlife." He said, adjusting his shirt. His chest was gradually shining with sweat. "Why wouldn't I?"

"You seem to fancy it a lot." Juliet added. "So much so that you can't help but to...*own* an instrument!"

"Yes, I happened to play a violin. It's funny that you know that." He said as he was slowly trying to get closer to the door. Juliet shrugged. "You know when I died in Italia, I've always wondered if Heaven were like all the tales we were told as children. Living in this world and finding a second chance, it inspired me to work on this poem. All I wrote was didactic and pastoral. But now, they are almost ethereal."

"Yeah." Ted said. "That begs the question; what were you really trying to do with those women we saw before? What song were you trying to play?"

"Just out of curiosity." I added, as my eyes were still looking into him. The two hostesses stood up and faced him as well. It was obviously that we were on to him this time. He wanted to get away. I saw that in his eyes. He stood almost frozen with his book, like a rat trying to get away when it was confronted with light. He suddenly rushed to his wardrobe, frantically opening it to find that the scepter was taken away. Pathetically, he glanced back at us.

"Um...my apologies. But if you excuse me, I believe that I...I need to settle some things." He said, hurriedly trying to open the door. Triggering my Blessed Eye, I stood up from the bed and used the stems of my mind to shut the door right in front of him. He turned around, staggered, and suddenly cowering to the corner of the room.

"I'm sorry, but what sort of things?" I asked as Ted and Juliet stood alongside me. Their blades were already ejected from underneath their sleeves. Juliet proceeded to tell the maidens to stand behind the three of us.

Shortly, my left fingers grasped at his wrinkly and supple throat, almost gripping into his jugular.

Activating my Apostle gauntlets, the blades ejected from underneath my right hand. I pointed the two blades underneath his chin. Ted and Juliet surrounded him, making sure he doesn't escape. In panic, he glanced at both of us while his body began shivering. "What sort of things? Hm? What things? Like selling nobles, priestesses, and innocent mystics to the devil? Like working with the Satanists? So many bloody possibilities!"

"Hold on now, dears. Hold on. It's not what you think! Honest!"

"Really?" Juliet asked as she pulled out the queen's scepter from her bag. I saw how his eyes pathetically widened like he saw a beautiful sunrise. "Then what's this? Why do you have this!? Tell us! NOW!"

"I...I can't tell you!" He cried. Juliet then placed it back into her bag.

"You're gonna have to, mate! Where are the others!?" I asked. I then shouted, "WHERE!?"

He said nothing. His hair was wet with sweat. The water dripped onto my hand. His eyes were frantically moving from one place to another. Suddenly, he spoke in an interesting type of tongue. He spoke with a hiss, "*Ka-les-mada!*"

My eyes focused on him and saw him looking at something else. As we turned, suddenly four Satanists materialized in the room. They had their swords ready. I suddenly felt a jolt pushing me back onto the floor. As I reserved my eyes back at Virgil, I saw him violently push the two maidens out of the way to get to the door. Ted and I both drew our handguns and proceeded to fire at him before he left. But the bullets slammed against the wall instead.

"I'll go after him," Ted said, undrawing his gun into his holster. "You two deal with them!"

"Take this back to the castle while you're at it!" Juliet said, tossing the scepter to Ted.

"You got it!" He then rapidly took off in a flash.

After I undrawn my handgun, Juliet and I unsheathed both of our swords and began to swing and strike at the Satanists.

Juliet and I finally fought side-by-side, back-to-back, and shoulder to shoulder regarding to one another as we both slaughtered the Satanists, seeing their eyes flash before us. Both of us swirled our blades with pirouettes. Juliet finished by acrobatically drop kicking the last remaining Satanist against the wall whilst I conjured my bow and flung a smoke-made arrow between his eyes. Blood flashed across the wall. The rest of the Satanists were left dead and quickly decomposing into black smoke. We were focused on killing the Satanists that we nearly forgot about the two maidens, who looked shocked and frightened. I began to quickly unsummon my bow and unsheathed my sword. Juliet unsheathed her sword as well.

"Go! Leave!" Juliet ordered as they complied hurriedly.

Shortly afterwards, more Satanists reappeared out of nowhere. They looked just like the ones who attacked in the Gathering, nearly assassinating Jesus, and kidnapping Sarah. Two of them had crossbows and the other three had muskets. Juliet and I eyed at one another. Our plan was to escape the place through the window that was just in front of us.

After we nodded at one another, satisfied with our quick plan, we both raced past the Satanists and burst through the open window, the sun brightening our eyes. We weren't surely where we going to land; either in water of the canals or find ourselves dead on the concrete.

Luckily, we found ourselves on a balcony. Turning around, the Satanists were prepared to fire. Quickly thinking ahead, we decided to scale on the side of the building to reach to the rooftop. It took us a good while to reach as quickly as we can. Scrapping down the limestone, we gripped onto every window frame, building rail, and balcony rams to jump and make our way to the top.

Soon, we got on top of the red tiled rooftop of the hotel, looking over the open sea of the city's rooftops, churches, temples, and towers. We began to sprint relentlessly across the surprisingly long rooftop of the building. I was running behind and on the left side of Juliet. But we stopped after we saw the same Satanists reappear. This time, they weren't alone. They were joined alongside with six other Satanists who each had their ivory crafted faussart swords erected. Three of the five wore white volto masks with the celestial sun emblem tattooed on it.

Juliet and I eyed at each other, tirelessly. It appeared to be that we didn't have much of a choice in the matter. I silently hoped that Ted was able to catch Virgil. But we knew that we had to make it through to reach for him. So, after Juliet and I nodded at one another, we both faced the Satanist herd. They were hungry for us.

Adjusting my hat, I unsheathed my sword from my shoulder holster once again. Juliet pulled her ring sword from her shoulder holster next to her left pistol. With that, we quickly charged at the raging Satanists approaching us. We both clashed; two Apostles against eleven Satanists. It became a composed and fluid feud between us. As I was swinging and blocking attacks, I tried my best to remember my training. I had to remember fighting those figments Ted used to help me. And I was doing as I did when I trained; I dodged and rolled underneath left and right strikes. I swayed in all directions to confuse and eventually strike down the Satanists.

With all her strength, Juliet dismembered one of their arms, sliced his torso, spun around, and used her sword to viciously detach his head. His headless body fell right in front of me. One of them tried to horizontally strike me with his musket, but I swayed to the right. I gripped the sword with two hands and cut his left leg. Then I gripped the sword with my right hand and slit the back of his neck with a backhand. Suddenly, Juliet tossed the other Satanist to my direction. As he was stumbling towards me, I held my sword like a baseball bat and swung his neck, severely slicing his neck. He fell right in front of me. I was

452 ~ KENNETH VIVOR

almost at awe at what I did. I know I had my fair share of violent outbursts, but I never thought I'd see myself doing something this vicious.
But it felt bloody good, I'm not going to lie.

We quickly looked at one another again, silently admiring our tech-
niques. We then ran across the rooftop and leaped from it. We shortly
landed on both feet in front of the canal, which staggered the public.
On each side, we saw more Satanists reappearing. Their macabre masks
were creepier than the last. We both ran and leaped from gondola to
gondola, post by post across the moving canal. Luckily it was crowded,
so we used the number of rowing gondolas and small boats to our
advantage. Unfortunately, we were oblivious to some of the gondola
rowers who fell into the water.

We then made it to the other street and ran past the crowd and
into the marketplace of the street. It was a very crowded and narrow
path straight down. With footsteps being so loud, I quickly turned and
saw that the three Satanists were coming after us. My heart pounded
and punched the inside of my chest, like it wanted to break away and
escape. Our Apostle skills kept up from getting tired easily, so that was
a bigger advantage. "Don't let them get to the castle!" They shouted in
their demonic and distorted voice. They really wanted that scepter. We
swiftly turned from corner to corner, as each narrow avenue was becoming distantly different. Let alone distantly crowded with food and
street stands.

As we ran past every building, a Satanist suddenly tackled me from
the side. I tumbled and fell onto the ground, crashed myself into a
flower stand. I looked up to the Satanist who looked down at me with
his gun barrel pointed at me. Suddenly, blood busted from his head
and his corpse fell upon me. The blood was pouring a bit on my face.
Quickly turning it over, Juliet came hastily to me and picked me back
on my feet. The smoke coming from her gun barrel implied that she
was the one who fired. As she undrew it, she held me by my left hand
to pick up the pace. Thus, we continued to run without looking back
or stopping at all.

The streets and city squares were gradually consumed with masses of Satanists and Arcadian Civil Forcers and soldiers warring against one another. The madness from Virgil was spreading like wildfire. Fiery burnings through the streets, rapid sieges plaguing the roads and other outbreaks seeped in the city like sap. We surpassed and continued to run. The herd of Satanists continued to bark for us to stop and surrender. They pounced on our tracks like wild hyenas.

Ignoring them, I remained my focus on the front. We sprang over crates and food stands. We both turned and saw that they were still on our tail, just six feet away from us. Juliet told me to follow her to the right side, making our way into the alleyways of the avenue. As we exited the alleyway, we approached another dock in front of another canal. So, then we turned left and went down past it. We weren't as quickly as Ted, but we ran faster than any average man or woman. Or any of the other spirits for that manner.

We then approached to the bridge that was over the canal. We scaled ourselves on the side of it and vaulted over the edge until we were on top of it. On the left corner of my eyes, I saw more Satanists reappearing. The two of us began to flee rapidly down the bridge until we were finally reaching to another place in the city. I saw that we were now in another city square, which consisted of basilicas and big palaces amid other typical buildings. Juliet turned around, as I did, and spotted the Satanists coming for us once again. Suddenly, she activated her Blessed Eye and raised her darkened right hand high. Above us, Alwyn, and a swarm of other birds of prey appeared and flew down and past above to attack the Satanists. They flew swiftly in their spectral forms and began to peck and bother the Satanists until they were gradually getting relentlessly mutilated.

"Let's go!" She said. I followed her. We were running and fleeing until we were heading towards a large basilica. Though different from the one Arianna was in, it was still magnificently huge and took up the middle of the streets.

"We've got to find Theodore and Virgil!"

"They can be anywhere in this bloody city!" I said, trying to talk whilst running with all my strength and endurance. We ran through the archways underneath the roofs of the palace until we were in the streets. Finally, we stopped and spun around, wondering if they were a way we can possibly find where Ted could be. Then Juliet quickly said, "He has to be in the castle! Let's go back there!" I nodded as we were taking off once again.

But as we were going until we later went into the depths of an alleyway away from the palaces, the reappearing Satanists stopped us. As we turned around to go back, another group of them reappeared. Juliet and I unsheathed our blades once again. All of them were equipped with large spears, faussart swords and crossbows. Unexpectedly, the voices came into my head.

"*Unleash the Shadowmacer. Do it! Let it flow and go with it!*"

I decided to listen for once. I disregarded the demanding commands of the Satanists, telling us to surrender. Then something else came into my head. I breathed in and out through my nostrils, closing my eyes. I felt my divine self that was placing its hand on my forehead.

Listen to what you fear
Listen to what urges you to shed tears
The shadows lurk to make its due
For the one who controls them is you

I triggered back to my Blessed Eye and suddenly felt unlimited energy flowing from within me. Then I opened my eyes and charged at one Satanist. As I fought and killed him, at the right corner of my eye, I saw a shadowy duplicate of me firing two arrows at the two other Satanists. Then I went for the other one and unleashed my Apostle blades, stabbing another in the jugular as blood combusted from it. Then another shadowy duplicate came out of me and used its sword and shield at another group of Satanists. Another shadowy reflection of me slammed one Satanist with a battle-axe.

Soon after, I exited the Blessed and saw that they were all lying dead all around us. I felt my energy reemerging inside of me. I looked down at my blade and saw it was adorned with smears of warm blood. It felt like I was daydream, except I was realizing it.

"Remarkable! You have a Macer too! You killed them all at once." Juliet said, staggered by what she had witnessed. I looked down at my hand and gripped it, chuckling briefly.

I smiled at Juliet. She smiled back until more Satanists running and approaching on each side distracted her. Lifting two arms, she radically materialized into a ghostly eagle and flew on top of the basilica. I turned to each side, seeing every raging and angry Satanists coming for me.

The minute I saw every projectile coming from each side, I gripped my hand and suddenly felt every molecule of my bodily system separate from my body. Shortly after, I suddenly found myself standing with Juliet on the roof of the basilica. She quickly grinned at me, implying that I have made another achievement. I was finally embraced with my shadows. And the voices.

When we saw the Satanists reappear on the roof of the church, we quickly ran once again. As we ran, I heard bullets flying past us and ejecting and ricocheting into the marble statues. We saw that the basilica we were on was integrated into a large palace. Juliet and I leaped and flipped from the basilica roof to the light gray roof of the palace. It was an oval shaped palace with spikes and statues framed around it. And so, we followed the circular roof as we then approached to the re-emerging Satanists once again. It was time to fight them on the go.

Soon, I ran towards one of them and summoned a shadowy halberd in both of my hands. After I impaled the Satanists with it, I unsheathed his sword from his waist scabbard, throwing it at the other Satanist in his head. The halberd in my hands then disappears. With my telekinesis, I managed to call upon the sword, dropped down the Satanist I just killed, and stabbed the other one in his neck. He was coming from the right side until I killed him.

Juliet, after getting smacked across the face by the Satanists, I raised my hand and forcibly lifted the bastard high from the roof, who suddenly stopped moving all molecules of his body. Thanks to Juliet. She

456 - KENNETH VIVOR

then – like a vicious wolverine – sliced open his torso with her Apostle blades, nearly spill whatever he had inside of him aside of the gore. Once I released him, he fell flat on his own puddle of blood plastered on the roof.

Surprisingly, I was almost slammed by a Satanist carrying a battle-axe. He looked to be at least ten feet. I swayed to the left. But he turned around and smacked me across the face, making me tumble to the ground and nearly letting my hat fly off. Attempting to use his axe on me, his arm was yanked backwards by Juliet's scarf. She pulled it back as he was struggling to fight with her. This gave me a chance to run up to him, cut open his knees until he knelt. With all my might, after Juliet removed her scarf, I slashed his throat with my sword. Gargling his blood and struggling for air, he fell forward. I collected my hat from the roof and placed it back on my head.

With that, we continued to flee. Once we reach the end of the roof, we both evaporated from the place to another rooftop during the city. All we saw was a large skyline of roofs and towers surrounding us. When we continued to run whilst performing precision jumps, we would land on each roof, making our way. At this point, we were just running through the entire city until the Satanists gave up. But being persistent, it wasn't going to happen.

Several more Satanists materialized in front of us as they didn't hesitate to fire their bolt action rifles. Whilst running, Juliet and I both undrew our pistols. Our guns were up and aimed at them. I held each grip with each hand and fired at each of them. The same with Juliet. With each intense recoil I felt as I fired, the Satanists were plummeting to their deaths. Though, it was difficult to run and shoot at once. One Satanist raged towards me. When he intended to swing at me, with one gun in my left, I shot his hand. With the other, I fired at his head.

Juliet ran towards one and disarmed one of the Satanist's guns. Placing him in a chokehold, she fired at each raging Satanists. Once three of them fell, she took the gun barrel to the held Satanist and pulled the trigger. Shredded brains pasted on her trousers, skirt, and stockings. But Juliet, being relentless and fed up, she didn't care. What mattered to her was getting to the castle; bloodied, dirty, or not. Thus, we continued to run.

Suddenly, on the other side of the avenue, we discovered the Satanists freely running across from us. They were running and jumping from roof to roof. Three Satanists were free running as well us whilst shooting their arrows at us. They even threw their shields at us, which functioned as boomerangs since they were coming back to them. The shields ricocheted over our heads, slowly discerning pieces of tiles from the rooftops.

We took advantage of the chimneys by taking cover behind them, including the much rectangular and wide ones. Juliet and I stood by one another, kneeling, and facing each other. I saw brittle bits of the chimney tearing and splashing due to the pressure of the flying metallic shields and burning bullets.

"What is it going to take for these buggers to leave us alone?" I asked frustratingly.

"We have to try what we can until they finally disperse!" Juliet said as she then conjured her bow. With the bow in her right hand, she took her left hand and wipe across the air. Four blue arrows were summoned and levitating behind her. She would take each one and fling it to an uncovered Satanist.

I drew my handguns once again and began to shoot at them. Whenever I shot them in the head, or into their hearts, they would fall like ragdolls and evaporate from Heaven. It was basic, but I felt my heart pounding nonstop. Anything could happen; one of which would end up with any of us getting shot.

Next to us, more Satanists were turning up. It was getting quite annoying at that point. Fed up, I stood up from cover and fired at them. Right. Left. Right. Left. I fired and the hammer struck the chamber in a repetitive but helpful manner. I swayed and danced away from their flying bullets going by my face. As I holstered my pistols into my holsters, I triggered into my Blessed Eye and conjured a shadow to swiftly take care of them. I watched as the shadow was duplicating itself in a rapid and eerily domino effect.

Afterwards, we saw a bright blue flash dashing like lighting and chain attacking the remaining Satanists. We saw each of them fall dead when they were spontaneously and abruptly attacked. Taking a good look, the light stopped flashing and it turned out to be Ted. Finally! He waved at us with the trademark shit-eating grin on his face. We both decided to traverse to meet with him.

Once we did, we were finally reunited. From what I saw, he used his scepter to wreck the Satanists as he was in lighting fast motion.

"So...that could've gone well." He jested, catching his breath as he held his scepter on his shoulder.

"You're telling me, lad." I said.

He then asked, "You guys are alright?"

"Aye, just about. And yourself?" I asked as I undrawn my handgun.

"Yeah! Just fought off the Satanists after I've dealt with Virgil!" He said. "No big deal."

"Where is he now, Theodore?" Juliet asked impatiently.

"Relax!" He assured. "I took him back to the castle! His ass is in the dungeon! We better go before they break him out!" With that, he summoned a vortex. But as soon as we turned around, four more Satanists were running towards us. The three of us quickly jumped into the vortex, which transported us into the interiors of a palace. The ornamented crystalized corridors were crowded with nobles, who were staggered after we exited the vortex.

We ran through the crowd nonstop. We shoved and pushed our way through before we saw more of the Satanists reappearing. The minute they unsheathed their blades was when people around us began to scream horrifically. We turned around and saw that they weren't going to slow down anytime soon. They wanted those papers very badly. We mindfully fought and ran simultaneously as they continued to cave it on us.

Soon, Ted created another vortex in midair. As soon as we speedily ran through, we ended up on the rooftops again. I saw that the castle was at the horizon behind the thickening afternoon fog masking over the city. The more we ran speedily, the more it angered the Satanists.

I heard more bullets and arrows swiftly flying over our heads and ricocheting behind our active feet. Reaching the end of a square rooftop, we leaped and slid down a sloped roof of another building. Upon the edge, we leaped and ended up going into the narrow interiors of an apartment building. My breath was hot and dry. The heat from the bullets were becoming evident by the minute. Gasps and screeches were passed from both sides as we rushed through every door, turned to each hallway.

Upon going straight down, we made a right turn and approached to the end of the hall. Luckily, there was another open window. Leaping through, we leaped from the balcony and made our ascension onto a long rooftop. I turned and saw that the Satanists were still chasing us hard, doing what they possibly could to stop us. But I didn't slow down despite my eagerly beating heart. The best part of Arcadia is that some buildings were built near one another. Thus, it was an advantage. After throwing down a smoke bomb, which we got through, Ted summoned and materialized duplicates of us to delude and lead the pursuing Satanists astray.

We began to scale down from the building we were on and slowly made our way to the streets. The Arcadian streets were open and expressive with the Satanists overconsuming the purity of the city. Herds upon herds, the common spirits of Arcadia ran in fear into one direction whilst the ongoing fight between Satanists and Fairies took course. It was a good way to make the pursuers lose us when we rushed through the crowd. And I recognized where we were when we were dispersing from the buildings and the masses.

We finally arrived upon the castle. But as soon as we arrived, it seemed too late. We came across an ambush that festered in front of the gates of the castle. Satanists and Pagan fairies were fighting against one another.

"Theodore, thank you." Juliet said as she was trying to catch her breath.

"No worries. Let's just deal with these assholes!" He said.

Our weapons were at the ready and we then charged towards the commotion. Once we knew it, we were engaged in an orgy of thrashing and slaying. Glancing on my right, I saw more Satanists in a line were rapidly approaching to the gates. They came and sieged towards us with swords in their hands and black smoke levitating from their eyes. Despite being in a very claustrophobic state, I made sure that my blade was only slicing our enemies. I briefly saw Ted pick up one of the Satanists' rifles and fired at each one whilst simultaneously impaling the other. Juliet jumped and twirled in midair as she made a roundhouse kick on each Satanist. Often, I closed my eyes to trigger my Blessed Eye, with two fingers on the side of my head. I mentally used cantation to possess a Satanist to go against his own without physically going into his body. I then resumed to the bloody reality and continued to swing my sword.

Everything felt like it was an ultimate disco party of death. It was clear that we were bound to make our own battlefields, despite not being actual soldiers. The alabaster concrete was already riddled with blood and decomposed bodies of Lucifer's fanatical followers. Good thing they would eventually evaporate to keep the roads clear and to not to provoke panic towards the common spirits. They were already devastated from what they saw. My sword made every slash and laceration. It proved how powerful the Redeemer was. I had to thank Michael for this weapon. It's not too big. Not too small. But it was good enough for me to carry and wield like I was a leaf in the wind. Reflecting my time at the foggy fields, I extracted it as I was embodying the blade.

After a few minutes of protecting the scepter from being stolen again, every Satanist has lied dead. Our clothes were almost decorated in their blood. But it was okay. It was okay with me. I wore it like a warrior. I could only imagine how my father felt killing enemy soldiers amid a hazy and crowded battlefield on the streets.

Soon, the guards led us to where the dungeon was, which was inside one of the gatehouses. Each layer had rows of cells, which made it look like a statutory penitentiary. I was getting an uncomfortable feeling of being put back in prison once again. Screams and cries of begging and pleading were sounded from every prison behind iron-incrusted bars.

They wore tacky and worn-out white gowns with numbers written across their backs.

Eventually, we reach near the end of the hall as we then looked and finally saw Virgil, huddling himself inside the dungeon. I bet he was the one who summoned all those Satanists at will. He knew that he couldn't fight. He knew that he was cowardly to fight us. Once one of the guards unlocked the door of the cell, they gestured us to go inside. As soon as he saw us, he was cowering against the cement-crafted wall on top of a plank nailed to it. His arms were spread across the wall. I caught notice of his knees. They were swollen and dislocated. In fact, Ted did a number on his face. His face was not only moist with his blood, but smeared purple and red shiners. He was almost dying, not that was an issue to me.

"Oh, I forgot to tell you guys. I did numbers. Just so you know," Ted said as he found the perfect moment to inform us on that.

"Please, I can't explain! I can't!" He cried, still sweating. He pathetically stumbled from the board to the ground. He was trying to pick himself up despite his busted knees. Closing all my fingers into a fist, I swung and decked him on his face until the back of his head slammed onto the wall. Approaching closer to him, I picked him up by his collar and slammed the back of his head against the wall again. Again, and again until blood soaked on the cold stone wall. I wanted to make sure he understood every lash I gave him.

"Oh, you're going to explain! Whether you like it or not! Goddamn pansy bastard," I said, unleashing my retractable blades and pointing it at his neck. "Where are the other accomplices?" He didn't speak a word. I quickly eyed at Ted. Soon as he stomped his scepter on the ground, it turned back into his pet python Penelope. She slithered passed me and slowly crawled on top of the seat, getting close to Virgil who was making terrible attempts to cower away from her. Of course, my blades were still pointed at his throat.

"Why are you working with them?!" Juliet asked with her hands attached to her waist. "You're not tough or smart as you made yourself! So, there's no point in escaping! Talk! Now!"

Finally, we got him to break and say, "Look, I did what I had to do to survive!"

"Survive. That's hilarious! Seems like you've done it willingly." Ted said. "We saw you have a Satanist violin in the wardrobe!"

"He promised me that I'd become a god! If only you see what he can do!! Who doesn't want to have that kind of power? You're lightkeepers, you'd know!" He said, nearly about to cry. "It seemed like a good opportunity. L...Lucifer saw to it. So, I agreed. But to gain that freedom out of that realm meant to...sacrifice my fellow nobles and the priest-esses! I didn't want to do it, but I had to! They were a lost cause to that opportunity."

"So, you sold out your fellow peers, the priestesses, letting them suffer there while you got out scot free to hide! You're far worse than just a coward! What were you going to do to those women back at the hotel?" Juliet asked angrily. When he didn't speak, as he continued to whimper. Juliet suddenly held me back from him. When I backed up, she came by him. Impatient and furious, she viciously stomped on his fractured left knee. When a scream burst from his open hot lips, she shouted like a monster, "Speak now, you worm!"

"I...I intended to have them help me channel the staff! That way, I can overthrow the queen, so I can become God through his eyes! I wanted to become king! He promised!" He cried. I was surprised that he was unafraid and very ready to tell the truth. I assumed that he thought we'd let him live afterwards.

"And you simply thought about this, ey?! Trying to sell them out...for you own motherfucking gain!" I asked angrily and disgusted, gripping my fingers harder onto his collar. I was seeing his eyes sporadically dancing about.

"Y...Yes." He said. "I...I had to! This was my chance to become greater than just a mere spirit! It was my chance!"

"That priestess...Bella...is young enough to be my own sister. Young enough to be someone's daughter. A sweet, innocent girl. Yet, you allowed her to be molested by monsters! And for what? Supremacy?! You're a piece of shite," I ridiculed as I got closer to him. "Just like that nonsense you said back there! Just a ruse to make us dumbed to see your true intentions! You're not going to get away that easily!"

"You do realize that he's using you as a host, idiot! He wants to rule through you!" Ted clarified and added.

"Host or not, I don't care! Just the mere fact of sitting on a throne and bestow all my orders was enough to interest me; regardless of what he wants! Arianna is a lost cause...like all the kings and queens here! Imagine...an afterlife that could be so better! Especially without the Covenant or any other monarch!" Virgil said. This gave me more prove that he was far from being redeemed. "That's what was on my mind! I can prove to Dante that I could be further from just mediocre living as a Chancellor!"

"Shut up!" I asked, "Where's the Phoenix, Virgil!? What's the Covenant!? Tell me everything! Now!"

"I don't know! I don't! I swear!" He said on a verge of tears with his soggy hands clammed together. "Please...this world is all I have!"

"So, did those guards and people you've murdered! So, did those you sold out for your benefits! For your greed! The Queen gave you a chance when you were ripped away from Earth! But now..." I said, preparing to make my first assassination. "...You've lost that chance!"

"Let me make it up to you all! Please!!? I beg of you! What would you prove by killing me?!"

"Life has had enough of you! That's what it will prove! Let's prove that, shall we?"

"No! PLEASE!!" He cried! But I ignored his plead and his tears, by finally injecting two blades into his jugular. Blood began to ooze from his wound where I placed it. His eyes were flashing with light as he was struggling and gargling his own blood that flowed down from his mouth.

"May you drown in the Abyss, you coward," I said with no remorse. I couldn't let him walk free for what he had done. So, I was glad to take his afterlife.

Once I released my blades from his throat, he plummeted to the floor and his eyes became blank and hollow. Blood continued to trickle down to his shirt, coloring it red. My eyes then caught something glimmering in his pocket. Inserting my hand into his pocket like a vulture, I pulled out what looked to be a silver pedant necklace, which was now riddled with blood.

It was a chained necklace with a pedant resembling a celestial sun with a star pentagon in the middle. The circle in the middle was pitch black. The rays were pointed colored with yellow color schemes. The black seemed to be crafted with the same mineral Sathanus wore for his armor. Perhaps he gained power with this pendant. I showed it to the others, who were puzzled when they saw this. After killing the Unicorn, this left us with two more to go, The Phoenix and The Angel. No Watcher was going to escape us this time. Never again.

Shortly after, we were led back to Arianna's room. We didn't know how we would tell her that a poet was trying to kill her. We didn't know how we would say it, but it would best to tell her anyway. Upon going into the room, I was staggered to see Jesus, Francis and the two Archangels with her. Jesus looked to be comforting and praying for Arianna to be healed. They must have been summoned.

When we were approaching, they took notice of us, and we bowed right in front of them.

"My fellow Apostles," Arianna said with a smile. "Jesus and the rest came to visit me. Is the Unicorn dealt with?"

I lifted the bloodied pedant I took from Virgil's corpse, making them awe at it. Francis came to me as I landed it in his hands. He eyed at it very carefully.

"Yes, Your Majesty. We discovered who it was: the poet Virgil." Juliet addressed, which made the entire room puzzle with doubts and denial.

"Virgil; Dante's friend." Jesus asked. He pointed at us. "Do you three speak true?"

One of the guards stepped in front of us and said, "What they say is true. He was hiding in the hotel this whole time to plot an attack on you, Your Majesty. He wore that pendant, giving him the powers to summon Satanists. He was formulating a plan to channel the staff and get to the Axis Mundi, I'm sure." She then went into her pocket and took out the two papers I gave to the maidens. She handed them to Jesus as he examined them both. I gazed at both Michael and Gabriel, who gave me looks of concern, hoping that I was correct. After examining and analyzing the papers, Jesus looked up in disbelief.

"You may go, thank you girls," Arianna said as the guards bowed and left the room.

"This cannot be!" Jesus said. "I...I don't know how I would tell Dante." He then gave the papers to Francis, who took a good look at them.

Francis then said, lifting the hanging pedant in one hand. "And we've seen pendants like this before. Mostly worn by loyalists of Lucifer to hunt down guardians. Or anyone who goes against the New Heaven. This is how they are summoned. These poor fools. Nothing but law dogs for the empire. How did he come about this?"

"Lucifer gave it to him," I said as I was slowly pacing across the room. "For he had promised him to become a god and ruler of The Summerland. He sold those mystic nobles and the priestesses upon it. He intended to steal the scepter, so he can overthrow you with the Satanists, Your Majesty. He also mentioned...something about...a Covenant."

"Goodness! That's blasphemous!" Gabriel said. "That means we have to be more vigilant."

"That means these spies could potentially try to overthrow the monarchs in the name of Lucifer." Francis concluded.

Arianna then regarded towards Jesus, "Should we warn the others?"

"I'm not sure. I have my doubts. I don't know if they would even bother to heed my advice. Or ask for our help. We've been divided since Lucifer's rebellions. And some of them are taking it very hard," Jesus said, contemplating with his arms behind his back. I wondered who the others Arianna was talking about.

"What others?" I asked.

"The other monarchs of the Promised Land." Francis answered.

"Virgil must have been told about us. Arianna and I once gathered the other four monarchs: Fergus Welles of Odin, Freka Abadi of Osiris, Shaolin Chara of Shàngdì, and Adrian Athans of Zeus. The Covenant of the Gods. Just as the monarchs that came before, as was my mother, each god of ours called onto us through vision to come together. We made a vow to unite and uphold protection for the Axis Mundi. Each winter solstice, we would come together with our scepters blessed by the gods to help strengthen the link to both lives and expand the evolution of the afterlife. They are the core gods who made this world before the others," Jesus explained. "But ever since the rebellions, and the Chancery's paranoia, they've been distant after we had to cut ties to keep our kingdoms safe. Arianna and I were the only ones willing to make the peace once again, even if we had to look after our kingdoms at the time. And still do."

"But I believe that giving them a warning would hopefully slowly bring us together at least. Just like...old times. Lucifer's empire is a big empire, and we need all the alliance we need to fend them off the afterlife's wellbeing. This...posse of fallen spirits seem to be coming for royals as well. Specifically, the Covenant. It's...slowly coming together. They're invading every facet of our civilization."

After saying that, Arianna sat up on her bed and said, "It's quite a shame Virgil attempted to murder me. I was fairly a fan of his works when her read them in our gatherings. Did he know anything about The Phoenix's whereabouts?"

"He didn't." Ted said. "But one thing is for sure; there can be others wearing those pedants that's giving them control and protection. Just to gain access to the Insignia without anyone in their way. Possibly, they could try to overcome the monarchs of the Covenant...maybe to overtake all of Heaven one kingdom at a time. Slowly growing an empire in their rule."

"I'll have to have the hotel closed for Arcadian Civil Force Investigation, just to find other evidence and to keep the hostesses and clients safe. Who knows what else Virgil has left? Why has he done this?" The Queen mourned.

"Because he was a coward! A devious rotten coward who only cared about his own wellbeing and living off the suffering of others! All he desired was power. Otherwise, why else would he sell those people?" I vented.

"The spineless fucker preferred to be a puppet than his own man!" Ted added. I nodded in agreement.

Juliet then pulled out the dragonfly Frask made and showed it in front of the Queen. Her eyes widened at the look of the device. I had to thank Frask wholeheartedly for what he did. Juliet then explained, "This, Your Majesty, is what we used to detect demonic energy at the hotel. It was built by Frask Douglas."

"He's a painter and alchemist in Celestia. Ted here happens to be one of his managers for their shop." Michael spoke. "For someone who paints on canvases for a living, he has a good eye for advance magic."

"I believe I recognize the coating." Arianna said, analyzing every inch of the machine. "These are made of rare bronze runestones from Jeremiah. They are made to be controlled by lightkeepers. Usually, they don't tend to share these rare items. How in Selene's name did he manage to acquire this from them?"

"He was a member of a secretive group of alchemists and painters called...The Neo-Romantic Society, I think it was. They often practice rare and advance alchemic magic." I said.

"Do you know if he made this one only?" Gabriel asked.

"He made two more...but those were just for testing." Ted said. "Why do you ask?"

"His genius might just save us and the prisoners of Hell," Gabriel said. "He must have had diagrams of this device, right?"

"He should. Probably tons. This was his most ambitious project. He has a lot more in store." I said.

"This might be the most advanced thing someone could do with magic." Gabriel said. He then eyed at us.

"Obviously, we wouldn't want to put pressure on him. He has his own business to pursue. Plus, we shouldn't drag him more into this than we might have done already," Ted suggested.

"So, what are you suggesting, Gabriel," Jesus asked him. "We must trend carefully with his help."

"There has to be other alchemists in the Promised Land. Jeremiah, no doubt. But some are residing here specifically." Gabriel said as he gazed at the device, studying every aspect of it. "I know little few."

Then Francis added, "There is a famous alchemist that came from my home realm of Bordham. Roger Bacon. He was a Franciscan friar and professor in my college and taught with his work *Opus Majus*, the work he had sent to Pope Clement IV in Rome of 1267 upon his request. He was a human then. He resides somewhere in the Promised Land as an astral. Especially after Bordham fell into ruin."

"He sounds promising. I never heard of him." I admitted.

"Of course." Francis said. "Ever since his time in the afterlife, he's been secretive, and I recently heard that he lives as a traveling nomad. He hasn't always been like that when I was a student. Perhaps if he's not too busy, I could possibly convince him to help build upon Mr. Douglas' work. It's just that he...often has us give him something as a token to work off from."

"That's fine. We can offer him goods. We could preserve what we have." Jesus added.

"He has expert scholars who are skilled in this line of work." Francis said. "Perhaps, this should give him purpose once more. He usually requires one or more things of importance."

Jesus then spoke, "If possible, I shall have the other monarchs to offer at least one piece of their possessions. We should be givers anyway. Maybe this would convince him to offer his assistance to invent upon dear Frask's contraption."

"But when the devices are built, how would we know if they are negative energy being utilized in Heaven?" Juliet asked.

"The Kaleidoscope. I have my own in this castle" Arianna said. "As soon as I heal, I can use that to mark where they could be."

"Of course," I said, concluding. "It's like using a radar."

Jesus then went up to Michael and Gabriel. "I'll need you to go back to the Main Chapel and contact Fergus, Freka, Adrian and Shaolin with the doves. We need to send them warning. And permission."

"I'm not sure of Fergus. He's usually always bothered of us. Freka, Adrian and Shaolin I could get behind." Arianna. "It's been long since we heard from them. But I'm sure they should be understanding. Whatever the case may be, we vowed to protect all the afterlife including that Insignia."

"What about us," I asked. Though I assumed that they were not going to use us for a bit. "What do you want us to do?"

"As of now, you just have to wait until we locate the satanic energy. Arianna should be able to tell you," Francis said. "You have our thanks for what you have done. Let us handle this case, you've done greatly."

"As a token of my gratitude, I've made a reservation for you three at The New Moon, one of the finest inns in Arcadia. It's the least I can do as an award for lifting Summerland off the Unicorn's curse." The Queen said.

"You've earned it," Gabriel said. "And we shall see each other again." I nodded to him.

"You three are dismissed for now. I'll have my guards escort you to The New Moon." She said smiling.

"Thank you, Your Majesty." We said as we were taking off.

"Oh, Gabriel," Arianna called for Gabriel. "I nearly forgot. I have something for the priestesses that you could give to them. Juliet, if you please." Juliet came up and took out the jar of honey the Queen previously gave us before. After handing it to her, she then passed it to Gabriel and said, "Please make sure they get this. The gods blessed it. Selene has blessed this. It should help them heal faster with grace."

"You have my word, Your Majesty," he said generously. "I shall be sure they get this."

"Thank you so much." She said. She then turned to us, "Oh...and you three may need to wash off the blood. You're a mess." We nodded as it was noted.

Soon enough, we were led to the inn, which was located on top of a large plateau far from the city. The building was looking out at the large seas scattered with large stone sculptures of Pagan figureheads. It felt like I was in a monastery because of its location. I managed to see Algor and Aventurine right after I reunited with them. Aventurine was placed in a stable integrated with the Inn.

I recalled a time when I was alive. I memorized the time I went to Florida with my family. I remembered being in a hotel like this. Kelley and I would both hang out at the balcony that exposed us to the open elegant seas with a line of trees nearby. This is what it felt like. Only...you guessed it. It was antiqued. It was ancient. But I was slowly getting used to it. Because I knew I had to; knowing that it was the life I had now. Yet, I was beginning to find hope in it.

During the mellow blue evening, I sat on a wooden chair in the balcony. We were on the fifth floor of the hotel. So, it was decent enough to get a good view. I was taking the time to play my guitar, my mother's gift. I had the notes for the Edith Piaf song she landed to me. I tried to play each note according to the instruction, but each mistake I made was mildly frustrating. I winced and sucked on my teeth. Perhaps it was because I was still thinking about everything that's happened. Nearly getting hunted down by the Satanists, discovering the Unicorn, using my powers, it was all crammed in my head. The least I could do now was to play my guitar with the cool breeze soothing my running nerves. The ocean being tossed around by the wind also helped, including the various cries of animals.

I looked back at the lined notes I had on the small table in front of me. Constantly looking back and forth at my guitar, I tried to capture the first notes. As I played, I messed up again. I winced in frustration.

"Stellar performance. Grammy worthy, I must say," A familiar voice joked. Turning to my right, the voice came from Ted who had his arms crossed and he leaned on the doorway.

Turning away from him to face the guitar, I said, "Thanks."

"Mind if I join ya," Ted asked.

"Sure, why not." I replied as I saw him walk past me to sit on the left side of me, the opposite side of the table.

"I got this baroque guitar over the holidays. My mother gave it to me." I said. "So...I'm just trying to play it."

"It takes time. It takes a bit of practice to learn." He said, leaning back against the chair, looking out at the ocean. He pulled out certain things from his pockets. Two white wrapped cigs. When he offered me one, I gave him an estranged look. He then said, "It's cake flavored herbs. Vanilla."

"Well...I do fancy vanilla cake," I said with a shrug as I stopped playing for now. I placed the guitar down on the table and received the cigarette. Once he lit up a match, he ignited both mine and his with ease. Regardless of my absence from it, it was almost a refresher to inhale vanilla toxins. I turned to him and saw him, very focused at the ocean glistening underneath the sheet of stars while inhaling and exhaling smoke.

"Y'know, with all that's been going on, you often forget how beautiful this world can be." Ted said. I nodded in agreement.

"It certainly is." I said. "The world we both came from was beautiful too. It's just that...we have the tendency to make it ugly." I continued to take a toke as my insides were consuming the vanilla aroma.

"I guess. I mean humanity was always destined to be incomplete, so to speak. But ain't that unique about us? There's beauty and ugliness in all of us. It depends on which path you want to go towards." After a dose of dancing smoke coming from his nostrils, he said smiling, "You've done good today, you know that?"

"We did." I said smiling back. "I told you, don't like being put in the bloody limelight all the time."

"I'm just saying." He snickered. Then he asked, "How did it feel? Killing Virgil like that? It seems like your first time. Still, you're a natural in this."

"It...It didn't feel like anything, in all honesty. Maybe it's probably because...I've held so much disdain for people that...well, it felt good in a way. Just to see people like this die. I don't know. I...went bonkers,

I fear. Maybe...because I'm not a good person." I tried my hardest to hide the fact that I have killed before. But not for the right reasons obviously.

"Nah, you're okay," Ted said scoffing. He continued, "These things just take sacrifice. I know it's an uneasy situation, taking lives. Let alone, taking afterlives. It takes sacrifice...to remove that notion that you must be too pure to live as a good man in life. A true man of God. But...tell that to those fellers who conjured those crusades...to justify that. Tell that to many who made that bold claim, only to go against it...time and time again."

"Fair point. I mean he knew what he was doing. And worst of all, he went with it!" I sighed after I smoked. "But even though I should be used to this by now, how do you stay committed and compelled to do this line of work? I don't even know how my father did it. Especially to what happened at the city. Nearly everyone died to our feud with those arseholes and that yellow-bellied bugger! This is what I feared. Not just my kin, but anyone caught up in this."

After he placed his two feet crossed on the table, he said, "Rest their souls. Truly. But...sometimes, it's never easy to save everyone at once. From my perspective, ever since I became an Apostle, I looked at how soldiers did this. Every range of them. Every tactic. And it may sound fucked up...because it is. But...when I kill, I think of it as...culling. You know what that means?"

"N...No, not exactly." After a toke, I proceeded to let them seep out from my mouth. My cigarette was halfway done.

"Think of it as being in a pack, a leader of the pack. Y'know, the typical predator and prey scenario! I chose to be the predator to wipe away the prey. Culling them." He then gazed at his crystalized blades, which propelled from underneath his sleeve. The cigarette resting between his lips. "Life, to me, is one big frontier. It's unpredictable. You either be hunted...or become the hunter. The wolf or sheep, and sheep are often victims. The monarchs who guard these lands help prosper. The problem is that the afterlife is nothing but a big forest to the Satanists and folks like them...who act as wolves. Making the monarchs sheep.

And preys cower in the side and ends up defenseless. Good as dead. But the predator...hunts. Just like Belobog...my ancestors' folk hero." Ejecting back his wavy blades by flicking his wrist, he then inserted his face to mine.

"Keep in mind, spirits here are guilty as hellish ones. They've done nothing but exploited heavenly magic in need to create little armies for themselves with drugs by using a fake pendant to summon them. Jesus saw this and made it punishable. At one point, Juliet, and I, alongside the Angel Paladins and Francis, had to infiltrate an alleged black market that was creating what we call artificial energies. They're a breed of spirits, who are either prisoners, traded victims, or...dead, given a drug made from emerald and amazonite to be reanimated into energy. Live ones would be deprived from all their senses and lobotomized into dull vegetables. These were our prime enemies before the Satanists. And it was easier before. Military forces needed our help to find them since they kept moving. Well, it was more so the assholes who made them. There were two noblemen, with what I would like to call edge lord tendencies, who plotted to overthrow the Oji Shaolin Chara in Tamashii No Ketsu Taba, his kingdom Takamagahara. They had over forty dead soldiers, who were resurrected not by their souls from the Void, but by the drug. They had ten workshops underneath sacred temples, villages, and monasteries in Akemi Creek. They were fronts for their business. We discovered where they were hidden and their inadequate plans to kill the king. And they threatened to kill more who intended to stop them. And believe it or not, regardless of what it was, it was the first time...I took a person's life. I asked myself...*is this how it feels.*"

He then looked out at the ocean again. He was finished smoking as he crushed the cigarette within his hand and threw it afar.

"Juliet felt the same way. Sure, it was something I was hesitant about at first. Still, I knew it was what I had to do, especially to stop them from running the market. Because before I pursued my assassinations, I began to think about all the times I was wronged, when I was alive. I thought about the things my dad put me through. The thought of what my aunt did to me. It made me realize things. About those assholes.

People who always get off in make other lives miserable, just for their own value. Just for fun without any effects. At that moment, I told myself...No, I was no longer going to be a prey. I will no longer be hunted. As an Apostle, I had to be the predator for once. I had to be the alpha wolf, defending his pack. I had to be the hunter. I had to cull evil. And so, after Juliet and I culled them, those places were saved. And soon, I had that nobleman killed...before he shot a woman and her children. With no restrain. No hesitation. Just his oozin' ghastly residue coating my jerkin like this...that's all what was left of him."

"That's interesting. I reckon...you do not believe in the ideal of heroism. You see it as a farce."

"Why shouldn't I? It's a childish illusion 'cause we're too scared of our flaws. The idealistic hero takes away what he truly faces in life. Not every hero does noble deeds to fit that standard because they are often faced with shit that contradicts that. I'm against the whole...black and white way of thought. I think heroes could be heroic on their own terms instead of living up to that status quo. In most cases, we do bad things to see good things happen. People tend to act as if they could do no wrong. They try to extract their favorite folk heroes so badly. But deeply, they sure as Judas's disloyal shit know that they are just as guilty of somethin'. Even the knights and the past Apostles were guilty of shit they weren't proud of. Only most were mindful. And to be that is to be mindful of our own condition. I mean...c'mon...we kill and hunt animals every decade for food to survive. We kill our trees and grass, forgettin' that they are living things too. So...I ain't sure why it's suddenly different when we kill one another. Especially when it came to self-defense or the defense for the weak? It's hypocritical, which is why I take no part of it. No one can go through life without that nature. I just intend to extract mine on the right enemies." He said as I nodded. He did have a point. "Besides, we have a long unapologetic human history of outlawing one another. One that is still in process, anyway."

"Well...what do we outlaw then?"

"Are you kidding me? Monsters...who pretend to be civilized. Monsters...who pretend to be men. I'm not saying to enjoy extracting violence like how I would...enjoy smoking, painting, gardening or...I don't know...fucking the hottest broad with the most elegant tits and ass. Far from it. We have a good message, but what we do to defend is not good. Still, we gotta quit actin' perfect than we actually are. Because we're not. I wish I was...but I'm not."

After toking in and blowing out the smolder from his mouth, he proceeded, "On the side though, I never told you how impressed I was; you've embraced your Macer." He said. My eyes widened in amazement. "That must have felt good, right? I told you...like pineapples."

"Aye." I chuckled to his pineapple analogy. After I smoked, I continued, "When we were traversing throughout the city, battling towards those Satanists, I didn't feel tired. I felt...more alive. Like I transcended through many planes. I...I know it sounds mad."

"What's wrong with being mad? It's a rational way of acceptin' life's true face. It's mad itself." He chuckled.

"I know. I just never imagined that they would make me unstoppable." I said with disbelief, still refusing to believe it. "The voices guided me through. The good ones. And it's weird...because it's still a condition that's been burdening me for a long time. Usually...I know people like me would get mocked or disregarded. I'm sure you feel the same."

"Truly. As someone with a range... I know how you feel. It's not fun to have at all." He said as he then engaged towards me. "But...I don't let it define me." He then rose from his chair and faced the ocean. But he said in sincerity, "I hope that I could be confident to express who I truly am. Not that I ain't comfortable with you or Juliet. But like I said, I don't want my faults to victimize me. And what you have shouldn't victimize you either. People like Lucifer or the Chancery love to think that they know you based on superficial information or some other horseshit. As if they have some form of control of your life and is eager to put you in a box. You shouldn't let them get away with that. They hate themselves 'cause they can't make a good life on their own. All you do....is tell them....to go fuck themselves. Don't let them play with your life, for it's yours and yours alone."

I nodded and absorbed everything he told me. And perhaps, the

476 - KENNETH VIVOR

guardians the voices referred to were themselves. Despite some of their ridicules and mockeries from the others, the other eight have helped me get far. And I was warming up to them. I knew that I had to live with the condition I had. I'm bounded to it. It's who I was. And perhaps, I had to accept the fact that I was not ordinary. It's the only way that I can ever separate myself from others. It didn't mean that I was above anyone. It just meant that I would never be what others want me to be.

It was clear that Ted managed to accept and embrace it. So, why couldn't I? But it made sense since Ted always came to be someone who didn't seek for everyone's approval. Not anymore at least. By hiding my true self, the one that got me killed in the first place, I suppose I was looking for an excuse to be seen as someone who came from a life of knighthood in accordance with my family and heritage.

As he was adjusting himself on the chair, he asked me, "Can I tell you something? I have to be honest about this."

"Go for it, mate," I said.

As he pondered down, he said, "I wouldn't want to live in a perfect world. It'd be less fun. I mean...for a species that worries about chasing perfection, happiness, and easy success, they end up making mistakes. Over and over. And we often don't learn from it. I wouldn't want to live in a world with posers pretendin' to be good than they are. Because when we rush to reach that phony inclination of a perfected world, you look back and realize that you've lacked any adoration for what was there and what you had. You forget to learn from it and make the best of it. And I'm guilty. Society has been giving all of us chloroform. Knocking us out. And people who don't wake up from that ...they're lost. Acceptive of the abuse. Sometimes...it's comical. Because really, what has it ever done for us than to break us and put us down into their conformity? Comical."

I nodded slowly, and I said, "That's very true. You're right." Inside, I felt ashamed of myself. Despite his suicide, Ted seemed to always stand true to his integrity. Yet, I threw mine away to become a criminal. I was haunted by my choices that were now trying to stop me from being the cavalier I wanted to be.

Soon after he left to go back inside, I thanked him for the conversation. Afterwards, I decided to pick up my guitar and play according to the notes. As I played, everything Ted told me traversed across my head. I looked out at the statue-riddled ocean, praying internally that it will get better.

Soon after I played my guitar for a long while, not realizing how late it was getting, I decided of go back inside. I saw Ted resting on the couch with his snake Penelope sleeping around him. Algor slept by him, presumably waiting for me. I can only assume that Juliet was sleeping in one of the beds in the other room.

Once I walked and turned to the right corner, I went and saw that there was indeed another room. It reminded me of those hotels where there were only two beds; meaning if you came with two people, one of them had to sleep on the couch. Except that the beds were slightly integrated to one another with a big rim and a drawer underneath.

Juliet was drifted into sleep. She had the white sheets over her body on the other bed in the right. So, I decided to sleep on the other bed, meaning we were both between a decent sized mahogany drawer. I placed the covers over my body, exhaling and slowly turning my eyes to Juliet. I was silently admiring her bleached hair from behind, as she sounded asleep. My eyes then caught the sight of her pendant lying on top of the drawer underneath the lamp. Picking up the necklace, I wanted to see the engravings of the pendant. I awed at the attention to detail the crafters put into it. The eagle was carved on Celtic floral design.

Sometime soon, I would very much like to meet Juliet's mother; even to bail out how drop down beautiful and intelligent her daughter was. I would also congratulate her for raising her daughter in such a bleak world. Eventually, I would like to introduce her and Ted to my parents. Including Kelley.

After I contemplated, I gently placed the necklace back on the dresser and paced myself underneath the sheets. I looked up at the wooden ceiling, contemplating for everything to be done right. And suddenly, the more I looked up, the more it prompted me to pray with my eyes closed. I silently prayed for everything to go well. I prayed for all of us to be okay. I prayed for my family's safety. I prayed that I would find meaning in this world. To truly become something better.

With that, I finally closed my eyes and waited until I drifted into a deep sleep. Suddenly, my body became paralyzed once again. I sensed every part of my body losing all feeling. Thus, losing my grasps of them.

XXX

Listen to Your Guardians

I was awakened by a voice. *"You still think you've gotten rid of us?"* My *eyes widened and saw that I was in a dark place once again. "You still think you're a hero in this story?"* I found my feet moist in the dark waters once again.

"I'm not trying to be a hero!" I roared back.

"Oh, but you are! Did you think just because you made it to Heaven, means that you would be redeemed? Meaning that you will get a second chance?! Any self-righteous hypocrite can do the right thing for the sake of an image! You have no chance! You know damn well you do not care for this war! You only want it done so you run like the coward you are!"

"You don't know me, alright? You will never know me!"

"I do know you! Because we are stuck together!" The voice said. *"You've made your choice, so there is no point in trying to become something better! There's no point in forgetting the past sins! There's no point in getting the life you want!"*

I then recoiled and covered my ears. I pressed on them very tightly until they were red. "Leave me alone! You cannot hurt me anymore! You hear me? You. Can't. Hurt Me!"

"I don't have to do anything! You're only hurting yourself! Continuously! You're still running away, hiding, from your nature! You refuse to face who

you really are! You think you're a man now! You think you are your parents! But you're still a child! With a lot to learn!"

I ignored the voice until it became muffled. But for some reason, I was still hearing it. So, I shouted, "That's not true! Stop trying to break me!" I even kept both of my eyes tightly closed. I wanted to make sure that I didn't see any darkness. I wanted light. But it was hard for me to wake up. In fact, I couldn't wake up at all.

So, once I opened my eyes, I saw that I was in a familiar place. It was something I remembered very vividly. It was a dinner room with a long rectangular table in the center. A fireplace was there, and the other side was facing two windows. Surrounded by porcelain-colored walls, I saw that I was in the diner room of the foster home in New York. I looked out at one of the windows, seeing all the cars, cabs, and buses passing down the road. The snow was falling and drifting through the air.

When I turned around, I suddenly saw myself summoned in the room. Pastor Gerald and Sister Ann were also summoned. And from the actions, I almost remembered that moment. I was nine years old and sat at the left end of the table, writing down something on a piece of paper. The two clergies were hovering over me with their arms crossed. One of them even had a cane concealed in his fist. I walked towards my younger self and took a gaze at what exactly I was writing down. What was I exactly writing for these clergies to look at me in an ominous way? Then everything was being gradually clear when I saw what I was writing at the time.

It looked very familiar and was written several times. Audi custodes tui. It was written over and over; at least one hundred to almost one hundred and forty times on each paper. I saw how my little right hand was blushing with red and the lashes from the swats I've gotten.

It made sense now. Everything became very clear. I remembered how I got that phrase to go on in my head.

"Audi custodies tui! Audi custodies tui! When you write this, I want you to engrave that in your head! To renounce those demons in your head! And the sins your dead family bestowed on you! You cursed this city! You and your grandfather! I'm sure you've seen the news!" Gerald said strictly.

I remembered he told me that. I felt every small spec of his saliva splashing onto my hair. I recalled the reason for them doing that to me. I was still sketching. Thus, they discovered my dark sketching based on my increased resentment for God. Of course, they saw them as demonic. They had my room confiscated until I fulfilled their wishes. Apparently, it was supposed to help me remove the voices in my head, which wasn't easy.

Mostly, I remembered how I felt very angry. I saw myself gradually getting angry by the sight of my body shivering when I was writing.

"*Your father's bigoted money isn't enough to fund this place!*" Sister Ann said. "*And it's worse when you're here! Who knew that that kind of selfish behavior ran in the family! Nothing but pseudo–God fearers!*"

"*You don't know my family!*" My younger self mumbled loudly.

"*What was that?*" The pastor roared. "*What did you say?*"

The boy didn't say anything. The room fell in brief silence. The boy continued to write down the phrase. Over and over. The led scratches echoed in the room.

"*For your information, we do know your family! We know what kind of filthy history you came from! You are not people of God! You're two-faced!*" Ann said. "*You have no chance! Unless you give your faith to our establishment. To our church! Like the children here. True children of God mind you!*"

"*Then stop forcing me!*" The boy shouted back at her. He was relentlessly yanked by his black hair and pushed onto the wooden floor. He was forcibly pinned on the floor. His lower jaw dripped with bile-taste blood. My eyes were widened. And I just stood frozen, staring at myself. It was like re-watching an old tape that I didn't want to see again. I was coming into grips of God completely leaving me. He wasn't there.

Once Gerald lifted the black wooden cane, he slammed it onto his head. The cane's crack echoed in the room, as well as the boy bailing his tears. Every smack he was getting made me jolts several times. I rubbed the back of my scalp and reflected at that painful moment. I still felt every slash, throb, and splinter from that cane. It was a relief to not feel that pain anymore. But after I was witnessing this, it brought the pain back. This was something I've blocked for a long time. Every inch of this place was supposed to be blocked in my head. Why in hell was it back in?! I wanted it out to move on!

"You're a piece of filth and a disgrace to God! It runs in the family! God won't help you! He has taken away your family, friend, and home! You have a chance to go to him alone, yet you failed! You still think you live in wealth! Think you could say or do whatever you want; I think not!" Gerald roared whilst constantly bringing down the cane onto the bruised flesh.

He ignored the boy's loud cries. He was even belted across his head at least ten to twenty times until he felt very numb. They even counted how many times they were striking. Every infliction of pain made me ache. It made me ill. I nearly had a panic attack from it. I felt as if I were still that shattered boy crying out for God to save me.

The old man continued to shout, *"You are a sinner! A cursed sinner! And until you give yourself to God, you will always be one! I want you to say it! And loud so that God could hear you before he leaves you!"*

"I'm a sinner! I'm a sinner!" The boy cried out as he continued to break. Teardrops damping the wooden floor.

"I think he had enough, Father Gerald! I think he learned!" Ann said as she crouched to take a good glance at the boy's tear-filled face. *"The next time you raise your voice again, the pain will be worse! And the next time I catch you drawing those drawings, we will break the devil from you once and for all! So, we will continue to pressure you until you become good in God's eyes! Until you invite the archangels into your heart and into that broken mind of yours! As a matter of fact,"* She got up and trailed off from the dinner room to the hall. Although tired from the physical lashing, the boy raised his head in wonder to what she was going to get. That was until she came back with five items. And I remembered what they were. I remembered vividly of what happened. That was also when she had my locket.

"...I notice how you and your family are very materialistic. And God despises materialistic beings! That's why they are dead and sent to Hell!"

"But those are mine! And my locket! Please, my sister..." The boy wanted to speak, until Gerald slammed his hand onto his head as he slammed

his face onto the ground. He began to taste his seeping blood on his bottom lip.

"To truly be redeemed is to make sacrifices! To suffer in Jesus's name! So, no more of these fantasy books..." Ann said as she went to the fireplace. With no hesitation, she threw the three books into the blazing flames. The boy's eyes widened with indescribable horror.

"...No more demonic drawings!" She threw my small green sketchbook into the flames, causing the fire to increase in rage.

"And no more jewelry!" She finally threw the locket, which got the boy to scream on top of his lungs and cry very loudly. He was flaying violently, as if he was having an epileptic seizure. Tears fell from his face uncontrollably. Soon, he flipped to his side as he proceeded with his dying tears and quiet sobs.

"Now as soon as you're done with your tantrum, you're going to sit in this room the whole day! You're going to finish your punishment! You will listen to your guardians; us! Not your dead parents nor your fake God! Then we'll see if you're redeemable. Then you'll have a purpose in this world being one with God! If I see another drawing, there'll be far more than lashes!" Ann finally left the room with Gerald, who had the door shut and locked. Soon after, the boy raced to the fireplace and picked up a wrought iron on the left side of the fireplace. With luck, he managed to pull out the locket that was burning hot.

It was encrusted with black markings and smears, especially on the pendant. The smoke was rising from it. The boy's face hovered over the locket and began to cry over it. I watched as his tears fell onto the ground near the necklace. I felt my eyes letting the tears come down my face until I was weak on the knees. Getting on both knees, I began to cry. My eyes were completely shut, concealing my vision in darkness, which I was thankful for. But the voice said, ***"Yes! Cry! That's all you're good for! Because you know it's true. He has left you! Everyone you loved left you! Because you're weak to face the world! You're weak to face life! Always on a run, on a rush, holding on to a desperate fantasy you cannot see nor have! So, go ahead! CRY!"***

Everything was coming back to me. I remembered how this was an everyday occurrence. This was my existence after my family died. This was what I had to endure. They prevented me to come in any contact, so all I did was pray for Harris to come back and rescue me. And he never came. I always felt safe with my family and Harris. I saw God whenever I was around them. But in these moments, and moments like this, I was on my own. They were always like this. They hurt the other children as well, but not the same as they did to me.

It was more hard coercion than violence. So, they had a clear bias towards me based on my grandfather's exploits. The God was no longer one I worshipped. I didn't see the God who would save me. I saw a God who took those I loved.

It made sense why no one had heard of the place I was in. They wanted their cruelty to be hidden from the public eye. And this was what I had to face ...until I took it upon myself to make my escape in the hollowest and snowiest of nights. I ran and surpassed through New York...to live on the dirty streets of Brooklyn. I would've used a phone booth to call Harris, but I was afraid of being tracked down. My mind was in panic of being hunted down. I was too scared to try to see it as an option.

But something else happened.

The room swiftly altered from being light to being dimmed with candlelight. It changed as I saw my young self-breaking down into ashes. The two clergies broke down as well, deconstructing before my eyes. But then screams and shrieks were heard about in the foster care. The staffs were seen passing through, getting the children into their rooms, and locking their doors for safety. More figures were materializing right in front of me. As I walked closer to the doors, which were open, I turned and saw that the hall was completely riddled with blood all over the walls. All the blood was smeared onto the portraits of great saints.

The white marble floor was decorated with decomposed bodies of the staff members. The sharp booms of the gun shots were heard in another part of the hall, which prompted the muffled cries of the children held in their rooms. In the middle of the hall, which was suddenly integrated with verdure and broken eerie construction, everything was coming back to me as I got closer. This was the time I exercised vengeance. Especially with Snake's help.

It felt like it was just yesterday when I bashed Gerald's head meat with his cane after stabbing him through his left cheek. The weapon he used on me. I battered and battered until the dove figurine was masked in his blood and specs of carnage. I was beating his head to bits. I've already done it to Ann as well.

What happened next reminded me of how unhinged this vicious act of vengeance made me. I saw myself get down on my knees, right next to his mutilated body. I swiftly opened his black shirt, exposing his under shirt. Upon tearing his under shirt, I grabbed a knife I've stolen from the kitchen. With that, not only I witnessed myself plunging the knife into his chest, but I also drew a deep line across until every drop of his blood was blushing and blooming from his wound. Again. Again. And again, until his chest was slowly demolished.

I stood up, witnessing my hands coated with blood and residue of his organs. Sweat showered and wetted my hair strands. I noticed how I ignored the cries of orphans who feared the loud booms of gunshots; meaning that Snake was killing the other staff members.

Looking back at it with my own eyes, witnessing what I did, it made me feel bad. They were truly terrible people who have wronged me, but they didn't deserve a painful death. Obviously, they had to be in the afterlife, but I didn't know where. I turned around and the voice came about. *"Doesn't the state of this place remind you of anything?"* The halls shifted from the children's home to...the school's hallway. It was as I remembered. Covered in blood. Floors riddled with corpses. Three of which were my family. Frighteningly, the voice then added, *"Doesn't this seem...familiar to you? It's ironic. You hated that shooter who bestowed death on your family. Or the girls who bullied your sister in school. Yet, it seems like you're no better than they were. No thought ran through your head of what those children had to witness, had to endure. You were so consumed with vengeance that you were oblivious to realize that you've became what you hated. Look at the path of death you left just because you wanted to be safe from the world! Because you choose to carry pain!"*

Tears came down my eyes. This couldn't be true. There was no way that I could bear to compare myself to that shooter. The shooter had no justification for what he did. But I did. "That's not true," I shouted.

"Oh, no?" The voice mocked me. The scene changes once again. This time, the entire hall was materializing into a much smaller room. The room was very familiar. It was a small bedroom inside of a church. I looked out the window that was next to the bed, seeing a much darker cityscape of New York City. So as soon as I turned around, something else was materializing before my eyes. An old man was knocked down. And he was being toyed and kicked over and over by a young man. I saw myself at the age of eighteen. And the old man who was knocked down and physically bullied was Harris. This was just six months ago when I was alive. Yet, it still felt like it just happened.

The boy then left and stopped after Harris advised him to think about how his life would eventually turn out. But he replied before he closed the door on him, *"Perhaps, except I don't plan to die today."* This is what he said, except that he did die. I ate my words now that I have witnessed it. And my heart was pounding slowly for seeing Harris, simply an old man, beaten up by someone who he practically raised after his parents. What was the voice trying to say? Why was it showing me things that I have done? Things I had experienced.

"This is who you are! This is what you chose to endure! You're not a hero or the victim! You are not the pure soul you intend to be. You are an heir of the Hospitallers! You are not what mummy or daddy pampered you to be! You are weak, faulty, violent, and dangerous to everyone you claim to protect! You are a heathen to those you claim to love! You only kill because it's an excuse to exercise your hatred! You are stripped from your humanity! And your petty attempts in reclaiming it, let alone bettering it, has failed! Do me a favor and face the facts. You have no chance of saving. Embrace it! Don't try to erase it! Don't pretend that all of this... didn't exist!" The voice said.

"You made them suffer! And you will do so again! You will damn

Heaven! You will damn your family! You will damn all! You are hopeless! You will always be alone! You are not of God! He hates you!! He hates you FOREVER!!"

"Leave me alone! Leave me alone! I'm not a failure! I'm not a monster!" I said over and over with my eyes closed. "I'm not a monster..."

"Kevin! Kevin! Kevin!"

I quickly rose and my eyes were wide open. I was no longer paralyzed. I turned and saw that it was Juliet who was calling for me. Her face was riddled with concern. I saw her right hand was on my left shoulder. I was breathing very heavily. I looked around wondrously, trying to make out of where I was as my heart was throbbing very fast. My breathing became frantic.

"Hey, hey, Kevin! Look at me," Juliet said as I felt her soft hands placed on both sides of my face. She got me to make my eyes look at hers. I focused trying to stop myself from breathing rapidly.

She said, "You're okay. Okay. Slowly. It's okay, dear. Take it easy. Slowly." I breathed in for five seconds. Held it in for three. And released in seven seconds. All whilst looking into her eyes as she instructed me.

I slightly looked away from her, but she made me face her. She told me to breathe slowly. As I did, I regained my consciousness. I noticed how my face was drenched with tears, in which she was wiping off.

She then glanced on the left side of me and said, "Theodore, fetch me water." I eyed back and saw that I've woken up Ted as well. I saw him take off to the kitchen.

"What...what happened?" I asked, trying to speak.

"You were having some sort of nightmare. But it sounded like it was much worse. You really scared me!" She said almost in panic. I saw Ted offering me a glass of water.

"You scared the shit outta us, dude! Here, this should cool you down." He said as I took the water and poured every drop down my throat. I gazed at his face, which was also full of concern.

"Thank you," I said to him. "What time is it?"

"It's only five in the morning. Almost dusk. Do you want to tell us what happened?" Juliet asked.

What was I going to do? I couldn't just simply tell them what happened. I couldn't tell them who I really was. I couldn't tell them what I did on Earth. What I witnessed made me afraid of who I was. A monster with an eerie imitation. I wanted to break down and scream the pain, but I needed to compose myself. I didn't want my sorrows to affect our task. I couldn't afford to muck up my position as a knight. So, I kept it to myself.

After I sighed, I simply said, "It's...not necessary. Just a nightmare."

"Are you sure?" Juliet asked.

"Aye. I'm sure. Honest. I'm sorry I worried you."

Juliet glanced at Ted for a good bit. Afterwards, she faced me, "Alright. But please remember...don't hesitate to tell us anything, okay?"

"Yes, of course. But it's fine. Really. Thanks guys."

"Alright." Ted said as he nodded and patted me on my left shoulder. "Take a rest, man."

I nodded back at him as he then took off. Juliet then stood up as her silk dress swayed across the floor. She then said, "I'm...going to make us some tea soon. Why don't you just go back to sleep, huh? Hopefully, you won't get another nightmare."

"I'll try. Thank you, Juliet." I gave her a sad smile. She nodded and took off. After she left, I saw that the skies were slowly becoming lighter blue. I was too scared to go back to sleep. I didn't want to relive those moments. So, I just simply lied on my back, trying to stay awake until the sun eventually comes up.

I wished I never lied to the Apostles, but I did it to protect them from my true nature. I was saddened that the light being didn't get rid of those visions. But I tried to let my father's words circulate in my head:

"Don't let your enemies make you into something you're not. Be guided by God, not man."

When the white cloudy morning was risen, I washed myself and prompted myself in my clothes, a grey jerkin over my white shirt and light grey trousers. Like before.

Soon, I was engaged in my hot beverage that Juliet prepared for us. It felt very good and warm inside of my mouth, especially tasting the mint flavor. So, I was trying my best to leave what I dreamt behind and tried my damnedest to consider it as simply a nightmare.

I came out of the room and see that Ted and Juliet were gleaming over a letter. Both were sat on the couch looking over a beige envelope, plastered with a purple wax marking. They finally unveiled it just as soon as I approached. They eyed back at me, hoping that I was okay after last night. Juliet asked, "Good morning, Kevin. How are you feeling?"

Stretching my arms over my head, I replied, "I'm fine. I'm okay." I walked over to the table to see what they were intending to read. "What are you reading there?"

"We just got it today," she said, looking back at the paper. "It's a letter from the queen's handmaiden. She's inviting us to attend the funeral...for the mystics. Their bodies were recovered."

"Right. That's no problem. Seems like there were those able to enter Hell. A slight chance that the toxin will be done. But regards to this funeral...we don't have any proper clothes." I said.

"They said that they're going to bring them to us in an hour. The funeral is in three hours." Ted said.

"Okay." I said gloomily. With my hands in my pockets, I then gazed outside of the window, which was glowing with the cloudy endurance.

Clearing her throat, Juliet called, "Kevin."

I turned to her. "Hm?"

"You know...it's...it's fine if you want to talk about...your nightmare." She said.

"I told you! I'm fine!" I said aggregately as I felt my crossed arms shivering. I sighed, as she looked almost saddened and worried. I then said, "I'm sorry. I'm fine. Really. It's just that there are more important things than to worry about me right now. I hope you understand."

"I know. I understand. But realize that you are just as important." She said after she sighed. "I think we should rest up before the funeral."

"I think that'll be good." I said.

I was still pondering in my dream. It was still lingering in my head. Everything that it was telling me. It's bad enough to attend a funeral for innocent people who weren't supposed to die (all because a coward like Virgil sacrificed them to Lucifer just so he can live).

But now I had to have this nightmare fester in my head. I decided to go outside just to look out at the ocean on the balcony. I was hoping that the blue wrinkles of the ocean could help get my mind off it.

Soon, the maidens of the hotel came into our room and gave us appropriate clothes to go the funeral. Juliet was given a long black dress with a headdress that had a veil. Ted was given black trousers, waistcoat, chemise, and a long coat. I was given almost the same wear as him. But I was already used to wearing black. Forgive me for the jest. Inappropriate timing.

Afterwards, they escorted us down to the ground level and to the front of the hotel. They prepared a carriage for us. It was a carriage, pulled by four brown horses. They were riding us from the secluded hotel all the way back to the city.

We arrived at the graveyard twenty minutes later. The green hills were decorated with tombstones and graves. Most of the land was populated with civilians; men, women and children all wearing black formal clothing. The horses pulled the vehicle from the gates to where the commotion was. As soon as we stopped, we were sent off. After we stepped off, we found ourselves whisk into a sea of people gracefully attending the memorial for her fellow citizens.

Up at the front, the people were surrounding several open graves made of glass. The queen herself was there, despite still looking very pale. She was in dark clothing as well, but of course it was more decorated with ornaments to easily identify her as superior. Inside the coffins were parsleys, flowers, incense burners and water. The priest was there, reading from what I assumed was a Pagan version of the Bible, praying for the lost souls to look after the brave individuals who had to endure being prisoners of Hell. No doubt this was borrowed from the likes of Valestone.

He spoke of how the nobles confidently contributed with the queen in their endeavors and tried to better the citizens of Arcadia; only to be betrayed by one of their fellow nobles. In the crowd, sobs and whimpers were heard. But it didn't distract us from hearing the priest speak highly of the eleven nobles who died: five men, five women, and one child. All of them were viciously murdered, in a way, by Virgil, in pathetic fear, madness and betrayal. This made me not regret what I did, knowing that he was going to get away with what he did. Even if it was a dark thing to do.

Each worker of the memorial placed glass lids on each coffin. They made sure that the smoke would be concealed and circulated around the bodies.

"May they be welcomed by the Gods and Goddesses." The priest finished as he closed the book. It was the cue for the crystal coffins to descend into their graves, sinking all the way to the bottom of the dirt.

Ten minutes later, everyone began departing from the cemetery, going back to his or her homes, including the priest himself who greeted the queen.

This didn't sit right with me at all. Seeing the noble kind struggle. Seeing the common spirits in constant fear for their loved ones. Seeing the Queen in distress. Once the other dragonfly prototypes are built and we find the two accomplices of Lucifer, we had to show them that we weren't going to take it anymore. We had to be strong. I didn't care how powerful he is. I didn't care about his noble agenda. Because of what he has caused, it gave me a reason to show how delusional and wrathful he was. We couldn't afford to have another wind-up dead.

After the priest was done talking to her, we took the initiative to talk to her. I hoped that she was doing all she could to get the dragonflies built. We were engaging to her on the hill. As she removed her eyes from the tombstones, she then eyed at the three of us as she suddenly took notice. With her hand elegantly held together, she gave us a soft smile.

As we bowed, we said, "Our Queen."

"Greetings, Apostles. I'm sorry that you have to witness this." Arianna said. "But I'm glad you were able to attend. You didn't have to. But I'm glad you did anyway."

"Nonsense. We're glad we came." Ted said. He glanced at the tombs of the nobles. "We're sorry about what happened to your city. I wish we made it earlier."

"Oh no. It's quite alright. Please don't ever blame yourselves for what Virgil has done." She said. "He has paid his due for betraying us. Attempting to overthrow me. These good folks he had killed will rest with Selene."

"Very good." I said.

"I am very thankful for everything you have done, despite how it resulted."

"It's no problem at all, Your Majesty. Forgive me for getting to the matter of things, but any luck contacting the three monarchs?" I asked.

After sighing, she expressed, "None unfortunately. When the Chancery threatened to expand Valestone into an empire, they didn't take that well. Right now, they're concerned for their kingdoms than to bother with a demonic legion. So...it's unfortunate, but I understand." Then she continued, "But upon checking the Kaleidoscope, I was told that one of them was in cahoots with the Satanists and Lucifer's Army. Fergus of Odin. I was given a letter."

"Fergus?" I recalled.

"Aye. He rules in Valhalla...north of the Promised Land." She informed. "Apparently, someone called The Fairy has provoked a civil war against him. Subpoenaing a demonic legion of monstrous Vikings."

"Just as we needed; another fuckin' Watcher!" Ted ranted. He sighed with a growl underneath. With his hands on his waist, he said, "Forgive me!"

"It's okay. I understand your frustration." Arianna said. "I believe the civil war is an advantage to steal Fergus's scepter from the Castle of Sigr."

"Damn! So, do Francis and the rest of Celestia's monarchy know about this?" I asked.

"They have to if this has been going on for a while." Juliet added.

"They do. Jesus even sent Michael and his soldiers to aid him. But Fergus strongly rejected. If I know one thing about Fergus is...he's damn stubborn sometimes. But I can't really blame him, in this case. He took the threat by the Chancery to have us moved out...too hard. Yet, he now generalizes Jesus as being as bad as they are." Arianna said. "Luckily though, this accomplice was direct and brash. Unafraid he seemed. He is called Rollo."

"Rollo. The first Viking who ruled Normandy as a human." Juliet informed. "What could he be with Fergus?"

"Apparently, he was one of Fergus's loyal men. His trusted lieutenant who protected the good folk of Sigr. He used to lead the Valhallians. But I think Lucifer convinced him just as he convinced Virgil. He's warring against Fergus into surrendering his power to him. Now it is Horik Druith who serves Fergus and sent me this. He doesn't even want my aid. No other kingdom."

I began to pace across the grass. I had my hands on my waist. I sighed, letting out my frustration. Even though it seemed like a step backwards into getting to the Angel, it seemed reasonable to take down Rollo before we got to the Phoenix. As Arianna put it before, at least he was apparently direct, which meant that I'd have more of an excuse to kill him.

So afterward thinking, I said to her, "Alright. We'll go after Rollo. But that's all there is to it, right? And soon, we'll go after the Phoenix."

"Definitely, we should do that." Juliet said. "From his silence, it seemed as though he was trying to contain the civil war. Preventing it from spreading across the Promised Land. He at least has unintentional nobility despite not wanting no part of the Covenant."

"Yes. Very well. Maybe it'll be a way to convince him to help us. But just be careful when you meet him. He gets very stingy when someone offers to help. Especially from Valestone."

"Well sadly, Your Majesty, we could care less." Ted stated. "We're still doing it for his sake."

"So, it's settled. Whether he likes it or not." Juliet added.

Arianna then glanced at all three of us before she took a glance over to the sea of towers of Arcadia. Her red pig tails blew along with the chilly wind. "You know, when I was just a little girl in the afterlife, I've always wanted to be a queen. I liked the thought of everything being accordant to my vision. To make a home for pagans." She then eyed at us. "But growing up in the monarchy, I nearly allowed that ambition and ideal cloud my mind that I was unaware of what my people wanted. My Father and Mother looked over this land and did it justly, allowing the spirits to live how they wanted to live. Making sure that they are always lively. Regardless of its mistakes."

She huddled us around to face her angelic face. "This is what Lucifer doesn't have, mindfulness. He's obsessed with his own principles that he isn't mindful of anyone else around him. I know that isn't your portion. But I pray to Selene that you don't falter into that trap. Be wholesome and open as you are now. Forgive me, I just thought I tell you this before you go. It's easy to forget."

"We dearly heed your advice, Your Majesty." Juliet stated with a smile. "Thank you so much for your hospitality."

"You are very welcome. Thank you for showing us a possibility for us monarchs to uphold the peace we had before." She smiled. "Please feel free to stop by Arcadia. The gates are always open to you." Lifting her arms to the skies, she said to us, "May the Moonlight of Selene bloom through you."

"And also, with you, Your Majesty." I said to her. After bowing, we both departed from the cemetery and back into the carriage that was kindly waiting for us.

When we traveled back to the hotel, which lasted for another twenty minutes, we were back in our room on the fifth floor of the hotel. It was a shame that we had to leave to get back to Valhalla. I would've loved to tour around the city, seeing the sights and seeing how different it was from Celestia. In a way though, we sort of did. But that was only because we were trying to escape the furious horde of Satanists. It wasn't enough. I would've also loved to see the throne room of Queen Arianna and feasted my eyes at the care they gave to the place.

But we had to go to Valhalla, especially to be there for the other residents who were possibly in desperate need of us. Especially for the priestesses. I just hope that the maidens and hostesses fed Aventurine enough for him to travel. Sooner or later, the entire room was empty. It was back to when we first came here; neat, nothing out of place, or anything odd.

Before we can go, I managed to recollect Aventurine from the stables on the first floor. He was gloomed properly and still has his tortoise pelt intact. He was still majestic as he was before. I had to be sure since I knew that we were departed from the mad task we had to fulfill.

Shortly after we got out from the hotel, we were sure to be ready to travel at speed to go to Valhalla. I turned around and made sure that everything was in the back on our saddles; our belongings and Algor. All three of us mounted on our horses. Algor announced his enthusiasm with his loud bark. I faced the slope that was previously leading us up to the hotel.

When I called out Valhalla, I triggered Aventurine to pull all three of us. It's the same thing that has happened before. Once we were gradually gaining speed and getting faster, we were soon traveling through the vortex.

XXXI

Valhalla Rising

After we made it through the vortex, we found ourselves traveling across a wooden bridge. Snow was falling and passing by our faces. In front of us was a large white crystal gate that was sided with large statues that were obviously Vikings standing proudly with shields and swords. And since it was in the north, of course it would be chilly. I mean, it was still January. So, to that degree, it made sense.

The compound was fronted with large gatehouses and towers, quite like what the Queen had in Arcadia.

Without delaying, we trotted to the front, hoping to see if they would allow us inside to meet King Fergus. Approaching further, we saw that they were two guards inside each tower beside the white stoned sculptures. They wore armor that was intact with fur pelts, most likely from the boars, bears and other creatures they hunted and skinned. We were truly in Viking country now.

"Halt! Who goes there?!" One of them shouted, forcing me to stop Aventurine from getting closer to the gates.

"We are looking for King Fergus!" Juliet stated on top of her lungs; the guards heard her voice.

"The King isn't here!"

"Well, where can we find him?" I asked.

"We're not telling you! He warned us about you! King Jesus Christ sent you three, didn't he!? Christ's pets."

My friends and I eyed at one another, not knowing how to answer that. But then I replied, "No. No mate, we came in our own volition. We intend to stop The Fairy."

"Ha, good luck with that! He's nowhere to be found here. The King's out in the Southern Plains, still warring with him!"

"Oy...you're not supposed to tell 'em that, idiot!" One guard ridiculed the other.

That was easy, I murmured to myself. "Where is that, the Southern Plains?" I asked soon after, hearing my voice echoing.

"Look, disregard what he said! It's not of your concern! Our king does not want any associate outside of Valhalla! Especially from Valestone!"

"We hear you're trying to contain a civil war. And quite frankly, consecutively warring against profoundly powerful demons isn't going to help. It's only going to have more of your men die." I spoke. "So...having three deadly and agile fellows like us can be your best chance of ending it when you allow us to decipher. Unless...you know...you want your king to die out there as well."

"You best watch your tongue, boy! These men, and the King, are willing to die for the Gods! You wouldn't know. You Christians and Catholics never do," he said, disregarding the fact that both Ted and Juliet are not of the same god as me.

"It's not an insult, lad! It's a mere observation at the task at hand. They're willing to die for your Gods, delightful." I said as I dismounted from Aventurine to speak to them generously. "But what about those who want you to come back? What about those families who want you to live? How do you think they will feel if they find them dying out on the battlefield? I'm quite sure that there are children in that city who are eager to be just as brave as their fathers; to heed their stories and be their legacies in their own fashion. Wouldn't be fair for them to live without them around if you ask any of us. Look, I understand. You have bitter resentment towards us...especially towards the lot at Valestone. But I assure you...allowing us forsaken vigilantes to help...would be a possibility of having all the heavenly kingdoms, including yours, to reconcile and unite as before. At the end of the day, we're all heavenly spirits here with common enemies. Enemies we seek to destroy before they outlive us all."

"He's got a point," Ted added. "So...will you let us help? Or will you continue to be stingy as hell?"

After pacing and hesitating, I watch as one of the guards faced us as I mounted back on Aventurine. Dastardly, he said, "Dammit, fine! If you truly are what you say, further away from this city, you should go down south and see a military camp, beyond the terrains. But don't tell anyone we sent you! And if our men or Fergus don't come back, so help us Tyr, we'll kill you ourselves with no hesitation!"

After an awkward silence, Juliet said, "Of... course. We'll be sure that won't happen. Thank you." With that information, I turned Aventurine around and all three of us turned away from the gates. Sooner we were away from the wooden bridge. We began galloping through the open snow-covered terrains, which overhead the mountains.

With that information, hopefully we could gain Fergus's trust. Especially once we kill Rollo for him. Truth be told, it was stunning to see Vikings before my eyes. I never thought that the afterlife was going to be the first place where I would see them. And if they exist in the afterlife, what else could be beyond these highlands and other realms.

On the way, we camped for two days with dying snow farther from where we were. Especially if the horses got tired. Ted and I would hunt for elks, deer, and bison while Juliet made their carcasses into stew. The bison pelt was used for covers. Whenever we rollout our bedrolls from our mounts, they'd summon tents made of yarn. And it was evidently useful, given how very cloth Valhalla was regardless of the snow being present on the mountain peaks.

The breeze of the cool wind would scorch into our skin despite our decent layers of cloth. But the fire we surrounded would give us warmth like a dying candlelight. But after we would drink and share funny stories of how good life used to be, I wanted to take the time to put my other gift to use, my journal.

I looked around, with an opened book with blank pages, to seek for something to replicate in the paper. I saw that Juliet was not asleep from the moonshine like Ted, who was lying flat on his stomach. She sat across from me as she stared down at herself grinding whatever herbs she had in a wooden manual spice grinder.

With an idea for my first piece to get myself back to sketching, I called, "Hey...um...Juliet?" Turning her eyes away from the grinder, she glanced at me and replied, "Yes, Kevin? What is it?"

"This...might sound a bit...strange. But I was wondering...would you like to pose...for a portrait?" I asked. She stood up and went from her sleeping bag to sit by me after placing down the grinder.

"You could sketch? I never knew that. Of course. Where do you want me?" After she questioned me, I saw potential in capturing her right by the fire. I wanted to capture her essence that would correlate with the light she represented. So, I then told her, "You could perhaps...kneel by the fire on my left over there."

"Certainly," she said as she was at my left and have her knees flattened on the cool grass and her hands placed delicately on top of one another. When she faced me, half of her face was colored by the fire. Dipping my goose quill pen into the ink, I began to look at her for a bit to keep her pose and the image in mind. *Perfect*, I thought.

Now, as much as I had bitterness towards him, I had to thank Father Harris for showing me how to elevate my sketches from basic figures to more realistic figures. As I swiftly drew her with the little flames, after outlining, I continuously looked just to be sure that I was capturing her right. I wanted this to be good for her. Though, I was surprised by how I still managed to sketch well. After such a long time. Sometimes, I was hoping for Ted not to eavesdrop and get any ideas. But he was asleep. I hoped he stayed that way.

Seven minutes later, I presented it to her as she got off posing. Her white - blue eyes widened, and her right hand covered her mouth as she witnessed my first drawing in fourteen years. Her kneeling by the fire as it lit up the darkness made of hatchings. "Kevin...this is gorgeous! This is very beautiful!"

"It's...yours, if you want it," I said, tearing it off from my journal and handing it to her. Taking another good glance, she looked up to me and said, "Of course. I'm sorry...I'm just...honestly ecstatic. No one has...really done a one portrait of me before. I hope you continue this endeavor. Thank you so much, Kevin."

I smiled and said to her, "You're welcome, Juliet. Thank you for posing. Even in the dark...you shine." When I said that to her, her freckled face blushed. And that blush was in my mind the whole night I slept comfortably.

Two days later, we raced across the kingdom's open but almost vacant country. On our way to the murky battlefield, we saw what was left of Valhalla. Broken down statues of the Norse gods. Decayed temples and holy places. Abandoned battlefields. Forsaken halls. I'd like to think that Valhalla was beautiful as well, until the rebellions came in the form of Ragnarök. It still was in a way. But just like a lot in Heaven, it could be better.

After drumming the hooves from valleys to leading the horses through murky forests, we were going up a meadow slope passing a streaming river. We suddenly saw a group of smolder and mist rising over the peak of the slope we were on. We also overheard faintly dialogues and barks from where the smokes were coming from. Of course, this caught our curiosity.

We eyed at one another to reassure that this could be where he can be. For all we knew, we were going down and further from the city as far as we could. This had to be where the war was most likely going to happen.

So afterwards, we were reaching on top of the peak, only to witness a sea of white tents all columned and riddled across a massive terrain. Of course, it was an ideal location to manifest a behemoth battle. Far out, there was an actual battle raging. Fire, murky mist, and a bloody flood of Vikings and flying Valkyries raging towards the collective mass of Demon Legionaries were all witnessed. But the king was yet to be seen. Vicious cries were bombarded. Smoke was coming from these large bonfires stakes that were scattered and inflamed with raging fires. On those stakes were darkened bodies that have been crusted by the flames. Some bodies were in a prone position with their lungs spread open like wings. It was too hazy to see everything. Juliet unleashed her spyglass from her satchel and observed the area, possibly to find the king.

"So...what do you think? Is our guy down there?" Ted asked.

"Aye, he is. I see him," Juliet said, putting her spyglass back into her satchel. "Let's go."

This prompted us to get down to where it was. After we dismounted, I decided to let Aventurine and Algor to make themselves scarce. I understood Algor's whine, but this looked very dangerous. And I wouldn't want him involved or Aventurine. At least when it was necessary. Ted and Juliet had their horses Newman and Violet disperse as well. We staggered down the mound.

Soon, we finally found ourselves sneaking quietly amid a rustling battle camp. I thanked Ted for bringing us behind one of the tents. We saw ourselves surrounded by tents inhabited by Vikings. We cautiously wandered a bit through the camp, which was nearly impossible to walk through. We hid and swayed from tent to tent, hoping that we wouldn't be seen. The entire environment was very hazy and raged with smoke because of the flames. I felt a bit warm by the heat that surrounded the place. But it was an advantage for us, so they would bother to catch us. Though, we had to cover our mouths to stop us from extracting a cough.

We knew it was wrong to trespass, but we had to see it done. They couldn't kill Rollo alone. But I did feel bad for seeing the soldiers already wounded and nearly dead. A lot of them were being carried on these white stretchers that were already coated in their blood. I was seeing myself embodying my father.

When we were walking through past the tents, we saw a commotion near the hill that was over watching the war-riddled steppe. It was gathered with a decent sized group of other Vikings who were armed with shields, swords, spears, crossbows, and longbows. They looked to be nodding. They were looking up to a man, who wore a bronze crown. Standing next to him was another brutish-built man with red hair.

He wore a furry dark brown cloak. His hair was a dirty white color. He had a white beard that almost reaches his chest. He looked to be Jesus's size, but a bit more muscular. His armor was decorated with Norse accent designs and had a face that looked to be Odin. By the look of it, I assumed that it had to be King Fergus.

As we engaged closer and closer, his voice was roaring with fury. He didn't sound angry. But he sounded courageous. I slightly saw the oversight of the war. All that was shown was fire scattered all over, along with millions of murky corpses, flagpoles and pikes rose high as they were planted on the ground. I saw the remaining Vikings and Valkyries trying to take on the Demonic Legionaries.

But I remained focused on Fergus, which I realized was giving a motivational speech to the remaining soldiers. As he was speaking, he paced left and right to make sure all his men heard him.

"I know all of you are scared! I know you all feel hopeless! I know you are exhausted! Agitated! Frustrated! Burdened by the loss of your brothers we have lost for the past few days! I am frustrated, saddened, and bitter as all of you! It is not my intention to send you to death! But we are Valhallians! This is the work of Hel! The attempt to have our souls broken! We. Won't. Let her get the best of us! We won't let the demons of Hel break our spirits! Do you know why? Because we are strong! We are brave! And most importantly, we are blessed! The Gods have blessed us! Only the Gods could slay the darkness! They are looking over our brothers in the Void! And they are with us now! And when we are blessed, we are strong! Do not give that turncoat Rollo the satisfaction, for he is no longer a brother. He wants Valhalla...he wants Sigr...he must go through us! And even if some of us will die today, we will dine with the Gods! We will do what it takes to protect this great bloody land!" Shortly, he raised his decorated sword from his waist sheathe in the air. "FOR VALHALLA!!"

"Valhalla!!" The Vikings shouted with their weapons in the air. Soon after, they all ran past him, going through the battlefield. And even though it wasn't my concern, but I truly hoped that those men heeded his words. I hoped that they would come back alive.

"Come on!!!" The red-haired man shouted as the others followed his voice. He raced down with his axe raised.

After all his men disbursed onto the battleground, he finally took noticed of us. I was stunned, but we expected it anyway. He scoffed when he saw us.

"I'm not going to bother asking how you've managed to get here. But I can only assume that you've come to enjoy the show?" He asked.

"On the contrary, we're here to help! We're Apostles of Valestone!" Juliet stated.

Sucking on his teeth, he said, "Valestone. Of course! Francis Bailey and that bleedin' Order of his! I thought I specifically asked that lass Arianna to tell Jesus we don't need assistance! Not ever! Let alone from knights!"

"We came in our own terms." I said. "We don't mean to trespass, but we need to stop Rollo! The Fairy!"

He then looked at us as if we were stupid. After he gave out a chuckle, he said, "I appreciate it! But if I'm ever in need to be biblically lectured, let alone taught by a couple of church school kids, or to have my beliefs even more demoralized and inferior, I'll make sure I send a dove. But until then, sod off!"

"Church school kids? Demoralizers? We're not that kind! We want him dead just as much as you do! With all due respect, we don't have time to debate beliefs!" Juliet said. She then walked up to the edge of the hill, pointing at the battlefield.

"Kevin, Theodore, do you recognize what those men are?"

Eying at each other, Ted and I walked up until we were next to her. We looked over and saw something peculiar. I recognized that those soldiers wore a special kind of armor. It was a dirty gold, which was mostly made of sunstone. The same kind of soldiers we saw when we were rescuing the priestesses. Almost the same as what Sathanus wore. It was no wonder why Fergus' men kept dying. *Good eye*, I thought to myself.

"Aye. They're Satanists! Lucifer's petty fan club led by Sathanus, the pilock! What's your point, lass?"

"These are not Satanists. They are Demon Legionaries of Lucifer, who are stronger and deadlier. They are working with those demonic Valhallians. They've grown stronger each time, not giving you a fair fight." Juliet said. "That's why your men kept dying. They bare the armor and wield the weapons of sunstone this time. Even if you manage to end one of them, it still affects you. Lucifer's right-hand enforcer Sathanus wears this!"

"You're crazy! We managed to have some of them burnt on the stakes, answering for all they could have done! But...we just don't know how they are coming all and about!" The king said in a frustrated tone. He looked over the overwhelmed battlegrounds. "It's like killing flies, only for more to come. They're nothin' but damn parasites! I've been trying what I can to contain it! But's it not easy! I don't understand...we've beaten them before! Just about."

"That's because they're summoned by Rollo! They've become power-ful. And sunstone is becoming impossible to outsmart." Ted said. Fergus turned to him. "Those assholes were Satanists you burnt. Probably going after us."

"Summoned? By Rollo? Out of all spirits! That's ridiculous! How?! By wishing upon a shooting star?!"

"My friend here is right, sir!" I added. "We killed someone else who was another puppet of Lucifer. He wore a pendant that allowed him to have the powers to summon Satanists and other monstrosities. All what is left is to find where Rollo is! And if you allow us to help, we can save your men! That'll mean that the summoning will stop. We could help one another. If not Angel Paladins, the Fairies of Summerland, then us."

He looked very skeptical. But he gradually softened his tone. Scoffing to himself, he looked over the raging seas of Vikings with Valkyries and Demonic Vikings with Legionaries furiously feuding once again.

"If you want your words to be in truth as opposed to just a mere speech for your men and women, we're your best chance. Otherwise, these blokes would die for absolutely nothing, I guarantee. No matter how inspired they felt. If you truly cared for the wellbeing of your soldiers, if you want them to go back to their families, you will allow us." I persuaded almost desperately.

It took him a good thirteen seconds to gradually heed our advice. After he sighed and grunted, he turned to me, "You bloody Christians always have a damn fancy way of using words."

"It's easy when it comes from the heart." I said. "I know how you feel! But...Jesus has faith in you! He always has! He didn't care for what you believed in. He admired your character. That's all that matters to him, regardless of all else! And not all of us are what you think!"

"Yeah...of course you aren't!" He scoffed sarcastically. I sighed and palmed my face.

"Heed this too, sir," Juliet said as she came from the edge. "If I nurse your men to health along with the doctors, will you allow my friends to find and kill Rollo?"

Shortly after silence, he scoffed and asked, "You...a nurse?"

"Yes."

"Huh...you look kind of...threatening to be a nurse."

"I get that a lot." Juliet shrugged.

"Right. And how fast can you heal these men?"

"These things take time. So not in five seconds, I guarantee." Juliet said.

"Well, I appreciate your honesty. And I suppose you two will get to Rollo," He said as he then faced me and Ted.

"He'll be on his ass for what he's done. You have our word." Ted reassured.

After sighing and mumbling to himself, he said, "Alright...fine! But best of luck in finding Rollo! He can be anywhere in this god forsaken spec of land! And if you can...bring me his head!"

Ted and I eyed at each other weirdly. I then asked him, "Isn't...that a bit barbaric?"

"Well, what do you propose we do, boy? Offer him church bread and wine? Sing kumbaya around a campfire? We're Vikings, for fucks sake!" He bloated. "I want the head of the traitor to be a symbol for those who would dare commit munity in the name of man!"

"If you say so." Ted said as he eyed back at me. I shrugged.

"Good! So, I shall be in the battlefield to hold 'em off! If you truly are what you say you are, I hope not to be disappointed!"

We nodded. We soon departed from the King to recall everything that's about to happen soon after. Truth be told, I was quite nervous of bypassing an entire land full of battle. At that moment, I had to ask myself what father would do.

The three of us looked at one another, exchanging looks that were implying that we were each wishing each other the best of luck. I kind of wished I stayed with Juliet to help her, but I know that I still had my task. And so, did Ted.

"You two do me a favor; don't die." She said generously.

"Trust us. We have no plans to die today." I said.

"Good." She turned back to the campsite. She then eyed at us. Her hands were inserted into her bag as she then pulled out the dragonfly device. She placed it in Ted's hands. "Blessings to you both by Anu."

"And with you too, Juliet." Ted and I said. As she departed, Ted and I walked over to the edge of the plateau, looking over the flood of an ongoing skirmish that was taking chunks of the land.

I took a deep breath and Ted asked me, "Ready?"

"Aye." I nodded to him. He displayed the dragonfly. I tapped into my Blessed Eye and pulled out my hand to levitate it. I felt the weight of the device without touching it. The eyes flashed white, and wings began to flap all about. It lifted itself in the air and began to fly over the battlefield. I placed my hand down.

"Think it's best to save your portal summoning, Ted. Let's save our powers for Rollo."

He nodded. I whistled to summon Aventurine and presumably Algor since I left him there. I know the lad has been longing to fight alongside me like before. And he can be very useful in this case. But I had to make sure that I didn't lose focus on the dragonfly that flew across the grasslands.

"Better put our masks on. This could get hazy." He said as we both summoned our masks. Ted had on his jester-like mask on once again. I had on my black and red bandana.

I then said, "Let's get to work, then. Shall we?"

"Yes...let's." Ted replied.

After Aventurine and Ted's horse Newman conjured by each side of us, Ted and I mounted on our steeds. I looked down and gave Algor a single nod. Afterwards, I whipped the reins repeatedly to made Aventurine go forward. Ted followed soon after. We found ourselves galloping down the hill and heading towards the debris and residue of the war-riddled grassland.

I was destined to get to Rollo that I was unaware of what I was supposedly going to get myself into. I'm essentially getting myself into a battlefield with an Icelandic pertlow and with an alvoton.

I suddenly saw a couple of Satanists from afar trying to shoot down the dragonfly. But I watched as Ted pulled out two pistols from his holsters whilst riding his steed. "Those fuckers are trying to shoot the dragonfly." Eying at me with fury, he said, "Make sure it doesn't leave your sight!"

"Right!" I said as I then eyed at Algor. "Algor, hang on!" I then brought my focus on the battlefield. To support Ted, I also drew my pistol with my right hand as my left held onto the reins. I proceeded to fire at each Satanist.

I saw that there was no turning back for now. I had to be sure not to run over or potentially murder Fergus's men. Luckily though, the grassland was widened enough and convenient for me to ride by as I followed the dragonfly. Beside the steed were two different states of individuals fighting each other. Jabbing, stabbing, spearing, and shooting with arrows and other fatal projectiles, this was all witnessed. All of it was in a foggy and toxic environment. I heard the loud booms of Ted firing his pistols at the charging satanic warriors. He shot the others who were intending to shoot the dragonfly. And even Aventurine got to shine in the field by violently swaying his hooves at the Satanists, although I didn't expect him too.

When I turned, I saw that some Satanists were one horseback, riding on these disturbed black misty horses that distortedly wailed. I warned Ted that they're pursuing us from behind. He made sure that each shot was précised at the heads, knowing that gut shooting wouldn't be enough. But I still had to focus on the way, although something lingered in my brain that most of these Satanists were warned about us coming for their puppet.

Going through the field of mayhem and insanity was lasting for fourteen to fifteen minutes; especially due to how big the damn field was. Even though I donned my scarf mask, I still coughed from the ashes, smoke from the fire scattered across the grass. I was hoping that we would reach there. But as far as I saw now, it was nothing but corpses of Viking soldiers, Valkyries, and Demons. Hurik was lost amongst the pool of bloodshed.

But soon after, it seemed like we reached the end of the battle. It was still foggy, but we made it out of the hostile battle. But I saw that the dragonfly was hovering near what happened to be a village far from the battle and was near the ocean. It seemed that we were on a land facing another spec of land from Valhalla. So, by that logic of the dragonfly stopping, it was most likely that the demonic energy was being utilized from there.

Before we would head down to the village, the dragonfly was leading us through a bloodied pathway into the burning woods. And yes, war was still prevalent. Ted and I looked back and saw that several Satanists were mounted on their horses, hurtling us down with bolt action rifles and crossbows. We both ran down straight the muddy path between the trees. We swayed and dodged every oncoming arrow and bullet that they fired behind us. I turned back and fired back whilst holding the reins of a rapidly running Aventurine. Ted undrew both his pistols and removed his saddle rifle, which was an arcane repeater that he had equipped on his horse's saddle. He began to fire at each Satanists, including their horses.

When the two Satanists launched from their horses and plummeted to their deaths, I turned back to the front. Ted whipped the reins and raced past me as he was galloping relentlessly throughout the woods. I raced by his side as we rode together and focused on the dragonfly's direction. At the end of the forest, which looked to be an opened stage, I saw light emerging. A way to the village.

Without any second thought, we raced down to the village. But further and further away from the woods, I saw that it was not as safe as we previously assumed. Perhaps from the overwhelming smolder that clouded my eyes. Most of the village's roofs were decorated in fire.

Once we went down there, as we were following the dragonfly, we were greeted with more carnage. Innocent common spirits were slaughtered right in front of us. Women were being shoved and tossed into their homes by their husbands. The Vikings of the village were doing what they can to make sure every innocent man, woman and child is left alive. Regaining energy in his guns, Ted tried everything he can to shoot the Satanist shadows of the Vikings. It looked like a traditional raid. And it was likely that Rollo was still intending to get the scepter. Perhaps, he needed to plunder first and have Fergus dead.

Suddenly, an arrow projected from nowhere and impaled into Aventurine's left shoulder. Wailing horrifically, he suddenly fell on the right side and in the middle of the streets. Thus, I felt myself launch from the saddle and onto the soaking mud. I felt my head go down and slammed onto the dirt road. Everything became fuzzy and heated. And my head very heavy, like I was getting knocked out over and over. Even my vision was jumpy and distorted. I felt my head leak with warm and wet blood. I felt it drizzle down my right eye.

As soon as my head was clearing up, despite seeing double, I picked up and place on my hat. I then turned and saw Ted trying to adjust his mask and getting down from his horse. Erecting his open hand, I quickly grasped it. When I asked if he was okay, he said he was. I went to Algor and helping him get up. Luckily, he was fine. But I then checked on poor Aventurine, whom had an arrow planted in his shoulder. Blood was streaming from his wound. He kept wailing and crying out. His eyes were staring at me in panic. I kept stroking his mane to calm him down as I was trying to remove the arrow. Grabbing hold of the arrow, I attempted to pull it out. But the creature violently flayed and roared. After I jolted back, I slowly stroked him to calm his running nerves.

Another arrow flew by and nearly hit me. Luckily, I conjured a shield from the Shadowmacer within me and blocked it as it bounced off. I saw that the arrow was coming from someone who was on a rooftop. It looked like a shadowy figure clearly holding a bow in his hand. Drawing out my gun, I tried to shoot the fellow. But he evaporated and dematerialized from the scene. When more Satanists appeared in front of us, I turned to Ted as he tossed me his rifle. Based on my training with them, I reloaded and fired round to round at each of them until they plummeted and succumbed to nonexistence. I tossed the rifle back to Ted as he grasped it with his left.

"Listen, you do what you can to go and find Rollo and the asshole who did this. Don't lose that dragonfly's sight." Ted said as he summoned his scepter whilst getting down from Newman. The horse ran after Ted spanked it and dematerialized from the scene. He wore the strap of his rifle over his left shoulder. "I'll hold my ground with Algor here, so Aventurine is protected."

"Right, just be careful! And don't let Aventurine bleed out." I said. "Take care of both."

"I promise." Ted assured. "Now go!"

With that, I took off. I sprinted with one foot after another. It felt like I was soon going to fall over due to the blotchy and muddy road. The dragonfly was still going straight the road, bypassing rapidly through all the flying projectiles that were coming from all directions. Some were even coming towards me. I had to truly find Rollo, wherever he had to be.

I eyed at the rooftops and spotted several more Satanists. I dissolved into black smoke and placed myself in one of the rooftops on the left side of the place. I came over to three more Satanists. They were relatively the same as I saw in Arcadia. I jumped while simultaneously striking one Satanist at a time with my unleashed Apostle blades. Leaping from on roof to another, I would jump from one bloke to another as I was still trying to focus on the dragonfly. Even using my cantation whilst on the move to see them take off aggressively.

After they were down, I got back to chase the dragonfly that was leading us to what looked like a military outpost that was overbearing the village square. It was raised with four towers on each corner of the square. Several stretched black and bronze tents were riddled and columned in the fortress with Vikings patrolling the grounds.

But in the big tent in the middle of the fortress came out a large man, who looked to be an inch higher than Fergus. His shoulders wore a white dirty pelt with iron shoulder pads. His armor looked to have leather and cinnabar. Underneath his helmet, his face was stern with three scars that ran across his face. His bracers were overcoming his hands. His dark brown hair was flailed by the wind. I knew right away that it was Rollo at his finest. The bloody turncoat.

All his men were gathering around him, from what I saw. It seemed as if he had something to say.

"I want this forsaken place to be purged! I want every supply and prize to be pillaged! I want every home searched! Make sure that every soldier and supporter of Fergus is dead! We will soon ride for Sigr for the scepter! Don't make me speak twice! Now go!" His roar prompted the men to disperse. He then descended back into his tent.

Given the excessive number of guards, it was clear that I would have to move through the place without being seen. I studied the compound as carefully as I can, analyzing every inch and sight of the place. But things became more complicated. It was difficult for me to analyze. One sight displayed a Viking patrol carriage coming out of the fortress.

A bright and red wrinkle was opening from outside the front of the outpost. Once the carriage exited, the wrinkle gradually dissolved. The dragonfly came back to me, with half of its wings torn off. As I grabbed hold of it, I studied the broken wings and saw tiny red sparks brimming from the wounds. I placed the device inside of my satchel. I eyed back at the fortress. This could mean one thing; a portal was surrounding the place. It could be the same portal surrounding Hell. I had to admire their tactics. Rollo must have known that we were coming for him. Whoever was telling him or Virgil about our arrival did their homework.

This made things complicated. If I go in there, it's most likely that I would instantly die. Therefore, I can't afford that to happen. I can't even use one of my range weapons to take him down.

Knowing that they would disintegrate, I continued to analyze until I eventually realized that the best thing to do was to find a way to somehow lure him out. I breathed. I allowed my body to be still to let the light within me flow.

The rain hails from the dead
The drops of beads colored red
But it falls for the love of what is true
That the blood of God reigns and is within you.

The voice from the trials came into my head. It came just as it did when I achieved my Shadowmacer. It drove me to bring out my hand, facing the fortress. I made sure that they didn't spot me. It was a good thing that I was far from their space. I tapped into my Blessed Eye once again, feeling heavy and hot in the eyes. I felt my veins suppressing and letting every cell traverse from my brain to the tip of my fingers.

Gradually, I witnessed something kind of unusual but brilliant. Water like smoke, which was blood colored, was blooming inside the grounds of the outpost. Some parts began to bloom with liquified blood and gradually flooded decently. Soon, I saw the towers streaming and leaking with blood.

The fog and moist red waters were flowing down and skating across. Loud crying was gradually coming up, knowing that it was working. The outpost was becoming overwhelmed and consumed with red mist that was nearly cloaking them, including Rollo's. Soon, it was coming from across every corner of the village square. Next, red droplets gradually levitated and multiplied by the numbers and stood afloat as if rain decided to stop falling.

Exiting my Blessed Eye, I saw my target shuddering and stumbling, unaware of where the curse was coming from. As if Moses intervened. From the look of the sight of soldiers screaming and running madly, it seemed as though that it was working. And blood-colored tree-like branches summoned, scattered and rapidly foliaged the entire square.

Including the Vikings who succumbed and had their skulls caved in. Some of them vomited violently due to its pressure around their throats. Like a faucet, blood was recklessly pouring from their mouths. Almost like the eye vessels...coming to a gruesome realization. I was in a strong state of shock myself. I just summoned murky fume mixed with waters and veins in the entire environment. Maybe the Demon Legionaries would be immune, but not the Vikings. That's for sure.

"You cowards! These are not behaviors of a Viking! You will gladly die for Lucifer and will be welcomed by fire!" Rollo roared with his sword and wooden shield at the ready. He came out of his tent and exited the fortress. His men followed him. "This is obviously the power of someone blessed by gods. But...not our gods. Different ones! If you want to prove your bravery, whomever you are, whoever summoned this madness, face me! FACE ME LIKE A MAN!"

If you say so, I thought. This prompted me to quickly dematerialize from the rooftop that I was on to the road of the village square. Luckily, he was out of the fortress, knowing that I would've died if it were otherwise.

I then faced Rollo who was with his men, readily holding their swords and shields. Although I was ready to take him out, I sincerely hope that I could still fight him regardless of being a bit undertrained for someone like him. He didn't seem big and frightening as Sathanus, but he was big for me.

But if David was able to take down Goliath with only one rock, then in the great spec of things, I could do the same. If anything, I saw him as an obstacle for me to go through. Almost like a wall I couldn't climb.

The Satanist Viking burst into laughter when he saw me. He clutched his torso armor with his hands to keep himself steady from laughter. As he stopped, he said, "There is no way a boy summoned this. All of this...just to force my hand!"

"Well... I did!" I said, swallowing my nervousness. I had to be confident. "And you're not going to get away with everything you've done!" I unleashed my sword, which was suddenly absorbing the floating blood droplets until my entire blade was completely coated and crystalized. My eyes widened in amazement, but I wasn't too surprised as I was about used to the otherworldly.

Rollo scoffed and looked at his men. Cockily, he told them to disperse as they did to continue raiding. He then glanced back at me with his sunken eyes.

"I know who you are! What you are! I was warned about you! Why would a pathetic Christian like you want to help these savages led by Fergus, huh? Why would you care to help him?"

"Because you betrayed him! You were his lieutenant! You served Valhalla! But you've become a dog for Lucifer! So, I have to take you down!"

"You say that I'm a dog! But Lucifer is the greatest ruler than Fergus can never be! He has a strong idea and principle to make sure that the afterlife doesn't die out...because failures like you want to have everything neutered to your liking. And you allow these godless monarchs profess on that! So, they send out puppets like you and your band of knights to destroy every chance of making a proper afterlife with order!"

"We fight to protect the livelihood of the innocence! And if I must,

I would die for these souls to live in peace without fear." I only said that to scare him. It didn't work, of course.

"Is that so?" He asked, gaining closer to me with his blade at the ready. "Well...if you care for them as you say...you will die for them!"

"That's what I just said, genius."

With that, he charged at me with his shield to knock me down. So, I got away from his strike. But then he quickly swung his blade, almost dicing me. I tried to remember Ted's intense training; a moment when we fought each other by the foggy terrains. It was nearly the same concept. Only, it was on a different level.

I made sure I dodged his attacks before I would constantly strike with my blade. He seemed like he was taking them well as opposed to staying down. He was possibly protected by the power of the medallion he was presumably given by Lucifer.

As we fought, the blood fog on the floor was pricked and splashed everywhere because of how much we were swaying and dueling across. I swayed amid the detached red rain with branches erecting like trees. I felt the hilt of his sword deck me in the forehead, making me fall onto the blood rooted concrete. When he intended to strike me with his sword and shield placed together, I rolled and dodged his attack. I unleashed my retractable blades and punctured them into his ankle, which make him recoil with a roar of agony. I then rose back on my two feet and held my sword in place, silently asking him to strike again. He lets out a monstrous roar as he sporadically ran towards me with his sword out. I made a horizontal strike down on his blade, messing up his attack by unbalancing his stance.

He attempted to bash me with his shield, but I jumped backward to avoid it. This obviously angered him. When I was caught off guard, he finally managed to push me onto the ground. I felt my hat flee from my head and my sword dashing from my hand. My body felt nearly tickled by the flow of the fumes. But I saw how it was all slowly dissolving into oblivion beyond. My attention was rapidly focused on Rollo who suddenly had an axe in his grasp. Attempting to slam me with the axe's blade, I quickly crawled back to avoid the blade as it slammed onto the ground.

I got up on my feet and managed to snatch away his axe when he was intending to swing it down on me. I found myself with a battle-axe than a sword this time. He blocked every strike that I made with his shield. He would often bash me with it, trying his hardest to knock me down once again. But not this time. This time, I was gladly taking every hit he gave me. I quickly witnessed the floating blood crystalizing on the axe's blade. I was not sure of its purpose. But it did integrate with the blood roots to move according to my swings, giving me a better chance at delivering heavy blows on his shield. It was slowly being dissembled and brittle.

Soon, we were connected: shield against axe. He kept pushing me aggressively. I eyed at my sword whilst struggling to maintain my stance. He used his right hand to go for his dagger that was holstered on his belt. I eyed at his face, full of fury and determination. I could tell that he didn't care who he would be killing. He would do anything to become a rightful king; despite being forced by Lucifer.

But he was smart in this scenario. With his strength, he made me sway to the front of the fortress and intended to push me, knowing that the toxic force field was there. I was getting near, stumbling to where it was manifested. I felt a warm aroma nearly consuming my head. It felt as though my hair will go in flames. Out of nowhere, I didn't know what was wrong. For some reason, I felt very dizzy as if I was going to faint. Maybe because of the fight or the fact that I had been flogged several times. But no matter how weak I was feeling; I was sure that I couldn't just be killed off like this.

With all the strength I had, I released and pushed him off me. I swung the axe to push away his shield. I then eyed at my sword lying on the ground. With the little power I had inside, I triggered my Blessed Eye to pull and levitate the sword from the ground into my left hand. When I grasped it, I felt his hands clawing onto my right arm. But it wasn't long when I began to impale the Redeemer into his chest. His eyes widened and almost went vacant. His mouth had a bloody leakage.

When I removed my sword, I impaled the blade into his torso several times. Soon, he dropped violently to his knees. He was grasping for air, struggling to maintain his soul.

Wheezing like a bloodhound, with blood continuously discharging from his jaw that drenched his beard, he looked up at me with disdain in his eyes. His eyes were on the brink of going out like a broken light blob. His soul was going to be removed. I dissolved my sword.

"I may not praise Lucifer's traditions. But...he was right! You placed yourself in a war.... you don't know shite about! This war is everlastin'.... because your kings forgot who they were! I wanted to change that! I renounced my faith to the Gods...because Lucifer entrusted me...to become the rightful king of Valhalla! It's a matter of enlightenment. To be what we were made to be. And you want to take that...away!" Rollo blubbered before he coughed fiercely. He tried to grab me, but I drew out my pistol. I marked the barrel on his head.

"Why did you get yourself...into this war, huh? Because you want to feel like a hero?! I hate to break it to ya, but there's no...such thing as a hero! Or a villain! You are just like everyone else in this world and the one we had; stupid...fools who make stupid mistakes! Only for them to suddenly make amends to feel...good about themselves. The only ones...who should be considered heroes are those who...are not godless! Weak, ignorant fools who create pseudo ideals and morals for their own aids... are not heroes! They're cowards, liars that abandoned the central principles that made us who we are! Who we were! They're unaware of their actions and are fixated in their false philosophies and pathetic beliefs. We were never meant to be...unique or special! We were made to be perfect...to serve the higher good willingly! Civilization would be simple if it was destined to be that way. Even if you kill me now...you are not...a hero! So...do what you have to do...in the name of your Order! But...you are not a hero! You...are fuckin' far...from it!"

What he said made me reflect to the nightmare I had. I tried not to let his words get to me, knowing what he was saying was just for me to stand down. Ironically, he was the one kneeling before me. So, the bloke was one to talk. That was an attempt at smart talk from someone who raided for a living.

After I've undrawn my pistol, I held the red covered axe, glared down at his face. I was breathing slowly, knowing that this was what would keep me alive. After contemplating, I got to him. I held the blade of the axe to his neck. First, I removed his helmet, revealing his demented face. Long dark brown hair with a relatively big beard was what he had. He also had three scars perforated on his face. He looked at me with anger, knowing that I beat him.

"Now that you're finished with your petty monologue, where... is... the Phoenix?!"

"I'm not tellin' you...shite!" He spat out his blood.

"So, you prefer to die?"

"I might as well. I'm close to the end! It'll take me back...to when I died a hero in Normandy! But even if I told you...what would you prove by killing all of us? Absolutely nothing! One of us...will get that Holy Insignia! And we will use it...properly! Your values are done! Jesus will be done too! So...go ahead. Become what you hate...and take my head to the deserter! I rather die like Tyr! I rather die! But...you're not a hero. You realize this, right?"

Scoffing, I said, "I never said I was. I'm just serving the fucking Lord."

I held the axe like a club. I used all my strength, the minimum I had, and swung the blade that tore into his flesh and broke through his neck bone. And the axe with it dematerialized. Once I knew it, his headless body fell on the right. As for his head, it rolled a bit far from his body, leaving a blood trail. Something caught my eyes when his body fell, the medallion from his neck.

After I went to pick it up, I examined it and saw that it was the same one Virgil wore. I figured that this is what he used to gain the powers of Lucifer. But with no courtesy for it, I threw it on the ground, held my sword to slam onto it, crushing it to bits. It was a shame, though. It was a beautifully crafted necklace. It was too bad that it represented something evil.

Despite suddenly getting dazed, I turned and saw that the fortress was disintegrating. So, did the force field around it. This meant that the Satanists would be gone for now. That meant that the villagers didn't have to suffer. That meant that the war was over. Fergus won.

But then I felt very powerless in my legs. Thus, I collapsed on the ground on all fours. I began to cough violently until blood was coming from my mouth like a water faucet. My head was feeling heavy again. To top it off, I was losing consciousness. Every sight became very woozy and smeared.

The weakness invaded me. So, I founded myself collapsing and lying on the ground. The faint shielded me from all the noise that went on about. I silently prayed to be found. I didn't want to be there anymore.

Later, I found myself slowly waking up. My body felt warm, as if I was laying on something soft and welcoming. I didn't feel anything stiff or rough. There was no sound of war cries, blades connecting to one another, or flesh meeting lead bullets. All I heard was a cool breeze passing by what looked to be a rounded room made of stones. I felt something stroking across my forehead. Something moist and warm.

My vision was progressively getting clear. I recognized some of the folks inside the room. Blinking constantly, I turned and saw that it was Juliet who was wiping my head with a wet white towel. On my left, I saw Ted leaning his back with his arm crossed.

"He's alive!" He said.

"Of course, I am." I said chuckling along with Juliet. I looked up into her eyes. I asked, "Where...are we?"

"We're in the Castle of Sigr, Fergus's castle. He had us brought here...since the war is over." Juliet answered as she continued to care for my head. "They're at the funeral, mourning for the soldiers. But he told us to stay so he can properly thank us."

"Oh. Okay." I said. As I was trying to sit up, I felt something etch inside my body. It was like a sharp pain, which felt like someone tugging and tearing my neurons. Juliet placed me back to lay me down.

"Don't try to get up." She suggested. "You need to rest. We'll leave tomorrow when you are fine and ready."

"Where's Algor and Aventurine?"

"Fergus had them taken care of by the stable workers. They're okay." She said as I was relived. I sighed.

"What...happened to me? I was doing fine...and suddenly...I fainted."

"It's because you got your head hit when you fell." Ted said. "When I was coming to get you, I saw an entire square, hazed with smoke and blood like trees. And I think the migraine fractured your chakras a bit."

"Really?"

"Aye. That's why you need water, food, and rest. Specially to rest your head." Juliet said.

"Alright. How...did nursing those soldiers go?"

Letting out a sigh, she said, "Not easy as I had hoped to be honest. But at least I saved those afterlives from decaying like the rest. We thank you wholeheartedly for helping us, Kevin."

"It's no problem." I said smiling. "I wouldn't have done it without you both."

"It's no prob, Kev. And good job cutting Rollo's head off! Juliet almost passed out when I crowded her with it." Ted jested.

"I don't know. Maybe seeing severed heads shoved at my face make me nauseous, Theodore!" She snapped at him. As she eyed back at me, she asked, "Anyway, did Rollo said anything about where The Phoenix could be?"

I sighed. "No, unfortunately. The bastard was so full of himself that he preferred to die than to give me a straight answer."

"Oh. Well, hopefully...as soon as we have more of the dragonfly devices, we should know then. They won't hide forever." Juliet said in the latter of high and low spirits.

"Definitely." I said as I glanced at the window, seeing the snow falling gently. Suppose this is where the wind was coming from. I felt Juliet finally removing the towel from my head, implying that she was finally finished.

She went to the table that was on the right side of the room. The table contained several jars with unknown herbs and substances. She went to put the towel back into a silver bowl.

"This entire bowl is full of your blood. You need to be more careful, Kevin."

"What can I say, I'm an unintentional masochist." I said to her. I guess I was always one with blood. I summoned blood-like magic and often let myself bleed. When I said that to Juliet, she grinned.

"A fetish of yours?" Ted jested.

I chuckled. "Why not, mate!"

Scoffing, he said in jest, "Okay! Whatever floats your boat, creep!"

"Oh...you won't believe this!" Juliet said as if something bright came into her mind.

She picked up and displayed a candle that was obviously used. "Good news. Emily was calling through this candle."

Ted then added, "Emily called and informed us about the priestesses. They're doing well. They're not yet cured from the cinnabar, but they're beginning to light up."

"She told us that Gabriel entertained them too and fed them the honey. So, they're returning to Arcadia to their families tomorrow. They're going to be given a chakra coach to help them remove the poison. We succeeded, for what it's worth." Juliet said smiling with all teeth.

It was good to hear that they girls were okay. I mean I already figured that they were, but it was good to hear from Emily too.

I also asked, "How is Emily by the way?"

"She's doing great too. Now she feels more confident to go back to class in La Divinum Estelle. She feels valued after talking to Lady Sarah." Juliet said.

"That's awesome!" I said smiling.

All I had to do was heal and to hopefully be good enough to meet Fergus again. I hoped that our actions would convince him enough to help Arianna and Jesus.

Later, I slept for a good two hours. It was midday already and I woke up to seeing Juliet and Ted fast asleep on chairs. If only there was another couple of beds for them to rest on, but I knew that something that convenient wouldn't happen. I saw how the skies were slowly mellowing down with the snow still drizzling from above.

Suddenly, we were all alarmed by the click and soft swoosh of the door opening, revealing to be Hurik himself. He looked to be very patched up after the battle. His left arm was wrapped over his neck. Ted and Juliet adjusted themselves as they both woke up. We focused on the red-haired man.

"The King awaits you." He said to us. "I must intend to other things, but you have...my thanks, Apostles. We are...grateful."

"You're welcome." Ted said before Hurik closed the door. He came to me and asked, "Hey Sleeping Beauty."

"You're one to talk." I chuckled as he proceeded to yawn.

"Do you think you could stand? Your energy is still rusty, but you should be able to move a bit." Juliet asked me. I looked back at her. I then replied, "I could try."

Concentrated, I removed the covers and gradually turned myself to a sitting position. I slowly got up, trying to regain my balance, and made sure that I was steady and still. Juliet and Ted watched me carefully.

It was not simple trying to adjust to the pain I felt traversing my spine, but I was at least feeling myself regain stability than before.

"Excellent. You can't use your powers for now, but it should take some time to recover." Juliet said.

"Thanks," I said smiling. "Now...let's see what Fergus wants from us."

We crossed from the room to the hallway this time around. There, we finally saw the king himself standing by the hall. His white hair still messy and wearing his armor proudly. He even emboldened the scars and bruises on his face very proudly. He leaned against the wall with his arms crossed. As soon as he took notice of us, he took off and came towards us. We felt small when witnessing him.

Scoffing at the sight of me, he asked, "By Odin's disaffected eye, you look like hell. Not the bravery kind that fought in battle. The kind that looks like you got plagued by Loki's wretched breath."

"Ha. I've gotten worst." I said grinning. "Um...I wanted...we wanted actually...to thank you for your hospitality."

"Don't mention it." Fergus said smiling. "I mean you've earned it anyways. You and your friends here. If anything, I should be the one thanking you. I should've known Rollo would be given such power. Let alone practice it in the southern village."

"He was apparently." Juliet said. "But he met his fate. I'm sorry he turned on you, Your Majesty."

"It's fine, lass. As much as I respected him, Rollo just didn't quite understand what it is we are striving for. He was my most trusted and loyal lieutenant...but he was always arrogant. Arrogant than me. He allowed that arrogance to consume him, believing himself to be justly." The king laughed softly followed with a sigh. He viewed three of us with his hands on his waist.

"For a couple of knights, you sure have Tyr's blood. You fought like true Vikings. Especially you, the way you removed his head." He said, pointing his finger at me. Hands back on his waist, he suddenly said, "But...you didn't really need to do that."

"Wait...what?!" My eyes widened. "But...you sounded sure!"

"You didn't need to, though. You see, I have this tendency to require something ambiguous when I get angry or agitated. I don't know. I just do it, I suppose. You're must bear with it. It happens." Fergus admitted, which frustrated me a bit to be honest. "I appreciate it, but you didn't have to put yourself into that."

"Really...? Well...fine. So where is his head now?" I asked him, swallowing my slight annoyance.

"At the bottom of the Frost Lake, possibly eaten by the Serpent." He said. "His soul, however, will be suffering in the Abyss."

"Fair enough, I suppose. I mean at least now your people, castle, and scepter are protected." I said.

"We're...sorry about what your men went through," Ted said. "How did the funeral go?"

"Fine. I didn't want to have to drag you three into it. Not that I didn't want you to join, but...I figured that you've went through enough shite. I just thought I let you rest. I'm just glad the others remain alive with us. Oh...and sorry if the place was uncomfortable. The other rooms were occupied." He said in a surprisingly humble way. "We're preparing a feast in the Valhalla Hall for tonight to celebrate the victory and...dedicate to our fellow men. And if you aren't in any rush, I was thinking that we could invite you...as a way of saying thanks. To lift spirits up and not be burdened by loss or Lucifer's bullshit."

"That'll be...brilliant. Wouldn't hurt to feast every now and then." I said. My friends nodded in agreement.

"Great." He replied with a smile. But then he also said, "I know that you also didn't stop the war simply because. I know you came since Arianna needs goods to offer them to...Rody Bacon?"

"Roger Bacon." We all said.

"Right...yeah...that. That bloke. Whoever he is. I should see what I should gather to send to Jesus. It's not much, but I hope it's worthy enough to get them to do...whatever Jesus has him doing this time."

"He needs to offer him goods to convince the friar alchemist to work upon a device that our friend from Celestia created. It's...supposed to be advanced magic beyond potions." I said.

"Advanced magic, huh? That's bloody ambitious." Fergus said. "Whatever we can do to help the others from Hel, I suppose." Before he took off, he said, "I'll have the maidens lead you to your rooms. At least the rooms we have available. I understand you'll have to leave on your journey tomorrow."

"That'll be lovely." I said.

Soon when it was later in the night, the festival has begun, and the stone castle was soon bloomed with lights and fire. Not raging angry fire, but mighty and persistent fire that blazed from the braziers that were in every hall of the castle.

Ted, Juliet, and I saw us in a great hall. All of us dressed in appropriate festival fashion to blend with the crowd. This was what Valhalla represented, a spiritual place for the brave souls. Men and women alike. Children too. The interior of the castle's hall almost seemed like a cathedral. It was a squared room with tables of food and drinks on every corner. Pork, roast, beef, lobster and ale, everything was at store for us to grub on. The ceilings were decorated with blue and white flags that displayed the Gods of Asgard.

The Gods that blessed these fine warriors. Everyone was there as the music was about to boom; friars, warriors, maidens, even the common spirits of Sigr. For a Viking, he seemed to grasp a bit from Jesus's values. And Fergus himself was there at the end of the square. Bestowed on his own throne, he was joined alongside a woman decorated with fur shoulder pads and a white crystal dress. Blonde haired and middle-aged, I came to know that this was his wife who was Queen of Valhalla.

Before we celebrated, he rose from his throne as we did with the other party members. He spoke generously about the soldiers who passed away. And even though it was right for us to mourn, he told us that they sacrificed themselves for us to keep our souls strong and faithful. Every emphasis he made would make the Vikings shout and release howls like northern wolves of the highest ridges. Bravery, strength, and pride for their heritage. The integrity of who they were is what the Norse valued. The ones who passed had strong souls and though they met their fates with Lucifer, they didn't die in vain. Along through the speech, he gave us a recognition in which we were enthusiastically applauded for ending the war and thus gained the respect from the Valhallians, Norseman and Norsewomen.

Once he was done speaking, we all raised our mugs and glasses high in salute and globed the red substance into our throats until they were empty. At least most of ours anyway.

It was a while since we had joy. And to be honest, it was needed. This conspiracy has nearly drained us of our energy and spirits to experience what we were missing. I at least knew that this was what would be Lucifer's intention anyway.

Three young maidens of the castle handpicked Ted. Giggling and gushing over him, he looked at us and shrugged with a chuckle as Juliet and I chuckled along. We saw him being dragged into the square floor to practice a folk dance that was acting out to the bagpipes, flutes, horns, hurdy-gurdy, drums, and psalteries. Everyone took part into dancing and jumping around in the center as the king would chuckle to himself, carrying his four-month-old child in his left arm.

I saw as Juliet rose from the bench we sat on, facing the dancing crowd. Eying her blue pupils at me, she glanced at me with a smile. It was the same smile that always aroused me. She quickly eyed at the crowd, hinting that she was asking me to dance with her in the group dance.

"Uh...no!" I said chuckling. "I'm no dancer. I'm a lot of things, but not a dancer."

"You have to dance at some point, Kevin. If you can sketch, you can dance." She spoke. "Don't be such a glop!"

"I'm not being a *glop*! I'm being honest! I'm just not good at dancing with others!" I said pointing my open hand to the dancing people. But I saw that Ted was certainly having a jolly time. I looked up at Juliet as her eyes stared back at me.

"We'll dance together then. Just you and I! Come on, you *glop*," She said. I felt her hand grasping my right hand as she pulled me from the bench. I found myself dragged and stumbling across the floor. My heart was pounding. It was the first time that I danced. I have swayed, but that was when I usually fight. But I never thought I would see myself dancing. Though I had a gleam of confidence since I was dancing with Juliet. Plus, she had us a bit further from where Ted was in the crowd. But it looked like as if I had no other choice. I didn't want to upset her. And she wanted me to feel good. I had to comply. Knowing that I never got to go to prom, I'd make this chance an exception.

Juliet had me face her and look into her eyes. She had me put my right hand on her waist while my other hand locked onto hers. My left fingers held her right hand. I felt her fingers hold mine. Thus, we began to sway and danced sporadically. "Watch as I do."

I found myself learning as Juliet technically had me in her control. I followed every sway and step she had us do. I suddenly felt my energy gradually reaching before me and all I had to do was to go with it.

"What are we doing?" I asked grinning and almost out of breath.

"Living, Kevin. We're living. Don't worry about anybody. Just try to pretend...it's the two of us. In an empty ballroom. Snow is slowly falling on our heads as we waltz. Just us. No one else." She said comfortably.

I nodded and that was what I was trying to keep in mind. All I had to do was to focus on her. Her smile. Her laugh. Her joy. All of that was what I tried to implicate. It went on for a good two minutes as the music was getting louder, colorful, and upbeat. I found myself dancing as if it was from the olden days. But it was satisfying when I was with her. I ignored and forced out the burdens as I looked into her eyes.

From clapping and locking our arms to spin, we didn't even take notice to the others who were staring at us and clapping to each beat of the music. Though I was a bit distracted, I found myself constantly locked in Juliet's eyes. Her eyes were locked into mine.

When the folk music was done, we were done dancing. I had Juliet by the waist, grabbing her before she fell to the ground. We found ourselves, posing for the applauding crowd. It appeared that we unintentionally gave them a show to watch. As we composed ourselves, we hugged and faced the crowd. We bowed elegantly and both snickered. For a first-time dancer, it was quite an experience.

Those hardships I carried prevented me to do something this surprisingly joyful. Something active as well. And it was thanks to Juliet.

"Ladies and gentlemen, the lovebirds!" Ted jested, which made Juliet and I blush intensely. I wish I would deck Ted, but I knew that this is who he was. But he seemed genuinely happy for us.

Suddenly, Fergus called for the three of us. He gestured for us to come over to where he was by his throne. I was curious to know what he wanted; either to make fun of my dancing or to introduce me to his wife and child.

When Ted, Juliet and I were away from the crowd, I met up with the king and queen. The queen named Queen Eira Welles greeted me generously. The white blonde-haired woman introduced me to their baby named Garth Welles. Wrapped with a brown quilted blanket, he had little blonde hair, just like his mother. But a lot of the whiteness came from his father. He even borrowed his eyes. I adored how he looked, seeing a natural baby born in the afterlife.

"My husband and I thank you three greatly for all you have done. You have brought us a new dawn for Valhalla." She said in a charmingly soft-spoken voice.

"You're very welcome, Your Majesty." I said.

"And quite lovely dancing. Especially from you two." Fergus said pointing at Juliet and I. "You seemed to woo the crowd. Tell me...what sort of dancing was that?"

"It's a dance I learned when I was alive in Wales with me mother." Juliet said. "It's one that I know mostly. Though some parts were still rusty, but at least Kevin and I managed." I smiled at her.

"But you were great! Quit being your inner critic. Really messes with your head," Fergus jested.

He then continued, "Anyway, I would like to have a word with you, Kevin."

He faced Ted and Juliet, "I'll get to you two shortly."

"Oh yes, sir. Of course." I said.

He rose from the throne and asked me to follow him. I watched back as I saw my friends talk with the queen. I saw that he was leading me to a much quieter room, which was on the other side of the center hall.

He led me to another hall that was decorated with portraits of the Gods. Swords, axes, and shields were displayed on the walls as an act of ornaments. The chandeliers were giving off a bright mix of orange and yellow light that was shining across the hall. But my mind was focused on what would Fergus wanted me to know. The music was a lot muffled and sober once the door was closed behind us.

"I...I wanted to talk to you because you seem to be a decent soul," Fergus said as he then eyed at me. "I wanted you to forgive me for my prejudice towards you. Especially when I spoke down on your beliefs."

"No worries. I didn't feel that was the case at all," I said. "The Order

I take part of teaches us a better way of maintaining our faith but to tolerance others. And I know the Chancery and those of God...demoralized yours...and we're sorry for that. We're not like them. I'm...not at least. Ted and Juliet are pagans. I'm the only God fearer, so to speak."

"That's good to hear. But I shouldn't have doubted you nor your friends. It's been difficult to keep the peace with Christ after that...you know. It's been hard to keep unity together like we used to. Valhalla committees feared the Chancery's judgment."

He then continued, "We were accused at one point of taking part of the rebellion, given how many demon Vikings there were that day. All in the name of justifying beliefs of an impractical paradise that is impossible to exist without problems. We mean to be our best. And yet, why is it we continuously strive to be perfect souls?"

"Perhaps, it's in our nature to. But all we could do is strive for excellence. Excellence allows us to continue...while perfection holds us back. I suppose that this is what Lucifer wants, though. He wants everything to be untouched, so he can have an excuse to exercise his power. Blokes would do anything to stop others from standing their own grounds."

"Aye. Which is why I still linger on why Rollo would have us plan out this seven-day civil war because of his munity. Let alone sacrifice his loyalty to the Gods. I didn't even know he donned a satanic medallion. I could've known. Not my best introduction, I'm afraid. I pray that Hurik does not do the same."

"It's fine, honestly." I said. "I'm just glad that we got rid of him. Now, this just leaves The Phoenix and The Angel."

"Right. And hopefully we'll have a chance to get those people back from the fires of Surt. All kings and queens of all faiths down there, I hear, have apparently renounced their services to their gods...to serve that pseudo revolutionary would-be lunatic! I mean...Hell has always been an empire, to be honest. But not under some fallen angel." He said.

He continued, "The one thing we don't tolerate is extremism. Well, I mean...we're barbaric, violent, pillaging scoundrels...no doubt...but even we don't bestow harm onto others who don't live like us. We are proudful men encouraged by our ancestors and the Gods, but we know how to be humble to others. Most of us anyway. So...I pray that you don't have yours taken highly to where it becomes immoral. Your beliefs are good in their own way. Maybe not the Catholics, but one of Christ himself. Just like this Order you take part of. They offer hope of the age of guardian angels truly reviving. Just as the age of Vikings thriving here in the afterlife. So, never renounce that goodness you have in favor of man...who's only intention...is to cater to their own zealotry."

"Of course." I said. "And that's something to tell your son. Obviously."

"Of course. Especially when the lad is old enough to become heir...in case I...well we would know. I want him to be a child first. Just as I must look after my kingdom, now more than ever. We've longed for a kingdom in which we could rule and serve the Gods according to our will. And I will be damned to have true heathens take that away from us. Thus, I want nothing but the damned best for Garth. Knowing what the afterlife has become. Still, I hope we could reunite the Covenant, make trade again, come together and...end Lucifer's horseshit crusade. Like the old days when they were bastards like 'im. If those stingy bastard Chancellors at Celestia allow us, that is...instead of intending to rule us. Hell, we thought about pillaging 'em at some point."

I nodded with a chuckle. He then looked at a portrait of him standing with his wife. It looked painstakingly beautiful, almost as if someone placed that effort into making it. Every stroke I noticed matched their features and highlighted their stances. Damn near perfect.

"So...you and Higgins, is it true that you are...lovebirds?"

Widened eyes in shock, I said, "What...no! We were just dancing and I...happened to be entranced. That's all."

"Hm." He said. "Your Polish friend seems to think otherwise."

"Oh, don't listen to him. He's just...being his delusional and random self. He's always been a jester." I spoke.

As he eyed at me, he said, "I have heard many truths from you today, Mr. Princeton. But that one...is a lie."

"How can you even tell?"

"I saw you blush from afar."

"What, you got the longest reach of vision in the world?"

"Kevin, I've been there before." Fergus said. "Almost the same scenario as tonight. Eira was a nurse when I first meant her during my first battle with the raiding Anglo-Saxon bastards called the Valentine Order from the land of Burgundy. Time to time, I would lay my eyes at her. Tell her who I was. Hell, even my true nature. She loved me for my raw honesty. I expressed myself...in a ballroom like this and I would be myself. This was something she loved. Often, men would become shallow and lie to themselves just to woo a woman. Some women do fancy being lied too, apparently. Unintentionally too. But not Eira."

"Wow." That was surprisingly true, coming from a Viking out of all people. "I didn't take you for quite a romantic, given what you are."

"Yeah...well, even Valhallians, as savage and righteous as we could be...can have some form of decency. Thing is you must embrace the fact that you have true feelings for her. And...you never know, lad! She may fancy you too and you don't even know it." He grinned at me. "If you don't tell me the truth, I'll execute you in the morning. I swear to the Gods. I'll chop off *your* head and sacrifice you to Odin. Swear on it."

We both chuckled. I then spoke with honesty, "Alright. I admit it. I do have feelings for her. Quite a lot. I just...I don't know. With everything that's been happening, I don't know how I can properly declare that to her. I don't want to seem like the typical anti-social teenager. And...I'm not that ...y'know.... romantic. I had...a pretty bad experience."

After he puzzled a bit, he said, "Romance...that's the last thing you want for your horizon. How about you ask her out on whatever astrals call it. It's like a gathering with only you and your partner."

"A date, you mean?"

"No...not the fruit."

"No. That's really what we call it. It's a date."

"They named a courtship after a fruit and calendar day? Well, astrals are certainly interesting spirits."

"Blame the synonyms, mate. Not me."

"Well, whatever. Why don't you ask her...*that*...and plan a perfect time to have it? Find her a perfect place for you to lay and adrift.

Somewhere where you could be your true honest selves without any worry of the world around you." He suggested.

"Right. I mean I have asked her before, but...I don't know. She did say that she'll consider it, but I'm not quite sure. That could mean anything. Maybe she'll change her mind, especially for what's been happening."

"Bollocks! If the lass said that she'd consider, that means she's up for it. Ask her again about this... date. And...be honest with her. Women love that. Most of them anyway. But she seems...very special. I never seen someone from Valestone this lovely yet...so iron-willed. You should've seen the way she was nursing my men when I came back from the battlefield. Sparling from left and right, tending the absolute shite out of them, she was. I was quite impressed with what she did. She reminds me of Lagertha, the shieldmaiden."

"Aye. She's the first in our Order. And she was a priestess once." I spoke.

"That makes sense. That sense of virginal prudence and iron-willed stance is what I saw in Eira as well. Though she was not a fighter such as I, she can certainly win with her mouth. Not that she wants to dis-integrate our virility, but to show something as strong as a sword. The most beautiful women...are those with the strongest hearts. It's beyond love itself, for the camaraderie of it thrive much further than the allure. And mind you, they're very rare these days. That is what I get with Eira. Back then and now. Friendship. So...this is your opportunity to cherish her; amicably and soulfully. Not in lust or fantasy. Don't ever let that pass nor desecrate."

"I'll heed that. Thanks, Your Majesty." He nodded.

Later that same night after I spoke to Fergus, I got myself to explore more of his castle. I realized that the festival was over, which lasted until the middle of midnight. As I explored every corridor, that was decorated with runes, symbols, and curves on the walls, I couldn't help but to think about what Fergus advised me. Like I said before, I truly did have feelings for Juliet. I just felt burdened by the Satanists and my earthly past. Two things that I try to rid from the world.

I strolled across every hall and saw that the people of the castle were already asleep. Some were still drifting themselves in the halls. Half of them were drunk from the wine and ale. Half were lounging and on the brink of making tender erotic love. Each of them was engaged in something. Reading, drawing, humming. I wasn't sure where Ted was. I would presume that he was still entertaining the maidens of the castle.

I suddenly felt a tap in the left shoulder. When I turned, as if it were a funny joke from God, Juliet showed up. She giggled adorably as I did. She looked very radiant in her grey vest and rolled up sleeves. Just as she did when we danced for the first time.

"How did your conversation with the king go?"

"Great. He was just...thanking us for what we accomplished." I said. "Where's Ted?"

"He's asleep in one of the rooms after we discussed with the queen." Juliet said. "You could say that wooing those maidens drained his energy more than his magic. Either that...or shit-faced by the ale."

"Right." After we both chuckled, I said, "So...where are you off to, exactly?"

"I got bored of staying in the room. So, I'm just...exploring to keep my mind moving." She said. "The level of care that was put into this castle is outstanding."

"Every castle is in this world." I admitted. I was thinking that this was a perfect time to ask her.

Do it! This is your chance! Don't blow it! Even the voices in my head (the good ones) were pressuring me to go for it. As annoying as they were. It seemed like the right time. There was no one relevant except she and I.

"We got two more, The Phoenix and The Angel. And finally, we will get to Hell and save those people." Juliet said. "We couldn't have done it without you, Kevin. I knew you were fit to be an angel. I...reckon you will return to your family when all this madness is done at some point." She smiled.

"Maybe...I'm still thinking about it. But...I'd like you and Ted to meet them soon. It'd be nice if you did, perhaps to have supper with them," I replied.

"I'd very much love to meet them. And thank them for raising such a man. You were great today, by the way. At the festival, I mean."

"Thanks to you. But you were better obviously."

"Oh please, you were getting way ahead of me. Surprisingly too. You're learning faster. Even than me. Fair to say the afterlife has done us some ounce of good. But...thank you." She said after she gurgled.

She then said, "I'll...uh...I'll see you soon, okay?"

"O...Okay. Sure." I stuttered like a bloody moron.

I watched as she was taking off with her hands behind her back. The voices continued to pressure me, telling me that I will miss my opportunity.

As I gulped slightly, I finally said to her, "Hey.... Juliet."

As she turned and stopped, she asked, "Yes, Kevin? What is it?"

"I was thinking.... remember when I asked you about hanging out together? You and me? I...was wondering if you would still consider it. Perhaps to...go...on a date?" After I asked, my heart sank low. I was unsure of what her response would be. I hope that I wasn't asking for too much.

But she slightly blushed. After it disappeared, she asked, "A date?"

"A...Aye." I said that, expecting her to turn me down. I know that I was setting my expectations high.

After she puzzled for a few seconds, she said with brightened eyes, "Yes, I remember. I'd said that I would give you an answer. Um...well.... sure. That would be...great. Do you happen to know when?"

"I'm not sure yet. But...it's just something for you to...consider. If that is alright with you, of course."

"Oh yes, no...definitely." She said almost nervously. She contemplated with her hands behind her back. "It's just...It's really funny. A bit convenient."

"What do you mean...convenient?"

"Queen Eira talked about it as well. When she saw...you and me dance." She said as she blushed. She slightly looked away from me. "I want to know something, Kevin. Do you really have feelings...for me? You can be honest."

"I'm not sure how you want me to say it."

"I just want to know."

After a sigh of defeat, I said, "I...I do, to be.... honest. I don't know how else to say it. There's just...something in you that I...can't help but cherish." I said. "What made you ask that?"

"I...I'm...just afraid, Kevin. I'm afraid of being used for nothing more than to be...disposable. Not that you would, but...it's something lingering in my mind." She said facing me.

"Of course not. I wouldn't bloody dare do that to you. Never."

After she slightly chuckled, she composed herself, "Forgive me. I don't think I told anyone this...but there is an in-depth reason why I dislike Lustina. Let alone working with her."

"Really?"

"I don't know how to tell you this, Kevin. But...I was...dating back to the days when I first became a nurse at sixteen. To a nobleman of the House of God and occasional bounty hunter. The son of one of the Chancery's Garett Pearson." She said. "His name was Evan. He was the man you saw I was talking to at the Gathering that night. I first met him when I was nursing him back to health...after he was riddled with lacerations fighting with manticores. He was kind, funny, smart, and...honest. He was charming too. Something out of a tale. At times, he'd pick me as his personal servant. And I was very blessed."

"Evan, huh?"

"Yes. When I expressed my feelings for him, he began to fancy me, and we began to go out for days. He seemed as if he genuinely did care for me as I did for him. But..."

"What happened?"

"I found out that he was cheating on me...with Lustina. I never realized until I caught him with her in his chambers one evening at the Homestead. I didn't know why...until he told me that I...I wasn't good enough for him. He complained about how prudent I was. There was a time he...he tried to pressure me. And he got fed up with me. And...it made sense when I saw him with her." She said almost tearfully. "She had the audacity to tell him more about my human life...and he was disgusted. Remember when I told you that...I was poor?"

"He didn't love you back...because of that? Bastard! The type of bloke who thinks he could do what he pleases because his dad is a Chancellor. Typical!"

"I know. Because I came from a poor life, because of my beliefs, that's why he broke up with me. He was disgusted by those who came from poverty. Let alone who are not of Catholics. He did Lustina in to satisfy himself .... since he'd feel shame for being with someone who once was poor and who's a pagan. It made sense then...I was his servant to make him feel good. Yet, he had no regard for what I wanted. There was no partnership. I was just an advantage. My whole life, my mother and I were nothing but advantages to them. My father. Those pastors. The nuns. The Chancery. Then Evan."

"Right," I said. "I'm...very sorry, Juliet."

"I've been paranoid about dating ever since. To be in a relationship. I realized that I was trying to find proper love, but...it showed that I was just too desperate. Longing to be loved truthfully since I don't love myself for being worthless, hopeless, or cowardly. I just waited for that opportunity to come to chance...since most of the men I knew only took advantage of me." She expressed. "I hope you didn't take my questions wrongfully before."

"No...of course not." I said. "I understand. I'm...sorry you had to go through that."

"It's fine. But thank you for understanding." She then said something else that stunned me. She spoke nervously, "I...I...don't how to say this, Kevin. But...I...I...actually...have feelings for you too."

I then responded dumbfoundedly, "Y...ahem...um...You do?"

"Yes. I didn't tell you because...I just didn't know the moment. I was too scared of what you would think of me. I'm a...very anxious person. I can't help it. Is it weird or...immoral to feel this way?"

"No...of course not. I...I mean I guess we both weren't sure how to approach it. Huh? Love is questionable in action than it is in words."

"Aye. I think I'm just afraid of being neglected again. I was afraid of not being good enough for anyone. That's why I hid it. But...you're different, Kevin. You see good in me, past standings. Most of all...you're very understanding. You listen. You don't condemn. You see me as more and treat me as if...as if I could be free from hell. You're probably one of the most understanding people I've met." I never knew that I did that for her. Nonetheless, it warmed my heart.

"The feeling's mutual, love," I expressed as my chest felt warm. After I hesitated, I held onto her hands. But I then continued, "I don't give a damn if you were rich or poor. I don't care whatever label you put, Juliet. Your kindness is what makes you special. You're honest, beautiful, funny, faithful, and strong. More than I could say about myself. You may not know it. But I'm sure Lustina wishes to be like you. And other women I've met who are shallow. They're just not as humble as you. That's the truth."

She smiled and glanced down. Her eyes were brightened, and her face blushed intensely. Afterwards, she eyed at me, "Kevin, that is one of the sweetest things that I've heard in a long time. But...I'm not sure if I can feel the same way about myself. You're just saying things I'd like to hear. I mean I'm not as perfect as people would expect of me. I can't even live up to Anu's goodness. I can't live up to a higher conscious if anything."

"You don't have to be perfect. That's shouldn't mean that you should be ashamed. It...makes you beautiful. The way I got you to sing again, you're getting me to...love again. I want to make things right in this life, Juliet. This includes cherishing women...like you. Unlike that bellend Evan. No offense." I said as I felt myself blush and getting warmer. Heat was traversing all over my body. "But I mean this. Truly. May God strike me if I'm bloody not. And if you do not wish for this to work out, I...I will understand."

As she was getting close to me, her face nearing mine, I felt her hand tenderly grabbing mine. Her fingers curling mine.

She looked towards me gently as she smiled, "You should show me then. You should think of something."

Her left hand was placed on my face. "Something in that head of yours."

Smiling towards her, I said, "Well...you're awfully close, aren't you?"

Chuckling, she said, "Why wouldn't I be? I needed to see the light."

"Of course. Do I...do I have your consent?"

"I taught you how to become an Apostle. Taught you how to fight. Taught you how to dance." She smiled. "Unless you want me...to teach you this too, Kevin Princeton."

"Sure...Juliet Higgins." I smiled and gazed deep into her blue eyes.

With that, both of our lips were finally connected. I tasted every bit of her inside as we began to embrace each other. When I closed my eyes, all I saw was darkness. But I felt her hands on my arms as I felt my hands on her waist. It was lasting for three seconds, but I couldn't get enough of her.

As we were done, we gazed into each other's eyes. I was entranced to her smile and the sensation she had on her face after we connected. I then said to her as I continued to hold her by her waist, "So...this is it, then."

"Yes." She smiled elegantly whilst slightly biting her lip. "How do you feel?"

"Uh...Pretty good actually!" I exclaimed in a whisper. I giggled a bit. "A...And yourself?"

I watched as her right hand came from my left arm and to my chest. "I feel...like this could be a second chance. To make this right. After we find those Watchers, get the mystics back from the Inferno, I think...we need to explore the horizons...between us. I think there is potential."

"Of course. Should...Ted know about us? Or anyone?"

"If *he* does, who cares? He enforced it somehow...like those soppy bachelorette parties," She joked. "Though he means well. For the rest, I don't care."

I chuckled along to it. As I released her from my grasp, she continued to look away for a bit. She then gazed back into my eyes and said,

"But...I've always felt that way. Perhaps it was a calling from Anu. Either way, I'm...happy it happened. So...I'll see you in the morning, Kevin. We set sail for Celestia."

"Of course. Have a nice night, Juliet. And...thank you."

"Thank you very much too, Kevin. I'll see you." She smiled as she was descending into the halls.

I sat down on the nearest bench in the hallway, pondering at what has happened. I was finally intimate with Juliet, the Apostle whom I had feelings for. And I pondered on how she even had feelings for me. I was astonished to where I chuckled to myself. Before I could go back to my slumber, I continued to ponder at it. Maybe there was a chance for me to make the relationship as good as it could be.

I hoped I did.

XXXII

Amends to be Made

Once we were all packed and ready to depart from Sigr, the Apostles and I were finally boarded on a Viking long ship back to Celestia. The morning was sky high and surprisingly brighter than the past few days. Unlike the ships I saw before, the ones with multiple sails, this ship I was on had one sail. A wooden decorated serpent was used as the figurehead for the vessel.

The sail was red with the face of a bearded man with a horned helmet. Each side had thirteen shields that were on the edges of the ship. There were thirteen rowers with large brown oars already drenched into the surface of the water. All crewmen were rapidly preparing to set sail. Beyond the sea we were to traverse were glaciers peaking from the sea's surface.

One of the crewmen told us that they had food, drinks, and enough supplies for us to survive since it was said to take a while to get back to Celestia. And plus, Aventurine was injured and tired. Speaking of which, Aventurine and Algor were both in the middle of the ship, confined in cages for their safety. They were brightened when they saw me again. Algor's tongue was drooling with his sliming saliva when he saw me.

As I crouched down, I told him, "Don't worry lad. It's only

temporarily once we reach back." I lifted myself from the ground as I finally met up with Fergus. He got down from the docks to the ship's surface.

In his big hands was a chalice, gleaming with diamonds and other dyed gems. He looked towards me with a grin that he was known for. Two other men brought in a large wooden trunk of what was most likely gold and other trinkets.

"This was my great grandfather's. It was said he never drank from this. I wasn't sure why. It's by the Gods. It was pure to drink from, apparently. But I think it's false." Fergus said. "So...I hope this would be good enough for that alchemist bloke to...do what he was assigned to do. Just don't convince him to drink from it."

I held the cup in my gloved hands. I looked back at Ted and Juliet who looked casually interested into it. Looking back at the Viking lord, I told him, "Thank you for this. I'm sure that he will take this very kindly."

"I'm glad you approve." He smiled. He looked at the three of us. "The chest is...my thanks to Jesus. And half of what inside...is yours. I shall tell my boy about you. I'll make sure of that."

"That'll be great, sir. It's an honor." Juliet said. "Thank you very much."

"I'm glad to hear it. And if you need aid, don't hesitate to stay connected. You have the accessibilities to our kingdom. May the Gods be with you three."

"Also, with you, Your Majesty." After we bowed, I watched as Juliet and Ted took off. Perhaps they were to lounge somewhere. Ted turned back and waved at three of the maidens whom he danced with yesterday. They giggled and waved back after he winked.

Before he departed, he then said to me in particular, "And make sure you tell me about you and...Higgins there."

"She said yes."

"My boy! Excellent. But always remember, the bond thrives further in amity, not desire!" Fergus said with a wink. He continued humbly and diplomatically, "Well...take care, Mr. Princeton."

"You as well, King Fergus."

And with that, we were gradually beginning to departure from the city docks. As soon as one crewman began to beat onto the drums, each punch on the drum's surface inspired the sailors to move the oars. We were waved back by the king and his wife.

My short experience in Valhalla was interesting. At that moment, I could say that Jesus was far from lying. The Promised Land was *completely* diverse. Culturally.

And it astounded me of how much Lucifer, and other spiritual beings like him, would want to take away that kind of establishment. Only to suit his needs. I guess all the worldly gods did unite to create a different world for us to roam. To truly feel united. Whether that was accepted or not.

Ten days later after sailing across the long river in between the mountains, we arrived back to the docks of Celestia. For a good while, it was finally good to be back. Especially after a long while since we formulated this plan.

The Apostles and I arrived at the Main Chapel, which one of the angel guards told us where they were residing. After giving us bags of rolics that were inside the chest, they were bringing the entire chest inside the castle. I inhaled the same strong aroma of candlelight that was casting mist across the decorated ceiling. They led us to the same conference room where we planned everything from the beginning of our journey. It looked much different in daylight. That was for sure.

Upon going in, everyone was there. It appeared that they were told about our arrival. Jesus, Mary, Francis, Michael, Bertha and Dante all were there. I guess Gabriel had already left along with the priestesses. All of them were sat around the long table. All of them turned their faces when they saw us come in.

Jesus rose from his seat and walked towards us. A smile ran on his face. It was his trademark smile. As he stopped right in front of us, the three of us kneeled quickly, politely saluting the humble monarch.

"It is done." Juliet said. "We've vanquished The Fairy in Valhalla. Rollo of Normandy. And Fergus thanked you with a chest of goods and materials."

"Very good, my fellow Apostles." Jesus complimented. "He didn't need to. But I'm very happy he was convinced. I'm very touched."

"We're very impressed that you went and stopped a civil war in your own volition." Michael said.

I then handed Jesus the chalice that Fergus gave to us. "This is what he had to offer to Mr. Bacon."

Jesus carefully analyzed and studied the item. But his eyes were lightened up with pleasure. The other representatives, including Francis, took interest. It was as if it they haven't seen anything from Valhalla. It could be possibly due to Fergus's strong independence.

"I hope this should do." I stated.

"No, this is excellent." Francis said as Jesus passed him the chalice. "This would do greatly. This should get him to progress it for sure." He then looked at us with a grin. "You three have done well."

We smiled back at him and thanked him greatly. Ted then asked, "So now what?"

"Now all I have to do is get to Mr. Bacon and offer him this and the other offerings." Francis stated. "And I would have to go to meet Mr. Douglas to ask him for more of the dragonfly diagrams. You three deserve a rest after everything. We'll take it from here. Trust us."

"Good work, you three. You're doing the afterlife justice yet again." Bertha said with a grin.

She then grinned at me and said, "Thank you for trusting in our forces, Kevin. And...in me. I hope this bond continues."

I nodded with a smirk.

"You are dismissed. And welcome back." Mary said. We bowed and were beginning to be escorted out by the guards.

But suddenly, Dante called for us, "Apostles."

"Yes, Chancellor Dante." We asked. We were wondering what he had to say.

"On behalf of the Chancery, we...are...graceful for what you have accomplished." Dante said in a surprisingly humble matter. Of course, he still had a stern tone.

"Thank you, Dante. We're...sorry about Virgil. I know he was very dear to you." I said.

"I appreciate it. And...indeed he was...at one time. But apart from his charisma, Virgil was a fool. Ever since he came here, he was always one to devoid from mortality and order. To live recklessly and dissolve to debauchery. Like any other libertine." He said. "I want to make this clear. We do not condemn freedom. Only when it does not coexist with wisdom. So do not make the same mistake. Now leave."

After we nodded, we took off.

Outside of the castle, Juliet then said to us, "I'm thinking of going to Goliath's Bay to help the herbalists. You two don't have to come."

"Why?" Ted asked.

"I...I think I know of an ingredient that could help build the toxin to get us to Hell. It just came to me." She spilled. "So, there's a chance that I won't be seeing any of you for weeks."

"What ingredient?" I asked her. She grabbed my hand and made me look into her eyes before releasing me.

"Remember when you first met me, and your body was intoxicated with something?"

When she said that, I suddenly dissolved the fog that was concealing my memories from six months ago. "Of course. The miracle pomme!"

"Exactly. I know it's a long shot, but I think we could be sure that the same case wouldn't occur for us. There should be some riddled on one of the islands of Ghai. So, I'm going to ask for a ship there."

"You sure you don't want us to come?" Ted asked. "In case if you...I don't know...come across more of the Satanists?"

"You two have done enough. This is something I must do alone. Plus, I know there some things you have yet to complete, Theodore."

"I do actually have to make some paintings." He said as if something in his head reminded him. "You know, just to help Frask. Just to also wait for those dragonflies to be built."

"Of course. But we should meet again soon. I promise." She said. Before she could go back to the castle, she and I shared a quick hug.

"I hope you'll be okay." I said after I loosened her from my embrace.

"I will. And don't worry about feeling alone. You should find something to do in the Khalservan." Juliet said as she then stared at her pocket watch.

She then gave a hug to Ted, which was rare to me. But it was still very sweet to see. After letting him go, she said, "I got to go before Jesus descends. I'll see you both."

"Okay...well...we'll see ya. Take care of yourself." Ted said. I watched Juliet stroll up the stairs and opening the doors to go back into the castle. It was just Ted and I for now.

"Not lovebirds, huh?" Ted had his right arm over my shoulder when he cockily said that. I shrugged it off me.

"Bugger off, mate!" I jested.

"I mean what can I say, you're the one who forced us to be together like some kind of fan boy."

"Either way, blame destiny." He said with a grin. He suddenly became neutral and told me, "I wish I had that true connection with Eliza. Would've been loving and true as yours with Juliet."

"You were too good for someone like her. And you still are," I said, my hand on his right shoulder. "I know you'll find someone too. You did inspire me. You inspired us both. I'm glad to be you friend."

"Thanks, man," He said with a humble smile. He then continued after pondering, "Listen, I might be back at my cabin for a few days to work on helping Frask. And maybe, he could repair the dragonfly device. You're free to join so that you wouldn't have to be bored."

"That's because you're often in and out, isn't it?" I jested.

As both of us began to walk from the courtyard, I then said,

"But...it's fine. I should find something to do. Maybe I'll think of what job to find."

"Sure, that'll be good. Not much stakes as of now anyway. Whatever you think its best, crumpets."

"Quit calling me that, mate" I said as I playfully pushed him. He pushed me back and we both chuckled.

"Theodore!" I said mockingly.

"Fuck off!" Ted replied with a scoff as we chuckled.

I never thought that it would feel good to go back to the Khalservan to rest. I got up back to my chambers. Nothing has really changed except the weather. It was much brighter than usual. It was good to see the sun gleaming in the sky once again and not cloaked behind the clouds all the time.

Upon going back into my room, I spotted a note that was apparently from Bella. Out of all people, it was surprising to see something from Bella, the young priestess whom we saved from the likes of Sathanus and Lucifer. The priestess who was finally happy and with her sisters back in Arcadia.

As I unveiled the paper from the envelope, I unfolded the note and began to study it. It was short, but very thoughtful and heartfelt.

Greetings Mr. Princeton,

I wanted to thank you greatly for everything that you have done for my fellow priestesses and I. We are in your debt and are very grateful for the comfort you gave us. Forgive me for writing this in a short period of time. But I wanted to find a way to thank you for making us feel strong again. We're going to get help from a chakra specialist. And we wouldn't have gotten through these dark days without you. I wish you and your friends the best. May Selene's grace bestow on you and your endeavors.

All the best,
Bella Summer of Arcadia

I just smiled to myself after reading what she wrote. Just by reading this, it made me feel as if I was doing some for once. I felt like I was doing something right. And mostly, I was just glad to know that they were okay and well. Especially Bella.

Soon after I read the letter, I plummeted onto the bed. I knew that I've technically rested during the hunt for The Unicorn and The Fairy. But we were always on the move. But knowing that we were halfway to getting the two other Watchers and finally Hell; I felt like it warranted a break. So, did everyone else who helped.

And I knew it would take a while, knowing that it would probably take a few weeks for the alchemist friar Bacon to develop upon Frask's project. And I knew that I had to wait until we discover where The Phoenix was. Juliet is traveling to Ghai while Ted is working on his paintings. And thus, I was left with nothing else to do. Nothing to do but pray to God that it would all be over since things were beginning to look up.

For the remaining days, I continued to train once again. I wanted to make sure that my powers were gradually getting advanced. And to stop myself from suffering from that random blackout, after unleashing my third power, I had to work upon it.

I took most of my time in the training room. It was the same circular room where I learned how to wield the Redeemer. The same training tower where it all happened.

To be a capable Apostle, to kill the two remaining Watchers, I had to make sure that I was prepared. Never in the life I once had has made me that eager to do the right thing.

I may have done terrible deeds, but I never lost my consciousness. I still had the Hospitaller in me. I was still a Princeton.

Four wool dummies were perfectly place in front of me. So, I would flip, jump, and acrobatically punch and kick in hopes to pass down pain on anyone who stood in my way. And I saw how much I was improving on my pirouettes.

Later, in the evening, Algor and I would also often visit the stables of the castle, mostly to check on Aventurine. I saw that his pelt was still fresh and that his wound was regularly getting better and better. The wound was wide and direct before. But now, it was concealing itself. This meant that if I were to go somewhere, I would have to ride on a regular horse. For Aventurine's safety, I could never bring myself to drag him into more danger. He was a rare creature in the afterlife, so I had to do what I could to make sure he was far from harm's way.

But when I was going on about my days in the Khalservan, a thought kept rushing through my head. And something was quite off with the Apostle Order. And perhaps Francis made it that way for a purpose. I wasn't sure what, but I'm sure that it was a noble choice. It lingered in my head to realize that plotting these assassinations was somewhat like a job. Only we weren't paid for it. It seemed more voluntary than an actual high paying job.

After one week, I soon brought it to myself to go and find Francis, which meant that I had to explore more of the castle. This time around, I managed to explore the much higher floors of the towers. And suddenly, I happened to stumble across a room that had yet to be discovered.

It looked comfortable. A fireplace was displayed on the left wall with two chairs in front of it. Behind the desk was a large window. And beside the desk were two bookshelves. The room was a little dense with the light of the sun decently shining through. The person on the desk was Francis. I realized quickly that this might be his office. He looked to be writing on something with a white puffy quill.

When he took notice of me, his head rose, and he said casually, "Ah Kevin, you've discovered my office. You wish to see me?"

After I reevaluated some things in my head, I said, "Sure."

"Why don't you come in?" He smiled as I stepped into his office.

On the left side of his room looked to be an average sized golden-framed flashy portrait. It was a representation of him in a classical-styled painting. With him were two women. The woman on the right looked to be slightly darkened, almost like who he told me about. She looked justly and beautiful. In the middle was a very young girl in a pink floral dress. The young one had to be his daughter Johanna. And the woman was his wife Catori.

"That was my...family." He told me, which I called. His chin was placed on his hands while elbows were planted on his desk. "Catori and Johanna. I miss them both. At least I have Johanna with me. But...I know that Catori is watching over me from the Void. She's with God. So, this painting is what I must remember her by. Seeing Johanna that young...brings tears. I only wish that...life wasn't too quick to take away her light."

Turning back to the painting, I said, "It's beautiful. But I guarantee she still has that light."

"Thank you, Kevin." He almost pondered their names. "I just came back from...seeing Roger Bacon, by the way. He and his students were residing at the White Dunes Desert in the Fields of Suns. I have good news."

"He agreed. Was he satisfied?"

"He was. And it was quite a relief if I'm honest." Francis said. "It's been very long since I was his pupil. And I know his intention was to stray away from civilization. But as soon as I told him, he was satisfied. He felt as though this would give him some spec of purpose. I have to give my deepest thanks to Mr. Douglas."

"Aye, he has a strong caliber for arts. I wish...I could excel in my passions like he does." I admitted. "I felt like I derived from that lately. A long while actually."

"You can find many opportunities here in the afterlife." Francis said.

"That's actually what I wanted to talk to you about. I had a question."

"Well, have a seat." Francis gestured his hand to the two chairs. I didn't hesitate to sit down. When I took a seat, I looked straight at him in the eyes. He then said, "What do you have in mind?"

"I wanted to know something. And I know it may be obvious to you. But the question is...do we get paid for every task we do by any chance?

Whether it's assassinating or things around that area? I remember that knights usually get paid back in the days by their leaders. Earthly ones I mean."

"Unfortunately, not these knights. Apostles do not get paid." Francis said. I figured. "Because the Order was brought up through the House of God, everything is paid off, including clothes, shelter, weapons, and so on. It is already funded by the Bridget Bank, which has funds used to help the weary and to hopefully build shelters and potential schools for guardian angels, when the monarchy wants it. I have some other ideas I mean to disclose soon enough. And because you are an Apostle, you can easily have access to places of royalty. And I know your family came from a wealthy household."

"Yes, I did. And they intend to send me and Kelley to Grand Arts Academy. They...just need to settle with more money."

"Right. I've heard of the place. There isn't anything wrong with money. Often, Apostles *would* be paid by those we aid. Usually a decent sum, especially by monarchs. But not always. And it is not our sole intent." He had a valid point there. "We are not mercenaries. And those warriors have a bad reputation, cursing the afterlife's standards with money as a sole motivation. And it's no better with the Satanists. Though, I knew of the order called The Masquerade Society; they were one of the knights for hire who practiced transfiguration. One I could think of. But not Apostles. Therefore, Ted and Juliet both have jobs on the side. Being an Apostle is more...voluntary. But I think you understand that by now, given what we do."

"Obviously." I said in agreement. "I guess I've been volunteering as an Apostle for a good while that I haven't had the faintest thought of getting a job."

There was a brief silence as Francis suddenly thought of something after he was puzzling to himself, "I've got an idea." He stood up from his chair and walked around to face me. I leaned a bit forward in curiosity.

"While I was talking with Jesus, he has told me of an opportunity for someone to be a...private bodyguard for Lady Sarah." He said. "He's been very concern for her safety. After all that's been happening, including the fact that she was nearly kidnapped and sold to Lucifer. Keep in mind, Sarah does fancy going out a lot."

"I wouldn't blame him. The Satanists can be summoned at any point in time. And any one of these so-called heavenly spirits could bear the pendants." I said. "So...whom did she ask for?"

"Well, perhaps it was just a mere coincidence or destiny. But she spoke very highly of you, Kevin. Especially how you rescued her. She preferred you, especially knowing that she knows Ted and Juliet had other duties." Francis said. "Jesus promises hundred bennies for every time she is properly protected. There were other nobles who were willing, mostly hired by the Chancery, but she turned them down since they were only in for the money and other...favors. It'll give you time to wait for the dragonflies to be built. So, do you accept the offer?"

"Why bloody not? It'll be good to see the Lady once again." I said. "And at least I'll have enough to feed myself, my family and Algor."

"That's excellent. I'll be sure to tell Jesus. Do you want to start tomorrow?"

"Of course. I'll be glad to. Thank you, Francis."

"You're very welcome, Kevin."

I then rose from my chair. "By the way, what were you writing there?"

"Oh...this?" He said gazing briefly at the notebook. "I'm just writing something I haven't written for a while before I go and send these letters of treaty to the kingdoms of the Covenant. I had ideas, so I must write it down before I must travel again tomorrow and return in a few weeks. It's...it's a memoir."

"Ha. Really? You can write creatively?"

"Yes, as a matter of fact. Wouldn't you believe that this is the first time in fifty years since I've written? Unbelievable, I know. I'm getting back into it. To get the adrenaline back. I have yet to give it a title too."

"So...what is it about exactly? During your youth of the past?"

"It's indeed about my past. About how I met Jesus after I left my home realm of Bordham, after it fell into ruin. And how I created this Order." He spoke. "I remember I was just a young man when I met him. He was humble and kind, just as he is now. He's always been like that. He always vouched for me. That is what I admired. Someone who can maintain his kindness in a conflicted civilization that prefers to be discriminative and cruel."

"Especially when he was crucified." I added. "I wish I knew how he did it. You know, not letting the world's bleakness get to him."

"Truth be told, I can't speak for him. All I know...is that even though he is a man, he was blessed. When the world turned on him, he had God to turn to. He trusted the stars than he did for man. He preached about the stars and what held them together. He was just a carpenter. But this carpenter became one of the most influential spiritual leaders of all time. He knew he was not a perfect man, but he chose to save those who were far from saving. When humanity offered him hatred, he brought them only love and understanding. That's what made him king soon after his mother. Because that is what they believed in. We all have the tendency to allow the world to break us. But the best thing is to manifest an unbroken soul. An incorruptible soul. And that's what he did. And it's why I intend to do right by him, for he has God in him."

"You're right." I said as I absorbed everything Francis said. "I think I'm going to train. Specially to prepare for tomorrow. I'll see you."

"You will, Kevin. I hope that you could write something as well. I feel you could inspire others as you inspired me. Through any art for that matter."

After he said that, I said, "I guess. I'll be sure to think about it. Thanks." I then left his office.

XXXIII

The Princess' Bodyguard

"It is good to see you, Kevin." Jesus said as I bowed right in front of him and his wife. I wiped my brow after riding from the Khalservan to the Main Chapel.

"It's good to see you too, Your Majesty." I said.

"I am thankful that you have accepted this offer." Jesus said.

"It's the least I can do. And I'm thankful for this opportunity. As if being an Apostle wasn't much of an opportunity if you get my meaning."

"Of course, Mr. Princeton." Jesus said. "Sarah plans to venture within Celestia. So, I want to assure that she is safe in your hands. It's just after everything that has happened, we fear for her being out there by herself. And we're very skeptical of some of the Civil Forcers, apart from Ms. June and Commissioner Cerviel. And we trust that you could keep her in great care when she traverses elsewhere."

"The thing about Sarah is that she is often very eager to be like her father. She goes out of her way often to explore the unknown to do noble deeds, which is not a bad thing at all. But the Satanists are a force of nature that could arouse out of nowhere in any second," Mary said. "We don't ever want her to get hurt."

"I'm sure that she would take great interest in being with me." I said. "I'll be sure to put her in great care."

"That's good to hear. Thank you, Kevin." Jesus said. "Sarah is currently at the garden of the castle. It's in the back. The guards will lead you to her."

"Thank you, Your Majesty. I shall intend to her at once." I said descending away from the monarchs.

It may not sound so surprising to some. But to me, it was. I got myself prepared for the most exciting opportunity in a long while. I finally had a job. And the best part was that it was simple. All I had to do was always guard the Lady. Although I wasn't too surprised, I was still quite astonished when Sarah considered me. Perhaps it was also an excuse just to see me and to hang out with me, which sounded more appeasing in my eyes.

I finally reached the terrace that was looking over the parterre garden of the castle, which almost reminded me of the one I saw in La Divinum Estelle. But it was much bigger, much lavish, and exotic.

As we were going down the stairs of the castle, I saw the Lady in her most extravagant dress. She wore a flowered white dress with a silky cloak. Her dark brown hair was down to her upper back. She looked more radiant than ever.

The two guards got her attention from picking white roses from the bushes and humming a hymn to herself. As she turned and saw us, she said to the guards, "Thank you, gentlemen. You may go."

The guards nodded and left me with her. I approached to her, still astounded by the sheer bloody scale. When I got to her, she smiled at me. And the shining sun was perfectly blooming on her sunny tattooed face.

"Your Highness." I bowed. Erecting her arm, she allowed me to kiss her by her small hand.

"Greetings, Kevin. Forgive me, I know it is cliché seeing a damsel picking from the gardens."

"No worries, Sarah." I said. "It is quite beautiful today than most. I wouldn't blame yourself."

"Quite right." She said as she looked over the big and most likely expensive orchard. Far out were the terrains forested with trees and hilltops.

"Word of mouth says that you've assassinated two of Lucifer's Watchers."

"Aye. It just leaves us The Phoenix and Angel."

"That is good. I'm sorry that I am usually not present during these formations. I cannot stand politics; especially in cases like this. Especially with Chancellor Dante pressuring me to be a professional."

"Isn't that the truth? But I've grown somewhat familiarized to it. That doesn't necessarily mean that I fancy it, of course. Just as killing." I spoke. I lounged both of my arms on the terrace fence. "Was there...anything you wanted to do in particular? Your parents said that you wanted to venture in the city. You often do so."

"Yes. I...I wanted your company, truth be told. And to show you around Celestia. It's bright and...somewhat dark spots," She giggled. She then continued, "The Chancery had other noblemen, but I chose you instead. They were in it for just coin. I plan to do some activities. We never got to be together often," she turned to me with a smile.

"Right. I'm in it for coin as well, to be honest. But not in that sense. You see, it's to provide for myself...and my family most of all. To help them get leveled. I'm thankful for the coin of Frask and King Fergus, but...it's still not enough to provide. Especially since I'm far from them."

"No, of course. Forgive me. I didn't mean it that way. It's just...most of the noblemen here and how they use it. They're not as good as they use to be. They've become immune to divinity, self-centered and boastful just to live off the Chancery's respect. And money...is usually the root despite being a necessity. They hoard it for themselves and their trivial pleasures."

"I understand. It's the dark side of nobility, I'm afraid. And...I'm sorry for not having the thought of hanging out with you. It's just with everything going on, it's been a bloody mess."

"Yes, I understand for sure. My father and mother have always been faithful, but they have feared for me recently." She said. "He felt that I needed someone to keep me safe."

"Your parents are good people." I declared.

"I know that. They raised me to safeguard and heed their actions. But at the same time, they raised me to think freely." She said. "I try to help others, especially priestesses, maidens, and angels to pursue this mindset. I try to be as good as my father, but it's...difficult when others try to stop you. Whether they intend to kidnap you, kill you or to remove your rank. Wisdom, love, and hope is all we can have. Yet, they are constantly lost through the darkness. Sometimes internally...because honesty and goodness scare us."

"That is true. Although, most of the time, external sources can cause such an impact on you." I said. "I know that for sure. I faced it."

"I'm sure you have. I'm sure everyone has." She spoke. "But...what do you mean by sources?"

"By that, your Majesty, I mean that your enemies are those who manifest who you are. As infants, we're given souls. Often, those souls are made in pain and result to evil. They inflict so much agony on you that...you're afraid to think for yourself. At the end of it all, you start to care about what they think. You start to be like everyone else. Become what the world wants you to be. It's like...they implanted a cancer that prevents you from staying true to who you are." I said almost depressingly. "Sometimes, I feel as though the world I had never gave us a chance to...to truly live our lives. Not even my family. And if it did, maybe I was either sheltered from it...or just blind to see it."

"I'm not an astral, but I'm pretty sure you did. It's just that others who had it chose to do despicable things to others. If anything, the civilization you call the western civilization is a cautionary tale for you to make a decent one here." She said with a smile. "And maybe it could be the same. But the difference between the two is that we are eternal beings. At least most of us. But we are still spirits. Therefore, we have a lifetime to change our ways. There's a double-edged sword in everything."

As I contemplated a bit, nearly getting my mind lost in the garden, I asked her, "Am I...doomed to change, Sarah? To be good?"

"From what you have done lately, I don't quite understand why you would ask such questions."

"I mean...it's just that...I have been carrying these burdens like carrying daggers on my back. The life I once had. A life I didn't want. And I thought that I would be free from those burdens, but they keep following me. Following me here. Whether it's the voices in my head or...or the dreams I've had." I said before I let out a sigh. "The truth is...I've been trying to...outrun this fight between the Apostles and Satanists. The heavenly against the hellish. I'm not...steady to help finish it. I want this to be in good terms, especially for my family's sake. But...it's as if I can't even help myself; given these illusions preventing me from being faithful. Or have a purpose. Just as...before. I suppose it's a reminder that seeking a purpose in life...or being whole...is a thing of the past. No true divinity. No personal faiths. No honesty. No atonement. It's all about obeying man's mock of nature now. Allowing rats to sit on thrones and live off suffering. Or rather...it's always been like that, and I couldn't see it. Nor believe it. And I cannot do anything about it, even as a knight. Because they have power...they have it all and I...and I don't."

"That's not true, Kevin. You *can* do it. There's just a lot of things in any life that are beyond our control. We are not in fault of that. You neither. But you could do what they can't do. A man who dwells in things he cannot control in life.... becomes his own enemy. He can only control his own life. The things he must make the future he sought for. In terms of those burdens, those are core enemies you are dealing with." She explained as she lounged her arms as well. "And it's okay, we all have them. I have them. My father and mother too. We all experience something; in life and death." She shifted her right hand towards mine.

I gazed upon her white grey eyes. "You're a good man. I see God bloom from you every day with every deed you do. You must stop undermining yourself...because you bring something that this world was missing."

"What is that your Highness?" I asked.

Thus, she replied with a soft chuckle, "Reconciliation with our dark sides. The truth and honesty about ourselves. That's my problem with people like the noblemen. The Chancery. We're so apt to be perfect that we forget to be in tune with ourselves. And the so-called *prophets* betrayed the word of God, betrayed his divinity and coerced people into their thought, making people ashamed for living on their accord. People like Dante are desperate to see God's face...not knowing that...he is here. He has many faces. You are only reminding us of that...especially with the Apostles. You must know that."

I smiled at her. She smiled back at me.

Shifting away her hand, she focused her eyes at the hazy horizon. She then said, "In the book of John verse 3, chapter 16, it was written that those who looked up to faith will have eternal life. Especially those who have faith in God. Anything divine, really. My father read this to me before. I was a child then. And he told me once that sometimes our enemies aren't always what we face. Sometimes...our enemies are within ourselves. To fight those we see, we must fight what is within us. To be vulnerable to God."

"To do that would be tough. They're like entities that make a living out of seeing others fall, including us."

"Yes, it would be. It's a cancer. A mucus. A plague that chooses not to leave." She said. "In order to be cured of that pain, we have to cut it. It may be difficult, painful even. But...it would be worth it in the end. Because we will become anew. I understand the need to go back to how things were simple. But we should change to be good. We should change...to be better. No matter what, we all must face life and work with it...not turn from it. Because living life away from the chains of man...you are free to be alive again."

"To be...redeemed." I said. I watched her removing herself from lounging. I then said to her, "You are extraordinarily wise for your age. They raised you well, which is obvious."

"You have my thanks. I mean...I must be as diplomatic as I can, given my position as Lady of the Promised Land. It's not always fun...but I embrace it. Even improvise." She admitted.

"I'm sure your father understands. There's nothing wrong with that thought. He cares about you deeply," I said.

"And I'm very thankful," She said. "Though royalty isn't fun as it looks. Sometimes, I feel as if I haven't done the House of God any favors, given of what has happened recently. I'm not as justly violent or agile as you are. I don't like violence nor to extract it, but I understand it's unfortunate purpose. I try what I can to have some relevance like my father. Serving communities, including priestesses or gypsies. Indulging to affairs of the state of Valestone...like the Gathering. I hope I am. Sometimes, I wish...I knew my grandmother...before she was killed. I dream to be just as good as she was one day when I become queen of this land."

"You are. And...I'm sure your father prefers for you to find your own way of preserving your life and not to follow his exact footsteps. It wouldn't take away the fact that he still loves you no matter what. Your enchanted exclusivity is enough to shed light into a world stripped by locusts. And your small duties are impacted. He just wants you to be young, especially since life can take that away. As for the queen who passed, she'd want you to be yourself. I would imagine that...because that's all you should be."

"T...Thank you very much, Kevin. Your words mean a lot." After she smiled at me, she then said, "I...I recall that time you rescued me. And I told you before that we weren't what you may have thought. You see what I mean now?"

"Aye. I realize that...your father was just a man who happened to be eternally blessed by God. But deeply, he's just like all of us. I'm sorry of what I said before. I was just on edge of being deceived, y'know."

"No worries. My father has been in your footsteps. He never claimed to be too godly. You saw how much he suffered on that blasted cross. But he saw what happened to the world and chose to save it. He didn't want nor asked to do it, but he had to prove that God's divinity existed. To save everyone from damnation." Sarah said. "He was lifted by the love he was given. When we're inspired by something, by those who do, even if it is small, we intend to do good things. It stimulates us."

I nodded, "You're absolutely right, lass. So...where should we go first, m' lady? What does this so-called *holy place* have in store for the both of us?"

She giggled and said, "How lovely, Kevin! You and your sarcasm. I plan to ride together to Samson Park, a grand public park in the city's district St. Joel's Clover." She said. "I hope that I won't delay you."

"Of course not. I've got time. I'm your bodyguard, remember? From what I could tell, I've got time. At least when Francis is not summoning me."

"Yes. Later in the evening, I'll be sure to have the banker from Judah Bank deliver bennies to me, so I can exchange to you. Sound good?"

"Yes, of course."

"Brilliant. Well, let's go." She said as I followed her away from the terrace.

The next hour, we reached the place on horseback. I guarded Sarah in the Samson Park. We were both galloping on our horses whilst taking in the lively space. And I didn't know if it was because I've lived in New York, but it really reminded me of Central Park. It formatted as like any park. Despite the little dense fog that swept across, it didn't stop me from admiring the trees that had silver leaves and trunks that grew glowing white veins. It reminded me a bit of Eastbound. The sun shined through the trees and spotlighted through the fog.

Couples lounged onto one another, looking out at the streaming water crossing underneath bridges. Children were running, jumping, and playing games with one another. Throughout the park, there were even several small bands playing good melodies. Flutes, drums, guitars, harps, lutes and hammered dulcimers were sounded. All of them were clustered into this manifested hybrid of joy. The strings were tugged respectfully as the antique nakers were beaten with clothed drumsticks.

One song that stuck with me was called *Noah's Ballad* sang by a band called *The Pure Harlots*. They were known amongst spirits for their darkly comedic songs based off the Bible such as *Golden Cow*. But

Noah's Balled was the most favored. It was the story of Noah, except the lyrics were obviously dark but were juxtaposing with the jolly and lighthearted melody of the instruments. It was making fun of those who drowned in the flood after Noah built the ark. And it was somewhat of a social commentary of how we are often arrogant to things we don't expect. The lyrics were in vain of....

All the others drowned very willingly
Knowing that their souls are truly free
All of them drowned in the water
While Noah and his kin happily sailed the sea
Hey, at least they didn't go to Hell
They drank good ale and rang good bells
When their souls found the Promised Land
They sang with a horse named Mister Hands

And a lot of the songs were like that too. A lot of them were catchy and unintentionally funny. But I guess it was the point. The songs really took it upon themselves to make light of the darkest bits of the Bible, which was both fascinating and eerie. Not to mention, it was good outside today. It was good to see the sun again. The snow was gradually melting in every corner of the park, slowing disintegrating into a cool chilling liquid.

It felt good to be a bodyguard, for I felt like I was protecting a celebrity. Or even the President. It gave me some pride. And of course, the children and elders will circle around us, greeting the princess.

Sarah would smile gently and gave them wisdom. There were times in which she reminded me so much of her father. From helping a crippled elderly woman to stand on her two feet to feeding the colored birds, I saw life in her. And that was what I was witnessing, life. With the war between the Apostles and Satanists manifesting in front of me, the battle-tattered nature of the afterlife being evident each time I journeyed, it nearly made me miss out on witnessing and experiencing what life could be again. Sure, there was talk of nonsense.

Dialogs ranging from whether the afterlife should or should not prosper with advance technology. Commentaries on whether Jesus should make peace with other kingdoms or not. Or become emperor. Or whether the afterlife needed democracies instead of monarchies. Or whether Heaven should be monotheistic instead of pantheistic.

I disclosed and disregarded, for I had little time to indulge in their petty opinions. I knew at that point that some spirits distaste the other kingdoms and dislike the pantheistic world. Still, I was just glad to be in a park. It was a park full of purities that never had the chance to be human or for the astrals who wanted to have that experience again. And for what it was worth, I was pleased to see men and women communicating face to face.

The benefits of a place with barely any advanced high-tech achievement bloomed that day. Though I was going to miss my iPhone, I was coming in terms with the loss, given how I was not a fan of some of the uses of technology from the world I came from. Especially social media or those intolerable five second videos.

Later in the evening, I managed to drop Sarah off to her home in the Main Chapel. And for the first day working, I could already tell that it was going to be not only simple, but it was also to be an honestly fun job. I really enjoyed being with Sarah. Seeing her not just as a Lady, but simply a girl. Today, she was a girl who wanted to live life normally.

Sarah was delivered the coin. She did as she was promised. Before I would take off, I thanked her gratefully. I thanked her for such a splendid time and for giving me this opportunity. Though I had other plans to make a living in this life, being a bodyguard was essential to me.

The next day, Sarah escorted me to another district in town. This time, she brought along her entourage. They were three flower angelic gypsies from La Divinum Estelle. And Magdalene's up and coming priestesses.

Scarlett Holiday, Hannah Clover, and Vivienne de la Cruz were their names. And they were charming and elegant as well. They were going to graduate soon after completing several years in the school. I learned from them that students are enrolled by the age of thirteen years old. They all graduate at my age, nineteen years old.

They obviously weren't angel guards, Civil Forcers, the knights or even Paladins. These angels were common as the other spirits. They often occupied as being singers, nurses, and keepers of nature and beauty. Hannah was a flower angel for love. Vivienne was a flower angel for peace. And Scarlett was a flower angel for harmony. And all three of them planned to become angels for humanity just like the angels that came before. They wanted to become guides for humans. Three of them were presented with floral drapes that reached their toes. Headdresses with flowers and floral cloaks over their heads.

I went with them to *Davidson*, one of the most active boroughs of Celestia ran by a work-centric baron named Ned Alexander. Manifested with red-tiled brick buildings facing one another, it was also the most trade-savvy boroughs, delivering and retrieving rich metal materials like gold and silver, rare crops, potions, expensive cloths, and healthy livestock. The streets were crowded with food stands, carts full of food and provisions for trade, and live entertainment performed by street performers. Just like the park, it was full of eccentric people who were enthusiastic about their businesses. Shopkeepers kept barking amongst the crowd all at once to advertise.

Dogs, barked, goats cried, cows mooed, chickens clucked, cats meowed, and pigs squealed and were being led across and around by farmers to exchange from workshop to workshop. And it was good seeing that for once, given what has happened for the past seven months. Not that I really expect a harmonic environment, but most of the workers I saw didn't seem to have a competitive nature. Sarah told me that some dealings would, instead, learn from one another and work independently to live up to their own financial standards; apart from a few bad eggs who take competition too far. There were stands of alchemists selling various toxins for decent prices as well. And some of the goods, items, armor, and wares came from other places in Heaven.

Sarah and the three angels were shopping for cloaks, pieces of cloths, dresses, trinkets, and tapestries under the brand name *Dream Fabrics*. There were pieces from Tamashii No Ketsu Taba, The Fields of Suns and even a Slavic kingdom in the Promised Land called Irij. Sarah fancied a diversity of clothes that weren't just from where she lived. And her entourage shared that passion in their own ways. I would often stand by just for them to wait for them and let them have their fun. And smoke every now and then.

During the night, we even intended a stage production of an adaptation of a tragic romantic fantasy novel, written in the afterlife by Katherine Tulip, called Graceless Flower. We sat at the third level row in the theater. And because I was with the Lady, we had special seats to see the stage at its majestic. The play was a tragic love story about how a woman committed suicide just to be with her lover after he died during a bloody war in Tamashii No Ketsu Taba. The women were obviously entranced by the story. But I'm personally fancy romance when it's used as a subtle subplot. But still, I enjoyed it for its production value. I enjoyed how entertainment in the afterlife set itself out to evoke reality to provoke betterment instead of being based of algorithms.

These were the things that I had to endure for the two weeks. Traversing from borough to borough in a royal carriage. From the quiet suburban district *Saint Rembrandt* to the historically luxurious streets of *Grace Hanover*, Sarah was blessed enough to show me how massive Celestia was as not just a city, but a megacity. It made me almost miss New York; despite it being a city of conformity. And because I was her guardian, she had networks due to her position. Like I said, it was simple. And by the time, I was already making at least one hundred and forty bennies. It probably wasn't much compared to how much Ted or Juliet was making. But at least it was a start. It was better than having nothing. It was decent enough for me to buy some food for Algor and a pack of tobaccos for myself. Obviously, I would have to work harder to earn a bit more.

By the next week I earned three hundred and forty. It was added to the coin I saved. I was continuing to guard the princess with her friends. I was able to use the money to purchase stored deer meat for

Algor. I was able to get certain green and purple herbs called *grensigs* to help Aventurine to heal. Even more so, I sent some money to my family as well as letters; promising them that I will provide.

I even brought and sent Kelley a stuffed *Captain McKriddle* doll. I sent father a red alabaster mug and my mother a beautiful pristine white pearl necklace. I was able to do something productive just to earn a living. To live as a functioning spirit in the afterlife, even if it meant to comply with heavenly society that was not too different from the natural world. But thanks to my experience as an Apostle, it was beneficial to what it took to be a proper bodyguard. I founded myself being more comfortable with Sarah and knowing a bit more of who she was.

A girl who happened to be the daughter of the Son of God. But also, a princess who just wanted to live as any woman who saw beauty in every inch of the conflicted world.

Today, we rode to a garden within the eastern depths of the city called *Green Haven*. It was like a park dedicated to collecting a vast number of plants to display and label them. I safely assumed that Sarah had a fascination with nature. She fancied everything that she saw. Hell, she'd often jump and skip daintily through the bushy mazes like she was a little girl. Including the angels. I followed them until we reach a dead end of the rose covered bushes. Sarah faced me and giggled with her dimples blushing a bit. The other girls giggled along.

"Being with you has been the most amazing days!" Sarah said as she playfully spun around with her arms out.

"Yes. You and your fascination with nature." I said with a little bit of jest. "And here I was thinking I was obsessed with adventure novels and other sorts!"

"Why wouldn't you be?" She turned and pulled me, getting me engaged into the rose covered maze. "Nature is a painting manifested. Nature connects with us and our souls. God is truly an artist, isn't he?"

"He truly is."

"Of course, I do not disclose Ted or Mr. Douglas. They are good in their own way, which is forever glorious. By the way, I am so content that you've met the three angels here. I always enjoy being in peace with my fellow peers." She said cheerfully.

"We are very thankful, Mr. Princeton," Vivienne spoke with a bow. Scarlett and Hannah nodded in agreement. And they spoke with very elegant Romani accents.

"Of course. So...spirits do care for humanity after all. I would think those angels would exercise their patrons only here."

"Truth be told, they only give humans guidance to prosper wisely as they appear as guides." Scarlett said. "Only the humans can choose to accept it...or to refuse that perception. But...we care. Especially God."

"That's good to know." I spoke. Sarah suddenly approached to me with open arms and made me embrace her. I hugged her back. Afterwards, the wingless sirens embraced me one at a time. Hannah said, "Thank you so much for this."

"You're very welcome, Hannah." I said as she finally released me from her embrace.

"If there is anything I can do, please don't dare hesitate." Sarah assured. "Your values are just as important. That's how we can create a fair land." I nodded with a grin on my face.

She then said, "The Chancery is wrong. So is Dante. Knighthood is not dead. It's alive and well. Always." I smiled gently to what she said as it lifted my pride.

I said to her, "I hope so. But I think it will be."

But then...unexpectedly, a deep voice rose from behind us, "Mr. Princeton." When we both slowly turned, the voice happened to come from a lone guard.

He was a middle-aged fellow. Equipped with his halberd in his left, he said, "You must be Kevin Princeton, I presume. You are needed by Ms. June."

I looked back at Sarah, trying to understand what I was exactly needed for. The angel entourage looked at one another, murmuring about the man. What would Bertha want from me at this time? Sarah stepped a bit further in front of me and asked, "What is the meaning of this?"

"I'm a part of the Civil Force Detective Agency. I'm afraid that the matters are confidential, Your Highness." The guard said nonchalantly. "I cannot say."

"Confidential?"

"Yes, madam."

"Regardless of who you may be, need I remind you that I am Lady of Heaven and daughter of Jesus Christ! Therefore, whatever you shall discuss should be direct with the House. No secrets. Or have you forgotten your profession?" She said sternly. I was very impressed with how authoritative she sounded.

"I haven't forgotten, Your Highness. But unfortunately, these matters are private according to Ms. June." The guard said in a stoic stern tone.

As I stepped aside of her, I said to her, "It's okay, Sarah. Bertha probably has something for me. Perhaps, it's an update on Frask's experiments or something. Why don't you and the girls ride back to your father in the castle? I promise to meet with you as soon as I'm done."

She gazed into my eyes with concern. She looked for reassurance from the other girls, who looked back concerned.

Although it was good to have someone concerned on my behalf, I knew what to expect from Bertha's flamboyant and strange ways of exchanging information with me. At this point, I knew what to expect. After she hesitated, she then told me, "Please be careful. It is strange for him to show up so suddenly."

"I promise," I said as I released her hands. I then approached to the bearded guard as I briefly saw Sarah taking off with her entourage.

"Be careful, Mr. Princeton," Vivienne said to me before she met up with the others.

"I will, lass. Don't worry," I said.

After I turned from Sarah and her entourage, I turned to the man and asked, "What is this about? I thought you hated us."

"Not everyone hates those who are angels. Bertha takes a liking to you. Let's get your peg so you can follow me. I shall lead you to her." He said as he began to trail off. I soon followed him.

In the next hour, after departing from the garden, I was galloping behind the guard.

Throughout the ride, I was pondering on how it felt bloody awkward for a Civil Force Detective to fancy me that much. He was leading me into a very interesting district that was further away from Celestia. It seemed like a normal colonial settlement, but a bit industrialized. I said industrialized due to some buildings being created from scratch. Fog from pending man-made contraptions in factories far out.

Men were bringing and sending off wagons upon wagons of logs, steel bars, grains, and shredded crystals. Scaffoldings were hugging around the deconstructed structures. Compared to the cities in Celestia, a lot of the buildings were made of wood and steel.

Compared to its monumental buildings, these buildings settled for less and thus were shorter. It looked a bit decent for a settlement. It seemed to be a local old town filled with brick-built mining cottages in Celestia. But far from the rest of the boroughs. Instead of the vanilla aroma that danced in other places, or the honest haze of beef from Davidson, slop stanched, tobacco smoked, and fecal matter was presenting its smell. It made me reflect my time in Brooklyn. I nearly forgot that Celestia was a city. And based on my time in New York City, cities are bound to have glaring flaws.

Some folks, however, looked to be dirty and couldn't let their eyes off me for some strange reason. Most women looked to be outworn and different from the Neotantrics. Most were half uncovered from the top. They looked at me seductively. Cursing, bantering, and flirtatious were rousing from them. Their dresses looked ritualistic and provocative and not virginal or prude like the Neotantrics.

To top it off, we trotted along the dusty road and came across a group of young men getting detained by the Civil Forcers. In fact, there were a lot more Civil Forcers here than there were in some parts of Celestia. But I continued to focus on the breathing of my temporary steed and at the guard. I was three foot away from him as I galloped down the sandy road.

Compared to some of the places in Celestia, I was surprised to discover that this was more of an old town than a district. I was not sure where the guard was leading me. I wasn't even sure why would Bertha want to meet me in a place like it. It seemed odd for someone as regal as her.

"What...part of the city is this?" I asked the guard as he rode on his greyish white steed.

"St. John's Township." He said. "Mining commune. It's a developing region after the rebellion. Ran by some cucked-up baron the Chancery decided to pick. Wouldn't say it's the best to visit now."

"How come, exactly?" I asked, even though I knew what kind of impression I was getting.

"An era of machine, civilization will soon seep. Local criminals, gamblers and other extremes take advantage of that in celebration. Particularly local gangs like the Astral Ghoul Boys. Ungrateful bastards feel disenfranchised just because the monarchy is spending money on the Paladins. They are unaware of their importance. At least it ain't a ghetto, for the most part."

"Well...why is it here in Heaven?"

As he randomly chuckled, he said, "Free will, lad. Reckless freedom. You must know by now that not everyone uses that privilege for good. That's the honesty about living here in Heaven. And...the price. The residents here are one of them. Trust me. There are other places worse like this in the city; Lightgate Union or Eranson. But this is the most prevalent...and often the most dangerous. Which is why we have the Civil Forcers in every corner. The king's humbled enough to see the good in scum such as the lot of them."

"R...Right." I said estranged. "So...are we getting somewhere? Where are we meeting Bertha?"

"She'll be just around...this corner 'ere," He said as he eyed at an alleyway nearby. "Best to hitch your steed here."

"A...Alright. Sure." I said as I dismounted from the horse and tied the reins onto the hitching post. I watched the guard as he dismounted from his. Both of my hands were soon inserted into my coat pockets as I casually followed the guard around the corner.

Upon entering a dense gap between two wooden buildings were four other guards. Three men and a woman garbed in the same uniform. But there was no sight of Bertha anywhere. So rightfully, something within me was telling me that something was already wrong. Why would he lead me to Bertha who wasn't there? Unless she made a delay once again, there was no excuse on getting me away from guarding Sarah.

Not to mention that the guards were staring at me strangely as if they were ready to pounce. My heart throbbed wildly. I felt my eyes leak with warm blood as I did before. Something was going on. Something happened for sure! The other guard whom I followed just stood in the middle of the alley.

"Where is Bertha?" I asked wiping my eyes. The guard turned to me, faced me with a smirk that suddenly curved on his face. "W...Where is she?" I asked again in doubt.

"She ain't coming, lad." He said as he suddenly jolted his head, which signaled the guards to gradually surround me. They stood with very threatening stances as they were armed with their swords. Then he said a familiar word, *"Ka-les-mada!"*

The guards began to engage towards me. They didn't give me enough time to unleash my sword. So, I unveiled both of my Apostle blades from my wrists. I began to counterattack them, unleashing all my strength to bestow onto them.

But I was overwhelmed. When I tried to attack, one guard snuck behind me and held his blade onto my throat. I ejected my blades into his eye sockets whilst kicking on other guard in front of me. I charged at the third one who was intending to strike. My retractable blades were connected to his sword. I tried to use my left to stab his torso. When I accomplished that, I felt something sharp enter the back of my neck. It didn't feel like the edge of a sword entering and exiting my jugular. When I removed it, I feasted my eyes at what look like some diabolical toxin concealed in a form of a long dart. As that happened, my vision became blurry. Everything around me began to slow down as if time was going to stop.

I fell flat on my face after I felt a sudden nudge that roughly put me out of my consciousness. And yet again, darkness was all I saw. I couldn't even feel myself being carried away. But I figured that I was lied to. I fell for it like a fool.

Clever trick, I suppose.

XXXIV

A Cage of Pain

"Goodness, what will it take for these methods to die? Would someone please remove the bag from his head?"

That was the first thing I heard when I was getting my mind to wake up. Everything was slowly becoming clear, but I found myself concealed in some brown potato sack. But I felt I was in a moving vehicle. I didn't know how long I was out for, but it almost felt like a long time.

As I felt the bag remove from my head, I saw myself concealed in a carriage. The interiors were lit with two lamps on each side. I gazed my eyes at three individuals who sat facing me. Two of them were black and gold-cloaked men with breastplates. Their hoods were so overbearing that I barely saw their faces. But in between them was someone astonishingly and frighteningly familiar. White creepily decorated mask with black detailed accents decorated and a dark furry pelt. Lucifer.

"Putting a bag over someone is getting a bit outdated. Even for me. Wouldn't you say, Mr. Princeton?" He asked in his somber voice.

Aggressively, I tried to move and attack him despite feeling very drained. My momentum was not in my favor, but I tried to fight. But I felt my wrists held tightly together by a rope. Including my feet. I was wrestling in panic, but the guard on the right held his gun at me. Lucifer held his hand to ease the guard's arm. My eyes spawn around, looking for something useful to use to escape and to warn the other spirits. Outside of the vehicle, I saw two people on horseback, supposedly guarding the carriage I was inside.

"The infamous...Kevin Edward Princeton. It's quite an honor to meet you, face to face. Or rather...mask to face." He greeted with a snicker. "Please, forgive me for the restrains. It's just a...precaution. I know what you're capable of."

"Aye, of course you do!" I said bitterly. He could only chuckle and grin behind his mask. But his differed colored eyes squinted.

"I'm sorry for the disturbance. Is there anything I can do to make this ride...pleasant?"

"Since you asked." I said almost in anger. "You can either tell me why I'm here or...you can be a good lad and let me out of here!"

He sighed and said casually, "The second option...I don't see that happening yet. But don't worry. You'll be out soon enough. However, I could do the first option. But...time is of the essence. Especially these days."

"What do you mean by that?"

"Oh...you'll know eventually." Lucifer teased. I felt my heart was throbbing nonstop and sweat damping my forehead. "I was invited...by the Angel. For a performance and search. I take interest in many spirits in the afterlife, specifically here in the Promised Land. It's good to see how it remains the same." He then pointed and wagged his finger at me. "But you...in particular...have perked my interest further."

"Meaning?"

"Meaning that you have a drive that inspires all." He said. "It's...quite inspiring to see someone strive to be good. Despite all the world's burdens you carry, you are doing everything you can in your power to make sure that your tasks are fulfilled." He said. "But...we both know that you didn't join just to simply appease the Heavenly monarchy or to resurrect an Order. Don't we? Hm. It's ...some mere agenda you have prior to your initiation. Just like me. And that is not a bad thing at all."

"Don't try to pull my leg, you plonker! You're just pissed from the fact that we killed two of your Watchers and foiled your plans! And when I'm out of here, I'll continue my hunt with the Order. And soon, those people you've imprisoned will be free from you!" I said in a determined fashion.

"You have nobility. I admire that. It feels...sudden...like someone woke up from an uninterrupted sleep." He complimented. "But *freedom*. That is such an interesting word." He gazed upon the window.

"Why do you have your puppets do your dirty work? Getting the scepters to the Axis Mundi? Afraid of getting blood on your hands?"

"That is none of your concern, I'm afraid. Oh, and I prefer blood. Most...definitely. Just not the way you think." He said softly. "It's funny how we often look at being free. It's...quite sad really. It could explain why the natural world was so...meaningless. It doesn't have to be, but it always chooses to. It could explain why we fail to save ourselves. Have you ever questioned the souls of humanity, Mr. Princeton? Have you...had the thought to question the Apostle Order for the days you were here?"

"What's that to you?"

"Simply just conversation. I sometimes happen to question the point of this conflict. What the ultimate endgame is. Apostles and Angels want souls to be inspired and free to redeem themselves. They want souls to elevate to the stars." He continued. "But do you ever find it funny how the same needs end up becoming...formulaic? It's almost unbearable. The souls of humanity are an interesting specimen. A lot of them intend to find an easy way to live life. They festered the natural world the Gods created with...these ideas and concepts that go nowhere. A lot of them are...artificial, pseudo and never grounded. Freedom is one of them. It's a very interesting one. It seems to result to more...chaos, hubris, condescendence, and disobedience as opposed to a courteous and professional civilization. You see, I always thought that people of all matter were sorely created to serve to manifest a world without sin, skeptics, or question. Not to have a life of their own. Because a gathering of different perceptions...could lead the world to die. Because when they are given the will to act as their own man or woman, act out their own accord, they become too prideful. Often animalistic than animals themselves. And it eventually leads them to think one is better than the other. They fight one another to see who would outlive who. Superiority complexes is what they have. They don't want perfected souls. They do not intend to be complete. They have no sense of humility nor honor whatsoever. And yet, you take part of a society of *knights*...that advocates this kind of behavior. Which is funny...considering how you detest people. Just as I."

When he said that, it prompted me to say, "We don't advocate chaos! But what do you expect? Not all souls are good! But some are! I don't hate all people!"

"Oh...but you do. Otherwise, you wouldn't kill our unit of militants and those who support the cause. You don't even bother to see any modicum of good in them," He spoke as if he knew me. It only yarned my nerves. "You just kill them recklessly. As if they were meaningless bugs. The Order has made you prone to do this."

"Because they've done nothing but hurt others by your orders! All in the name of your false crusade! They won't listen to reason because you've literally built them that way. Ordering them to kill those who don't falter to your twisted philosophy! Without any question! What do you expect me to do? It's not as if you care for them! I don't know why I am even telling you this! You wouldn't understand!"

"I don't know why you told me to begin with." He said as he almost choked with laughter. "It's almost as if...the Apostles has influenced you greatly. You grew close to their flawed creed. It appears that you've grown close to this Order and the members within it. One of them you've befriended. One of them...you've loved. And you've assisted others into putting our plans in jeopardy. And you honestly think you have a chance of saving because of that. You've become prideful...as if everything is going as you hoped for. Redeem yourself from your mistakes by forgetting your past sins to become anew. Forget the world you once came from to make this one right, the life you could have. It almost reminds me of someone I knew. Abraham.... Darius, the third Apostle."

"Francis told me of what you did to him! How you broke him,

pained him, and made him carry his burdens to the point of taking his own afterlife! If you think you'll do the same to me, you have another thing coming!"

"I'm impressed. Often, someone who faced me will cower. Especially knights. But...not you. I like that. But you and Abraham are obviously quite different. Although, he too wanted to forget his past. You see, unlike you, Abraham...lacked pride. So...he came to me to become stronger. He came to us to become redeemed from his mistakes; one of them being how he violently assaulted his childhood friend he was once engaged with. A Russian herbalist. Although he was never confident, he was honest with others. Especially her. The Apostles were the only ones who saw light in him. But...he felt like they championed his mistakes...instead of perfecting him. They expect him to move on and better himself. But he didn't want to do that. He joined because was desperate to devoid any semblance of who he was. He was willing to sacrifice it...to be saved from humanity. His humanity as well. So...he came to join our flock. And yet, he felt burdened by our... *procedures*. And we knew what we were doing. For his own good." Lucifer looked back at me.

"Abraham failed to learn from his suffering. And because he didn't face his burdens, he failed to learn from his mistakes. He failed to trust me. That is what I ask from my followers. I was the one – the only one – to save him. Just as I have saved others. I wanted him to embrace who...he...was! I wanted him to remember what he did and to have his mind fester with the burdens he placed on that woman! I wanted him to plunge in a stream of shame, pain, self-hatred, and guilt to arise...free. I wanted him to be caged in pain to be given forgiveness. To earn his precision. A magnum opus in a form of a soul made by me. But...he took his own afterlife...because he couldn't handle it anymore. And there was nothing I could've done to stop him."

I sat against my back and pondered on what he explained. I still didn't know what he was trying to explain, as if he was intentionally trying to break my mind. As if it weren't already broken.

"Unlike you, Kevin, at least Abraham was able to accept his true nature. No pride in his life. A failure longing to be saved. A degenerate trying to envision what he couldn't have," Lucifer said.

He then continued, "No one is free. We love to think that we are. We admire the thought. Free from sin, from shame, from consequence, confusion, circumstance. Free from life. But we aren't. And there's a reason for this. We saw how it looks. How it works. Freedom...has the tendency to bring the absolute worst from people. This means that they are endlessly doomed to reach true salvation. The only way to be good...is to become more than mere individuals that go on these mind-less odysseys that lead to more unfulfilled questions about existence. It's the matter of having our natures, burdens that made us imperfect and limit us from creating a true paradise, forgone. It's funny how people think they are individuals, yet they are quick to seek someone to idolize. A messiah. Someone to think for them since they cannot do it on their own. They're no different from the wildlife. Only they act...*civilized*. So, this idea of freedom is simply...a myth. A dead tale we tell ourselves at night to keep us hopeful for an artificial concept that has yet to exist. Like the dead tales of knights in shining armor. And frankly, it's about time to accept our true purpose."

Suddenly, I saw the guard on the right pass him a syringe. It looked to be a dark red substance inside. Almost like blood. He then spoke with the syringe in his fingers. I felt the grasp of each guard. They held me tight to make sure I made no movements. One of them palmed his hand onto my scalp.

"This is what I am going to teach you tonight, Kevin." He said softly but eerily. "I'll teach you how *not* to resist pain. I will show you how to accept your burdens and sins. To own them. To let them break within your heart and cripple your mind. To be concealed in a cage. And once you've learned that...you will be free from that cage. You will be free from your pride. You'll be given a new soul. You have such strong potential...for great things, Kevin. Superior things."

I suddenly watched the needle insert into the flesh of my neck. My eyes felt jumbled. I stared into his eyes. "You just have to work immensely hard for them. Now...I hear that Apostles are good in their dreams. Let's put that to the test, shall we?"

I struggled to regain my consciousness. But I suddenly saw myself almost sinking into the depths of some hellish part of my mind. It almost looked to be the trials of my mind, but it had a different intention.

This was a strange feeling I felt. I felt like I was dreaming; yet my body was fully awake and always moving. My mind felt as if it were paralyzed, meaning that I couldn't use it. I couldn't move an ounce of my body. I didn't feel any pain. I couldn't see with my own eyes of what was happening. But I was concealed in a red place. Just like the trials from the initiation. Far out, I saw mountain ranges. And soon, I saw a village. A lot of the buildings were overshadowed with darkness.

The village looked to be something that I should remember. I just didn't quite understand which one. But something did catch my eye. I looked far out, and it took me a while to conclude that the village was threatened. It looked to be an uncalled skirmish taken place there. I wasn't just going to stand by and allow those innocent people get slaughtered, whether I was in control or not.

I ran down the slope to get down to the place and liberate it from this darkness. I came down and eventually got to where it was. The roofs were decorated with tremendous fire. The fire looked obscure, almost smoke like. The Satanists were there, jabbing and thrashing their blades onto the men, women, and children. All of which were only making a living.

I unleashed my sword from my strap and began to charge at each one. I began my massacre by thrashing and slaying my blade onto every single Satanist I saw. And I did it with no question. No thought traversing my brain. But in the back of it, I did wonder why Lucifer would bring me here to crucify his crazed followers. With every dead body count increasing rapidly, I wondered if he was just allowing this to happen. Not to mention that even half of the Satanists I wrestled with strangely died willingly. Perhaps it was to show their strong deluded faith to Lucifer.

It was a long fight. A long one-man battle. Lasting for sixteen minutes or more. I went through every house tirelessly to make sure that every Satanist screamed in panic as they saw me. I wanted to make sure they squealed like pigs in a slaughterhouse. After everything they not only put me through but putting others through hell in the name of their god. Regardless of what nonsense came from Lucifer's mouth, I was not going to allow that to let it get to me. And when I would soon be done, I will come for him next. And Hell would have to look far for a new ruler.

I managed to make it into one house. I found myself inside the interior. Presumably some kind of living room. Two Satanists shockingly got down on their knees with their hands clamed together, wailing towards me. Their red wispy eyes stared at me with a sense of desperation and fear. Being fueled with hatred I had for what Lucifer just did to me, why would I show them mercy? Why would I show mercy to those who took part of an order that advocated benign control all in the name of creating a new heaven? A new heaven in their eyes? A new heaven where they were the masters? A new heaven where life itself was bent to their will?

With no hesitation, I swung my sword against their throats as they simultaneously plummeted to the hardwood floor. Their blood pooling all over. I breathed heavily, letting out all my hot angry breath. Letting out the entire stench they bestowed from inside. Suddenly, the corpses dematerialized into sand. I looked carefully, curious, and unsure of what was happening in my eyes. I couldn't make out of what was happening.

Suddenly, the door behind me creaked open. I turned with my blade at the ready. Surprisingly, it turned out to be Lucifer. I stood wondering why he would be here. He came inside the house with his hands slowly clapping. Each clap echoed inside the house. My eyes were now focused on him. He was joined alongside two more individuals; Sathanus and a woman with bleached hair; whiter than Juliet's. The woman appeared to be wearing some black formal dress and bared hair and skin that were pale as snow. Her dark eyes were circled with dark eyeliner that was smeared down her face. She wore a tiara with a white rose pedal connected to it. She had roses attach to her celestial waist sash. In her hand were the violin and the bow.

"Pride...cometh...before...the fall!" He said gleefully as he was then eying at me. "Pride definitely comes.... before the fall!" He then gestured his hand to the corpses, suggesting that I should have a look at them.

When my eyes glanced back at the corpses, it eerily turned out that they weren't Satanists at all. Their clothes were different from the Satanists I fought. They were casual. Normal. My eyes widened, and my entire physique shook uncontrollably. I gazed carefully in hopes to find out that it wasn't them I slaughtered. I knew them. I knew them too well. And that was scary. A man and a woman. Despite the obscure surroundings, the interior of the room gradually began to look familiar.

I looked back at Lucifer as he was just simply nodding his head. I looked back at the two people and realized who they were. Everything was becoming clear. Overwhelmed, I plummeted to my knees in front of the two corpses. "My...my..." I couldn't finish as I was struggling very much to compose myself.

My...parents. I murdered them. "No...no...Mum...Dad!" I cradled them in my arms as I was soaked by their blood.

"Yes. The two people who cared for you dearly. More than anything in this world and the one they had. Yet, you killed them. Your father's ironclad bravery...gone. Your mother's angelic voice...gone." Lucifer said with a snicker. He even went around me just to approach the table. He grabbed the red mug that concealed a hot beverage. It was still warm. It was the same mug I recently sent. The masked man lifted his mask just to get a sip. He then followed and said, "I told you that I was going to teach you how to accept your burdens. Perhaps not everyone knows who you really are. Not yet anyway. But they will now. A rich boy turned street thug with cold blood, with nothing to lose...but his humanity." He began to chuckle behind his mask after he sipped the beverage. Soon he said, "I'm proud of you, Kevin. Excellent performance. You passed your task greatly. Not only you became what you hated, but also you did it willingly. But...tell me. You honestly thought it would go your way after you joined this war? Hm? Hm? That you will return and be in this sanctuary to relive glory days? Expecting mother to put food on the table, to play with sister...or to work with father? You thought that everything would be normal? That's what it's all about, isn't it? Getting a life...you never got to have? Tell me...is it?! It. Is. Not. Knightly. To be silent. So, speak!

"No.... No, I thought.... I didn't mean...," I wondered horrendously for Kelley. She was nowhere in sight. I just continued to hyperventilate, refusing to believe it. "I...I'm sorry...I.... didn't mean..."

"Yes, you did. You did mean it. You did. You had negligence. You were blinded by your need to play make believe....to find a place...to seek approval...by playing this grandiose angel they built you up to be. To be saved, you need prettily words to feel safe in your conceit. Because deep down...you hate yourself. Therefore, you hate others." Lucifer finished what I wasn't going to say. A manner in mockery. He chuckled, "I know what keeps a soul strong, Kevin. And I know enough to see it plummet as soon as the things that made them stronger...that makes them safe...desecrate. You don't truly love your parents as you think you do. You do not care for the Order, your friends, or those you call allies. You want them to make you feel good...give you faith, sanctuary, and a purpose...since you cannot do all that on your own. They don't depend on you. You depend on them. You do! I've seen your type. The self-pitying squire ambitious to prove himself to the world...but ends up doing it for nothing. Especially a squire from false prosperity. You had the power to stop your true nature, but you chose not to. You gladly accepted it. Quite surprisingly. Now, all you must do is to embrace it. Let it fester...in that broken head of yours."

Placing his right hand on his chest, he said, "I, on the other hand, aim to give you a new soul. It's what I do. A soul with no modicum of your nature, but one where it could...cooperate in creating a sound world. A good world...without stupid mistakes like this. But...go ahead, redeem yourself for nothing. That's okay. I'm coming for the others as well. And...for the Axis Mundi...once I get one of the scepters. I don't care which."

Before he took off, leaving me hopeless, he said, "It's a shame. Loving family you had. Lovely home they have here too. It highlights...love that has yet to be fulfilled. The thing about the truth...is that it's upsetting. But you come to accept it, knowing that you cannot escape it. When I became an emperor of Hell....it made sense to me. No one gives demons much credit. Angels only pamper you for lofty false hopes...blinding you.... while demons tell the truth of who you are. Perhaps you should come to accept that this world, and the world you had, don't quite accept people like you anymore. God has truly left and cursed you and your family. I mean...look at the world you came from. They've abandoned the values of the God...you still serve somehow. And from what it looks like...it seems like you have too. Not that I blame you, for God has failed when he made humans. Their essence. Their humanity. What did he expect when humanity turned their back on his son? Exactly. If this'll make you feel any better, join them in the Void." He looked deeply into my tearful eyes and made sure that I was one hundred percent focused on his darkening eyes and said, "My words will flourish....my reign will thrive. And when my legends are heeded...our new heaven...will survive. We will survive. And you will too when you allow us to reshape your soul. Until we meet again, Kevin Princeton." He strayed away from my eyes and looked down at the mug. He suddenly tossed it across the room, spreading the beverage across the floor. I jolted to the shattered sounds that pierced into my being.

As he took off, he whistled to himself. I recognized the tune, which I came to realize that he used it in a mockingly jest. *'Suddenly, there's a valley...where hope and love begin.'* I was so frantic to shout for Kelley. I wanted to roar out. Tell her to run and find somewhere safe. But I was so overwhelmed with everything. To the point where I almost felt nothing but purgatorial numbness.

"You should've known what you've signed up for when you joined this war." Sathanus said. "Now...you'll know the pain warriors feel. You'll know the price for redemption, boy. You will."

"It is...what it is...my child. No one really heals...unless you submit to the hand that feeds you. You cannot escape your nature or the nature of others. You can only change them." The woman said as she held the violin and began to play. It was the same macabre tone that controlled the priestesses. And now I was a victim to it. The music played until I found myself drowsing once again. My mind and body both ending as I descended. I laid sideways and watched with blurry eyes two soldiers armed with rifles.

"Search for his sister. The pest should be here somewhere. We'll feed their corpses to crows...right after I do the mother in." Those were the last faint words I heard from Sathanus. And that moment when my body was turned, facing the floor, and I felt myself being hardened and pinned onto the cold wooden floor. That feeling of being pinned crawled back into my spine and made me feel even more powerless.

My head felt as if it were being clawed with sharped fingers engraving into my scalp. My arms and legs pinned harshly on the floor. I was too exhausted, poisoned, and numb to comprehend even fully what was happening to me. I glanced at my mother's corpse being pinned down on the floor...with Sathanus going on top of her. It was what I saw before I slowly dozed to blackness.

Mum. Dad. Kelley. I failed you once again. And I'm sorry. I'm so...so sorry.

Soon after, I gasped for air and found myself concealed in something dark. It felt rusty, dirty, and uncomfortably tight. There was only one little hole on my right aligned with where my right eye was. I looked out and saw only tall grains. It felt overwhelmingly hot like being in a sauna. I tried all I can to make certain movements, but I was really confined in whatever box I was concealed in. I saw that I was half naked and strapped from my clothing and my weapons. My wrists felt naked without my blades. Everything I had was gone and nowhere to be seen. Physically, I felt very sick. Not to mention very sore. Especially my arms, legs, and backside. Especially my backside. In fact, darkened bruises were printed on my arms and legs. My entire energy drenched from me.

"Help me! Somebody please! Help me!! Get me out of here!!" I shouted as I stomped my feet against the crate. I bellowed from my throat, "HELP ME!! SOMEBODY! PLEASE!!"

"No one is coming to save you!" That voice. It came back to invade me. *"Not after what you did!"* When he said that, more of them joined alongside:

"Look at what you've done! Look at what you DID!!"

"You killed them all! You did this! This was worse than the school shooting!"

"You did this! This is all your fault!"

"AAAAAAAAAAHHHHHHH!!" I screamed on the top of my lungs, desperately crying out to escape from this infernal ridicule. I continued and continued only to come to the fact that all I heard was the sound of my own voice. No one was surely coming to save me from this confinement. The only thing I saw through that hole was grass.

And that was about it. When all seemed lost, my head banged the ceiling. Again, and again, I bashed my head onto the oak top of the coffin. I barged constantly and saw the sight of my own fluid imprinted on the wood. It grew and grew with every tireless barge. I felt the blood slowly curving around my eyes and down pass my lips. I tasted the bitter warm runny after it was streaking down my face.

After I was diligently screaming and banging, I knew what I had to do. And knowing that my mind was finally in my favor, I triggered back to my Blessed Eye. I had to find somebody to get me out of here. And I knew whom as well.

"T...Ted...Julie...et...! H...Help me! P...Pl...Please! I.... I don't know...where I am! Please save me!" I frantically shuddered after I spoke through my mind, hoping they felt my need for them in their intuitions. After I was done, I instantly resumed back to my reality.

I prayed frantically but silently that they would receive that message. I didn't know how they would find me. I didn't know which one, but it had to be somewhere in the Promised Land. Or just Valestone. Not in Hell, for sure.

For an hour, I was still confined inside the wooden box. I felt the scorching radius enter my body and infesting into my nerves. I was completely drenched in my own sweat. I had no one around me. Not my parents. Not Kelley. Not even my friends yet. I was left alone and far from Celestia with the voices accompanying me. Roaring into my pounding temple.

There were moments where I believed that they were real. It felt as if they were physically with me now. For the first time in a while, I reluctantly came to agree with the other eight shouting ceaselessly in my mind. It was my fault. I killed my own parents and presumably left Kelley to die. I killed those villagers. With darkness concealing me – with only one little glimmer of light – I was forced to embrace those images until I came out. It felt like I was beaten all over again. It was as if Pastor Gerald and Sister Ann were shouting at me again. And at times, I heard their voices too.

"We told you to listen to your guardians! To listen! You made your choice. Save your pathetic tears!"

"You wanted to forget your sins! You wanted to forget the world! You wanted things to be normal again! It's never going to leave! Just as you will never be good! Your burdens will always follow you! You will always be sinful!"

The heat was getting so high, loud, and impaled in my mind that its inflamed brainstem like tonsils. My heart was beating relentlessly and cruelly. I start to hear a lot of other things that I didn't want to hear. The image of my dead parents festered in my head. I began to see it, and had it face me; almost like someone stapling a picture of it and having me face it.

There were instants of where I thought I heard crying. Hysterical crying was coming from all around. And I knew that it was from Kelley. She wasn't there, but her voice was! It was loud enough for me to believe that she was there!

"Why did you kill them, Kevin? Why did you tear our family apart? I thought you loved us! How could you? HOW COULD YOU??" I felt her hot angry breath splashing onto my face. Her tear cries crept into my ears.

"Kelley, my sister. My dear sister. I...I'm so sorry." I said tearfully as I led myself to slowly break into moans and sobs.

"Don't cry for us, Kevin." I heard another voice.

"M...Mother?"

"Yes, my child. We are with God. We are in peace. And we want you to join us."

"I'm...so...so... sorry for what I did to you! It...It wasn't me...it..."

"Shhh.... It's going to be okay, my child." Her voiced coddled me. *"It's going to be alright. Just come to us and we will be together."*

"But...what about my duties? My...life here?"

"They will be fulfilled by someone else. We are not wanted by the natural world. Or by the afterlife. We're not wanted anywhere anymore. You are tired and sad, my dear child. My sweet little boy. You did all you could for this world and we're proud of you. Now it is the time for you to rest. Please, come to us. Your father and I are waiting for you. We miss you. Just...breathe. Breathe. Breathe."

I inhaled and exhaled. Again. And again. The veins within me slowed smoothly as they were calmed.

"I will, Mum. I will...I will come to you this time. I will," I said after I breathed.

I then began to shed more tears and continued weakly, "I'm...I'm so tired. I can't take it anymore. I can't!"

"I know, my child. Don't cry. My little boy." She said.

She continued, *"Meet us in the Void...and you will be in peace. You will finally be free and safe...in the live we could have together. Believe us. We will be together...like before."*

For almost two hours, I laid inside. Hopeless and feeling un-welcomed, this is what I felt. I couldn't bear the fact that Lucifer won. I couldn't have allowed him to win. Otherwise, this would mean that I would put the entire Promised Land at risk.

My face was cover in the debris of dirt that scattered. Blood drenched the middle of my face. Tears circulated around my eyes. Sweat kept my entire body moist, scooted and sticky. My eyes felt heavy with the heat streaking inside my head.

I tried to keep myself better by humming the Mountain Lullaby. I still remembered the tune. I remembered the lyrics. But every time I would try to hum an ounce of it, I would often be pushed to tears.

I was weak. And maybe this is what the Satanists wanted. This was what Lucifer wanted. This is what the other eight voices wanted me to accept. I just wished I listened before...instead of believing that I was changing for the better. I failed to be my parents. My bloodline. I failed to return. I was a rotten deluded criminal, through and through. A spoiled child seeking love from the world. I couldn't change that. I couldn't be good.

But out of nowhere, I overheard sharp barks coming from the outside, distracting me from my thoughts. They thundered the box I was in. The barks soon became a prolonged howl. It was all muffled, but I made out the fact that it was a creature. Though the creature did sound very well known to me. I almost recognized it.

Followed by the howl, my name was being called, "Kevin! Kevin!" The voice was feminine. The other sounded, "Kevin! Kev, where are you!?"

My little interest suddenly lifted as I recognized who they were. Who could possibly be coming for me? I turned my eye to the hole and shouted on the top of my lungs, "Ted! Juliet! I'm here! I'm in here!"

"Oh, my goodness! Kevin!" I recognized Juliet's slightly broken voice. I heard footsteps gradually approaching to where I was. With only grass in my sight, I saw slight movements of it being impacted by what looked like a large brown paw.

"Quick! Help me open this, Theodore!"

"I got you! Hang in there, Kevin!" Ted told me.

As I watched the lid of the coffin being adjusted and lifted, I saw something inserting through a little crevice. It looked to be a white silver blade of some sort. Up and down, it went as it was togging and playing with the coffin door. Once the door began cracking open, a sheet of light was shooting through the crevice that began to get bigger.

With that, the door was finally lifted open, and light beamed towards my face. I got up and gasped heavily. I felt the wind passing by and my vision was very blurry. To my right, I saw my friends. I watched as Juliet unsheathed her sword, which explained how it opened. Algor quickly came to me and traversed his big tongue all over my face, which allowed me to see more clearly again. I saw that I was surrounded by a large mass of tall grass. The mountain ranges stretch further ahead with the sun peaking between.

Soon after I stroked Algor, I felt Ted and Juliet's arms lifted me up from the hellish box. They both embraced me as I embraced them back.

"We're so sorry, Kevin! We're sorry!" Juliet sobbed behind me. I felt warm droplets coming from her eyes washing down my exposed back.

"How...did you find me?"

"Algor led us here. It took us forever! We've never been to this place before!" Ted said fixating his eyes at the flat plains. Turning to me, he said, "Come, we gotta get you out of here!"

After our embrace, he placed my arm around his shoulder and was leading me to ride with them on one of their steeds. My legs ached and the joints in my feet felt yarned and caved in. Ted asked, "Can you walk?"

"It...It hurts!" I winced as every move I made etched a nerve in my ankles and my lower back.

"We're so sorry we didn't get you in time," Ted said with sincerity.

"I'll have a look at you as soon as we get back!" Juliet said as she was clearing off from her sobs. She was mounting onto her grey white spotted thoroughbred. Ted got on his red chestnut horse. With all the momentum I had, I grasped his arm to hop aboard on the black leather saddle. I wrapped my arms around his waist. On his saddle, he had a large brown bag.

"Don't worry, we recovered your stuff. They were thrown in a lake." Ted said. Once he whipped the reins, we began to gallop away from the sight.

XXXV

The Souls of the Martyrs

When we rode back for two and a half hours in silence, we reached back to the Khalservan.

I was bathed and had my wounds cleaned. My head was dressed in a bandage to heal my forehead. I was clothed in casual comfortable clothes made of loose linen. I was so hungry that I feasted upon a bowl of beans, rice, and tilapia that they had prepared for me. I didn't really say much of a word to them during those moments. So, every interior I entered was filled with silence. All I did was fixate on everything that occurred. Everything that happened was still manifesting in my head, as if it were happening again. And it was something that I just couldn't express.

I was soon in my bedroom with Ted and Juliet looking out for me. They told me that Francis and Michael were soon coming to check on me as well. And all I felt was utter guilt for letting this happened.

Juliet sat beside me on the left side of the bed while Ted sat on a chair next to her. I felt something inside my heart being grabbed and pulled. And I was almost beginning to breathe. So, I wrapped my arms around Juliet's waist, holding her close to me. I felt her arms around me. Her hands were gently placed on my head. I was almost ready to cry, but I had nothing left to cry about. Maybe they were held back. I hoped they did.

As the door creaked and quickly opened, I released myself from Juliet. I saw that it was Francis and Michael rushing inside with their eyes consumed with panic.

"Oh, thank goodness you're alright!" Francis exclaimed as he approached to me. His eyes were looking into mine as his hand was on my shoulder. He wrapped his arms around me, and I cuddled him back. "I'm so sorry, Kevin! Are you okay? Are you hurt?"

"It's...just my ankles. Juliet... took care of them." I said weakly.

"That's good." Michael said, as he checked my temperature by having his hand on my neck. When he removed it, he then took off to the door and closed it behind him. "You'll be okay."

Francis looked back at me and said, "We will let you rest, Kevin. Definitely. But if you can, tell us exactly what happened. Jesus wondered where you were and wanted to see if you were okay after Sarah left you."

I began adjusting to composing myself to speak to Francis. I tried to hold myself together before I could breakdown into pieces. After I took deep breaths, I began to speak while avoiding trembling, "I...I was doing what I was supposed to do. I was guarding the princess until...one of the Civil Forcers called for me to meet Bertha! He led me to...a place called St. John's Township."

"Okay," Francis said. "So, what happened from there? Did you see Bertha at all?"

"No...no. It was a trap!" I said. "I was sedated into a deep sleep. My energy was completely drained from me and...suddenly...I was captured by Lucifer in a carriage. He was invited...by the Angel. He was leading me to Corinthian County. And then..." I felt myself getting choked up. My eyes were watering quite quickly.

"It's okay. Take your time, Kevin." Francis said while putting his hand on my shoulder, grasping it to assure me. "Tell us what happened next, so we can find a way to help you."

"It's okay, Kevin." Michael added.

Overwhelmed, the tears managed to escape my eyes, "He...He...drugged me...with cinnabar. I wasn't...in control of myself. It felt like I was...like I was sleepwalking. But I wasn't. It felt like...like a lucid dream. In this vision, I thought that the...Satanists were slaughtering everyone and burning...the county. So, I slashed at them to save the county. At least...that's what I thought. Not only I killed...those people, but I...I killed my.... my...my own parents! My family!" I then said through sobs, "It's all my fault! It's all my fault!"

I felt overwhelmed by Juliet's embrace. I then said very weakly, "I was so powerless! I tried to fight, and I failed!" The following were just sobbing. I clutched onto Juliet as my cries were muffled. I cried, "I made a promise to come back! I made a goddamn promise! Now they're gone forever!"

Francis was reluctantly taking in my cries. Everyone did. I wept as if I were still a child. I wept as if I was still being beaten at that foster home. Nonetheless, I wept.

"Hey. Hey. Look at me, Kevin," He said softly, getting me to look into his eyes. His eyes looked just as broken as did mine. But his magnetism was enough to give a comforting smile, assuring me that everything will be alright. "Listen to me, none of this is your fault. Okay? It's not your fault. You couldn't have known. We all could have. And we will get to the bottom of this. You understand that, right? Tell me you understand. Breathe...calm yourself...and tell me."

It took me a couple of seconds to compose myself. Inhaling and exhaling rapidly. After I sniffed and slightly coughed, I said to him, "I...I...I understand."

"Good. That's good." He smiled sadly. "Now...do you know if you sister Kelley is still alive?"

Sniffing up my stale and wiping my slimy nose, I answered, "I...I don't know. The next thing I remember is Sathanus...and that woman...they used the violin on me to...knock me out. All I knew was they were planning to...capture her too. But...I think she's alive. I pray."

"How did the woman look like?" Michael asked.

"She had...white hair. Short hair...down to her neck. She wore some kind of ...black bridal headpiece with a veil and a white rose. Her dress was black and...formal."

"*Lilith.*" Francis said to Michael. So that was her name. Francis then asked, "What happened after they knocked you out?"

"The next...I was confined in a very hot box. Every part of my body felt weak and sore, as if I...I was...I don't really know much of what happened after that. In my home...I felt someone...a Satanist maybe...pinning me onto the ground. But...I don't remember anything else. All I knew was that...Ted, Juliet, and Algor got me out. But...I still felt nauseated." I said as I let out another hot breath. I left the room in silence. All eyes were gazing at one another. Juliet closed her eyes a bit. Ted bowed his head in distress and murmured to himself.

After releasing a sigh, Francis then turned to Michael and said in command, "Bring me Bertha into the Main Chapel. I want her to answer for this. And send the Angel Paladins to help the remaining villagers at Corinthian County. Tell the baron that it was all a big misunderstanding. Kevin had no intention to do what he did."

He then faced Ted and Juliet, "First thing tomorrow, I want you two to make sure you find Kelley Princeton and get her somewhere safe. Get her out of Valestone somehow. It's not safe here anymore."

"Of course. Most likely she flew away from the scene in fear." Juliet said. "But what will you do?"

"I think Michael and I need a word with Ms. June. That is if we can find her. At this point, I don't care of what the Civil Forcers or the Chancery says. This is...very bad! How the hell did Lucifer just slip under us like that?! Seems like the Angel is the most dangerous of our targets." He said, but he was still regarding his trust onto Michael.

He then looked back at me and put his left hand on my shoulder and said to me, "Hang in there, Kevin. Alright? We will resolve this. You will rest for the remaining days. But I need you to be strong. Okay?"

I nodded at him. Mostly I did it just to give him the satisfaction that I would be okay. But it was an excuse for me to cover up how incredibly scarred my heart was. I watched sadly as Michael and Francis took off.

Before they left, Michael nodded at me as he proceeded to close the door behind him.

"Do you wish to be alone, Kevin? I wouldn't want to pry." Juliet asked in sorrow.

I hesitated a bit since I didn't want to make them feel awkward or bad about my state of mind. And I wanted company, but I mostly wanted to ponder on this myself. So, I weakly said as tears carelessly drove down my face, "Yeah. Yes...I wish to be alone. Thank you very much, guys. Truly."

Juliet and Ted rose from my space and were slowly walking towards the door and ready to make an exit. Ted turned to me, with gloomy brown eyes. His eyebrows flexed downwards, "Listen, Kev...if you wanna talk...we're always around. And uh...is there something you want us to tell your sister when we see her?"

I gulped to sink more tears from my eyes. But they escaped once again. I finally said, "Just tell her...that I'm sorry. Tell her...that I tried."

After gazing at one another, Juliet said, "Okay. We will tell her. Take care, Kevin. Things will get better. We promise. I...I love you." They both left the room with sad smiles. The door clicked shut.

I was finally by myself in my own room. But all I had to think about was how bad things quickly became. What this all because I joined this war, I wondered. I knew that I have done great things for the Promised Land.

But I should've seen this entire thing coming. Yet, I didn't. I was naïve and prideful to believe that he would stay quiet and afraid after we killed Virgil and Rollo. But this just made everything else complicated. Maybe I should've helped Bertha, but I was inclined to believe that everything was fine after she helped them. But I was blinded. And now, I've allowed it to affect my family. I did it. I dragged them into a war without thinking they'd be hurt by it. Something I wanted to prevent.

I was fully convinced that Kelley didn't deserve to have a brother like me. And because of what I did, something inside me was telling me that she would resent me. I wouldn't blame her. Even more so, this would mean that The Phoenix and The Angel would presumably become more powerful than ever. All because of what I did. Kelley loved our parents the most. Especially me.

My heart was scorched. My mind was still reduced to those memories. I couldn't sleep throughout the night. I just lied down on the bed until the lights of the sun broke through the curtains. My eyes were very baggy, heated, moist and heavy. Heated and moist they were because of the tears that couldn't be held back. So, my face was left dry, course and crusty. My mind was left dry as the juices vanquished.

I was just conflicted. And both my heart and mind were leaning onto this decision. A decision that my mother herself was setting up for me. And perhaps it was true that I was never accepted by anyone or anything. I wasn't accepted in the world I was born in. Nor was I accepted in the afterlife. It seemed like every good I tried to do for those who wanted to preserve safety; it would always fall back on my face. It would result to destruction. I failed as a son, a friend and as a man.

This prompted me to finally reveal myself from the covers to get back on my two feet onto the hardened oak floor. But then I had very quick images of what I've witnessed and what I felt. The unwanted illusion of Sathanus attempting to force himself in my mother's corpse made me skid and rush to the sliver bucket in the corner as I emptied my stomach.

The bile came roughly from my mouth like a faucet. After wiping my mouth, I then stood up and limped over to my desk, ignoring the pain I felt, and grasped at my notebook; one of my sister's Christmas gifts.

Pulling up and adjusting the chair, I sat with my pointed knees underneath the desk. I proceeded to open the book, curled my fingers onto a white quill, dipped it into an ink jar and began to write down whatever came to my head. And I wrote in hopes for anyone, including Ted or Juliet, to understand and to accept the fact that I caused what happened to happened. I hoped that they would understand that they were better off without me.

I wrote down about how I was sorry for existing. I felt as though that everything that I sought would eventually collapse. And I believed that when I am gone from this life, it wouldn't be any different at all. I knew that I shouldn't have dragged myself into the war.

God has left me once again, when I was on the great verge of giving him a second chance. Only to realize that he was truly gone.

Soon after I finished writing what came to my mind, I tore it from the book and placed it flat on the desk. I reached for my box of chocolate cigarettes and a tiny box of matches from the corner of the desk. Soon, I rose from my chair and proceeded to stray away from my room, closing the door behind me until I was back in the empty gothic halls.

Despite my aching pain, I walked down right until I managed to go back down to the main room. From there, I exited to go and find the stables to retrieve Aventurine. Turning right, I reached around the courtyard until I reached the open stables. There, I found Aventurine. His black pelt and structure were still intact and looked to be healed after getting wounded.

Upon waking him up, despite his snorts and whines, I managed to get him up before I could saddle him. Hopping onto him, I managed to keep my balance as we turned to get away from the Khalservan. Aventurine walked fine as I rode him. I appreciated the caretakers for doing their duties. I was called to stop by the guards as soon as I trotted, but I refused and didn't listen. *"Mr. Princeton! Mr. Princeton! Stop! Mr. Bailey said that you need rest! Mr. Princeton!"* I heard them call from the distance but ignored them.

I went further and further away until I descended into the forest. The more I rode, the more I grasps the sound of the skies thundering. Soon, I was feeling the moist drops coming from above. Regardless of the leaves being tossed around by the chivalrous winds, I still felt, as it was a way to make fun of my state of mind. Either that, or I was taken back to how I died. I felt everything coming back to me when I galloped Aventurine across the leaf and twig infested grounds. Flies buzzed around my ears as I aggressively swayed my hands to push them away.

It took me twenty minutes to approach towards the exit of the forest. It revealed a steep cliff overlooking the mountain ranges and other group of forestations. The Promised Land was surely a fine and vast place. It was too bad that I couldn't make it worth living in it. I dismounted from Aventurine and analyzed my cold environment. When I saw how wide it looked, I was too invested. All I thought about was going to my parents and leaving all this hurt behind. All I thought was going to the mist I saw in front. Perhaps then, I would be saved from sin by being one with the mist. One with the wind.

I coldly told Aventurine to disperse so he wouldn't stay there. When I was intending to reach the edge of the rocky structure that was before me, I heard snorts and the whizzing from him.

It was one of the last things I wanted to hear. I rapidly turned to him and shouted, "I said go, stupid, bloody animal! GO!" When he saw me point my finger, he sadly left and began to dematerialize from my sight. I busted out a sigh from my guts and bowed my head in shame.

I then turned around and began to go up to the tip. The mountains were masked with heavy packs of clouds that were under a gloomy blue firmament. As soon as I felt the wind blow through my hair, I knew then that I was closer to the clouds. I looked down and was briefly stunned to how deep it was. If my calculations were correct (which was most likely not), it looked to be at least ninety feet down into whatever abyss it would lead me.

My hands reached into both of my pockets and pulled out my box of cigarettes and matchbox. I only needed one of each. So as soon as I had one brown cigarette in between my pink lips, I lazily threw the rest of them off the cliff. I then scratched the match until little fire sparked. This got the cigarette to burn, which prompted me to inhale its smolders and blowing it to join with the clouds.

Though the chocolate flavor wasn't enough to lift me up internally. I threw away the burnt match. And I just began to inhale the smolders, intending to corrupt myself. I ignored the tears streaming down my face, the soft rain drizzling and continued. I inhaled the smolder for a good while. Every time I proceeded; I remember how warm it felt. I remembered how bad it smelled. But it was sensational. And it helped coped with the falling shards of water.

"You should've done this a long time ago." One of the voices expressed. *"At least you know better now. No one will ever accept you nor your failed legacy. God has left you. Accept it."*

After the rain washed off the tears, I stared blankly at the clouds and mountain ranges. And what better way to go than to smoke? Now I knew that I was done for. I was in my own mind now, trying my best to block out everything that surrounded me. The songs from the birds. The leaves blowing. The bugs creaking about. This urge to be one with nature. Becoming a knight. Accepting my true nature. I've managed to block all of them.

And the voice of my father appeared. *"Join us in the Void, kiddo. Accept that this world won't accept you. You tried. And I'm very proud of you."*

"I will join you, father." I said as I stood on my two feet. I was slowly reaching to the rocky edge. I was hesitant because I never thought I would die that way. But then I remembered how horrifically I was shot as a human. I felt every piece of lead enter and fogged the inside of my body. So, jumping off wouldn't be any different. "I will join you," I repeated.

I flicked the cigarette from my fingertips as I watched it glide down the side of the cliff until it disappeared into the fog. I closed my eyes and kept the darkness to myself. I intended to ignore all my surroundings so the pain would be nonexistent. I closed everything to finally be with them both.

The Lord giveth and the Lord taketh. He might as well take mine again. He takes. And never gives.

"Kevin, stop! Don't you do it! Don't you dare do this," I heard a voice. It wasn't in my head. It was outside of my sacred temple. I peeled my eyes and gradually turned only to meet with three people who couldn't let me go. I saw Ted, Juliet and Francis getting off their mounts. All three of them attempted to get closer to me. Distraught and concern was riddled in their expressions. From afar and through the showers, I saw water in Juliet's eyes.

"You don't have to do this, Kev. We can solve this together!" Ted said. "We can resolve this!"

I scoffed and said after, "I figured you saw the note. What is there to resolve?"

"We'll talk! Dialogue! You don't have to take your own life!" Ted said. "When you are confident enough, we can talk!"

"Listen to Ted, Kevin! We're here for you! I know your heart is still scarred from what happened! But we can't let you do this!" Francis said. He was getting close. But he hesitated as soon as I was having my right heel over the edge.

"Why? Don't I have the free will to do it? Aren't we *ghosts*?"

I then turned my back on them, facing the mountains. "What's the point of living this life...trying to be better...if the horrors in my mind never allow me? What's the point of doing all of this...if I keep making mistakes? I failed. I failed the Order. I failed Kelley. My family. I...failed myself. I thought that I could...make this life better. I was willing to give it a chance. But...it's all the same. This is the end...and my only chance to outrun it."

"This isn't the end, Kevin. You can still make it better!" Juliet said choked up. "You were poisoned by Lucifer. It wasn't your fault! He wants you to do this! Don't you understand? Please look at us! Please! For the sake of Anu, Kevin! You have a sister!"

When I turned to her, I said, "I do understand, Juliet. I understand that he was right. I'm...doomed to change. I'm irredeemable. It's clear that I will never be accepted. Good people will always suffer. And evil people...well, it seems like they will always thrive with ease. No matter how much I fight it. And...that's something that I must accept. I was never meant for Heaven. And no one will care. People never do. I died before and nobody gave a shit! I might as well die again! This is what they want! This is what they push me to do!"

"Who cares about other people?! Why do you care so much about what everyone else thinks?! We care about you! Your sister cares about you! That's all that should matter. Live life for yourself, not everybody! Tell us about your past, anything, and we wouldn't treat you any different, Kevin! I swear it! Please, you don't have to do this! We could help you," Juliet said weakly with tears hastily running down her face.

"Help me? Juliet, I've been deceived many times by those who thought they knew me based on lies! I've been deceived by God again! This constant abuse on my kindness made me into something I'm not! And I'll never be the same ever again because of it! And I'll never get the life I wanted!" I cried.

"Everyone gets deceived, Kev! Bad things always happen to those who are good and sincere. And it always will. It sucks, but it is what it is. But that don't mean you have to put up with them. It's just what some people are because they're broken, and they set out to break others to feel comfortable with their shitty lives! And we ain't responsible for what they do to us or themselves! But think about your sister! She's still alive in this life!" Ted said reassuring. "All you have to do is be there for her!"

"She hates me, Ted! She does! I know it." I said coldly.

"How would you know that? Huh? Those voices in your head are trying to convince you that you're a failure! She knows that it wasn't your fault for killing the villagers and your parents!" Ted said.

He continued, "She knew that it wasn't your fault. She understood what was happening to you! That you were under his curse! She doesn't want you to inflict the blame on yourself!"

"It doesn't matter anymore! Okay? It doesn't! She's better off without me! You're better off without me! Everyone is."

"Kevin...if you do this, you'll give Lucifer and his flock the satisfaction!" Francis said. "We are this close to getting to the Watchers and rescuing the folks from the Inferno! And do you know why...because of you! Instead of focusing on your failures all the time, think of the good things you did! Those priestesses from Arcadia, especially Bella, would've been dead if it weren't for you! Virgil and Rollo would've gotten away with their deeds had you not exterminated them! Sarah is recovered because of you! Emily is going back to school because of you!

Mr. Douglas is confident in his alchemic work again because of you! I told you...that you were my second chance to make things right after the Twelve Apostles. After...Abraham."

"Oh.... yeah. Lucifer told me...about Abraham. How he...was a lot sinister than you made him out to be." I said. "How you accepted him...even though he had beaten his own friend!"

"Do you know why I accepted Abraham despite what he had done? Because he was a good man, not just because he was my friend! I saw it in him. He was willing to change. Abraham couldn't control himself, which was why he did what he did! And he hated himself for it! I wanted to help him deal with his anger. I wanted him to stop loathing himself. I wanted him to better himself and value who he was. I couldn't just let him to ponder on the fact that what he did was terrible...because everybody does! No matter how they mask it!" Francis almost spoke out of frustration. But then he said sadly, "He only took his afterlife because Lucifer corrupted him. He made him dwell too much on his failures. He was victimized constantly so that his soul could break! Lucifer tested him. He's testing you, Kevin."

I said nothing else. I was just eager to leap from the edge of rock formations, praying that I had a death just as painful as with my human life. I just wanted nothing more than to punish myself. Maybe then, I would find true heaven in the Void. A true afterlife.

I then said, "Hmph. All of this sounds like is all about how you feel, not about me. I understand, though. So...you could stop trying. This world...is just like the others. Hell, I don't know if it's even real. Maybe I'm...back on Earth...deemed as a loony...already forgotten."

"That's not true! This world is real! This life is real! What about those dreams you could get in this life? What about the chances you could take now?!" Juliet said.

She was getting slowly but closer to me. Her arms and hands were alerted and tense. "You're a good man driven by a pain that has to be understood. You just need to be open about it...like you were open about your love for me! Don't hide it anymore! Just tell us how we could help you thrive! Tell us how we could help you! And Francis,

Theodore and I are saying these things because you are important to us. Not just as an Apostle, but as a man! A man! The love you have for your family always lifts us! You made a difference for these people we've helped! And you still can! You could still make a heaven in your life! And we will help you! We owe that to you! To your sister and your parents! We're truly sorry that they died...but that doesn't mean that you should! So, please...please...don't jump!"

I felt a light slowly awakening in my mutilated heart. I looked outward deeply, silently questioning what would happen if I were in the Void. All I thought about how this was a chance for escape. An escape from life's systems, laws, conflicts, and its romanticism of seeing me in pain. But then I thought how it would not only be a disservice to those I love or came to love, but a disservice to myself.

"Kevin, please...don't do this...," Juliet said whilst she suddenly stood and shivered. After she hyperventilated, she suddenly sobbed grimly and quietly behind her hands. My heart sunk and weighed when I saw her that way.

I watched her break down, frightened and defenseless, as if I truly did matter to her somehow. It was frightening in a way, since I knew about some of the men she had to deal with. Yet, I stood out to her...in terms of love. I watched as Francis stroked her back in a gentle manner, which led to him wrapping his arms around her. Her face sunk into his chest as he held her tight to soothe her.

"Look at Juliet, Kev. She loves you very much. She's crying like this because you're her first true love. The person who truly understood her and helped her love herself," Ted said as he looked at me.

He continued, "You gotta have a strong soul, no matter what. Think about those who do care about you, who want the best for you. Not those who don't. Not the world. You have a sister. And right now, she needs her brother. I hate to break it to you. Sometimes, we can't escape our past nor recreate what we wanted it to be! But we can be better than those things. We could grow to make a life we can have now. That's how you could honor your parents! Honor them in name!"

After he said that, I suddenly felt my eyes slowly filled with tears.

Releasing Juliet, Francis then added softly, "Please, Kevin. I'm already haunted by what happened to Abraham, my home realm, and my wife. Those I lost. The friends I lost. I'm haunted every day. I don't wish for this to be the case for you too. We never gave up on you. And whether you know it or not, God never gave up on you. Please ...don't give up on us. Don't give up this new life he has given you. He gave you this life. It's real. And I promise we will make it work. I swear! Please, give us a chance!"

I looked back at the cloudy highlands whilst overhearing Juliet relentlessly crying her eyes out. My eyes still felt warm with water welling within my eyelids that soon escaped. Ted then said, "Let me ask you this, Kev; if this is what you really want to do, ask yourself this first; do you want to go through life gripping on what it could've been? Or do you want to see what this new life can be?"

I really thought about what he asked. I really did. And he was very right. I couldn't do it. I couldn't kill myself. I couldn't leave them. Not my friends. Not Kelley. Especially her. I was her brother. I had to make it right for her. I had to live for her. I had to make it right for myself. And I couldn't cut this new life short. For once, I had to see a reason beyond what I wanted from it.

Thus, I got away from the edge and stormed down to embrace Juliet in my arms. I felt her embracing me too. My eyes were shut closed as I felt warm tears coming down my face alongside the rain. "I'm so sorry! Please don't cry for me," I wept. I soothed her wet wooly jacket, calming her.

We both stared at each other with tears in our eyes. We continued to embrace one another. I grasped the sloppy inhales of Juliet's running nose by my right ear. With her red eyes closed, she locked her forehead onto mine.

My wet eyes closed. I continued to embrace her in my arms as she embraced me.

XXXVI

Irons Sharpens Iron

Once I was back at the Khalservan, all I did was rest and get dried. There was a chance that I was still terribly affected by the toxin Lucifer put inside me to sedate me into becoming his mindless weapon. I pondered in bed, wondering if my powers would soon come back to me. I recollected what I had done in the evening. I was still baffled by how I intended to do the same method as Ted and Abraham did to themselves.

Later in the evening, Bailey was kind enough as always to check upon me. His face was wrinkly than ever. And because of everything that has happened recently, I didn't blame him. His eyes gazed at me, displaying comfort as he asked, "How are you feeling?"

"I'm...getting there, I suppose." I said as I briefly glanced at the loaf of bread and grapes on my desk that Juliet gave to me in kindness. She even gave me the same toxin she gave me before.

I then turned to him, "Juliet offered me something just to fill my stomach."

"Yes, I see that." He said gazing around the room. Briefly gazing at my desk, he said, "That's very dear of her." He then smiled at me and said, "I'm very pleased that she cares deeply for you. And it's wonderful that you're together. Aside of her hardened nature, Juliet has always showed sensitive kindness...even towards some who don't deserve it."

"That's true." I said humbly. "Did you...get any word from...Ms. June?"

"Yes. She said that she didn't order that Civil Force Detective to fetch you. She claimed that he had gone rogue. She offers condolences to you for your family. So, she is leaving the city for now to investigate at the county."

"Right." I said after letting out a sigh. I didn't really care for what she was going to do. But I did appreciate her for the condolences.

"And Ted told me to tell you that...your sister is safe. She's with...my daughter Johanna. She'll be looking after her in the Happy Hunting Grounds." Francis said.

"That's good to hear," I said humbly and very relieved. "Thank you so much."

"It's no problem. I'll let you know about her." He then said after a quick pause, "I know this may be a bad time to disrupt...but I was hoping to talk with you a bit?"

"Of course." I said. "Come in."

"Thank you, Kevin." Francis said. He welcomed himself into my room whilst heading for my desk. From there, he grabbed hold of my wooden chair and place it right next to me. He was on my right side of the bed. He sat with his hands clammed together as he began to let out a sigh.

"What is there to talk about?" I asked curiously.

"I wanted to give you more...of a clear explanation of why I had people like you and Abraham in the Order. I believe I wasn't too in depth...as I would have hoped." He said. He then eyed at me and spoke, "You know, it would've been much easier to just...reject Abraham and completely have him out of our lives. To completely disregard him from our Order. It wouldn't be the first time either."

"What do you mean by that, exactly?"

"You see ...this entire war – if you could call it one – between us and Lucifer all began with a disagreement between him and Queen Mary.

He was her royal protector at the time." Francis said. "They had different ideas...of how they wanted to help the souls of humanity. They had different visions for the afterlife. Mary was moved by her son's actions on Earth and thus believed that souls could be lifted and inspired to elevate through experiencing the life of a spirit. You know why humans are considered as God's most favored creatures? He loves everything, of course. But he loved the essence of human nature because your kind is the first species to have the ability to create and destroy in an endless cycle. It's a unique species that has a duality of nearly everything. He embraced the notion of souls being developed. Because he knew that no one else could ever get to his level. And...it's for the best. He wanted the humans to experience their lives and to expand in another. He embraced excellence in which humans often strive to achieve greatness in every decade. Lucifer didn't take that kindly. He believed that we could get to that level of God. He wanted spirits to...be superior to God. All it would take was to remove their natures. Not to strive through life and find great and unknown aspects of it, but to serve beliefs not made by the gods themselves, but man who feel above nature. That was his notion of creating universal peace. This led to him to lead this... mutiny against us. Conducting a bloody massive rebellion with half of the fallen Angelic Paladins. He became very unethical...which was why he was exiled to Hell."

"And...how did Jesus feel about that?"

"Regretful actually. He was bitter towards the Chancery. He was not king at the time it happened, for he only wanted to serve as messiah and husband. But he and Lucifer were very close before I came to Heaven. He wanted to have Lucifer compromise in good terms without resulting to a war. But..."

"It did anyway."

"Right," He said in reluctance. "So...why am I telling you this, you are wondering. Well, it's because it has relevance to why I had men like Abraham in the Order. It's because I still saw good in him. He showed me, breaking down in tears for repentance. I usually don't quote it much, but in Proverbs 27:17, it reads.... iron sharpens iron, and one man sharpens another. I chose to build him to lift his soul. I couldn't just break him. You see, I was inspired by Jesus's view on people. His love for everyone, whether good or bad, is not just a romanticized one. Although there are elements of it. His love means to understand. Just as forgiveness. His acceptance for others for their imperfections that brings out who they are and what makes every individual special. Especially those who seek guidance to discover their own potential in life...without being burdened by their past or to falter to the same evils as their enemies."

"With all due respect, I'm not sure what does this have to do with me."

Letting out his breath in the air, he then said, "A lot of them are corrupted badly because of their past. That has the tendency to bring out the worse from them. Some enemies we have are troubled by their past. But they aren't willing to be better. Nor to seek help...even when it is offered. They use their own troubles as an excuse to destroy every-thing else. But for those who are, he never hesitated. Remember one of the Apostle guidelines I told you? One of our most prominent?"

After I pondered and thought further back, I realized that it was a while since I remembered. But I suddenly had it come back to me. Thus, I answered, "Love the dark, praise the light."

"Exactly. I'm glad you remembered." He smiled. "We acknowledge that we are deficient. And a lot of us come from very rotten up-bringings. But that shouldn't mean that we should feel bad for them. They shaped us to be who we are now. And sometimes, it shapes us into being not only good people, but better ones. Just like what Ted said today in a professional way. We can never forget our past. We can never forget what we've witnessed; whether it was getting involved in a traumatic event...or a crime we ourselves committed. These are memories that stick with us forever. We shouldn't be let down by these burdens. Instead, we can be better than them. We shouldn't be broken down and become consumed with them. We shouldn't carry shame or hurt. We should be built up and enthused to do just."

"What about the Satanists? Do you think they can be redeemed...despite what they are?"

He pondered on it, trying what he can to avoid contradicting himself, since it seemed hard to see them as human. "The Satanists...they...they believe that they are already saved. They're saved through Lucifer. That's the problem. They praise and celebrate a broken creed. They're monsters made to look as if they are human. But they were sorely made to be monsters. It's in their nature to win against everyone so they themselves can prevail. They hate themselves and allow Lucifer to play into their dignity. He encourages self-hatred just so they could devote their broken poise to him. He has no care for them whatsoever. They don't even care for one another. It pains me deeply to end them, given how they were built. But again, we didn't ask to be dragged into their war. They must conform...because they are afraid of living on their own, knowing that they will be beaten down for acting as folks with minds of their own. So, they feel safe when he leads them. They chose to commit those actions all in his name after being delivered. But...I believe...he himself could change. I want to believe that a least one of them can be good. I'm quite sure there are. But they get murdered right away for disobeying Lucifer's twisted laws. It depends on him to remember why he was loved in the first place. Why he was valued. It's between him and his god, I suppose."

"I'm not sure. He was sure as hell giddy when he used me to..." I wanted to shout out for what he did. But I restrained myself. So, I decided to let out my breath.

"When you told us that.... the good people will always suffer while evil people will thrive, I believe that's the idea of any life, Kevin. It's free will. Those who choose to justify their sins live easily. They're the ones who bury their heads in the sand and prefer to be given everything without taking actions. They want to live in complete bliss, just so they wouldn't have to face hardship. They always settle for less because they are afraid of taking risks. But they are the unhappiest...because they had nothing fulfilled. They lay on their beds as they contemplate and woe over their regrets of what they could've done. Those who are good, however, suffer because they knew that if they wanted to live, they had to accept nature's true face. Yet, they're often the most content. The ones who look back on their lives, as they lay on their beds and smile. They were happy for having something to live for. The darkness we endure makes us brighter. And although bad things should ideally never happen to good people, it always does anyway. But it makes us into better individuals. Suffering, to them, is an opportunity for everlasting growth."

After breathing, he continued, "Lucifer saw you do something good. And thus, he wanted to make you fail so he could succeed. That's what enemies tend to do. They bully us into failure so they themselves can conquer. You nearly gave them the satisfaction when you intended to kill yourself. But...I'm glad you thought it through. It shows that despite your broken heart, you indeed have a strong soul. Stronger than he could ever have."

"All thanks to you. So...why exactly are you telling me this?" I wondered.

"The other deal you gave me...I feel that hiding this truth from Ted and Juliet is hurting you because you don't wish to be rejected. Especially Juliet." Francis admitted humbly but in a firm matter. "But this is who you were, Kevin. Your past built you this way. But that doesn't mean that you shouldn't be ashamed of it. Ted spoke about his. So, did Juliet. And they aren't ashamed. Our past and burdens shape us. Look at the scars on your face...when you were attacked. Scars show us what we have been through. And they heal slowly and overtime, they stick with you."

I then slowly stroked my face as my fingertips touched the smooth strikes that were covered by dried skin.

"These scars may be ugly. Coarse. But that doesn't mean we should be ashamed. It means that we can embrace them, learn from them and grow." Francis spoke. "And when we learn from our upbringing, we can be free to become greater. It's the only way we can let them go and leave them behind from the place you once knew."

I let out a sigh of reluctance because I knew what he was already going to ask of me. I then asked just to be sure, "What do you suppose I do? Tell them that I'm a criminal? Tell Juliet I slept with a prostitute and murdered her soon after?"

"Just tell them the truth. Think about it. You've grown to them. Therefore, you should feel comfortable about telling them. I know it's hard. But if you tell them who you really were, why you joined the Apostles in the first place, you will be set free from these burdens. They will understand, for they are still learning to accept their faults."

My heart began beating after all the assumptions that traversed my mind. I didn't know what to think of it. But I felt from being tense to slowly calm as I felt his hand grasping my right. I looked up at his sudden gloom demeaner.

"I know how it feels to...to wanting to know true answers about life. Becoming what others expect you to be to validate themselves...since they can't do that on their own, I know that pressure too. My father and mother pressured me...all my life...to follow their ways to be truly accepted by God. To dishonor them meant that I dishonored God. They disowned my older sister for...wanting to seek and understand every-thing beyond what they taught. Her and I were ostracized for being who we were. I forgive them though. You have no idea how blessed you are to have such an understanding and loving family, Kevin. I'd killed to have that. And I'm sure a lot of children feel the same. But I want you to know this; just because they are not always here with you, does not mean that you are alone. They're in here," His right finger pointed at my chest before removing it. "You're still here. Your sister too. You carry their principles and extract them in life, just as I did when my home was gone. It's the only reason why I even made this Order. To remind people like you... that you are not alone. Remind them of their better selves. Their angelic selves, something this world is afraid of now. So, in case you've felt any pressure of being here, I'm sorry...if I ever pressured you. I...I just thought to make it known. I'm very sorry. I should've been there to help those villagers...and your family. I...I failed. I feel foolish not knowing."

"It's...alright. It's okay. You couldn't have known about what happened. You had to consult with the blokes at the Happy Hunting Grounds. And as for me becoming a knight, you just wanted to help me. You got me out of that cell. You saw something in me...that I refused to see in myself. I guess...I was desperate to think that I could...be free. To change a world, revive a life I never got to have. I identified...with the knights and you. I know how it feels to...feel as if what you do is never good enough for anyone. Lucifer...was right."

I turned to a concerned Francis and said, "I did hate myself. I hated myself for not being as brave as my father and ancestor nor spiritual as my mother. I hated not being a good brother. I hated not being good enough for God. I hated myself for having these hallucinations. These episodes. This infernal sickness. I caved in...and became a bloody criminal! And...I thought that if I became an Apostle, I...I would be saved to be perfect. I thought I would do what I couldn't do as a human. Perfected since I hated who I am. But it won't make any change. I mean...look at me. Look at...us. We're cavaliers...in an age that doesn't want us around anymore."

After pondering on my words, he spoke, "I understand. But...that's not how it works. Even guardians weren't perfect. You cannot expect things to change vastly, even with your actions. Not everyone will serve God as the guardians did. And that is fine. You cannot expect to be completely sound. Because it's the laws of nature. I value you, Kevin. You're an empath yearning to see the good in everything, despite nature's truth. Most think that their evils are good, believing that they could change nature through coercion and molding every being they see. Someone like a knight or dame, however, embraces nature. Works with it. A true guardian accepts the flaws of others. Including his. I'm very glad you value and honor your parents and bloodline. You could honor and love them, because they are a part of you, but...don't be like them. Be *yourself*...and find your faith to fulfill your life. Take what they taught you and forge *your* path. I know that we as guardians are obliged to protect others. But in terms of giving them what they want, you don't owe them anything....to make you feel as if you're not good enough.

You're good enough to those who believe you are. Most importantly, you are good enough for God. You're not in life to be someone's possession or champion. You're in life for yourself and whatever world you choose to make. Some folks have an intent to make you hate yourself. They get off to it. Never surrender to that kind of behavior. You understand?"

I sighed and said, "I...I guess. Thank you...very much. But...what about The Phoenix and The Angel?"

"Don't worry about them. Your mission is to take care of yourself. The Phoenix and The Angel will be dealt with accordingly. Especially the Angel. Michael is interrogating Bertha today just as yesterday." He said. After he sat silently a bit, observing my room, he suddenly turned to me, "I...I just want to let you know...that we're here for you. You are a bright, good, and loving young man, even if you don't see that. I admire your wisdom...and your courage to make a difference. And I don't wish for any evil to take that spirit away from you. Or to corrupt you. I may not be as good as your father or mother. But...I will always be there for you. I owe that to them. And I owe that to you...for allowing me to help you. Even if you didn't have to."

"Thank you, Francis." I said with a clogged throat as I felt the urge to embrace him as he embraced me back. After a good minute, he stood back and leaned back on his chair. I noticed how moist his eyes sockets were as he quickly wiped his face and sniffed a bit.

"Very well, I should let you rest. I will see you again." Francis said standing from the chair and putting it back where he got it. "I'm going to meet with Mr. Bacon tomorrow to have the dragonflies tested and flown. And I must travel again to the Happy Hunting Grounds to see if the herbs will be traded to the herbalists."

"Do you think by then we should get the Phoenix and the Angel? Once they are found?"

"Most definitely. But I don't wish for you to worry. All I ask is for you to heal. You went through enough." He humbly said with a soft smile. As soon as he finally reached the door, he turned to me before leaving, "You're a great Apostle, Kevin. A good spirit. A good descendant. And most importantly, a good brother. You're more angelic than you think.

I implore you to never forget that. There's not much to prove...only for you to know that."

"I'll try. I promise. Thank you, Francis." I smiled softly back at him. As he nodded, he finally closed the door on the way out of my room.

I leaned back against my pillow and pondered. Most of the atmosphere was taken it by the mildly loud snorts and snores coming from Algor. I looked down and saw how curled and deep asleep he was. I continued to ponder and recall everything Francis told me. I even had another thought to apologize to poor Aventurine after I enforced my anger on him. I hoped that he was well fed and would soon forget about me shouting at him.

And soon, I found my eyelids getting heavy and my mind slowly going to rest. My body felt as if it were dead. So, I decided to join along and rest my head on the fluffy pillow. I hoped that I could heal properly so I could help my friends get to the Watchers and to save the people from Hell. Soon, I would make martyrs of those who supported Lucifer and what he strived for.

When my eyes closed, I drifted into my consciousness and silently prayed for everything to be forgotten, including my intended suicide. I prayed for things to get better.

The next day, I got back to exploring the Khalservan. I wished I were feeling better as soon as I can so I could continue to be a bodyguard for Lady Sarah. Not to mention that I was always bored of it. I was always bored without Ted or Juliet. I felt bored and nauseous still.

During the quarter of the day, I continued to play catch with Algor outside of the castle. I needed to keep myself a bit active. After letting Algor off, I began to look over the mountains and I couldn't stop myself from thinking what just happened yesterday. The cloaked mountain peaks were sustaining the skepticism and engaging me with an ethereal expression. The mountains were dense and far out of range, yet I remained my focus on the hairy horned brute that happily handed me over the tree branch I threw.

Later, Algor and I visited the stables within the castle's walls. I was hoping to meet with Aventurine to see if he was okay and not hurt. I saw within the stable that the white maned stallion was eating out from the tin bucket. His eyes lit up as soon as he took notice of Algor and I. It was good to see him treated well. And to always see him healthy. I came to him and stroked onto his snout. Upon hearing his snort, I then embraced him in my arms and apologized to him in silence. My ears caught his snorts vibrating through his woolly neck.

Soon after my departure, I was inside in the Khalservan and having the time of my life to myself in the Common Room. I sat across the blazing fireplace and continued to be overwhelmed by what has happened. I watched the embers take off up to the chimney as the flame blazed and silently cracked. From letting go of these burdens to letting my parents be in peace, there was something within me that was strangely shifting as I was thinking. It wasn't a bad feeling, but it seemed neutral. In fact, it was almost relieving.

All I had to do was to tell my friends the truth. I had to show that I was not perfect. I had to show that I was refusing to move on from a world I didn't get. This was something I must accomplish. And I was somewhat grateful for Francis for suggesting me that. I was just not sure how to do so. And I was just a bit scared. I felt my right leg quiver and shook.

Suddenly, my ears caught the noise of boots slowly creaking through the halls. A group of them were being sounded. I turned around to see a group of people coming into the room. Ted and Juliet were inside, but alongside with surprising guests; Emily, Frask and Sarah. Both Frask and Sarah were astonished by every inch of the interior. Emily wore a white cloak with floral design. And Sarah wore a blue and white dress.

"Oh, hi Kevin." Frask said with a smile. He quickly came to me with open arms and lifted me off from the ground. I hugged him back.

"Ha! It's good to see you too, Frask!"

"I know! It's been a while!" Frask then turned to Ted and Juliet after letting me go. "Ted was just bringing me here for the first time. So...this is where all the magic happens. Literally."

"Yes." I said. I then saw the Lady coming towards me and hugging me tightly. I hugged her back.

"Kevin, I'm so sorry." She said almost tearfully. Then she began examining my state. "Are you alright? This is all my fault. I've shouldn't have..."

"No no...it's quite alright, Sarah. It's not your fault. I'm the one who should be sorry."

"No! This is my doing! I should've known there was something fishy about that guard!" Sarah said shamefully. "I didn't know he was an imposter."

"It's fine. Really." I then saw Emily approaching and hugging me. I hugged her back.

"I never thought I would see you again, Kevin."

"It's good to see you too, Emily. And I like your new cloak."

"Thank you." She said with a cheerful smile. "Lady Sarah has gotten me to be a part of her entourage after my studies in the school!"

"She's loving the school very much, now!" Sarah said.

"That's very brilliant, Emily. I'm very proud of you." I said with a smile. "You worked very hard for that...so you deserve every award."

"All thanks to you, Ted and Juliet. I do not wish to know what I would do without you." She said as she wrapped her arms around me once again. I softly began to stroke her and embrace her.

"You're very welcome, lass." After I said that, she let me go. I got around to get away from the heat of the fireplace.

"I don't know if you heard." Frask joined in. "But...Roger Bacon...out of all alchemists...is going to build upon my dragonfly projects! Isn't that amazing!?"

"It is." I said as I was trying to be enthusiastic without letting the burdens overwhelm me.

"How are you feeling," Juliet asked me.

I let out a sigh and said, "I'm fine. It's just that...I'm trying to get myself together, that's all."

"Ted and Juliet...they told us what happened," Frask said. His voice sobered from his usual optimism. "You saw Lucifer. Didn't you?"

I turned to both Ted and Juliet, almost glaring at them for trying to involve the three of them into what I almost did.

"Look, Kevin...we got them here to give you a sense of closure and comfort. I know you've always felt alone. But..." Juliet said.

"Look, I appreciate it, guys! I do! But you didn't need to do that! I don't want everyone else to know!" I nearly yelped. "I thought we're not supposed to bring others to the Khalservan! Emily, I understand. But Frask and Lady Sarah?"

"It's fine, man! Francis asked us to do so before he went off to see Roger Bacon and to get to the Happy Hunting Grounds." Ted said with a reassuring gesture.

"What don't you want us to know, Kevin," Emily asked.

"Lucifer had him kidnapped and..." Sarah couldn't finish. She nearly gagged from what she was trying to say. I had begun to be nervous. "...he made him slaughter most of the county folk, including...his parents."

"I'm...so sorry, Kevin." Frask said humbly. "It must have been horrible. That's...really unfortunate."

"Aye, it was. But...there's nothing I could do about it now other than to get to those bloody Watchers of his!"

"No! Not until you've rested!" Juliet said sternly.

"I don't need rest, Juliet! I'm tired of resting! I don't need special treatment every day!" I said almost in frustration. "I'm tired of letting others suffer or die because of my damn mistakes! And these three shouldn't be dragged into this!" I then turned to face the fireplace.

"But it wasn't your fault! We've talked about this! When will you get that...instead of trying to be stoic, self-loathing or tough?" Juliet asked in frustration.

"Until I finally right my wrongs for once!" I said.

"Because that worked so well last time, right?!" She retorted. I sharply turned to her and paced myself to her personal space. I was starting to have heat burning for what she shouldn't have said.

"What are you trying to say? Huh? That I wanted to kill my parents and those people? Is that what you're saying, Juliet?"

"No..." Juliet let out along with a sigh. "I didn't mean that. I'm...I'm just saying that you need to stop putting burdens on yourself and think of others for a change!"

"But I have! I've tried! And yet, I make mistakes constantly! And I get belittled! Only I deserve it!"

"Because you won't let them go! You won't accept that you've made mistakes like everyone else! That's your problem! And you thought by taking your own life...it would solve your problems!" Juliet yelled towards me. "We want you to care for yourself and for you to feel better! We brought Emily, Sarah, and Frask to give you support...no one else! So be goddamn thankful that we had you in consideration as above other things, including them!" Juliet then let out a sigh. She looked down with her hands locked on her hips. I felt stunned and almost petrified.

But then she stood back and pondered gloomily, as if she regretted what she said.

"You were trying to...kill yourself," Emily asked as she turned to me with eyes full of disbelief and sadness. "Why in the great heavens would you try to do that to yourself? Don't you know how important you are to those who love you? Who want nothing but the best for you?"

"Not when I suddenly muck things up and they turn on me, like everybody else! It doesn't concern you, Emily. It's done! You wouldn't know! And you shouldn't!" I said, still boiling from the inside.

"Hey...she already knows about the Apostles. So, does Frask and Sarah! We're friends here, Kev!" Ted said in a humble but strict tone. "We need to stick together and act as one."

"Like the Satanists, right," I asked without thinking. It just came out from my mouth.

"Horseshit! You know what I mean, Kev! I mean that we gotta show consideration for one another, not to hold each other back because of our personal burdens! You need to chill, dammit! Realize that not everyone is against you! Stop that bullshit!"

"Guys...guys...please..." Sarah implored to keep the room at ease until the only noise was the ticking coming from the clock in the right corner of the room.

Sarah then faced me and asked very humbly, "Kevin, what don't you want us to know? Just...tell us. Please."

After I pondered and let out hot air from my mouth, I felt like I was prepared to give my reasons. But I was sure that it would be disorganized. I then said, "I was trying to kill myself...because I felt the burden of losing my parents again. I always felt like a monster who can't do anything right. No matter how hard I try."

"A monster?" Frask asked with concern. "What could you possibly think of yourself as monstrous? Lucifer is the true monster! You did great things for the Promised Land, Kevin. This was just an unfortunate accident that happened too quickly. You weren't in control of that. Don't be too quick to beat yourself up."

"It's not that simple to feel content with yourself. I haven't...always done great things, Frask. And I was always enforced to face them." I said. "When I was a human...I was six years old...when my family died as humans. They were shot...right in front of me...by a shooter in school. We were a happy family. A wealthy family. But being a family was sorely richer and fulfilling than wealth. I never really had true friends because of how the press portrayed my father. They wanted to stop us, using news outlets and newspapers as weapons. Making a narrative to condemn my father just because of the mistakes of my grandfather who was mayor. But we had to stick together and to never let anything tear us apart. That was why I wanted to help make his campaign a reality. So...my family were the only people in the world I could trust. I owed them that for what they did for us. They gave me a reason to embrace the world, despite what it was. But...when they died, I...I felt lost without them. I couldn't let them go. It got to the point where I couldn't even go back to school without having to pass out or have these sporadic psychotic episodes or...to cry, shout or just...break apart. My father's friend, Father Harris...a pastor.... he kept me in his care with my family's inheritance. I was homeschooled by him. Despite feeling hurt, he was giving me hope in the world. He was trying to teach me...to see the best in everything, no matter what. He taught me to have faith in God. He was the only reason why I still had to believe in a hopeful life, even without my family."

After I coughed a bit, I continued, "It was only five years later when he sent me off to this foster home to deal with his work. A Catholic foster care for orphaned children that my father helped financially before he died. He couldn't let me stay with my step-uncle...since he rejected me. He had business as a chaplain for the army. He was called to help. So...he made me stay there. At first, I thought it was a good place. I felt homesick, sure. But I was trying to maintain myself. It wasn't long when I came to realize...that the place was hell. I felt betrayed...when Harris never came back. Even if I was prevented from making contact, I hoped for him to save me. He was the only one left I trusted in the world. I considered him a part of the family. These two clergies would beat me constantly. Audite custodes tui is what they told me every day. It was something to remember. They wanted me to be pure...in God's image. The God they made to scare me into hating myself. They said that they would help me cure my illness...but it only destroyed me. They abused me and mocked me for the family I came from. And these voices...were enhanced because of it," I said pointing towards my temple.

"One night...I snuck out from the kitchen window...with all I needed to survive in the streets of New York. I ran away and disappeared for thirteen years. I was under the wing of a bloke named Snake. He was my only friend. Perhaps, I was a fool to trust him, given how I lost all hope in people, but he showed me that I could. Not only he taught me how to fight or to use my environment... he showed me more of what the world really was. How...deceitful, condescending, and fraudulent people can be. Soon, I abandoned God. I abandoned the idea of making a perfect world. I scammed and robbed. Instead of bettering the world or making a life within it, we had to escape it. We wanted to escape, but we had to get money. Along the way, I killed to extract my hatred for humanity. I killed a prostitute named Talia Greyhill. I went back to the foster home with Snake. And we slaughtered the faculty of the place, neither aware nor caring for the crying children. I murdered the two clergies who wronged me out of vengeance. Stabbed them both to death. So, we killed eleven people in total...while most of them lived. And a couple of weeks later, Snake got me to get some money from my family inheritance to pay off one of our rivals to make peace. I saw Harris again...after thirteen years. We...we had an argument about everything. He threatened to call the police after the crimes I've committed. And it...ended with me...punching him until he gave me the money." I felt the tears filling up my eyes. And my voice was starting to choke up.

"I just took the money...without any consideration for him. Not only I lost my family, my home. Now, I lost my friend. Another unwanted sacrifice made to escape civilization. The next day...Snake and I got arrested and were sent to a federal penitentiary. They were going to send me to a psychiatric ward...after discovering that I was...I was...mentally ill."

I then swallowed and began to talk normally. And I noticed how silent and petrified they were to hear all of this for the first time.

"Harris came and stopped by to tell me that...he was leaving to Chicago. He...felt like he did a bad job...being my guardian. And...I didn't forgive him since I felt betrayed. Several weeks later, Snake busted the both of us out thanks to a riot that broke out. We were chased all through the city until we reached Ramapo Mountains, that's where my family and I used to camp most summers. Both of us planned to run away to Iceland; just to hide and...live in peace without...people somehow. But the police got to us...and they shot me down."

Afterwards, I let out a sigh and finally said, "I know you're thinking Kevin, you're a monster! You're an irredeemable creature of the night! But this is who I was! And I loathe myself every day for it. I just pray that it shows why I...I wasn't too eager to talk about it. I don't ask for empathy nor pity, just...for you to know."

I saw concern in their eyes, especially Juliet's. My heart sank, and I felt my insides tremble and stutter. I was truly hoping that they would understand.

"You went through a lot, Kev! That's...that's rough. I'm sorry to...hear about all that." Ted said humbly.

"I'm...so sorry, Kevin. I really am. It...it makes sense now. But...do you know if...this girl...Talia is in the afterlife now?" Juliet asked, gloom overwhelming her tone.

"I dunno, if I'm honest with you." I said. "I believe so. If I ever do meet her, I would...apologize for what I've done to her. That is if she is willing to forgive me. I won't be burdened if she doesn't,"

"Man has inflicted so much pain on you. And it forced you to do evil acts." Emily said.

"No, man didn't do it, Emily. I did this...to myself. I should've been better than what man's laws wanted me to be. I failed to stand out because I lost faith in...in everything; God, people...myself. I joined this Order...to be saved. But the nightmares I had, and the voices, they wouldn't let me move on. It's as if they want me to embrace my faults and make me feel worse than I already do. When I think I could escape them, they come back. I... I just ...I've said too much, Emily." I sighed.

"It's fine now, Kevin." Sarah joined. "Your soul was very broken before. But you have been lifted. Don't you realize this?"

"I never realized it. Sometimes...it's hard to tell. My soul was broken many times I've lost count. It's hard to let go of pain." I admitted.

"But you have, Kev. Seems like I ain't the only one hidin' scars." Ted snickered a bit. "The world most of us came from makes us do fucked up things. Francis told me that it could do that to a person. But that doesn't mean that we are doomed to change. I don't know about you...but I'm a firm believer in redemption. Redeeming yourself is one of the healthiest things that you could do. Accepting your mistakes is what makes you human, not avoiding them or forcin' them out. And look here, man...you ain't the only one. I fucked up when I was an Astral Ghoul Boy after I died. And I fucked up for committing suicide; for hurting the *one* who cared for me the most through hard times. We've all lived the bright and dark side of being human."

He then faced the other fellows and asked Frask in particular, "Frask...you might have done things you weren't proud of."

"I did actually." He then sighed and said in a regretful tone, "Before I ascended to Jeremiah, I died in a car accident because I was in a fight with my brother Brian on the phone. I died before he did. It's very petty. And pathetic as hell. But the fight was over...a girl that we both liked. But she became my girlfriend soon after and...Brian got jealous. We haven't talked since. He's somewhere in Heaven now. But if I can ever see him again, I would totally want to make amends with him. That is...if he is willing to do the same."

Ted then asked Juliet, "Juliet...I'm sure you messed up on a whole lot."

"I was possibly irrational when I decked Lustina's face...after how she treated the priestesses. It felt good, but now that I thought about it...I felt like it was wrong. I know she wouldn't care to listen. She never did. But if I had dialogue and I was stern with her, perhaps she would take that in some semblance of consideration. I was too fueled with anger when she mocked them. I've always had trouble trusting others, opening my heart. I've bottled up my emotions and it destructs me. But...I try to be better at being hopeful and welcoming. I try to be calm and wise, even though it's not easy to forgive your enemies. I can't help my angst sometimes."

"Emily." He then asked her.

"Well...I know it was wrong for me to hide out in here instead of going back to school. But ever since I went back, I did things that I never thought that I would do. And because of the dedication I've put in my studies, I'm now a part of the Lady's entourage. I'll become a good inspiration to those who always feel as if they cannot reach their greatness."

Then Sarah spoke out, "I never said that I was perfect. As a child, I always wanted to be like my father and my grandmother. To be in their image. But...it only made me dismiss my uniqueness in favor of being targeted."

Sarah then turned to me with tears in her eyes and said, "It was my fault for leaving you, Kevin. I should've been more watchful of that guard. And I shouldn't have gone far. I just...I just wanted to remember what made this place so grand without having to think about this war all the time. I hope you could understand and forgive me."

"I...I do understand. It's not your fault, Sarah." I said humbly.

As I saw her wiped her eyes before the tears could commence, I said, "But I'm thankful that you've said that."

"What does this tell you, Kevin? Sure, some of these are petty. But they are still mistakes." Ted continued. "At one point in our lives, or afterlives, we've all had our souls crushed and torn from us. We all have the tendency to just... give up. We get irrational when that happens. We get crazy to where we don't have a proper way to channel it. So, what can we do? Well, we can own what we did. We must look at our upbringings. But the most important thing to do...is to let go of those burdens and move on. To do great things. It's easy to let it get to ya and carry it until you die or live a miserable person. That's what our enemies want from us. Either to fail or to become a part of their hive mind of misery. Despite how different our sufferings were, they're still considered as pains. And they brought us together. Because what we went through...what all of us went through...no matter how petty or traumatic...we can rise above it. We can prove them wrong. We could show them that we won't be followers because we will become leaders. Shepherds, not sheep. We'll always be the head and not the tail. We have to be leaders of our own legions."

Soon, he turned to me and said, "You were too focused on being saved. It's not a bad thing, but your problem was fearing failure. You feared doing wrong based on your past. And it's bad for your nature. Being an Apostle is not at all about being perfect. It's about owning our scars because it's who we are. Instead of worrying about being perfect, be adventurous. Instead of seeking gratitude from the whole world, be grateful for those who do. Instead of avoiding or trying to escape life, work through it and make it into your best portrait. Instead of hating yourself, love yourself. Having those ideas in mind don't make you self-ish because you have nothing to prove yourself. You have nothing to ask for...because you have it already. You're on a journey. And it ain't always clean. But that don't mean that you should give up on it. That

Kevin you spoke of...ain't the Kevin I fought and connected with these past few months. What happened...don't define you no more."

After I absorbed Ted's encouraging words, I began to ponder.

Perhaps there was more to redeeming myself. It was more than just being saved, remaking glory days or being absolved from sin. It was an ongoing odyssey for growth within an endless cycle of life's laws. I had to accept that my journey to my divine self would be slow and messy.

Perhaps there was a true reason why I was unintentionally blessed with an eternal life. Or to end up in Heaven. And I should not take that, nor the afterlife, for granted. I did that before. I needed to do what I couldn't before. And I had that chance to do so with the life I have.

I was slowly coming to understand that the afterlife was not a place to go back to how things were. It cannot revive everything. It was a place to go forward. I had to move on from what I couldn't have to make a future of what it could be. I loved my parents. But I'm not them. And I was sure that they wouldn't want me to be like them. They wouldn't want me to go through this life burdened by what I couldn't have.

"Theodore is right. You are not alone in this journey for the stars, Kevin," Juliet said as she then got to the cabinet next to the father clock and fetched a bottle of wine and a steel cup. The others got an extra cup as well. Pouring down the wine to quench our thirsts, she then offered a full cup for me. "We're all in this with you. We just have to be strong together."

"Aye. We must. We have to." I said as both of our cups clinked against one another's.

XXXVII

Third Time's A Charm

Eleven Weeks Later...

The wetlands behind the Khalservan were lit with the powerful arms of the sun. The leaves were bloomed by it. They were yellow when it was captured. Other sounds were crickets chirping in the grass, the birds crying on the branches of the trees, and the cries, wails and snorts from other unknown wildlife heard from afar. I felt moist in my ankles since both of my feet were intact on the ground. I crouched within the tall green reeds that were populating across the grounds. I felt Algor's hot breath breathing against my face.

I had my bow and arrow prepared, stalking whatever creature I can find. This was the sport I decided to do after I rested for days. Specially to help the chefs to cook. To be a smart and calculative Apostle, I had to practice my stealth. And when Ted and Juliet were residing at Tamashii No Ketsu Taba to get the Phoenix for one month and a half, I spent a partial of each early misty morning, stalking, hiding, and contemplating. Despite the annoying flies and mosquitoes buzzing near my ears, I had to remain my focus.

I analyzed my surroundings, recalling my intense training from last year. I recalled my place here with Juliet. I remembered when she showed me the mechanics of the gauntlets. I remembered how she helped me train with the bow. And it was fair to say that over the months, I've grown accustomed to it.

A roar suddenly slightly caught me off guard. Algor crouched and growled silently. The steam forced itself out of his mouth.

"I know, lad. I see him." I assured the brute with a whisper. My eyes caught a strange animal that was six meters away from where I was. The pelt was red with brown stripes. It had the body of a stag, but four of its legs were a hybrid of vultures. Its head looked to be replaced with what could be some reptilian creature. It had a round scaly structure with blue eyes and a decent sized snout. It had pointed ears on each corner of its head.

Like a raptor, it croaked and squealed. It was drinking alone by the river, which was my luck. I looked back at Algor, giving him a stare of warning. I got him to listen to each command. If the creature were to run, I would have to use him to my advantage to get him.

I turned back to the creature and paced myself as quietly as I could. I stopped immediately as it was alerted by the water being toggled by my movements. I waited for it to remain its focus on its beverage, feasting its tongue on swamp water. My hand still grasped to the bow with my right fingers togged on the string. Soon, it got bored of looking out and decided to drink again. Unaware of our presence, it was. And it was good for us.

As soon as it was focusing and drinking, I slowly rose and summoned the arrow between my fingers. I pulled back until the arrow's crest was near my cheek. I steadied the point at the neck of the animal, maintaining my balance and keeping it still.

Quickly, I began to breath in and out, so I could be able to remain calculative and collected in mind. Once I was done, my eyes sharply opened, and I suppressed the arrow to fly across the tall grass. Quickly, I saw the arrow impale into the creature's neck. The sight of it being impaled into his muscle startled it and he stammered away from the river and fled back into the woods.

This prompted Algor and I to sprint. My eyes never left the

creature's current state. I watched as it was still running sporadically. It even began to wail in such a way that it's cry would reach into your heart and tear it out. It was clinging to its afterlife by its sounds. And it was so scared and helpless to where it even picked up its own pace.

I whistled for Algor to go ahead of me. I watched as he ran on all four, swaying and tossing the swampy water aside. I watched as Algor finally confronted the creature and clawed all his teeth into the creature's neck. Wrestling it, the creature was still clinging on for dear life. It cried hysterically like a child. Soon after a few seconds, the creature was down with blood trickling down from the wound Algor left on it.

I approached to get a good look at the creature. The blue eyes were in fear and terror. I didn't know what to make of it. When I practiced, all I was thinking about were the Satanists. I didn't see it as just a mere strange animal. Algor came by and stood next to me, looking over the creature struggling along with prolonged wailing.

I ejected the two blades from my left Apostle gauntlet and kneeled in front of the dying creature. I looked into his eyes and saw how much he was suffering with this continued blood loss. I didn't want it to die painfully. I placed my mindset to rest to give the creature a proper offering. I felt awful, for the creature didn't do anything aside of just living.

I impaled my blades slowly to stop it from struggling. My entire hand was moist with its blood. I looked back at the creature and saw how its eyes stopped dilating. It became shallow and hollow. It was still blue, but not pure as it was before. I whistled for Aventurine to materialize by my side.

"I'm so sorry, mate." I said to make myself feel better. And for it to travel with the creature. An innocent but valuable creature.

I began to undo a knife from my scabbard to severe the limbs of the creature to bring to the chefs. I yanked off the joints as I removed the limbs. The strings of meat yarned with blood as I pulled. Next, I slid the blade across the torso and proceeded to remove its internal organs as more blood began to seep out.

I promised them that I'd help, despite the condition I had and my recovery. Francis told me that victims like me would recover from three to four months. But I wasn't going to let what happened – or what might have happened – stop me from saving those from having the same fate. I grasped from the times I finished meditating; I was seeing more of what I was; more than just a sketch artist. More than just a son. I was a *fighter* because I never gave up. Because I kept going after I fell. Because I would do anything to protect those I love. All what was left was to fight against the *right* enemies; especially given how I saw that the only way to escape the war I got myself into was to see it through. No matter how long it would take.

This is what I reflected on as I hunted: the balance. The burdens, this addiction to escape and the hatred I had towards myself were keeping me off it. Although it was generally never easy to be balanced when life consecutively tests you.

After I severed its legs and neck, I placed them all in sacks that were dangling from Aventurine's saddle. The peg snorted dynamically when I placed each piece of meat in the hanging potato sacks, now soaked with blood.

Suddenly, another cry was heard from afar. I was very far from where I was that the only way, I could track it was to follow where it came from. It was soon followed by a group of grunts; all of them were coming from the right.

"Come on, Al!" I said as I mounted on Aventurine and galloped along the path to follow the voice. I went and wrestled my way through every standing bark, stomped across every twig and fallen branch to save someone who was clearly in distress.

Soon after I reached to the plains of the wetlands, I saw where the noise was exactly coming from. It turned out to be a man. He looked to be stripped from his armor, which could mean that he was one of the guards. I nearly vomited when I saw his intestines being toggled, mutilated, and roasted by a group of vultures. These vultures wore brown and white feathers. I dismounted from my steed to find a way to scare those demonic birds somehow.

Algor barked to catch their attention, but they weren't listening. They were fixated on the organs of the poor fellow. I unleashed my pistol from my shoulder holster and suppressed the fire towards the sky. They were scared off by the pistol's echo. Sheathing it, I quickly approached to the guard. I saw that his arms and legs were impaled with hardened metal nails. His face was riddled and drenched with stripes of blood coming down from his forehead and his soaked blonde hair.

I removed each nail from his body part despite him yelling out to express his pain. I got on my knees to look at him in the eyes. His eyes were cloudy with a sharp spark of light, meaning that he was dying.

"Who did this to you?"

"The...the.... Satanists...are..."

"The Satanists? Why...who summoned them?"

"Please...do not...be deceived...by her!" He said whilst violently coughing blood.

"Her? Who do you mean, lad?! Who's her? The Angel?"

"Don't...let...her..." His face instantly became pale. The light in his eyes diminished and became hollow.

"Dammit!!" I yelped. I looked back at the man. With care, I gently closed both of his eyelids. "Rest in the Void, dear sir."

I stood up to begin my short investigation. I examined the other bodies, which wore the same outfits as the man I just saw. A lot of them were mangled with their organs exposed. The blood that was leaving the pile and colliding with the streaming river implied that their bodies were still fresh. The torture was recent. Their hands and feet had the same results and wounds.

Soon after my investigation, I called out for the guards to help me bring their bodies back to the dungeon of the Main Chapel. I needed a clear examination. And I knew that someone like Juliet would be very good at it, given how she was a surgeon. It was a good thing her and Ted came back.

"Hm...yes, these are just recent." Juliet said as she analyzed and gazed over the pale bodies on the wooden table, which was in the dungeon. "It seemed like...this happened earlier." Juliet gazed at me, Ted, Francis, and Michael. "It seems that they didn't simply have their intestines plucked out. The ruptures of their torsos, it seemed like the Satanists did it themselves. They opened their stomachs as bait for the vultures."

"What were you doing out in the wetlands, Kevin?" Michael turned to me.

"I was hunting with Algor and Aventurine to give to the chefs. I heard shouting and...it came from him." I said, pointing at the poor corpse.

"Wait! Oh God! These are guards from the Main Chapel!" Francis exclaimed softly. "And you are sure that this was the work done by the Satanists?"

"Apparently. He told me not to be deceived by *her*?" I said. But suddenly, a thought just came to my head. I instantly asked, "Do you think that...the Angel...did this to them? Or someone working with him?"

"It could be." Ted said. "We were able to get and place the Phoenix under arrest, by the way."

"Turned out it was Oji Masayoshi from Tamashii No Ketsu Taba." Juliet added. "But you'd figure we would see the Phoenix with the Angel. In the city or any other."

I suddenly was taken by surprise by the monk walking down the stairs and entering the room. "Mr. Bailey! You are needed upstairs."

"Why for?" Francis asked, stepping in front of us.

"It's the Queen, Holy Spirit. She wishes to see you! It's urgent!"

With no hesitation, Francis took off upstairs. And thus, we all followed just for curiosity. It was very unusual for the Queen to come to the Khalservan, being how it was an independent base of operations.

Finally, out from the underground of the castle, we were at the large doors of the castle. There, Mary was indeed there alongside the other guards who held halberds. She wore a red cloak with white underneath. Her silver jewel crown was still intact. She turned to us with her eyes full of what looked like fear and a bit of confusion. In her hands was some sort of large dark red book.

"Mary, what happened?" Francis asked.

"Jesus's scepter.... it's been stolen!" She said frighteningly. "And Sarah and Mr. Douglas are gone!"

My eyes widened as well as the others. Francis then asked, "What?! Are...are you sure?"

"I speak truly, Francis. And the guards who were meant to guard the scepter went missing. And I made sure that Sarah was stay put in the castle! After Jesus's sermon, they went missing! So, I tried what I can to find her! I sent out every guard and Civil Forcer! And...I discovered something in the ledger."

She hurriedly opened it in panic. "Look here!"

Francis came to overlook and fixate at the page the queen opened. He squinted in question and asked, "What in the heavens are these markings?"

"I do not recall these markings in the ledger. Look at how many noble houses of Heaven were supposed to be next for the Satanists to hunt. They could be responsible for the stolen scepter and Sarah and Mr. Douglas's confinement!" Mary said as she then presented us the page. I was stunned to see a bunch of names. And it took me back to how this all spiraled and where it could eventually end up. It showed a long list of noble houses that were circled and checked off.

"Three of the forty-five kingdoms are next. Freka of Aaru, Adrian of Elysium and Shaolin of Takamagahara." Mary said. "It implies that someone was using this to format a plan for Lucifer...to send agents to steal the scepters. Specifically, from the Covenant of the Gods. And look here..." She pointed. "Only few of them from each house were granted freedom from Hell to become so-called puppet rulers; Virgil, Rollo..."

"Yet, no one from Celestia was freed. This is strange." Michael said.

"Sarah was almost sold by someone from this kingdom. Virgil sold the priestesses and other mystics from Arcadia. And Rollo sold as well from Valhalla. But no noble was free. What does it mean?"

"Look... Oji Masayoshi Chara is the Phoenix! He was freed as well." Juliet said as she pointed at his name. "It's the son of Shaolin! When we captured him, we rescued his little sister Ojo Li Chara, the princess. He was trying to exchange his own sister for the scepter to Lilith. He intended to sail to the Axis Mundi."

"It's a good thing we stopped his ass!" Ted said. "But the problem is...who the Angel is. Seems like he's left."

"Your Majesty, do you recall letting someone borrow the ledger?" Michael asked whilst facing her.

"I never let anyone use it!" Mary said almost defensively. "I always have it locked in our chambers. The strange thing is that there was no sign of a break in. I've had every noble and soldier interrogated within the castle yet again! The Satanists must have appeared and reappeared behind my back!" Afterwards, she slammed the book closed in frustration and held it. The book closing echoed the gothic halls. "I feel like we're getting nowhere to the bottom of this conspiracy! It's spiraling constantly with all this betrayal! And Sarah has been stolen from us again! If anything happens to her, God forbid..."

"Don't worry, Your Majesty. We will solve this." I said humbly, trying to calm her nerves. "We will get Sarah and Frask back. And the scepter."

She let out a big sigh and said, "Thank you, Kevin." After she patted my shoulder, she then said afterwards, "Jesus is rounding up the Civil Forcers and Paladins to search through the city. I know it is farfetched, but I believe that we should work more closely with Ms. Bertha June. And her forces."

Ted then asked, "Are...Are you sure, Your Majesty?"

"The herbalists of Goliath's Bay have yet to create the toxins and the soldiers are locking down the Main Chapel to protect the temple from being entered." Mary said.

She continued, "We have no other choice, I'm afraid. Our best guards disappeared from their tasks."

"I suppose you mean the guards who were guarding the scepter. They were found...dead," Francis said gloomily.

"Wait...how? What happened? How do you know this?" Mary asked.

"Kevin stumbled in the wetlands and saw them. They had their intestines and other organs fatally plucked out by vultures. It's a terrible sight." Francis informed. "One of them told Kevin not to be deceived by her."

"The Angel. They could mean...her. Or him," Mary echoed the word weakly. She was becoming pale.

She then said in panic, "I don't know! I don't know anymore! This would mean that he is closer than we were led to believe. We have no choice but to seek Bertha. Somehow, I think it's Lilith who's the Angel. She has to be!"

"Let's pray not! Let's just hope we could find Bertha fast. Despite her acts and fits, she could be our last chance to retrieve what we lost. Especially in Corinthian County." Francis then faced Ted and Juliet, "You'll need to go to the Civil Force Department and look for Bertha."

"We will." Juliet said. Francis then eyed at me and said out of nowhere, "That is...if Kevin truly feels ready. It's up to you. There is no shame if you wish to rest."

With no hesitation and a bit of faith within me, I said, "Let me go fetch my stuff. And my hat."

We later rode in a carriage to the police station. And on a side note, it felt good to wear my traditional Apostle gear once again.

The Civil Force Department happened to be on another district in Celestia known as Paul's Grove. The carriage driver led us to the small district that was connected to the main avenue of Celestia, which I soon came to know as Branch of Hope. It was a two-way street and obviously different from the other districts in the city. At the middle of the road was a large stone sculpture of a bearded man garbed in a robe holding a book close to his chest and holding a sword up in the air. The roads were still populated by the carriages. At this point, it was nothing new. I've seen worse roads in New York to get used to the hustled city. And the roads were consumed with Civil Forcers and Paladins storming through and checking every building in the neighborhood.

When I turned to see Ted's face, I sensed skepticism on his face as he looked out of the window when the carriage was still moving.

Once we finally stopped in front of the building, presumably to be the Department, I thanked the driver. At least I knew that I had Ted and Juliet with me in case I do something irrational or act unprofessional. I never thought that I would come to a day when I need to visit the police. The building was mildly big and rectangular with pointed towers and seven levels. Walking up the stairs, we met two guards who allowed us to pass despite us being Apostles. Supposedly since we didn't bother to tell them. Or they knew that the queen pardoned us.

Once inside, I couldn't help but get flashbacks about how I was placed in prison. The only difference is that they were fashionably dressed in the same armor the two angels wore – who happened to chase me when first got here. They were heavy, but not so much. A lot of them zigzagged throughout, perhaps investigating Sarah's kidnapping. They were even interrogating several noblemen and women in small rooms.

We stated our business to find Bertha to one of the Civil Forcers. By her voice, this gave me the notice that she was not willing to answer. It was an elderly woman. But a very well-built woman. She gazed at us with stern amber eyes surrounded by her soppy and slightly moist face.

"Ms. June is not here today. She is at the Isles of Ghai to investigate. So, I wouldn't stop by her office if I were you. Let us handle this matter!"

Of course, she wasn't here. Why would she be? And of course, the well-built stingy woman wasn't going to allow us. After all, we were self-righteous vigilantes to them. So, on our way, we quickly formulated a plan to break in into her office. I didn't exactly want to be caught picking the lock, even though it was right to interrogate as an Apostle.

We traversed through the cold interiors of the station until we stumbled into the bathroom in the hallway, hoping it would be big enough for my friends and I to huddle. We didn't want them to witness our power, especially Theodore's. And this was the only way to get answers since the Civil Forcers weren't going to allow it.

Ted summoned the portal into a shadowy cloaked office. Thus, we went through, hoping that this would be her office. After the portal closed, we examined and analyzed the place. It was stuffed with shelves on each corner. We found ourselves standing behind her desk. And like any office that belonged to the police, the shelves and drawers were scattered, scrambled and messy with papers and other potential evidence. Though, it was a nicely crafted office full of antiquity.

"We need to be quick, so they won't get any ideas." Juliet warned.

Without backing out, I searched through her desk. Restlessly, I wrestled and placed down files upon files. Ted and Juliet both looked at the shelves and drawers. I focused back on the files and skimmed through them, hoping to find something relevant. There were files about the priestesses, which could mean that she was trying what she could to resolve what happened.

Juliet skimmed through every shelf and opened every book, which was most likely irrelevant. Ted did the same. And it was getting tiring.

For a few good minutes, we've searched and analyzed. And so far, they were irrelevant. A lot of the files we collected and skimmed through revolved around petty to important criminal felonies, mostly committed by residents of St. John's Township. Yet, there was nothing regarding the Satanists.

But I came across something that made me stop. I pulled out a list of what looked to be names and illustrations. Underneath were apparently Civil Force Detectives who were investigating villages and in charge of the caravan. John Tillerson, Emily Downes and Richard Owens were the three that worked with Bertha apparently. I recognized them, for they were the ones who jumped me in St. John's Township. One illustration looked very familiar: a middle-aged man with brown damp hair. It looked to be the same Civil Forcer (or Watcher undercover) who strayed me from Sarah. It turned out that he was named Reginald Era. They were also Watchers with aliases such as The Wolf or The Nightingale.

Then below was another list. It listed all the villages; from Bartholomew County to Leviticus Epicenter to Corinthian County, there were marked with the letter *x* next to each individual village in Valestone. The only one that was checked off was Corinthian County. And I was estranged to know why it was in one of Bertha's files.

I turned around and continued to observe. My brain was starting to conjure veins in my temple. I read that the purpose was to find the Holy Insignia's true power, which was in a form of a crystal shard hidden within one of the villages. And Corinthian County turned out to have it. My mind began to severely analyze everything as the jigsaw puzzle pieces were coming together. I thought about all the times Bertha has urged me to work with her in stopping the village burnings. Perhaps to destroy the damn crystal shard.

Though, Ted soon came to me with a paper that looked to be recently crumpled.

"Kev, I could be wrong, but it's seems like it's a letter to you. From your dad...but it looks like he wasn't finished." Ted said as he handed me the note. I placed the file on my side and began to briefly read what it had to say;

Kevin,

This is your father! If you happen to get this by some miracle, please listen to me. Whatever you do, do not trust her! She will deceive you and plans to use you against us! She has brought Lucifer. Works with him. Whatever you do, do not trust....

The letter father attempted to write stopped. I'm not sure who he was talking about at the time, but I saw that the date was when I murdered him. I knew this because of how he hinted at the fact that this woman was using me against them. If only I understood what he wanted to tell me.

"Wait, what's that," Juliet asked as she came and pointed at a small beige envelope that apparently was next to my right foot. I looked very carefully and slightly recognized the wax seal's shape. It resembled a circle with swirly rays surrounding it. It reminded me of the medallion worn by Virgil and Rollo. Why did Bertha have this? I wondered if she was using this as evidence.

Juliet had the envelope in her hands as I stood back on my feet to see what it would unveil. She opened and pulled out the folded paper.

"What is that, Juliet?" Ted asked.

"It's some...it's a letter." She answered as she began to unfold it. Her blue eyes became lighter and gradually adjusted in concern as soon as she read out loud;

My dear Bertha,

You have used your power well. Because of your loyalty to the Empire, we are enthralled to be in your debt and to put you in our fold. Bring the Scepter of Christ, the alchemist, and the Lady to the Isles of Ghai. I will be sure to be there to help channel the power of the Bright Star and baptize you. As thanks for your contribution to our congregation, we will award you great power and blessings to overthrow the Covenant monarchs of the Promised Land to conjure an empire under your rule by having the Legionaries to conduct a cleanse in Heaven. And soon, the entirety of the afterlife itself.

May the Bright Star Guide You to the New Heaven, my angel.

Sincerely yours,

Lilith

"My goodness!" Juliet cursed towards me.

"What happened, Juliet?" I asked.

"It's a letter...from Lilith! This...whole time...it was her! Bertha! She's the one who summoned the Satanists. She's the Angel! And now she's going to the Isles of Ghai! To Goliath's Bay! She's...She's planning an assault!"

"That's where the herbalists are! We have to go there now!" I exclaimed. "Sarah and Frask could be in danger!"

"Let's go!" Ted said, summoning the portal for us to exit. As we went through, we were back in the bathroom.

Next, we presented this to the commissioner after we apologized for breaking into her office. We gathered the evidence, which put every Civil Forcer in the office in complete shock. And those feelings of shock were justified. We told them that we will go there first to see if we could find Sarah and Frask.

As soon as we left the station, we reached the docks in hope to catch the latest ship. On the way, Juliet contacted Francis through telepathy by tapping into her Blessed Eye, asking permission for us to go after Bertha. Exiting, she claimed to us that it was okay with him. Especially since Juliet still had the horn to summon the Angel Paladins for assistance. I nearly had forgotten about that.

When we reached the docks infested with large ships, I looked far out to examine how long could we exactly travel in a matter of time.

"We're never going to make it out on one of these ships! We have to get there as fast as we can!" I exclaimed. Then a thought got to me. Aventurine. Especially since he was a peg. But the problem was how would I have Ted and Juliet fit. Aventurine had a very short spine for three people. So, I wouldn't want to sprain his back.

I turned to my friends and said, "I think I'm going to go ahead of you two! I'm going to summon Aventurine to fly me to the isles!"

"No problem, Kev! Think we should be able to get our pegs after we warn Francis!" Ted said.

Juliet then came up to me and gave me a hug. Next, she said holding my face, "Be careful! We'll be behind you!"

"Will do! I promise!" I spoke. Whistling as loudly as I could with the whistle, the blackened and white maned horse summoned from a materialized cloud of wispy smoke. It was a good thing that he had a saddle on him. It was oak-colored leathers with satchels and extra rifles holstered.

As I hopped on, on both sides of my eyes, I saw big black wings made from wispy smoke creeping from his back. My heart pounded a bit loudly as I would have never thought that I would start flying right away. As a human, I did fly on a plane once. My father even flew Kelley and I on a biplane he used to have in his home, owned by *grandfather*.

But the thought of me not only flying, but controlling the flight was nerve racking if I were honest.

But there was no time to ponder on my fears and worries. I had to get to the isles. So, as I whipped the reins, Aventurine rode and galloped to the end of the docks. What I had to do was to pretend as if I were galloping on the ground. That way, it should work for flying as well. My heart fell and stumbled as Aventurine began lifting us off from the edge of the dock.

Soon, I was finding myself gradually going up and far from the docks of Celestia. I looked down, almost hurling up by the large view of the city. The winds flew past my face like an air conditioner.

I regained my focus on the front. I saw myself flying rapidly across the large body of water on a flying horse. His large ghostly wings thrust us forward, fighting against the wind. I sunk my hat to make sure that it just didn't blow away from my head. I briefly gazed down, vastly admiring the clearness of the waters despite being very far up near the clouds. And all I had hope, as I flew on Aventurine, was to find and locate the Isles of Ghai. With any luck, I should be able to spot where I was once stranded when I first came to Heaven.

"Kevin!" The voice called. I turned my head and finally saw Ted and

Juliet each on their own pair of winged steeds. Juliet rode on Violet who had grey wings. Ted rode on Newman who had red wings. They were a bit far from where I was, but they were still flying relatively fast.

"We're nearly there! There should be a couple of islands with villages on our left! One of them Goliath's Bay" Juliet shouted behind. "You're doing great!"

"Thanks! I hope so!" I focused back on the way. So, with any sense of faith, I should be able to locate a string of islands amid the ocean.

We were passing the time flying across, until we conclusively saw what looked to be the isles. It had to be. There were twelve land masses scattered about, forming a circle of some kind. Most of them were completely forested with trees and mountains. The others were popu-lated with buildings. It was surely not a city, but I did see some form of civilization being displayed.

As we were finally coming down, two large ships caught my eyes. These two black vessels with golden sails were docked near the beach. The sails had the same Satanists emblems imprinted on them. The beach looked very crowded due to something happening. Could this be Bertha there? And hopefully Sarah was safe there.

"We'll land on one of those roofs!" Ted said as he flew past me to follow him. Juliet flew by as well.

We began to sway our companions to land on the rooftops. There was a chance that the Satanists were at a look out. Presumably, Bertha must have told Lilith and the Satanists about us coming. So, they could be alarmed the minute they saw us.

We flew down to a temple that was looking over the town. It was on top of a tall structure of rock. Once we finally landed and felt the wind ease down, we got down from our rides. I made Aventurine disburse from the roof as Ted and Juliet had theirs disburse as well. Thus, we sported our masks.

The island was beautiful. Surrounded by other landmasses, in my mind, I admired it. The streets of the settlement below us were crowded with Satanists, who looked to be threatening the good villagers into following them. They were armed. And their faces grew with black smolder. The buildings below were down a slope and below the town were a crowded beach. This had to be it.

Seeing that we were far up from the town itself, through Ted's manifested portal, we entered the floating ripple until we finally found ourselves on one rectangular rooftop. To get down to the beach, we rapidly and rapidly killed the Satanists without being spotted. Going down from rooftop to rooftop, tower to tower, it was clear that the entirety of the place was completely deserted for the Satanists to temporarily occupy.

It took us a while to get down and jump from the top to the bottom whilst swiftly killing them without alerting anyone. And it was new to see Ted use his shortbow. But as soon as we reached the boardwalk, we both hovered over the fence and landed on the hot sands. We've reached the beach. And so far, we didn't alert any of the Satanists. And thus, Lilith was bothered. At least not yet anyway.

We were confronted by a crowd. It was as if we were amid a public execution, whether as sick entertainment or for an instruction conducted by besmirched officials. And I was hoping that Bertha wasn't killed, because I wanted to be the one to do it. I pondered about the thought. All this time, I was lied to. I was manipulated. Made a fool. But not this time. She was going to pay for what she did to me. And those she has hurt.

"I fuckin' knew not to trust her! And not because she's a ginger!" Ted whispered.

"Especially how she intended to intervene in our missions. Forgive me, Theodore." Juliet said to him. "I should've known. She played all of us for fools!"

"We all could have known." I said. "I just wish I saw it coming sooner. I thought...I thought I could trust her."

Ted, Juliet, and I then began to contemplate at one another to approach the display stealthily.

There was a crowd of men, women, and children (most likely herbalists and mages) being confined and guarded exclusively by the

Satanists. They had their rifles, swords, shields and spears. Like a square, they surrounded the crowd who were facing the front of where the two large ships were anchored.

"I know you want to kill her. But before you do, we must know why she did this." Juliet warned. "Just...put her in her place somehow."

"I'll...try. I'll try." I said reluctantly but stoically. I had the urge to kill her, but Juliet was right.

"Be careful", I said to them both as they nodded at me.

Juliet and Ted separated from me to deal with the Satanists silently. They were faster than me, so it was very clear. Ted wished me luck on getting Bertha and rescuing Sarah and Frask. And plus, I had them to aid me if anything went to hell.

After I took a deep breath, letting out every breath of burdens from my heart, it was time. It was a good thing I didn't wear something too obvious, so I could be inconspicuous.

I began to walk through the gathering, making myself briefly one with the swarm. The villagers had a range of emotions and thoughts going through their heads. I was curious to what they were witnessing. But the more and more I was getting closer; a voice from the front was beginning to sound very familiar to me. It's a soft, young, and kind sounded womanly voice.

"Oh, great Morning Star of the Inferno and New Heaven, we are gathered here today...to witness the rebirth...of your greatest servant...Bertha June."

I kept gently pushing through the people as the voice was becoming more and more clearer than before. It sounded almost like Sarah.

"She has done your bidding...and thus, is ready for your eternal blessing..."

I felt like I was getting closer and closer to the voice. It wasn't long when I shortly got to the front of the crowd. I was stunned to what I was witnessing before my eyes, a ceremony.

At the end of the beach was a white marble archway built on the water. The archway was decorated with white flowers with an overwhelming amount of olive branches twisting and twirling around the arch. Beside the archway were two marble statues of angels with their arms raised. In the archway was Lilith and Bertha. Lilith was placing Bertha underneath the water that had a blood like substance in it. On the side, Sarah had a scroll in her hands as one Satanist soldier held a gun to the back of her head.

"Her greatness will shine amongst the afterlife. Her greatness will lead us...to the New Heaven that our god, Lucifer, has in store for us." Sarah reluctantly continued to read. "Lord Satan bless her and give her eternal strength...to overcome her enemies and false leaders who are fronts for harbingers."

When Bertha was finally pulled out from the water, she began breathing rapidly. Her face was wiped and coddled by Lilith who then said, "Welcome us."

Clapping and applause were sounded from where I was. My guess was that they were threatened to do so. Despite the guarded exhibition, this was my chance to get to her. I was no longer going to hesitate. I knew what I had to do. So, I raced past the crowd and was reaching for the baptism. Behind my mask, I was baring and hardening my teeth. I hardened my fists until they were rock solid.

Upon reaching to the water, I finally managed to get myself between the two women. Pushing Lilith aside with my left arm, I reserved it back to violently grab hold of Bertha's collar. I saw her hands holding onto my arm. I looked into her eyes and had my blades unleashed from my right hand. A smile curved on her moist face, which made me hardened my teeth.

"Do it." She told me. "I'll never tell you."

Hesitation was non-existent in my mind. I felt bad for not heeding much of Juliet's advice, but the red head was giving me no other choice. So, I began to lunge my blade near her throat, remembering all of what she has put me through. But a strong tingly stroke suddenly traversed across my arm. I was trying to stab her, but it seemed like my arm was held in place. I felt my entire body freeze suddenly. My beating heart was beating very slowly. I felt like it was being grasped and squished.

I gazed on my right and saw the black-haired woman playing the violin on the beach. But how was it possible? I assured that I've rested enough for me to flourish my soul.

Things got more complicated when Sarah was carried and had a pistol pointed underneath her chin by the guard.

"H...How?" I asked. "How...are you...doing this?!"

"Poor boy...a part of your soul still remains...broken." Lilith said. "You thought that you would be clear from this pain you carry? That's not how it works. It's already broken...and there's nothing you could do. Thus, I have you in my hand."

I spat at her, "Fuck you!"

She began chuckling as she then stopped playing the instrument. Finally released from its power, I let go of Bertha to regain my energy. I let out several violent coughs into the water and saw my hat leave my head.

I then saw her lift her hand. This prompted the Satanists at the beach to hold their fire against the villagers. Whimpers and gasps of despairs were expressed from afar.

Putting her hand down, she then said, "I want this to work out, Mr. Princeton. I wouldn't want to do this. I really wouldn't. But...the minute you recover and inject those blades into Ms. June's throat...is the minute the good folk here dies. As well as Jesus's precious daughter and this fellow painter here."

They left me with no other choice. I was in a dilemma. As much as I really wanted to put an end to Bertha's afterlife, I had to let her live for now. Mostly, for the sake of the herbalists, Frask and Sarah. I wouldn't be any better if I just let them die. So, I decided to focus on my breathing, slowly and steadily regaining my energy.

"Very wise decision, Mr. Princeton." Lilith said. She swayed her head to the guards. I saw them approaching me. Next, I felt both of their hands tightly grabbing on each arm, pulling me away from the water and back to the sand. All I did was face her with disdain as she glared at me. I watched as Bertha was getting herself out from the water as well.

Her black eyes glanced over to the soldier, who in response bowed. She then said, "Kill him...find his friends and do the same."

My heart sank deliberately.

"Wait..." Bertha yelped. She walked and stumbled a bit to get to Lilith's ear. The white-haired woman leaned to gain something secret from Bertha's mouth. I was puzzled yet applaud that she would let my friends and I live. But I was mostly confused on what she would be saying to her.

As soon as she was done whispering, Lilith then said as she passed the violin and rod to her, "Very well."

She was crossing over to face the crowd of herbalists, mages, and other magic users, men women and children. Sarah stood and watched very cautiously and frightened, still held against her will. So did Frask. She spoke with an almost bombastic tone; "I will spare each and every one of you...if you would be kind to offer this young man the toxin you've prepared."

Everyone was dead quiet. Nothing was sounded aside of the waves being tossed and the seagulls crying and yapping about in the water blue sky. One young woman came out from the crowd as she pulled out something from her satchel. She was a young red-haired woman with a yellow dress. In her left hand was a small glass vial of some purple substance.

Lilith nudged her head to where I was, silently demanding her to give me the toxin. The young woman focused back on me and was hesitantly walking towards me with the vial held within her grasp. As soon as she approached me, she cocked off the quark and passed it to me as soon as the Satanists released me from their grasp.

"I'm...sorry if it's a little...messy. I'm not sure if...if I got it right." The young herbalist explained.

"No worries," I said as I began to chug onto the small vial until it was completely empty. I felt the liquid sizzle in my throat. I even tasted the bit of the miracle fruit I ate before. I had to make sure that I was controlling the toxin just, so I wouldn't get drugged again. But a few seconds was enough for it to take effect. My body was gradually feeling extraordinarily warmer than usual.

Soon, random images were creeping into my head. I wasn't sure what it was, but I couldn't make up on what was happening. But I was almost losing control over my own body. In some accounts of flashing, I saw myself concealed in darkness, screaming hysterically and hyperventilating. I saw my arms banging onto something.

I dropped down on all fours, coughing out slimy blood that was drizzling from my lips. The more I was doing it, the warmer I was getting to the point of feeling like I was nearly bursting into flames.

"Take him on the ship. We'll have something special in store for him." Lilith demanded.

She then demanded the other soldiers, "Prepare to save Heaven."

I felt my arms being held once again. I wanted to call for Ted and Juliet, but my intuition was telling me that it was already too late. I didn't want to think too deep to where I was presuming that they were already dead. Plus, they were more experienced Apostles, so I had hope. As my weakened body was being strutted and dragged away from the crowd, despite my blurring vision, I saw the large line of Satanists preparing to suppress fire towards the villagers, including the young herbalist. Lilith then said with ease, "Screw it. Let them have it!"

"Wait...no! No...Stop!" I cried. But the rifles of the Satanists already alerted my ears and boomed. I constantly tried and tried to wrestle away from the grasp of the two Satanists guards.

Perhaps they were using my broken soul towards their advantage to slow me down. I still heard the screams of somebody being locked in a cage. Or concealed in a box. A very fiery hot box with no infliction of air. Maybe the toxin was meant to turn out this way.

And because of its powerful heat beating within my chest, I began to pass out slowly. At this point, I've lost count on how many times I blacked out or got knocked out just to end up somewhere different. Frighteningly but strangely, it took me back to the times where I would blackout as a student because of the horrors I've faced. I would see quick flashing images of myself throwing intense tantrums in classes or falling in the middle of the halls.

It was clear that a part of my soul was broken. But I wasn't going to let Lucifer break me completely. If anything, this was an advantage to release those nobles from Hell. I wasn't sure how, especially without Ted or Juliet. And I truly hoped that those who were met at the end of the Satanists' powers were going to rest in the Void.

All I could do was avenge them. Just as I was avenging my family, friends, and all I've lost, neglected, hurt, or turned away. It was time for true amends.

XXXVIII

The Holy Land of Darkness

Five hours later, the warmest flash traversed away from my body, and I felt nothing but slight frostbites that woke me up. My eyes adjusted to realize that I was on the deck of a ship. The crew yelped and shouted, but in very crude and almost demonic tones. I slowly stood up and felt my arms restrained yet again. This time, my wrists were wrapped with rusty iron shackles attached to chains. I saw myself stripped into my white chemise shirt. My weapons and outfit were yet to be found, but I felt like they were obviously confiscated.

I saw myself sailing by crooked mountains and misty forests manifested with nearly broken-down and dried pine trees. All of them underneath a discolored blue sky. In fact, pretty much everything else seemed very discolored, devalued, and dehumanized compared to what I saw from Heaven. It had very saturated blooming shades. Swarms of unknown flying beasts swirled and flew around mountain peaks. Most likely, they could be dragons, but I wasn't quite sure, even given how the mist wasn't much help.

Nature was no longer saturated with hopeful greens, but very depressed greens surrounded by a hollow afternoon mist. The air was smeared with ashes and another toxic smolder that was creeping into

650

my nose. It's basically how I once saw the world I came from; devalued of something that was supposed to be beautiful.

My tiring eyes then slowly fixated at the river that was leading us to a large city that was far from where we were.

Straddled by the sight of decomposed torn hands were clinging onto the ship. They banged and scratched the ship, leaving scratch marks onto it. It made me ill to see malnourished and skeletal fingers desperately cling onto the ropes of the vessel. On top of that, the moans and cries came from the abyss, misunderstood due to the water.

Afar, like I said, looked to be a city. In ways, it almost looked like Celestia. But the towers I saw looked sharp and unwelcoming. But it was clouded by the rainy mist.

"I know you are longing to know why."

I turned to the voice on the left and recognized it. The same snooty voice that now irked me after letting everything that happened lead to that moment. I saw the same long red hair that reached down her upper back, covering her neck. She still had the same Civil Forcer outfit too. She turned to me with a neutralized look on her face.

Irrespective of my restraints and very low energy, I rapidly charged at her. But I found myself falling back by the chains that happened to be engraved onto the ship's board. I tried wrestling to break away. I needed to enforce every form of pain on the woman for what she had done.

Getting closer to me with her hands behind her back, I asked her through my hardened teeth, "Why? Why would you do this? Jesus and the others...they trusted you!! My family trusted you!! *I* trusted you!!"

"And you have the full right to be angry." She said, calmly as usual. It only made me my skin gradually tense and warm. "But...you don't have the full right to be appalled by this. And trusting me was your first mistake."

She then faced the riverside. I then asked, "What is that supposed to mean? Is this what we should expect from a Civil Forcer? Betrayal??"

I was sure that she heeded those words, which resulted to her

652 ~ KENNETH VIVOR

shivering a bit. She then said, "I'm not...a Civil Force Detective. If you've worked with me like I asked, you would've understood my true motive. You would've gotten a clue. But you did the opposite of what I asked, meaning that you didn't take me seriously. And it's not your fault. You thought that you were doing good."

"This whole bloody time...it was you! You initiated this war! You summoned the Satanists! You got those mystics sold in this god-forsaken realm! You conducted those attacks on the villages! You made me kill my parents!"

"And I'm glad for that! You act as if they were nothing but saints for a dying legacy. They were just as guilty for their sins. Blinding you into seeing the good in humanity. Shelling you in a box you refuse to get out from. Your love for them is a weakness than it is a strength because you refuse to look at life that beholds to you! There's more to it than the petty values they taught you."

"They may have been flawed, but who isn't? At least they were always willing to do good...which is more than I could say about you! I should've known! I feel like a fool! You're the Angel...all this time! You've gotten those people killed! And you didn't give a damn! Why did you even work alongside Virgil, Rollo, and Masayoshi?"

"I never did! It was never about them! It was about my devotion to an actual savior!" Bertha said. "Virgil, Rollo, and Masayoshi treated this like a game. All of them begged to keep their afterlives. They were willing to do anything to get out from this place. So...out of pity, Lucifer had each of them sell out their fellow mystics from their noble houses in Heaven as an exchange not only for freedom, but also to rule over the Promised Land. That promise got into their heads...and they wanted to evidently control everyone. They were casualties of this unwarranted war, not knowing that they were vessels for Lucifer to get to the Insignia. So, they had to go somehow."

She began to laugh a bit. Then she said, "It's hilarious how men would do anything for that kind of affluence. So eager and ambitious, yet so reckless, brash, and naïve. Never collected and intelligent as women. I only had you kill Virgil and Rollo to stop them from getting in my way.

To them, it's just a typical heist for power. For me...it's to elevate greatness. I conducted the curses in the village...in hopes to find the shard. Lucifer has granted me to get to the Axis Mundi only. But what was missing was the shard; a crystal that held the Holy Insignia's true power. After tirelessly searching disaster after another, it turned out that it was hidden...underneath your family's lovely home in Corinthian County. I destroyed the villages, using a spell book, enchanted by darkworker magic. And those Civil Force Detectives were scouting for the shard. The Watchers was my idea from the start all those fourteen years, only Lucifer gave us pardon. Unfortunately, the same for someone like Virgil. I wanted your help to find it after helping those villagers settled in Corinthian County. You're the kind of astral I needed as an accomplice, not another gullible boy dragged into that order of fake angels. Mr. Jefferson and Ms. Higgins were lost causes already succumbed to that flawed way of thinking. So, I wasn't going to get anywhere with them. You were meant to be different. But...you didn't take me seriously. So, I had to do what I could...to make you *cooperate*."

I then roared at her without holding back, "How would my parents know about a bloody shard underneath their house?! How would anyone know?! You didn't have to kill them!"

"Oh, but I did, Kevin. I had to kill them," Bertha said with no sign of care in her voice. She still sounded as if we were friends. "The minute I reveal the shard, the risk I would take by having them as witnesses. Let alone the entirety of village folk. No spirit here should hoard that kind of power. Let alone in the comfort of their own home. Jesus wasn't clever enough to hide it elsewhere. Yet, he is one with God. A weak god."

I nearly vomited in rage for what she said, but I composed myself to regain my focus on Bertha. "So...you summoned the Satanists. On the day that we met."

"I had to do what I can to get that staff. I had to do what I can to get the shard. You got in the way. But at the same time, you gave me an opportunity. And I gladly took it. Just wished you did the same for me."

"What about that night that you were supposed to meet Sathanus at the deserted alchemist lab…to channel Satan into Queen Arianna's scepter with the priestesses? What happened there?"

"I was looking for the shard. Those scepters could be used to enter the temple. I mean it makes sense. What better way than to steal from the Covenant of the Gods? But Jesus's was more integral to the Holy Insignia. So, I left the Scepter of Selene with Sathanus as I did reconnaissance in the Main Chapel; gaining intel on how to get that staff without entrance and the perfect timing. Specially to have him summon Satanists to rid Michael and the Angels. But I knew that Jesus's was more significant. Thus, I disregarded that heathenistic staff and focused on getting the shard before his scepter. Still, Virgil seemed desperate to have the same official leadership. So was Rollo. So was Masayoshi. They were out for themselves. If anything, getting you to kill those men gave me time to do all of this. You did me a great favor. As naïve as you are, you always did make a good errand boy." She said, which got my blood to boil intensely.

But this resulted to me feeling the tears suddenly coming down my face. It wasn't in sadness, but I was so consumed with disdain, disgust, and bitterness. Virgil and Rollo's deaths were pointless. Don't get me wrong; they had to die for what they did. But why would they work under Lucifer knowing damn well that one of his supporters basically used them as bait so we could stay out of her way to let her do her deeds?

"Why are you doing this? Why couldn't you just tell me the truth?" I asked.

"I was always an ally of Lucifer. From the very beginning. I only subverted the Promised Land…to cripple Jesus's power from within. And it was somewhat easy…knowing how dependent the Chancery was to the Civil Force Detectives. If I were a regular Forcer, my actions would've been public. And I didn't want that!" She admitted with a hostile voice. "From what I've seen from the heavenly monarchs, it's no wonder why Lucifer has such displeasure. Those kings and queens – if you can call them that – fail to take the afterlife seriously. Especially Jesus. You would think after he was basically sent to Earth, only to die by the hands of man, he would reconsider his place and strengthen it. Bestowing his powers among humanity to be perfect in the eyes of God. But no. He goes on about wanting spirits to find their own faiths and their own ways to be better. But to what end? Just so the souls of humanity could continuously make mistakes. The same mistakes? Just so we can accept them for who they are?"

She then glanced at me and said, "I'm doing this...because we are better than this, Kevin. We don't have to be just mere flawed spirits living until we eventually become adrift. We can be perfected beings. A perfected civilization. Isn't that what you want? To forget the past. The burdens? The voices? The sins? Those leaders of yours are only holding you back from the potential of escape to a new heaven. They think that lifting your soul, building it up, could help you achieve enlightenment and greatness? That is crazy. Souls can't be lifted. When a child is born, you cannot build its soul. You give it one. A better one. That's what we are, Kevin, eating, shitting, sleeping and clueless impulses for civilization to mold. Dogmas exist to keep our lives strong. Not chakras or any petty self-loving nonsense! And you could either let swindlers mold you...or those who could only tell you the truth."

"What truth? Huh? What damn truth?"

"That even souls are flawed. And they can only be completely reset to be flawless. Admit it; the world we both had was manifested with a cultivation that disregards morality. And we cannot have that with the afterlife. We're better than this. We cannot just stop at being good. We need to be better. And all we can do...is to trust in Lucifer. He knows. He can lead us to a true better world. A world that someone like Jesus could ever dream of. But chose not to. We can have a world...where it doesn't have to worry about change or progression because we would all be perfect under one glorious divinity. No wars. No injustice. No prejudice. Just everlasting peace. You see, it was no accident when Lucifer left Heaven divided and destroyed, for his intention was to rebuild it...to where it makes sense. To rebuild and manage the afterlife...to what it's meant to be. Not another Earth. Not another cursed species. You could thank Eve...for being tempted by the Abyss to damn the Earth and its species. Lucifer intends to fix it...in his way, of course. That is why...we must support him."

That creed again. That false creed. I was getting really fed up with hearing it. Fed up with how hypocritical it sounded. How is it they can use these noble ideals as a front for sinister means? At least the Apostles and all of Heaven are genuine with not only their words, but also their actions. I saw that for the months I was in the afterlife. So, it sickened me to see these blind followers of Lucifer see themselves as righteous individuals.

If anything, this was something Arianna warned me about. How unaware they really were. They don't see the damage they've made on the afterlife and those within it. "And your way of...achieving this...new heaven that you have planned for all of us...is to kill someone's family? Other families? Most of them astrals who only simply want to live again?" I asked.

But she scoffed and said, "Ugh...spare me the self-pity and faux morality. Don't you ever get tired of that?"

"Don't you ever get tired of lying to yourself?" I then asked, "Why did you stop Lilith from killing me? You could've had us killed, but you didn't."

"I've always had a fondness with you. Especially the day we met." She said. "You and your friends are clearly bright. You were just...misguided by those who thought they could help you. You cannot become leaders, Kevin. Bees cannot work on their own volition. We are all servants to the higher good. And it should remain that way. Which is why...as soon as we get to Dolorem...you will be offered a choice; to renounce your faith to the heavens and to your own personal spirit.... to become the servant of a much brighter leader who could show you light. Or...to die with your faith. Look, I'm sorry that your family had to die another death. I truly didn't want them to. I had a war start to end. It would've ended this trivial everlasting battle had we worked together. But... you've gotten yourself into the wrong side. And well...you only have yourself to blame. You've been trying to live two different lives at once, Kevin. It's unwise. To live in divinity, let one of them go. Otherwise, you'll be stuck in this purgatorial middle to find out which life you want. The life of a knight.... or just a son. An angel...or a legacy in a cursed family. Make a choice."

She then sighed and continued, "It's too bad that it has to come this way. I wish we didn't fight. I wish we could both come to a...consensus. A singular understanding...that souls can only be reshaped with new souls. So...the only way to do that is to have the entire Apostle Order wiped out completely. And it wouldn't be the first time. We did that to every scout that wields a blade and acts as a hero. You see, we could easily handle with the militaries of those kingdoms. They are blessed by those pathetic gods of theirs. But knights... are the biggest threat. Because of what you teach. You venerate continuous death, chaos, and upheaval. And we will make sure...that your existence...is dead! For good!"

Her saying that frighteningly reminded me of when the Satanists slaughtered the Twelve Apostles and every other order of knights who tried to save the spirits of the afterlife. From her unapologetic conde-scending tone, it's as if she wants history to repeat for her own gain. They wanted to succeed again. I wasn't going to let them. Especially knowing that despite the many losses of souls the afterlife suffered, it didn't take away the fact that Lucifer lost. And this wouldn't be any different.

I looked out and saw that we were getting closer to the city of antiquity. It looked to be a city build from pride. A selfish pride. I then said to her, "You think that I would ever join...after what you've done to me? What you did to others?"

"That's for you to tell Lucifer, not me. Ask him that. I'm just his servant."

'A slave is what you are,' I thought to myself as I mentally prepared my mind and soul. I had the sense that she didn't even love herself, given how she dismissed the concept of seeking a divine self as *self-loving nonsense*.

I really couldn't understand what would be in store for me in the city of Dolorem. I figured that as soon as I reached the place, I would be wanted dead. As well as my two friends.

We sailed passed two epic sized stone statues of two winged men, each of them holding a bible in one hand and a spear in the other. They were a gateway to Dolorem, an empire waiting around the corner. At the far mountain ranges was a city stretching from left to right, mostly manifested with towers, big cathedrals, and mosques. The river was becoming more of an ocean, still riddled with wayward souls sobbing hysterically from the bottom of the dark depths.

Approaching the docks, we finally boarded soon after. One of the guards managed to unhook the chain from the lock. I almost felt my wrists being torn by the shackles. I was almost pulled and restrained like a dog. A creature used for their experiment, continuous torment, ridicule, and abuse.

As I was being confined and forced out of the ship's deck, I retorted towards Bertha, "You will regret this! When I'm free, you'll finally meet my blade."

"I look forward to it. Because as soon as I channel Jesus's scepter, and I reach the Axis Mundi, we'll see who will regret it at the end," She said with a smile. She gazed at the guard, jolting her head that implied for him to escort me. I instantly focused my eyes at the front, seeing Dolorem for the first time. I wasn't sure what state this city was on, but I was sensing pride from all over. Every monument and sculpture of Lucifer himself proved that. It was truly a beautiful dense street, but it was only a front for something sinister.

The glares and stares of the inhabitants and citizens of the supposedly great city welcomed me. All of them were on each side, clearing the road for the legionaries to pass through. Compared to Heaven, each man and woman wore nothing but pallas and stolas of all the same gold and black colors, representing their state. They all looked physically lifeless as if all hope was instantly strapped away from them. Yet, they looked compelled to liken to the awaiting paradise their Lord had in store for them. But it felt less like a city and more of walking through a psychiatric ward. From their white blurry eyes, it was clear that they were sedated and voluntarily unmindful of their grim surroundings. Even some of the children looked very malnourished and sadly close to death despite the great well-being of their parents. They smiled at me grimly, anticipating for my death. Yet, they still looked sickly. And some of the men looked deformed, disfigured, and brutalized to the bone. Yet, any demonic being with authorized positions looked well fed and bulked as opposed to the folks they supposedly served. Even though it was clear that they didn't care for the well-being of their subjects; only what they could do for them. It smelled of wet dirty ashes and resent in the air, pus, or any bodily fluid.

It could explain why they had so much disdain for me, even though there was nothing I could do. They could speak of it to their messiah. But honestly. Was this Lucifer's idea of a paradise? Starved children? Deformity? Guideless ignorant fools? Unfair forced labor to break them? People who fundamentally loathed themselves and feel unworthy? A world that gratifies and sensationalizes pain, a lack of real piety, victimology and suffering without any urge to be the least redeemable? A collective of deranged and sickly spirits who take pleasure in having their dignity stripped from them in the most unjust and unholy ways? Like what happened to those priestesses? Like what happened to me? Despite the glaring flaws, seeing the horrid display before me, with the little time I had, made me grateful for not being ascended there. It made me cherish what Heaven tried to be. It was one thing to live in a decent world with bad eggs here and there. Living in an entire world manifested with nothing but toxic beings who believed in a magnificent and beautiful lie was another.

As I passed every surprisingly clean building, avenue and corner that was leading me to the palace, I was pondering of everything that would happen to me at the very moment. I glanced at every ornamental poster, embracing their leader's agenda. Promoting his agenda. His words will flourish. His reign will thrive. And when his legends are heeded, our great world will survive. That's all they wrote. Like what I heard from several Satanists I fought. I felt so confined and out of my comfort. Especially knowing that I was getting closer and closer to the Dolorem Palace. Whatever I was to meet, I had to keep myself guarded. The Satanists intend to break me just as they did before. And I cannot let them. Not again.

The Palace was built with plenty of tall towers with very extended rooftops integrated with the towers. It was on a slope a bit away from the city. Still despite feeling very tired, exhausted, and close to falling, I was forced to still walk. Upon facing the fort surrounding the castle, I was presented with crucifixes on each side. The poor victims, some with molted and ashen bodies, their heads donning animalistic skulls, were ripped from their souls. Perhaps, they were immolated. Obviously, they were nailed. But given this was Hell, it was clear that Lucifer's crazed followers had fun being creative with their methods.

Some bodies were sunken from all their blood. And it was evident as I spotted large gapping lacerations on each of their arms. I could only assume that they suffered blood loss and slowly died soon after. A lot of their crucifixes had sinner carved on chopped off planks that were then nailed onto them.

"That's gonna be you up there. You and your fellow knights," One of the guards said with a snicker. A way to mock me.

As soon as we got to the gates, I was handed over to two guards. They wore dirty stag skulls and black cloaks. They held halberds in their hands while both grabbed my arms to drag me into the castle.

Soon enough, I was in the citadel of demons posing as men in armor. They seem like they were men, but I knew better to realize that behind those animalistic skulls were monsters. In front of the door looked to be a familiar man. A giant man with heavy armor. It looked almost a lot like Sathanus, but he seemed like he wasn't. The man was bald headed and brutally scarred on his face. He donned a small scruffy beard that was a dirty orange scheme. And his eyes were dark, sunken, and hollow. Just like his heart.

I wasn't quite sure whom that was until one of the masked guards called, "We have him, Sathanus!"

That was Sathanus. It was surprising to see him without his helmet. He certainly looked very unsettling, but I held myself together to not show fear. They were all opposing and expected me to be scarred.

Grasping his sword's handle holstered on his belt, he said, "Good. Bring him to Lucifer...perhaps he should know better now. Soon, he should join his friends if he acts up."

After going up the stairs, I finally faced the enforcer and looked him in the dark eyes. I made sure to show all resentment towards him. But in the inside, as soon as he mentioned friends, I automatically figured he was referring to Ted and Juliet. Thus, I was relived to realize that they were okay after all.

The demon grinned and scoffed at my attempt at being intimidating. He then said, "You know...even in death, your mother was a good use for...bodily frustration. Too bad it was on a wooden floor and not under the sheets. As for your sister, Bertha hopes to sell her to me. Seventy bennies she cost. I'm very eager...to have her apart of my collection, now that we know her brother...is a lightkeeper. Getting the short end of the stick surely runs in the family it seems. Especially in your case." He laughed along with the other soldiers.

So, it was true of what happened to me and my mother. And now the bastard planned to buy my sister.

After heeding how he had his men really defile my mother and I, I then said with resent, "That's quite a lovely face you've got, Sathanus. It'd be a shame if someone made it uglier...than it already does."

His face twisted with disgust as I suddenly felt a sharp jab at the bottom of my abdomen. I winced and cried out my pain, coughing a bit. Sathanus's sword handle was erected, which was the result of my wounded stomach. He bent down and said, "Don't think you could make those retorts here! You're in Devil Country now, you molested mongrel!" I ignored his angry breaths as I was trying to endure the pain in my abdomen.

"Get him out of my sight already." He demanded as I was soon dragged away from his eyes.

Soon after we passed through the decorated halls and made our way to the staircase, I was getting close to meet a cloak worn man out on a balcony. I presumed that it was obviously Lucifer, perhaps still masked and hiding his monstrosity. I was still feeling aching due to Sathanus' tantrum being exposed.

When the guards were presenting me to the man, I felt their hands forcibly integrated onto my shoulders. I didn't have control of my knees, which meant that I had no other choice but to get on all knees to face the wrath of a wannabe savior. My eyes gazed at the look of his muscular back, which had the Satanist emblem tattooed on his back.

His masked head slightly turned, and he said through his muffled voice, "It's honorable to see you again, Kevin."

Growling behind my teeth, I said sarcastically, "Likewise."

He turned and faced me, "See that you've...come to an understanding of your mistakes. You didn't take your afterlife. I'm quite impressed. Who convinced you? Jesus? Francis?" He scoffed, "It doesn't matter. I don't really need to know. I came to realize...that you prefer to look up to liars to justify your existence. Or to build upon your life. I'm surprised that you don't seek vengeance."

"You...You made martyrs...of my parents. Of those people!" I gritted through my teeth.

"Now...let's not get it twisted. I didn't create martyrs. It just so happens that people unknowingly succumb to death. I don't intend to make martyrs, Kevin." He said. "I intend to create life with new perfect souls to prepare for the Pure World. That way, no one would have to be martyrs. Do you know of the Hermetic principles? It's the ancient systematic principles of self-mastery made by Hermes Trismergus, one of Jeremiah's more adequate philosophers. One of the principles that stood out is the Principle of Rhythm. The heavenly kings rose from arrogance...but fell to ruin. The Apostles and this race of knights rose from pride...but fell to demolition. And you rose from your pride...but lost you human life and lost those who made you. All of this has a purpose, Kevin. To truly break that cycle of life, you must be willing to make sacrifices. We cannot say that we want peace and yet commit the ill actions we claim to be against. Actions must be taken. And to do so...is to give up our desires and self-preservations. Losing those we love, the things we love, allows us to see life more visibly. Thus, making us wiser. We have to let go...to truly be one with divinity."

"Why won't you just kill me? You've broken me. You might as well." Truthfully, I didn't mean it.

He responded with a laugh, "Why would I kill you? The intention from young men, trying to be strong, is awfully hilarious! No...I see a possibility in you, in all honesty. I truly do. It's why I wanted to see you."

"You see the potential of me being a mindless weapon of yours."

"No...not a weapon. A voice." Then he said this as he was passing by me, "Spirits can be good, Kevin. They just need someone to help them tap into that potential to be their very best. And just like humans in general, they need...a competent and merciful god that won't let them down anymore. A god that won't lie to them, spoil nor deceive. And...I'm willing to give you that chance to seek the rightful guidance."

"Why? After everything you've done?! Why would I ever join you?" I shouted.

"Because...like a god, I could make things possible." Lucifer said as he then extended his left arm, clawing out his hand. I turned to see something taking form in the middle of the hall. Two people were materialized right in front of me out of greying wispy smoke.

The two people were a man and a woman. Both looked to be sickly pale and fully stripped off any clothing. I wasn't aware of who they were until I studied their faces carefully. My eyes widened soon after I was realizing who they were. Mother and Father. But both of their expressions were blank and almost lifeless. It was really them standing there. But I couldn't fall for that. Lucifer knew that I would probably give him the satisfaction for joining his cause by having my parents brought from the Void.

Angrily, I said as I turned to him, "You think that I would allow you to...bribe me like this?"

"By you killing your parents, and those you've murdered, I tested the shard, used my scepter and gave them new vessels with their souls intact. This thing is even too powerful for my own scepter. Who knew that it could possess even the most fragile of ornaments? Obviously, with the Insignia, the effect would be more impactful. They'd be...re-molded. Body and mind." Lucifer chuckled. He then said to me, "Your mother and father are willing to welcome you in the new heaven, Kevin. They came to understand what it is we are intending to do. We want the same as the Apostles and the whole of Heaven, but something more. An Eden. A paradise. Think about it. A family reunion in true paradise. Wouldn't that be beautiful?"

"We *had* a reunion in paradise. And you took that from me. You plagued us...as if we weren't plagued before just for wanting to live a good life by serving God! You're just a monster masking himself as a savior. Like every other maniac hiding behind a label of goodness. Like every being that stole our human lives," I said.

"Would a monster go out of its way to bring the two people you hold dear back from the Void?" Lucifer asked. "I care about souls. I care about you. Imagine what great things you could do for the afterlife with a perfected soul. Imagine an afterlife where all are united under one God, with no conflicts, divisions, or confusion. Imagine...only one single truth being abided."

He then strolled back to the balcony and extended both open arms, "This...world...could open hearts and minds to the possibilities of honed souls. It doesn't need to be a world of suffering, hurt and damnation, but a united world in general. Every inch of this universe...infused within a nation. A world in unity and not division. An Eden that is untouched by broken men with power. All it takes...is to accept this commitment and make that sacrifice. To allow me to have that

Insignia...so we could become one great civilization. It's the only way to salvation. To work hard for it. Just like how both of your parents had to work hard...to escape the Void. There will come a time...where I will eventually succumb to death. Thus, I need someone...such as yourself...to continue my crusade. I still sense that resentment for human behavior in you. You were one the right track. You could still be. All it takes is sacrifice."

I looked back at my parents. This time, I had to really analyze them. The reason was because I noticed something immensely different about them. It made sense of how they looked to be born once again. I watched my mother's eyes. They were now misty and looked very saddened. It was almost like she was afraid. And so, did my father. Their bodies were shaking minimally, almost as if they were trying to shake off some sort of force that was preventing them from being free. Tears even began to stream down their faces.

"So, what shall it be, Kevin? Do you want to become redeemed with a pure soul...or do you prefer to have this broken one instead?" He asked, as I was still concentrated at my parents. "Do you want me to save you from your burdens? Your past? Your curse? Make the right choice. You don't have to see yourself as the criminal you once were. You don't have to be burdened anymore. You could be free in the life you've always wanted. You could leave that sinful life behind...in favor for a new one."

Something didn't sit right with me when I saw them. Their bodies seem pseudo in comparison to how I knew who they were. So, I told him, "Those are not my parents."

"Why of course they –," Lucifer intended to speak until I cut him off saying, "You're using their trapped souls in these fake vessels...just to get to me! The same bastard who damned me for not letting them go in their home where I had to be complicit to pain! Isn't that funny?! Now you intend to use them as bribery! You're desperate! You're a liar!"

"I'm a god, Kevin! Gods never lie!" After he took a deep breath, he said to me in a diplomatic matter, "Besides, the Apostles only pampered you to believe in your own self-righteousness. Whereas they, and others like them, have done nothing but infested the likes of true goodness with their debris full of lies and false ideals. And yet...you fight for them. What have they ever done for you? Huh? What have they done? Tell me."

I pondered within. Deeply. Soon, I spat out, "They showed me things that I've lost. They've possessed things that you will never understand. They reminded me of what it meant to truly live with God. They showed me how an imperfect man could still rise and do what is right. Not just for his honor, but for everyone. They accepted me, regardless of who I was and who I am. They showed me what the afterlife could be without monsters like you! That's what they've done! And I will do my damnedest to return the favor for everything they did for me. I don't need a new soul, especially from you! I'll never become your vessel! My whole life, my family and I have been burdened by devils, preventing us from living the life we wanted to have! Tangled in their destructive opinions and conflicts! And I always had to accept it, not do anything about it, like a good boy as it continuously tainted my mind! But now, I can. This life, the Apostles, is my new life now! I get to determine it! To flourish it! And no religion, empire, society, or harbinger will ever break me or kill me ever again! You will never destroy me! You will never take this soul! This soul...is who I am!"

After he stood pondering, he let out a muffled sigh and said, "That's...quite a shame. I thought that we could come to an understanding. So...you prefer to be a martyr, I see." He turned back to lounge himself on the balcony before he made an order. "Very well then. Take him to the chambers and lock him up...like the *criminal* he is. He prefers to act like one...he could die as one."

I heeded that word, criminal. But I wasn't going to let that word define me anymore; because for the first time, I was defining who I was. Not my parents or the others. Because I was not them. I was no longer my past. I was the future. For what it was worth, I was choosing to live by God.

I felt my arms getting grasped once again as I was forcibly pushed to walk away from Lucifer's back. I was set on what I wanted to say to him, and I didn't regret any part of it. But I did hope to see if Ted and Juliet were okay. And I had yet to see where the nobles were held captives.

As I left, I was overhearing muffled yelps of pain that was being restrained. I heard what sounded like blades meeting the flesh. And that what I would realize that they were using them against me. They were sorely created just to be disposed when they had no use anymore. I gripped and hardened my cuffed fists.

The elk skulled guards took me to the bottom of the castle, which seemed more like Hell than what I witnessed. The cells were circled around a hole in the middle of the dungeon. And the pit looked to have a behemoth herd of relentless red eyed rats swarming and running. It was darkly lit with simple torches hung on the walls, giving little light. A lot of cells were displaying nothing but terrifying methods of pain and confinement. Women in the cells were worse off, especially when pregnant. I watched as most of them were having their fetuses forcibly removed as they made unforgiving leakages all over the dirty concrete floors. The men, and children, in other cells were receiving lashes as the sharp leather whips met and integrated into their flesh. Some were tied to posts as they received rounds from the firing line from Legionaries. Some were inside wooden tubs of what looked to be fecal matter. All the madness and putrid nature was what too much to gain. I bought into the notion that the poor blokes refused to compromise to Lucifer's new heaven.

One of the guards leading me even spelled it out for me, "Those who dare give in to defiance...are nothing more than scum...who deserve to be treated as such. Defiance against the New Heaven...will not be tolerated."

Soon, I was presented to a much larger cell room, facing the other cells across the pit. Surprisingly, it was full of men. The men were shackled onto the walls and lounged on their backs against the murky greying stonewalls. It reeked of blood, sweats and most likely melted fecal matter that roasted underneath the hot blazing sun. As I walked past all the chained victims, I was already feeling the toxin take effect. With such a humid and moist atmosphere, I already was sensing dampness all over my body. I couldn't help but reflect on that day in the box. But I had to know that it was over now. I was still a living spirit. At least for now, anyway.

Shortly after, they roughly pushed me against the wall and forcibly sat me down between two other victims. One victim was a man who was not only stripped of all his clothes, but also had horrible scars presumably by fire. The other had wet dark black hair. But with the little light that was shimmering, it turned out to be brown.

The guards raised both of my arms and had my wrists shackled against the wall. Soon, they both stormed out of the cell and closed the iron bars on all of us.

My ears then caught a voice; "K...K...Kevin?" A faint whisper sounded.

I turned and studied the bloke next to me since it was right by me. I almost recognized it. When he slowly raised his head, his hair bangs were moist and covering his eyes. On his face, he grinned a bit.

"Wait...T...Ted? Is that you?"

"H...Hey." He replied faintly.

Relieved by sighing, I said, "You're okay. Thank God! Thank God, you're alright!"

"Glad you're okay too!" He said as he swayed his head to move his hair strands. "I thought they got ya! We tried to get you, but...we were ambushed when the Satanists and Legionaries were summoned before their mass assault. After those...poor herbalists..."

"I...I know. But.... where's Juliet?"

"They're...they're questioning her. Trying to get something out of her before sending her to her cell," Ted said. "But she's okay. Hopefully."

"Frask and Sarah?"

"Rescued by the Civil Force, luckily. But...it's becoming crazy in Heaven. She really blindsided us...as everything was goin' on!"

I looked around desperately, finding some way to get us out of there.

"Once I find a way out, we have to save Juliet. And the mystics if we can find them. We have to go back and save Heaven!"

"Well, it's going to take a helluva long while for our sorcery to come back. Usually...three hours or so. So...we might as well wait until we reunite with Juliet somehow once we're brought to the Coliseum. Hopefully, we could come up with a plan. Somehow."

"Sathanus will have our stuff?"

"Most likely in his chambers within this fuckin' castle," Ted said. "As for the mystic nobles, they work as slaves. The Satanists are having them channel their magic into...a podium of some sort they made to use the Insignia. Mostly alchemists and spellcasters to exploit their magic for their own gain by using their runes and knowledge, knowing that the Insignia is a heavenly scepter. All of them are confined by a darkworker magic Lilith manifested for them to prevent them from escaping. They're underneath a cathedral called Holy Temple of Sammon in the middle of the woods...far south of Dolorem's forests."

"Bloody hell! So...aren't we in a layer, or what?" I asked since I was more familiar with Dante's interpretation of the Inferno.

"Nah...you're thinkin' of Dante's interpretation. In the afterlife, the seven sins of Hell are scattered as kingdoms. Were in the kingdom of Superbia, the land of pride. Juliet and I planned to go find the nobles while you go and get Bertha, stopping her from channeling Jesus's scepter and getting to the Axis Mundi Isles."

"Sounds like a plan." I said. "Let's just hope that it could work."

"Let's hope so." He said. "So, all we can do...is wait for the execution to start."

"It looks like it." I realized. But I wasn't going to lose faith. Not this time.

I asked Ted, "Do you think...that we could still save them? Sathanus's maidens?"

He narrowed his head down and slowly shook. He said, "It's too late for them. The way I see it...the only way they could be free...is a merciful death. They've become vacant. Internally. Plus, it's been a long time since the rebellions. What a damn mess he's made of them!"

I sighed heavily, embracing the sad inevitability. But after I mustered up, I then asked Ted, "So...how did you know all this? About the mystic nobles being trapped?"

He replied, "I overheard two guards talking about them. They were talking about using the female mystics...as comfort women. It's a sick thing, man!"

"I agree," I said in pure disgust. I then told him, "Lucifer...he tried to convince me into becoming his...vessel."

"That's why they took away our powers. They hope to insert dark-worker magic in us. He knows that we're the last lightkeepers. He just wants to exploit us just like the rest. That's all." Ted stated, which I agreed to that obvious obligation. "We ain't giving him shit."

"Amen to that," I agreed.

XXXIX

Live by the Sword, Die by the Sword

After three hours, I didn't realize that I drifted into sleep until I felt something tug at my left foot. I scoffed and woke up to two elk skull wearing guards, looking down at me like I was a helpless stray dog.

"Rise and shine, you piece of shite! Get up!" The one guard grasped my right arm and pulled me off from the ground. They undid the chain from the wall and began to tug me like an animal.

Soon, I found myself outside of the castle as the very gloomy skies bloomed against my eyes and temporarily blinded me. To make matters worse, not only I was surrounded by many pike and spear holding guards. But also, one of them came in front to place a potato bag over my head. And all I saw from there was nothing, but dried yarn tied together.

I felt myself getting tossed forward, pressured to move despite my blindness. I still felt my wrists getting torn from the bones as the chains were aggressively pulled. I grunted and groaned, but of course I was ignored. These were demon soldiers we're talking about here.

As soon as I was forced to stop, I heard a carriage. The wheels were trammeling onto the cobble stone roads. Something was creaking open. Thus, I felt a guard tug on the back of my shirt and shuffled me into something shaky. I assumed that I was inside of a wagon.

"Anyone dares to communicate with one another, or to conduct some bloody conspiracy, and we will dismember you on the spot!" One of the guards warned with a horrid tone in his tongue.

When that warning was surely heeded, I felt something moving away. I was sure that we were inside of a wagon. And I was accompanied by prisoners who were due for execution. I was hoping that I was with Ted, knowing that both of us were together.

Throughout the ride, I contemplated about our plan and how it would turn out to be. I was never a perfect strategist, but I would hope that the plan would be executed in any way that would work. All it would take is to retrieve our things, call for assistance (preferably, the Angel Paladins if we could) to rescue the nobles, and for me to stop Bertha from getting to the Axis Mundi. I had to pray that all of that would be checked off.

It took up a long while for the wagon to finally stop at someplace. The more we drove, there were constant angry and savage roars heard gradually. As I felt the holt of the carriage, it implied that we were at our destination. All I heard from there on were cries of the crowd. An angry crowd indeed. I barely heard my own breathing or the quiet whimper from someone next to me.

As something creaked open, I felt my arms getting yanked from the wagon. I found myself struggling to stand as I was forcibly placed on something coarse and scarce. Finally, I felt the sack removed from my head and I was welcomed by the brief bloom of sunlight.

When it disappeared, I was presented a massive arena with six levels of benches. One podium on the right side held ten men with deco-rated clergies and draped elites of Lucifer's congregation. I saw myself surrounded by some of the finest folks of all Dolorem. The men and women all sat and stared down at us, shouting down and barking toxic nonsense on all of us. They carried pikes with various skulls and other absurd scepters. In the middle of the arena were four large wooden crucifixes. And all I thought about was one of my dreams I previously had. The arena was surrounded and heavy with soldiers who carried pikes and flag spears, all of them colored black with the golden sun emblem in the center. They waved along with the breezing wind.

When I was pushed forward, I turned to my left and saw a familiar person a bit distant from me. White, blonde hair. Slim but voluptuous form. White shirt with light blue trousers and opaque stockings and black boots. I widened and recognized Juliet. She was alright, but her face was full of justified fear.

Her eyes looked darkened and almost half awake. I called, "Juliet!"

She turned to me with fear and her blue eyes lit up, "Kevin!"

"Move it, you shit bird!" I felt my back getting pushed forward as the guard roared. It meant that I had to not delay the inevitable. While moving forward to the crucifix, I looked back and saw Juliet. She was also forced against her will. I nodded at her, silently but hurriedly assuring her that things will get better.

After the guards were preparing the crucifix, they guard behind me forced me to face forward and lie on my back. My head unfortunately connected to the hardened wood of the crucifix. My arms were tugged to be far apart, and I felt my wrists being wrapped around by scratchy worn-out rope. I looked up at the sky, silently asking for my powers to return somehow.

I had my body revolting against my will, meaning that the crucifix was adjusting itself to be held up. From there, I saw that I was at least eight feet from the grimy grounds. In front of the arena archway, we apparently went through were four individuals all mounted on their steeds. Lucifer, Sathanus, Lilith, and bloody Bertha. In her right hand-held Jesus' scepter. Beside them, of course there were two other armed soldiers.

I watched as Lucifer got down from his black steed with gold accents and began walking towards us. But he stopped at his tracks, all just to hear the sudden roaring praise and adoration barked from the crowd that was angry not so long ago. He raised his arms in a messiah like manner, swaggering as if he was truly something meaningful to the people. But all I saw was a self-righteous coward hiding away behind a mask.

I turned to my right and saw that Ted was the last one to be carried up on the crucifix. When he rose, his arms were confined by rope as well. He turned and eyed back at me, his brown wet hair masking half of his face. I looked back at Lucifer and saw that he was silencing the crowd by gesturing both of his arms downwards.

The crowd gradually grew silent. He began to pace back and forth with all eyes focused on him. Lilith, Sathanus, and Bertha all watched him as well, eager to hear what he had to say.

"Rebuke the beast among the reeds, the herd of bulls among the calves of the nations. Humbled, may the beast bring bars of silver. Scatter the nations who delight in war," He began his homily with a scripture from Psalms, presumably justifying his course of action. He then said afterward, "My children, I bring you the rebuke of a national phenomenon. I bring you all here to witness the reckoning upon the harbingers of confrontation!"

The crowd shouted loud praises. They drummed into my ears. They chanted, *"Your words will flourish. Your reign will thrive. And when your legends are heeded, our great world will survive!"* Over and over, they said it. As I glanced down on the left below us, there were two guards preparing something. One guard had a sharp iron spear in his grasp, the other held a blazing torch and caressed the spearhead with its flames.

"The omens...the heretics...they claim to tolerate different beliefs! They claim to be accepting and take things with honor and sincerity. But Jesus Christ...the so-called *Son of God*...son of the Virgin Queen...the false redeemer...sent here his band of knights...these sorry excuse for angels.... on a fool's errand to destroy us! They've come to destroy all we have built! They come to destroy our plans for a new heaven to be fulfilled!" Lucifer roared behind his mask.

He continued to roar, "That treaty he has sent me a long time ago...was simply a way to shut us up! What does this tell you, my children? What does it tell you? He doesn't want peace at all! He means to destroy it like he always does!"

From there, all I heard were boos and angry barks from the crowd. They acted like gullible dogs, forced by harsh demand to like, and dislike. To conform and not to act like individuals with brains. And though I was obviously far, I felt their strong shrieks and monstrous roars from all over.

"But I hold myself to be an understanding spirit. A humble man. An angel. I know better than to take away afterlives simply for disclosing the potential for something grand for the afterlife. But this has been the conflict for years. It has rested, but it grows hungry. Impatient. It wouldn't die. I realize now that I am the true redeemer who will lead all to a true hereafter. A true paradise that is just around the corner. All it takes...my children...all it would take...is to rebuke this...eternal illusion that has led us astray from true eternity for too long now. And this illusion came to form as walking specters dressed as knights. Only I can lead you to what is true, astray you from what is not. One way or another, our plans for achieving peace will be content...even if it results to hellish carcasses lying on muddled pools of their own creation. We will hide no more, my children. This war has begun. Right on schedule! Angels from the grounds...Demons from above! And in the end, we will be the ones to rise! We will prosper! We will thrive as our empire thrives. And when we do, when every defiant spirit is put down like hopeless diseased mongrels constantly clinging onto the bitter bits of the life they have left, the afterlife will be OURS to preserve! It will be in OUR hands! And the New Heaven will become one nation...under one GOD! Those who choose to obey will forever prosper, while those who rebel will succumb to eternal suffering! And even if today, Satan forbid...I am taken down on this very spec of land, my words will traverse into every one of you to heed and act upon my words and practice them, no matter what! To chase down the harbingers who intend to get into our way of heaven! Because I will unite this broken discord once and for all to seize the goodness the afterlife has lost! And it starts...right...here!" He finished his homily by holding out his arm at Sathanus.

When the heavy built enforcer unmounted from his steed, he

approached to one of the guards. He was given the heated spear. Grasped and hardened in his right hand, his first victim was a crucified man who was right next to Juliet.

I couldn't make out his feelings from afar, but his constant loud whimpers and shrieks were enough for me to sympathize for a man begging for forgiveness. A pale, middle aged, innocent, and red headed fellow, I was not exactly sure what he did to get to where he was. Possibly for having a mind of his own.

"This redhead is guilty of straying away from our principles for secretly sharing the filthy words written by Christ to the noble mystics! Worse than treason! After all we provided!" Sathanus roared as his words were echoed. "But...now you'll know the consequence of having a prideful mind of your own. Would you?"

I saw him towering the burning spear near the man's face. The man screamed and choked up tears, "Please, I'll obey! I'll obey!! I'll OBEY!! I beg you, please!! Please!!"

Sadly, his pleas were ignored. Without any remorse, nor brief hesitation, the bull-skull worn captain injected the spearhead into one of the man's arms. It hissed when it planted into his flesh. There on, the man shouted and screamed on top of his lungs. I looked away, knowing that it would be troubling to see. But I unfortunately had to hear the man's blood coiling and incapacitating cries of intense pain.

My eyes were shut. But the scream stopped with the blade severely crushing itself into supple flesh. With curiosity, I opened my eyes and saw that the man was already dead. His pale freckled body was drenched in his fluid, which was rushing down very quickly. From afar, I saw that his lacerated wrists were deepened and burnt by the spear. The murky colored body fluid from his lacerations drenched and cloaked the sides of his naked torso.

The crowd cheered, whistled, and even laughed. They laughed hard, mocking the poor man's screams. My heart sank, and my mind rushed to think of something to stop Juliet, Ted, and myself from meeting the same fate.

But I felt my skin grew even paler as Sathanus approached to Juliet. I sensed and briefly saw genuine fear in her eyes. I was hearing her whimper under her breath. He then said to her in the most baritone voice, "Either you comply and obey, or you allow your flesh to meet this spear. It's your call."

She said nothing. She just stared at the fuming spearhead with her mouth opened. Her chest was rapidly going back and forth. Sathanus shrugged and placed the spearhead towards her left wrist. Her eyes were brightened, and her chest moved hurriedly despite being confined on a cross.

I felt horrendously nervous. But somehow, I was beginning to feel energized. It was as if my blood began to run normally again. What did it mean? It meant that I had an opportunity. And I thought of it as time was being of the essence. After I turned to Ted, who looked nerved by the display, I then shouted, "Wait! I choose to comply! I'll obey!"

The crowd grew silent. Their cheers turned to murmurs. And all eyes were focused on me.

"I would like...to join your flock! I...I understand now." I said in a hurried tone, giving them the satisfaction that I was genuine. "I understand...what I must do to earn...my salvation!"

Sathanus scoffed and said with a dismissive tone of voice, "You're bluffing! It's a trick!"

"It's not a trick! I promise! I'm telling the truth!" I said. "I wasn't...thinking straight before. Take me down from this crucifix and I promise to prove it! I will. I would like a blessing from the Morning Star! I truly wish for it. I am being truthful. I swear. I wish to embrace him!"

After I spoke, everyone began to murmur to themselves. Some were even mockingly making amateur orgasmic noises to satirize my need of embracing Lucifer. What was obnoxiously loud was met with confusion and skepticism. But I saw Lucifer pacing around a bit. Afterwards, he finally said, "Take him down from there."

I grinned. This meant that it was going well. All I had to do was to play it out and to expect anything. So far, it was going as planned. Surprisingly too. As a criminal, I did fancy myself a pretty alright conman.

After I was taken down, it was a relief to be off from that contraption. I began to walk towards Lucifer. But I briefly turned to the crucified Ted and Juliet, who looked rightfully confused. With haste, I quickly winked at them with my right eye, assuring them that I knew what I was doing. I hoped, at least. I had to make sure I didn't arouse any suspicion from the guards.

I turned to Lucifer and watched as his arms were out. He was ready for me to come into his embrace. He was ready for me to allow him to come into my heart. Behind his mask, I only assumed that its genuine glee.

As soon as I approached his personal space, both of his gloved hands were on both of my shoulders. He looked down at me with his different colored eyes. I looked up at him. I quickly glanced down at his wrist and saw that next to his sword's ivory hilt was a dagger. I looked back at him and smiled.

"I am happy you have thought it through, despite our differences." He said. "I know that we can both achieve greatness in our New Heaven. And you will honor your parents."

"I'm happy too. Thank you." I said. To put his guard down, I suddenly wrapped my arms around his slim body frame. I began caressing his back to deceive him. Once my right fingers felt the hilt of his dagger, I was lucky to realize that it was a loose holster. I felt him embrace me into his arms.

"I will give you purpose. I will flourish your soul. I promise." His soothing voice concealed lies. I was willing to eradicate that the best way I knew how.

When I pulled out the dagger hastily, I said in a whisper, "In your sad broken dreams."

With no hesitation, I injected the sharp blade from his back. He grunted next to my ear. He whispered faintly, "My words...will flourish. My reign...will thrive. Soon, you will understand your wrongs."

"I have. And always will," I said after I shook and ejected the blade from his chest. As I pushed him off me, I watched him struggling to stand. His eyes widened in surprise. I came up and impaled the ivory blade near his heart, missing his heart. I didn't kill him. But I allowed him to suffer. He deserved to suffer, for he reminded me of every wrong I faced.

He quickly clutched both of his hands onto his wound and fell on his knees. He glared at me with faint eyes and blood stroking down from the bottom of his mask, implying that he was drizzling from his bottom lip. Next, he fell facing the sand.

The crowd roared and shrieked in fear. And from there, what was meant to be a public execution was quickly descending into madness. I looked around as the people of Dolorem gasped and looked down. Some rose from their seats. Some fainted.

I looked down and saw that the guards were rounding up to surround me.

"He's wounded! Take him back to the castle!" Sathanus roared in demand. Two guards quickly came to Lucifer's aid and cradled him in their arms, exiting out from the coliseum's arena. I watched both Lilith and Bertha exit from the arena as well. Dammit! I thought in my head.

Sathanus looked back at me and roared from his lungs, "Get that fucking heretic! Get him! *Ka-les-mada!*"

I saw myself surrounded by Satanists, all of them holding out their spears and swords at me. I was surrounded with a bloodied dagger. At this point, I figured I was outnumbered, knowing that my friends were still trapped.

Thus, I called upon the Shadowmacer to consume me. Triggering my Blessed Eye, I allowed my shadows to flow through me. With a shadowy sword gripped in my right arm, I summoned the eight shadows to aid me. I swiftly slain and came down on every standing soldier that was in my path.

Soon, I began to take down each guard as quickly as I could. And I was doing so by using Lucifer's dagger. Amid insanity, several Satanists reappeared. They all stormed towards me. As I charged forward, I jabbed at every standing Satanists that came for me. With haste and the urge to get to Ted and Juliet, I smoothly engaged with one Satanist at the time, ending each one. And maybe it was either my anger or my training, but I saw that I was creating deep lacerations on their stomachs and chest.

One of the Satanists charged at me. But I swiftly eyed at him and threw the dagger at his head. I then took one of the other Satanists near me and circled my arm around his neck. Lifting my left hand, I used my cantation to pull out the impaled dagger to come forth. I watched it fly out from the dead Satanist's skull as it simultaneously swiftly slit the other Satanist's throat. Soon, I curled my fingers around the handle and slammed the blade into the throat of the other Satanist I had wrapped around my arm.

As soon as three Satanists plummeted to the sands, pooling and soaking blood, more demons and Satanists were rounding up to attack me. I looked up and saw Ted's triggering his Blessed Eye. Soon, the entire ground was materialized with light blue ghostly forms of actual Polish knights. This angered and distracted the Satanists and Legionaries. They began to be engaged with the ghostly forms, giving me time to save both Ted and Juliet.

I ran toward whilst conjuring two wispy smoky blood daggers in both of my hands. Hopefully with these, I thought, it should discrete the ropes holding them up.

But when there were approaching soldiers, I would summon, control, and wield the blood clots from the ground; either to trap or strangle whilst holding the daggers. I felt in control of them as if I were still practicing surrounding myself with mountains in Heaven. I conducted them in a rhythmic manner.

Right after I wielded, I launched the summoned knives at each crucifix and watched them impale near the top of their heads. My eyes widened at the wispy smoke turned into clot roots, crawling down, and deconstructing the crucifixes. What was hardened became hollow, shaky, and shallow in an instant. Ted and Juliet shook themselves off the binds. When they were able too, they both landed on their feet like two agile felines.

I finally reunited with them and quickly embraced them as they were thanking me. After I released them, Juliet held up her arm. Alwyn began to take form on her forearm. Soon, she launched the hawk eagle from her arm. Flapping his majestic wings, Alwyn swung around and swirled all around the arena until he finally flew off from the coliseum.

"Don't worry, Alwyn will track down Bertha," Juliet said. "We have to go to the castle."

"Right," I said.

With no hesitation, all three of us didn't bother to look back. We both rapidly sprinted from the sands of the arena until we made it our through the archway and back onto the ugly cobblestone roads. It was a good thing that we were still in the city of Dolorem. Yet, we were far from where the castle was.

We were suddenly watching large herds of pike and spear wielding soldiers round up in the open streets in front of us. There were two different herds coming from both sides. Luckily, it was a crossway street. The three of us were presented with Roman marble buildings. It was our cue to take off and run.

So naturally, the three of us raced down the street until we were in between the lined-up buildings on each side of us. The common spirits of Hell were straddled and devasted by us, but mostly unnerved by the number of angry soldiers raging through the streets like rats, overwhelming the roads. I remained my focus forward, swerving and dodging moving wagons and carriages.

But what came to my head was to take the chase to the rooftops. So, once I saw a two-horse drawn carriage approaching. I eyed at Juliet and Ted on each side of me. After we nodded at one another, we each swayed on the right side of the carriage and grabbed onto the rim until I saw myself on top of it. And on my left was an opportunity.

After I flew off the carriage, I grasped the edge of the orange tiles. I managed to pull up my upper body. Soon after, I saw both Ted and

Juliet doing the same. We both sharply looked over the open ocean of rooftops, grotesque towers, domes, and mosques. Far down the horizon was the castle. It looked to be a distance drawn far from where we were. The milieu was dusty and masked with smoke. It was going to be a challenge, but it was worth overcoming for the sake of the nobles, the Axis Mundi, and the afterlife. We began to run and leaped from roof to roof. Some roofs we ran on were narrow, flat, and slanted, making us down with ease and haste.

Suddenly, something surrounding us was ricocheting from the dark orange tiles. Luckily, we covered ourselves with our arms. I briefly gazed up and my eyes widened to the flying swarm of demonic soldiers with bolt action rifles shooting down at us. Their backs had black wispy smoke wings, lifting them up from the ground.

It didn't stop us from running to our destination. We were approaching towards the edge of the roof and slid on our backs. Once there, we leaped towards the balcony of an apartment building. We were suddenly running through a luxurious interior habited by whom looked to be hellish looking aristocrats. My beating chest and loud breathing was enough to make me ignore their screams and gasps.

We approached another balcony in front of us. Once we leaped from there, we landed, and dive rolled onto another rooftop. When we thought we were lucky, suddenly three Satanists materialized in front of us with their swords and rifles drawn.

All three of us charged and raged towards them until we were each connected with one Satanists. The one I was engaged with tried very hard to take me down with his rifle's bayonet. I swayed and swiftly dodged every strike he intended to make. A final strike allowed me to disarm his weapon. I held the rifle with both hands and slapped the Satanist across the face with the rifle's butt. Flipping it forward, I impaled the bayonet into his neck. I hastily snatched the pistol from his waist holster and pulled the trigger as the bullet fired through his head. He struggled and gargled his blood and plummeted to the ground. Ted and Juliet had already ended them as well. We all sensed more bullets raining down at us, giving us a chance to duck behind a large chimney that was next to us. Looking up, we saw that there were more demons hovering over us.

When they continued to fire, Ted held out his hand and stopped the firing bullets, freezing them in midair.

He then said to me, "Give it here!" Confused at first, I realized he meant the rifle, which I didn't realize that it was still gripped in my left hand. I didn't hesitate to toss him the rifle into his open hands. Once he recoiled and reloaded the bolt handle, he aimed at one of them and pulled the trigger. Despite being a satanic weapon, it didn't stop Ted from showing off his sharpshooting skills. I know we were undertrained, but we had to fend them off somehow. Regardless of it not taking affect.

While he was firing, he briefly used his trigger-happy hand to conjure another floating ripple, a portal. He told us to go through, assuring that he will continue to fire at the demons. Using their own weapons against them. As Juliet and I jumped into the ripple, Ted joined along as we all ended up landing on top of the roof of a cathedral. We were underneath a line of flying buttresses.

We continued to run as the castle was getting a bit nearby. But it was still very far from where we were. So, there was still some more obstacles to run over. A door was slammed behind us. What caught our attention were several more Satanists busting from the cathedral's roof and storming towards us. Of course, we ran and fired our way through by using their weapons against them. Not because we wanted to cower, but because we had little time for conflicts.

But as we were approaching, seeing the sun still cloaked behind the greying skies, more demonic soldiers hovered and blocked our path. A whole row of them swarmed and prepared to fire their rifles and crossbows. All made of energy. We staggered and stopped on our tracks, but we had to think about the Satanists who were behind us as well.

We quickly eyed back at them. When we turned forward, I swiftly caught Ted materializing another portal below us. He had to be tired at that point. We both looked up and saw the soldiers preparing to fire. As soon as they fired, we already jumped down into the ripple. I was hoping that the arrows and burning bullets had hit the Satanists instead.

We found ourselves landing on another rooftop amid the bustling and soldier riddled city. This time, we were getting very close to the castle. We didn't stop. We continued to move down. Below us, the roads were still swarming with soldiers pushing through the people. They pointed their rifles at us and began to fire. Black bullets flew upwards next to us. It didn't slow us down.

We leaped from one rooftop to an alleyway between two buildings. We zigzagged against each wall until we towered ourselves on top of the flat service. On the roof we were on, one Satanist was summoned. But Juliet swiftly summoned her energy longbow and fired at his head until he fell backwards and off from the roof.

We darted sharply and saw the draw distance getting closer to where we needed to be. We began to scale down the building we were on. Once we saw the road, we landed on our feet. We continued to take off. We were approaching a marketplace.

We were running very eagerly in hopes to be far from the reach of the soldiers as they were angrily ordering us to stop. We took the chase through the tunnel on the right side of the building. And because of the number of city folks were wandering on the streets, curious about the commotion, we got lost through the people.

As we were free from the crowd, we saw ourselves in the middle of a bustling road. Each side of the road had carriages running through. And right out there was the castle, looking down upon that very hill. We looked back and saw that the soldiers were continuing to come relentlessly in numbers.

We were eagerly running tirelessly down the crowded road. By the time we were almost out of the city, I felt my feet getting yarned a bit. But I had to be strong. And I couldn't stop now because of the bloody demonic army on our tail. And the Satanists wanted our heads as usual in promise of some fake reward.

We saw a passing wagon and hijacked it as Ted hopped onto the driver seat and pushed off the driver. "Sorry," he cried. He began to whip the reins for the horses to gallop faster and faster. We swerved from corner to corner depending on how many soldiers there were to get us. Juliet and I were fending off the best we could. The entire streets were swarming and swarming with soldiers and Satanists.

As we went finally racing from the last alleyway all the way to the palace, we happened to be exactly back into the war encampment where I was before. We rode faster until we busted through the gates and back inside of the encampment. The horses wailed and snorted fearfully after we quickly got off, finally in front of the bloody door. But it was still shut closed. But Ted and I managed to burst through, only to meet with...and you might have seen this coming...more bloody guards.

Whilst going through the hallway, we were dodging and jumping over upcoming halberd swings and spear jabs. At one point, as we were approaching the crossway stairs in front of us, Juliet tapped into her Blessed Eye and called upon her large flock of ghostly vicious birds that materialized from the wispy smoke. They surrounded and began to jab their diverse beaks into their helmets. We finally made it through. Working our way up the stairs, we turned to the left as we made it through another grotesque hallway.

Going down the hall, there was another crossway. Juliet came in front, presumably since she knew where our stuff was located. And without our weapons or gear, we would be useless. So, once we reached the end of the hall, Juliet led Ted and I to the left. There, it was leading us to a spiral flight of stairs. As we spun going up, we finally reached another hallway. This time, we were apparently heading towards a large door in front of us.

"It's in here! Hurry!" Juliet said in a rush. As she and I pushed through, Ted was the last one to enter. We founded ourselves in an office with another level above us. It was Sathanus's enclosure. On the desk in front of us were our things. As soon as Ted used a spear from the model of a demonic knight statue, he used it to block the door. It didn't take us very long to put on our outfits and use our weapons.

"We only have a few minutes! We can't delay!" Ted said as he was hurriedly putting on his jerkin.

"Aye, no kidding," I said as I was finally dressed and had my weapons, including my pistols equipped. I placed my hat on my head, making sure it didn't leave my head this time. I then asked, "But what are we gonna do?! Those soldiers are on us like bloody wolves!"

"I've got an idea," Juliet said as she was also dressed. She inserted her right hand into her satchel and pulled out something I've quite forgotten about. An ivory war blow horn with the angelic engravings. I slightly widened my eyes.

"You're sure that the noise will reach from here?" I asked.

"It should, I hope." She said. In a hurried manner, she placed the mouthpiece between her pink lips and blew into it. The horn made an ominous roar that sounded both harmonious and somewhat threatening all at once. It made the room shake a bit. When she was done, the noise was still going on for a good three minutes.

"Think that should reach them. This is some calling call." Juliet commented.

Boom! Boom! Two bangs made us jolt a bit. The cavalry was already here. But luckily, the spear was strong enough to hold the door shut. Ted insisted on manifesting an arcane mine from his satchel as a trap in case they entered. The three of us sharped our eyes at the second level floor. Alas, another opportunity was blessed upon us. We rushed around the desk and took the time to scale ourselves up the column to reach over the balcony. I was still holding on to each ledge, trying to stop myself from looking back and slowing down. Unconsciously, all I wanted to do was rest. But I knew I was not going to let myself to continue to let the Satanists win.

BOOM! BOOM! BOOM! The door sounded again. By the time we would leave the room, perhaps they would enter and find us. So, it prompted me to finally meet the Apostles who were already on the second floor.

We finally rushed through the door that was right in front of us, presenting us another hallway. We turned to the right, trying to find a way out of the palace now that we were equipped.

As we were reaching the other end of the hallway, we stumbled and stopped. What alerted us this time, you may ask? Several armed soldiers were already in the left side of the grotesque hallway, scouting out for us. This time, they were accompanied by three skinless, relatively massive, and red eyed hounds with teeth shaped and sharp like talons. Unfortunately, our footsteps have caught their attention. Including the hounds. We didn't hesitate to go towards the right side of the hallway. The loud barks of the hellish looking hounds were enough of a motivation to take off as quickly as we could. There was no crossway this time. The end made us turn to another right.

Juliet suddenly unleashed something from her satchel. Three silver eggshells, engraved with floral designs, were in her left palm. She slammed the shells in front of the soldiers and the hounds. What it did was burst into sparks that swiftly grew into flames. It was a good diversion for us to escape.

Finally, after we made a sharp right, we were approaching to an open door. We had yet to find out where it would lead us. Soon, the light bloomed in front of us. We were outside of the castle and discovered we were in the battlements of the palace.

Knowing that there was no way to simple jump, we ran towards the left side of the battlement. But as soon as we were closer to escaping, a herd of soldiers blocked the path and held out their spears. We quickly decided to go back to where we came from. But of course, another group of soldiers rounded up and blocked that path as well.

Obviously, we founded ourselves surrounded. Each group of demonic soldiers held out their spears and were gradually gaging at us. While Ted drew his arcane revolvers, Juliet and I unleashed our wands and transformed them into swords. We wanted to be as threatening as they were. We couldn't show fear.

To the right of us, Sathanus was seen hurriedly pushing through the soldiers. When he was finished pushing through, he drew his dirty golden pistol and cocked the hammer back, making the engravings glow across his barrel. I sensed that his dark eyes were glaring down at us.

I held up my sword and stood my ground.

"Did you honestly thought that you were going to get away...with what you did?" The captain asked, pointing the gun's barrel at me. "But look at you now...surrounded and trapped like the rats you are. You will conform, one way or another. Either to our cause...or death itself!!"

"Did you really think I was to join you? You're wrong!" I said with retort.

"I admit that you had us fooled. Including myself. No knight or Apostle has ever done what you did. I must say, I'm impressed," He said. "But now that you've had your fun, I believe an apology is in order."

"Why should I apologize...to a fallen angel...who had innocent spirits die? Just to pursue this...fake ideal crusade?" I asked through my teeth. But he began to chuckle behind his helmet.

He then stopped and said, "You're right. The same innocent spirits who casted him aside...whereas all he wanted to do was to change for the betterment of the afterlife. You're the one who stabbed him. And for what?"

"You allowed it."

"It won't be the first time I've put your Order to rest. But all could be fine. This discord we have could be arranged and united...if...you...comply," Sathanus said in a more ominous tone.

Ted suddenly got in front of us and pointed both gun barrels at him. He cocked both hammers and said, "We ain't givin' in. We're never givin' in. So, go fuck yourself, you kutas (**dick**)!"

Sathanus swayed the barrel from me towards Ted. He ordered, "Put those away, Yankee boy. You know you aren't brave enough to shoot us. You don't know how to use those."

"They came from my holsters. So, you wanna bet, pal?"

I appreciated Ted's bravery, but he knew that he was no match for a beast like Sathanus. At least not now. So, I took it upon myself to walk and stand behind him. And Juliet stood right next to me. The beast was coming closer with his pistol still pointed at us. His finger was tempted to put the trigger.

A laugh busted from under his helmet. He struggled to keep his composure. But after his laugh lasted for a few minutes, he said, "You pathetic little shites, the three of you! You are willing to die for one another....to protect your precious Order. To protect your friends. To protect your ideals and kingdoms. Meanwhile, there are many of my men...many of us...and yet, only the three of you in a dying society. Two heathens...and a false man of God. Once we're done with you, we'll kill your kings and queens as well. Including your mentor. Your age...has passed. It's been done for centuries. Get over it."

"That's when you're wrong," Juliet said, standing in front of us with her sword almost near him. She said, "If you think you will repeat history by wiping all of us from the afterlife, you're gravely mistaken. You may have taken out the ones who came before us. Taken down all knights. But they went down...destroying your crusade! And we will do the same!"

He chuckled and briefly gazed upon his soldiers, possibly asking himself *'Can you believe this?'*

He then asked her, "Is that so, lass? You, on the other hand, are as brave as a rancher girl. Stupid, heathen bitch. What makes you think we won't destroy you?" He blatantly placed the barrel on her forehead, making me eager to fight him regardless of his size. He then asked eerily, "Why are you still shaking...if you're not afraid? Hm? Huh? Why is that?"

Despite her body shivering a bit, she kept her composure and retorted back to him, "We don't kill to validate ourselves. To justify our cruelty! Let alone prove ourselves as worthy warriors, who are nothing more than fragile boys trying to be stone cold men. You think you're a man! But you're nothing but a disgusting coward!"

Anything that challenged his character riled Sathanus. I was very proud of Juliet of what she said. But as soon as he lifted his pistol backwards to pistol whip her face, I jumped forward, unleashed my blades from underneath my right wrist and impaled them both into his strike. Blood was drizzling and soaking through his gauntlet.

"AHH! You little shit!" He shouted. Suddenly, I felt his right hand grip my neck. Dropping my sword, I nearly felt my blood stop circulating inside of my skull. I was choking upon my own saliva. I gazed at Ted and Juliet. Both were held against their will when they intended to save me.

Another tug on my jugular made me focus into Sathanus's dark eyes filled with blood coiling rage. He then said, "One way or another, you will comply! You...are just a degenerate thug from the streets. You'll always be a degenerate thug! Self-righteous scum looking for meaning! Only Lucifer could give you meaning! You know it! Every man and woman here know it! Hell has longed for a leader to lead us to a better afterlife where peace is a manifestation! And no one will take him away from us! Not even a mongrel like you! We have eyes everywhere! Don't think you could run or hide in sanctuary! Your friends...your sister...you'll never be safe. Not in Heaven! Not anywhere in the afterlife! I promise!"

Suddenly, I felt him release my neck from his confinement whilst simultaneously witnessing a sudden burst of greying smoke forming and blasting through the battlement.

I felt my hat leave my head. And I barely saw what was happening. But as soon as I was whooshing away the smoke with my panama hat, I sharped my eyes to the left up and saw some shadowy collection of winged men in the skies. They held rifles, bows, spears, swords, and diamond shaped shields that were glazed with hardened stain glass.

But the smoke was clearing from my eyes, and I saw that the men were indeed winged. They were armed with bolt action rifles and arcane bows, firing down like a wild rainy storm at the demons in front of me who were plummeting to the ground like dolls. I stood up with my sword picked up from the ground and I turned at the front of me. Two justly built men were fighting alongside one another. One of them had long light brown hair with bronze armor. The other had short black hair with a man bun, donning silver armor.

I analyzed very carefully and slowly recognized both angels. My attention was caught by two arms grasping me on my feet, until I realized it was Ted and Juliet helping me up. As I adjusted on two feet, I looked over the battlement and saw a large herd of the same army.

This time, some were raging through the city on horseback. Some were sieging through one their feet. Over their heads were long spears, some with gold and blue flags attached.

I turned my attention to Archangel Gabriel, who's armor was already soaked with blood. He smiled and asked, "Are you three alright?"

"Well, apart from having the entire Demonic Legion on us, yeah. We're doin' good!" After Ted said that I watched as Michael was finishing off Sathanus by knocking him cold with the hilt of his sword. He turned to us and hurriedly came to join.

"What did you do to make them so upset," Gabriel asked.

"Kevin stabbed Lucifer in the chest, for starters. He's injured," Juliet said.

"Well...that explains a lot." He said to us, "You did wonderfully. Rash, but wonderfully. Good job for calling."

"Thank you," she said. "But what took you?"

"Apologies," Michael said. He then gazed up at the swarming angels. "As you can see, we needed backup. Heaven is beset with a big assault by Lucifer's army right now! So, we have to go back to help stop it!" He then faced us once again and asked, "Any chance you know where the mystics are trapped?"

"There trapped in an underground dungeon, underneath a cathedral by the name of Holy Temple of Sammon!" I spoke.

"And Bertha?" Gabriel asked.

"She has the scepter! She's already headed to the Axis Mundi. But I've tracked her down with Alwyn," Juliet informed. "We need to stop her before she gets to that staff!"

As Michael was pacing quite quickly, given the warring state, something has made him stop in his tracks. He then said to Ted and Juliet, "You two will go with Gabriel to rescue the mystics from that cathedral. Worry about that now!"

He then looked at me and said, "Kevin, you and I will go after Bertha. From there, I'll force the demons out from Heaven. Chances are that she might be there already."

Before I would go with him, I came to Juliet. We both quickly hugged one another, and she said holding my face, "May God be with you, Kevin. Be safe."

"You too. Come back safe!" I said as I released her.

I then gave a quick hug to Ted and released him. I said to him, "Come back safely, lad."

"We will. Just worry about getting that scepter back! With the shard! It's about time you suck it up and be a goddamn hero!" Ted said with a grin. I nodded.

And as he and Juliet were running with Gabriel through the warring battlement, Gabriel shouted, "Good luck, Kevin. See you back in Heaven!"

I nodded. I turned back to Michael as he gave me a small grin.

Suddenly, a bloodied soldier was limping towards Michael. His hair was nappy and wet with sweat. His face riddled with specs of blood and dirt. He said to Michael, "Sir, we sent some more soldiers to meet you at the Axis Mundi. Just as commanded. But our numbers here are decreasing extraordinarily here! Somehow, the demons are growing in power! What do you suggest?"

Before he said anything, Michael took one good gaze at me. His hand was on the weary soldier's shoulder. He said, "Try to stand your ground! As best as you can! All of you! Once I reach Heaven, I'll be sure to send more reinforcements!"

"Yes, sir," he said as he ran and disappeared in the crowd. Michael took another glance at the sky. The extra layer of omnipause smoke and cloud were disintegrating, making the angelic swarm clearer to see. He soon whistled and called upon his horse as it summoned right next to us, distinguishing the mist to reveal the steed.

"The skies are clearing up. Are you ready, Kevin? This is going to be bloody." Michael asked me.

"I can't think of another way, sir." I said. He had me mounted on the beautiful crystal-colored stallion as I saw its wings burst. After I sheathed my blade back into my satchel in wand formation, I held onto the reins.

"Make sure you catch up and hang tight," Michael said as he dived off from the battlement and flew up into the air. Whipping the reins, the horse wailed and galloped across the bloodied battlement. My heart pushed back as the steed hopped over the battlement and had us swoop over until I saw that I was vastly distancing from the battlements. I looked over the pristine streets of Dolorem and saw it infested with a full siege seeping through.

As soon as we descended into the grey bleak skies, I flew through the powerful and wildly brutal flying swarm of angels and demons colliding in feud. Wingless angels on flying pegs pointed and fired their arrows and energized bullets from their rifles. Their shots thundered the clouds like lightning. The winged soldiers fought and thrusted their spears and swords towards one another. Vice versa.

Some angels and demons fell into the desperate watery abyss of the ocean. There was just a lot to take in. I felt the thrusts of winds pushing me back. I held on to my hat despite the rushing wind's attempt of making it fall. After we flew through the madness, we hovered until I was whooshing from Dolorem through the gargantuan gloomy misty mountains. I made sure that I was behind Michael, who was soaring very fast.

Soon as we have flown for three minutes, Michael has made us soar from the corrupted land across the dark waters. It was not pure or crystal blue as it was in Heaven. It was a much darker blue. A depressing shade. The more I flew across the wide ocean, the closer we were getting to two pillars that created a wispy smoke-filled portal. Perhaps this was our way out to get to Heaven.

Without any sign of slowly down, we were already getting towards the brightness. I slightly squinted my eyes in hopes to avoid blindness. Beautiful and blissful, but bright. Bright enough to eventually light a fire. And I knew from then, we would eventually go and stop Bertha. We had too.

XL

⟨⟨⟨⟨⟨⟨⟨⟨⟩⟩⟩⟩⟩⟩⟩⟩

The Axis Mundi

Once we finally exited from the other side of the portal, it felt refreshing and relieving to see the crystal water again. It was good to see that the skies were moved by angelic white clouds. We were still flying for miles to get to the Axis Mundi, which was said to be in the central plane of Heaven's oceans. But even they were also plagued with a raging blazing feud between angelic and demonic ships. Soaring past a forest of erected masts with massive sails of each faction, I glanced down and saw each ship firing at one another, bursting into fire, and seeping slowly into the watery void.

The chaos was surely sent by Lucifer based on the doings of Bertha. I had to stop her. I had to stop her alone because she chose to make it personal.

Soon, I was beginning to see pointed towers that were reaching towards to clouds. And landmarks were taking form when we were gradually approaching. I began to see other marble Roman and Greek columns parallel to one another that created portals, scattered in the ocean. In the middle of all of it were the Axis Mundi Isles.

A circular sentiment gate was surrounding the singular marble and pointed tower. It was almost the shape of the exact shard Lucifer stole. By the land, two Satanic ships were already boarded. And the bloody front gate doors were broken down. So, the place was swarming and patrolled by Demon soldiers and the Satanists.

As soon as I saw Michael land, I descended the winged stallion to land on its crystalized hooves. As soon as I dismounted and patted the horse, I ran by the left side of the gate to stray away from the eyes of the Demons to meet Michael. We had to come up with a plan. As soon as I landed on two feet, I looked up at the gates wall, which was fourteen feet above my head. Michael was in discussion with the ten soldiers taking cover behind the wall, hiding out from the Legionaries until they had to wait for his command to attack.

He turned his face to me and approached removing something from underneath his tunic. In his right hand was a small olive-shaped vial filled with reddish liquid. He said to me, "Take this. It's likely that Bertha has already made the place surrounded by cinnabar energy."

"But...I passed out the last time I took it."

"It is the cinnabar in your soul that battled against it before. Don't worry, we shall have a chakra professional to help you remove it once this chaos is settled. Hopefully, since they are often hard to come by," Michael said as he handed me the glass vial.

Concealing in my left hand, he then said to me, "Kevin, whatever happens, you have to make sure that Bertha does not – at all – get through that door! And when you get out, you must never...ever...speak of it. Not even to Ted nor Juliet!"

"Right. Of course. But what about the soldiers in the front?" I asked.

He looked back and suddenly had his hand reach for his holstered sidearm. He looked back at me and said, "I'm going to make a distraction...me and my men here...while you find your way inside by subverting through without being caught. You think you could do that?"

I nodded nervously. But I swallowed my nervousness and said, "Yeah. I can."

"Excellent. Thank you, Kevin." Michael said, patting me on the shoulder.

He the continued, "And...I know this was such a toll on you. I know it's a bad time to say this, but...I was told that you were intending to kill yourself. I thank God wholeheartedly that you didn't go through with it. We've lost far too many good people in our days. We cannot afford to see you lose yours. Your life is precious and important. You're a good young man, Kevin. You're not alone and we'll always be beside you. Remember that."

"Thank you, Michael," I grinned and nodded.

"You're welcome. Best of luck. And be careful, yeah?"

"I will. You too," I assured him. He nodded and swiftly ran with his right hand on his sword handle. This gave me time to quickly analyze and plan my way into the tower.

The Satanists were most likely guarding the front that I saw from above. The fields looked to be twelve acres apart from each other. What I could do is to furtively get my way inside.

So, I began to scale my way up the wall. I propelled myself forward with each large step I made with my toes. Once I was finally making my way to the flat surface of the wall, I looked over and saw at the broken gates at least fourteen demonic legionaries standing around and armed with long rifles. Behind them were eleven Satanists patrolling the front of the temple's front. It looked to be a fortress at that point. All I saw was the lone Axis Mundi temple.

After the quick analyzation, I saw that they were one Satanist below me. I got myself up to sit on the wall. I quickly opened the vial to take a sip from the Fahrenheit tonic. What I feared more than the Satanists was the force field preventing me to enter. So, as I chugged away, the vial was already empty. My tongue consumed the same warm minty tingling sensation I tasted before. After three seconds, I was starting to feel warm. The tonic was taking form inside of me.

"Argh," I winced as the tonic was still corrupting my broken soul. But it was no time to endure the pain.

So, as I looked down, I stood on my two feet and balanced myself. Flicking my right wrist, the two blades came out from my gauntlet. It was a good thing that the armed Satanist didn't sense my presence despite the wince I made.

Once I studied his movements to see if he was to meet my eyes,

I crouched and leaped from the wall. Landing on him, I got him plummeted to the ground. With no holding back, I swiftly impaled and removed my blade from his neck. His blood was pooling by his head and shoulder. I looked up to see the remaining Satanists, unaware of my clean kill.

I saw that there were bushes surround the side of the tower right by the flight of side stairs.

Bang! Bang! I heard gunshots from the distance. I watched as it attracted the fourteen soldiers in the front. This meant that Michael and the Angels finally fired. A skirmish was soon to begin. Thus, I had my own priority. The massive battles at sea became distant as the thundering cannons and cries became faint. As soon as the soldiers were disbursing away from the front gates, I continued to swiftly pace myself with the decomposing body in my arms. No time for distraction.

The Satanists looked to be interested but knew that they had to hold their position. Once I was nearing the bushes, I quickly lifted the corpse and threw it in as it disappeared into the leaves. The more I saw of the tower, the more I realized how much of a behemoth it was. I looked up and saw that the point was almost penetrating the Void.

So, I began to swiftly make my way up the side stairs, making sure that I was not caught. I looked over and over, hoping that the Satanist's body wasn't caught. I knew that it will eventually disappear, but I wouldn't want to risk seeing the body.

Shortly afterwards, I made it up to the temple. The clear marble stone was becoming more and more prevalent the more I witnessed its painstaking detail. I looked over and saw that the Satanists were still roaming around. Some were still curious about the commotion. I saw that four Satanists were disbursing from the temple's front to check in with the soldiers.

Luckily, this gave me a chance to enter. But to distract them, I raised my hand and summoned one of my shadows from the Shadowmacer. The wispy dark obscurus looked into my eyes, waiting for my order. I pointed to the Satanists and said facing it, "Deal with them." The shadow swayed and dashed away with a sword in its hand. When he was away, I felt a part of my head beginning to bang against my skull. For now, I had to endure it.

I turned and faced the large door that was before my eyes. I took a deep breath, hoping I knew what I was doing. With no turning back – at least for now – I opened the doors and entered. Upon entering what looked to be a very large room, it didn't take a while for me to hear the cries of pain and anguish from the remaining Satanists.

Once I entered, the door did not hold back from closing itself. But I was surrounded by nothing but silence. I thought about my dreams as if they were coming to a reality. Although, I did hear something liquifying that was traversing through the place. In fact, my boots were becoming wet due to having them implanted in moist ground.

But out of nowhere, it was no longer becoming dark. It was gradually lighting up than it should be. Floral, horizontal, and lavish lines were all colored light blue. All of them were traversing and tangling on these larger-than-life pillars that were all scattered in the dark room. And the place was somehow flooded with dark waters.

Intrigued and estranged, I removed my sword and held it for precautious reasons. In case some semblance of Satanists was ever to show up. I was walking towards the middle in between the decorated pillars. I couldn't stress how small every place in the afterlife made me feel. And the interior was no exception.

It took me a while to get to the other end of the temple, which looked to be where I needed to go. Despite the sogginess I felt in my boots, I paced myself through the heightening waters. I needed to get there quickly. When I was approaching to the entrance, I stopped on my tracks and quickly took cover behind a pillar. I spotted four Satanists, presumably looking out for Bertha while she tried to enter. They were armed with rifles. The other two were far at the entrance. Just so if they were unaware of my presence, it was good for me to sneak behind and kill them with a clean stab. I only wanted Bertha's attention.

With my cantation, I extracted my soul to possess one of them to stab the other next to him with his dagger without making a sound.

After I disbursed from cover, I bent both of my knees and slowly stepped closer to the others. With each tedious step, I made sure that the water did not make too much noise. Only droplets. Unleashing my retractable blades from my right, I began to pace myself moderately quickly. And before they could even notice me, or to alert Bertha, I already impaled the blades into their necks. Blood shot and oozed down their necks whilst they gagged and gasped with blood pooling in their jaws.

They dropped in front of me. I finally went into the big room. At the end, I saw someone with noticeably long red hair. At the end of the bridge displayed what Francis once described a large door with a golden watching eye. And the person lifting the scepter – presumably Bertha – was intending to have it opened. Beside the bridge were two flowing waterfalls, falling to whatever abyss lied ahead.

I walked over to Bertha. The shredded droplets of the water were pasting themselves on my stubbled face and onto my hat. I paced myself quickly to her, feeling warmer. Either it was the Fahrenheit tonic taking effect or it was simply my distaste and anger towards her.

She has already channeled Jesus's scepter due to the crystal illuminated with a dark reddish color. Her face suddenly turned when she noticed how quiet the Satanists were. And that was good. This meant that it was me and her this time.

Her head sharply turned to me with amazement. She was stunned to see me. Her face seemed faded. But then she smirked and said,

"Hello Kevin."

"Hello Bertha."

She quickly eyed at the door and back at me, she said, "I see that you've came to the Axis Mundi."

"I have," I said as I held my longsword's hilt with two hands.

"Lovely place, isn't it?"

"Aye...it is. Which is why we shouldn't be here. I wouldn't want to spill your traitorous blood all over these grounds," I said.

I continued, "But if I have to, I will."

Flattening her lips to a neutral expression, she dropped the scepter next to her. She then faced me and said while pointing at me, "Alright. Of course. You call me *traitorous*. Why is that? Because what I say is true? You call me traitorous, but I am only doing what I could do to make the afterlife prosper well! To make sure it doesn't fall in the hands of those with no integrity!"

"You don't care about the spirits! None of you do! You see the afterlife as an opportunity...for your own gain!" I snapped at her. "Your stupid narrative!"

"You may see it that way! Your *free will* depends on it! But you are too blinded by that *free will* to realize that we're fighting for something! Like what you are fighting for," Bertha said from afar from where I was.

She continued, "Only we are fighting for purity and peace, not just for our own pleasure! It's obvious that you haven't learned anything; given how you deliberately stabbed Lucifer! You think that you're a *hero* for that?! You think that you're redeemed?! You think because you stand alongside those who claim to be holy...means that you are reaching salvation?! You're gravely mistaken!"

"I don't need a lecture from you anymore! And I sure as hell do not wish to be a part of your new heaven!" I said, tightening my grip on the sword. "I'm not trying to be a hero! I want to do what I can to stop this world from meeting its third fate! Something I couldn't do for where I came from! Now surrender! It's over!"

She didn't heed my order, which echoed inside the interior. "You are quite the errand boy I figured you were," she ridiculed. She unsheathed her rapier from her waist scabbard. She then said, while she was suddenly choking up, "You think you're the only one who has his soul broken by people?! Try getting kicked out by your own family because you were an accident not meant to exist! Try struggling to find your place in a world where everybody blindsides, deserts, or uses you for themselves, forgetting your existence! Try asking God for a better life, knowing you can't do it on your own, no matter how hard you try! Only for him to turn on you too! As my parents and everyone else did! Leaving you to face the world alone...until you can't take it anymore!

You think you're the only one...who wanted to escape humanity? Your humanity? When you dwell into that kind of darkness, when you allow that broken soul to...desecrate...it only makes you stronger when you earn a new one! When I saw you that day; I saw myself. The person I never got to be. The potential I never gotten to tap into. I saw who I was...and what I can become. What I could obtain. I saw a second chance to instigate someone like me to a cause beyond themselves."

As sorry as I felt for her, I was honestly disgusted by her attempt to use it as an excuse for her heinous crimes. In my mind, all I thought about was ending it. So, I said whilst holding out the sword towards her, "You had my parents killed...when they only wanted to live again! You tried to sell my sister for money! You killed all those people! You cursed those villages with your obscenities! You and your posse used the C.F. D. as a front! You caused this madness! And now, you expect me to give a damn about you?! You've lost my concern and trust!"

"I didn't ask for your concern! Nor your trust! I don't need them! I only ask for you to understand why I am doing what I'm doing! Lucifer understands what souls need to be! He made me stronger. Made me smarter. He accepted me, acknowledged me. That's why I joined his empire. It was bad enough to be concealed in humanity's mistakes. But the afterlife is better than that! Better than falsifying its noble notions! My whole life has been nothing but molestations, false hopes, and loneliness, all of which I couldn't do anything about! But now I can! I could show that I exist in this world! We could show them, Kevin! The afterlife can be so much better...when everyone submits to the New Heaven. And all could be done...by the Insignia that is behind this door!"

"I'm not giving you any chances of going inside that room!"

She chuckled and said with a smile, "This is so hilariously pathetic. It's quite lovely, I must admit. Seeing someone give orders! That someone who was once a criminal. A human criminal who slaughtered countless people, scammed unwitting folks, defied the law, and screwed a whore...only to later kill her!"

"I don't need you to remind me of who I was! I lived it. Accepted that it happened. I've left that life behind and chose to be better! You're the one using your dark life as an excuse for your crimes! You're the one who won't change! Only way you can...is to surrender that scepter and the shard! Now!" I warned.

"You better ask in a polite matter, little boy."

"It's not a request! It's a demand! Get over yourself already and just surrender!" I shouted. I then followed, "You're no better than the others! Because what you did to...to us...what you did to me...is unthinkable! You're no bloody different!"

"You don't know me! Why should I bend backwards to a feeble Jew who made a pointless sacrifice as a human? For all this talk about peace and harmony, he sure as shit doesn't give a damn about that! He doesn't care about peace! He doesn't want to cleanse the souls of humanity! He only wants to see them tear each other apart like brainless animals! Like what they have always done! Lucifer, however, has an exceptional vision for the afterlife! And I gladly approve of that and support it! So would my ring! Either you understand it or cut loose!" She had herself already engaged to fight.

She continued, "And I will see his vision fulfilled, one way or another! I will have the life I deserve! In this world and the next! If I must die for my faith in a paradise, then best to reign in hell...than to serve in heaven!"

After I notched my neck, I said to her, "As you wish. I'm done talking to you."

Soon, both of us raged at one another with our blades erect. Thus, our blades connected and generated white sparks with each hit. While blocking every big strike from her blade, she did a pretty good job of keeping me unbalanced. But I would always position myself, never compromising. Never putting my guard down.

I ran and leaped toward her with the blade. She slashed on the side of my blade with fury, making me unbalanced. When I got back, I did a back stroke on her torso. Luckily, she swayed around it. I still had my blade pointed at her. We stood and studied each other, the mist of the ongoing falling waters between us. The mood was quiet. The only sound near me was my own breathing.

Shortly after the ten seconds, I let out a roar and jousted my blade once again, in which she blocked my strike. We continuously connected and smacked out blades in lavish ways. As we were continuously slaying at one another, we kept spinning as we were placed on difference sides.

Whilst striking at her with one hand, she kept using one hand to parry my strikes. I parried hers as well. With one big strike down, I was able to block it. But we held our blades like glue to the point where she was even trying to gradually push me off the edge of the stone bridge.

But with all my strength, I pushed her back and made her stumble backwards. I began to engage with her and continuously slashed at her with the blade despite her blocking every strike. Learning from my training, I swayed my sword with ease. But my strikes would almost always come out strong and précised.

Once again, I made her spin to the same spot as she was before. I ran up to her and we continued to integrate our blades. Both of us swung at each other like relentless bloodthirsty soldiers. We swung wildly. Each strike continued to summon quick orange sparks. I felt my frustration rising, knowing what kind of person she was. What she has put me through. The strikes became very hardened. Again. Again. And again. Right until the blade came down onto hers, disarming her weapon.

Dropping her sword, she briefly gazed down almost in defeat. She angrily breathed in heavily and glared at me. She suddenly positioned herself with both of her arms guarded. It was only fair. So, I decided to unsheathe the Redeemer. Just like her, I also held my fists up. We both stared down at each other's souls, waiting on who would make the first move.

Without holding back, she hopped two times towards me and began to throw three punches. Right, left, and right again. I blocked all three using both of my forearms. Intending to throw another punch, I blocked and held that one. Soon, I threw a left punch at her temple and made her head sway to the left. She regained herself and composed her stance. She decided to engage with me again and intended to throw a right blow.

I dodged and weaved away from her strike and dodged underneath her leg spin kick. I leaped and attempted to throw a left blow onto her skull, in which she blocked it. Just as we fought with swords, we connected our forearms and intending to punch one another. Until one of us meant one, that is. But as I fought, I was taken back to my human days, where I fought in the streets of Brooklyn. Snake taught me once to make sure that every move I made would manipulate and confuse my opponent. And it couldn't be more evident if it tried.

At one point, we both tried to strike at our legs. But I swiftly grabbed her second attempt at kicking me, I held her by her ankle and used my left hand to slice her thigh with my Apostle blades.

"Augh!!!" She yelled and stumbled back. Holding on to her wounded leg with her right, she quickly got used to it and decided to engage with me. Every punch she threw, she kept yelping like a hound. She then took my upcoming blow at her and twisted my arm. I let out a yelp in pain as she yanked it around my back and went close behind me.

I felt her hot breath next to my left. So, I stomped her toes with my bootheel. She screamed, and I turned around. I turned around to face her and adjusted my left arm, which was working fine. Despite feeling tired, I ran towards her and tackled her to the ground with her arms flailing upwards. I found both of my bent knees over her chest. I faced her down and glared down at her with disdain. I began to throw every punch with the short amount of strength I had within me. Left, right, left, and right. Occasionally, I made an upper cut onto her chin. Her face was becoming gradually bloodied. But to be fair, so was mine. Bertha was a cunt, but she knew how to fight. But I thought about everything that happened. Thus, it built up each blow I made.

Again, and again, I strike at her until her face was gradually riddled with purple and blue smears. Her temple and forehead were drizzling with blood. She tried to block my other blow by grasping my fist. However, I pushed her left arm aside and continuously punched her hand against the ground. She shouted in pain as she felt her joints snapping from within. I quickly drew my arcane pistol and cocked the hammer back, preparing to fire at her head.

I saw her grin with her lips with four lines of blood drawing from her jaw. I felt a sharp pain in the groin, and it made me recoil off from her. I rolled on my back and felt my hat leave my head once again. I sat my head up and saw Bertha struggling to stand on her two feet. This gave me a chance to shoot her.

But I looked back and saw that it was at least two feet away from me. I thought if I could reach it, maybe I could shoot her. However, as I looked back at her, I saw that she was already standing. She stood with her gun barrel pointed at me.

I ignored her, thinking that she was bluffing for me to stay down. But as soon as I was just trying to go for the pistol, *BOOM!* I already heard a sharp and swift sound hitting against my flesh. Particularly between my torso and pelvic bone. "Argh! Dammit!" I felt the pain growing sharply and traversing. I looked down and saw that the bullet Bertha fired hit near my torso. I felt the blood oozing from the wound.

But it didn't stop me from trying to get my gun. But she was walking towards me whilst undrawing her gun.

She said to me, holding her injured hand with the other, "Why don't you just give up, Kevin? You know...what it has...to be! Everyone you came to love will become a part of this new heaven! And your sister...she will forget about you...once we get her into our flock! The Apostles won't always be there for you...because the only way to restore the afterlife to its true glory...the way it should be...is to wipe them off. Worse than the last! To let your flawed faith...die...while ours will endure. Unless...you obey the New Heaven."

I ignored her words and concentrated on reaching to my gun. As I dragged myself, she continued, "Give up and understand that only Lucifer can give you meaning to all of this! He could save you from your past! Jesus can't save you! Nor Francis! You will be deceived...just as I was! There is a true afterlife around the corner! A true place we could call paradise!"

As she was closer and closer to me, she was already looking down at me. I watched as she lifted her left foot and stomped on my wound very hardly. I yelled out, "Argh!! Augh!" The pain was unbearable. I gripped my hands tightly to make myself sustain the pain, praying that it will vanquish.

"And you are not going to stop me from getting there!" With one final squeeze on my wound, she released her foot. The pain in my torso was getting worst, as if something was on the brink of falling off. Embrace the pain. That was something that rang in my head. And thus, that is what I did. I had to embrace it for now.

So, I reached out my right arm to reach my pistol. My fingers touched the tip of the pistol butt. As soon as I curled my fingers, I made sure that they fully grasped around the handle. My index was placed on the trigger. And luckily, I saw that the hammer was still cocked back, meaning that it was prepared to fire.

Slowly and steadily, I pointed the barrel at Bertha, who was limping to the scepter. I intended to kill her for all she did, but something within tirelessly was converting my finger to stray away from pulling the trigger. Perhaps, this anger I had was being controlled by my light. I heard a loud gasp that echoed in the temple. I suddenly saw Bertha drop to the ground face down. I held onto my bleeding wound with my left hand. I felt it continuously flowing from my torso until it reached down into my trousers, soaking it. I had to see what was going on with her.

After undrawing my gun, I took my time to stand up. But when I stepped up on one foot, I winced to the pain that bloomed. My hand still on the bleeding wound. My head felt wildly massive because of the blows I received. I was drowsy enough to not care about picking up my hat. At least, not right at the minute. My focus was to get Bertha.

I dragged my numbing right arm as I walked near her body. Clinging onto my bleeding wound, I saw that she was still crawling to get to the door, like a dying insect. She was breathing rapidly. After I was near her, I bent down on one knee and turned her over by grasping her shoulder. She stopped crawling as she was trying to grasp for air. Her mouth drizzling a curtain of blood. And her eyes were gradually whitening. "The energy of the...Satanist...it's etching into my core," She faintly said as she was constantly taking her last breaths.

She continued, "Why...didn't you shoot? A light bloomed for you not to go through with it, I presume."

"Believe me. Watching you suffer like this...is more effective. There are monsters.... far worse than you...that are need of my attention. Like that bloody posse of yours...for instance." I hated saying that to her. I really did.

She investigated my eyes as she chuckled. And somehow, they were still full of pride. She coughed at me and asked, "You don't know what it is you're doing. Do you? Every mistake you make, it's going to slowly destroy the goodness.... we intend to preserve! Doesn't that mean anything to you?"

"Your so-called goodness...is only an excuse...to insure conformed suffering in damnation. You're no revolutionary. You're no crusader. You know exactly what you're doing. Don't kid yourself!"

"You still don't know...or seem to care! All this death you conducted...in exchange for your salvation. I only hope it pays off in the end," she said.

"Even on the edge of your life, you still talk."

"Because...there's so much I have yet to say..."

"You always have something to say, Bertha," I said.

She smiled with her bloodied teeth and said, "This is good. Trust me on that."

"It better be. Seeing how you won't live for much longer."

She breathed deeply, allowing the air to enter her body. After her eyelids opened, her eyes were becoming foggier. She said, "I loved...life, Kevin. I loved what...it could be. I loved our world. I always did. I always will. It's dear. But...I hate who we are. I hate our species for what they did. Humanity is an illness to life. And to carry it to the next life...is truly unthinkable. We hold ourselves back. Pushing away what could truly be fruitful. Faithful. Seamless. I don't believe...in progression. Steppingstones. Or anything that excuses war, justifies crimes, or fetishizes every despicable, cruel, or inherently evil piece...of man. Something that brings out the worst...from people. I've always...prayed to God...for a flawless life. To be perfect...myself. To have breakthroughs from circumstance. We all have the tendency to let things die. Principles. Morality. Beauty. We try to keep all of them alive...knowing that there are those, such as yourself, who want to see it destroyed."

"You should've worried about being that hope you wanted from the world, no matter what, instead of expecting it to be perfect in your eyes," I said to her.

Her eyes somehow were shifting in a narrow portion as if she was coming to regret everything she did.

"But that's what I've always wanted. It's what keeps me going. In this life...and the one I had. We can't let things die. They're apart of us, don't you see? I allowed God to be with me, hoping that he will show me that world. To show me that light. I sacrificed for it. I worked for it. All alone. But...he turned on me. Like he turned from the world he created. Like he turned on both of us...making us damned!"

"I felt like that. I felt like he turned on me as well. But I realize that God did not make life that way. We do that...to ourselves. We always have. And it's most likely...that we always will. I wanted a perfect world too. I distasted humanity for their faults. I included. And maybe I still do. But this world made me finally understand my nature...and the nature of others," I expressed. "No one could ever be as good as God. No one is perfect. But we could always be what he wants us to be. Better versions of ourselves. For better or for worse, life cannot exist without us...because that is what makes it special. I'm convinced that some are far from salvation. But even they don't deserve this."

"I appreciate your spirit, Kevin. But it doesn't matter now. I was close to an actual Eden. A paradise where peace is not meddled by broken men. Even if it risked...being in the Inferno. I will be...remembered. My posse will continue my masterpiece. My mark...my blood...will be painted across all the afterlife's history. You, on the other hand, will become scum rotting away in the street of some god forsaken neighborhood."

"No one will remember you. Lucifer doesn't care for you. He sees you as an asset. A means to an end. He's not capable of love. Don't you get it!?"

"You may see it that way...," she said before she coughed. Then she continued, "You're the one who doesn't get it! Who cares whether he's capable or not? I know what I want in the end. But he is loving. You just don't want to understand him. After what he went through with Jesus, it's no wonder why he did what he did. It's justified."

"It's no excuse...to have eight million spirits die for nothing! It's no excuse to put the afterlife in such a state!"

"Ha...You act all superior now just because of your knighthood! But we are just the same. I know. It's...overused to say this. But it's true. We both fight. We stand for something. We put ourselves on the line for our principles and faiths. The only difference...is that we fight for a faultless world...whereas you fight for a flawed one," She breathed.

"Well, I thought I wanted to fight for a perfect world. But now, I rather fight...for an imperfect world...than an empty one...destroyed by wicked conformity. One man's paradise...is another's damnation. We may not be...equal in... worldviews. In color, status, or nation. But our very existence...all of us...and what we do for life.... how we serve life...is enough to be considered as such. That's all. Learning from agony...is what will set us free. That's what you said. Only unlike you, I choose not to cut corners. Only to do the right thing. As an heir of the Hospitallers. As a Princeton. As a man."

After she pondered and coughed, she spoke, "It doesn't matter now. We could talk on and on like politicians...with heads up their asses! But when I'm gone...those who support him...they'll come for you. Now more than ever. They'll have your head for what you did to their leader. They'll come here and have the same intention for that staff. And when everything...all around you...begins to break before your eyes...only then...you will finally understand. And it will be up to you...to accept him...or to cast him aside." She continued to cough violently. Blood shot up from her mouth. She then said, "Don't forget. He was...one of you. He felt how you felt. Saw what you see."

"So were you. At least...I thought you were."

She leaned her head against the floor and breathed again. Her breathing was clogged by the amount of blood she was losing. She eyed at me with eyes, suddenly full of concern. Despair. She said to me, "You've sold your soul...in exchange for deliverance. To the wrong folks. There are things...you don't know. But you will. You will. You will know your value. It's easy...to forget what you've been through...when you are given new blessings. Cherish them, seeing that they are easy to lose."

She breathed once again and finally said before she passed, "Welcome...to the afterlife, Kevin Princeton. I only wish...we could've been friends...in this place." With one lasting breath, gasping from exhaustion, her eyes were left open. Her mouth wide open. And the light shined from her eyes. Soon, it became vacant. Hollow.

I took it upon myself to close her eyelids. I then said to her, "May God have mercy on you. Hopefully...you'll find that perfect world."

Soon, I looted through her pockets. In her jacket pocket, I felt something hardened and small. When I pulled out my hand, there it was: the shard. I didn't stop. So, I placed the shard into my pocket. Next, I went passed her corpse and grabbed Jesus's scepter.

Finally, I began to depart with the shard and scepter. I grabbed back my hat on the way out from the temple entrance. All what was left was to get Michael to get Bertha's body out from the place. And the force field around the island was probably gone now.

It was a bit of a downer to not see how the Holy Insignia looked like. But it was probably for the best. Not even I wouldn't want to put myself into having full power. Not even to witness all its glory. It stood right where it belonged. Untouched by the hands of zeal.

What Bertha said stuck to me. I really wished she was my friend too. She did good things for my family and the others. I just wished she didn't do what she did just to create a perfect world.

I prayed to shatter the falseness of a universal paradise that blinded Lucifer and his followers one day. There was more to the battle than I thought. All to determine the fate of the afterlife.

I hoped to do what I can to stop it. All of it.

XLI

The Fifteenth Apostle

Two Weeks Later...

The shard has finally been returned, though I had yet to know what Jesus planned to do with it. His scepter has returned as well, kept, and held in the shrine safe and heavily guarded by the most brutal and unforgiving soldiers. And Sarah and Frask have been safely returned to their homes. Ted and Juliet returned safely after the mystics were returned.

The assault was eventually stopped by Michael but cost the lives of most of the soldiers in every position. My wounds were treated, but the pain was still prevalent. It was not an easy two weeks to get everything relatively normal. But I suppose nothing will always be easy. Even with others.

It was certainly not easy to get over those who passed. It still hurts. Let alone to watch with your own eyes. I'm sure it wasn't easy for Jesus, knowing that it was hard to keep promises as both messiah and a king. Especially a king.

Today, the Main Chapel was decorated and bright. It was still early as dusk was slowly dying. The people of Celestia were mandated to join the funeral. It was a day where we watched the spirits who only wanted to live pass on to another place where they could rest. A place where they could live as stars. A place where they would come together and unknowingly create constellations.

It was their day today.

So, I sat alongside Francis and faced Jesus from the left side of the room. I obviously wore dark clothing; but it was somewhat lavish and resembled to what I wore as an Apostle. Of course, my friends were there as well; including Frask himself. They were also well-dressed. The interiors were moderately dimmed with the light from the pink-orange sky as the stained-glass windows painted the room. The sun was still asleep.

Jesus spoke with grief in his tongue. After he sighed, he began, "We come here today...to watch our fellow men and women...shift their spiritual counterparts into what they truly were, stars. Within all of us, there is a star that blooms like a flower. A light that shines like the sun. And the last thing we want for the stars we have...is to watch them die. Let them burn. To watch them fall into the darkness of the abyss. Great men, women, and children have passed today. Common spirits who only wanted to live their lives, whether they were pure spirits, shifters...or astrals. Though, we may not know their intentions, end goals, or who they were, God knew. And God watches us from everywhere. Through everything and everyone. The cross...I sacrificed myself on..." He then pointed to the large stain glass window behind the three thrones.

It showed a large cross decorated with floral engravings and down the middle showed the chakras shaped as diamonds. "...signifies every-thing. Sure, to someone like Lucifer...or Pontius Pilate...or our fellow Chancellors here...it signifies what they consider as justice. Nailing those who are casted as criminals. All because they prefer to be in their echo chambers. They have their way of looking at it. But to me, it means a lot. Faith. Resurrection. And Love. In this world, we are alive. We continue to live. To thrive. These signs of the cross must remain alive as well. And people like Lucifer intend to tear it apart. He wants to...break our souls. Succumb to something worse than death. Unfortunately, my great people, this...everlasting conflict that I have regretfully taken part of...has officially begun. A conflict that I have tirelessly tried to protect all of you from. One I want to end for good. A task I intend to continue...now more than ever with the Covenant of the Gods. Because it has cost the many lives of these great souls of humanity. It is time...that I come very honest with you. I am the Son of God, one of the high kings of the Promised Land...therefore, I mustn't lie to all of you. The Gods has made us monarchs to be honest. I mustn't lie. I must be honest."

He let out a deep sigh and said, "The Axis Mundi...consists of a scepter that once had the power to control the core minds and hearts of humans and spirits. To resurrect souls from the Void or the Abyss. An ultimate key to create paradise. I channeled it to become a celestial plane for the afterlife to connect to humanity. Many have said that I am not for peace. Many have said that I am not for harmony. I am called a fraud or a shadow of what I used to be. None are true. I am for peace. I am for harmony. I condemn the zealous actions to obtain both. I condemn people suffering to be pure by removing their humanity. I condemn leaders who don't see their people as men and women with hearts, minds, and souls, but sees them as projects for their immoral societal experiments. Leaders who falter God's grace. Leaders who play with lives like a fiddle. I condemn all of it. That is why I channeled the staff. My fellow souls, we must understand one of the truths of the afterlife. This place belongs to the gods. But the lives are yours. We all have our odysseys, our visions for inner peace and harmony. We all make choices that build us on who we are. We all have dreams, wants, needs. We all have our own lives and ways of honor. We all have our gods within us. Our own heavens and hells. And I would just be as corrupted as Lucifer if I were to take those away from you. A world that seems imperfect is what makes it genuine...special...and unique. Because it allows us to grow constantly in faith. To grow closer to the divine. Not to kingdoms, empires, rulers, nobles, but God himself. To expand and bolden who we are. To consecutively better ourselves for legacy upon legacy. To seek for something greater beyond man's need for elitism. Beyond our outer wants to satisfy our inner needs. It is why I am your king. I rule to keep the wisdom of faith and freedom alive. I couldn't care less for power. That should go for everyone. So today, all of us should honor these lost stars. They didn't deserve to meet their fates. But now, God has them in his care. And right now, they will glimmer in the sky. And their songs of stars will last forever…and ever. Thank you all. May God bless you eternally."

It was over. These were good words. Prettily words to lift the citizens and to put the souls to rest. Soon, I got up to reunite with my friends. But at that token, I was thanked by the Civil Force Commissioner Cerviel, this bucked up, uniformed and brown-haired fellow, for what I did. And he thanked Ted and Juliet as well. Surprisingly and unexpectedly, we received gratitude by most of the people inside, which was more than enough to warm my heart. Including the soldiers.

The Chancery too. Only I sensed no true sincerity from them. Especially from Leviticus Himlin. I was glad to determine who was genuine and who was not. Still, I chose not to care. I was not obliged to admire nor care for those I saved. Outside of my circle, the spirits were no different. I cannot hope to help them. I could only, hopefully, guide them to help themselves.

However, as if a part of my brain popped in my head, I was coming to realize what I've become. A herd of insights traversed my mind like a cow herd riddling across the great gold plains of wheat. It was almost a bittersweet feeling, being gone from a world that was essentially going to hell to begin with. But a world that I knew. A world I wished I had time to make right as I somewhat did in the other.

I almost choked up thinking about it; every event I've been through. Whether they were lucid dreams or even the darkest moments. It was enough for me to ignore the time going by as the funeral was over and the common spirit folks began disbursing from the Main Chapel's interior. Suddenly, a familiar voice said, *"You've been trying to live two different lives at once, Kevin. It's unwise. To live in divinity, let one of them go."* Bertha. Her voice. Her last words. Somehow, they haunted me.

"Excuse me," I said quietly as I disbursed from the throne area and into the halls of the castle. There was something I had to recollect on my own.

After I went up the spiral stairs, I was already back in that marble walled hallway. The same I remembered when I broke in. It was still a bit saturated from any color because the sun was too shy to rise. But I presumed it would shine now.

Once I was making my way down the hall, I placed my head on the nearest wall on my left. I gazed upon one of the doors I was nearby. A doorway that led to a room I haven't been in for a long while now.

Once I faced the door, I looked left and right and hoped that I wasn't watched. Or followed. So, I swiftly went inside the room. Specifically, the Kaleidoscope Room. The room in which I could only know about the Earth's whereabouts.

I stood and faced the large round flat fountain. The dark waters were still and subtle. I didn't bother to use the mechanisms to see the kaleidoscope better. So, I slowly but swiftly paced myself forward. I was gaining closer and looked down at the very still water. Upon it, there was my reflection.

Harris claimed that he would never forget me, but have I forgotten about him? That's what I asked myself. Of course, I had to figure it out.

After I hesitated a bit, I moist my left hand and manifested ripples. The once still waters were shifting into a lake of bright stars, displaying those various galaxies in the universe. I pressed into the Milky Way, and there I saw the planets all within the ether.

And when the kaleidoscope shifted, there it was; the world I knew. The world I came from. Earth. There it stood still. Beautiful and disgusting, like a beast with the most exotic of pelts. A vulture with the most extraordinary feathers that came from the sweetest cosmos and nebulas. Funny how I wanted to escape that world, not realizing how I much I was missing the goods thing I had there. Not realizing how my life could've turned out if I didn't die.

To be fair, it wasn't the planet itself I wanted to be free from. It was those within it. It was the *world* they wished to make.

I swiped the water right and the kaleidoscope zoomed me into the

Earth. And as if it read my desire, it focused on the many continents and states. I swiped, and it zoomed into America. Specifically, New York. It was raining from a much lighter blue sky. Perhaps, our worlds shared the same sun. The same stars. It was good to see the city never sleeping. It was good to see that they've forgotten about me.

But I wanted to see my grave one last time. I knew that I was gone from the world forever. But I needed answers for those I honestly cared about to be okay. Harris, a pastor who was unaware of my suffering. Snake, a criminal who unintentionally led me astray. Both men who meant well. I hoped they were okay.

As I watched the cemetery, there were indeed some folks mourning for their losses. There were two individuals near my grave. One of them wearing a grey fedora and black overcoat. The other wearing a navy hoodie. I zoomed and went above their heads, eavesdropping to what they were discussing.

"So...*what is your real name*," the older man asked.

"*Gale. My real name...is Gale Kennedy*," the young man said. And he sounded familiar too. And surprisingly, so did the old man.

"*And you are Father...Harris. From St. Charles Borromeo Church, right?*" Gale asked. My eyes widened.

"*Yes. I used to preach in this city. But...God spoke to me about...exploring horizons. A calling, of some sorts*," Harris said in a gloomy tone.

Gale was scratching his heel with his shoes. Both of his hands were inserted in his hoodie pockets. He then said, "*You know...Kevin...he spoke highly of you at one point. When he was with me.*"

"*Really? That's good to hear. But...I understood his anger. I turned my back on him.*" Harris said.

"*Don't feel like that, man. I mean...you didn't know he was suffering. And...he was prevented from making any contact by them foster caretakers. All them kids were. Some fucked up shit. Good thing they have the place shut down.*"

"*Thanks be to God. But I still should've known. I...I thought I was helping him.*" Harris sorrowfully said.

"Me too. I'm...Look man, I... I'm sorry...about what I did to him. What I made him do. It was my fault that he died. I'm...responsible," Gale said in low spirits. "I thought that I was helping him too....in a way."

"You led him astray and succumb to your level. Despite that, I'm...I was just glad at least he was safe until...until his fate," Harris said. "Still, you're forgiven."

Both facing the grave, Gale then said, "You know...I had a conversation with him. I talked to him about...my mom and dad. How I left them both to...live on my own, because...I was tired of being lied to. Especially when it came to gods...or God himself. I used to think that...God made this world cruel on purpose."

"No. God didn't make the world this way. We did. We did this to Kevin. We did it to his family. The people in this world don't want to take responsibility anymore. We seem to blame external things, or one another, instead of looking inward ourselves to be better. And...I'm guilty of that," Harris said.

Before he continued, he suddenly began to choke up and spoke on the verge of tears, "I...I just miss them so much. This family...meant the world to me. Kevin's father was always such a good friend. My best friend. And...And I let him down."

Gale removed his right hand and patted Harris' shoulder. He said, "You did all you could, man. Don't beat yourself up. Kevin told me that despite feeling abandoned, he remembered the good times. Like that one time...he told me that you took him to the Radio City Music Hall for Christmas. The same place he went when he was with his family. And the time you...you both prayed and sang in the church. Or the time you taught him to draw. He only felt sad when you left him...because...he missed you. Maybe in his heart, he still...loved you. You were the only one he could trust, and he lost faith when he was prevented. You know what I mean?"

Harris then said, "That's very nice of you to say that, Gale. I'm...so glad he remembered those things." I was already feeling my eyes gradually getting watery. I remembered those good times.

"I just...I just ask God to welcome them...in Heaven. They deserve it. They were such a good family to me. Say what you will about their beliefs, their history, but...they represented things I felt were lost in this world. Their history wasn't perfect. But then again, what family is? Even so, they tried to be good. They had a sense of veracity and nobility. A family who wanted to bring good to a world that...only wanted to push them back and destroy them. And Kevin... unfortunately...gave in to that hatred." Harris said.

"He's in peace now, man...away from that bullshit. Away from these assholes. He was a cool dude. And...I'm gonna do right by him once I'm finally out of prison for good. Leave that other life for good," Gale said as his head turned to Harris. "I owe him that. Truly."

"God bless your soul, Gale. I understand that the burdens of the world took a toll on you as well. And you and Kevin wanted to live free from that. It was a wrong way of doing it, but...I understand. At least...for what it was worth, you were a good friend to him," Harris said. "I hope that you will find opportunities. A steppingstone towards the right path."

"I hope so, man. But I know it's gonna be a helluva long time. I'm considered a savage in this country, just as my ancestors were. And from the looks of it, I haven't done any favors to remove that stigma. Hell, I was told at one point by a fed that...my kind should've been removed from America by now...along with the others."

"I'm...so sorry about that, Gale. But there is still time. You could still change. And I'm glad you're considering it. This may be silly to ask. But do you...still plan to go to Iceland?"

"I'm not sure, bro...I guess so. This country is a shithole anyway. But to go there to lay low.... I just thought that it'd work at the time. Some movie bullshit I thought of. Are... you gonna be good?"

After releasing a sigh, the pastor said, "I should be. I'm only here for a few days before I go back to Illinois. Mourning for this family was a priority for me. I felt like I had to."

"I see. That's good you did that." Gale said. After looking at his wristwatch, he said, "I have to go. My time is up to go back to the big house. But it was cool meeting you, Harris."

"Likewise, Gale. And I pray that you reconcile with your family." Harris shook hands with the former career criminal.

Before he took off, Gale continued, "Thanks, man. And...take care of *yourself, man. The world's gotten enough dudes to carry burdens. Don't be one of them."*

"I'll see that I won't. Thank you, Gale. Take care."

With that, Gale began to take off from the graveyard. He was far out from the frame. Harris stood alone at my grave. Suddenly, he pulled out something from one of his coat pockets.

He investigated it with two hands; a piece of paper concealed in plastic to keep it from getting wet. He then said, *"I remember you gave this to me...after I left. I hope this drawing...goes with you; to show that I have never forgotten about you. Even if you thought I did. It hurts my heart whenever I see this illustration you made when you were only six...because I wished that things could've worked out between us. I pray that we will meet each other again and start over. For I know that anything with divinity is holy. God bless...your little soul."*

He crouched and placed the drawing onto my gravestone, stood on his two feet. After he stared at it for a good second, he disbursed from the gravestone. I forgot what the picture was. I remembered I gave him a drawing before I left to go to the orphanage.

As I zoomed into the grave, I saw that it was decorated with banquets of roses and sunflowers. And with the flowers displayed a drawing I remember I made. A drawing with me and my family with Harris and Jesus. The day I drew this was the day Kelley got that pirate playset.

I had a quick flash of images going through my head. I was recalling that early morning when I stood at the doorsteps of that foster care. I gave Harris that drawing, and he accepted it with no hesitation. He said that he always felt as if he were a part of the family anyway. He was thankful and promised to keep it with him. And we both hugged before he took off with Mr. Blackwater driving the cab.

Harris never forgotten about me. He had evidence to prove that. And yet, I've forgotten about him.

"He is still alive! He is! And he must be found again!" His voice crept and made my body grow cold. It was an unfair fight, battling tears.

As the picture gradually disappeared into rippling dark water, I stood back from the Kaleidoscope. My heart was becoming weighted, and my eyes were becoming wet. I was overwhelmed with all kinds of feelings. Happiness. Sadness. Regret. Guilt. They all took a big toll on me. And the burdens awoke within me once again.

I leaned against the wall next to the door and slid my back down. I sat until my knees were at the level of my face. And with no holding back, knowing that I had a big empty room to myself, I bent my head down and expressed nothing but sorrowful sobs.

How could I ever set a good example for my sister? How could I ever meet Harris again and tell him how our parents have met their fates far worse than the last? How could I ever tell him of the evils that still lurk through the afterlife? These questions spun across my head. If anything, it only made me cry hysterically to the point they echoed in the room.

"I...can't...I can't do this alone. I...I can't be alone! I don't want to be alone! I can't! Please," I cried to myself. Possibly praying, I wondered. "I don't want to be alone anymore! I can't do this alone! Please!" I continued to cry as my sobs echoed the giant room.

"But you are not alone, Kevin. You are welcomed and forgiven. There is no need to cry anymore." A voice said. This prompted me to rise on two feet. As I wiped the tears that circled around my eyes, I saw that the voice came from Jesus. He closed the door behind him and faced me with a gentle smile on his face.

"Who was crying? I...I wasn't crying." I said as I knew I was lying to myself.

"It is okay to be honest," the Son of God said to me. His thumbs wiped both line of tears that were flowing down my face. "There you go."

"F...Forgive me, Your Majesty. I didn't mean to come in here. I...I just needed to be alone for a bit."

"You shouldn't apologize. I've always figured you were fascinated by this place," Jesus said. He gazed upon the Kaleidoscope fountain. "It's a beautiful place. A way to know about the natural world's whereabouts. And something touched your heart to make you conceal all sorts of sentiments. And the tears were a way to express them. It's a wonderful feeling."

As I let out a defeated sigh, I said, "Aye...it's something like that."

"Yes. And by the way, you don't always have to address me as...Your Majesty all the time, Kevin. Just call me Jesus. I won't condemn you."

After I let out a soft chuckle, I said, "Okay then. If that is...okay with you."

"I wouldn't have said it otherwise. But...I feel like something is burdening you. Do you care to tell me?"

After I sighed, I then expressed to him, "I...I saw an old friend of mine. Two of them...actually."

"Yes, Pastor Harris and Gale Kennedy. An unlikely duo that came together and mourned for you. You have good people down there," Jesus said. He then walked over to gaze upon the waters. I joined alongside him.

"You felt before as if he abandoned you."

"Aye...but he hadn't. He always thought about me. All this time. And...I turned my back on him. I was so selfish," I said on a verge of tears. I tried aggressively to hold them back.

I cried, "Damn selfish! I was so inclined for a perfect life that I had no regard for what I had. For whom I had! All I had to do was wait! To wait for him!" I proceeded to try to vanquish the sobs from my system.

"I'm sure. Truly. But then what? You would gladly endure the manipulation you unfortunately sustained? It's one thing to discipline. It's another to hurt based on... resentment. No child deserves to suffer that way. You'd put up with that again?"

"No! I...I just...I wish things turned out differently than they did! I wish I never made those mistakes!"

"You have sinned, but who hasn't? A man who embraces his sin and tries everything to normalize it is one thing. But a man who knows he is sinful, understands his limitations, but longs to be saved is another," Jesus said as he looked back at me.

He continued, "They are there to only push you back. But... you could overcome them. We're not at fault for what others do to the world nor what they do to us, but we could be better than what it doesn't have to be. I could...only assume that you felt...neglected by me as well."

I turned to face him and said after I pondered, "God abandoned me that night. We devoted every prayer. Every fast. My family, my heritage, our faith, our lives, our deeds...they weren't good enough. I know that I'm not...the only one. But...I had to pressure myself to prove my loyalty to him. And it exploded."

Jesus's face became a bit down and full of gloom when I said that. He then said, "I know...it has been hard on you...to find faith again. I hope that...you do find it within your heart. I'm very, very sorry, Kevin."

I nodded in silence. But I saw his arm reach for my shoulder. I looked up into his eyes and he said, "But...there is something that you haven't discovered yet, Kevin. Something within you that you've looked over...when the burdens plagued your mind...pressuring you to be inclined to a sound life you never got to have."

"W...What's that?"

He whispered, "Your God."

"Really?"

"Yes. I know Francis taught you this, but I feel as though it should be reminded. All this time...you had God. You were just hurt to see him. Too burdened by the devil's illusion to see his signs and wonders. But...he worked through you. You did all those wonderful things here...because the God you wanted...the God you thought left you...he was with you. You take the love from your mother, the honor from your father, and the joy from your sister. And you didn't know it. But...I saw all three of them. When those bright green eyes looked up at the foggy morning sky, I knew that something bright enlightened within you. I knew that others like you would take a chance to make a true difference in this godly-made universe."

"So...what are you saying? Is my God the same as yours? The God you served?"

"He doesn't have to be. He could be that star angel you merged with. God is everywhere, works through everything and everyone. There is a war in everyday life with goodliness and evil going against one another.

Life is like that in general. It's an endurance test to see how you will hold
on to your faith. Moses, Samson, and all others had God work through
them when they were challenged. And their acts were written. Noah
and his family would've drown had he not do the will he was asked by
God. Moses wouldn't have saved his people from bondage in Egypt had
he not looked up to his God. David wouldn't have slain Goliath had he
not call upon his God to give him strength of a thousand men. Each of
these men...had their own intimate relationship. Because they each had
him. But when they did their deeds, it was clear. We have a god...just as
we have a light. We also have demons...just as we have darkness. They
coexist for a reason. And the reason is to learn from your mistakes to
seek guidance. You see God in those who want nothing but good for
you. In this world...and the one you had."

I pondered more into it. It was bewildering, but at the same time
satisfying. I never thought of it that way. Then again, I was taught
this by Francis. Perhaps, I've nearly forgotten about it because of what
happened. Like he said, I just needed to be reminded. I then asked,
"It's that simple. It should be...but why do some people make it hard
for others?"

He removed his arm and palmed his face down. Facing me, he said,
"It comes down to power, Kevin. Man's fundamental drive to prestige.
They use God's grace...as a front to apply fear into others...just so they
would submit. History has men who practiced this since the beginning
of time. Some people just think they have all the answers to being one
with the divine, disregarding that they have a lot to learn. Instead...it's
the deadly competition to decide which would be the supreme doctrine.
And that notion treats people like projects and property, which is what
I condemn. It is true that no world cannot live without order. But it
gets to a point where these leaders lose touch with nature and think
they are above it. Thus, they refuse to see humanity in others. I've seen
enough of that in Earth. I find it disgraceful that most of them...even
use my own words as a protection for their own wicked acts. And...it
hurts because I would never condone those crimes. God's words are

meant to be worshipped, heeded, and practiced wisely. Yet, they riddle my words, my name, and God...in poison. And it is very sad. Men have this urge to rely on their full trust to other men to define their lives. Most of them led them astray because they only see flesh. But God would never do that to them. All it takes is to have a blessed eye to look past the flesh to truly see who or what is divine and what isn't. Those clergies hurt you badly. I saw it through this Kaleidoscope and asked God to bloom within you. Because all I saw was them destroying that spirit."

I was choking up once again, trying to fight myself from breaking down again. "They...they destroyed...my faith," I said choking up. I felt Jesus embrace me in his arms as my head felt his chest. His hand caressed my head as I felt more lines of tears leave my eyes. "I tried to worship you...to be saved. But I feel like a curse," I sobbed, which made him silent a bit as he was just enduring my soft cries.

"You are not a curse. Children are sadly exposed to darkness very often. Those people...all they do is prey on your fear. It is never easy...to give men a chance to seek divinity their own lives. The world you came from made it hard for people to nurture themselves. It is never easy to teach. Even I need guidance," Jesus said. I felt lines of warm tears etching down my face.

He continued, "I do not wish for anyone to think that it is a sin...to experience what makes them whole. No child should ever be condemned and told they will go to Hell for not being what they were forced to be. I came down as a human to teach those to reconcile and revive their essences, not to unleash the light's feeble brother."

He then looked into my eyes with his hands on my sunken shoulders. "Those people who hurt you...are sentenced to Hell! And all others like them. They will never hurt you again. Ever. They are not of God, but the Devil."

I nodded whilst sniffing and composing myself. I placed my head downwards. But he lifted me up and said, "Faith is calling to you, Kevin. You still have a chance. It is not the end...just because you're a spirit now. It's like waking up in a new day to pursue in your new endeavors. I don't believe in death, but growing stars. Follow the stars of the universe, not the embers of machines. My sacrifice was not for someone to become Christian, Catholic, or what have you. It was not to make you perfect beings nor to worship me. My sacrifice was to give people a chance to seek for divinity on your accord. And those should never be condemned. Because God doesn't condemn. He welcomes, whether someone accepts it...or casts it aside."

He was very right. I nodded and was completely calm than before. He continued, "As much as I am resentful towards Lucifer's ill actions, he does have a point about suffering. It is indeed something to learn from. But it shouldn't be fetishized. It shouldn't be dwelled with. He just doesn't understand. He's not awake."

"It's the bloody company he keeps as well," I added. "It felt good at first, but...I...I feel bad for what I did to him. But...I just can't seem to see goodness in him yet. Neither his network. It's hard to practice love...in the face of evil."

"I know. But even so, that is why we must protect this everlasting glory, Kevin. We must keep it thriving. Stand its ground as best as we can. I seek to improve our monarchy," Jesus said as he proceeded to remove his hands from my shoulders. We both looked up and saw that the sky was becoming brighter and pinker. All the stories of Jesus being forgiving were true. How is it that he could see the best in Lucifer, despite all he did to the afterlife? It astounded me. I just hoped that Lucifer could see the same in Jesus.

"I am blessed to have a wife and child. I am blessed to serve God and give these spirits eternal hope, the best way I can...just as my mother had done. I am glad to protect them. I'm blessed to having to meet you too."

He gazed down upon me and said, "Your mother and father were great people as well. They didn't deserve that suffering the second time. I promise to honor them in name. I owe them that...for staying true to their faith. And they are with you. Do you believe that?"

As I nodded, I said with a grin, "I hope so. I want to believe it. I do." I then asked him, "Will my soul ever be saved again?"

"It has, Kevin. It has always been saved. You just needed to discover it. You must stay true to it...and live for God's divinity. Right now, you need to learn to love and forgive yourself to nurture it. You need to be in tune with your balance to cope with flaws you have. You need to look forward and face your new life. God loves those who accept and better themselves. But I've always known that you were strong. You take it from your parents. You and your sister both. Most parents are sadly not like them, which is why you are here...to bring that light to a world that needs it right now. In your way, not just theirs. The afterlife has lost itself to Lucifer's invasions and his obsession of making sin a beauty. But people so blessed as you are doing well to make it thrive again. And I'm proud of you. Truly."

As I smiled with a brightened face, I said to him as I embraced him in my arms, "Thank you very much, Jesus."

"You're welcome. Thank you for having faith, Kevin," Jesus said as he held onto me warmly. I felt very light than I should. It was such a good feeling as being in a nice hot tub. It was the kind of warmth I had yet to feel for a while now.

After we hugged, I asked, "But...what will you do with the shard?"

"I might have it broken apart. I still wish for no spirit to lay their hands onto it. I feel responsible. I had no idea the county was built on that very place we hid it. But...it won't stop Lucifer from trying to take control somehow." Jesus said.

"I hated hiding the truth about the Insignia from the common spirits. But I did that for their own good. And now...there's a chance that some spirits will intend to go after it."

"Not if we're around. I guarantee you. We may be the last, but we're not dead. And you have the Covenant of the Gods...to protect this world's integrity."

As I looked back, I faced him and said, "I think...I would like to say farewell to my sister. Before she goes. I wish... she could stay with me."

With one hand on my shoulder once again, he looked at me and said, "I understand. I believe it's for the best for now. Unfortunately, this kingdom has become a target for Lucifer. Someone that dear and young doesn't deserve to be in the crossfire. Especially after she was almost...sold. She deserves a better life away from conflict. The Hunting Grounds has energy I wish Valestone had. It's the only way you could protect her. But...it won't last forever, for you will be together again. Whether in the flesh or in spirit. Tell her that she is blessed. And you take care, Kevin."

"I will. Thank you, Jesus. You as well." I said as I departed from the room.

When I got out from the Main Chapel, the courtyard was crowded with many individuals. All of them huddled around one another. Some even recognized me and congratulated me. I was thankful for their responses, but my priority was to see Kelley. I figured that she would be in Celestia to intend the funeral, especially for our parents.

After I made my way through the gates, I walked across the bridge. I turned to my right and saw how bright the sky was becoming. The sun found it in its heart to light up and start the day. A day in which I didn't know how it would turn out. But I didn't wish to know.

When I went down the bridge, I witnessed several carriages already disbursing from the front of the castle. I faced down the other side of the street with lined up trees. As I was finally seeing the carriages, wagons and horses disbursing, it revealed one carriage that was drawn by four horses.

I recognized Francis from the back, hugging someone. Her arms were around his waist. And next to the young woman was Kelley. She was dressed in a formally black made dress. Francis stopped hugging the woman and patted Kelley on her head.

This prompted me to go across the road to finally reunite with her. As soon as I was coming over, it didn't take long for her to turn her eyes at me and curve a smile across her face. I watched her with widened eyes as she swiftly ran towards me and jumped at me with open arms.

As she embraced me, I embraced her back. My head lied on hers as I felt her warmth.

"So...you're Kelley's big brother Kevin," The woman said to me. As I released Kelley from my arms, I faced her. The woman looked to be in her mid-twenties with dark hair. She wore a purple dress with a black cloak over her shoulders. Her skin was pale, her face riddled with light brown freckles. With her arm extended, her hand was open. "She told me all about you. How good of a brother you are."

As I shook her hand, I asked, "Thank you. But...who may I call you?"

"Johanna. Johanna Bailey." It was her. Francis' daughter. It made sense to why he was hugging her. After I shook her hand, she said, "I hope my father didn't burden you too much. He could do that to a spirit."

"Hey," Francis joked back. "Don't listen to her, Kevin. She just doesn't like being told what to do. That's all."

"That's true," She jested. She then said to me, "You have my thanks for...saving the afterlife from being eradicated. I couldn't imagine what it was like. I know it was hard to...save all lives."

"It was. But...I understand that this line of work requires sacrifices. Even unwarranted ones." I said. I then said to her, "I...thank you whole-heartedly for looking after my sister. You know, she...she means the world to me. And...it's hard enough, now that...y'know..."

"No worries. You also have my dearest condolences. It's never easy for someone to have full responsibility for their sibling. It's usually very...easy with parents," Johanna said. "I never had a sibling, but...I empathize with that notion. I'm glad that my dad was able to help you. I love him for looking out for others, for me, including himself. He's not perfect...but I love him for that."

"Aye, I'm thankful for him." I smiled at Francis. He smiled back at me with his hands in his pockets.

"Well, I must take off. Jesus needs me to set up a session with the Chancery," Francis said as he hugged his daughter by her shoulder and kissed her head. I could only imagine what Jesus would tell the Chancellors. "But...I shall see you in the Khalservan, Kevin. Very wonderful work today."

"Thank you. And we will." I watched as he took off.

"Take care, Kelley." He said to her as he began to disburse into the crowd. Kelley waved back at him.

I turned and faced Johanna. "This Order you take part of...it means a lot to him. He tries everything to renovate it. To keep the afterlife alive. I'm thankful that you are making his vision come true."

"I know. He's a good man for that. And...he saved me."

She looked around a bit and read our faces. Kelley and I. She knew that we had so much to say to one another. She proceeded to say, "Kelley wanted to talk with you before she goes. So...I'll wait inside. Pretend I'm not here."

"Of course."

She faced Kelley, who responded with a nodded, and departed to the carriage. I faced Kelley. I knew, within my heart, that she was hurting. It was one thing to lose her earthly life along with our parents. Losing them in a world of eternal living was another. And it could really break someone's mind. I knew it did it to me. I knew she didn't want me to blame myself, but I still felt responsible.

"You saved us. You and your friends. Even if it did come with carnage," She said almost coldly but humbly.

She smiled, "I'm proud of you, big brother."

"Thanks. I did what I could," I expressed. "It wasn't easy. But then again, it's not always easy."

"Yes, I bet." She said.

After she pondered, she then said, "There's been something I've been thinking for quite a while now. For the months we've been in this world. The years I've been here. I don't really know how to put it. I don't want to sound...selfish...but...maybe that world we came from...we were too good for it. They didn't want us. At all. Maybe...they're just used to living in their own filth and don't intend on getting out from it. Or...maybe it's because of the kind of world it was. What we tried to bring to it, they don't want it anymore. Or...maybe I'm just talking out of my ass."

After I chuckled a bit, I replied to her, "No. You're just...thinking.

A lot than you should be. It's normal. It shows you're...growing up, which...scares me sometimes."

"Who knew right? In the afterlife, no less. I guess that's what losing family does to you," She said. I felt a bit saddened when she said that.

"How's the Happy Hunting Grounds so far?"

"A good place, Kevin. Friendly people. Great food. Warm homes. A place I'd expect a sanctuary to be. It beats running from village to village. I thank your friends for getting me into a carriage there...after I ran away from those Satanists trying to get me," She said. "Johanna is loved there. She's very blessed."

"She is. I'm glad that she's looking out for you."

Kelley looked a bit down and continued, "I was afraid, you know. That you would die too. I heard you...you couldn't take it anymore. You wanted to end it all."

I sighed and said, "News travels fast, I suppose."

"No. Um...Mr. Bailey told me himself. About what happened. But I sincerely hope you realize...that it wasn't your fault."

"I know. I just...I want to know why. Why is it...we get torn apart by circumstance? By evil? By death? It's as if we're cursed somehow. It's as if we'll be cursed forever."

"I guess that the devil himself could work through most people as well," Kelley said. "This place is no different is what I'm saying. Even if we have eternal lives."

Her face suddenly brightened, and she then asked me, "Remember one summer...our dad was hosting one of these parties with war veterans he helped? And...when Mr. Blackwater wasn't watching, we'd both sneak into mom's recording studio. With instruments, records, and stereos."

"Mind you, that was your idea. I didn't want any part of it. You knew how sensitive she was about us entering without permission," I said with a bit of jest. "We were grounded several times for it."

"No offense, but it was a boring party! Maybe because I was just a stupid kid, and I didn't bother to get the occasion. Or...I distance myself from hearing about the ideals of war. But I digress. I remembered we both would play music on one of her record players. Dead Can Dance, of course. But...I also remembered a song by Elton John...*Your Song*, I think it was."

"Aye, I remember. Quite vividly. You loved that song so much."

"I did. I still do. Mum always told me this; there's a reason behind every song. It could be based off...anything. And...the message could be taken in however form imaginable. To me, that song...describes how strongly we survived. In that life and the next. We had each other, Kevin. I'll be honest with you; I was never good with other girls my age. And I know it's odd since I seem more...outgoing in nature. But...I find myself alive and well with...women who were older than me, like Mum. Being together...as a family...that's what always kept me going. Being with you in school always made me go through the day."

Suddenly, she began to choke up a bit. She then said, "And...I just thought that...maybe...it could last forever. I thought we could look out for one another...protect each other...from a world that wants to erase our bond. Mum...and Dad. All they wanted to do...was inspire. They wanted to be the embodiment of goodness. To see goodness in everyone." Tears suddenly welled up in her eyes. She then said with a choked-up voice, "And they got killed for it. In two worlds. And my brother...has been hurt for...wanting to do good."

"All I could say is I'm sorry, Kelley. I never meant for all this to happen," I said to her with gloom arising. I felt my insides tremble. And my heart grew heavy and pulled down. I felt my heart etching, seeing Kelley that way. Her smile disappeared. And what was left on her face was a cold drowned emotion.

She had her head down and her shoulders tightened. Her hands were clammed together to her chest. As her eyes closed, her teeth gritted. She tried to stop herself from breaking. So, I held her into my arms. Suddenly, I heard her begin to cry on my chest. Her arms wrapped around me.

"I hate seeing our family torn apart, Kevin," She sobbed.

"I know," I said. "It's okay. It's okay. Don't cry."

"I...I should've fought! I saw what those...monsters did to you! What they did to Mom! To Dad! I.... I was trying to get help, but those...monsters were coming for me! I was a coward. I'm so sorry," She said weakly through her sobs.

"It's okay, Kelley. You did the right thing to run. You couldn't have done anything. It was just...it happened so fast. It was impossible to stop it." I released Kelley and saw her face was already drenched with her tears.

"Our legacy will stay alive. Even in this new world. This new life. I promise you."

As she sniffed, she said, "I wish...I was strong. I wish I was brave. Just like you."

"You are brave. Braver than...me." I said with a gloomy chuckle.

I then jested, "You always were a fighter. In your own way."

She let out a small chuckle and sniffed her nose. After she wiped her teary eyes with her hand, she said, "People are just so...vile...and cruel! Sometimes...I hate them! All of them!"

"I know. I...I know. But...not all of them are like that. Some...some people are possibly just as confused as we are. Probably scared, mad or...lost. Trying to make sense of life, I suppose. They're fighting battles of their own. Some win and some lose. And...that's okay. But don't worry about them. Worry for yourself. You need to." I said to her. "But it's best for you to be with Johanna. It's much safer. Trust me."

"You...You're right. I suppose it's for the best." She suddenly asked me, "How...How does it feel? To kill so...easily? I know it might have been hard at first...in Brooklyn. It risked a fragment of who you are."

As I pondered on that question, I wanted to give it a good thought. Specially to set a good example to her. So, after I've thought about it, I said to her, "Well, It's never an easy thing. Taking a life. Or an afterlife. It's not a fun thing to do. But...the way I see it, we're dealing with deadly forces. Ominous snakes that wither through the garden, desecrating everything it touches. And it could come from anybody. Anything. So...when I...eradicate those snakes, the garden is safe. Protected. Pure as ever. Most snakes are poisonous. So, I exterminate that kind. The irredeemable. Ones who never think about the consequence. I'm given no choice. No options. Just...that golden moment to do what's right, even when it seems wrong. But to protect the flowers I love, to keep them blooming underneath the sky, to see them...relish and thrive in their own spec of dirt which they rest upon...I take that golden moment to destroy that snake. Poison is meant to be doused...disposed.... before it spreads through the garden. It took me a while, but it made me accept that...we're not as pure as we'd like to be. There's more to life than what we once believed in. What our ancestor believed in. I think our parents were seeing that too."

She looked down a bit and said, "Heh! I always known you were poetic, Kevin. You make it sound so...simple. And just."

"Well, there's a double-edged sword to everything, Kelley. Nothing is ever one shade of color or ideal. That's how I see it anyway. At least...now I do."

"Kill...or be killed, I guess."

She looked down once again and asked, "Will we see each other again? It just...feels like we're separating for good."

I said to her, "Of course not. It's best for you to stay safe. It's not safe with you around me; in my line of work. Not yet. This life...this is what I chose, Kelley. To protect you. And I'm going to fight on behalf of you. In honor of our parents. Our bloodline. But...these demons...they'll be coming for me for what I did. Any so-called *heavenly* spirit could be a spy for Lucifer, especially to hurt me. Bertha's gang is still out there too. I don't wish to think about them getting you. I...I need you to be strong for me now. I promise to write to you every single damn day. I need you to be happy again, as happy as you can be, and live your life. A strong life. Like a pirate."

She nodded with lines of tears coming down from her eyes. She smiled a bit as soon as I said the word pirate. I wiped them both with my hands. I then said to her, "You're the only semblance of family I have left in this world, Kelley. I cannot lose you too."

After she pondered, she cried, "I...I'm going to miss Mum and Dad! It's going to be so hard without them when it was getting easier again!"

"I know. I'm going to miss them too. It's not going to be simple.

There will be times of failure. I know it. But by God's grace...we will get through it. It's only the beginning of our journey in this new life. It's like waking up...from a nightmare."

"I suppose...there's always a chance to start over, even if...it's not what you want," She said as she was clearing from her sobbing state. "I guess after what we've been through in both worlds.... I just...I don't know what God wants from me anymore. What he wants from us. We try to do good in his name, but he punishes us...for no reason."

"I don't know either. I still don't, even as an Apostle. Maybe it's not about what he wants from us. But what he wants for us. I...I hope I could see that. But I know we will. We must. And we will always be together." I then showed her the locket I was wearing around my neck. Her eyes widened a bit and her face bloomed with light. "Because I have you in my heart and mind...to keep me hallowed. To make me love my humanity. To face...life again."

We both began to hug out every burden that was holding us back like puppets. After we embraced ourselves, we held hands and looked into each other's eyes. Her eyes were brightened than they were before. And I felt warmth crept into my heart once again when I saw her smile. "And I love the doll, by the way. Thank you. It's so sweet."

"Of course. Take care of yourself, yeah? I love you very much, lass."

"I love you, too, Kevin," Kelley said as she hugged me back. After-wards, she stood back from me and took another good glance at me before she retreated into the carriage with Johanna waiting. As she was going up the steps to sit inside of the carriage, Johanna popped her head to see me and said, "I promise to continue looking out for her. I owe you that much. Hope we cross paths again, Kevin Princeton."

I said with a reply, "Hopefully. Thank you very much. Take care of yourself too, Johanna." With that, she closed the carriage. Shortly after, the horseman whipped the reins and had the four strapped horses pull the white carriage away from the gates of the Main Chapel. I stood and watched as it rode passed by me to the left.

I watched as Kelley had her face at the window. She smiled and waved back at me. I smiled back and waved, assuring that things would truly get better. It wasn't long before I realize that the sun was already set. The carriage disappeared into the bustling big city of Celestia.

Around me, I saw as the entirety of folks have disappeared and went back to their homes or jobs. But I truly did hope that what Jesus said, what my friends and I did, would truly impact their minds and think about what they have seen on that day. I didn't seek to be a hero. I just hoped that my actions would inspire them to help the afterlife.

With my hands placed into my pockets, I simply walked back to the Main Chapel. Just as an excuse to go and meet up with my friends.

A very weird but depressing way to start the day, I thought. But how could I make it become better throughout? That what I had to think about.

And I pondered on my conversation with Kelley. Without realizing it, I made a vow. A vow I made with everybody. In a world that was dying, this was a chance for me to revive it. I had to keep my soul alive. My sister alive. Our legacy of Edward Carter alive. The Apostle Order alive. And every innocent folk had to live.

What was lost could be found again. And throughout the pondering, this was something I needed to believe. I got into the Order. I chose to have that purpose. And I chose not to escape it. Because there wasn't a way out. I could only finish it, no matter how long it may last. To do that, I had to be alive to see it. It was the only way.

Later after I reunited with Ted and Juliet, we hung out in the city today. For the first time, we were trying to act like common spirit folk.

We tried taking consolations. I tried to get over all that happened. It wasn't simple, given what we went through. Especially for Juliet, who was more fearful and haunted by what we faced and endured.

But today, we mostly had our little fun in Samson Park in the center of the city. From getting set portraits by the river to just simply walking throughout the park, it was good to be alongside common spirits occasionally. It was good to not worry about the Satanists for once. It was good to not have their blood splattered on us.

And not that it mattered, but we were applauded by some of the folk in the park for what we did. Especially for what I did as I was called the *Spright Assassin* by some folk. So, we appreciated it.

But when the skies were becoming damper with yolk yellow smeared with a rageful orange, being how we spent the entirety of our time in the park, we rode back to the Khalservan.

The more we rode a long while to the Khalservan, it took us until sundown to reached there. Unmounting our horses, the monks were leading us to where we had to go. Seemed like they were waiting for us.

The interiors were darker than they should be. But I believed that it was a special occasion that they were hosting. Certainly, it wasn't a birthday party.

Going through the halls, the monks were leading us to a much familiar place. A place I thought that I would never see again. The ritual room. While unexpected, I was still correct about it being an occasion. But I had yet to know. But Ted and Juliet seemed too.

In the front stood Francis, Michael, and several Virtue Elderlies. All of them were cloaked. In Michael's hands was a decorated sword. It was a bright white crystal with a golden cross guard. The grip was glazed with diamond shards with the hilt made of a crimson crystal.

"Mr. Princeton, Mr. Jefferson, and Ms. Higgins come forth please," Francis called. His voice echoed the room.

After we eyed at one another, we soon came down passed the friars who were making a gateway. An extension to my place in this new heaven. As we all met with Francis in front of us, he said to us, "Please kneel."

We both kneeled on one knee. Our heads were bowed. I had a sense of excitement running through my body. I was giddy for what was to happen. My right arm was bent to be placed gracefully on my knee. I caught a glance of Michael coming down with the sword erected. All silence, there was nothing but the blowing growls of the fire being blown by the wind.

Michael first said to Juliet, "Dame Juliet Hosea Higgins, as the Thirteenth Apostle, the first in this generation, you have served your duty in keeping the Order in balance. In times of cruelty, you have stayed true to bravery, kindness, love, and humility. You are now knighted and regarded as an Apostolic Noble. *Put on the whole armour of God, that ye may be able to stand against the wiles of the devil.*" As he said this, he placed the blade on each of her shoulders.

Shortly after, he got to Ted and said, "Sir Theodore Beckett Jefferson, as the Fourteenth Apostle, the second in this generation, you have served your duty in keeping the Order in integrity. In times of falsehood, you have stayed true to honesty, loyalty, creativity, and friendship. You are now knighted and regarded as an Apostolic Noble. *He that walketh uprightly walketh surely: but he that perverteth his ways shall be known.*" Like Juliet, he also knighted Ted with the sword.

I let out a deep breath as soon as Michael arrived towards me. He then said as I was feeling the blade come down on each shoulder, "Sir Kevin Edward Princeton, as the Advanced Apostle, the third in this generation, you have served your duty in keeping the Order in reconciliation. In times of doubt, you have stayed true to honor, reclamation, honesty, and faith. You are now knighted and regarded as the Fifteenth Apostle. *And when he was demanded of the Pharisees, when the kingdom of God should come, he answered them and said, The kingdom of God cometh not with observation: Neither shall they say, Lo here! or, lo there! for, behold, the kingdom of God is within you.*"

Although I was a bit below Ted and Juliet, it didn't stop me from feeling honored. It made sense for Ted and Juliet to earn it, being how they came before me. And I knew eventually that I would be good as they were.

As soon as Michael went up and stood next to Francis, Francis then said to us, "Rise, Apostles."

All three of us rose on our feet. We glanced at one another and smiled. Francis came down to me to face me. He then said with his hands on my shoulders, "You have reached to the pinacol. I am proud of you. All of you. This honor you receive is not by me, but by all the Gods in the afterlife...as they all vow to be with you." He pointed out Ted and Juliet. Focusing back on me, he then said, "This is just the beginning of your new journey. And you have the Apostles to stand beside you. And the afterlife...will be moved by you. And you are keeping the Order alive. Therefore, you are keeping the afterlife...alive. We wish you all luck as you continue those endeavors. Congratulations."

"Thank you, Francis," I said with a smile. He then had all three of us face the friars, guards, chefs, and every person bringing liveliness to the Khalservan. Including Emily and Sarah whom I didn't knew were inside. All of them stood proudly and looked at us with adoration and just.

Francis rose his hands and said, "With the Satanists returning, the Demons rising, and Lucifer's crusade thriving, this is the beginning of all what would stand. The beginning of what would be his downfall. It will take time and hardship to get through. But we have our Gods on our side. And with these three honorable knights, we will stand proudly and lead our enemies astray! May God empower them! May their hymns.... last...forever!"

The applause has surrounded the entire ritual room.

Kelley was right. It felt like something out of a fairy tale. I never thought that a young man born in the early 90s in modern day England, who moved to New York, would go to the spirit world, and become knighted. Knighted. The life I had, the entirety of it, I have fantasized about that moment based on the stories I read as a child. Only for them to come true in this strange reality.

I presumed that it was how I imagined how my ancestor felt when he swore his loyalty to his legion.

As I said before, I intended to make this new life right, this time. I expect it to be harder, knowing a bit of what it is like. But with the sorcery I had, with the Apostles by my side, and Kelley, my ancestry and my family in my heart and mind, I didn't expect to be put down now.

My soul may have been broken and poisoned, but it will be resurrected soon enough. I promised. I was broken. But as my mother once said, there are two different broken men. Thus, I chose to be the second.

But as of the current situation, my friends and I decided to celebrate the occasion. Specially to lift ourselves up after the morning. And what better way to do that then to stop by Litler's.

The night was young. The stars of the spirits glittered the mellow blue sky. The city lights of Celestia shined across the horizon. And Litler's was bustling with singing, dancing, drinking (and possible drunk), and talking. My Apostle friends and I drank alongside Frask. With glasses in our hands, we celebrated. We feasted. We have gone gold. And I've become a legend. Therefore, I drank like a legend. My apologies for the last sentence.

Frank came up to us with his hairy elbow on the desk. With a smile, he asked after a chuckle, "So, what is the special occasion for all of you to drink like Vikings from Valhalla?"

After Ted took a big slurp from his keg, he wrapped his right arm around my shoulder, holding me close. "My boy's graduated, man! He's hit the major leagues! We all did!"

After laughing, he said, "Splendid! Splendid! But...c'mon, lads. Eh! I know exactly what Francis has you three doin'! Just remember...you are the super knights of this time! You gotta watch your backs for folks tryin' to take ye down! What you've done ain't enough for your kind to be squandered by that blasted Chancery!"

Juliet slurred, "Oh...I hear that they are in big trouble! Trust me, sir! I'm possibly tipsy! Aye! But I know enough to distant good and bad folk! Especially if they are or are not cultists! Disappearing and reappearing every now and then!"

I chuckled. And it was clear that Juliet was having a bit of a good time. And it was well-deserved for all she did. And she was even cuter when she was tipsy.

Frank then looked over at Frask and said, "And you're the owner of *Potter and Clay*, aren't ya? I've seen you time to time. Brilliant work!"

"Oh, well...yes. I am. Thank you. But it's called *Frask and Ted's Shop of Divine Wonders now.* Kevin here gave me the idea for the name," He said with his left fingers around the keg's handle. His keg was half empty.

"I'm celebrating two occasions. The House of God giving me good word of mouth for my shop...and I've sold eleven thousand paintings over the course of six months! My biggest sale yet!"

"Woohoo...yeah!!" Ted cheered with his hands clapping against each other. He got all of us, including the crowd, to cheer for him. Frask shielded away with a smile.

"Couldn't have done it without you, Ted!"

"No problem, man!' Ted clanged his keg onto Frask's.

Frask then said, "And...an additional third occasion I'm celebrating this night for...is because of you three together. Including you, Kevin. Today, you made this average painter and alchemist... a hero. And...I just wanted to say...thank you wholeheartedly. Truly!"

"You're not average. You've earned it, mate! Cheers!" I clicked my keg onto his. So, did Juliet and Ted.

"It's good that you've done it," added Frank. "I was thinking about purchasing one of your works actually. I'm hoping to fresh up this dirty arse place! Making it more fashionable for business! Honest business! Ain't always a bad thing to renovate, right?"

"Absolutely right. And I mean the money would be enough to create more inventions. I'm even thinking about getting more hires," Frask answered before he rashly drank the ale from the keg. I drank a bit from mine.

"Asshole! What, I'm not good enough for ya now, huh?" Ted joked.

"Obviously. Nah...I'm kidding around. But I don't know...I see some horizons is all. And I plan to reach them," He said as he then pulled out four bennies from one of his pockets and placed it on the desk. He then said, "I know it's thirty. But because of how good it was...I'm paying extra."

"Thanks a bunch! You have a nice night, Mr. Douglas! And congrats again!" Frank said as Frask took off and waved back at us. After I waved, he went out from the saloon and disappeared in the bustling streets.

I turned back to my friends, and they gave me smiles.

"Well...I shall leave you three. Wouldn't want to ruin your occasion with my wretched breath!" He laughed.

"It's no problem, Frank. Thank you," I said. I watched as he was collecting Frask's money before getting engaged with another group of fellow spirits.

"So...Kevin, as the Fifteenth Apostle, what would be your first course of action," Juliet asked before she drank away.

"Fifteenth Apostle. I like that. It has a nice touch to it. Heh heh. Well...I plan to do my somewhat knightly duties, for starters. Stopping bank robbers, criminals, fanatics, whatever comes to mind. Hell, maybe I'd save a princess from a fire breathing dragon if I have too. I understand that not all demons come from Hell." I said. "But lately, I was thinking about resuming...with my other talents. Talents I've abandoned for quite a while now."

"Being a writer, right," Ted asked me, figuring out one of my passions.

"Maybe. I was hoping to be an art therapist. But writing isn't a bad thought either. I could write a book. I had a couple of ideas. One of them being stories about how negativistic people would unintentionally ask for an apocalypse amongst their lives. You know...because of their apparent hatred for a valued honest life. I feel like it's sometimes an excuse to do what they want; be it pretending to have morals. Or condemn those for having differing minds. Or...to piss in someone's mouth in public. Because they can, I suppose. I don't know."

As Ted chuckled, he said, "Now that...I like your honesty."

"Ah... good to know," I said cockily as he and I clanged both of our kegs and drank all our drinks. I felt the cool raspberry taste of the ale I was given. We slammed our kegs onto the desk. Releasing bitter air from our mouths.

I added, "I'm not saying that I'm better before any smug bastard assumes I am. I'm just putting words out there that they can be helped to fulfill that empty void."

"That's a very rash view on emptiness, Kevin. But...you're not too wrong about those kinds of people," Juliet said. I nodded.

She added, "They are just figuring their purpose, I suppose."

"Who isn't," Ted said in agreement.

"I mean...they aren't. But I applaud those who try. Not to a bunch of losers who give up and force others...to do the same."

After he took another sip, he then said to me, "You know, the Satanists will come for us. Especially for you... for what you did. They'll become more powerful. We'll be on the run from their immoral law whilst fighting them off. It won't be easy with prices on our head. No Apostle did what you did. I don't... mean to scare you."

"I know," I said a bit nervously. Perhaps knowing that now it would make me have a lack of rest. Or sleep.

"But don't worry. You have us, the Apostle Order, and the House of God to protect you. Especially your god," Juliet said with her left hand on my right. I looked up to her and smiled.

"Thank you," I said as she smiled back. "I just hope we could make a difference. I know it takes time."

I watched as Ted suddenly pulled out his pocket watch. After he opened and gazed upon the ticking time, he then closed it and said to us, "Hate to break it up to ya. But...I've got an important appointment."

"An appointment? With whom?" Juliet turned to him. I faced him as well.

"Uh.... just a couple of old friends, that's all. I forgot to tell ya. My bad. But...it shouldn't be too long," Ted said.

After Juliet sighed, she said with caution, "Okay, but...you better come back to the Khalservan safe, yeah?"

"I will. Jeez, quit playing mama bird for once," Ted said as he came down from his stool. After he paid with a couple of bennies to one of Frank's children, Bo, he said to me, "I swear, this woman sometimes! Well, I'll see you, Kevin. Congratulations again. And...thanks for...being an awesome friend to me. It means a whole lot to me."

"Aye, of course. Thanks to you too, brother." Ted and I pounded our knuckles against one another. He passed me and patted Juliet on her shoulder before he took off. Thus, he too, disappeared into the streets.

It was only Juliet and me. Both of us were slumped onto the desk.

Tired and exhausted by everything we went through, I watched as Juliet gulped up the rest of her strawberry ale.

"I have a feeling those old friends of his are the *Astral Ghoul Boys*," Juliet said.

"The less I hear about his...appointment, the better. Perhaps, it was only a matter of time before he'd finally dealt with them."

"Aye, that's true."

"This is what he does though. But...I think that is why I am so fond of him. He's not afraid to stay true to himself anymore. At all," She admitted. "I wish I had that mentality."

"I know. That's why he's a good man. He's not like one of those blokes who pretend to be someone they're not...just to fit in. I know I fell into that deception before. Criminals, fanatics, conformists have made a massive haven of the world we had...and forced us to stay by playing to our fears. It's inevitable to fall into that."

"We all have that tendency. It just depends on how we get out from it; I suppose."

"Aye. Rather lay on a meadow of boring lambs...than a den of vindictive lions." I nodded.

She then said, "I...I have some herbs, actually. Chamomile. I often use them to help the patients I take care of. I had them collected from the rarest parts of Eastbound, I'm sorry it took so long. I would offer them to you now, but only when you want. It's in my nursing hut if you ever want it."

I nodded as I took in the information, "That's very generous, Juliet. Thank you. Maybe it won't completely get rid of the voices, but...it'd be something to help me cope with them, at least. I'm sorry I didn't tell you of them." She nodded with a smile.

"I understand. It's too personal for you. Still, you should tell me if they are getting worse." But then her face narrowed as she was pondering on something.

But soon, she asked me, "Can I ask you something...personal?"

"Of course, Juliet. Anything."

She then continued, "I know you are new. And it's too early to ask.

I'm one to always think ahead. Blast my mind. But...is this life...being an Apostle...is it something you want to become? Have you thought about being...something more?"

I then asked, "Hmmm...Have you thought about it?"

"Oy, I asked first." She said with jest.

"I'm kidding." I began to ponder. And maybe she was right to ask that. I know there was more to this life than to be an Apostle. So, I then explained to her, "I'm...not sure what else is there for me if I'm honest. I mean before...I felt like I didn't really have much of a purpose anymore...apart of doing acts to escape life's law. But when I became an Apostle, I feel like...I do have one. I made friends. I saved others. I've broadened my mind. I identified with almost everyone I came across. And I felt guilty. And... I used to worry about death, knowing that at some point...I had to rush through life to become who I wanted to be before it was too late. I didn't take time to enjoy life correctly. I know I will eventually become an art therapist...or something of art, but I know that there is something I could become, Juliet. Something more."

"And you will," Juliet said. "Being an Apostle is a start. You could still be a knight, but still pursue a dream. One of which brings out...who you are and what you could be."

"Aye, you could. I mean...everyone always said that...life is too short. It may be true. I used to think that. Most of us astrals did at some point. But...here, now I know that...I shouldn't have to worry. I shouldn't have worried about death. Because...we don't die. We could live. And continue to live. And now, I have so much time to appreciate the beauty of something flawed yet something so real. I wish I knew that before. At my lowest point, I didn't want to kill myself. I just didn't want to live anymore. I wanted to escape living. But now I realize that there's so much more to life in general...that I didn't bother to see. And to make the very best of it on my own accord. I only wish I've known all of it before. It was because...I felt like I was dying in that world. But...I'm alive here."

"I know. Being that we both came from...repressed upbringings, false religious caretakers, and all, they were right about one thing about this place; you get to live eternally. The only difference is...is that they won't be coming here anytime soon. Given how they were towards us. And even if they did, they wouldn't dare mess with us."

I chuckled, knowing that it was true. And it was ironic. They claimed to be holy, yet they did the most unholy things to us. And now, they've failed. I'd figured that they truly wanted us to go to Hell. But we've beaten them to their own game.

"I do hope that I will eventually grow to this...new God...knowing that the other I praised is sadly dead. I realize that the God I served is...not the same as my parents nor my ancestor. This one...was waiting for me to see him. I hope he could truly save me...so I could save others who are hellbent to man's mockery of life. But...I thank him for giving me this eternal life. And I plan to spend these days with people like you," I said as I then casually held onto Juliet's hand on the desk.

She gazed upon my eyes with her glittery sky-blue eyes.

I continued, "All I want now...is to enjoy this moment before another. Humans and spirits are not perfect. They both seek. They seek to grow. But there is...one thing we do differ. Humans live for life. But spirits.... we live forever. We live forever."

She softly gripped onto my hand and covered it with the other. She bent her head and looked down a bit. I slowly lifted her soft skinned chin with my other hand as she smiled at me.

"For a lad with sixteen voices, you have a way with words." Juliet said. "But...you're very right, Kevin. And...I'm happy that you chose to be in the Order. I'm glad...it did something for you."

"I wouldn't have met you otherwise," I said as she began to blush. I then asked as we released both of our hands from one another, enduring the touch we had. I asked her, "Now.... I told you my bit. I believe it's your turn. Do you plan to be an Apostle for long?"

After she pondered a bit, she said, "Not for long. I plan to move east somewhere in the Promised Land. Raise a farm, perhaps. Maybe with me mum. To truly be in peace as I am surrounded by mountains. Away from the likes of people for a bit. Don't get me wrong. I love being an Apostle. It's the best thing that's ever happened to me. It's just that...I feel like this land...has so much more to offer. But I don't want to dream too much about it. I want to enjoy today and see where it leads. But it's what I envision. I know...it sounds quite boring."

"You're right, it does sound boring." I joked as she gave me a playful sneer. She slapped my right arm.

"Heh, I'm kidding. I hope you find that quiet land. It sounds...peaceful. Free," I said. What she wanted sounded a lot of what I would've wanted when I would be in Iceland.

After I gulped, I then asked, "Would you...want me to be there with you? To raise a farm...or to bring life to the land. Like having a kingdom. Being king or queen. God...I'm rambling! Forgive my poor attempts of being romantic. I'm not.... really good at this."

After she chuckled, she smiled and said, "Me either. I'm...not even sure if I ever will. But we don't have to be. We could do our best. Being that...our lives are eternal; we still have time. Even with what we already had...before Valhalla." She said as she then paid several bennies from her pocket.

She then said to me, "Speaking of which, the night is still young. Do you still wish to go on that date? I already paid for us both."

"I thought we were dating...since we basically know one another now."

"I mean...a real date, silly boy," she smiled. "I know a place. Besides, you don't know much of me yet."

A grin grew on my face. And thus, I replied, "What are we waiting for?"

We both smiled at each other and got up from our stools. After we said our goodbyes to Frank and his children, we were back in the streets. As Juliet mounted on her thoroughbred, and I mounted on my pertlow, we began to ride away from the narrow streets until we began to hastily traverse throughout the city until we were soon to get past the homestead and possibly the Khalservan.

The night I have been longing for had begun. As soon as we passed the Khalservan and Joseph's Homestead, we began our date at a very familiar place. It was her perfect place. Her favorite one to date. East-bound. Even after those hectic months of stopping fanatics from getting their hands onto a staff, it still illuminated relentlessly in the night. It was still something out of a fable that we read in our stories. Instead of the temple, we went behind it. We were presented a large lake surrounded by trees and were fireflies danced across. We resided in a structure of eight marble pillars carrying a glass dome decorated with stained colors of purple, pink and yellow flowers. The marble ground we stood on had white candles on each corner of the gazebo.

Later, surrounded by candles shedding their lights, dimming with darkly lit orange flames, Juliet and I danced. It was after I played my guitar for her.

We held each other close and swayed across the floor. In our minds, we pretended to be at a royal ball.

And I pictured it very vividly. It was a heavenly white room with big marble pillars surrounding us. A chandelier made of diamonds and crystals shackled above our heads. And snow fell around us as if winter couldn't sustain its sanity. Nor patience. We were in an enchanting gazebo looking over the glossy lake under the darkened sky. But it was a good thought.

Anything thought was better than to worry about who to assassinate next. Or who or what to run from.

We slowly spun and swayed back and forth, each of our hands held together. Juliet's face locked onto my shoulder. I held her close, protecting her. Shielding her from worries. Sheltering her in bravery.

I quietly said to her, "Juliet, I'm...I'm...I'm sorry."

"You're sorry? What could you be sorry for...exactly?"

"You know. For making you...cry that day. When I was going to....," The words were too hard to express. So, I furthered explained. "It hurt me to see you that way. I just...I never knew I mattered that much to you."

After she was quiet, she said to me, "It's okay. I didn't even know...why I had that breakdown. We've only met a year. Perhaps, it was

my anxiety commencing. Or...perhaps it was the moment I...had something boiled up inside. I feel like it was the first in a long time...when
I opened to someone. In terms of love. I had to grow in a place where
I had to keep my feelings to myself and not to show it. Knowing that
no one would ever understand except my mother. But...I met you. I saw
how honest you were...about everything. I've always found it hard to
be honest because of this...fear of being hurt. But you brought out the
whole of me I haven't felt. It's something I'm still working on. As well
as my faith. I feared losing you because...my love for you...is a way of
saying thank you for...for all you did for this world. And for me. You do
matter because...of the kind of man you are. And when I help you...to
open yourself and trust in your life ...I feel like I help myself. It helps
me heal and...opens me up to a new light. You are the new light."

When we faced each other, I looked into her eyes and suddenly
saw a tear lining down from her right eye socket. I wiped it from her
face. I felt her hand leave my waist and caressing the left side of my
scarred face.

"I didn't feel welcomed before," I admitted. "My whole life, I tried
to find where I belong. I thought that I did with only my family. We
wanted to find a home. But...I've met you. And you welcomed me.
You've helped me all this time. It's my turn to help you." Her face went
over my left shoulder and stayed. I held her closer by her waist.

I whispered, "You don't have to feel afraid anymore. I will never
leave you. I promise."

She said nothing. But soon, after placing her hand down, she replied,
"I'm glad to be that angel for you, Kevin. I'm happy the afterlife...is
your home."

As I contemplated, I said to her, "It's...weird and corny to say this;
but...you seem like something out of a dream. Yet, we're from the same
world. I feel like I saw you...like the angel I've missed in my life." After
she chuckled softly, she looked at me once again.

I felt her cool soft hand on my face. She then said to me, "You're
the knight I've dreamt about when my mother...told me those stories.
Stories I hoped would become real...in my own life."

"I'm glad to be that knight for you, Juliet. And I'll always be that knight."

"Just not a white knight," She said as I chuckled.

She smiled and suddenly asked as she gazed at my eyes, "*Audite custodes tui*. I think it's about time to listen to the right guardians. Ones of God. The father of Christ. Not the imposter made by foul clergies and their churches."

Snickering, I replied, "Definitely. I'll still serve God. Just not man's God. I will never associate with their imitation of him...ever again." She nodded with a grin.

She then said, "I'm sorry for...what I said to you on the day when Emily, Frask and Sarah were in the Khalservan. It was very uncalled for. It was...in the heat of the moment."

"It's quite okay. I'm sorry as well. We were all in that moment. This is what Lucifer, and his congregation wants us to feel. To feel angry, sad, and hopeless. But we will rise and step against them. Especially with you. And our love will be stronger. And our love will revive the glory of the Order. The glory of the afterlife. Our worlds will be together."

Thus, we began to stop dancing and hugged. Her face laid on my right shoulder.

Given what we've been through, we had to escape. Only unlike Talia, I understood her demons plaguing her. She understood mine. I never forgot it. Both of us caressed and cuddled on the marble ground as we extracted our vulnerability towards one another. I didn't denounce doctrine as an excuse. And it didn't lead to what one would think. Because it was the moment where we both had no care for man's manipulation of everything anymore. I didn't even care for the crusted cinnabar anymore. I cared about being with her. The daisy that was blooming into an orchid under the starry sky.

Later, we soon found ourselves sleeping together under the dome. Hours and hours flew by like a flock of birds. Yet, the night that was young dawned. I loved her. Her hair. Her face. Her smile. Her temple. Her skin. Her eyes. Her friendship. And her honest nature. A mutual moment with no acute action.

It was very unearthly to comprehend my love. After we woke up around three o' clock, giggled for what we did, stared at the starry sky, we went outside of the gazebo. Mounting on our steeds, we rod. Yes, it seemed to be a short date. A short night. But it was something I was never going to forget.

Epilogue

The sky was no longer bright. In fact, it was growing up. They were smeared with pinks, blues and white. And the mountain peaks continued to get shined upon by the sun's glowing flare. Before I could start a new day as living as a spirit, I took the morning to visit Jacob's Cemetery. I heard that my parents were going to be buried there. I wanted to truly say goodbye to them. I wanted to let them be in peace. I rode on Aventurine and had Algor run alongside me. Ted and Juliet were both kind for riding alongside me.

Before I went there, it was nice of Emily, Ted, and Juliet to collect the appropriate baguette of flowers to offer to my parents. They got me a collection of mayflowers, Tuscan sun perennial sunflowers, roses, tulips, and daisies. The Tuscan sunflowers were my mother's favorite. She used to plant them in our garden. Thus, I hoped it would go with her into the Void.

Soon, Algor, Aventurine, the Apostles and I went towards the western meadows of the Promised Land. And with the sun brightening upon the tall grain grasses, the mountains standing broadly and tall, with the trees peaking from afar, it was just more of an emphasize of how majestic the afterlife was. This everlasting conflict had made me not appreciate it as much. But as soon as all of it is over, like Juliet, I would love to live in a place far from civilization. It reminded me of the Ramapo Mountains; a place where my family camped. The last place I remembered.

Jacob's Cemetery was just far up ahead. It was up a hill. And when I was approaching it, I was beginning to see little tombs. It was no ordinary graveyard. Upon entering through the archway supported by the gates, I saw the entire acre of land riddled with burial vaults. Not just simple tombstones. Tombs big enough to fit two or four coffins inside. All of them made from white marble. I supposed it made sense. I was guessing that this is where they would put offerings and other trinkets for the dead spirits to take. Ted and Juliet decided to wait at the gates. As I rode slowly through the graveyard, I tried searching for where my parents were buried. When I rode, all I did was ponder. I pondered on my previous life. With my entire family with me. I thought about that drawing I drew once and what it could've been. I wanted it so badly to work out. I wanted to love the world I came from. But circumstances compromised with my expectations. I'm sure my parents felt the same. I knew Kelley did. And whenever I thought about the good times, my eyes would gradually water.

I searched and scanned, used my eagle eye to spot the vault. But in the far right, as I explored, I saw the Princeton name carved on the white marble. I dismounted from Aventurine and began leading him to the burial by holding onto the reins with my left hand. The flower baguette in my right. Algor's heavy breath panted next to me when he was walking by me. I looked around and witnessed others spirit folks, making amends, and speaking with their losses. As I stumbled in front of the vault, I looked left and right. The statues of virtuous angels standing on each side. I let out a deep breath and hitched the reins onto a post to keep Aventurine still. The pertlow clapped his left hoof against the grass in impatience. I told Algor to stay put and keep watch at Aventurine. Shortly after I caressed his fluffy head, I pushed my way inside of the vault. The darkness that concealed the glass coffins were soon shrouded by the morning lights.

In the tomb were two candlesticks in front of each coffin. Uncovering my box of matches, which I use to smoke with, I ignited each candle stick surrounding their glass coffins. And the more it shined, the brighter it was becoming. The interior was immersing with a bright soft orange lighting up. In between the coffins was a table with an empty vase with floral engravings on it.

I first focused my eyes on my mother. I laid my eyes upon her and anchored my elbow over the coffin. I vowed to never forget everything she taught me. I would never forget what kind of person she was. A guitarist who played for the poor, using her angelic voice as a front for passing hope onto others who had none. She did the same for the after-life. She suffered. She strived. And she provided what she can for this world. And the world we once had.

Her scarred skin was paler. Her lovely eyes shut closed. And both of her hands were crossed over with a rosary in her hands. She was surrounded with flower pedals, white silk mantles, oil jars and chalices. Trinkets like jewel necklaces and basil herbs were scattered around her as well. Love was one of her strengths. It was something I never knew I had from her. I had it all along. All I was doing was hiding it from the Earth.

After I gazed upon her, I took it over and gazed upon my father's, who had it the worse. I vowed to never forget what he told me. A war veteran and aspired humanitarian who was trying to make the world we had better. Whether it was faltering into the likes of war. Or to succumb to the media outlets, just for the sake of protecting not only his family. But to also protect our good name that was tarnished by our grandfather's mistakes. A name that was antagonized by a collective group of people who preferred to, as Kelley placed it, live in their own filth. I never forgot his courage. His strive to stay true to himself when others tried to bring him down to their level. His courage to not follow his father's footsteps.

I saw him in the coffin as well. His arms were crossed with a rosary. His eyes were closed. His skin pale as the stars. And just like mother, he was also surrounded by flower pedals and white mantles. The herbs surrounding his spiritual corpse were rosemary leaves. Honor was one of his strengths. He always put the family first before himself. And it was a virtue I had as well. A virtue I cannot fail again.

Jesus was right. I had all of those within my soul. Yet, I've hidden all of them to favor a world that never accepted me. A world that didn't accept Ted, Juliet, nor others. A world going to hell. And enough was enough for hiding who I was. And I had enough of favoring the worse just to belong. I've had enough of having a false belvedere of what was good or bad. Despite the deep thrive I had to kill the Satanists who poisoned my soul, violated my pride, and made me kill the whole of Corinthian County, despite my vow to kill Lucifer for what he had done, despite the words of Bertha, I placed my vendetta aside and silently swore to my parents.

I would honor them in name. I would love them in name. And I would never ever fail Kelley in blood.

I pondered. I thought about what I had to really say. I soon said from my heart after I exhaled, "I lived three lives. One was partial. One not very good. This third life, I will make it right. For all of us. This is what I'm choosing. I know that you are with me. I need you beside me; no matter what. I promise to keep our values alive. To use what you taught me, I will keep those alive. I promise to face life again. You gave love and honor to this world. And the world we had. And God will bless you and reward you eternally for it. He will give you the peace you deserve. I love you both. I love you. May God...look over you. Amen."

Afterwards, I placed the baguette of flowers into the empty vase. I faced the illuminated candle lights surrounding their glass coffins. It was not an easy thing to see them go again. It was not easy the first time.

My shoulders were suddenly overwhelmed with warm touches. As if some formation of love and honor stood behind me, I heard voices. "*We love you, Kevin. We will always be there for you. And Kelley. We love you both,*" Mother said.

"*This life is yours now. Live it well...for God is with you,*" Father said.

I turned moderately quickly, only to see no one else. Only an open door. The sun was still gazing its light upon me as if I was on stage. I turned back to see my parents for one last time. Taking my last chance to leave my sanctuary to rest to make one of my own. I took a good glanced, asked God silently to keep them safe in the Void. As well with the others. After I inhaled and expressed a deep sigh, I took it upon myself to leave the tomb. Allowing my parents to finally rest. I closed the door behind me and turned around. Algor sat on all fours, panting excitedly at me. Aventurine huffed and snorted. With both hands on my pockets, I just grinned and chuckled to myself. I said to them "Why don't we go back, shall we?"

I went to unhitch Aventurine. Next, I got up onto the saddle by going up the stirrup. Mounting myself, I sat on the leather saddle. I glanced over at the peaking gold sun once more. Soon, I used the reins to move Aventurine away from the marble vault.

When I was dispersing from the graveyard, alongside Algor, I began to pace Aventurine quickly. I began to gallop quickly down the meadow, forestalling for a new day to come up from the afterlife. Alongside my new best friends, we rode alongside one another across the golden plains blown and tossed by the morning winds.

It was not a normal life. But it was still a life. A life I chose not to escape, but welcome. A life I chose to thrive...longing for what is to come. It belonged to me.

And it always will. Forever.

CPSIA information can be obtained
at www.ICGtesting.com
Printed in the USA
BVHW031036060722
641372BV00014B/154/J